# THE
# CRADLE
# OF ICE

## TOR BOOKS BY JAMES ROLLINS

*The Starless Crown*
*The Cradle of Ice*

# THE
# CRADLE
# OF ICE

## Book Two of the Moonfall Saga

# JAMES ROLLINS

TOR PUBLISHING GROUP
NEW YORK

THE CRADLE OF ICE

Copyright © 2023 by James Czajkowski

All rights reserved.

Maps provided and drawn by Soraya Corcoran
Creature drawings provided and drawn by Danea Fidler

A Tor Book
Published by Tom Doherty Associates / Tor Publishing Group
120 Broadway
New York, NY 10271

www.tor-forge.com

Tor® is a registered trademark of Macmillan Publishing Group, LLC.

The Library of Congress Cataloging-in-Publication Data
is available upon request.

ISBN 978-1-250-76674-8 (hardcover)
ISBN 978-1-250-89046-7 (international, sold outside the U.S.,
subject to rights availability)
ISBN 978-1-250-76675-5 (ebook)

Our books may be purchased in bulk for promotional, educational, or business use.
Please contact your local bookseller or the Macmillan Corporate and Premium
Sales Department at 1-800-221-7945, extension 5442, or by email at
MacmillanSpecialMarkets@macmillan.com.

First U.S. Edition: 2023
First International Edition: 2023

Printed in the United States of America

0  9  8  7  6  5  4  3  2  1

TO VERONICA CHAPMAN,
*who started me on this road long ago.*
*I continue to follow the guideposts you left behind.*

*When the world stopped turning,*
*new lands were born.*

Steppes of
Giants

Lands of
Aglerolarpok

Eldgossi Isles

Boiling
Bay

THE ICE FANGS

Tartok Plains

Blackstone

Trader's
Ferry

Amik

Agate

Braidlands

CLOUDREACH

Keel Break

Anvil

Shrouds

Pilatuk

NORTHERN
HENGE

Eitur

Flint

Butcher's
Bay

The Twins

Of

Tatret
Lake

RIMEWOOD

Azantiia

Hel'sa

Chalk

Dalalæda

Savik

Bay of
Promise

CLIFFS OF LYRIA

Salt

Guld'Guhl
Territories

Fiskur

LANDFALL

Swamps of Myr

The Wastes

Tangleweed
Sea

THE FIST

Shield Islands

The Great
Gras

Kingdom of Hálendii

SOUTHERN
HENGE

Dödwood

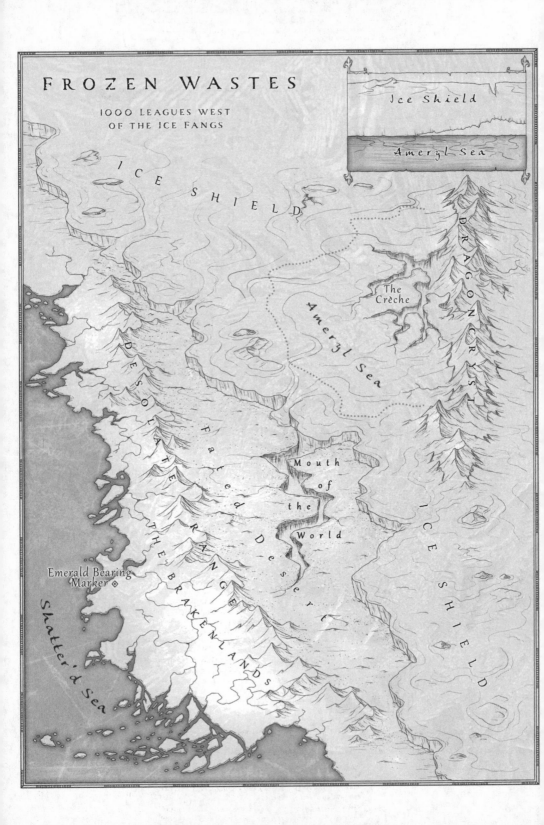

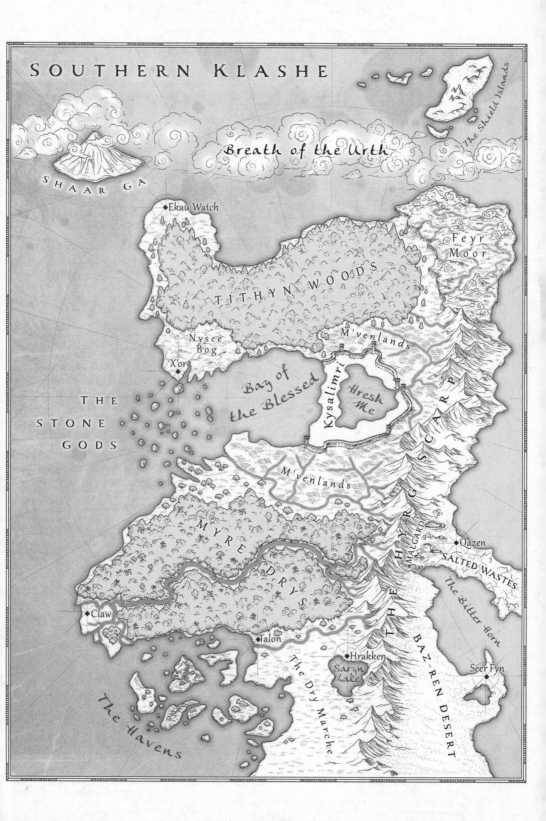

# THE
# CRADLE
# OF ICE

I sit frozen in place, a hand hovering over crisp parchment. Trepidation grips my heart, saps my will. My hand trembles. I seek any excuse not to continue her story. I make bargains and sift through arguments in my head. What difference would it make in the end? Who will read these words? Who will study the scribbled sketches of a past fallen into shadows? There are none who remember her, none who could recount the cost in blood, and strife, and misery.

Still, I must forge on—not for some future reader, not even for myself.

But for another.

She still stares at me from the sketchbook propped near the window, where each day's first light shines upon her ashen hair, the scowl of her lips, the jeweled blue of her eyes. That heavy gaze dares me to tell her story. It weighs upon me, burdens me, reminds me of a promise I made long ago.

Still, I have held off, resisted her. Two seasons have passed me by. I used that time to return to what I previously wrote, to scour for truths that escaped me with the first telling, details that might have portended what was to come. I reread how a beclouded girl regained her full sight, a cure found in poison, how she fled both prophecy and the king's legions. I saw how fate and folly drew the pieces of some grand game of Knights n' Knaves to her: a second-born prince, a broken knight, a recalcitrant thief, a figure sculpted of flowing bronze, along with countless other minor players. But none less than her winged brother who had come to share her song and heart, binding the two closer than any siblings.

Still, that was just the beginning.

The first tale was one of innocence, where even hope could be found amidst the bloodshed. It concluded with the forging of a purpose, a union to defy prophecy, to seek to melt the amber locking the Urth in place and set the world to turning again, to thwart the doom found in one word: moonfall.

What comes next is far harder to relate.

Worse yet, to write it is to live it again.

It is the story of innocence lost, of trust betrayed, of hope banished. It makes a mockery of what was written before. Even now I can hear her winged companion wailing in the dark. It is a pained chorus of bridle-song that binds me even now, that ices my blood and freezes my hand in place.

I do not wish to tell this story, to live it again.

*Still, in the dawn's light, she stares at me from my old sketchbook. Those eyes were painted with an oily crush of azure shells, but power resides there even now. As I meet that gaze, it breaks through the spell that binds me, enough for me to loosen those cold words trapped inside my chest.*

*So I begin.*

*I have languished for two seasons in my attic croft, which is auspiciously fitting—as where I pick up her tale, the same time has passed for her.*

# ONE

# THE ICE SHIELD

*Whenne frost burns skinne, who ken tell ice from fyre?*
—Found in *The Kronicles of Rega sy Noor,*
account from the first explorer beyond the Fangs,
who vanished during his second expedition

# 1

Nyx held her hand up against the brilliant swath of stars. The warmth of her breath misted the icy darkness, obscuring the view enough to make it look like some spellcast illusion. Alone atop the middeck of the *Sparrowhawk,* she gazed at the wonder above. She had never imagined such a radiant glittering existed beyond the sun's glare.

*Then again, how could I have known?*

As the wyndship continued its westward flight under the arch of the night's sky, she recognized how small her existence had been until recently. All her life had been spent within the Crown, where night was but a dimmer gloaming of the day. She pictured the bronze orrery in her old school's astronicum, where the sun was represented by a spherical kettle of hot coals around which tiny planets spun on wires and gears. She pictured the third orb—the Urth— driven by the orrery's complicated dance. As her world circled the sun, it never turned its face away. One side forever burned under the merciless blaze of the Father Above, while the other was forever forbidden His warmth, locked in eternal frozen darkness. The Crown lay between those extremes, the circlet of lands trapped between ice and fire, where the life-giving love of the Father Above nurtured those below.

*And now we've left it all far behind.*

She shifted her hand toward the reason for this perilous flight. With the cold numbing her bare fingers, she measured the full face of the moon, as bright as a lantern in these dark lands. She tried to judge if its countenance had swollen any larger, searching for evidence that her prophecy of moonfall could be true. She again heard the screams from her vision, felt the thunderous quake of the land—followed by the deafening silence of a world destroyed as the moon crashed into the Urth.

She could not tell if the moon's face had grown any bigger, but she did not doubt her poison-induced prophecy from half a year ago. Alchymist Frell had confirmed the same with his own measurements, in scopes far more precise than Nyx's fingers. According to him, the full moon had been growing incrementally larger, more so over the past decade. The bronze woman, Shiya, had even assigned a rough date to the world's end: *No longer than five years, maybe as short as three.*

Nyx felt the pressure of that narrowing time line. It weighed like a cartload of stones sitting atop her chest. Even when resting, she often found it hard to breathe. Their group had spent the tail of summer and most of autumn in preparation for this journey into the dark Frozen Wastes. They dared not rush their efforts, especially when so little was known about these icy lands. And now with the winter solstice rapidly approaching, they still had hundreds of leagues to travel, with time ticking rapidly away.

Despairing, she lowered her arm and slipped her fingers back into her fur-lined gloves. Since crossing over the mountainous Ice Fangs—that jagged barrier of snowy peaks that marked the boundary between the Crown and the Frozen Wastes—they had seen the moon had waxed and waned three times over. Thrice, Nyx had watched the dark Huntress chase the bright Son around and around. Each time the Son showed his full face again, Nyx had snuck away, like now, and climbed to the open deck of the *Sparrowhawk* to judge the moon's cold countenance.

Still, that was not the only reason she had abandoned the warmth of the ship for the frigid ice of the open middeck.

She shifted along the starboard rail, craning past the girth of the ponderous gasbag that obscured most of the sky. She searched for the telltale sickle of her brother's silhouette against the stars. Her ears strained for his call through the darkness. She heard the ice cracking loose from the huge draft-iron cables that linked ship to balloon, but all else lay quiet. Even the flashburn forges that propelled the vessel through the air remained silent, their baffles sealed against the cold, trying to keep the warmth locked inside the wyndship.

For most of the journey, the crew had relied on the current of the westward-flowing sky-river to carry them ever onward. The ship's forges certainly could have hastened their flight, but their supplies of flashburn had to be conserved, even with the extra tanks welded along the *Sparrowhawk*'s hull. They needed enough fuel not only for the trip out across the Wastes, but also for their return if they were successful in their quest.

She leaned farther over the rail, scanning the sky, her heart pounding slightly harder.

"Where are you?" she whispered through her scarf.

As she searched, the wind brushed the loose strands of her dark hair about her cheeks. The breeze no longer carried any hint of its former warmth. She pictured the twin rivers that flowed across the skies. The higher of the two—through which the ship traveled—carried the scathing heat of the sunblasted side of the Urth in a continual westward flow before returning in a colder stream that hugged land and sea. It was those two streams—forever flowing in two different directions—that blessed the lands of the Crown with a livable clime. Hieromonks believed it was due to the twin gods, the fiery Hadyss and the icy giant Madyss, who blew those rivers across the skies, while alchymists insisted it was due to some natural bellows created between the two extremes of the Urth.

She didn't know which to believe. All she knew for sure was that this far out into the Wastes, that hot river carried little of its life-giving warmth. And from here, their way would only grow colder. It was said that if one traveled far enough out into the Wastes, the very air turned to ice.

Knowing this, she searched the stars for her bonded brother. He needed these brief flights to stretch his wings and escape the tight confines of the *Sparrowhawk*'s lower hold. But he had been gone far longer than usual. Concern constricted her throat. Her limbs shivered from more than just the cold.

*Come back to me.*

As Nyx kept her vigil, the chime of the second bell of Eventoll echoed up to her from the ship's interior. She shivered in her coat, drawing its hood tighter to her cheeks. Her teeth had begun to chatter.

*He's been gone a full bell.*

Both frustrated and worried, she stared down at the spread of broken ice far below, reflecting the silvery sheen of the full moon. Finding no answers in the unending landscape of the Ice Shield, she stared upward again. She hummed under her breath, casting out a few strands of bridle-song.

"Where are you?" she sang to the stars.

Then she felt him: a tingle at the top of her spine that spread a warmth across the inside of her skull.

Relief escaped her in a misty exhalation.

"Bashaliia . . ."

A massive shadow swept low over the balloon and out in the sky before her. As the Mýr bat's wings cleaved across the starscape, he angled over on a tip and spun back around. With that turn, the tingling warmth grew into a soft keening, less heard than felt, a slight vibration of the bones in her ears.

She danced back from his approach. As he dove, his wings spread and cupped the air, slowing him. She retreated farther to make room. Luckily, she did. When he ducked under the gasbag, his claws released a massive haunch of some large beast. The chunk of carcass—easily a hundred stone in weight—bounced and slid across the deck, leaving behind a steaming trail of blood.

Bashaliia then landed himself. His claws skittered across the planks, digging for purchase, before finally coming to a stop.

Nyx sidestepped the gore and rushed up to her friend.

His wings folded around her, enveloping her. Velvety nostrils found her cheek. His warm breath panted over her. His body was a flaming hearth in the cold. She nestled into that warmth. Her fingers rubbed the dense fur behind one of his tall ears. Her other palm rested on his chest, feeling the thump of his heart. The beat was already slowing from the exertion of his hunt.

"Bashaliia, you mustn't be gone so long," she scolded softly. "You had me worried."

He hummed back his reassurance.

As he did, her fingers dug into his pelt. She appreciated how thick it had grown. His body had quickly adjusted to the cold—amazingly so. She was not the only one to notice. Krysh—the alchymist assigned by Frell to accompany them—had noted the changes: the extra layer of fat, his shaggier fur, even the thickening of Bashaliia's nasal flaps. It was as if the bat were mimicking the baffles of the ship's forges, narrowing all openings to keep heat inside. The alchymist had also leeched blood from her friend and reported changes there: *an increasing volume of red cyllilar matter, accompanied by an ever-protracted time for his blood to freeze.* Krysh attributed the latter to the appearance of ice-resistant chymicals, agents that still stymied identification. His conclusion: *It's as if the creature's entire form is rapidly changing to fit his new circumstance.*

Nyx wished the same were true for her.

Even encased in Bashaliia's warmth, she shivered. They needed to retreat below. She lifted her chin and softly sang, letting threads of bridle-song slip from her to him, sharing her desire to return to the warmth of the ship.

He briefly drew her tighter, using his long tail to reach around and scoop her closer. His heavy musk enveloped her. Despite his bodily changes, his scent remained a constant. She drew that musk into her lungs, letting it become part of her. It smelled of briny salt and damp fur, underlaid by a sulfurous hint of brimstan. Despite the passage of time, he still carried the scent of the swamplands with him. It reminded Nyx of her own home in those drowned lands, and all she had lost.

Her dah, her brothers, Bastan and Ablen . . .

*All dead.*

She drew in a deep draught of Bashaliia's musk, using that scent to stoke her memory. And not just that past shared with her family, but one that lay further back, nearly forgotten. She could picture little of it. It was a time made up of smells, tastes, touches. As a babe, she had been abandoned in the swamps after the death of her mother. She would not have survived that harsh landscape, but a she-bat discovered her and took her in. Nyx was nursed and sustained by the massive creature.

*And not just me.*

Nestled under those same wings, a small furry brother had shared those milky teats.

Her finger dug deeper.

*Bashaliia . . .*

His scent, the warmth of his body, served as a reminder that she had not lost *all* of her family during that horrible summer. She wanted to keep him close, to stay here longer, but she knew they both needed to retreat below.

She placed her palms against his chest and pushed out of the blanket of his wings. The cold struck her immediately. Frost already crusted the outer edges of Bashaliia's tall ears.

"Let's find us a warm stove and hope its coals have been freshly stoked."

She turned toward the raised aft deck and the doors that led down into the lower hold. Before she could step in that direction, the doors to the forecastle banged open behind her. She spun around, startled. The flare of lamplight momentarily blinded her.

Bashaliia's wings snapped wider, defensively, as he responded to her distress.

She lifted a calming hand to him, recognizing the intruder through the glare.

"Jace?" She struggled to understand his arrival. "What are you doing here?"

She knew her friend and former tutor despised the cold. Still, he headed toward her, huddled under a thick blanket, his breath huffing streams of white. He kept a wary eye on his footing as he crossed the frosty planks of the deck.

"There's something I wanted to talk to you about in private," he said. "Something curious, maybe important. Then Graylin caught me as I headed up here. He's ordering everyone to the wheelhouse. Darant spotted something ahead. Something worrisome from Graylin's grim tones."

"He always sounds grim," she reminded him.

"Mayhap, but we'd better hurry. Especially since he doesn't know you're up here alone."

"I'm hardly alone." She patted Bashaliia, who had tucked his wings in again.

"I don't think Graylin would take any solace in that detail."

Nyx knew Jace was correct. Despite their confinement in the swyftship, she and Graylin had grown no closer. The man might be her father, but then again, he might not be. Still, he continually sought to assert some manner of control over her. She rankled at his ever-present shadow and searched for any moments to escape it.

*Like now . . .*

She recognized that it was not only Bashaliia who needed a respite from the ship's close quarters.

Jace frowned at her, his lips set in a familiar firm line whenever he was confronted by her obstinance. "If Graylin ever learns that I knew about your little sojourns onto the open deck, he'd yank the beard right off my cheeks."

She reached over and tugged at the drape of red curls under his jawline. "It seems secure enough to me."

He pushed her hand down, a blush rising to his cheeks despite the cold. "Let's keep it that way."

She smiled. "The heavier beard does look good on you. It seems both you and Bashaliia are growing furrier with each passing league."

His cheeks flushed a deeper crimson. "Like him, it's not for *looks,* but to keep me warm."

She shrugged, casting him a doubtful glance. "Help me get Bashaliia below, and we'll head over to the wheelhouse."

He gruffed under his breath, but she saw him comb his curls back into place after her ruffling. As the wind caught and parted his sheltering blanket, she also noted how else her friend had changed. Where Bashaliia had added a layer of warming fat, Jace had trimmed down. During the voyage, he had been sparring regularly with Darant and Graylin, honing his skills with both fist and ax. Additionally, as the ship's larder was tightly rationed, he had shed a fair amount of his bulk.

Still, there was no removing the scholar from this novice warrior.

Despite his plain desire to escape the cold, Jace crossed toward the bloody haunch left on the deck. "Where did this come from?"

"Bashaliia's been hunting," she explained.

He squinted at the hoofed end of the carcass. "Three-toed and white-furred. He must've taken down one of the martoks. Though from the leg's small size, one of their yearling calves." He reached to the pelt and pinched up a bit of moss, which glowed faintly in the dark. "Fascinating. We should bring this leg to Krysh and see what else we can learn about those giants that roam the Ice Shield."

Nyx disagreed. "It's Bashaliia's kill. He clearly needs more sustenance than can be found in our thinning stores. In fact, he should probably hunt more often before it gets any colder."

"True." Jace straightened and rubbed his belly. "The more he can sustain himself, the slower our larder will wane. I'll have a couple of the crew drag the leg below and salt it down."

"Thank you."

As they headed to the aft deck, he stared longingly at the haunch, but with a hunger born of curiosity. "Who imagined such massive creatures foraged these frozen lands?"

Nyx understood his interest. Through the ship's farscopes, she had spied the massive herds of martoks ranging the broken ice fields. The shaggy, curl-horned bulls looked to stand as high as the third tier of her old school. The cows were only slightly smaller. The herds appeared to feed on tussocks of phosphorescent moss that grew across the ice, ripping up sections with their tusks. Krysh—whose decades of alchymical interest focused on the Wastes—had studied dried samples of the same plant, collected during rare excursions by foolhardy explorers. He said it was called *is'veppir* and claimed the cold foliage was more related to mushrooms than mosses.

"Who knew such life could exist out here?" Nyx said, and stared to the west. "We'll soon be beyond where anyone has ever set foot."

"Not necessarily." Jace's voice lowered with a studious distraction that was as familiar as Bashaliia's musk. "I've been reading accounts of those who dared venture beyond the Fangs. *The Kronicles of Rega sy Noor. The Illumination of the Sunless Clime.* Even a book that Krysh claimed was stolen from the Gjoan Arkives, a tome that dates back seven centuries. It's what I found in those pages that I wanted to discuss with you, to talk it over before I brought it up with the others."

By now they'd reached the double doors that led off the deck and down into the ship's hold. She tugged the way open and turned to him. "What did you find?"

"If what's written is true, we may not be alone in the Wastes. There could be other people."

She scowled in disbelief.

*That's impossible. Who could live out here?*

Jace held up a palm. "Hear me out, and I'll—"

The entire ship jolted under them. Thunder boomed across the clear skies. On the starboard side, a flume of flame shot from the lower hull and across the sky. Chunks of draft-iron and shattered wood exploded high above the rail. A few pieces came close to ripping through the balloon. The blast shoved the *Sparrowhawk* into a hard spin. Strained cables screamed and twanged under the sudden assault. The deck canted steeply.

Nyx lost her footing, but she kept a grip on the door.

Untethered, Jace slammed hard to the planks, hitting his chest. He slid across the icy deck away from her. Half tangled in his blanket, he gasped and clawed and scrabbled to halt his plunge.

"Jace!" she hollered, and dropped to her backside. Maintaining her hold on the door, she shoved out a leg for him to grab, but he was already out of reach.

Bashaliia lunged past her, flying low. He dove at Jace, falling upon him like a hawk on a rabbit. Claws stabbed through the blanket. Jace cried out in pain as those sharp nails found flesh, too. Then with a single beat of wings, Bashaliia wrenched back to Nyx with his captured prize.

"Get inside!" Nyx yelled, and led the way.

With alarm bells echoing throughout the ship, she fell through the door and crawled down into the short passageway. Bashaliia tossed Jace after her, then clambered in behind them, ducking low and squeezing through.

Jace groaned, sat up, and leaned his back against the wall. "What happened?"

Nyx stared past the open door. By now, the *Sparrowhawk*'s spin had already slowed, the deck leveling again. The flames had sputtered out, but a smoldering glow persisted on the ship's starboard side.

She faced Jace, swallowing hard before speaking, fearful of even voicing the possibility, knowing the disaster it portended. "One of the ship's forges must've exploded."

## 2

It didn't take long for Nyx's fears to be confirmed.

She stood beside Jace in the crowded wheelhouse of the *Sparrowhawk*. Everyone gathered around a pock-faced crewman named Hyck. Time had weathered the old man down to tendon and gristle, but his eyes still shone with a sharp fervor. He was a former alchymist who had been defrocked ages ago and now served as the ship's engineer.

He rubbed a rag between his hands, trying to erase a residue of greasy flashburn from his palms but only smearing it around instead. "Lucky it were only the starboard maneuvering forge that blew. If it were the stern engine, we'd never be able to limp our way back to the Crown."

Nyx shared a concerned look with Jace. She knew the swyftship had three forges, a pair to either side and a huge one at the stern end of the keel.

"Have the fires been put out?" Darant asked.

"Aye," Hyck answered. "First thing we did. Flames be the greater danger here than any blast. Your two daughters be surveying the rest of the damage, seeing if there's anything to be salvaged."

Darant paced the breadth of the wheelhouse. This was the brigand's ship, and any damage it took was as if it were to his own body. His face remained a dark thundercloud. He kept a fist clenched on the hilt of one of his whip-swords. A dark blue half-cloak flagged behind him, a match to his breeches and shirt, as he pounded across the planks.

Graylin lifted a hand. "Does this mean we'll have to turn back, return to the Crown?"

Hyck opened his mouth, only to be cut off by Darant. "Sard we will!" the pirate exclaimed, half withdrawing the slim blade as if ready to attack anyone who challenged him. "This li'l hawk might have a damaged wing, but she can still fly true enough. We can compensate for the loss of the starboard forge. Like Hyck said, our stern engine is what matters most. We continue onward."

Graylin turned to Nyx. Concern narrowed his eyes, allowing only a hint of silvery blue to show, like a vein of ice in his rocky features. There was little other color to be found in the man. It was as if the legend of the Forsworn Knight—a tale that wove Nyx and Graylin together in tragedy—had turned him into a book's etching, a figure drawn in shades of black and gray. His dark hair and scruff of beard were salted with white. Some strands were weathered by age; others marked the sites of buried scars. Yet, not all of his old wounds were hidden, like the crook in his nose and a jagged weal under his left eye. They were all testaments to his punishment for falling in love and breaking an oath to the king of Hálendii.

A growl rose. While it didn't flow from Graylin, it might as well have. It expressed a mix of frustration and anger. The knight's shadow shifted farther into view. The vargr's amber-gold eyes glowed out of coal-black fur. Muscular haunches bunched, ruffling the tawny stripes buried there, like sunlight dappling through a dark canopy. The vargr's tufted ears stood tall, swiveling back and forth, seeking the source of the danger that had set everyone on edge.

Nyx hummed under her breath and wove over a calming thread of bridle-song. It wound into the rumble of that growl, tamping down the vargr's guardedness.

Graylin tried his own method, resting a calloused palm on the beast's shoulder. "Settle, Kalder."

The vargr swished his tail twice more, then sank to a seat, but his ears remained tall and stiff.

During her brief connection with Kalder, Nyx had sensed the wildness constrained in that strong heart. Some mistook Kalder to be a mere hunting dog, one obedient to Graylin. Nyx knew their attachment ran deeper, a bond born not only of trust and respect, but also of shared pain and loss. The memory of Kalder's brother, lost half a year ago, still echoed inside that stalwart chest. She heard whispers of chases through cold forests, of a warmth that only a brother curled at one's side could bring.

Kalder's edginess was also likely due to the months of confinement aboard the *Sparrowhawk*. Such magnificent beasts were never meant to be caged.

Graylin turned from the group and stared out the row of forward windows. "Darant, I trust your faith in your ship, but perhaps caution should outweigh conviction in this regard. If we lose the *Sparrowhawk,* then all is lost. Rather than rush headlong—"

"No!" Nyx blurted out.

As everyone turned her way, she refused to shrink under the combined weight of their gazes. She remembered the three turns of the moon it had taken them to get this far. To return to the Crown would take just as long. And they'd still have to make the crossing again to return to this spot.

"We'd lose half a year," she said. "We can't afford that. We must reach the site Shiya showed us on her globe."

"We understand," Graylin said. "But Shiya also told us we had at least three years, maybe five, before moonfall became inevitable. We have some latitude for cautiousness."

"No. No, we don't."

"Nyx . . ."

She shook her head, knowing a good portion of Graylin's restraint was born of concern for her. Pain shone in his eyes. While she might not be his daughter, she was still the child of the woman he had once loved. Graylin had long believed Nyx had died in the Mýr swamps, only to have her miraculously resurrected and returned to him. He clearly did not intend to lose her again.

But she dismissed his concerns. They did not matter.

Instead, Nyx pictured the shimmering mirage of their world cast forth by Shiya's crystal cube. An emerald marker had glowed deep in the Frozen Wastes. That was their destination, though little was known about it. Not even Shiya could guess what lay out there, only that the site was important. For any hope of stopping the moon from crashing into the Urth, they had to set their world to turning again, as it had countless millennia ago. Somehow that glowing marker was vital to accomplishing that seemingly impossible task.

"We don't know what we'll find out there," Nyx warned. "Or how long it will take to pry answers from that mystery. We can't risk any further delays. For as much as we know, we may already be too late."

She kept her face fixed, both to show her determination and to hide the deeper part of her that hoped they *were* too late. If they set the Urth to spinning again—something that still seemed incomprehensible to her—it would herald its own catastrophe. The world would be ravaged in that turning tide. Shiya had shown them this, too. The massive floods, the quakes, the storms that would rip around the planet. Millions upon millions would die.

Nyx understood this fate was far better than the eradication of *all* life should moonfall occur. Yet, in her heart, she could not dismiss the untold suffering that would result if they were successful. She knew it was necessary, but she kept a secret hope guarded close to her heart.

*Let those deaths not be by my own hand.*

"The lass is right," Darant said. "If we turn around, we may never make it back out here again. War is brewing across the Crown. Back when we left, the skirmishes between Hálendii and the Southern Klashe had been worsening. Coastal villages raided and burned. Sabotage and assassinations. On both sides of the Breath. Who knows what we'll discover if we return? We could become trapped and embroiled by the fighting. And don't forget your old friend King Toranth, and his Iflelen dogs. They're still hunting us. Best not we give them another chance to close that noose."

"Still, those arguments don't take into account what lies *ahead* of us." Graylin pointed at Darant. "Even before the explosion, you had me summon everyone to the wheelhouse because you were already worried about the path of our flight from here."

Nyx glanced to Jace. She had forgotten how Graylin had ordered everyone to gather here. The explosion and mayhem had diverted all attention.

"What's wrong?" Nyx asked. "What lies ahead?"

"See for yourself." Graylin led them toward the arc of windows fronting the wheelhouse. The view looked out across the moonlit fields of broken ice. "The navigator, Fenn, spotted the danger earlier through the ship's farscopes. But you can see it plainly enough now that we've sailed closer."

The group spread out across the bay of windows. Nyx searched below the ship, but the view looked the same as it had for months. The full moon's brightness reflected off the ice, casting the world in shades of silver and blue. Huge swaths of *is'veppir* moss, aglow in hues of crimson and emerald, etched the frozen landscape. As she squinted, she made out swaths of darker dots. *Martoks,* she realized. They gathered into vast herds, sharing warmth, moving slowly.

Nyx frowned. "I don't see what—"

Jace gasped next to her. "Look to the horizon."

She shifted her gaze out farther. The ice spread all the way to the night sky, dappled in bright stars. She shook her head, still not seeing anything. Then she realized that the stars did not reach the ice. They vanished high above the horizon line. Her vision shifted, or maybe a drift of cloud cleared the moon. Then she saw it, too. The world ended at a line of jagged peaks, blocking the stars and their path ahead. The range of mountains, all black and sharp-edged, thrust high out of the ice, forming a shattered rampart.

"That must be Dragoncryst," Jace said. "The peaks were named by Rega sy Noor in his *Kronicles*. During his first overland expedition two centuries ago, the explorer sighted them from a distance but couldn't reach them. He named the range because the mountains looked like the crested back of a great sea creature bursting through the ice."

"He's not wrong about that," Darant grumbled. "But this beast may prove more troublesome."

"Why?" Nyx asked.

Graylin answered, not turning from the window, "The peaks don't just breach the ice, but also block both sky-rivers."

Nyx pictured the high warm winds driving them westward and the colder flow running eastward, hugging closer to the ice.

Darant turned to the ship's navigator, who was bent over the eyepiece of the *Sparrowhawk*'s farscope. "How's it look, Fenn?"

The navigator straightened and turned to face them. He was young, likely only seven or eight years older than Nyx. He was lithe of limb, with white-blond locks and green eyes that suggested he might have some Bhestyan blood, a people who dwelled on the far side of the Crown—though he refused to talk about his past. Still, he was also the least dire of the crew. He always had a ready smile and a boundless well of jokes.

That smile was gone now. "It's worse than I thought," Fenn said. "The skies are roiled into a huge storm that sits atop those peaks. I wager that tempest never subsides, forever powered by the war of those contrary winds."

"Can we cross through it?" Graylin asked. "Especially with one of our maneuvering forges gone?"

Fenn glanced at Darant, who nodded for the navigator to speak his mind. Fenn sighed and shrugged. "Only one way to find out. No one's ever sailed over those peaks. We'll be the first."

"That's not necessarily true," Jace corrected.

Everybody turned to him.

Jace explained, "Rega—the explorer knight who named those mountains— set off on a second expedition, intent to cross the Dragoncryst, only this time he traveled by air, in a ship called the *Fyredragon,* named after those peaks."

Fenn's eyes twinkled, showing a gleam of his usual amusement. "Aye, but as I understand it, he never *returned* from that second trek."

"True," Jace admitted dourly.

Nyx nudged him. "You should tell them what you told me outside on the middeck."

Graylin stiffened with shock. "The middeck? Nyx, what were you doing outside?"

She ignored him. "Tell them, Jace."

Her friend nodded and faced the others. "I've had plenty of time to read through most of the historicals that relate to the Wastes, recorded by those rare few who dared travel into the ice. One claims that there are clans of people who live beyond the Dragoncryst."

Darant grunted sourly. "Who? Who could live out here?"

Jace's brows pinched with concern. "According to *The Annals of Skree,* a book secured from the Gjoan Arkives, they're *a chary tribe of daungrous peple who abide amidst dedly beasts and gret monsters.*"

"They sound delightful," Fenn mumbled.

Jace turned toward the storm-riven horizon. "It is said Rega read the same tome and set off to search for those tribes during his second expedition."

"From which he never returned," Fenn reminded them again.

Before anyone could respond, a clatter of boots and raised voices erupted from the other side of the wheelhouse. The door to the main passageway burst open, and a flurry of figures rushed inside. They were led by the bronze figure of Shiya. Though sculpted of hard metal, she moved with grace. The shining glass of her eyes took in those gathered in the wheelhouse. From the dark stains marring her modest shift, she had accompanied the others to survey the ruins of the flashburn forge. They had likely leaned upon her considerable strength to help search the wreckage. As she entered, the lamplight reflected off the contours of her face, but her expression remained unreadable.

Those who came with her were far less stoic. The stocky form of Rhaif hy Albar—the Guld'guhlian thief who had rescued the bronze woman from the depths of the mines of Chalk—came around Shiya's left side. A litany of curses flowed from his lips.

"What's wrong?" Darant asked, stepping closer.

Rhaif stemmed his tide of profanities and waved to Shiya's other side. "Best your daughter tell you."

Glace crossed around the bronze woman to meet her father. Her almond complexion was flushed darker. She shoved a braided blond tail behind her shoulder with one hand and held forth her other palm.

"We found this buried amidst the ruins of the forge's fuel assembly."

They all gathered closer. A knot of dark iron lay twisted in Glace's white-knuckled grip. It looked like a black egg that had burst open. A bitter smell of burnt alchymicals accompanied it.

"What is it?" Nyx asked.

Graylin scowled. "A stykler."

Nyx gave a small shake of her head.

Jace explained. "A shell packed full of iron filings and glass that turns molten."

Glace kept her eyes upon her father. "Brayl and Krysh are already examining the other two forges, to make sure there are no more bombs hidden there, too."

Nyx stared down at the blasted object. "A bomb?"

"Not just a bomb," Darant growled, and glared around the room. "It's sabotage."

# 3

GRAYLIN GRIPPED THE hilt of his sword. He sought to center himself with its strength and familiarity. Heartsthorn had been in his family for eighteen generations. The blade was as much a part of him as his own arm. Still, his clasp was so hard that the silver thorns of the sculpted pommel stung his palm.

"We have a traitor amongst us," Graylin growled to the trio of men gathered around a scarred ironwood table.

He had already sent Nyx below with Kalder, to bed the beast down in the quiet of the hold. The earlier commotion and anger surrounding the revelation of a saboteur aboard the ship had riled up the vargr, setting him to growling and snapping at everything. Only Nyx could control that wild heart. Jace had gone, too, accompanied by Shiya to guard over them.

Afterward, Graylin had retired with the three men to a small chart room off the wheelhouse, intent on continuing their deliberations in private. A single lamp hung from a chain overhead, illuminating the cramped space. The walls were covered in hundreds of round cubbies crammed with curled scrolls of countless maps. Atop the table, a drawing of the Frozen Wastes had been nailed to its surface. A sextant rested atop it, along with a sheaf of papers with scrawled calculations in charcoal, marking the labors of the navigator.

Rhaif leaned against the door, making sure they weren't interrupted. Or maybe he was simply resting his back. The knees of his leggings were stained black. He reeked of smoke and burnt oil. His fiery hair, grown lanky and long during the voyage, lay plastered with sweat after helping with the wrecked forge.

"A traitor with us," Rhaif spat sourly. "As if we don't have enough trouble."

"Live long enough, and you learn life is nothing but trouble," Darant commented. "Still, the alternative is worse. So best get your joy where and when you can."

Graylin frowned over at the man. "You're taking this revelation of a saboteur in our midst in fair stride."

"I'm a brigand. For me, betrayal and duplicity are as common a commodity as coin and sword." Darant leaned his fists on the table, his eyes flashing with fire. "But don't get me wrong, I'll flay whoever damaged the *Hawk*. That I'll not abide."

The final member of the gathering cleared his throat. Alchymist Krysh was bent over the pinned map with his head cocked to the side, but his thoughts were more likely on the new threat. He glanced up, revealing sharp gray eyes.

"We must consider the possibility that the saboteur might not be aboard the swyftship," he said, straightening to his full height.

Krysh's complexion was burnished copper, like a sunburn that never faded. His long black hair was tied into an oiled braid, a match to the dark robe of his order. But he was also no frail scholar. He stood a handsbreadth taller than Graylin, and though into his fifth decade, he kept his body well muscled. And no wonder. The man had grown up among the rugged ranchlands of Aglero-larpok, which notoriously hardened its people into leather and bone. Beyond that, Graylin had learned only an abbreviated version of the man's history, but Frell insisted Krysh could be trusted.

Despite that reassurance, Graylin's suspicions jangled through him, stoked by the sabotage.

*How much do we really know about him?*

Rhaif pushed off the door and stood straighter, one brow raised quizzically at the alchymist's statement. "Krysh, the saboteur must be aboard the *Sparrow-hawk*. Someone had to plant that stykler, yes?"

Krysh nodded. "Certainly. But a stykler is uniquely designed. It can be packed with a smolder fuse, a cord wound tightly inside and coated in insulating amalgam. Such fuses could be lit and take up to a year to finally reach the bomb's combustible core."

Darant's eyes narrowed. "Are you saying someone could've planted it aboard my ship before we left the Crown?"

"It's possible. At least something we should consider. The saboteur could have set a long fuse, wanting us to travel far across the Shield before it blew."

"Stranding us," Graylin muttered.

Darant rubbed his chin. "Krysh could be right. Back at my camp, our preparations for this voyage dragged on. Word could've reached the wrong ears. I know all too well how any trust can be broken under the weight of enough gold."

Rhaif looked little convinced and waved at the pirate. "But according to your daughter, the other two forges were not tampered with."

"Aye," Darant agreed. "Brayl wouldn't have missed anything. She's got sharper eyes than any eagle. And with my two daughters now guarding those forges, they'll remain untouched."

Graylin understood the thrust of Rhaif's inquiry. "If the stykler was hidden before we launched, why cripple only the portside maneuvering forges? Why not take out all three? Then we'd be stranded for sure."

"Maybe they wanted to keep us from reaching our destination but not kill us outright," Krysh offered.

Rhaif huffed. "So a saboteur with a conscience."

Krysh shrugged. "Or maybe the intent was to force us to limp back. Where we'd be captured and interrogated once we returned to the Crown. Whoever is trying to thwart us might not know our goal, and if we died out here, that knowledge would be lost."

Darant stood stiffer. "All the more reason we keep going, I say."

Krysh looked across the group. "Before we make that decision and despite my angle of inquiry, I must caution that I *do* believe the saboteur is still aboard the *Sparrowhawk*. As much as we all might wish otherwise."

"Why?" Graylin asked.

"The most likely scenario—which is usually the right one—is that the traitor damaged only the portside forge because he wouldn't want to die by his own actions. Gold seldom buys martyrdom."

"True," Darant said.

Krysh continued, "I also find it significant that the saboteur waited until we were faced with crossing the Dragoncryst before making his move. He probably thought crippling us now, with such rough winds ahead, would surely drive us back."

Graylin nodded at the alchymist's logic. It seemed Frell had chosen well in picking this man. "If you're right, how do we root this traitor out?"

"We don't," Darant answered.

Graylin scowled over at them.

Darant explained, "We're crewed with thirteen men and five women. The traitor could be any one of them. Or even *more* than one. To ferret out the culprit or culprits would be next to impossible."

"What do we do, then?"

Darant shrugged. "We trust in the saboteur's love of his own life—as demonstrated so far. I'll keep my daughters guarding the forges, but I suspect they're safe for now. If the traitor acts again, it'll likely be in a manner that doesn't end up getting the bastard killed, too. We'll have to be ready for that. To keep a wary watch on those around us."

A loud knock drew their attention to the door.

"We're nearing the mountains!" Fenn called through to them. "Another bell and we'll be at the edge of the storms. What's your orders, sir?"

All eyes fell upon Darant. The pirate waited until he got nods from everyone, making sure he had unanimous consent—or maybe he wanted to be able to spread the blame if the decision proved disastrous.

Darant shouted to Fenn, "Warn the ship! We need every loose feather of the *Hawk* pinned down before we get to those mountains."

The pirate faced the group again, pressing the back of his thumb to his lips in a Klashean bid for luck. "Saboteur be damned, we *will* make it over those mountains."

Rhaif looked dubious. "Even if we make it, what'll we find? Remember that lad's warning from earlier. Of *daungrous peple* and *gret monsters*."

Krysh slowly nodded. "If those legends prove true, a traitor amongst us will be the least of our problems."

Arkival limne of
Martoks
(native to the
Ice Shield)

# TWO

# A PRINCE IN EXILE

*Kysalimri—the Eternal Citi of the Southern Klashe—is
the oldest settlement in all the Crown. Under its deepest
roots lies stone & iren that herken to the Forsaken Ages,
dread'd seeds of a time lost to historie. But from those seeds,
a gret city grew, spreadyng from the Bay of the Bless'd to
the foot'd hills of the Hyrg Scarp, crossyng hundreds of
leuges in everi direction. It is less a mark on a map than a
kingdom alle its own, divid'd by ancient walls, but unit'd
by blood & purpose. It is sayd: if Kysalimri æfrer falls, so
will the world.*

—From the eighty-volume treatise,
Lyrrasta's *Geographica Comprehendinge*

# 4

THE SECOND-BORN PRINCE of Hálendii struggled with his chains as he crossed toward the rail of the pleasure barge. The silver links ran from Kanthe ry Massif's ankles up to the collars of the two chaaen-bound escorts who trailed behind him. Even after spending a full season in Kysalimri, the Eternal City of the Southern Klashe, he had not acquired the skill necessary to fluidly match his stride to those bound to him.

His left leg tried to reach out, only to be brought up short by his chained ankle. He flailed his arms in an entirely unprincely manner, attempting to catch his balance, but recognized it was a lost cause. He fell headlong toward the deck—then a firm hand gripped his shoulder and caught him. His rescuer chuckled as he drew Kanthe upright and helped him over to the rail.

"Thanks, Rami," Kanthe said. "You just saved me from breaking this handsome nose of mine."

"We certainly cannot have that, my friend, especially with your nuptials only a moon's turn away." Rami nodded toward a raised dais in the center of the wide boat. "Of course, my sister, Aalia, would not tolerate her beloved to be so marred on her most perfect of days."

Kanthe glanced across the deck to the velvet divan. Sheltered under the barge's sails, Aalia im Haeshan rested atop a nest of pillows, seated on one hip. She was a shadowed rose, adorned in silk robes woven with golden threads. Her oiled braids, as dark as polished ebony, draped her shoulders. An embroidered bonnet bedecked in rubies and sapphires crowned her head. Her black eyes stared askance, coldly, not even once glancing toward her betrothed.

Kanthe studied her. It was only the fourth time he had laid eyes upon her since arriving on these shores. *My future bride,* he lamented silently. While only a year older than Kanthe's seventeen winters, she looked far more mature, certainly more than a prince who had fled to these shores, a prince considered to be a traitor to his own people.

Contrarily, Aalia was held in the highest esteem. It was evident by those who kept her company. Twelve chaaen-bound knelt around her, six to a side. The dozen, like Kanthe's two escorts, were cloaked under robes, their heads capped in leather, their faces hidden behind veils tucked into their neck collars. Such Klashean *byor-ga* garb was required of the baseborn when outside their homes. Only those of the single ruling class, known as the *imri,* which meant *godly* in their tongue, were allowed to show their faces. The hundreds of other castes had to remain covered from crown to toe, apparently deemed too unworthy for the Father Above to gaze upon them. This applied also to the Chaaen, who were schooled at the *Bad'i Chaa,* the House of Wisdom, the sole school of the city, an establishment notorious both for its rigorousness and cruelty. The higher you were among the *imri,* the more Chaaen were bound to you, serving as aides, advisers, counselors, teachers, and sometimes objects of pleasure.

Resigned to his fate, Kanthe turned to stare across the Bay of the Blessed.

Rami kept to Kanthe's side. Aalia's brother was accompanied by six Chaaen of his own, three to a side, chained one after the other. Rami im Haeshan was the fourth son of the Imri-Ka, the god-emperor of the Klashe. He was considered of lesser rank among his siblings—unlike his younger sister, Aalia, the emperor's sole daughter, who was held forth as the empire's greatest treasure.

*And I'm to marry her on the night of the winter's solstice.*

He wiped sweat from his forehead with the edge of his gilded sleeve. Unlike the Chaaen, who were required to wear the *byor-ga* garb, he had been decked in a *gerygoud* habiliment, which consisted of tight breeches shoved into snakeskin boots and a sleeveless tunic, all covered in a white robe with long-splayed sleeves that reached his knees. A cap of gold finished the outfit. It was the clothing of royalty. The Imri-Ka had granted Kanthe honorary *imri* status shortly after he had arrived here.

*A better welcome than being thrown naked into a dank cell, I suppose.*

Though with each passing day, he wondered if such a fate might not have been better. He heard the shuffle of Aalia's entourage as the emperor's daughter rose from her divan. She crossed toward the ship's opposite rail, plainly avoiding him.

The royal assemblage had spent the sweltering morning gliding across the Bay of the Blessed, winding among the Stone Gods, the thirty-three isles and outcroppings that had been carved into representations of the Klashean pantheon, all thirty-three of them. Rami had tried to instruct Kanthe on the deities' names and their respective domains within the holy hierarchy, but they all blurred together.

Rami remained determined and pointed ahead, toward a stone sculpture of a naked man with a rather prominent appendage between his legs, who carried a pudgy baby under one arm. Flowers and baskets of offerings lay festooned about his stone feet.

"Here comes Har'll, in all his majesty and prominence." Rami lifted a brow toward Kanthe. "He is our god of fertility."

"It's certainly plain *why* he gained that reputation." Kanthe waved past the statue. "Mayhap it's best for now if we give him a wide berth."

Rami laughed. "I'm sure you will sire many children. I've seen you in the baths. While you may not be as blessed as Har'll, you will make my sister very happy."

Kanthe coughed at such frankness. His face flushed hot. He tried to stammer away his discomfort. He still flustered at the ease with which the Klashean discussed such matters openly, with nary a bit of shame.

Unfortunately, Rami wasn't done. "Of course, that applies to *anyone* you'd share your bed with."

The man's fingers slid down the rail to touch Kanthe's hand, the invitation plain. It wasn't the first hint that Rami would like to explore their relationship beyond their already warm friendship. Rami was a couple of years older, but Kanthe sensed nothing predatory or manipulative. It was simply an open invitation.

Kanthe had already known about the changeableness of Klashean relationships, both inside and outside of wedlock. Hálendiians ridiculed such behavior and considered it further proof that the Klasheans were immoral. Kanthe had always found such an aspersion to be hypocritical, especially considering the abundance of whorehouses throughout Hálendii, not to mention all the men and women indentured into sexual servitude. Even his father kept a palacio of pleasure serfs at Highmount.

If anything, Kanthe found the openness here to be more honest. He had talked to Frell about it in their rooms. The alchymist had theorized that the fluidity found here might have something to do with the Klasheans' strict caste system, one that was rigid and overly complex.

*When one screw tightens, another often loosens,* Frell had offered.

Kanthe patted Rami's hand and turned to lean against the rail. While Kanthe had been in these lands for a season, he still hadn't found his way to becoming that *loose*.

Rami grinned and took a matching position against the portside rail. He clearly took no offense at Kanthe's rejection. Aalia's brother likely had no trouble filling his bed. He was tall, straight-backed, with the same handsomely dark eyes as his sister and a complexion like steeped bitterroot with honey. But more importantly, Rami had proven to be a good friend, acting as guide and teacher on all matters Klashean. And if Kanthe was honest with himself, Rami's attention was flattering, a boost to his own esteem.

Especially considering Aalia's abundant disregard.

Kanthe glanced across the barge. Aalia stood on the starboard side, shading a hand over her eyes to stare up at the next god gliding past their boat.

The purpose of the morning voyage had been for Kanthe and Aalia to spend time together, to converse politely under the gaze of a trio of chaperones, to perhaps get to know one another before the solstice. Aalia had only spoken one word to Kanthe: *mashen'dray,* which meant *step aside.* He had been blocking her view of one of the Stone Gods. He also noted that she used the word *dray,* an appellation when one addressed someone of a baseborn caste. It seemed not everyone was willing to accept Kanthe's honorary *imri* status.

Kanthe couldn't blame her.

*No one who truly knows me would consider me "godly," certainly not the Illuminated Rose of the Imri-Ka.*

He gave a shake of his head. Even as a prince of Hálendii, he was held with little regard in his homeland. For all his life, Kanthe had lived in the shadow of his twin brother, Mikaen, who had shouldered out of their mother's womb first, earning his birthright, destined from that moment for the throne. As such, Mikaen had been doted upon and cherished, readying him for his fate as future king of Hálendii.

Kanthe had a far less illustrious upbringing. He was delegated to being the Prince in the Cupboard, whose only use in life was to be a spare in case his older twin should die. His lot was to sit on a shelf in case he was ever needed. Still, to be of some usefulness to the kingdom, he had been trained at the school of Kepenhill, to prepare him to serve as future adviser to his brother.

*Not that such a fate will ever come about now.*

As he stood at the ship's rail, Kanthe flashed to Mikaen lunging at him with a sword. Despair weighed heavily at this memory. Worse, it hadn't been the first time that Mikaen had tried to kill him.

Kanthe sighed, still finding it all hard to fathom. As children, the two had been boon companions, as close as only twins could be—until their destinies inevitably pulled them apart. Mikaen was sent to the castle's Legionary to be trained in all manner of strategy and weaponry. Kanthe was expelled beyond the castle walls to Kepenhill, forbidden to even wield a sword.

A gulf eventually opened between them. How could it not? They became as different as their faces. Though a twin to Kanthe, Mikaen looked as if he had been sculpted out of pale chalkstone, sharing their father's countenance, including his curled blond locks and sea-blue eyes. Kanthe took after their dead mother. His skin was burnished ebonwood, his hair as black as coal, his eyes a stormy gray. He was forever a shadow to his brother's brightness.

*And now here I am, exiled among the kingdom's enemies.*

Kanthe had thrown his lot in with Nyx and the others, intent on stopping the doom to come. He searched the skies and spotted the full moon sitting near the horizon. It shone within the smoky haze of the Breath of the Urth, which marked the boundary between Hálendii and the Southern Klashe. The haze—made up of ash and fumes—rose from Shaar Ga, a massive volcanic peak that had been erupting for untold centuries, creating a natural smoky barrier between kingdom and empire.

Kanthe tried to imagine what was happening back in Azantiia. He suspected word of him reaching these shores had made it to Highmount and his father, King Toranth. Such a landfall would be taken as a betrayal, one to be stacked upon the others. They would assume Kanthe was siding with the Southern Klashe as war drums grew louder across the northern Crown. But again, that was not why he had come here.

He scowled at the smoke-shrouded moon.

*It's all your fault.*

As if scolding him for this thought, a blast of thunder boomed in the distance and echoed across the forested shores. It was so loud the waters of the bay trembled.

Kanthe straightened, shaken out of his dreary reveries. He stared up at the clear blue skies, then down to the northern horizon. A patch of the Breath's haze had darkened, blackened by fresh smoke—but the new pall hadn't been belched out by Shaar Ga.

Kanthe's hands tightened on the rail. He took a deep breath, trying to catch a whiff of what he suspected, but the distance was far too great. Still, he knew the source of that thunder. He had heard its telltale blast before.

The captain of the barge hurried over, closing upon Rami, who stood as stiff-backed as Kanthe. The hulking man carried a farscope in hand and held it forth.

Rami took it and extended it to its full length. "What is it, Ghees?"

"Looks to be coming from Ekau Watch," the captain said.

Kanthe recognized the name of the large outpost on the northernmost coast of the Southern Klashe. He stepped closer to the others, drawing their attention.

"I fear someone must've dropped a Hadyss Cauldron over there," Kanthe warned, picturing the barn-sized iron bomb named after the god of the fiery underworld.

"Are you certain?" Rami lifted the scope to one eye.

Kanthe shrugged. "Not long ago I had one nearly dropped on my head." He then added a more worrisome note. "If I'm right, it takes a vessel the size of a warship to carry such a fearsome weapon."

Rami leaned over the rail with his scope. "I don't spot any wyndships. But that pall is dense. And flames are already spreading into the neighboring woods, churning up more smoke."

Rami lowered the farscope and turned to Ghees. "Get us back to Kysalimri."

The captain bowed brusquely, then hurried away. Rami gave Kanthe's shoulder a last squeeze, then rushed after the man.

Alone now, Kanthe stared toward the horizon. He rubbed his shoulder where Rami had gripped him, plainly offering Kanthe reassurance.

*I don't deserve it.*

He remembered his earlier reverie, wondering what had been transpiring in Hálendii. He was now certain: word had *indeed* reached his father of his son's betrayal. While the tremble in the bay subsided, Kanthe's breath grew heavier as he feared the worst.

*Did my coming here push my father over the edge? Is this the result?*

He couldn't know for sure—but one certainty settled like a stone in his gut. He stared at the smoke, at the distant spark of spreading fires.

*This act means war.*

# 5

KANTHE FOUGHT TO keep his seat in the jolting carriage. He gripped the edge of the bench with one hand and pushed his princely arse more firmly into the pillowed cushion to hold himself in place. The coach was an open one. Winds from their swift passage through the streets of Kysalimri whipped his hair and buffeted his royal garb. He used his free hand to keep his gold cap in place.

Across the carriage, Rami bowed his head near one of his advisers. Though the elder's features were presently cloaked by his *byor-ga* headwear, Kanthe knew the man. Within the palace grounds, the Chaaen were not required to cover their faces. The gaunt man's name was Loryn. He served as Rami's counsel in matters of the court. The rattle of wheels drowned their words, but the pair were undoubtedly discussing the explosive incursion to the north.

Kanthe turned away with a groan. Armed horsemen, a cadre of the royal guard, flanked the golden carriage. Ahead of them, another gilded coach rattled over the cobbles, carrying Aalia and her dozen Chaaen. Beyond them, the entourage was led by a war wagon, prickling with crossbows. Archers watched every shadow for dangers. More swordsmen in light armor crowded the middle of the wagon. Even the horses wore plates of metal. A second war wagon trailed the parade, guarding their rear.

Kanthe should have felt well protected, except he caught the glares from the nearest soldiers. Though their faces were half hidden by drapes of thin mail, their narrowed eyes glinted with accusation.

*They blame me for the attack.* Kanthe could not quell his own sense of guilt. *I should not have come to these lands.*

Still, Kanthe suspected the soldiers' wrath was stoked by suspicions that he may have had a more direct involvement in the attack to the north. The nearest horseman bowed his chin so he could spit into the street near the wheel of the cart.

None but Kanthe noted this act. He lowered his hand from his cap and tightened his fingers into a fist.

*I don't even have a weapon to defend myself if I am attacked.*

Gloved fingers touched his knee. "Do not be goaded," the Chaaen seated next to him warned.

Kanthe glanced at the man. Violet eyes, framed by black brows, stared through the slit in the draped *byor-ga* coif. The man's complexion was a few shades darker than his own. Kanthe forced his fingers to relax, reminding himself that he had an ally here.

Pratik had once been chaaen-bound to a royal merchant until half a year ago. While traveling abroad, Pratik had been pulled into the fold of those who sought to prevent moonfall. The Chaaen had escorted Kanthe to these shores. After the prince had been granted *imri* status by the emperor, Pratik had been assigned to Kanthe. Silver chains led from Kanthe's boots up to the man's collar, the iron of which signified his scholarship in alchymy.

Unfortunately, Kanthe had been gifted another Chaaen, too.

He glanced past Pratik to the figure sharing their bench. Brija sat stiffly, her usual posture. Kanthe swore the old woman's spine had been fused into that position. Her collar was silver, marking her studies in religion and history. She served as Kanthe's aide in matters of Klashean language and customs. Though he suspected her true role was to spy on him and report back to the emperor.

"King Toranth must be furious that you fled here," Pratik said, drawing back Kanthe's attention.

"That was made plain enough this morning. My father was always quick to anger and even swifter in his punishments."

Pratik leaned back. "To drop such a fearsome bomb as a Hadyss Cauldron atop Ekau Watch, he is determined to make his claim on you clear, to demand the emperor hand you over."

Kanthe exhaled heavily. "My father was never a subtle man."

"No matter. The Imri-Ka will never relinquish such a prize as you."

Kanthe glowered. "I don't think anyone ever considered me a *prize*."

"You are sworn to the emperor's only daughter. To give you up, the Imri-Ka would lose honor. Not just him, but his entire Haeshan clan." Pratik nodded at Rami and waved toward Aalia in the next carriage. "His Illustriousness would never let that happen."

"Then war is inevitable."

"Not just inevitable. With that fiery act, it's already started. For now, we must consider how it affects our plans."

Kanthe frowned, reminded that he had not come to these shores just to get married. While Nyx and the others had flown off in search of a mysterious site deep in the Frozen Wastes, his group's mission was twofold. They were assigned to search for further knowledge out of the ancient past, from the Forsaken Ages, an era that predated known history. Pratik claimed there were rumors of unspoken prophecies, portents from the past that spoke of a coming apocalypse. It was whispered that ancient tomes held in the royal librarie— the Abyssal Codex—offered insight into those prophecies. The collection was buried under the private gardens of the Imri-Ka and guarded over by the Dresh'ri, a mystical order of scholars.

Agreeing to this marriage had been one notch in the key that could open that forbidden door. From here, it would be up to Pratik and Frell—the alchymist who had accompanied Kanthe here, his former mentor from school—to gain entry to that librarie. Frell had already been in contact with an emissary of the Dresh'ri. Still, it had taken months to gain an audience with that sect. It had only been granted this morning. Pratik had wanted to be present, too, but the Chaaen could not refuse to escort the prince on the day's sojourn across the Bay of the Blessed.

Still, it was not that aspect of their mission that concerned Pratik. "If war breaks out, it will be much harder for us to reach that buried Sleeper."

That was this team's other goal. Kanthe pictured the shining crystal globe resting in Shiya's bronze palm. An emerald glow had marked the spot in the Frozen Wastes that Nyx and the others sought to find. But a blue dot had also shone on the globe, within the Crown itself. It lay south of Kysalimri, beyond the Hyrg Scarp mountains. It marked the possible location of another figure like Shiya, a living bronze construct, one of the Sleepers left by the ancients to help guide the world should doom threaten. Unfortunately, Shiya's memories—stored in a repository beneath the Shrouds of Dalalæða—had been mostly shattered, leaving her with only dregs of knowledge from the past. The hope was that if they could wake this other Sleeper, its memory might still be intact.

Pratik sighed loudly. "I do not imagine Emperor Makar ka Haeshan will allow his newly wedded daughter to have her grand procession across the lands, celebrating the nuptials and introducing all to her new husband. Not with a war being fought."

Kanthe knew that had been the original plan: to use that royal procession to reach the site of the blue blip. It lay outside the city of Qazen, a fortuitous location, as it was tradition for the newly wedded, especially among the *imri*, to seek the counsel of the Augury of Qazen to foretell the future of their union. But not everyone was pleased with the fortunes spoken by those oracles. It was said many a marriage ended there, well before it even started, with countless bodies buried in the neighboring salt marshes.

*Maybe I'll end up there, too.*

"If we're in the thick of war," Pratik continued, "we may need to concoct another excuse to reach those lands."

Kanthe glanced over. He noted Brija tilting in their direction. The old Chaaen was surely attempting to eavesdrop on them, likely stymied in her effort by the near-deafening rattle of wheels and the pound of hooves.

Kanthe leaned closer to Pratik with a slight nod to their curious neighbor.

"Best we save such a discussion for another time. If we're lucky, my father won't disturb my nuptials any more than he already has. Time is running short. The winter solstice is almost upon us."

"It's still a full turn of the moon away," Pratik reminded him. "But you're right. If we could get ahead of your father's plans, before war fully breaks out, then our original strategy could still hold. To that end, we must plead with the emperor to move up the date of your wedding."

Kanthe swallowed hard, glancing across to the other carriage. "That's not what I meant—"

Pratik ignored him, sitting straighter. "Maybe as soon as this week."

Kanthe slumped back.

*What have I done?*

# 6

Lost in his own worries, Kanthe winced as the midday bell rang out across the city. The incessant clanging ached the bones of his skull. He groaned heavily. He was arse-sore and sunbaked, but their carriage had finally reached the blue expanse of Hresh Me, the city's central freshwater lake. The Klashean name roughly meant the *Silent Mouth* or *Hungry Mouth.* The exact translation depended on whether one rolled that R across one's tongue or not—though, he was still unsure which was which.

*I really should study harder.*

Their procession of carriages mounted the shoreside road that circled the lake. The emperor's palace lay on the far side, seated atop a hill. The walled grounds occupied a landhold as vast as most cities. In the center rose its hundred-spired citadel. The fortress was so expansive that it took a multivolume series of atlases to map its countless rooms and passages. Many of the baseborn caste lived their entire lives there. They were birthed within its walls and eventually burned in the crypts below it.

Kanthe shuddered at the thought and turned away from the lake. He studied the passing spread of Kysalimri. The Eternal City of the Southern Klashe could be a country in and of itself. It spread outward from the Bay of the Blessed, encircled by a concentric series of walls, each marking the passing of centuries as the city grew. Thousands upon thousands of white towers pointed at the sky, all crafted of the same white marble, all set ablaze by the sun. The stone had been mined from the neighboring eastern mountains of the Hyrg Scarp. It was said a score of the Scarp's peaks had been worn to nubs to build the Eternal City.

Kanthe did not doubt it. During his seventeen years, he had never set foot in Kysalimri. He had certainly heard rumors, been shown maps. Still, nothing had prepared him for first setting eyes on the city. He had considered Azantiia, the royal seat of Hálendii, to be vast, but a hundred Azantiias could fit within these walls.

The royal entourage slowed and skirted away from the lake again as they reached a bustling dockworks that blocked their way. Fishing skiffs and larger barges crowded the piers. Gulls and crows screamed in an unending chorus. The winds carried the scent of spilled fish guts blistering in the heat.

Kanthe was relieved when their carriages swept away from the shoreline and back into the shadowed edge of the city. The temperature dropped, and the air quickly cleared of the stench. Shops lined either side of the road. Bakeries scented the air with yeast and cinnamon. Open braziers roasted fish, sizzling fat and flesh.

Kanthe's stomach growled, reminding him he had barely touched the spread of wares afforded him aboard the pleasure barge this morning, too discomfited by the presence of his betrothed. Unfortunately, their coaches didn't stop at any of the cookeries. They still had a long way to go to reach the Imri-Ka's palace.

The group continued onward without slowing—until an overturned hay wagon blocked the way ahead. Bales littered the street. A dehorned ox had been sliced free of its tethers and shook its head, as if denying the accident was its fault. Figures in *byor-ga* robes fought to right the wagon using a long pole.

As the carriages neared, a few arms waved, begging for assistance.

Their pleas were ignored.

Once the golden shine of the carriages came into view, the men in the street fell to their knees and raised the backs of their hands to their foreheads in clear obeisance. A few sang praises as they passed. Or maybe it was prayers. Here in Kysalimri, the line between royalty and godhood blurred.

Aalia failed to acknowledge the deference, apparently deaf to the litany of praises, or so inured to the homage that it meant no more to her than the cries of the gulls by the docks.

Kanthe frowned.

*It seems I'm not the only one unworthy of her attention.*

The procession jostled past, taking a side street to skirt the blockage. After a time, the motion of the carriage lulled Kanthe again. He settled back into his seat. His eyelids drew heavy, his chin sinking to his chest. Then the carriage bumped sharply, tossing him fully out of his seat. He landed hard on the bench, clacking his teeth together.

"Hold tight," Pratik warned. "This stretch runs rougher."

By now, they had reached a section of the city that looked in ill-repair. The cobbled streets were missing countless stones, creating a rutted and pocked path. The homes on either side looked long abandoned. Windows were boarded up, or simply broken clean out. Bony-ribbed curs scurried from their path, vanishing into alleyways and barking at their passage.

The carriage rattled past a house of worship. Its steeple had collapsed long ago, crushing the chapel beneath. Kanthe stared at the ruins. He seemed to be the only one noting any of this. The soldiers kept their gazes fixed forward. The pace of their carriages grew swifter.

Kanthe cast Pratik an inquiring glance.

"Kysalimri may be the Eternal City," Pratik explained, "but the same could not be said for the populace. The birth rates have fallen over the past two centuries. All the city's white marble may gloriously reflect the sun, but the shine only hides the slow rot beneath. Vast swaths have fallen into ruin. It has been four centuries since the city had to expand its outermost walls to accommodate growth."

"I've heard no whisper of such a decline," Kanthe said, shocked. "Not even from my teachers at Kepenhill."

"No one talks about it here. And certainly not when abroad." Pratik nodded to the soldiers, who all focused forward, seeming to refuse to see what lay to either side.

Past Pratik's shoulder, Brija stared toward them. Her eyes glinted coldly through her veil's slit. She surely did not appreciate Pratik sharing such insights.

The old woman was not the only one to overhear their conversation. Rami leaned forward. His six Chaaen, who were spread across two benches, looked conspicuously elsewhere.

"It's true." Rami pointed to an abandoned row house with a guttered roof. "Such a regression remains a challenge to confront, especially when my father refuses to acknowledge it. Sadly, he seldom leaves the palace grounds. During my nineteen years, he has stepped out its gates no more than a dozen times. Mostly to travel to his Augury in Qazen."

Kanthe recalled his dismay at the thought of the members of the baseborn never leaving the palace citadel. Apparently, the Imri-Ka was equally trapped, though of his own volition. Still, it made Kanthe despair.

*I'm to marry into this family—maybe in as little as a week. Gods above, spare me such a fate. Or at least buy me more time to figure a way out of it.*

As if the gods heard him, a loud blast shattered the day. A fiery sun exploded ahead of them. The concussion threw Kanthe back into his seat. Rami was knocked to the floorboards as the carriage horses reared in their traces.

Kanthe raised an arm against the blinding flash, shielding his face.

He caught a dark shadow cartwheeling high amidst the flames.

*The war wagon . . .*

The armored coach flipped twice in the air before crashing against a neighboring building. Soldiers shouted, men screamed, smoke rolled over their carriage—but not before movement drew Kanthe's eyes.

Figures cascaded down the walls to either side, dropping from the rooftops, scurrying down ropes. More shadows appeared in windows, drawing bows into view.

An ambush.

A horse slammed into their carriage, panicked and riderless, its tail on fire.

It bounced off the cart and fled away. Their own tethered mounts reared and crashed in their traces, shaking the carriage. Two broke free and thundered off through the chaos. The other two were felled by a barrage of arrows.

Kanthe cursed his father, picturing the earlier explosion to the north. Apparently that attack's intent wasn't just to herald the advent of war, but served as a feint, a distraction.

*To get to me.*

# 7

KANTHE SEARCHED FOR a weapon, determined not to be killed—or worse, to be captured and dragged back to Azantiia. Better a swift death than a slow, torturous end in the dungeons back home.

A cordon of mounted soldiers regrouped and surrounded their carriage. Shields were raised over the coach's occupants—and not a moment too soon. Arrows and crossbow bolts peppered the ironwood and steel. Men fell from their saddles, giving their lives to protect their royal charges.

Behind them, the war wagon in the rear thundered up, drawing abreast of their carriage, but in the narrow confines, it could go no farther, could not get past their coach. Archers fired at the attackers. Crossbow bolts sparked off the white stone. One arrow severed a climbing rope, sending an ambusher tumbling to his death. But more attackers had reached the street, driving forward, wielding curved blades.

It was only then that Kanthe realized his mistake, his self-centered folly.

The ambushers had their faces bared, which was why he had thought they were the king's assassins. After so long in Kysalimri, he had grown accustomed to seeing everyone around him hidden under their *byor-ga* robes. Only these attackers, with their features uncovered, were clearly Klashean, defying the royal edict to cover their faces. Their only adornments were stripes of white paint across their eyes. Even their weaponry—the curved swords— was foreign to the kingdom's legion. A few attackers also wielded thin whip-swords, a unique blade whose flexibility was a guarded secret among Klashean metalsmiths.

The truth struck him hard, setting his heart to pounding in his throat.

*They're not after me.*

The arrival of the war wagon had driven most of the attackers away from Kanthe's carriage—or more likely the assailants simply retreated toward their intended target.

Rami shoved next to him. He had hiltless throwing knives in both hands. His bared wrists revealed rings of sheathed blades strapped to his forearms. "We must get to my sister."

Kanthe searched through the smoke and smolder. The other carriage lay on its side, catching a brunt of the earlier blast. Soldiers guarded over it, protecting the Illuminated Rose of the Imri-Ka, who huddled within. Bodies lay strewn across the cobbles, both friend and foe. Another soldier dropped, an arrow through his throat.

Aalia's protectors would not last much longer, especially as the attackers focused their assault on that carriage.

In the narrow street, their own coach blocked the war wagon from reaching the others. The archers aboard it dared not shoot in that direction, lest a stray bolt should strike Aalia. Recognizing this, soldiers were already leaping from the wagon to cross on foot.

Bowmen in the windows rained death from on high. The soldiers did their best to cover their heads with their shields. Still, they were held at bay by the barrage. More bodies fell.

"This way!" Kanthe yelled, turning to the opposite side of their carriage from the trapped war wagon.

He took a step, ready to leap over the rail, only to have his left foot betray him. He fell headlong, striking his chin against that rail. He landed hard and twisted around with a scowl. He had forgotten he wasn't a free man.

Pratik dropped beside him. "Hold still." He reached to Kanthe's boots and undid the chains that bound the prince to his two Chaaen.

Rami had already shed his own anchors and helped Kanthe up, taking care of the blade in hand. His friend's eyes were wide and glassy with fear. "Aalia . . ."

"I know." Kanthe turned to Pratik. "Get this carriage out of the way. We need that war wagon freed if we hope to escape."

Kanthe didn't wait for acknowledgment and leaped out of the coach.

Rami followed, landing beside him in a crouch. "How do we reach her carriage?"

It was a fair question. Smoke choked the street, but it didn't afford enough cover from the archers in the windows. The soldiers recognized this, too. The handful still alive in the open had forsaken trying to cross the distance. They huddled under shields, trying to protect themselves not only from the bowmen above, but from the crossbows wielded by those on the ground. They were pinned down in a wary stalemate.

Across the way, Aalia hid under her toppled carriage. Only five of her defenders remained, crouching in the coach's shadow, their shields raised.

One of the last soldiers, a lithe woman in light armor, bore a whipsword in each hand and a small metal shield strapped to each forearm. She knocked aside a crossbow bolt with a clang of steel. Dead bodies lay piled before her, creating a macabre rampart, defying anyone to cross over.

"Aalia's bodyguard," Rami gasped. "Pray she can protect my sister long enough."

Kanthe tugged on his friend's arm, drawing him in the opposite direction. "Not that way."

# 8

With Rami at his heels, Kanthe rushed behind the carriage to a fallen horse. A soldier lay crushed under the armored steed. Kanthe stopped long enough to unhook a crossbow hanging from the saddle, along with a quiver of feathered bolts. He felt a thousandfold more confident in his plan as he gripped the weapon's ironwood stock.

As a second-born prince, he had been forbidden to wield a sword, but that hadn't stopped him from learning to hunt with a bow. He had been trained by the best, a Cloudreach scout of cunning skill and agility.

He remembered one lesson now.

*When hunting dangerous prey, your best weapon is the shadows.*

With bow in hand, Kanthe ignored the fighting in the street and ran low toward the neighboring ruins of a line of row houses. He climbed through a broken window, scoured long ago of any shards of glass. He took a breath to help Rami through while letting his sight adjust to the darkness.

"If we stick to this cover," Kanthe whispered, "we can cross forward through these homes and come up behind your sister's carriage."

Rami nodded and pointed deeper into the structure. "Such households usually share a common courtyard in the back. We could pass more quickly through there to reach the home closest to Aalia."

"Good."

Kanthe headed through the dilapidated structure. The upper level had partially collapsed, creating a deadfall of beams, planks, and broken stone. Rats and other squeaking vermin fled from them. Webs stuck to their faces and clothes. The place smelled sharply of spoor and old piss.

Kanthe glanced back to check on Rami. The prince of this realm showed no hesitation or squeamishness to be climbing through such filth. His face remained a mask of desperate determination. Rami grabbed a fat rat by the tail and flung it away without a wince. Kanthe liked the man all the more— resolute now to firm up their friendship if they survived.

Together, they forged through to a low-roofed kitchen with a soot-blackened stone hearth in a corner. A far door hung crookedly, letting in more light. A peek through revealed a rear garden. It was overgrown with weeds, thistles, and thorns. A lichen-scribed stone ring marked an old well.

"Stick close to the wall," Kanthe warned. "In case anyone on the second floor is watching this side."

Rami ducked after Kanthe into the yard. They flattened against the wall. As they edged along, his friend readied his blades, flipping them across his fingers. He was likely testing their weight, limbering up his joints, or maybe it was a way of dispelling his nervousness. Either way, the silver knives seemed to appear and disappear at will.

They continued through the weeds and over broken roof tiles to reach the abode nearest Aalia's carriage. He glanced to Rami, getting a confirming nod that passing through this home was their best chance.

Kanthe led the way, squeezing through a door that gapped open. He took a breath to steady himself and let his sight adjust again to the gloom. Echoes of the battle outside reached them. Screams, shouted orders, clashes of steel.

"Go," Rami urged.

Kanthe continued through the home's kitchen. At least this place was in better shape. The second floor remained intact. He passed stairs leading up. His ears strained for any sign of lurkers above. But the fighting outside made it difficult.

He ducked lower and exited into the main room at the front. Broken furniture lay strewn about. A pile of ashes and partially burnt wood suggested someone had once used this place to camp from the cold.

Rami grabbed his shoulder, hissing low. He pointed upward. A thin trickle of dust streamed between the rafters, seeping through the floorboards above. *Someone's moving up there.*

Kanthe cursed himself for focusing on the floor, the piles of ashes. He carefully shifted a couple of steps to the side, edging toward a ragged hole in the ceiling. While the upper level was mostly in place, a corner of it had given way. He made out the slightest flickering glow up there, noticed only as the light shifted in the gap's direction.

*Have we been heard down here?*

Kanthe positioned the butt of his crossbow to his shoulder. A bolt was already in place, strung taut. As he neared the hole, he lifted the weapon to his eye, aiming intently. He tilted his head enough to flick a look at Rami, willing his friend to hang back—then froze.

A shadow shifted behind Rami, at the threshold of the kitchen. Someone had come down the back stairs, moving silently to come up behind them. A sword flashed in the darkness.

*Ambushed yet again . . .*

Maybe it was Kanthe's look of shocked horror, but Rami reacted, moving as swiftly as a striking serpent.

His friend dropped a shoulder and, without even seeming to glance backward, flung his arm behind him. Silver flew from his fingertips. The blade found the man's throat. The cry was a strangled gurgle as the knife all but silenced the attacker.

It was quiet enough for Kanthe to hear the tread of boots overhead. He swung around as a figure leaped through the hole, a cloak flared wide, a sword in hand.

Kanthe still had his bow at his cheek and squeezed the trigger. He kept his grip tight as the twanging release threatened to shake off his aim. The bolt pierced the attacker's left eye before he even landed. His legs crumpled under him, followed by his body.

Rami joined him. Kanthe grabbed another bolt from his quiver and fitted it in place, cranking the string taut. They watched in all directions, but no other attackers appeared.

"Must've been all of them," Kanthe whispered.

They rushed across the rest of the room and reached a window that had been partially boarded shut. They peered through a broken slat. The back of Aalia's toppled carriage lay directly ahead. It was impossible to tell how many defenders remained.

The only one in sight was Aalia's lithe bodyguard, who still danced on the cobbles, fighting two attackers. The pile of bodies around her had grown. But the feathered end of an arrow waved from her left shoulder. Her face ran with blood, not all from her attackers.

Another assailant rushed across the street to join the fray.

The woman could not last much longer.

*Not without help.*

Kanthe shifted his crossbow to the gap, aimed with a steadying breath, and fired. The bolt found its intended target. The running assailant's head snapped back, carrying his body with it. The figure crashed backward.

Rami had shifted to the door by now. It had been roped shut, but age had turned hemp to mulch. His friend slammed his shoulder into the door and burst out into the open. He rushed for cover behind the overturned coach. He made it safely, likely due to the thickening smoke—and the fact he and Rami had already dispatched the two men upstairs.

Kanthe followed, struggling with his weapon, fumbling for another bolt. As he reached the street, he spotted an abandoned bow, likely tossed here when the first war wagon exploded. A leather quiver lay steps away amidst a scatter of arrows.

He smiled at this smallest of good fortunes, not knowing which god to thank. He tossed aside the crossbow, glad to be rid of it. "Sod that."

He scooped up the bow and gathered the arrows back into their quiver. He caught three between his fingers. He gripped their shafts firmly as he straightened. Rami nodded to him, then rounded the wagon, ready to go to the aid of the bodyguard.

Kanthe followed at his heels, stringing the first arrow in place while still holding the other two between his fingers.

Their sudden appearance from behind the wagon caught everyone off guard. Rami dispatched one of the bodyguard's attackers. Kanthe took out the other. Together, they flanked the woman, who stumbled back a step, breathing hard.

More assailants rushed forward.

Kanthe had already shifted his wrist to fit the second arrow to the bowstring. He drew and fired. As the shaft flew, he fixed the remaining arrow in place, pulled hard, and let it loose. The two arrows struck true, dropping two figures.

Beside him, Rami twirled and spun, flashing silver through the air.

Screams followed, blood arced high, more bodies fell.

Kanthe fumbled with the quiver over his shoulder. He grasped three more arrows between his fingers and pulled them free. Before he could fit the first one in place, a leather-coated arm lunged before his face. A crossbow bolt clanged off steel, ricocheting off the small shield strapped to the bodyguard's forearm. She shifted forward, ready to defend them both.

Kanthe concentrated on the bowmen up in the windows.

Rami dispatched swordsmen on the ground.

The battle waged for what felt like forever.

Kanthe found himself gasping. He wiped sweat from his eyes. His fingers ached. His shoulders burned. He searched his quiver, only to find it empty. Likewise, Rami had snatched up a curved sword after running out of knives.

Kanthe risked a glance to his friend, read the fear there, confirming what he knew was true.

*We can't win.*

Then a loud crash drew all their attention to the left. Horses reared and snorted, tossing their armored heads. The war wagon burst past the other coach. Before it did, Kanthe saw Pratik leap into the wagon from the other carriage. The Chaaen carried an ax in both hands. The man must have chopped the carriage free of the weight of its dead horses and finally maneuvered the coach out of the way.

The armored war wagon thundered toward them.

Archers fired in all directions, driving back the attackers.

The huge cart drew to a stop amidst a clatter of hooves. A door opened on the wagon's side, revealing a steel-plated cabin hidden beneath the open battle deck.

Now protected, Rami turned to the toppled carriage. Aalia crouched far under it. A handful of her chaaen-bound nestled with her. The others appeared dead, having used their own bodies to shield the Illuminated Rose.

Kanthe went to Rami's aid. He helped get the Chaaen up and moving, while Rami unchained his sister from the dead. They hurried to the wagon, where soldiers hauled them inside.

Kanthe offered his hand to help Aalia up.

She slapped his arm away, looking past his shoulder as if he were not even worthy of her gaze. "Do not touch me," she spat in Hálendiian, plainly able to speak his language all this time.

Kanthe balked at the heat of her rejection.

Rami winced and assisted his sister into the wagon. He offered an apologetic shrug to Kanthe as he passed. "She's frightened."

Kanthe caught a glare from Aalia before she turned away. It wasn't *fear* shining on her face. He easily recognized what it was.

*Hatred.*

He sighed and followed her, accepting his fate as best he could.

As he did, a stray crossbow bolt sliced past his ear, close enough to shave off a few strands of hair. He ducked to the side and searched in the direction of the attack. A figure appeared down the street. The man lowered his weapon and stood tall, fearless, his dark face bared to the sunlight. His strong features—firm jaw, wide cheekbones—could be considered handsome, especially his bright violet eyes, rare and prized among the Klashean. The only blemish was a scar that ran from brow to cheek, crossing through the white paint over his left eye.

That gaze fixed on Kanthe.

The man's expression was easy to read.

*Hatred once again.*

The figure lifted an arm and slashed it low. Upon this signal, the attack ended. The *pinging* of arrows and bolts went silent. Figures vanished in all directions, fading into the shadows. The man, clearly the leader, turned and followed.

"Hurry," Rami warned, and held out an arm toward Kanthe.

He grabbed his friend's hand and allowed himself to be pulled inside the wagon. Rami guided him to a bench. He dropped heavily, exhausted in every measure of the word.

He closed his eyes, picturing that figure on the street.

Only then did he remember one detail. As Aalia had slapped his hand away, she had been staring past Kanthe's shoulder—in that same direction. He had thought her too disdainful of him to be worthy of her gaze. But maybe she had also spotted the leader out in the street.

He shook his head, too addled to contemplate it all. He only knew one thing for certain. He pictured the expressions shared by Aalia and the attacker on the street and accepted the truth of this day.

*I seem to be doing what I do best.*

He sighed loudly.

*Creating more enemies.*

# THREE

# DAGGERS IN THE WIND

*Know this! The strum of a bard's lyre can awaken mem-*
*oris, stir the blode, give rise to teyrs. It moves a listener in*
*gentle ways. But bridle-song—which soundeth as sweete to*
*the ear—cuts through blode & bone. It does not move; it*
*grabs! To be bridled is a fist in the skull, leavyng no roum*
*for thought, will, or dremes. Best to put a knife to one's ear*
*than heed that Sirenes song.*

—Taken from the sermon of the Hapric cleric
Clea ja Raan III, whose followers cut out the tongues
of hundreds of bridle-singers; some claim he was gifted
himself, using his song to sway those to carry out
his bloody will.

# 9

NYX SAT CROSS-LEGGED in the gloom of the *Sparrowhawk*'s lower hold. She kept her eyes closed, not that there was much to see. Lamp oil was as precious as flashburn aboard the swyftship. Only a pair of lanterns lit the cavernous space, and one had been commandeered by Jace.

Her friend knelt nearby. He hunched over the tome on his lap, a text secured from the cabin he shared with the alchymist. He mumbled as he read, something she always found endearing, as if he were arguing with the long-dead writer. He sought further knowledge about what might await them beyond the Dragoncryst, but she suspected he also needed to distract himself from the more immediate danger.

She appreciated that.

A moment ago, word had echoed to them from the ship's highhorn, the metal tubing and baffling that ran throughout the wyndship. In less than a bell, they would reach the mountains. Darant ordered every crewman to their posts. All others were to secure themselves in their cabins, less to protect them than to get them out from underfoot.

She had already decided to weather the storm and mountain crossing in the hold. She wanted to be near Bashaliia and Kalder, to calm the two during the tumult to come. Jace had informed Graylin of her plan when he went topside to fetch his book. She had been surprised the knight hadn't returned with Jace to shadow over her. But Nyx already had a guardian far stronger than any man.

Shiya stood a few steps away, unmoving, not even breathing. She had become a statue again, a figure sculpted of bronze.

Graylin also likely knew that any evacuation must pass through this hold, where he could easily collect her. The *Sparrowhawk*'s two tiny sailrafts, miniature versions of the larger wyndship, were stanchioned in the hold's aft, their snubbed noses pointed toward the stern doors that could open to the skies. If the *Hawk* should become compromised, those two rafts would be the only means to abandon the ship.

As she waited, she hummed softly, a vibration of throat and breath. While Jace spent chunks of his day sparring with Graylin and Darant, Nyx had been honing her control over her bridle-song, a gift carried in her blood, passed down through generations.

Half a year ago, she had learned its true source.

*Bashaliia—or rather, his brethren.*

Lost in the depths of time, the ancients had instilled in his breed a heightened ability to communicate, to wend many minds into one, to form a vast, cold intelligence. That consciousness was likewise preserved and protected by its spread throughout the colony, where every individual was a poisonous fortress of strength.

The Mýr bats had been devised to be living sentinels, stationed to monitor the Urth over the passing millennia, to watch for any dangers, and, if necessary, to wake the Sleepers buried around the world.

With her eyes still closed, Nyx cast out threads of power. They brushed against Shiya, one of those ancient Sleepers. Her kind were nonliving sentinels, artifacts crafted by those ancients, instilled with the same potent bridle-song.

Through Nyx's gifted touch, Shiya grew into a torch in her mind's eye. The enormity of the woman's power was nearly incomprehensible, not just her strength of limb, but also the well of energies throbbing inside her. Shiya was a living furnace, one meant to warm the amber of this world and get it turning again.

But *how* to do that remained unknown. Time proved more powerful than the will of those ancients. Many Sleepers were lost, crushed under miles of ice or blasted by the heat on the Urth's far side. Even the Sleepers' librarie of knowledge had not survived intact, leaving Shiya potent but confused, a powerful weapon but one without an enemy to point it at.

It was up to Nyx and the others to fill in the gaps, to weave this frayed tapestry of history and knowledge into something whole and understandable. The only clues were the location of the emerald marker hidden deep within the Frozen Wastes and another on the Urth's other side, out in the lands forever scorched by the Father Above's merciless and unending gaze. Though much knowledge was lost, Shiya sensed it was vital to reach the site in the Wastes first. But no one, not even Shiya, knew why.

Without any other Sleepers to guide them, their group had no choice but to attempt this journey. Still, there remained a small hope. Shiya had discovered at least one other Sleeper who appeared to be intact, though still slumbering. The artifact lay deep within the Southern Klashe. Others of their original party—Alchymist Frell, Prince Kanthe, and Chaaen Pratik—had left to search for that Sleeper. But with no certainty of their success, Nyx and the others had to risk crossing the Wastes.

*But what will we find?*

Nyx let her tendrils of bridle-song sift away from Shiya's bronze form. She tightened her throat, pitching her hum wider. As each thread reverberated back to her—bouncing off the stacks of crates, off the edges of barrels, even from the curves of the inner hull—a picture of the cavernous hold formed inside her. The space spread from bow to stern, buried under the bustle of the upper decks. With her eyes still closed, she gained a shadowy, wispy vision of its full breadth and entirety.

She smiled at the familiarity of that vague sight. For all her life, until recently, that was all she could see of her world. She had been afflicted as a babe with a clouding of the surfaces of her eyes, which dimmed the world into just shadows and muted colors. Even now, she still found a measure of comfort in that familiar darkness. It was her past, her home, all she had known until recently. Then one of Bashaliia's brethren had come to her defense during an attack, poisoning her in the process. The envenomation cleared away that cloudiness, an affliction tied to those great winged beasts, while also inflaming the latent gift in her blood.

Much like Shiya, Nyx was a Sleeper awoken.

Some called it a miracle, assigning it to the blessing of the Mother.

For Nyx, it was as much a curse. The brighter world was often too much to bear. The gift of bridle-song still frightened her. She barely understood it, but with practice, she had learned to sharpen her focus.

Through the echo of her song and the weaving of her threads, she could discern the life hidden around her: the scurry of mice amidst the crates, the scritch-scratch of crickets, the flutter-buzz of flies, even the casting of a spider's web. Each was its own song, and when she could find a harmony of her own to match, she could orchestrate that melody: get a furtive mouse to slip into slumber, lure a cricket to rub its legs into a chorus, trick a spider into changing the lay of its web.

This last ability was called *bridling*, to bend lesser creatures to your will. The rare few who shared her gift were greatly valued. They could ensnare massive sandcrabs to pull loaded trains across the desert, bind dogs and cats into loyal hunting companions, break horses to saddle and reins. Nyx found such control to be distasteful, somehow wrong—yet, she could not deny a measure of attraction to it. The power was undoubtedly seductive.

*Perhaps because I had so little control over my life up until now.*

Disheartened by this reverie, she opened her eyes and let her song die away, winding the threads back to her. As she did, a few strands drifted over Jace. Through that brief touch, she read his concentration. It smelled like a smoldering hearth. She also sensed his fear, which felt like air after a lightning storm.

He glanced up from his book, as if sensing her attention. "Nyx?"

She shook her head, shaking away the last vestiges of her gift. For a moment, as her bridle-song faded and with his eyes upon her, she smelled something musky wafting from him, a rose in fresh loam.

"It's nothing," Nyx mumbled.

Still, her cheeks heated up. She knew what this last scent portended. It marked his desire. *For me.* Reading and exposing his private heart felt like a violation.

Luckily, Jace didn't press the matter. He straightened, working a kink out of his neck with one hand. With the other, he lifted the book from his lap. "I think I've delved as deeply as I can into what lies beyond the Dragoncryst. All I'm finding are tales, each more outlandish than the one before it. This one claims that there's a great sea hidden in the Wastes—which is clearly absurd. Maybe my time would be better spent—"

The ship jolted hard, swinging sharply to portside. Crates and barrels creaked and groaned against the thick nets securing them in place.

Shiya closed upon her and Jace. Strong hands latched on to both their shoulders. "Stay close, stay low," she warned, her voice calm but firm.

As the ship shook and vibrated, she dropped to one knee, anchoring herself and the two of them—and not a moment too soon.

In a few breaths, the *Hawk* became a sparrow in a gale. The ship made sudden rolls or whipped wildly side to side. Nyx gasped, her body flung to and fro within Shiya's grip. She bit her tongue, drawing blood.

Jace reached over and grabbed her hand. Her fingers latched hard to his. She shared a worried look with him.

Darant's voice echoed to them through the highhorn. "We're in the brunt of it now! Grab your arses and hold tight!"

# 10

For what seemed like an eternity, the *Sparrowhawk* battered its way through the storm. The ship got flung in every direction. The winds grew into an unending howl, aching ears, pounding chests.

Nyx's shoulder ached within Shiya's grip. Jace held on to her hand just as tightly. Nyx tasted the iron from her bitten tongue. Her heart thundered in her throat. She pictured the ship shattering into pieces and raining across the Dragoncryst.

*When will this end?*

She was not the only one nearing the breaking point. In a neighboring stall, Kalder rose from his nest of hay. The vargr's nose pointed toward the hold's rafters. His throat rumbled with a chattering growl of distress. His tail slashed the air.

On the other side of the hold, Bashaliia squeaked softly at her, seeking reassurance.

Nyx tried to stand, to get closer to him, only to be knocked down as the nose of the *Sparrowhawk* bucked upward.

Outside, the winds rose into a low roar, accompanied by louder booms as gusts struck the ship. The draft-iron cables groaned under the strain, adding to the cacophony. The cavernous hold trapped and amplified the noise.

Nyx regretted her choice of refuge. With no windows, it was impossible to judge what was truly happening. She was not the only one disabused by this circumstance.

Kalder's growl turned into a wail. By now, the vargr had crammed himself into a corner of his stall. He braced under an overhang that served as his den. His legs were splayed wide for balance, his head low.

Bashaliia fared somewhat better. He hunkered with his wings outstretched. He swayed in place, his sharp claws latched deep into the planked floor. Still, he keened his panic toward her.

She knew she needed to calm both beasts lest they break free of their respective stalls and injure themselves. She took a deep breath and hummed in her throat and chest, stoking her bridle-song. She fought for the focus necessary to wield her gift. Amidst the chaos, she faltered. Her humming stuttered. The threads of her song dissolved before she could wield them.

*I can't do this.*

The *Sparrowhawk* heaved hard to the side, swinging high. She feared it would spin full around. Shiya's fingers tightened with bruising force, pushing her and Jace lower.

Jace kept hold of Nyx's hand. He winced, but his eyes shone hard. He nodded toward Kalder and Bashaliia. "Help them!" he shouted.

She let her worry show as she looked back at him.

*How?*

Jace must have read the question on her face. "You can do this! Search for what calms *you*. Share it with them."

*What calms me?*

She squeezed her eyes shut, seeking those moments when terror had gripped her—which were plenty of late. But she had found little solace in those moments, only bloodshed and loss. She searched further back. With her eyes sealed, she fell more easily into her past, to when she was near blind. She remembered a girl, barely six, shaking in her bed, blankets pulled to her chin, as the invisible world thundered and boomed.

*Much like now.*

Back then, as the shutters banged and the winds howled, another had entered her room. A palm came to rest on her chest. A voice rose in a soft song that somehow quieted the rest of the world. Her dah sang a lullaby to her, to quell the terror inside her, to reassure her that all would be well.

She had nearly forgotten that moment, but as the memory filled her, calming her even now, she sang those simple words, a lullaby never forgotten, each syllable etched deeply into her.

> *When gales blow and boats do rock,*
> *    I am here, right beside you.*
> *    So, close your eyes and know it true.*
> *When lightning flares and thunder booms,*
> *    I am here, never to part.*
> *    So, calm your breath and be still your heart.*
> *When hail pounds and rains do flood,*
> *    I am here, to protect you ever.*
> *    So, be at peace and rest forever.*

As she sang, she found her focus, anchored in the past but still present. She wrapped her bridle-song into each lilt of the lullaby and let it spread outward. She infused each tendril with the sense of security, with the reassurance of her dah's timbre, the warmth of his palm over her heart.

She extended her reach across the hold, the threads glowing in her mind's eye. She found Kalder and warmed those cords through his panting chest. She let them gently wrap around his panicked heart. Other strands reached past his wide, glassy eyes. She teased his memories, conjuring up times of calm and peace. She burnished and brightened those with her song.

—*of milk warm on the tongue.*

—*of the pile of littermates safely ensconced in the curl of tail and belly.*

—*of a brother running alongside a trail, two hearts shared.*

—*later, a nest made of blankets atop a soft bed, shared by three, bathed in each other's scents until all become one.*

She felt the heat fade in Kalder's blood, his heart slowing its thunder. His heaving chest became a steadier pant. She didn't allow him to drift too far into a peaceful slumber. He still needed to be alert, to protect and brace himself, but hopefully now he had more control, perched on firmer legs, attuned more alertly.

She shifted her attention toward Bashaliia, but some of her song must have already reached him. He hunched low. His wingtips balanced on the planks for additional support. His eyes, like hot coals, glowed back at her. He mewled toward her, extending his own song and melding it with hers. Though they were still apart, it felt like a warm embrace.

She allowed herself to sink into it. Cocooned within the glowing strands of bridle-song, Nyx felt the outer world faded around her. It became just the two of them. And while she drew comfort from this, it was not wholly returned. In that intimacy, she discovered threads, less bright, infused with a sad longing, a pining that traced deep into Bashaliia's heart. As with Jace earlier, she knew their meaning. Her winged brother had lived all his life within a communal collective. He was always part of a greater whole.

*But no longer.*

Months ago, the ship had traveled beyond the reach of his colony. Even the frighteningly cold intelligence that existed both within and without the colony could no longer commune with him.

*He is alone out here.*

It worried her, too. She had lost Bashaliia once before, when he was much smaller, but that vast intelligence had preserved her brother's essence before death and passed it into his current form, returning him to her. That was no longer possible at this distance.

This worry frazzled her song, shredding that safe cocoon.

The world returned with all its thrashing and rolling, with its howls and booms. Only now, reminded of Bashaliia's fragility, she felt her fear sharpen. The threat of the storm had new meaning for her.

*I cannot lose him again.*

Perhaps sensing her distress, Bashaliia's soft mewling grew into a shrill shriek.

Even Jace jerked with alarm. "What's wrong with him?"

"I don't—"

Then she heard it, carried on the wind, piercing the storm's roar. It felt like daggers cast through the winds, slicing through the hull. It was bridle-song—only hardened into spears.

She gasped under the assault. She had never felt such strength—or at least not in months. For a moment, she thought it came from the great mind of Bashaliia's colony, somehow breaching the distance to reach them.

*But why?*

As that force grew around them, raising the small hairs on Nyx's arms, she recognized her mistake. The power grew into a massive wave ahead of them, filling the world. She cowered before its dark immensity. While the intelligence of Bashaliia's colony had been cold and immovable, what Nyx felt here was something fiery and malignant, all hatred and enmity.

Bashaliia's cry turned into a scream.

She swung toward him. For a breath, she saw him writhing within a net of fiery threads. He fought it with his own song buried in that scream of rage, shredding it apart.

*Someone's trying to bridle him.*

Nyx struggled to stand, to go to his aid.

Shiya's hand tightened on her. "Help me."

Nyx turned to see Shiya fighting the same assault. Only now did Nyx realize how sluggish she felt. Her limbs had gone leaden. Jace's hand dropped from her slack grip. He slumped in Shiya's embrace, his head lolling to one side.

*Jace . . .*

Nyx's vision narrowed to a point. Still, she felt Shiya cast out her own song. Her bronze form vibrated with the effort, her chorus laced with fury. Her threads wove into a glowing shield around her.

Nyx swallowed the numbness from her throat and hummed forth her own song. She added her voice to Shiya's. Their two choruses struggled for a moment, then settled into a tentative harmony, though Nyx suspected even that success was due to Shiya's skill. Focusing harder, Nyx bolstered their efforts. The shield slowly grew stronger, forming a shell around them.

As the two forced it wider, Nyx found her strength returning. Her voice grew firmer. The shield hardened and extended, pushing against the assault.

Safely ensconced within the shell, Jace groaned and stirred, shifting upright again. He rubbed his eyes. "What . . . what happened?"

Nyx couldn't falter from her song to answer. She knew Jace could not see the war waging within the hold, nor the shield protecting them. Still, he was no fool. He glanced between her and Shiya, likely recognizing the strain of the song they shared, though unable to determine the necessity of it.

Nyx glanced over to Bashaliia. He continued his own fight, but the assault shifted its intensity away from him and over to the protective shell, lashing it even harder. Nyx turned to Kalder, who appeared unaffected, as alert as always.

Nyx risked adding words to her song, to communicate to Shiya. "Whoever it is . . . they're targeting those aboard."

As proof, the bow of the *Sparrowhawk* dropped precipitously, tilting the ship toward its nose. A set of barrels broke loose from their netting and rattled away into the darkness. Nyx and Jace would've followed, but Shiya still anchored them.

Nyx pictured everyone in the wheelhouse succumbing like Jace had just done, bridled into oblivion by that malignant song. She wouldn't have thought it possible. Those gifted like her could sway lesser beasts, but the minds of men and women were too multilayered and complex to bend. Even some beasts were too clever to successfully break.

"Can we extend this shell around the entire ship? To protect everyone?" Nyx sang to Shiya, though she suspected this was an impossibility.

The bronze woman confirmed with a shake of her head.

Nyx grimaced and pointed toward the spiral stair that climbed out of the hold and up into the main ship. "We must get to the wheelhouse. Carry this shield to the others."

"I'll go with you," Jace said.

"No." She pointed behind her, sweat beading her brow. She struggled to sing and explain. "If we lose the ship, those sailrafts are our only hope. Free their tie-downs and get ready to winch the stern doors open."

Jace nodded.

Shiya intoned a warning. "The shield. If Jace leaves its protection . . ."

Nyx had already anticipated this danger. She loosened enough threads to reach across to Bashaliia. She infused her intent.

*Protect Jace.*

Bashaliia had already proven himself capable of thwarting this assault. Her brother understood and whistled sharply back, extending a winding coil of energy toward Jace.

Nyx turned to her friend. "Do your best."

By now, the *Sparrowhawk*'s plunge had steepened. The winds had grown into a wail. The ship shook and rattled. Dread sharpened to a pain in her chest.

*How long before we crash into the teeth of the Dragoncryst?*

With no way of knowing, she pushed down her fears and pulled free of Shiya's grasp. "Let's go."

# 11

RHAIF CLUNG TO the maesterwheel of the *Sparrowhawk*. He braced his legs to hold himself in place as the ship plummeted in a steep dive. He fought to haul back on the wheel, to draw the nose of the ship up. He had seen Darant do it before, but the wheel's piston refused to budge. Ahead, through the curved windows, he watched the jagged teeth of the Dragoncryst rush toward him.

He came to a flurry of conclusions with each panicked beat of his heart.

First and foremost . . .

*Someone should've taught me how to fly this sarding bird.*

To either side of him, figures lay collapsed across the wheelhouse's planks. Except for Darant, whose body snored between Rhaif's legs, where the pirate had fallen after he dropped from the ship's wheel.

Second thought . . .

*Be careful what you wish for, you fool.*

After being trapped aboard the *Sparrowhawk* for so long, with little else to do but win a few brass pinches from some of the crew, Rhaif had chafed at the confinement, the boredom, the blur of one day into the next under a sunless sky. He had prayed for something to break the monotony.

*And look what that got me.*

Sweat ran in cold rivulets down his face, stinging his eyes. His arms ached from his struggle with the wheel. He grimaced at the certain death rushing toward him. His bowels clenched in his belly, giving rise to a third conclusion.

*I really should've used the privy before we hit these winds.*

At the moment, he fought his bladder as much as the storm. And like with the battle in the air, he was certain to lose this fight. He searched for relief, for some help. Graylin had fallen to the planks steps away. Others of the crew slumped over the secondary controls, which consisted of screwlike wheels and levers of unknown function.

He cursed them all, reaching a fourth and final thought—and probably his last:

*Why me?*

He had no idea why he had been spared whatever witchery had befallen the crew. As everyone began staggering and dropping, Rhaif had felt the world lurch around him. His vision spun and blurred at the edges, as if he had swilled flagons of cheap ale. Then a melody had suddenly filled his head. It was not some bawdy ditty, though that would've matched the drunken spiral of his senses. Instead, it had been a lullaby, one his mother had sung to him many nights. She had been a member of the Kethra'kai tribe of Cloudreach, whose bloodlines were rich with bridle-song.

Unfortunately, while Rhaif carried the gift, it was a pale shadow, watered down by the Guld'guhlian blood of his father. Still, he caught inklings occasionally: spotting the wisps of golden strands wafting from a skilled singer or, even rarer, catching a sense of another's inner world when he brushed past them. It was what probably made him such a skilled thief. Then moments ago, as his mother's lullaby had risen in his head, it had cleared away the muddling miasma that threatened to drown his senses. The world had stopped its spinning.

*Not so for the others.*

When Darant had fallen, Rhaif had rushed for the maesterwheel—not that he knew what to do. As the squall of winds tore at the ship, all Rhaif could manage was to hold them steady, to fight the wheel with each gust and bluster of the storm. But he could not pull them out of the dive. He didn't know what he was doing wrong. He feared his stabilizing efforts were only quickening their plunge.

Through the windows, he spotted his fate. The serrated tip of a peak filled the world and grew nearer with every breath. It looked like the *Sparrowhawk* would be impaled atop it, skewered straight through, from bow to stern.

To avoid such a fate, Rhaif yanked the wheel to the right. The *Hawk* rolled in that direction. Slowly, too slowly. The roar of the winds grew to a wail. Draft-iron cables shook under the strain, tremoring the entire ship.

*C'mon, c'mon, c'mon . . .*

He prayed to every god of the northern pantheon—and wished he knew all thirty-three of the Klashean gods, too. The only name he skipped was the dark god Đreyk, whose sigil was a *horn'd snaken*.

*Feck 'im. I'd rather die than owe that daemon a favor.*

The view out the windows skewed ever so slightly. The mountaintop tilted away. Rhaif's lips tightened to somewhere between a grimace and a smile. *Thatta girl.* By now, he practically hung off the maesterwheel, adding his weight, trying to force the ship into a harder turn. It seemed to be working. The peak slipped farther to the left. Still, it would be close.

The *Sparrowhawk* plummeted toward the rocky crag. It was all black and encrusted with ice. Savage gusts scoured crystals from the stone, creating a glinting haze that traced the winds. It would've been beautiful if it wasn't so deadly.

The swyftship dove through the ice storm. It slipped past the jagged moun-taintop, but its slope rose high to the left, like a dark wave frozen in place. The *Sparrowhawk* skidded sideways down its slope. A wide valley opened past the mountain, though more peaks rose beyond it.

Rhaif didn't have time to worry about those.

His prayers turned to curses.

*Maybe those'll work better.*

For a moment, it appeared so. The slope fell farther back. Rhaif huffed out his relief—until an outcropping appeared ahead, a dark shoulder of the mountain. Rhaif hauled on the wheel, bracing his legs for more leverage, us-ing every muscle in his back.

Knowing there was nothing more he could do, he squeezed his eyes closed.

A splintering crash shook the ship. He heard something tear away with a screech of draft-iron. He pictured one of the outer flashburn tanks ripping off its welding, taking part of the hull with it. A fresh howl of winds echoed behind him, confirming his fears.

Still . . .

He opened his eyes. Outside, the mountain was gone, replaced by the sweep of the icy valley. "We made it," he gasped out, ending in a near-manic chuckle of relief. "We made it."

But he quickly sobered, knowing it was only a momentary reprieve from death. The ship continued its dive toward the valley floor. He glanced back toward the roiling howl of winds where the storm had broken into the ship.

*Maybe I should've added Ðreyk to my prayers.*

As he stared, the wheelhouse door banged open, and a blazing sun pushed into the space. He gasped and let go of the maesterwheel. He lifted an arm and blinked away the glare. It took him an extra breath to recognize the familiar golden haze.

*Bridle-song . . .*

For him to see it so brightly, the power behind it must be immense. The wielders appeared, rushing forward.

Shiya and Nyx hurried toward him, half sliding down the slanted floor. Their fiery blaze spread outward, reaching the walls, where it vanished from his weak bridle-sense.

He could not find his tongue to even voice a question. Around him, the others stirred on the planks, quickly waking from the witchery afoot. A hand grasped his ankle, then another his calf. He stared down as Darant climbed his body. The pirate's face stormed from confusion to fury.

Darant got his feet under him and shoved Rhaif away. Glad to be relieved of duty, Rhaif stumbled aside—only to trip over the leg of another waking crewman. He fell hard onto his backside. Darant grabbed hold of the wheel and seemingly took everything in with a glance—of course, brigands didn't last long if they weren't ready for the sudden thrust of a sword at their back.

"What've you done to my ship?" Darant bellowed, while waving the others to their stations.

Rhaif shrugged. "Thought I'd play captain while you were all napping."

Graylin rushed to Darant's shoulder. "We need to get higher before we clear this valley."

"I see those mountains ahead of us as plain as you can," Darant groused. "Just gotta get 'er nose up first."

Darant shifted his legs. One foot reached under the console and pressed a pedal near the floor. The pirate pulled on the maesterwheel, and its shaft slid smoothly on its pistons. The slant in the floor began to level as the bow rose.

Still on his backside, Rhaif leaned on an elbow, looked under the wheel, and groaned.

*Ah, so there's a pedal . . . someone really needs to tell me these things.*

Darant bellowed to the others, "Set that stern forge to blazing! We're getting our arses out of here!"

Nyx sidestepped Graylin as the knight came protectively toward her. She pointed toward the window. "Hurry! Something's coming!"

# 12

NYX STAYED CLOSE to Shiya in case the woman needed her voice. For the moment, the assault upon the ship had ebbed—though the threat remained. She felt those dark energies probing and gliding over Shiya's glowing shield, focusing there.

Nyx stared out into the windstorm.

*Perhaps the wielders have grown wary by what confounds them.*

With the attack concentrating on Shiya, more of the ship's crew woke from the bridling slumber. Shouts and orders echoed all around her, both across the wheelhouse and through the highhorn to the rest of the ship.

Nyx kept one hand on Shiya's arm, using her bronze form as an anchor in the storm. The *Sparrowhawk* continued to tremble and rock, forging a hard path through the howling winds. Nyx stared past the windows, searching for the source of the bridle-song. Though the onslaught had waned, she sensed the dark strength out there, like thunderclouds stacked across the horizon.

*And we're heading right toward it.*

After shaking off the slumber, Darant had fought the *Sparrowhawk* high enough to clear the mountain range beyond the wide valley. By now, they had crossed most of the breadth of the Dragoncryst. Only a few jagged teeth of the range still cut across their path.

Graylin stuck to the brigand's shoulder. "Perhaps we should heed Nyx and turn aside from whatever's out there. Try another approach. Circle south or north."

For once, Nyx agreed with the knight.

Darant was not so easily swayed. "Our starboard hull's gutted. We're taking in cold winds faster than our coals can warm. I need to find a place to land and get that hole patched quick or we'll freeze to death. For now, we've got a bit of tailwind, and I need every scrap of help the gods can give me."

Fenn reported from his navigation station, bent over his farscope. "Dense ice fog ahead, just past the mountains, filling the skies. Probably churned up by the mix of warm and cold winds."

Nyx squinted at the view. Stars glinted high over the last of the peaks, but near the horizon, a wall of mist washed away their twinkling shine. It looked like the cold fog rose higher than the *Sparrowhawk* could climb. Trepidation pebbled the flesh of her arms.

*We mustn't go in there.*

She opened her mouth to voice this aloud when the wheelhouse door slammed open behind them. Cold blew into the room, accompanied by the muffled roaring of winds from the back of the ship. Hyck and Brayl hurried inside, bundled in fur coats. The grizzled engineer's lips were nearly blue. Darant's daughter shouldered the door shut, then turned with a scowl that looked frozen in place.

"Definitely not repairing that gaping rent from the air," Hyck reported. "The damage ripped out a whole cabin, along with a big corner of the kitchen, taking with it one of our stoves."

Brayl stalked forward, shaking ice from her dark braided locks. Her face was as grim as her report. "We can't account for two of the crew. Griss and Pyle. Quartermaster Vikas reported the two were headed for the kitchen to warm their bollocks after a spell out on deck."

She let them all picture what must have happened. If the two men had succumbed near that stove, they would have been unable to save themselves when the hull was breached.

Darant glared over at Graylin, as if daring him to ask again about turning aside.

Graylin simply crossed his arms, not taking up that challenge.

Nyx let go of Shiya and stepped closer to the two men. "Whatever attacked us, it's sheltering in that ice fog."

"Are you certain?" Graylin asked.

Nyx cast out her senses, tuned to the energies of bridle-song. "It . . . it feels like a black corruption snaking through those dark mists."

All eyes turned to the spread of windows. During the brief exchange, the *Sparrowhawk* had crested over the westernmost row of peaks. The last of the rocky crags vanished under their keel. The storm winds quickly abated, winnowing down to a few gusts. The swyftship settled into a smooth sail.

Ahead, the mists erased the world. The fogbank rose to the stars and spread unbroken to the north and south.

"We mustn't go in there," Nyx insisted.

"No choice, lass," Darant said. "I need a place to land. And soon. We can only hope the fog keeps us hidden long enough to find a spot." He leaned his mouth to the highhorn. "All crew. In a quarter-bell, we glide silent. Even a whisper after that, and I'll have your tongue."

Nyx gave the pirate a worried look, which he noted but ignored.

Graylin shifted closer. He glanced at Shiya, then back to her. "Do you have any inkling what's out there—or when they'll renew their attack?"

She shook her head. Shiya kept the blaze of bridle-song around the wheelhouse. It frazzled along the walls, as if the ship were already burning in a golden fire. It wasn't until this moment that she realized the assault upon the ship had stopped. All had gone quiet, as if the enemy had decided to match Darant's strategy.

"They've ceased their attack," Nyx whispered. "At least for now."

"Maybe they retreated," Darant offered hopefully. "Decided we're too much for them."

"No," she assured him. "They're biding their time."

"Until what?" Graylin asked.

"Until this."

The *Sparrowhawk* slipped into the mist's edge. The world vanished around them. As it did, the last of the winds died, too. Even the gusts ripping through the hull breach grew muffled. A dismaying silence settled over the ship.

Darant didn't have to remind the crew.

Everyone knew the truth.

Nyx reminded them in a whisper, "They're out there."

# 13

A HALF-BELL LATER, Nyx found herself posted beside Shiya again. Heeding Nyx's recommendation, the bronze woman had let her song die away. Nyx had feared that the blaze of Shiya's shield would be a beacon in this fog.

Rhaif kept vigil on Shiya's other side.

No one dared speak.

Graylin turned and looked hard at her, his silent question easy to read.

*Anything?*

She gave a small shake of her head. Her hand reached to Shiya's elbow. If another attack struck, the pair of them would have to act swiftly. Still, the waiting stretched to a dagger's edge. Her breathing grew heavier. Her eyes strained as she searched the featureless fog. Her stomach felt another swing of the ship.

At the wheel, Darant slowly circled the *Sparrowhawk,* spiraling them lower and lower. Blinded by the fog, he dared go no faster. Fenn kept watch under their keel through his farscopes, searching below. But it was as if the world had vanished entirely.

Nyx shifted her feet. By now, her sight had adjusted to the gloom. The mists faintly glowed in the moonlight. This far into the fog, the ship's windows were pebbled with droplets, obscuring the view. Nyx wiped similar beads of sweat from her forehead.

She studied her damp fingers with a frown.

*Something's not right.*

She let go of Shiya and passed to Darant's right. She reached out and placed her palm against the alchymically hardened glass.

The pirate glared at her, hissing low, "What're you doing, lass?"

She turned, her voice the barest whisper. "It's warm."

Darant thrust out his arm and dropped his hand next to hers. His brows shot high. His voice gasped a bit too loudly in surprise, "She's right!"

Nyx moved back. Her understanding of the world outside shifted. "It's not ice fog. It's not *fog* at all." She swung to the others. "It's *steam.*"

Graylin came forward to confirm the same, which irked Nyx.

*Why can't he trust my word?*

Fenn spoke softly from his station without lifting his eyes from his scope. "Must be some monstrous source of heat under us."

"And we're dropping straight toward it," Rhaif groaned.

Other crewmembers gathered by the windows. Fearful of what awaited them, everyone searched below.

Except for one.

"Beware," Shiya warned, her voice ringing sharply. Her face stared upward, as if her gaze could pierce through the roof. "They're coming."

Nyx felt it then, too. Since entering the steam bank, she had sensed a well of power ebbing and surging through the mists. It had kept a wary distance, but it now surged toward them from above, like a dark wave crashing upon a foundering raft.

She hurried to Shiya's side, pulling in a deep breath as she rushed. Shiya arched her back and sang, her voice as firm and bright as the bronze of her skin. Strands of bridle-song webbed quickly, knitting back into a shield. Nyx added her voice, focusing hard to push her pounding heart out of her throat.

She quickly found her harmony, bolstering Shiya's efforts. Together, they expanded the sphere of their protection out to the walls. Golden fire again sheltered those within the wheelhouse. She clenched a fist, bracing herself. She waited for the attack, for those dark spears of bridle-song to pound against their shield.

But that was not the threat.

Graylin stumbled with a gasp from the window. A large shadow swept past the ship's bow and vanished below them. Nyx caught the barest glimpse of scalloped wings. Her blood turned to ice at the sight. Her song faltered, fraying the edges of the blazing shield.

*It can't be . . .*

Then another shadow swept into view, hanging there for a breath, before snapping huge wings and shooting high. There was no denying the truth. The form was shaggy-pelted, with a shorter tail, but they all knew that creature.

"It's a bat," Rhaif said. "Like Bashaliia."

Nyx knew the thief was wrong.

*It's nothing like Bashaliia.*

More shadows shot and glided through the mists, staying high, barely discernible through the steam's pall.

"What're they doing?" Rhaif asked, drawing closer to Shiya.

The answer came as the ship gave a hard shudder, settled for a breath, then jolted again. Draft-iron cables whined and twanged outside.

"They're bombarding our gasbag!" Darant yelled. "Ripping into it."

Nyx craned her neck, staring upward. She knew swyftships like the *Sparrowhawk* were built as fighting vessels, faster and more agile than the giant warships. To withstand assaults, their balloons were compartmentalized into sections. A swyftship's gasbag could take several tears and still stay afloat. But there were limits to how much damage it could withstand.

"Hang tight!" Darant said as he shoved the maesterwheel forward.

The ship's bow dropped, sending the craft into a steep dive. Nyx's feet slid, but she grabbed hold of Shiya to stop herself. The song died in Nyx's throat, but the bronze woman did her best to keep a shield up. Nyx cast her senses, brushing against the fiery hatred flowing through the steam. So far, that power stayed out there, rather than being cast down upon the ship.

*Maybe their earlier assault burned through the bulk of their bridling energy, leaving them no choice but to attack physically.*

Darant spun the wheel, sending their descent into a tighter spiral. The sudden maneuver tossed Nyx to the side. She lost her grip, but Rhaif caught her. He pulled her back to Shiya, while also holding fast to the bronze woman.

"Can you call them off?" Rhaif gasped, speaking both to Nyx and Shiya. "Convince them we mean no harm?"

Nyx stared upward.

Shiya answered Rhaif, "They will not listen."

Nyx knew the woman was right. The colony out there might be distantly related to Bashaliia's, but something had malformed them. She sensed nothing like the cold astuteness of the swampland clan. What swept through the skies was feral, savage, but plainly still cunning—as this ambush demonstrated.

Despite Darant's efforts to shake off the haranguing flock, the ship continued to quake and rock. Nyx swore she could hear fabric rip as more of the balloon was torn by sharp claws.

*We're not going to last much longer.*

Graylin voiced the same, closing upon Darant. "It's hopeless! We must get to the sailrafts! Pray those smaller vessels can slip past that horde."

Nyx expected Darant—ever proud of the *Sparrowhawk*'s ability and his own skill—to dissent. She was wrong.

"Do it!" Darant flashed his gaze right and left, to the secondary stations, to his daughters. "Glace and Brayl, get Nyx and the others into those rafts. Find somewhere to hide in this steamy clag."

Glace stepped toward the man. "Father . . ."

He thrust an arm toward the door. "Go. I'm not giving up on the *Hawk* just yet."

Darant turned away, dismissing his daughters. Ever obedient, the two women closed upon Nyx and the others. Their faces were hard masks of concern.

Nyx spoke as the pair reached them. "I left Jace in the hold. He should've readied the rafts by now."

Behind them, Darant bellowed orders through the highhorn, divvying up assignments. He called back as they headed away, "Once free of the ship, dive fast! I'll do my best to draw the bastards off."

Nyx gasped as her skull suddenly burned. The small hairs danced across her skin. She glanced back as a huge shape flew into view. It struck the window with a resounding crash. The hardened glass splintered. The bat perched there, claws digging deep into the bow planks. Wings battered at the ship. Its ears lay flat to its skull, while fangs gnashed at the glass, smearing its surface with poison.

Those black-diamond eyes, though, never shifted. They glared straight at Nyx, tracking her as she fled with the others. For a breath, she sensed the horde-mind staring through at her. The cold malice cut into her skull—bringing with it a single thought, no words, only intent.

But it was clear enough.

***We will break you.***

# 14

HUDDLED IN THE hold of *Sparrowhawk*, Graylin grabbed Nyx's arm. Fear forged his fingers into iron. The others had already boarded the two sailrafts. Bundled in a thick coat, Nyx stood beside Bashaliia at the foot of their raft's ramp. She had wanted to wait until the last moment before leaving the beast's side.

"Get aboard," he ordered.

Even sheltered behind the sailraft, he had to yell. The *Sparrowhawk*'s massive stern door had been dropped flat, sticking out of the ship like a tongue, poking into the steamy darkness. Graylin kept watch on the skies as the ship spiraled deeper into the mists. The air stank worrisomely of sulfurous brimstan. After so long in the cold, the heat flowing into the ship felt oppressive.

"Now," Graylin pressed Nyx.

She kept a palm on the bat's cheek and glanced over. "Are you sure we can't take him with us? There's room."

"Barely, and we've gone over this. He's better off on his own and can follow us down. He's certainly far more agile than any raft. If anyone can escape those monsters, it's him."

She sighed and leaned her brow against her brother's bowed head, saying a final good-bye.

Deaf to bridle-song, Graylin imagined the energy passing between the two. In that moment, Nyx looked so much like Marayn. The tenderness in the girl's face, the steel in her eyes, even the edge of fury in the set to her lips. It all stung his heart. He prayed that he could take better care of her than he had her mother, a woman whom he had loved more than his own standing, his own blood oath, his own life. Still, Marayn had died in the Mýr swamps. He had failed her in the end, abandoning her in a futile attempt to lead the king's forces astray.

As Nyx straightened, he searched her face for features that matched his own, but all he could see was Marayn. Nyx might be his child, but he could not know for sure. He had shared Marayn's bed—memories of which were forever etched in his heart—but so had another, the man to whom she had been indentured. She had been raised among the pleasure serfs of King Toranth's palacio, becoming the sovereign's most beloved treasure. The king had forbidden any other man from touching her.

But Graylin had broken an oath and trespassed where he shouldn't have, bringing ruin to all. The guilt had become as much a part of him as his scars and calloused bones. Still, the gods had granted him a measure of absolution.

He stared at the young woman before him. He didn't care if she was his daughter or not, only that she was Marayn's. He'd treasure even this small part of the woman he once loved.

Bashaliia finally backed away from the ramp, fluttering his wings loose.

Nyx stared after him, her expression pained. "Be careful. Stay close to us."

With matters settled, Graylin herded Nyx up into the small hold of the sailraft. He looked over at the other craft.

As he watched, its stern door snapped shut. Rhaif and Shiya were already inside. The immense weight of the bronze woman had limited the number of crew it could carry. Darant's daughter Glace manned its controls. The only others aboard were the engineer Hyck, along with a pair of brothers, Perde and Herl.

Brayl called from the wheel of Graylin's raft, "Seal us up! My sister is ready to launch!"

With a grimace, Graylin rushed into the hold and grabbed the crank handle just inside. Using all his shoulder strength, he wheeled it around and around. The stern door slowly rose behind him.

Inside, Nyx crossed to Jace and Krysh. The two of them had hauled in a crate of hastily packed books, tomes apparently too precious to leave behind. Graylin didn't care. If nothing else, the volumes would make good kindling for a fire.

On the other side of the hold stood two more crewmembers. Fenn leaned over Brayl's shoulder. The navigator gestured and talked rapidly, likely planning for their descent. Looming over them was Quartermaster Vikas. The woman stood a head taller than Graylin and massed twice his size. She was all muscle and grimness encased in leather armor. She carried a broadsword, one so lengthy it had to be sheathed across her back.

More passengers could've been crammed in here, even with Kalder's hulking size aboard, but the rest of the crew, numbering eight or nine, had opted to remain on board, to help Darant in his own escape. They all knew their only hope of completing the journey—or even returning home—depended on saving the *Sparrowhawk*.

Brayl elbowed Fenn back, snapping at him, "Give me some sodding space already. I know what I have to do."

Graylin recognized her ire was not directed at the navigator. She rankled at having to abandon her father. Still, the two sisters were the best pilots aboard the *Hawk*, possibly even better than Darant.

*We need their skill.*

Jace suddenly yelped and jerked back. He pointed toward the bow window. "They've found us!"

Graylin twisted around to see what had provoked the young man. Outside the swyftship, a pair of shadows swept through the steamy mists. Until now, the beasts had been harrying the gasbag and upper deck, ignoring the lower stern.

No longer.

One shadow cartwheeled through the air and dove toward the open deck of the *Sparrowhawk*. It landed on the dropped door outside. Claws skidded across the planks. Its leathery wings were held high, its head low. It hissed, baring teeth, likely wary at the strangeness of the ship's interior. Its sheer size—twice that of an ox—drew all their breath.

"Launch!" Graylin gasped out. They could not risk the enormous creature damaging either sailraft. They had to go before the beast got its bearings.

Another realized the same.

A resounding twang sounded to the left. The other raft shot out into the mists like a wooden bolt. It sailed far, nearly vanishing. Before it did, a small balloon exploded from its top, snapping taut, catching the craft before it plummeted. Small jets of alchymical fire burst from its stern forge, propelling it into the cloak of the mists.

Startled by the launch, the massive bat had flapped to the side. It now blocked their path. Fiery eyes turned upon their vessel. With a deafening screech, it lunged at them, claws reaching.

"Go," Jace urged.

Brayl held off, rightly so, voicing her concern. "If it rips into our furled gasbag . . ."

Graylin understood. *Better to be trapped aboard the* Sparrowhawk *than risk a deadly plunge in a damaged raft.*

Nyx moaned and shoved a palm to the roof. "Don't."

Gray frowned, confused—then a shadow sped over the top of the sailraft.

Nyx's arm dropped leadenly. "Bashaliia, no . . ."

Her brother dove upon the huge attacker, striking hard. The two tumbled and twisted away. The enemy screamed and thrashed, surprised by the ambush. Despite the disparity in size, Bashaliia drove the beast out of the stern. The pair fell away, tangled together, lashing at one another, then vanished into the steamy mists.

Nyx fell to her knees. "No . . ."

Brayl didn't wait. "Hold tight."

Everyone snatched for hanging loops of leather. Graylin abandoned the crank and grabbed for one of them. The raft's stern door remained a quarter open, but it couldn't be helped. They dared not wait another breath.

Brayl pulled a lever, and the raft snapped forward, thrust by the launch cables. The craft blasted out of the *Sparrowhawk*. Graylin lost his footing and swung from his loop. Kalder skated on his paws across the floor, bumping into him. Nyx, still on her knees, toppled over, but Jace grabbed a fistful of her coat and held her in place.

Graylin's stomach lurched as the cast-off raft plummeted for a long spell. Brayl clearly wanted some distance from the ship, from what swept through these mists. Then a small blast sounded overhead. Graylin pictured the balloon bursting taut above them. The raft's plunge stopped short, hard enough to rip his fingers from the leather loop.

He kept his legs under him and twisted around to peer out the gap in the stern door. He glimpsed the *Sparrowhawk* as it was swallowed by the mists. Shadows chased after the ship, then they disappeared, too.

Brayl ignited their stern forge. Blue-orange flames spat out into the steam. The fire sputtered a moment, then roared into a steady blaze. The raft sped faster now, fleeing in the opposite direction.

Nyx stood up shakily and stumbled toward Graylin at the door. "Bashaliia?"

Graylin searched the skies. "I don't see him."

She joined him, even allowing him to put an arm around her. She trembled as she stared out.

Graylin tightened his arm. "He'll find his way back."

Nyx's next words were a whisper. "But where are we going?"

Silence settled over the hold, all lost in their own thoughts. Then the raft veered sharply portside, throwing Graylin and Nyx to the side.

Brayl cursed behind the wheel.

Fenn gasped.

Graylin turned in time to see the raft skirt away from an icy cliff that filled the world on that side. Dark blue meltwater streamed across its surface in countless cascades. He crossed toward the wheel, gathering the rest with him.

"I don't understand," he said. "Have we circled back to the fringes of the Dragoncryst?"

"Impossible." Fenn leaned closer to the window. "I'm navigator enough, even in this steamy clag, to know we've not done that. This wall of ice . . ." He glanced back to everyone. "I think we might've fallen into some massive seam or rift in the Ice Shield."

Jace cringed. "Should we head back up, try to sail clear of it?"

Fenn looked higher. "I can't even see the top."

"There's no going back," Brayl declared. "We'd burn through our reserves trying to climb that far. And we all know what awaits us up there."

Krysh joined them and pointed down. "Whatever lies below us must be the source of the steam. When we crested over the mountains, the sheer breadth of those mists had been impressive, spreading at least a hundred leagues to the north and south. And there's no telling how *wide* it might be. If this is indeed some rift in the ice, it must be colossal."

"Then what do we do?" Jace asked.

"We continue down," Graylin said. "Like Brayl said. There must be a bottom to it."

Jace shrugged. "If so, I guess it'll at least be warm."

Nyx ignored the ice cliff. Her gaze remained high, her thoughts easy to read, as was her fear.

Graylin placed a hand on her shoulder, reassuring her again. It was all he could do. "He'll find us."

Nyx simply repeated her earlier words. "But where are we going?"

He gazed down into the steamy depths of the chasm.

*I wish I knew.*

Arkival limne of
Raash'ke
(native to the
Ice Shield)

# FOUR

# THE FORBIDDEN EYE

*Littel beyond rumour is known about the Abyssal Codex,
the shadowi librarie of the Dresh'ri. It is sayd that those
who have seen it are blind'd. Those that spayk of it have
their tungues cut out. Those that trespass be gutt'd most
foully. Only one truth is beyond questioun: the dred wisdom to be found there is as much a wepen as any sword.*

—From *Travails of the Southern Klashe*
by Heraa hy Rost, who, seven years later,
would suffer all the tragedies mentioned above—
his ravaged body recovered from a salt well
in the city of Qazen

# 15

As the second bell of Eventoll rang through the palace, Kanthe sank gratefully into the steaming stone bath. Soothing salts and other alchymical compounds had been ladled into the waters, along with redolent perfumes. He didn't know if any of it was efficacious in healing his wounds, only that the salt burned all the scrapes and cuts that he had sustained from the ambush.

Still, he lowered himself with a grimace until only his face remained above water. He stared up at the dozens of oil lanterns hanging overhead, all aglow, casting flickering beams through starlike perforations in the tin. He closed his eyes, trying to center himself.

After the events of the day, he and Rami had been interviewed by the emperor's counselors—a trio of stern-faced elders—to the point of exhaustion and irritation. The three had drawn out every detail about the attack from the two young men without offering any information in return. Likewise, each soldier, archer, and guardsman was equally interrogated, but with much less civility. Several were rewarded with silver wreaths for their bravery; others were scolded and led off at swordpoint. No doubt the head of the guard would have been executed for allowing the royal party to be ambushed, but the man had died in the explosion, which was probably a godsend. His death out in the city had surely been less painful than what he would've found down in the emperor's dungeons.

Notably absent from the proceedings had been Aalia herself. Once their war wagon had reached the palace citadel, she had been rushed away, along with her surviving Chaaen. Even in the bath now, Kanthe could not shake the fury in her face, directed at him, as if he were to blame for everything.

The slam of a door echoed across the tiled bath chamber. Kanthe sat straighter with a groan. Pratik entered, accompanied by Frell hy Mhlaghifor, the alchymist from Kanthe's former school. Both men's eyes fell upon him. From their expressions, the day's inquiries were not yet finished.

Frell stopped at the edge of the wide bath, hands on his hips. He towered over Kanthe. He wore his usual alchymical garb of a belted black robe. The only addition was a silver circlet crowning his dark ruddy hair, which had been braided into a tail that reached his shoulders. From the shining circlet hung a thin veil—gauzier than the typical *byor-ga* of the baseborn castes. It marked Frell as one of the Unfettered, a foreigner to these lands. The veil was presently drawn aside, revealing a stern scowl, his typical expression when looking down upon Kanthe, his former student.

"Seems trouble is drawn to you as surely as flies to shite," Frell commented.

Kanthe grunted tiredly. "But in this comparison, am I the fly or the shite?"

"Neither, in fact," Pratik interceded. "I suspect the morning's ambush had nothing to do with *you,* Prince Kanthe. They were clearly after the princess."

"It was a bold strike," Frell admitted. "As the only daughter of the emperor, she would be a prize above all."

"That is, if the attackers succeeded," Pratik added. "It cost them eighteen men in the failed attempt to grab her."

"But who were *they?*" Kanthe asked.

Pratik frowned. "From the attacker's white-masked eyes, they are no doubt members of the *Shayn'ra,* meaning the *Fist of God,* a faction of heretical fighters that have plagued the Southern Klashe for over a century—though clearly, they've grown bolder of late."

Kanthe pictured the leader standing in the street, undaunted by the failure of his ambush. "But what do they want?"

"To sow chaos and discord. With the ultimate goal of ending the rule of Klashean god-emperors and returning the land's riches to its people."

Frell snorted. "Or more likely to simply usurp Haeshan and take his place. History is rife with such fighters who espouse freedom, but in the end, prove to be as despotic as those they take down."

"Mayhap." Pratik shrugged. "The Haeshan line did indeed destroy the Kastian clan five centuries ago, who wiped out every heir of the Rylloran tribe prior to their rule. Still, we should not underestimate the *Shayn'ra,* especially now."

"Why's that?" Kanthe asked.

"I suspect the attempt to grab Aalia was stoked by your father's attack to the north. They likely sought to take advantage of the bombing to make their move. They must've hurriedly staged that overturned wagon in the streets to push us into their trap."

Kanthe winced, remembering the toppled cart, the recalcitrant ox, and the men struggling to right it. *I hadn't even considered they were part of the attack.*

"And even in their haste," Pratik added, "the ambushers came close to succeeding."

"All too close," Kanthe mumbled, noting the sting of his wounds.

With a heavy sigh, Pratik shifted over to the steps that led down into the bath. Here in the palace, the Chaaen had shed his *byor-ga* habiliment and wore only a knee-length tunic and sandals. Apparently, even such clothing was too much to bear. Pratik shed out of his tunic and kicked off his sandals.

As Pratik stepped down into the bath, Kanthe looked studiously elsewhere—

not out of shyness at the man's nakedness. Kanthe had grown accustomed to the lack of modesty found indoors here. Instead, he was discomfited by the Chaaen's disfigurement, by the lack of manhood between his legs. Not to mention the crisscrossing of white scars across his dark skin and the iron collar forever fixed to his neck. All were testament to Pratik graduating from the *Bad'i Chaa,* the House of Wisdom.

Kanthe had thought his own tutelage at Kepenhill had been stern and demanding. It paled in comparison. While his school had discouraged trysts, demanding purity, the House of Wisdom enforced it by clipping their first-years. Worst of all, those who failed to move upward were executed. Those that survived were rewarded by being indentured to the *imri* class, to forever serve as chaaen-bound advisers. Most of the time, when Pratik was fully clothed, it was easy to forget the misery hidden beneath. Only now, that harsh history was undeniably bared.

It all served as a stark reminder that Kanthe was on foreign soil, about to marry into a culture that still appalled him in many ways.

*Maybe the* Shayn'ra *have a point . . .*

As the Chaaen settled into the steaming waters, he seemed not to notice Kanthe's discomfort. Pratik's features remained placid, as if he readily accepted such cruelties as a part of life. Instead, he remained focused on the matter at hand.

"That all said, the ambush on the street has me less concerned than the bombing to the north by Hálendiian forces," Pratik reminded them. "If war breaks out, we'll never reach the site of the Sleeper buried near Qazen."

Frell crossed his arms. "Perhaps the assault upon the princess may serve us in the end. We may be able to use that attack to move up the wedding date."

"How?" Kanthe asked.

Frell rubbed the shadowy stubble on his chin, clearly reappraising the situation. "Emperor Haeshan needs this wedding to take place. He's already announced it. His will is considered that of a god among the people. He will lose face if the wedding doesn't happen."

Kanthe's stomach churned queasily at the thought of rushing the marriage.

Frell continued, "We might be able to convince the emperor that if something were to happen to Aalia, the thwarting of her wedding would further denigrate His Illustriousness. Such a threat might sway him to move up the date of the nuptials."

Pratik shook his head. "Such reasoning will fail. Emperor Haeshan has already reinforced her protection. He'll keep her confined to the palace and under heavy guard. He'll not risk the chance of a second attempt by the *Shayn'ra.*"

Frell frowned. "But—"

Pratik cut him off. "The winter solstice is too important. On that day, the full moon will shine high in the sky with the sun at its lowest point. It is a rare event, considered portentous among our people. Emperor Haeshan will want his only daughter married under such an auspicious moon. It will take far more than a failed kidnapping to move him off that date."

"Then what will?" Kanthe asked, doing his best to hide his dread.

"I will need to ponder it further," Pratik admitted. "But it might aid our cause if you could convince Rami to support this change of plan. Perhaps you should bed the prince, after all. It might help us. He is considered quite skilled, it is said."

Kanthe's face heated. "I . . . I've already agreed to marriage. Isn't that enough?"

Pratik ignored him and turned to Frell. "If we do succeed in changing the date of the wedding, we must consider our *other* mission here in Kysalimri."

Frell grimaced. "To search for what knowledge lies hidden in the librarie of the Abyssal Codex."

Pratik nodded. "If the wedding date is moved up, we'll have less time to accomplish that task." He waved toward the door. "To that end, how did your audience with the Dresh'ri go this morning?"

Frell shrugged. "I met with Zeng ri Perrin, their head inquisitor, along with two elders. Over the breadth of the morning, Zeng pressed me about my past, my training, my lines of study, settling on the most important question: *what knowledge I sought among their ancient tomes.* I thought it best not to prevaricate, especially as I wouldn't be able to hide my line of inquiry once I gained entry. So, I told them the truth—that I sought apocalyptic prophecies from the time of the Forsaken Ages."

Pratik nodded. "It was wise not to lie. The Dresh'ri name means *Forbidden Eye.* It is said the eldest among them can read the truth in one's words."

"How did they respond?" Kanthe asked.

Frell touched the crook of his left arm. "Still unknown. After the questioning, they leeched blood from me, then left, saying they would inform me of their judgement later."

"I imagine the bloodletting will be used for an oracular reckoning," Pratik explained. "To further judge you. Did they offer no other hint of their assessment?"

Frell paced the edge of the pool. "At the conclusion of the questioning, Zeng consulted with the other two Dresh'ri, who hadn't spoken all morning long. I overheard one phrase, only because it was repeated twice, once by each of the elders before they left."

"What phrase?" Pratik asked.

"If I made them out correctly, it was *Vyk dyre Rha.*"

Kanthe scowled. "What does that mean?"

"I don't know," Frell admitted. "But one elder spoke it like a curse. The other whispered it reverently."

Pratik had shifted straighter in the water. His eyes had gone huge, showing too much white. *"Vyk dyre Rha,"* he whispered.

Frell focused on the Chaaen. "You know those words?"

Before the Chaaen could answer, a low rumble rose all around them. The waters of the bath trembled and shook. The lanterns overhead swayed. They all held their breath until the disturbance settled.

"Another quake," Frell whispered dourly. "It's the third since we arrived on these shores."

Kanthe knew what worried the man, what the alchymist believed this portended. Frell had shared his worries with them: that the gradual approach of the moon to the Urth was the source of these disturbances, a sign that moonfall was growing ever nearer.

Kanthe tried to discount it. "I asked Rami about it. He said the Southern Klashe suffers such shakes with fair regularity."

"Not with this frequency," Frell countered. "I reviewed stratigraphy archives at the *Bad'i Chaa.* Going back centuries. The quakes have been growing stronger and more often. Even the recorded tides seem to be rising higher, especially over the last two decades."

Kanthe shook his head. Whether Frell was being paranoid or not, there was nothing to be done about it. He returned to their prior discussion, facing Pratik. "Back to this *Vyk dyre Rha* that Frell mentioned . . . what do you know about it?"

Pratik remained quiet. He had to swallow twice before answering. "It's a name. In ancient Klashean. It translates as the *Shadow Queen.*"

Kanthe and Frell let the Chaaen collect himself, sensing he needed a moment.

"I . . . I only heard it spoken once before," Pratik said, his gaze far off. "By a scholar at the *Bad'i Chaa.* He was my mentor, an alchymical historian who studied the Forsaken Ages. One day, he drew me to his private scholarium. He claimed he had come across a single mention of a god-daemon in one of his alchymical texts—the *Vyk dyre Rha*—but the creature was not part of the Klashean pantheon of gods."

Kanthe pictured sailing through the Stone Gods out in the Bay of the Blessed, each atoll carved into the likeness of those celestial beings.

"My teacher believed he had made an important discovery and consulted with the Dresh'ri. He went down into the Abyssal Codex to continue his research—and was never seen again. Later, his name was stricken from the House of Wisdom, as if he had never set foot there."

Frell frowned. "Strange. What did your mentor's text say about this Shadow Queen?"

"Little beyond terror. It is prophesied the daemon would gain flesh and form and bring about the fiery end of the Urth. But I'm convinced the Dresh'ri know more, that they lured my teacher down into their librarie to silence him forever. He must have kept quiet about sharing this knowledge with me. Or else I would've surely suffered the same fate. Since then, I've listened discreetly but learned nothing more. Just rumors that the Dresh'ri worship a god—one that bears no sigil or symbol. The name is never spoken, so I can't be sure, but I've long suspected—"

"That it's this *Vyk dyre Rha*," Kanthe said.

Pratik nodded and stood. Despite the heat of the bath, his skin prickled with cold bumps of terror. He faced Frell. "You must *not* go down to that librarie, even if you are invited. Refuse. Say you've decided to pursue another angle of study."

Frell remained silent, but Kanthe knew his mentor. If anything, this story stoked the alchymist's curiosity. The Abyssal Codex would lure him—as surely as a fly to shite, to use the alchymist's earlier words.

But considering Pratik's warning, Kanthe knew a more apt analogy. No matter the danger, his teacher would be drawn there . . .

Like a moth to a searing flame.

# 16

FRELL PACED HIS sanctum afforded him by the emperor. Beyond the chamber, he shared the larger spread of rooms with Kanthe, but this space had become Frell's private scholarium.

After the discussion in the bath chamber, the three had gone their separate ways. The prince had left to seek out Rami and attempt to win the young man to their accelerated timetable. Pratik had disappeared to see if he could glean anything further after Frell's interrogation by the Dresh'ri. The Chaaen had connections throughout the sprawling citadel, ears who listened for him.

Alone now for the past three bells, Frell intended to pursue his own investigation here in his study. The space was a quarter the size of his scholarium at Kepenhill. He missed his old place, which was centered around a giant bronze scope that he had used for his astronomical studies, a scholarship that had confirmed the slow and incremental swelling of the moon's face over centuries of time, warning of a pending apocalypse.

*Moonfall . . .*

Remembering the earlier quake, he stopped at a window to stare up at that threat in the sky. According to the Hálendiian faith, the moon was home to the twin gods, the bright Son and dark Daughter, who continually chased each other around and around, waxing and waning the moon's countenance. Presently, the silvery face of the Son glowed full in a sky that had dimmed to purple with the last bell of Eventoll. The sun itself was currently out of sight, shining near the horizon behind the tower.

Frell had been studying the sky's celestial dance for the entirety of his scholarship at Kepenhill. Astronomical studies had always fascinated him, going back to his earliest days as a child. He rubbed his left shoulder, where a family brand had been burned into his skin, marking his heritage. He hailed from the cold northern steppes of Aglerolarpok, at the westernmost edge of the Crown, where the sun would sink most of the way each winter, allowing the glittering arc of stars to reveal themselves, offering a glimpse of the hidden void and its vast mysteries. As a boy, he would often climb atop the roof of their family barn and gaze in wonder at the splendor, sometimes even seeing the radiant shimmer of the Veils waving across the northern horizon in hues of emerald and blues.

Such a life seemed forever ago, not even his own. His family had owned a horse ranch, raising the hardy and prized Aglerolarpok ponies. Oftentimes, he swore he could still smell their musky sweat, the heavy drapes of their manes. The odor seemed to rise off his own skin, as if his young body had been inescapably steeped in the brine of their scent.

*Still, that was ages ago . . .*

He turned his back to the window.

*How simple life had been back then.*

The rhythms and pace of those days had been comfortably routine: waking as the sun showed its full face, moving ponies to their pastures, the ever-rolling cycle of foaling seasons. It seemed like another person's life, something he read in an old husbandry text.

When he was only eight, he had shown enough promise that a teacher advocated for him to seek a spot at one of the Hálendiian schools. His mother's face had shone with such pride, while his father had simply looked relieved, perhaps happy to cast his seventh son aside, a son who was more dreamer than horseman. Frell was tested and accepted into the Cloistery of Brayk, a school deep in the Mýr swamps. After he had risen through its nine tiers and gained the black robe of alchymy, he had moved on to the school of Kepenhill, becoming the youngest member of their ruling Council of Eight. It was there he met Prince Kanthe and where his studies revealed the danger hanging over their heads, a threat that would be confirmed by the visions of a young girl.

*And now, ever a wanderer, I've moved on yet again to the Southern Klashe.*

He shook away this reverie and crossed to his wide desk. Its surface was piled with dusty books and stacked with brittle scrolls. Some he had carried with him—mostly those astronomical treatises concerning the moon—but others he had culled from the libraries across the vast city of Kysalimri. He had even ventured into the *Bad'i Chaa* to search its shelves. The school's librarie was easily tenfold larger than the one at Kepenhill. Still, he had been happy to leave the House of Wisdom, a dreary and solemn city within a city. To him, it appeared to be more a prison than a school. Few would meet his eye; none would speak to him. Then again, he had to wear his veil, marking him as an Unfettered. Even out in the streets, he had been shunned, as if brushing against him might lower one's caste, a system so complicated he still failed to understand it fully.

Pratik had tried to illuminate those mysteries, to explain how each citizen served as a cog in the vast machine that was Kysalimri. They each knew their place, their duty, and took solace in their role. And maybe he was right. Most seemed resigned, if not happy with their fate, having a task they could take pride in. It was said that the *oil* that fueled this city was the *blood* of its people. And despite his personal misgivings, it had worked for eighteen centuries.

Kysalimri remained the Crown's oldest city.

It was also home to the land's most ancient scholarly order—the Dresh'ri—who were centuries older than even the daemon-worshipping Iflelen back in Hálendii. The Iflelen cabal adored the dark god Đreyk, whose sigil was the viperous *horn'd snaken.* Blood sacrifices were burned at His altars far below Kepenhill.

Frell frowned, weighing Pratik's earlier warning.

*Do the Dresh'ri have their own dark god—or in this case, goddess—whom they worship?*

He had not even considered this possibility but did not doubt its veracity. And not just because of Pratik's assertion. Another had made a similar accusation once, long ago. It was why his thoughts had drifted into a melancholy past. While studying at the Cloistery of Brayk, he had been befriended by the head of the school—Prioress Ghyle—who hailed from the Southern Klashe. After events of the past summer, where she had helped Nyx and her allies, Frell had heard rumors that the prioress had been dragged in chains to Azantiia, where it was believed she was executed.

Frell closed his eyes, trying to squeeze back a heartbreak that was wrung with guilt.

The two of them had shared countless long evenings, deep in conversation, often deeper into their cups. They had discussed philosophy, esoteric theories of alchymy, even heretical talks of religion. Pratik's earlier words stirred up an old memory, one that haunted him now. Prioress Ghyle had been discussing how the dozen Hálendiian gods found their counterparts in the Klashe, only spread across thirty-three different deities. With her words slurring, she had insisted there were actually thirty-*four* gods among the Klashe. He had challenged her, but she had grown pensive. He still remembered what she claimed next.

*Some gods are too shadowed for the light to reach them, especially when they're buried under the gardens of the Imri-Ka.* And she offered a warning, too. *Pray that such a god never claws free of the darkness. It will mark the end of the world.*

At the time, Frell had dismissed her drunken ramblings as some incredulous fable.

But no longer.

Standing at the desk, he shifted a tome out of its stack and brushed dust from its cover. Gilt lettering spelled out FA MADBA ABDI'RI, which translated as *At the Altar of the Eternal Eye.* It was the oldest written history of the Dresh'ri. The cover depicted the scalloped wings of a black bat with a golden eye in the center, the sigil of the secretive order.

Frell ran a finger along the symbol, reminded of Nyx and her companion.

He wondered how she and the others were faring. He had no way of knowing. All he could do was focus on his own task.

He had already scoured this particular book, hoping it would help him better understand the order. It claimed the Dresh'ri were the founders not only of the House of Wisdom, but of *all* the Crown's schools. Which could be true. While each school was unique—some freer, others stricter—they basically adhered to the nine-tiered structure. Further bolstering this assertion, the Dresh'ri maintained their order's strict number by getting first pick of the Wisdom's graduating scholars, overriding all other claims. It is said even emperors bowed before the Dresh'ri.

Of course, wilder assertions peppered the book, some clearly fanciful: that the Dresh'ri could commune with the dead, conjure up spirits, bend others to their will with a single breath, even craft unique alchemies out of blood tailored to that person, from love spylls to specialty poisons.

With a slight chill at this thought, Frell rubbed the crook of his arm, where his own blood had been leeched away. Pratik claimed it could be used to better judge Frell. He hoped that was all they did with his life's blood.

Pushing down that worry, he picked up the book, intending to read through it again, to search for any inkling of this *Vyk dyre Rha,* this Shadow Queen, haunting between its lines.

*I must know more before I dare venture into their librarie.*

AS ANOTHER BELL chimed away, Frell struggled to keep his eyes open, thwarting his best intentions to read all night. The lines of text blurred; his chin bobbed toward his chest. Seated in a chair by the window, he finally closed the book in his lap.

*Enough . . . I'm learning nothing new.*

With a groan, he stood. His legs wobbled with his first steps toward his desk. He was only thirty-seven, but he suddenly felt like an old man. As he caught his balance, a whiff of a familiar scent struck him. He stopped and inhaled deeper.

*What is that?*

It smelled of summer-parched hay and the warm musk of a mare ready to breed. He lifted the edge of his robe and sniffed at it, believing it rose from his own skin, his Aglerolarpok past rising up again—but all he smelled was his own sweat and wool that needed freshening.

He straightened and searched his sanctum.

*What strangeness is this?*

The aroma drew him toward the room's closed door. With each step, the odor grew stronger. He spied wisps of smoke trailing under the door and into his chamber. Fearing Kanthe might have left coals burning in a hearth and started a fire, he hurried to the door and opened it.

Smoke wafted over him, carrying that same scent. The room beyond was fogged into obscurity. He stepped forward but halted at the threshold, fear icing through him. Despite his hesitation, he drew a deeper breath, unable to stop himself. The scent of home was too alluring, calling to the boy who ran the fields and fought off ponies with a stick, pretending it was a sword.

The world swam around him, weakening his legs.

Past and present blurred.

He slumped toward the stone floor. As he did, shadowy figures rushed through the smoke, coming toward him. They were robed in white, with cowls embroidered in gold.

*The Dresh'ri.*

He fell to his back, his limbs gone leaden. He tried to lift his head, but it was too heavy. He lay flat, only his chest moving up and down, drawing more of the alchymy into his body. Though the view spun, he remained awake. He could still smell his past suffused in the rolling pall, taste it on his tongue. Only his muscles refused his commands.

Hands grabbed his arms, his legs.

Unable to fight them, he was lifted from the floor and carried out of his sanctum.

*Where are they taking me?*

A face appeared before him, leaning close. The man's embroidered cowl had fallen askew, revealing a familiar forked beard, hawkish nose, and dark eyes. It was the Dresh'ri emissary who had questioned Frell.

Zeng ri Perrin spoke quickly. "Frell hy Mhlaghifor, you've been judged worthy to enter the Abyssal Codex. It is an honor beyond words. Especially for one exiled to our lands. Take comfort in this invitation."

Relief and hope swelled through Frell, but it was dashed by the Dresh'ri's next words.

"But know this—once you enter, you will never leave."

# 17

KANTHE LOWERED THE long-stemmed pipe from his lips and stifled a
cough. "Oof, this leaf is strong," he said. "My heart is pounding in my throat.
What's in it?"

Rami smiled, showing the full whiteness of his teeth. "Tabakroot, snake-
weed, and a pinch of ramblefoot."

Kanthe rested the pipe on his knee, careful to keep any ash from his polished
boots. In fresh trousers and an untied shirt, he felt overheated and overdressed
on the private balcony.

Rami wore only a loosely belted robe, showing the swatch of hair across his
chest that climbed his throat and formed a close-cropped beard that looked
as if it had been painted in place. The Klashean prince had also sought a bath
after the trying day and remained barefooted. The curls of his hair had dried
disheveled, adding a certain rakish charm to the young man.

Kanthe found it hard not to keep Pratik's earlier suggestion out of his head,
about bedding Rami. Especially when the Klashean prince spent considerable
time lounging in his cushioned chair, with one leg up, revealing far too much
of what lay under his robe. Still, even with the lack of attire, Rami showed no
attempt to seduce Kanthe.

Instead, after Kanthe had arrived here, the two had shared a small meal of
braised duck and spiced beans and a bottle of Aailish wine each. Afterward,
they had retired to the balcony overlooking the city to smoke and perhaps
finally broach the subject for Kanthe's visit.

Rami had refused to talk about the wedding while eating, deeming it inap-
propriate conversation. Klashean custom frowned upon discussing anything
beyond the trivial while breaking bread. Instead, they had talked animatedly
about hunting—an affinity they both shared. They even shared stories of their
childhood, finding much in common. Both were sons who had no hope of
ever sitting on the throne, whose only expectations were to bolster their more
illustrious counterparts. In Rami's case, that was his eldest brother by a decade, Prince Jubayr.

Rami took a deep draught from his pipe, holding it in for an impossibly
long time, then steamed it out of both nostrils. He pointed the pipe's glowing
bowl at the swirling smoke. "All our fine leaf is grown from the royal farms

out in the surrounding M'venlands. We should go there sometime. It is quite striking when all the fields are in bloom."

Kanthe took this opportunity to broach the subject of his visit. "Maybe we could stop there during the royal procession following my wedding."

"Indeed." Rami lifted a brow. "Does that mean I'm invited to go along? My sister may have a say in the matter."

Kanthe muttered as he took another tentative draw on his pipe, "I think if Aalia had any *say,* she'd call off this wedding."

Rami smiled. "She'd never go against my father's wishes. Your nuptials are too important to the empire. Both now and in the future, especially once she bears you a son."

"Ah, someone who could claim by blood the throne of Hálendii." Kanthe understood the situation all too well. "Still, that iron in the fire might take forever to heat, if it ever does. A war must be won, and a certain brother set aside."

Rami shrugged. "My father strategizes beyond the moment. Like ancient Kysalimri itself, our people abide and are ever patient. Any stratagem, like our finest wine, is best appreciated when it has time to properly age. Nothing should be rushed."

Rami's gaze lingered a touch too long on Kanthe, silently hinting that the Klashean prince was willing to wait for what he wanted, too.

Kanthe turned away and cleared his throat. "Speaking of rushing. Plainly the situation between kingdom and empire is about to become more dire. I see the emperor is already mobilizing his own forces."

Kanthe pointed beyond the balcony railing. The breadth of Kysalimri—a forest of marble towers and spires, some topped in gold—sprawled to the horizon, shining under a full moon and aglow from the low-cast sun. It was breathtaking and intimidating in equal measures. It appeared to have no end. It was as if the city were the world, and the world were this city.

Hovering over it all, a fleet of four ponderous warships slowly moved across the city, carried aloft by their giant gasbags. They dwarfed anything in the Hálendiian forces. The ships themselves were armored in drab draft-iron, but even at this distance, the rows of ballistas and cannons glinted in the low sun of midwinter. And if that weren't enough, each ship was flanked by dozens of sharklike hunterskiffs and fox-nosed swyftships. The entire fleet headed north, ready to defend the coastline after the kingdom's attack. Perhaps they'd even sail through the smoky Breath of the Urth to reach the southern shores of Hálendii and retaliate in kind.

"War will soon be upon us," Kanthe continued. "Perhaps it might be best to firm those ties that will bind our two lands together sooner rather than later. Come the winter's solstice, it may be too late."

Rami shifted to lean on a shoulder, facing him more directly. "You wish to hasten your marriage to my sister?" The Klashean prince must have read the hesitation in Kanthe's expression and pressed the matter. "Is this something *you* truly desire?"

"It . . . it could best serve everyone."

Rami's eyes narrowed. "Does that include you?"

Kanthe knew better than to lie to his friend.

Rami leaned back with a heavy sigh. "Is that why you came here this Eventoll? To petition me for this cause?"

"Yes," Kanthe answered bluntly. "But that does not mean I don't value our friendship—our future kinship. But I know my father too well. He must've learned of the coming wedding, and he'll set fire to all the Crown to stop it. But if I'm already married, it will take the winds from his sails."

"Or it may make him even angrier."

"True. But if there's even a chance to stop an all-out war, we must attempt it. To change the nuptials is a simple act that could be rewarded with a quelling of hostilities. At least for a time. A spell long enough perhaps for diplomacy to work."

Rami took another long draw on his pipe, exhaling slowly before speaking. "You say you know your father well. As I do mine. The emperor is like a mountain, not easy to move. Once he has stated his will, it will prove difficult to shift off that date."

"The winter solstice . . ."

"Let me confide in you." Rami's eyes found Kanthe's again. "Not only is that day auspicious to my people, the emperor consulted with the Augury of Qazen, a prophetic wyzard who has my father's ear, more so than any of his thirty-three Chaaen. He holds much sway over the emperor."

"I know someone like that." Kanthe gritted his teeth, picturing Shrive Wryth, a corrupt Iflelen swine who forever whispered in his own father's ear.

"I suspect the reason the emperor seldom leaves the palace citadel is because of a warning from the Augury, though I can't prove it or dismiss it." Rami scowled deeply. "It was also the Augury who selected the date of your nuptials."

Kanthe sat back with a groan. "So, Emperor Haeshan will never budge."

"Like the stubbornest ox."

Kanthe sagged, mostly disappointed, but also slightly relieved. "Thank you, Rami, for sharing this confidence."

"You are most welcome, my friend. But I must ask the smallest of favors in return."

Kanthe swallowed hard, knowing what was about to be requested of him. He tried not to glance toward the bedchamber door, struggling to think of a gentle way to dissuade this payment.

But that was not Rami's intent.

"I shared a truth," the Klashean prince said, "now I must ask for one in return."

Kanthe exhaled with relief. "Anything."

Rami sat up, turned, and faced Kanthe. "*Why* did you all come here? You claimed your self-exile was to escape persecution for traitorous acts that were falsely laid at your feet."

Kanthe's limbs went cold. He came close to dropping the pipe and had to clench it harder. A few bits of glowing ash fell from the pipe's cup. None of them had shared the true reason why their group had ended up here. Apocalyptic portents were rarely welcome, especially during times of war. That had been proven true back in Hálendii, where all their attempted warnings only led to bloodshed and death.

Rami leaned closer. "The reason you truly came here?" His eyes glowed brightly, shining with a sharp cunning that he had kept hidden until now. "What does it have to do with the moon?"

# 18

CARRIED THROUGH THE gardens of the Imri-Ka, Frell took in deep breaths. Each inhalation of fresh air cleared his head. The spinning world resettled into some semblance of order.

Still, his body refused to obey him. He felt the iron grip on his arms and legs by the four Dresh'ri who bore him, but his limbs could not fight them off. He couldn't even raise his head, which hung crookedly from his shoulders, bobbing with each step through the perfumed grounds.

Gravel crunched under sandals. Tailored bushes rushed past him. Thorns from purple empyrean roses snagged at his robe. Water burbled in stone fountains. Lanterns glowed in the shadows of the high-walled courtyard.

He spotted others in *byor-ga* habiliment who scurried from their path, servants who surely knew better than to speak about what they had witnessed.

The group finally reached a tall marble archway in the center of the gardens. A pair of knights flanked the entrance, holding the chains of massive war dogs, who snarled in threat. But none of them made any effort to stop or question the cadre of Dresh'ri led by Zeng ri Perrin.

Frell was hauled past the threshold, but a pair of black iron doors blocked the way. Zeng lifted a white staff, embossed with ancient sigils, and the doors swung inward, welcoming the return of the librarie's guardians.

By now, the fresh air had cleared enough of the numbing alchymy for him to focus more acutely. Beyond the doors, the group entered a small stone antechamber. It appeared to have no exit. The seven Dresh'ri crowded in tight, making room for a latecomer, another member of their order.

No one spoke.

Zeng shifted over to a lever on the floor, grabbed it, and hauled it down. The ground bumped, then shook. Frell had enough control of his body to gasp as the floor began to descend, accompanied by the sound of rushing water.

Frell could not stifle his amazement.

*Some pressure-fueled artifice . . .*

Still, he should not have been surprised. The Klashean alchymists outstripped all others when it came to sophisticated mechanisms and innovative craftworks.

As the floor dropped, an elongating well stretched above him. The stone walls were polished smooth, impossible to climb.

It reinforced Zeng's earlier warning: *You will never leave.*

The torchlight from the entrance overhead had become a dull, distant glow by the time their descent halted. Another iron door opened. A familiar and welcoming smell greeted him. The scent of dust, dried leather, and dusky parchment. It was as familiar as home. He knew what they were about to enter.

*The Abyssal Codex . . .*

Frell was carried down a short hall and into a lantern-lit cavernous space. His breath caught in his throat. He gaped at the sheer breadth of the place.

The domed ceiling rose so high that its apex vanished into shadows. Shelves climbed nearly as tall, densely packed with tomes and sealed scrolls. Ladders scaled those heights. A few cowled scholars perched on the rungs. They were illuminated by tiny lanterns strapped to their shoulders. Across the vast expanse of the place, small stars twinkled in the distance, marking other Dresh'ri.

Despite his pounding heart, he could not help but be awed, even humbled. The shelves vanished into the distance, overwhelming his senses. This librarie dwarfed even the one at the *Bad'i Chaa,* which had been massive.

As he was hauled along, he could not determine if the space was once a natural cavern or if it had been dug out of the rock. The shelves seemed to radiate out from a central core, which he was being carried toward.

His eyes rolled all around, trying to take it all in. He wished he had control of his neck to better view the extent of the Codex. Curiosity competed with fear.

Then the shadows shredded overhead. A flurry of tiny black wings swept down upon them. Their group was assaulted by a high-pitched squeaking; their robes were spattered by foul droppings. Then the horde dashed away in a coordinated eddy.

Frell tried to follow their path back into the shadows, recognizing the winged creatures.

*Bats . . .*

This was confirmed by Zeng, who dropped back to pace alongside Frell and waved his staff to chase off the last strays. He must have sensed his captive's confusion.

"Since the founding of the Codex," the Dresh'ri explained, "a colony has been preserved here. It is their home as much as ours. They serve as steadfast caretakers, helping to protect our treasures. Throughout the centuries, our winged brethren have feasted upon all manner of pests that risked damaging our vast bounty of leather and yellowed parchment."

Frell felt both disgust and amazement at this shrewd accommodation. He also remembered the Dresh'ri sigil he had found embossed on the book back in his sanctum. It had shown the wings of a black bat with a golden eye glowing in the center.

*Was this the source of that symbol?*

"Of course, sharing this vault with these agile hunters requires a few precautions." Zeng leaned closer and pointed to the side, toward a cluster of desks draped in leather, their surfaces daubed in guano. "And certainly a fair amount of mopping."

Frell had already noted the many servitors shuffling through the shelves, cloaked in drab *byor-ga,* which made the resplendent white of the Dresh'ri stand out all the more. Like the city above, the subterranean librarie appeared to be an equally ordered world, structured by the hierarchy of its caste system.

The group finally reached the Codex's core. At its center, a spiral stair led downward.

As he was lugged toward it, Zeng assured him, "We do not have far to go. The Venin awaits."

DESPITE HIS ATTEMPT to stay focused, Frell grew dizzy as his bearers carried him down the tight spiral of the staircase. Their descent wound round and round, revealing a surprise.

*The Codex extends down here, too.*

The group marched past level after level, where more shelves spread out from the stairwell. He counted ten tiers by the time they reached a set of black iron doors sealing off the bottom. He was dumbfounded by the sheer enormity of the librarie.

All the knowledge of the world could be hidden down here.

*And maybe it is.*

Frell also noted that each scaffolded level appeared to shrink in size as they progressed, as if they were climbing through a pyramid balanced on its point.

*And now we've reached that buried tip.*

But what was here?

Zeng stepped to the door and rapped his staff three times. After a long breath, iron scraped loudly, and the doors swung wide. Firelight flickered from inside, dancing their shadows across the walls of the antechamber. A warm mist swept outward, redolent with incense.

Frell held his breath, fearing some other disabling compound in that scent, especially as the paralyzing miasma had begun to wear off. His fingers and toes now tingled and prickled. He could even slightly wiggle his digits, but it took great effort.

Zeng turned to the others. "Take him to the altar."

Frell's heart pounded harder.

*Do they mean to sacrifice me?*

He was carried over the threshold and down a short flight of stairs. The fire-light grew brighter with each step. He sensed the weight of the librarie stacked overhead, all pressing down upon this small chamber.

A quiet chanting rose around him as he entered.

His bearers finally stopped and dropped Frell to his knees in the center of the room. Hands propped him up, but he could finally lift his own chin.

He nearly fell back in shock.

The small chamber had been carved out of rock, exposing twisted and sundered beams of ancient steel. Some claimed that the foundations of Kysalimri were rooted in the past, going as far back as the Forsaken Ages.

*Is that what I'm seeing?*

Between the protrusions of steel, shining emerald veins cut through the stone, glowing a poisonous hue, forming a noxious web. It spread outward from the far wall, where twin pyres burned, smoking with unknown alchymies.

A stone altar stood between the fires. Atop its slab rested an open book, as wide as his outstretched arms. It appeared to be an illuminated manuscript, one that was likely centuries, if not millennia, old. The exposed pages revealed painted figures crouching and leering amidst lines of faded text. The images seemed to move in the flickering light.

Frell swallowed hard.

*If such a tome was sequestered down here, it must be more precious than all the books above.*

He tried to study the open pages. He was scholar enough that desire flared through his fear.

*What is written there?*

Unfortunately, Frell could not move any closer. Plus, the book was not unprotected. It had its macabre guardians.

Surrounding him, like spiders in that glowing web, a ring of cloaked and cowled sentinels stood watch. Both men and women. They were dressed in Dresh'ri garb, but clearly the gathering was something far more inimical. All their eyelids had been sewn shut. Their ears sculpted into sharp points. Their nostrils splayed open and stitched wide into place. Even their teeth had been sharpened to points.

With horror, Frell recognized the purpose of this mutilation, the appearance sought by the disfigurement.

*They've been carved to look like bats.*

# 19

FRELL CRINGED IN horror at the ring of figures surrounding him.

It was from their lips that the chanting rose. Their singing grew louder. He fought to clap his hands over his ears, but his limbs still refused his command. He knew what he was hearing. He recognized the hum resonating behind the intonations. The sound ate at his skull, danced fire over his brain.

Frell's senses swirled, making it hard to think, frazzling his focus. Still, he knew the truth about these mutilated men and women, the gift carried in their blood.

*They're bridle-singers . . .*

Zeng came before him, bowing to each of the figures, then faced Frell. "The Venin welcomes you. Seeks your guidance."

The Dresh'ri lifted a palm and blew an ashy powder into Frell's face. Surprised, he could not stop himself from inhaling it. The dust burned into his sinuses. His lungs convulsed, as if trying to reject the poison.

He gasped and coughed, doubling over. He clawed at his face—only then realizing he had control again of his limbs. Still on his knees, he sat straighter, no longer propped up by his bearers. He lowered his hands and stared down at his palms, which still trembled and quaked.

A fine mist of the powder hung in the air.

*Not poison but antidote.*

Zeng touched his shoulder. "We know what you came to seek, Frell hy Mhlaghifor. Even what you keep secret."

Frell tried to shake his head, to deny, but he could not. The singing, the alchymy in the smoke . . . it all ate at his will.

Zeng waved his staff. Two of the Dresh'ri crossed to the twin pyres. Each threw fistfuls of silvery powder into their respective fires. The flames burst higher, dancing toward the roof on either side of the altar.

"Behold!" Zeng sang out. "She who will end the world and start it anew!"

His staff pointed to the image revealed by the flames. It had been painted across the far wall behind the altar. The glowing emerald veins emanated outward from it. The depiction looked smudged out of soot and drawn with black oil, or perhaps even smeared from the shadows themselves.

Frell gasped at the sight.

A huge full moon rose high on the wall. Silhouetted against it, a black beast with outstretched wings dove toward the altar. Its wings turned to flames at the edges, dancing in the firelight cast by the two pyres. A dark rider sat astride the creature, as hunched as the beast itself, both staring toward those in the room. Only the rider's eyes were pools of that vile emerald, which shone even brighter now, glowing with menace.

"Here is the *Vyk dyre Rha*!" Zeng intoned.

Before Frell could stop himself, he revealed that he knew that forbidden name. "The Shadow Queen . . ."

Zeng swung toward him. The man's face was a mask of adulation, approaching madness in its intensity. "We know the Iflelen search for a girl who commands one of the great Mýr bats, a beast of astounding size and malignancy. Someone you have communed with."

Before Frell could respond, Zeng lifted his staff high.

The Venin around him responded, singing in unison, in ancient Klashean, carrying with it a frisson that set Frell's heart to thundering in terror. He covered his ears, but he could still hear them.

*"Vyk dyre Rha se shan benya! Vyk dyre Rha se shan benya! Vyk . . ."*

Zeng pulled one of Frell's hands down and leaned closer. "You cannot deny Her. You know it in your heart. We all can see it. Listen and know it to be true!"

The chanting continued. *"Vyk dyre Rha se shan benya! Vyk dyre . . ."*

Zeng's eyes shone feverishly as he translated. *"She is the Shadow Queen reborn!"*

The Venin continued to sing, adding new words, infusing the weight of history and certainty. It rang with prophecy.

Zeng stayed close, reciting along with the singers. *"She who would be reborn one day, in flesh and form. Burning away all that She possessed, leaving only darkness and savagery behind. A dread being who will spread fiery ruin in Her wake, until all the Urth is consumed."*

Frell leaned away, wincing. The bridle-song grew to a gale in his face, driving the conviction of their portent into his bones, rooting it deep.

Zeng did not let up. "Tell us who She is, where She hides!"

Frell knew they meant Nyx, but even in the storm of their faith, he could not believe it. Still, he remained dulled by the alchymies, seduced by the bridling. He fought to stop his tongue, to strangle his breath, but he could not.

"She . . . She is . . ."

Zeng pressed him. "Tell us."

"Nyx . . ." he gasped out, the words tumbling unbidden from his tongue. "Daughter of a slave . . . bound by blood . . . molded by the bridling of a shebat. She is like . . . like no other." He spoke what was in his heart but what he had never dared speak aloud. It was a terror he held deep. Tears spilled down his cheeks. "She is an empty well . . . waiting to be filled. A vessel destined for a power like no other."

He knew this to be true. Back at the Shrouds of Dalalæða, Shiya had claimed Frell carried some trace of bridle-song. The ancient Sleeper believed it was that gift, calling from his blood, that drove him to study the moon in the first place. He had wanted to dismiss such a statement, but he could not. When Nyx sang, he had sensed the untapped power inside her, a near bottomless well.

*If it should ever be filled . . .*

He shook his head, afraid even now to face that terror. It was one of the reasons he had agreed to accompany Kanthe and Pratik to these lands. Down deep, Nyx terrified him. He lifted his head and stared across the altar at those glowing eyes. Flames danced at the edges of his vision.

Certainty firmed inside him.

*She will become that dark god.*

His shoulders shook. A sob escaped him, knowing another truth.

*But she is our only hope.*

Bowing to this conviction, Frell fell to his hands and shared what he knew was true. "Only she can stop moonfall."

Zeng was not satisfied and leaned to his ear. "*Where* is She? Where is the *Vyk dyre Rha?*"

Frell did not fight answering this question, satisfied it would do them no good. "Beyond your reach. Far out into the Frozen Wastes."

"Where?" Zeng pressed him, nose to nose with Frell. "Tell us where. We will know if you lie."

Frell sagged, his head hanging, sweat draining from his face, mixed with tears. He didn't need to fabricate a story. He told him the truth. "Even I don't know."

Zeng straightened, his face gone purple, his fingers white-knuckled on his staff. He pointed its length at Frell. "Then you are of no further use to us." He turned to one of his brethren. "Kill him."

The Dresh'ri stepped forward, freeing a dagger, which flashed brightly in the firelight. As he approached, Frell didn't move from the floor, too defeated, too cowed.

*So be it.*

His executioner stepped before him. He grabbed Frell by the hair and yanked back his head, baring his neck. The blade lifted high.

Before it could fall, a length of steel burst from the man's chest. His body stiffened in shock and surprise. The dagger fell and clattered to the floor. The Dresh'ri screamed as the blade was withdrawn and his body shoved aside.

Another Dresh'ri took his place and snatched a fistful of Frell's robe. "Get up!"

Frell obeyed, wobbling to his feet, struggling to understand—then he spotted the violet eyes and iron collar hidden under the Dresh'ri cowl. He coughed in shock.

*Pratik . . .*

The Chaaen tried to shove Frell toward the door, brandishing his bloody sword all around. "Run!"

Frell resisted. He twisted away from his rescuer and stumbled back to the altar. The heat of the two pyres blasted his face. The dark countenance of the Shadow Queen glared down at him.

"What are you doing?" Pratik hollered, panic rife in his voice, swinging his sword wildly.

Frell reached to the sacred book resting open atop the altar and dragged it toward him. He and the others had come to the Southern Klashe to learn more about ancient apocalyptic prophecies. He glanced up to the full face of the moon rising behind the Shadow Queen, then down to the illuminated pages.

*I can't leave this book behind.*

Before Frell could close its heavy cover, one of the Dresh'ri broke past Pratik's guard. The man grabbed the book, cursing loudly in Klashean. The two wrestled over it for a breath. Still too weak, too addled, Frell knew he'd lose this battle.

In desperation—though it went against all his instincts as a scholar—he lunged and snatched a fistful of pages. He ripped them free, desecrating the ancient tome.

Perhaps shocked by the act or unbalanced by Frell's sudden relinquishment of the book, the Dresh'ri stumbled away, prize in hand. The man's hip struck the edge of the altar, spinning him around. With a cry of horror, the Dresh'ri fell into the pyre on that side. Screams echoed out of the flames as the man's body thrashed—less to free himself than to protect the book.

Both causes were lost.

The flames cast higher, licking the edges of that dreaded prophecy painted on the wall. Smoke rolled thickly, reeking of burnt flesh.

Frell clutched his stolen pages to his chest as Pratik reached him. The Chaaen grabbed him and pulled him toward the steps leading out. He waved his sword, holding the others at bay.

"Run!" Pratik repeated.

This time, Frell obeyed.

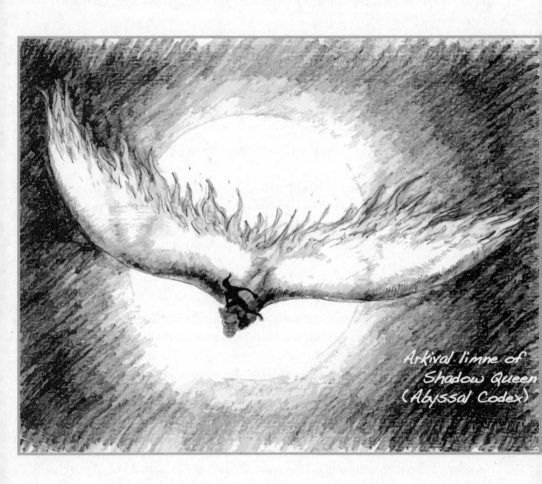

Arkival limne of
Shadow Queen
(Abyssal Codex)

# FIVE

# A SHIVER OF SHARKS

*First, know Noor was a bastarde of a knyghte. Ruthless in his ambicions, relentless in his convictions, dogg'd in his pursute to cross the Dragoncryst—but worst of alle, was his unswervyng belefe in his owne misbegotten notions of what laye b'yond those ici peaks. Second, know this. I miss my frend & he did not deserve such a cold end to his tale. Still, I suspect he would hafe it no other waye.*

—From the addendum in the second edition of
*The Kronicles of Rega sy Noor* (added by the cartographer
of the first excursion, who refused to accompany
Rega on his catastrophic second expedition,
where ship and crew vanished into ice)

# 20

DAAL WADED OUT of the Ameryl Sea and planted the butt of his fishing spear into the red-sand shore. He leaned heavily upon it, drawing deep breaths after his long dive. His wet skin steamed on the cold beach.

He stared across the expanse of the sea, its waves oiled in every shade of green and deeper ameryl, a shimmering mirror that vanished into the distance. The waters spread under an ice cavern that stretched hundreds of leagues wide and twice as deep. Its roof spanned half a league above, and its bottom delved to unknown depths, to forever-dark regions guarded over by the Dreamers.

A few rocky islands dotted those waters, but most of the land was an endless beach that spread along the sea's edge, framed on the other side by a towering ice wall that climbed into the mists. Directly overhead, the world of ice broke into a sky so distant and cold that few dared venture there.

*Only death lay above.*

Down here, the Crèche protected life, a cradle that nurtured all.

Daal swiped the dampness from his brow.

Across the sea and above, a warm fog hovered high, rising from regions of boiling waters. The steamy mists swirled across the high glacial roof. The ice's steam-smoothed surfaces and spearlike sickles glowed through the fog, bright with shining lichen and draped with phosphorescent frills of fungi.

Exhausted, Daal let the net slip from his shoulder and drop to the beach. A few black ablyin shells rolled free.

"I'll get 'em," Henna called from behind him. His sister trampled through the sand village she had crafted while waiting for him.

He smiled at her. She was only eight—half his own age—but she had sprouted tall already, testament to her mixed Noorish blood. She remained all kelp-armed and skinny-legged. Her long dark hair, threaded with the green strands of her Panthean heritage, remained wild and unkempt. In another four or five years, those locks would be shorn to mark her maidenhood.

*I'll hate that day.*

He combed fingers through his cropped hair, a match to his sister's blend of ebon and ameryl. His bare chest was fuzzed the same, defying his prayers. He had tried shearing the humiliating growth off with the sharp edge of a shell, but mostly ended up slicing his skin. He had wanted to match the smooth skin of the other men, those of pure Panthean blood—not that it would've helped much.

He lifted his hand before his face, spreading his fingers, frustrated by their meager webbing. He dropped his arm and shook his head. Even his ears were too large, sticking out too wide and rising to the barest point. But he was not about to try clipping those. It had been easier when he was young, when his hair was longer, and he could mask the Noorish blood that ran through his veins. But some aspects could not be so easily hidden. Like the unmistakable shine of his blue eyes. Even his sister bore the ameryl eyes of their father, a pure Panthean, like most who lived in the Crèche.

He was happy for her, if not a little envious.

Henna finished gathering the shells and fought to drag the heavy net across the sand. He moved to help her. "We're two leagues from home, Henna. At this pace, we won't get there until the morrow."

She scowled at him. "I can do it. I'm not a baby." She freed an arm and pointed at the green froth of waves. "See to Neffa before she crawls out here and scrapes her belly on the rocks."

His sister was right. He shouldn't neglect his friend. He held out a palm toward Henna. "I'll need one of those ablyin."

She brightened, fished in the net, and threw a shell at him. Despite her determined attempt, it landed in the sand between them.

"Good try."

"I meant it to go there." She returned to hauling the net.

With a shake of his head, he crossed over and picked up the large shell. He reached to his belt and freed a steel dagger, one of his most prized possessions, gifted to him by his father when his hair was shorn of its childhood. He used the blade to shuck the ablyin open and tossed aside one shell. He balanced the other in his palm, exposing the meaty mollisk flesh. He took a moment to tweeze out a few spitworms that squirmed across its surface and cast them away.

Satisfied, he stepped back to the lapping waves.

Neffa had beached herself to the height of her withers. Still, it meant Daal had to wade waist-deep into the surf to reach her. His sealskin breeches, snugged tight to his thighs, had nearly dried, but Neffa awaited her reward.

Anticipating it, she bounced a bit on her forelegs, casting forth more waves from the winged webbing of her limbs. As he approached, he had to be careful of her spiral horn, lest it spear through him in her eagerness.

He reached and offered the open shell. Neffa leaned forward and gently lipped the treasure, slipping out a pink tongue to scoop the mollisk from its shell. Her sharp teeth gnashed it with a grunt of pleasure. Puffs of steamy mist expelled from the twin holes flanking her horn on top.

Daal smiled and slid a palm along her smooth gray cheek, using a finger to rub the folds around her right eye. "Who is the best orkso in all the sea?"

She rumbled deep. He mimicked the same, casting out the contented grumble back at her, letting her know how much he loved her. For a moment, as he did so, a wave of deeper sensations swept through him. Certainly, he smelled her wet hide, her humid exhalations, the fishy odor of her breath. But he also felt the rough sand under her soft belly, the pound of two hearts, one in the chest, the other near the tail. Even a deep well of her tenderness.

Startled, he stopped his warm grumble, and the sensations dissolved out of him.

*Strange . . .*

He wanted to dismiss it all as his pure fancy, manifested by his affection for her. He had grown up alongside Neffa, bonded at a young age to be partners in the waters. They had weathered storms, both out at sea and through the trials of his life. Over the years, he had inklings of similar impressions, but never *this* strongly. And it hadn't been just Neffa. All the shoals of orksos responded to him like no one else in the Crèche, not even the Reef Farer, who led all the clans.

He took pride in this talent. While he might be teased, sometimes harshly, for his mixed blood, none faulted his ability with the orksos.

*And not just with those grand creatures.*

He swallowed, chasing away that thought, but not before he flashed to dark waters, being dragged down by Neffa during a hunt, his ankle tangled in a saddle loop, a shiver of Kell sharks diving upon them, then—

"No . . ." he gasped aloud.

Henna stopped tugging on the net. "Then you take it," she said, misunderstanding his outburst.

Daal cleared his throat, blinking away the memory. "I . . . I'll fetch the net in a moment."

He waded to Neffa's flank and loosened the neck straps to free a small leather saddle from her back. He flung its wet length over his shoulder and patted the orkso's side. Neffa craned her head around and settled an eye on him. She wheezed out her concern with a sharp spurt from her nostrils.

He patted her again. "I'm fine. Now you get yourself back to the village. I'll meet you at the pen. I might even have a couple more ablyin shells that don't make it to the feast."

She eyed him hard, silently exacting a promise for him to do just that. With a grunt, she shoved with her forelimbs and slid into the deeper waters. She tossed her head, sweeping her horn high, then dove away.

Daal waded back to shore. He collected his net and spear and waved its forked end down the beach. They still had a long way to hike. He had chosen this remote spot to hunt for ablyin, where the kelp forests ran tall and the reefs were seldom scoured. His father had scolded him for hunting alone, but there were few in the village who were willing to join him. Still, to somewhat appease his father, he had taken Henna—not that she would be able to rescue him, but she could at least point to the spot where he died.

They set off down the beach.

By the time they were halfway home, passing a stone plinth in the sand, carved into a large karp balanced on its curled tail, Daal's feet had begun to slow.

Henna ran ahead, chasing crabs that danced from their path. He tried to remember when he had so much useless verve. He was already exhausted. It didn't help that each step toward home added weight to his shoulders. Out here, away from the curled lips and the dismissive slights, he felt far freer. No longer watched or pointed at.

Plus, this eventide marked the first night of Krystnell, the celebration of the god of the hearth. It opened with a festival of dancing, where young men and women gathered from all the villages and sought their mates.

With his hair shorn, marking his manhood, this would be Daal's first year when he could offer himself. Not that he held out much hope.

Old shame burned his cheeks as he walked. He'd had a single tryst half a year ago, a woman two years older who was soused on saltberry wine. They had fumbled in the dark, him more than her, at the back of a fishery. He barely knew what to do. He could not even breathe, all the blood rushing from his head, swelling him hard. She had stripped him, laid him on his back, come near to mounting him—then backed away in disgust, pointing between his legs. *All that hair,* she had said. *Like matted kelp. I can't do it.* She had grabbed her smock and fled, leaving him humiliated and even more ashamed of his Noorish blood.

Days afterward, he caught other young women eyeing him, snickering behind their hands to one another. Some had looked upon him piteously, a few with matching disgust.

As he dragged his feet, Henna continued her determined crab chase. By now, she had nearly vanished into the fogged distance.

"Slow down!" he called to her.

Despite his reluctance, he set a faster pace. He had closed half the distance when hard thunder echoed off the cliff that framed the far side of the beach. He feared an icefall, a constant danger, when slabs of the frozen cliff would come crashing to the beachhead.

He dropped his net and pounded across the sand. As he ran, the thunder grew into a strange roaring, like that of a dragyn out of old stories. Moments later, reinforcing this conceit, the steamy mists overhead turned ruddy, then fiery.

He fled after Henna, who had stopped, looking skyward.

Directly over her head, something dark, riding those flames, dropped out of the mists. It looked like a fishing scow. Above it, a great bladder shook and rattled amidst dark ropes.

He sped faster, toes digging into the sand. He reached the site and dashed under the descending keel. The air burned hotter.

Daal reached his sister, scooped her up, and dove out of the craft's path. He rolled across the sand with her. The strange scow struck the beach hard behind him. The flames roared an extra breath, then coughed into silence.

Daal got up, retreated, pushing his sister behind him. Once far enough away, he planted his spear and leaned its trident toward the danger.

The scow steamed and ticked on the beach, one side half jammed in the sand. The bladder above it teetered drunkenly. Then a stern door crashed open. Figures staggered out. Men and women. Strangers all. They did not seem to note him frozen on the beach.

Daal gasped as some great beast, shagged in dark fur, stalked out with raised hackles. It sniffed the air, then burst through the others, coming straight at Daal and Henna.

A gruff voice barked a harsh warning in a tongue out of the distant past.

The beast skidded on its paws. It kept its head low, ears high, snarling, baring fangs.

Daal kept his spear pointed at it.

A small form joined the creature, coming forward and resting a hand on its shoulders. It was a young woman, dressed in strange clothes. Her hair was a pure fall of shadows. Her blue eyes, flecked with silver, shone at him. She hummed under her breath, both to beast and to him.

As she did, Daal noted a glow emanating from her, limning her in a golden light. He found his throat vibrating, instinctively trying to match that harmony.

"Nyx . . ." a tall man warned, coming forward with a sword.

The woman ignored him. Her eyes continued to shine at Daal. Similarly with Neffa, he sensed more than he should have.

*Whoever they are, they mean us no harm.*

Daal lowered his spearpoint a handsbreadth and rose from his crouch.

Henna stayed at his hip. "Who are they?"

He shook his head.

The strange woman suddenly flinched. She stepped back and stared up at the dense mists, craning her long neck. A laugh of relief escaped her, stoking her glow brighter. "Bashaliia . . ."

Daal searched the mists and spotted a shadow sweeping downward, vague at first, then clearer, forming dark scalloped wings. He gasped. Such wings haunted the nightmares of all in the Crèche.

The creature dove into full view, revealing its true nature.

Daal hollered in terror, *"Raash'ke!"*

Henna screamed and fell back into the sand.

*You will not take her.*

Daal leaned a shoulder back and threw his spear with all his strength—aiming for the heart of the daemon.

# 21

NYX HAD ONLY a moment to react. From the corner of her eye, she had seen the young man—barefooted and bare-chested—throw his spear. As it sailed overhead, she cast a single note of bridle-song at Kalder. The massive vargr, already primed and tensed, reacted to her plea.

The beast leaped from the sand, leading with his open jaws. Kalder snatched the spear from the air. As he landed, his teeth snapped its length in half. With a sharp growl, he tossed the pieces aside.

Nyx turned to the two figures in the sand. The man had a dagger in hand now, guarding over a small girl. His eyes were huge, his lips fixed in a pained grimace of determination. His gaze focused on Bashaliia, who circled above and keened his distress after the attack, perhaps sensing the tense tableau below.

Nyx pined to Bashaliia, warning him to stay high. She lifted both palms toward the two strangers. She understood the young man's terror. The sight of a Mýr bat diving out of the steaming fog had to be unnerving. She remembered her own first encounter atop the ninth tier of the Cloistery.

"Do not fear." She flicked a glance up. "He's a friend."

The man did not look convinced, likely didn't even understand her.

She rested a palm on Kalder and waved to the others, giving Graylin a hard stare to hold back. The knight had his blade drawn, ready to protect her. Shadowing his shoulder, Quartermaster Vikas carried a broadsword in both hands. To the side stood Jace and Alchymist Krysh.

She heard Jace mumble in awe, his eyes as wide as the young man's, "There *are* people in the Wastes."

Krysh reminded him, quoting from the Gjoan text, *"Daungrous peple."*

Behind them all, the *Sparrowhawk*'s navigator, Fenn, remained with the sailraft, looking more amused than distraught. He had been waiting for Brayl to finish her inspection of the raft for damage.

Nyx focused back on the young stranger, whose attention never left the circling shadow of the bat. She placed a palm on her chest. "I am Nyx," she said, stressing her name, then lifted a hand to point high. "That is Bashaliia."

The man glanced at her, then back up with a shake of his head. *"Nyan, ba raash'ke."*

She frowned, remembering him using that word before. *"Raash'ke?"*

He shoved his dagger toward Bashaliia, clearly adamant. *"Raash'ke."* Frustration dimmed his terror. He used his free hand to feign ripping his throat with his fingers. His gaze twitched to Jace and Krysh. *"Daungrous."*

Nyx stiffened in surprise at his use of the old word. *Does he somewhat understand us?* At the same time, she realized *who* he thought Bashaliia must be. She pictured the shaggy-furred, blunt-eared versions that had attacked them and drove them down here.

She shook her head and pointed again at Bashaliia. "Not raash'ke. Friend."

She knew there was only one way to convince him. She backed a distance away and sang to Bashaliia, welcoming him to land, only well away from everyone. Bashaliia swept high once more, keening in distress. She reassured him in kind.

Finally, he sailed down. As he landed, he canted his wings wide, wafting sand. He then tucked his wings and wobbled on his legs to her side. She nuzzled his head and rubbed his ears. He leaned closer, mewling for comfort. His velvety nose sniffed at her, his breath warming her skin. Her fingers discovered damp spots and came away crimson.

*Blood . . .*

She cringed, picturing him wrestling with one of the raash'ke. He had survived, but not unscathed. She sang soothing chords, calming his heart, promising him he was safe.

*But is that true?*

She faced the young man, who looked aghast. She didn't know how well these people knew those bats who haunted the ice, but she ran her fingers along Bashaliia's ears, extending them to their full height. Her other palm ran down the sleek fur of his chest.

She fixed her gaze on the man. *"Not* raash'ke."

He finally lowered his dagger, looking more confused than relieved. The small girl tried to round his hip and come forward, drawn with the bright curiosity that only the youngest possessed. The man held her back.

*"Nyan, Henna."*

Nyx left Bashaliia to draw nearer again. She placed a palm on her chest once more. "I am Nyx," she repeated.

The man licked his lips and rested a hand to his own. "Daal. I be Daal."

Krysh stepped closer, too. "I think he comprehends some rudimentary version of our language."

Daal scowled at the alchymist. "Mother teach us. Makes us learn. To be"—he frowned for the words, then discovered them—"proud of our blood."

Nyx struggled to understand. *How could this be?*

The answer came from the girl, Henna, likely the young man's sister. She shifted clear enough of her brother to lift the long locks of her dark hair, which had strands of green woven through them. She picked out the darkest sections and pointed at Nyx's black hair.

"You Noor. Like me."

Jace stiffened with a gasp.

Nyx looked at him. "What?"

"These two." His eyes grew even wider. "They have Noor's blood."

She still did not understand, frowning at him.

Jace tried again. "Rega sy Noor. The knight who captained a ship out here over two centuries ago—and vanished." He pointed to the brother and sister. "I think these are his descendants."

NYX KEPT CLOSE to Daal as his sister crept toward Bashaliia. The young man had sought to stop her, but Henna had kicked him soundly in the shin. As the girl extended her arm, her eyes glowed with childish longing, full of curiosity and wonder.

*"Car'ada,"* Daal warned her, shifting closer, one hand on his sheathed dagger.

Nyx touched his arm. "She's safe. He won't hurt her. I promise."

Daal kept his place but didn't lower his palm from the dagger's hilt.

Steps away, Bashaliia bobbled back and forth on his legs, which drew a small smile from Nyx. Back when he was no larger than a goose—before he died and was resurrected into this larger form—he would prance like that whenever excited. It was a reminder that despite his large size, he was still her little brother at heart.

Henna reached a palm up to touch his chest. *"Gree ly resh!"*

Nyx glanced to Daal, who looked a year or two older than her and stood half a head taller. This close, he smelled of salt and a sweaty musk. "What did she say?"

Daal glanced over to her and translated. "He very warm."

Nyx was momentarily captured by the ice of his eyes, so blue they were nearly silver. She realized she was staring and glanced aside. "He's still probably overheated from his battle. Making him extra warm."

Earlier, while they had tended to Bashaliia's wounds, using a salve that Krysh had in a healer's satchel, Nyx had offered Daal a sliver of their tale, of their encounter with the raash'ke. She wasn't sure how much he had followed. She had also introduced the others, though she sensed him growing overwhelmed—not that she could blame him. Jace had practically peppered him with questions, trying to understand everything at once, his history, what life was like down here, and on and on.

Finally, Nyx had drawn Daal aside to give him a moment to collect himself. It also let the others attend to the sailraft and assess what to do next.

Though Graylin seldom let his gaze drift too far from her.

Still, it had seemed to work. Daal had grown more relaxed, even curious, asking questions about Bashaliia, about where they had come from. Again, she kept it as simple as possible. Longer conversations would have to wait.

Henna giggled brightly, drawing back her attention.

Towering over the girl, Bashaliia had bent down his whiskered muzzle and snuffled the crown of her head, then both cheeks. He whistled and nickered at her, taking in her scent, inspecting her with bridle-song.

Henna squirmed all the while, wearing a huge smile. *"Gree heelee!"*

Daal grinned himself, for the first time, like the sun piercing storm clouds. He squinted one eye, clearly trying to think how to explain. Then he lifted his hand from his dagger and wiggled his fingers along his bare rib cage.

Nyx understood. "Tickles. He's tickling her."

*"Yee."* Daal nodded. "Tickles."

Graylin waved to her, indicating it was time to regroup.

Nyx held up a palm, asking for a moment more. She turned to Daal. "Would you like to meet Bashaliia yourself?"

He considered it, took a breath, then nodded. "Henna not scared. Bad for me to be."

His sister heard him and waved insistently. *"Yee! Da mist."*

Nyx went with Daal, guiding him to Bashaliia. Henna backed away, her eyes still huge with excitement and awe. Once close enough, Daal lifted an arm. Bashaliia leaned forward to sniff at his hand, then bowed his head and pushed his crown into the man's palm. The bat's ears folded back, flat to his skull.

Nyx's brows pinched. She had never seen Bashaliia grace a stranger like that.

A soft warbling nicker flowed from the bat's throat.

For a breath, Daal matched it, only more melodic, likely without realizing it. His hand glided over Bashaliia's head, his fingers combing the fur between those ears. The man's eyes drifted half-closed.

*"Gree resh,"* he murmured, confirming his sister's appraisal of the bat's warmth. He let his arm drop and backed a step, his melody going silent like a snuffed candle. He stared back at Bashaliia. *"Gree prel . . ."*

Nyx pressed him. *"Gree prel?"*

He looked at her, his eyes brighter. He struggled for a breath, then pointed at the arc of ice that glowed through the steamy mists.

"Shines," he said, translating. "He shines."

Nyx studied Daal as he gazed at the distant glimmering. *Had he noted the aura of bridle-song that rose when the two had touched? Did he carry the gift?*

She hummed deep in her chest, casting out glowing tendrils toward the mystery standing in the sand. She tried to read him as she had Jace back in the *Sparrowhawk*'s hold, when she had inadvertently brushed strands through her friend, exposing his private heart. Back then, it had felt like a violation, but she could not stop herself now. There was something different about Daal, more than just some nascent bridle-song in his blood.

*But what?*

She sang her strands toward him—but once near, they dissipated into a misty cloud and wisped away. She shivered in shock.

Daal glanced at her, his expression unchanged. He didn't seem to be aware of what had happened. His gaze flicked to Bashaliia. He stared a long moment. His next words were strained, edged with apprehension.

"*Gree nef oshkapi, hee miss'n Oshkapeers,*" he whispered, turning his attention to her. He swallowed, clearly trying to explain. "He . . . *oshkapi* . . . dreams . . . deeper than all, like the Dreamers of the undersea."

She shook her head. "What do you mean by—"

He grabbed her hand, looking haunted. "No go there. Ever."

She tugged herself free, struggling to understand.

Graylin noted their brief tussle and strode toward them. "Are you all right?" he called to her.

"We're fine," she assured him, knowing Daal was only expressing concern. *But about what?*

Graylin waved to her. "We should be going."

She wanted to argue, but from the distress in Daal's eyes, she simply nodded, dropping this mystery for now. "Will you still take us to your village?"

"*Yee,*" he agreed.

Nyx knew the plan was to reach his home. Daal was not the only mystery they had to solve. Their group had waited on the beach, keeping close to the sailraft, off-loading essentials, all the while hoping that there might be some sign of the other escaping sailraft and its occupants. Not to mention the *Sparrowhawk,* which was last seen fleeing into the mists, drawing off the pack of raash'ke.

As she joined the others, she gazed up at the mists, shimmering under the glow of the encrusted ice.

*Where are you all?*

# 22

RHAIF CIRCLED THE beached sailraft for the sixth time, but nothing had miraculously changed since the *fifth* time.

He stared at the stretch of sand, dotted by thorny bushes with crimson berries that were surely poisonous in this landscape that only the undergod, Nethyn, could appreciate. Everywhere he looked, the strand extended to lapping green waters.

"Why did you have to land us on an island?" Rhaif complained, turning back to the raft. "We're trapped here."

The pirate's snowy-locked daughter, Glace, stalked atop the sailraft, wading through the ruins of their shredded gasbag. Its remains draped and hung over the raft, like a god's dispirited cock.

She glowered down at Rhaif, her almond skin darkening with anger. "Be thankful you're in one piece."

Hyck, the *Sparrowhawk*'s engineer, crouched up there, too, inspecting the wreckage. The scrawny man had stripped off his shirt in the humid heat, showing all his ribs. He fingered a ragged rent in the balloon's fabric, then tossed it aside. "No sewing this back together."

"Don't matter," Glace said with a hard scowl. "We have no way to inflate it. And we only have dregs of flashburn left in the raft's forge. We're not going anywhere."

"Then we're stuck," Rhaif groused, swiping the sweaty strands of ruddy bangs from his brow. "And with nothing but salty water all around, we'll be sucking on pebbles before long."

The twin pirate brothers, Perde and Herl, hauled out the last of their supplies, stacking crates and barrels in the sand. It hadn't taken long. In the rush to flee the *Sparrowhawk,* they hadn't had time to stock their provisions. The pair had also shed their roughspun shirts, showing wide chests and a splay of tattoos over their backs, depicting various scenes of carnage and debauchery, likely preserving the histories of their respective exploits. It was the only distinguishing feature between the two, that and Herl's crooked nose from an old break. The two Gyn-sized behemoths both hailed—or rather escaped—from the closed and walled-off Hegemony of Harpe. They certainly had the typical Harpic jaundiced complexion and pinched eyes.

Herl had noted Rhaif's complaint. "Aye, the thief is right about sucking on pebbles. We have only one barrel of water."

Perde shrugged. "But *two* of ale."

"Well, at least you all prioritized correctly," Rhaif conceded. "We can get drunk before we sweat to death on this god-fekked island."

He scanned the mists.

The fog hung thicker on one side, where the waters boiled and spat, giving rise to heavier steam. Far overhead, the world was roofed by ice, the underside of the mighty Shield above. Through the hot mists, the surfaces glowed in hues of crimson, blues, and emerald, shining from crusts and drapes of moldy growths.

Rhaif only knew the source of illumination because their raft had gotten too close to that jagged roof. Earlier, while descending into the massive rift in the Shield, Glace had guided their craft away from a cliff of ice that rose on one side. She feared colliding with it, especially when near blinded by the fog. That avoidance sent their vessel gliding into the mouth of a vast cavern hidden below the Shield. Apparently, it must have melted into existence countless millennia ago, creating the mineral-rich, salty sea below.

They hadn't even been aware they had swept into that cavernous space until one of the roof's fangs of ice ripped into their gasbag, sending them into a wild, spiraling dive.

Even now, Rhaif hadn't completely caught his breath. His heart continued to pound in his chest.

Still, despite his grousing, Glace *had* saved them all. She had staved off their plummet long enough to spot the sea under them—only it had been bubbling and belching with steam. The heat had come close to boiling them alive, like crabs in a stewpot. Glace fought the raft away from the danger, spotted a beach ahead, and aimed for it, believing it was a shoreline. They crashed here, gouging a deep groove in the sand and rock, cracking a gaping rent in the keel.

Only after bailing out did they recognize their error.

It wasn't a shoreline, but the crest of a sickle-shaped island. The sandbar stretched half a league in length and a fraction as wide. Except for the scraggly bushes, it appeared barren.

"How are we getting off here?" Rhaif asked.

Hyck clambered down from his perch and offered an option. But from the engineer's sour expression, he wasn't confident in his plan. "We have two axes. Maybe we can hack free a section of hull and create a raft. Make oars out of other planks and row free from here."

Rhaif scowled, pointing out the largest flaw in this endeavor. "And go *where* exactly?"

Glace looked equally unconvinced. "We don't know if those boiling waters encircle us. We could cast off and be overwhelmed by the heat or fumes."

Rhaif wiped his brow again. The air reeked of sulfur and bale-breath. It already stung his eyes and burned his nostrils.

"But worse," Glace added, "we don't have enough rope to rig a stout enough raft. Especially not one that could carry all of us."

She looked toward the one member of their group who weighed as much as Herl and Perde put together. Rhaif turned to where Shiya had stopped along a curve of the island. The bronze woman stared out to sea.

Shiya must have overheard their discussion. "I detect firelight in the distance."

Rhaif crossed to her, drawing the others with him; even Glace leaped deftly to the sand. He searched the dense fog but saw no flicker of flames.

"Where?" he asked.

Shiya pointed out into the mists.

Rhaif squinted but still failed to see anything different in that fogbank compared to the rest. He glanced at the others. "Are my eyes too old? I see nothing out there."

They all shrugged, equally confused.

"It's there," Shiya insisted. "Flickering flames. Many of them."

Rhaif trusted Shiya. Her glassy eyes were sharper and capable of seeing the world with a perceptivity far beyond any of them.

"How far off?" Glace asked.

Shiya turned to the woman. "I cannot properly discern."

"Could it be the others trying to signal us?" Rhaif asked. He pictured both the sailraft that carried Nyx's group and the *Sparrowhawk*.

Hope surged through him.

"I do not know," Shiya admitted. "But you are correct about these waters. They're dangerous. I can hear other regions bubbling and spewing hotly out there."

"Then what do we do?" Hyck asked.

She faced him. "I will walk there."

Rhaif took hold of her arm. "Shiya . . ."

She turned her glassy blue eyes upon him. "I have no need of air. My weight will keep me to the seabed, allowing me to cross. Though it may take time. I suspect some of the magma vents could damage me, so I will have to keep clear of the worst of them."

Rhaif swallowed, struggling how to convince her otherwise, but he also knew she was right. With this heat and foul air, they couldn't risk staying on this island for more than a day or two.

"I will do my best to fetch help here," she said.

She stared at the group, awaiting their agreement.

They all shared worried looks, but no one objected.

Rhaif let out a strained sigh. "Just be careful."

Shiya's eyes glowed softly upon him. She lifted a hand to his cheek. Her palm felt like the warm flesh of any woman. The curling strands of her hair, a dark bronze, wafted gently about her brow. Her skin swirled in hues of rich coppers, from pinkish to a darker red, especially her lips.

Rhaif lifted his arm and covered her hand with his palm. He remembered when he had first set eyes upon her, deep in the mines of Chalk. Seeing her ensconced in her glass bed, he had thought her a statue come to life by some god's miracle.

*But no longer . . .*

They had spent months aboard the *Sparrowhawk* in each other's company. He already knew she was far more than simply the masterwork of some skilled artisan working in bronze. After so long together, he recognized her unique intelligence, her true compassion, even the humor infused into her form. While she might not have been born of womb and blood, she was as much a woman as any other—only more so.

Rhaif swallowed hard, hating to see her leave. After so long together, he could not dismiss his heart. He had grown fond of her, as he would any woman of flesh and bone. He even desired her. She was beautiful beyond words, his dreams given form.

Sadly, he knew she couldn't return his base cravings, but that did not lessen his tenderness for her. She recognized his affections, even returned them in her own fashion. She would often sing in his cabin, stirring the bridling gift in his own blood, a heritage from his mother. In those moments, shared together, it felt as intimate as an embrace.

She lowered her hand. "I will be back," she promised him, easily reading his apprehension.

He stepped away, letting her go. He struggled to clear his throat, then called before she turned away. "Bring back ice."

She grinned at him. "Or course. I know how you hate warm ale."

He smiled in turn.

*How well she understands me.*

With a wave, Shiya waded into the sea. He stared as her form slowly sank into the waves—then was gone.

* * *

RHAIF SAT IN the sand, dreaming of a long cool bath. He'd kicked off his boots and soaked his feet in the lapping water. At least the sea was cooler than the air. A single tin cup rested next to him, pushed into the wet sand.

*Maybe I can learn to appreciate warm ale.*

In his head, he tried to guess how long it would take Shiya to reach some distant shore. She had already been gone a while. Still, he had no inkling of how far off her destination might be or even the pace that she could maintain while navigating a seabed, especially one that was a maze of fiery vents.

As he lounged in the heat, he tried to imagine what it must look like down there. He pictured his homeland. He grew up in the smoke-shrouded city of Anvil, the hub of the Guld'guhl territories, a dry and inhospitable land of mines and diggings. Along its northern coast lay the Boiling Bay, named after the many volcanoes, large and small, that steamed in those waters. He imagined the seafloor here much like that, a Boiling Bay flooded over, drowning those scores of volcanoes.

Still, he quickly shook that thought away. It only stoked his worries. Shiya might be sculpted of bronze, but even metal melted in the hottest of furnaces.

He reached for his cup, determined to acquire that taste for warm ale. As his fingers closed on it, a melon-sized rock floated to the surface of the water. He had heard how pumice stones, spewed from the throat of Boiling Bay's volcanoes, dotted its waters, sometimes forming great floating rafts of rock.

Intrigued, he sat straighter—until that rock opened its eyes.

He gasped and scooted on his backside away from the surf. The rock lifted from the waves, revealing a long, snaking neck. Its jaws gaped open with a sibilant hiss, showing row upon row of jagged teeth.

*Feck this place . . .*

As he fled, more creatures sprouted from the waters. They formed a swaying forest behind him, rising out of the sea. Their necks pulled muscular bodies, lined by overlapping ridges of armored scales, from the waves. They came rushing ashore atop powerful legs, claws digging into the wet sand.

Rhaif turned and fled up the face of a dune. His bare feet slipped and slid, but he didn't slow, chased by that hissing chorus. He crested the dune and spotted the crashed sailraft ahead.

Herl and Perde sat atop crates, playing a game of dice. Nearby, Glace leaned over a map she had taken from the *Sparrowhawk.*

As Rhaif dashed down the dune, he hollered, "Hyck!"

By now, the others had noted his panic. The engineer, who had been lounging with a pipe, sat straighter, then stood up, shading his eyes.

"Those axes!" Rhaif shouted to him, remembering Hyck's plan to build a raft.

"What about 'em?" Hyck asked.

Rhaif waved behind him. "We're gonna need *both* of 'em."

He watched their faces go shocked and knew the slavering pack had topped the rise behind them. Herl tossed his dice aside. Glace ducked into the raft, hopefully going for a weapon. Hyck followed her.

Rhaif glanced over his shoulder. One of the creatures had a lead on the others, some bull version of the beasts. As it came down the far side of the dune, it lowered its head and flung high its tail, an appendage tipped by a spiked fan. From its end, a rain of darts shot toward him. They peppered the sand around him.

A sharp sting struck his upper thigh, but he ignored the pain and ran faster.

Hyck reappeared and tossed an ax to each of the twin brothers. They caught the hafts in midair and ran forward. Behind them, Glace dashed out of the raft's hold, sword in hand, and sped past the brothers. She was lithe on her feet, a blur of black leather, appearing to fly across the sands without disturbing a grain.

"Down!" she ordered him.

Rhaif didn't need the warning. The pounding in the sand was more than enough. He flung himself headlong, skidding on his chest across the sand.

Jaws snapped where he was—then shot over his sprawled body.

Steps away, Glace dropped to her knees and slid toward him. She stopped with Rhaif's head between her thighs. She swept her sword high and cleaved the neck of the beast. Its head continued onward, chased by a fount of blood.

A large dead weight shoved into Rhaif from behind, further burying his face into Glace's fork. The severed length of neck, still squirming in death, fell heavily over his back. Hot blood soaked him.

Glace scooted back and hauled him to his feet. "Get into the hold!"

To the side, Perde and Herl had dispatched two of the creatures. Swinging bloody axes, they charged toward the others.

From the top of the raft, Hyck shouldered a crossbow and fired a dart that struck an eye of a beast that had just crested the dune. Its neck writhed, tossing its head about, then collapsed to the sand. Its body rolled and tumbled down the sandy slope.

The rest of the pack—responding to the scent of blood, the sight of the dead—trumpeted their distress and thundered back around. They retreated for the safety of the water, vanishing over the dune.

Still, Rhaif hobbled toward the raft's hold, his leg on fire. His hand probed and found the impaled barb. He tried to tug it out—then screamed, falling to a knee. It was barbed in place. He fought to stand again, but his assaulted leg would no longer hold his weight.

He rolled onto his hip.

Noting Rhaif's distress, Hyck leaped to the sand and ran to him. Glace backed there, too, but kept her sword ready, facing the dune, prepared if the beasts should regain their bloodlust and attack again.

Hyck dropped next to him. "What's wrong?"

Rhaif twisted enough to show the end of the barb sticking out from the meat of his upper thigh.

"Hold still," the engineer warned, and removed a dagger from his belt.

"What are you gonna—"

Hyck sliced the back of Rhaif's leggings, exposing buttock and leg. Blood welled and ran into the sand. The pain continued to spread, a fire eating away all control. He lost hold of his bladder, soiling himself and the sand. His stomach cramped. Agony strangled his breathing into gasps.

Hyck pointed the tip of his dagger at the blood. Where it welled out, it had begun to boil and go black.

Glace passed her judgement. "Poison."

# 23

FROM A ROCKY rise on the beach, Graylin surveyed the village ahead. It climbed in a labyrinthine maze from the water's edge up to the towering ice cliff. Hundreds of lanterns flickered, along with flames that rose from pots and urns.

The entire town looked like a conch shell cut in half and splayed open. It spread in convolutions and curves, all in hues of red and ocher. It looked sculpted in place—and likely was. With no trees growing in these lands, the homes, walls, and structures—some climbing as high as four or five tiers—had been formed out of the sands and turned into stone by some strange alchymy. All the roofs were thatched with dried kelp, casting a greenish hue that matched the neighboring waters, adding to the look of a seashell cast out onto the beach.

Only this shell wasn't empty.

Laughter and shouts echoed across the sands, accompanied by the strum of strings and a merry beating of drums.

"Krystnell," Daal said at his side. "Festival. Start at eventide."

On Graylin's other flank, Fenn shrugged. "If we're gonna drop in, what better time than a celebration?"

Graylin kept his palm on the hilt of his sword, but he kept Heartsthorn sheathed. When they entered the village, they needed to avoid any outward sign of hostility. He wanted no misunderstanding. He glanced at Daal.

*Like before.*

Nyx had taken Bashaliia over to a nest of massive boulders that offered shelter in a small cave. They would leave the Mýr bat hidden there until after their introduction. Quartermaster Vikas would remain behind, guarding over Bashaliia with her broadsword. Along with Kalder. The vargr would also surely strike terror into any villager who spotted him, so he had to be left behind.

In addition, Krysh would stay there—to attend to Bashaliia's wounds that had started to bleed again during the trek here.

It took those conditions to convince Nyx to leave Bashaliia's side, but Graylin did not want her out of his reach.

*Not in these strange lands.*

The plan was to enter the village with a small party, to make their introduction less intimidating. In addition to Nyx, Jace and Fenn would come with

Graylin. Still, despite his desire not to appear threatening, he intended to protect Nyx.

Jace had slung his double-headed ax over his shoulders. It was a formidable weapon, forged of Guld'guhlian steel, shafted in unbreakable stonehart. The young scholar had become quite deft with it after months of training aboard the *Sparrowhawk*.

Likewise, Fenn carried a pair of Bhestyan half-swords at his hip. Though he might be a ship's navigator, no one aboard a pirate's vessel wasn't ready to fight. And the lad had trained with Darant, a swordmaster like no other. Even Graylin had honed his skills by sparring with the captain.

Daal had also sworn to help shield Nyx, while his sister, Henna, promised to hold Nyx's hand, to further demonstrate their lack of menace. Not that it required any oath-taking on Henna's part. She hovered around Nyx like a bee to a honeyclot.

Graylin had prepped one last safeguard. He had left Darant's daughter Brayl back at the sailraft. She had been tasked to ready the small ship, to strip the raft to its essentials, lightening it enough for the reserves of flashburn to be sufficient for one short flight—certainly not out of the Crèche, but hopefully to safety. If necessary, he'd hold the entire village at bay to give Nyx a chance to reach the sailraft.

A scuffing of sand drew Graylin's attention around. Nyx approached with Jace, but she kept glancing back toward the covey of boulders.

Graylin crossed down the rise to meet her. "Are you ready?"

She nodded, but it looked unconvincing.

Henna dashed forward, all but shoving Graylin aside, and took Nyx's hand. The girl dragged her forward. *"Kee won."*

The child's bubbling enthusiasm drew a smile from Nyx. "All right," she said. "How can I refuse such a determined invitation?"

Graylin studied their small party, taking measure of each. He'd have preferred to enter the village with a king's legions, but this group would have to suffice. He turned around and led them up the rocky rise.

As he scaled the slope, the world grew strangely darker. Graylin rubbed his eyes, believing something hindered his vision. But from the others' slowing feet and squinting gazes, they also suffered the same.

Except for Daal, who had continued onward, then stopped.

He frowned back at them. "What amiss?"

Fenn pointed upward. "Look."

Graylin craned his neck. The radiant shine glowing through the fog had dimmed, as if smothered by a thickening fog. The emerald and reddish hues had faded away, leaving only shimmering swaths of blue that looked like a spangle of stars in a night sky.

Daal followed their gazes, clearly baffled by their confusion. "It be eventide."

Jace gaped upward and offered an explanation. "The luminous lichen and molds . . . they must dim on a regular basis, some natural tide phased to the turn of a day."

"Eventide," Daal concurred.

Fenn smiled in wonder. "Amazing. Maybe these clans use those lights to help navigate their world like we do with the sun and moon."

"We can explore such mysteries later." Graylin pointed ahead. "Keep going."

As they crested the rise, the village glowed in the darkness, its hundreds of flames shining brighter down below. Daal had told them his town was named Iskar, which simply meant *Hook*. There were another dozen or so villages spread along the coastline, covering the span of the giant rift that split the Ice Shield. One town even sat on an island out there. This entire world of steam and sea went by the name of the Crèche.

Daal set a faster pace. A ringing of stone bells broke out, echoing across the sand, accompanied by cheering. Music ramped up, bright and joyful. A large central plaza near the water's edge flared even brighter as a ring of bonfires ignited.

"Krystnell starts," Daal explained, and guided them away from the sea. "Home this way."

He aimed for the darkest corner of this convoluted shell, where only a scatter of lanterns glowed. The plan was to take them to Daal's family, his mother and father. To make landfall there first. If they couldn't convince the young man's family of their group's best intentions, then any hope of gaining the village's trust was doomed to fail.

Plus, Daal had assured them his mother was far more fluent with *the Noorish tongue,* as he put it. Graylin's group would need a skillful translator if they hoped to gain the cooperation of the townspeople.

They finally reached the outer edge of the village of Iskar, where a few homes had crumbled into a rubble of sand and rock, as if the magick that had sustained them had given out. Though, more likely, it was from mere neglect and the passing of time.

Daal rushed them down dusty, narrow streets, taking one turn, then another. They passed dark homes, all low-roofed and hunched. A few had candles burning inside, which gleamed through tiny windows, so crude they were barely translucent. Still, the light cast the glass into the pearlescent glow of a clam's lining.

Daal swept an arm at the empty street. "All go to festival."

Graylin suspected that wasn't the full explanation for the lack of people in this corner of Iskar, but he didn't press the matter. He didn't want to slow Daal with questions.

The same could not be said of Jace. The former student ran his fingertips along one of those sculpted walls, clearly appreciating its sinuous curves. "Astounding. How did they accomplish this?"

Graylin scowled at him.

"And look at this," Jace said, slowing to peer into one of the waist-sized urns that held a single flame dancing atop what appeared to be a hollow reed full of holes. It sat imbedded in a pool of oil that floated atop a jellylike substance. "It must be some type of fat or melted wax."

Daal nodded back. *"Whelyn flitch."*

"It smells sweet enough," Fenn said, sniffing deeply as they passed. "Like mulled wine."

Only Henna seemed to understand the urgency of the situation, though from a different perspective. She tugged on Nyx's arm to keep her new friend moving. *"Kee won!"*

Graylin agreed, motioning to all. "Keep going."

They finally reached a modest home that looked well-kept, with windows brightened by clusters of candles. Two small fire-bowls flanked the woven-reed drape that served as a door. The flames danced cheerfully, as if welcoming all.

The firelight highlighted an arc of stones that set off a patch of sand. The grains had been combed into an intricate pattern of triangles surrounding a five-pointed star with a crossed set of arrows atop it.

Jace stumbled a step as they approached, then hurried forward. "That sigil . . ." He stared back at them. "It's the family crest of Rega sy Noor."

Nyx drew closer, awe in her voice. "Then you were right earlier, Jace." She stared at Henna, then over to Daal. "They're his descendants."

Daal made an exasperated noise and urged Jace and Nyx back. He held up a palm. "I go first. Better to . . ." He squinted, struggling for the words.

Nyx filled those in. "To prepare your elders for our unexpected arrival."

Daal's features pinched, clearly not understanding.

Graylin just waved. "Go on, then."

Daal nodded and crossed to the door. With a final worried glance back, he ducked through the drape.

Graylin waited with the others—then the shouting began.

\* \* \*

DAAL WINCED, WEATHERING the storm, praying for it to end. His father stood before him, red-faced, furious, saliva flecking his lips.

A finger stabbed at Daal's chest. "It's well past eventide," his father scolded hotly. "Did you not hear the bells? Krystnell has started. We should be there. With all the village. Yet, we wait and wait and wait, not knowing where you and your sister were. Your mother was about to rouse searchers. On Krystnell of all besotted days."

"Da, listen—"

"No more excuses, Daal! You've been fretting about Krystnell for months. I know that's why you're so late, hoping to skirt the festival dance, to put it off another year."

"That's not why I'm late," he said, growing angry himself. Though, in truth, his father wasn't entirely wrong. Daal *had* tarried down the beach for that very reason. If he had left promptly, he might've never met the others.

*And maybe that would've been for the best.*

"Then why?" His father leaned close, his ameryl eyes shining with frustration.

His mother finally spared Daal, touching her mate's arm. "Let him speak, Meryk."

With just her touch, some of the fire snuffed out. His father sagged and waved dismissively. "What then, Daal? Why do you drag your hairy arse in here so late?"

His mother scowled. "Meryk, there's no reason to be crude or to disparage your son's Noorish nature. He can't help it, any more than I can. Do you find me so distasteful for the blood I carry?"

Daal stared gratefully at his mother. Due to her Noorish heritage, she stood a head taller than his father. Her oiled hair was as dark as ebonstone. Her eyes matched Daal's, as blue as polished ice.

His father gently touched the back of his hand to her cheek. "Of course not, Floraan. You remain as beautiful as when I first met you."

She leaned into his hand.

Daal knew their history. It was rare for a pure-blooded Panthean to forsake their family and muddle their lineage with the Noor. At least for the past century.

Prior to that, it had not been uncommon. For decades after Skyfall—the day when the Noor had fallen through the mists and crashed here—the two clans had mixed happily. The striking nature of the Noor, who hailed from lands both mythic and fantastical, had stoked curiosity and interest. The newcomers, with their strange customs and skills, had been welcomed into villages, into homes, into beds. But as time passed, that uniqueness wore off, the differences chafed. The Pantheans—who had lived here since the first melt—grew to resent the mingling with the Noor, thinking it diluted their purity. The Pantheans believed their bloodline had been whetted by the steam and ice into their best form. Consensus grew that the Noor befouled it, weakened their lineages.

So, the two grew apart. Those with Noorish blood were relegated to lower duties, held with little regard, forbidden from positions of authority. Still, the Noor persisted, finding comfort among their own, sharing rituals that went back to Skyfall, preserving their language and taking pride in their heritage.

When his father gave his heart and blood to Daal's mother, he had suffered gravely for it. He had been cast off and exiled by his family, forbidden from ever returning to his village. Still, despite such a fall, he had never once expressed regret for that decision, even while raising a son as headstrong as Daal.

His father sighed, calmer now, but his expression remained disappointed. "Let's start anew. Why are you—"

The door flap shoved open behind him. Henna jammed her head through. "Have you told them, Daal? We've been out here forever."

Daal waved her back, but she just stuck out her tongue.

His mother drew nearer, her eyes narrowed. "Who's out there?"

Daal took a deep breath. "Henna and I met some strangers. Far down the beach. After I was done gathering ablyin for tomorrow's feast."

"Strangers?" his father asked. "From another village?"

"Well, yes, I guess."

"From where?"

"They're Noor."

His mother perked up, stepping forward. "Our blood? From what village?"

Daal swallowed. "From outside the Crèche."

His father huffed with exasperation. "Don't be absurd. Out with it. Where are these strangers really from?"

Daal took a step back and pointed up. "They plummeted out of the mists. Like during Skyfall." He stared at his mother, pleading to be believed. "They hail from the homeland of the Noor."

His father rolled his eyes. "What fezzy nonsense is this? I raised you better than that, Daal."

Henna, still in the doorway, lost what little patience her small body could hold. She entered, dragging Nyx by the hand. The others followed, crowding in behind them.

His father's mouth fell open. He backed away, sheltering Daal's mother behind a raised arm. "What daemonic mischief is this?"

Nyx bowed her head, speaking Noorish. "No daemon, I promise you. Just tired strangers needing help."

Henna hopped up and down on her toes. "And, Ma, you must go see Bashaliia." She swept her arms wide. "His wings were this big."

Daal covered his brow with his palm. "Henna, you're not helping."

# 24

NYX SAT AT a small stone table. The benches were slabs of the same, only softened by cushions. A spread of toasted loaves and jams had been offered to them. The fare tasted both strange and familiar. They washed it all down with a sweet wine.

Jace picked at his bread, his nose close to the crumb. "I'd swear it's made out of barley and rye."

Daal's mother—Floraan—corrected him as she laid down a platter of moldy cheese of some form. "Sea oats and fermented algae," she said. "An old Noorish recipe."

Fenn spoke around a mouthful. "After months of hardtack and salted meat, this is wonderful."

Floraan smiled, her skin aglow in the firelight, her eyes bright. She used a palm to flatten the fall of a simple moss-green shift that reached her knees and was belted at the waist. Her short dark hair, oiled tight under a thin net, was adorned with small pink blossoms. She had clearly been dressed for the festival, which was well underway. The pound of drums and the strum of distant strings reached them, along with sharper bouts of laughter.

With a final nod to them, she returned to where Graylin stood beside a firepot with Meryk. Daal's father proved to be nearly as fluent as his mother. Still, Floraan assisted with translation when needed.

Nyx and the others had left it to Graylin to offer a skeletal version of their story, leaving the meat of the matter for later, especially avoiding the subject of Bashaliia.

Daal's father was currently admiring Heartsthorn, the knight's sword. "Such craftsmanship," he murmured, and handed the blade back. "We have mines to the north. Learned to smelt from the Noor who came. But it is rare, treasured."

As their talk continued, Nyx stared about the table. Henna sat next to her, burying her bread under a thick slather of jam. Jace flanked Nyx's other side, staring toward the ongoing discussion, trying his best to eavesdrop, clearly wanting to be part of it.

Across the table, Daal leaned on an elbow next to Fenn, attempting to explain to the navigator about the construction of their boats. "We weave kelp.

Same as roof. Make layer and layer when wet. Then let dry in forms. Orksos pull. Or we ride them deep."

"Orksos?" Fenn asked. "What are they?"

Nyx wondered the same, but before Daal could answer, Jace drew her attention. He nodded toward Meryk.

"These Pantheans," he said, keeping his voice low. "They clearly have lived here for millennia on end before Rega crashed his ship into the Crèche. Did you note the webbing between Meryk's fingers, rising to the first knuckles? And their smooth, wrinkleless skin. Even their ears are small and pointed and cleave tight their skulls, not unlike sealkins back home. And the color of their hair. The same as their neighboring sea. It's as if their bodies were honed over time to match this harsh watery landscape."

Nyx eyed Daal's father. He wore skintight breeches and flat sandals. A loose shirt, silken and shimmering in hues of green, hung to his waist. Its deep-cut collar revealed much of his smooth chest. His dark green hair was pasted flat, carved around those small ears. On closer inspection, she noted his clothing looked finer than Floraan's, made of a richer material. Still, his shirt appeared threadbare in spots and frayed at the edges, clearly from long use. Yet, to her eye, it still hinted at a wealthier past.

As if sensing Nyx's attention, Meryk turned and led Graylin and his wife back to the table.

Floraan waved them all up. "If we hope to gain the village's help to find your friends, we must be off. The Krystnell courtship dance starts soon. It will grow chaotic after that."

"Also, too much wine will have flowed by then," Meryk added. "Best to reach the Reef Farer before that happens."

Daal let out a low groan at the mention of the dance, which raised a scowl on his father's face. Still, they all stood up.

Graylin shifted next to Nyx. "Stay close to me."

Nyx rankled at the terse command, but she recognized they had *all* better stick together.

*We don't know what sort of welcome to expect.*

DESPITE GRAYLIN'S ORDER, Nyx found herself striding alongside Daal's mother through the curving streets of Iskar. She was drawn by Floraan's warmth and maternal love. The woman held her daughter's hand, nearly swinging Henna high with every step.

Nyx studied the two from the corner of her eye. She had never known her mother, Marayn, an escaped pleasure serf. Graylin had shared stories, extolling on his beloved, often in melancholy tones, about her beauty, her compassion, her strong-willed nature. Nyx had pried everything she could out of him. Still, those stories had been Graylin's history, not Nyx's. As much as she wanted to, she could not draw any true warmth or connection from these accounts.

Orphaned and raised by a swamper and his two boys, she had never known a mother. While her dah had lavished her with love, she had still felt a hole in her life. She had thought it was from not knowing about her past, about the mother who had given birth to her. Yet, now that she had filled in those gaps, it still failed to squeeze that hole any tighter. If anything, that knowledge only made what she had lost hurt more acutely.

Next to Nyx, Henna giggled and gazed with glowing affection toward her mother. Floraan, in turn, leaned down and kissed the crown of her daughter's head.

Nyx smiled sadly, mourning what had been stolen from her.

On her other side, Jace drew her attention, pointing up. She was grateful for the interruption.

"Over in the Crown," he said, "alchymists believe it's the Father Above—the sun—who grants life, that sets seeds to sprouting and leaves to spreading. But here, in this sunless world, I wonder if the glow above casts down some fraction of that sustaining essence. Or maybe all this life is fueled by those hot gasses expelled through the steam. Or some combination of both."

He sighed loudly, longingly. "I could spend forever here."

"Let's hope that doesn't happen," Nyx warned. "We still have farther to go and more to accomplish."

Floraan heard them. "Fear not. If need be, you could find a good home here in the Crèche. It might take some adjusting. Both for you and for us. Following Skyfall, the Noor—your people, my people—were not immediately taken to the Panthean bosom. Mishaps and misunderstanding took many lives until some semblance of peace was achieved. It took time for the Noor to accept that they would not be rescued by their own people and to learn to live in harmony with the Pantheans."

"And that's what brought about peace?" Nyx asked. "Abandoning the hope of rescue?"

"That and perhaps a prophecy."

Nyx shared a look with Jace, then returned her attention to Floraan. "What prophecy?"

Floraan smiled and waved to encompass their group. "That the Noor would return one day." She reached and gripped Nyx's hand. "Though I suspect that *prophecy* of your return had less to do with hope and more about *necessity*."

"What do you mean?" Jace asked.

"Such a rumor served to protect the Noor, both in the past and now. Early on, Pantheans had come to recognize that the Noor had talents and knowledge that far surpassed theirs. If they believed some future clans of Noor might return, especially in force, they dared not eliminate us or risk retribution."

Nyx's feet slowed. "So, it was *fear* that truly brought both sides together."

Floraan laughed brightly. "Only in part, my dear. It is a hard life here. It takes many hands, working together, to ensure everyone's survival. That's *necessity,* too. But that's not all." She nodded to her husband. "Sometimes it's simply love."

Nyx continued in silence, digesting everything. Pangs of guilt gnawed at her. Graylin had shared much of their group's story, but he had never explained about the threat that drove them all into the Frozen Wastes.

*Moonfall . . .*

If Nyx and the others should succeed in their efforts to set the Urth to spinning again—an impossible enough task—this side of the world would turn over and over again to face the sun. Eventually, the Ice Shield would melt and drown this world.

Nyx stared at Henna, then over to Daal. Ahead, music rang louder. Drums thumped, strong enough to be felt in the chest. Laughter and merriment flowed. It all sounded joyous, full of life and hope.

For Nyx, it only stoked her despair, making it harder to breathe.

*We came here seeking their help—but their only reward will be death.*

Daal's father finally turned to them. "We've reached the plaza. I will strive to get the Reef Farer to listen. Berent is a hard but fair man. Still, let's pray he's in good spirits."

Nyx followed, ashamed and suddenly unsure which outcome she'd prefer.

# 25

GRAYLIN CLIMBED THE rear steps, which led up to a raised dais that loomed over the open plaza. Meryk and Floraan flanked him. Behind, at the foot of the stairs, Nyx stayed with Jace and Fenn, along with Daal and Henna.

Gaiety and raucous laughter echoed everywhere. Large hide drums thundered along the curved walls, except where the plaza met the sea. Horns made of huge, curled shells trumpeted in harmony, accompanied by all manner of ornate string instruments.

As he headed up, he gazed out to the sea, where boats of various sizes rocked alongside a half dozen stone piers. If he squinted, he could make out pens cordoned off in the water, fenced in by what appeared to be floating weeds. Large creatures milled within, piercing the waves with their long horns.

*Strange . . .*

At the top of the steps, a pair of guardsmen in sleek leather armor, with helms bearing small wings, came forward. They blocked the way with crossed spears tipped by steel tridents.

*"Rel'n dar waa?"* one asked.

Meryk moved closer and pointed toward where a small-framed man—the Reef Farer—lounged in a reed throne, adorned with shells and gilded ornaments of silver and gold. Other simpler chairs dotted the stage, occupied by a handful of people who chatted amiably together.

*Likely his family.*

A woman in a neighboring seat idly held the Reef Farer's hand. She tilted over to whisper in his ear, but her gaze noted Graylin. Her eyes widened with surprise, then narrowed with curiosity. She leaned closer to the throne, her lips moving, but her eyes never left Graylin.

Ahead, Meryk appeared to be arguing with the guard.

Floraan explained. "It seems Reef Farer Berent is not in the mood to entertain strangers. If he knew *how* strange, he might change his stance. That's what Meryk is trying to relate."

One of the guards stared Graylin up and down, surely confounded by his tall boots, heavy cloth trousers, and fur-edged vest over a long-sleeved tunic. Still, those spears refused to part for them.

The impasse was broken when the Reef Farer waved one of his subordinates over, maybe a nephew or cousin. Words were exchanged and the way was opened.

Meryk led them across the dais, accompanied by the two guards. Once near the throne, Meryk dropped to a knee and bowed his forehead to the back of his hand. Floraan did the same, so Graylin followed their example.

Seated in a casual fashion, the Reef Farer nodded at each obeisance. Berent was clearly Panthean. His smooth complexion made it hard to guess his age, but his hair had gone a silvery gray, speckled with green, contained within a circlet of white stone adorned with emeralds, rubies, and sapphires. The jewels, aglow in the firelight, matched the hues of the daytime skies.

As his eyes settled on Graylin, they slightly narrowed, shining with a reserved interest. Berent then turned to Meryk and waved for him to speak, to explain this intrusion and the presence of this stranger.

Meryk sat straighter and spoke quickly.

While this discourse continued, interrupted by occasional questions, the woman seated next to the Reef Farer kept her focus on the newcomer to the village. Graylin had been informed by Meryk that she was Berent's consort, a woman named Ularia. She was a carved figure of white marble, and from the dark emerald sheen of her short locks, she was far younger than her consort. She wore a long shift, as pale as her, but laced with opalescent pearls. Her gaze shone with cunning intelligence.

It took much to intimidate Graylin, but he still broke that gaze first.

He turned to the plaza. The celebrants below ignored the events transpiring atop the stage. Wine flowed freely. Music chased dancers across the plaza in complicated patterns that involved much twirling and sudden stops that ended in claps. They all appeared young, finely dressed, with sweat shining off their faces, both from the exertion and excitement. More dancers waited at the edges for their go. Meryk had explained this was a suitors' dance, where mates were sought, allowing blood to be stirred across the many villages.

Floraan touched Graylin's arm, drawing his attention back. "Reef Farer Berent would like to speak to you."

Graylin turned to the throne and gave a respectful bow of his head. The leader of these people rose from his seat and crossed forward. His lips had thinned. Doubt shone in his eyes. He appraised Graylin, perhaps trying to determine what manner of ruse this was. He reached and ran a finger along the fur edge of Graylin's vest.

Berent cocked his head to the side. *"Weh sin'k fay nah?"*

Floraan translated. "He wants to know what manner of beast this came from."

Graylin glanced down. "Fox. The ruff of a fox."

Floraan swallowed, then whispered, "We have no word for such a creature." Still, she turned to the Reef Farer and tried her best. *"Gree fay fox,"* she offered, stressing the foreign word.

He nodded, looking little convinced. Graylin suspected the man believed this was some elaborate costume, some festival joke to amuse the gathering. In fact, Graylin had battled enough opponents to know the Reef Farer was losing patience, tipping into irritation, even anger.

Before matters worsened, Graylin offered one way to convince him that they were not from these lands, that his clothing was not a fabricated ruse. He held up his palms and eyed both guards who flanked them, then ever so slowly slipped his sword from its sheath.

One of the guardsmen stepped defensively forward, but Berent waved him off. The Panthean's eyes narrowed with curiosity, maybe avarice, as the full length of the blade was revealed.

Heartsthorn glowed in the firelight. Its silvery length was inscribed with twining vines heavy with grapes. The decoration celebrated Graylin's corner of the Brauðlands, a roll of hills cooled by the shadow of Landfall's cliffs, where his family's vast vineyards spread.

Berent stepped closer again. The tip of his tongue licked the edge of his upper lip. Graylin read the desire and turned the blade and balanced it across his palms. He lifted it high, then lowered the treasure into the Reef Farer's hands, so the man could inspect its authenticity.

Graylin glanced over to Meryk, remembering how the Panthean had mentioned the rarity of fine-wrought steel here. No one would forge such a treasure just to play a trick on the Reef Farer.

Even his consort, Ularia, rose from her chair and came closer. She had finally found something of interest greater than Graylin for the moment.

When the Reef Farer looked up again, there was no doubt in those eyes, only amazement. He asked a question, which Floraan shared.

"He wants to know where your great ship lies. He would like to see it."

Graylin hesitated for multiple reasons. First, the small sailraft would surely disappoint. And second, he still wanted to keep its location secret, in case things turned sour and their group needed a fast escape.

Berent spoke quizzically again, sounding like he was repeating the same inquiry, only his timbre had hardened.

Graylin knew he had to be careful. His group's presence risked upsetting a delicate balance that had stretched back centuries—to Skyfall, as they called it. Since that time, he imagined little had changed in the Crèche. The Pantheans were likely unaccustomed to surprises or sudden changes in circumstance.

Meryk pressed Graylin, reinforcing his leader's interest. "I would like to see this ship, too."

As if summoned by this request, a roaring echoed off the sea, like thunder rolling in from a storm. It grew louder with every thud of his heart. All eyes turned to the skies as the mists turned to fire. Music went discordant, then fell silent.

*Oh, no . . .*

Graylin knew what was coming.

Lit by a rush of flames, a massive shape plummeted out of the steamy mists, swirling fog in its wake. Above, the shreds of a balloon whipped and tore at the skies, as if clawing for purchase. A portion of the gasbag remained intact, doing its best to hold the ship aloft. Flashburn forges cast out a maelstrom of fire below the keel.

But it was not enough to stop the plunge.

The *Sparrowhawk* fell through the air and crashed into the water, just missing the ends of the piers. A huge wave blasted outward, ripping boats from tethers, shredding through the fenced pens. The swell struck the shore and washed halfway across the plaza. Dancers and musicians were flooded in all directions.

Out in the water, the *Sparrowhawk* heaved high after sinking to the depths of its deck rails. It bobbed crookedly, casting forth more waves. Beneath it, fires burned undersea, then went dark.

In the plaza below, people screamed and yelled, trying to rescue those flailing in the tides. Confusion reigned.

But not up here.

A sting poked Graylin's neck. He turned to find the Reef Farer holding Heartsthorn at his throat. Fire sparked those eyes. The man's lips curled into a sneer of fury.

*I'm about to die by my own blade.*

But the worst was not over.

Darant had not come alone.

Fresh screams of terror rose from the plaza. Ularia covered her mouth and fled back. Graylin followed her gaze skyward.

High overhead, black shadows shredded free of the steamy fog. They cartwheeled and spun through the air, diving toward the sea, determined to pursue the crashed ship. More and more appeared out of the mists, creating a dark thunderhead that descended toward the village, drawn by the noise and firelight.

The Reef Farer gasped their name like a curse. *"Raash'ke . . ."*

Arkival limne of
Orksos
(native to the
Ameryl Sea)

# SIX

# A Palace in Panic

*Ne'er flee from adversiti—for whil the bolden maye die wenn they stoppe, the feerfull must ne'er stoppe renning.*

—Attributed to Plina im Kastia

# 26

STILL SEATED ON the balcony of Rami's rooms, Kanthe recognized the shock and disbelief shining on the Klashean prince's face. Rami's pipe had long been forgotten, its fiery leaf gone cold.

Kanthe had just finished explaining the true reason he and the others had come to Kysalimri, to the lands of the Southern Klashe. Rami had clearly suspected something was amiss. The prince had somehow discovered their interest in the moon—but he did not know the full extent of the danger.

Now he did.

Rami sat straighter, choking to speak. "You . . . You all believe the moon will come crashing down upon us? It's not some jest? That the Urth will be destroyed."

Kanthe had held little back of their story. He even raised Frell's concerns about the growing frequency of quakes and more turbulent tides. Still, he suspected that the others would not be happy with all that he had shared, but with war threatening, it was time to loosen the tight clamp on their secrets.

*We need an ally here, or we will fail.*

That was part of Kanthe's justification for including Rami in their secret endeavor. But deeper down, it was mostly born of Kanthe's growing discomfort at having to lie to a young man he considered a friend. Plus, the weight of all the secrets had become a boulder sitting on his chest. He had needed to unburden a portion of it, even if it meant placing that weight on another's shoulders.

Kanthe studied Rami's face, his dark eyes. The prince had gone stone-faced and unreadable.

*Did I make the right decision? Or have I ruined everything?*

With no indication of what he was thinking, Rami dumped the cold contents from his pipe's bowl and set about tamping in fresh leaf. He lifted the pipe to his lips, and with a flaming taper, he set the leaf afire as he puffed it brighter. He leaned back, took a deep inhale, held it, then let it ease out in a long curl of smoke.

Only then did he turn to Kanthe. "So what do we do?"

Kanthe lifted both brows. "You believe me?"

Rami shrugged. "First, I see no benefit in fabricating such a story. If anything, it makes you sound mad. Second, as the fourth-born prince of these lands, few consider my actions. It wasn't hard to sneak into your alchymist's chamber and note his peculiar line of inquiry. The moon and apocalyptic omens."

Kanthe's eyes widened. "Wait. You broke into Frell's sanctum? Without him ever knowing?" He was both shocked and impressed. Frell had placed all manner of wards to detect anyone meddling with his books or work.

Rami lifted one hand. "Back in Hálendii, you used your idle time to become a skilled hunter. Whereas my interests here went beyond knife throwing." He wiggled his fingers. "One of my Chaaen descends from generations of thieves. After some training and diligent practice, my trespasses now go unheeded. In fact, there are few locks I can't tickle open."

At this last boast, Rami's gaze settled upon Kanthe with the slightest of smiles.

"Can you teach me how to do that?" Kanthe asked, envious of such a skill.

"I can teach you many things." An eyebrow arched. "But as much as that would give me great pleasure, let's return to the question at hand. What can we do to stop this moonfall if it's to truly happen?"

Kanthe weighed whether to let go of one last secret, but he had committed himself to this path. No reason to stray from it now. He leaned closer. "There's something important, nearly miraculous. It may be hidden in the southern reaches of your lands, an ancient artifact that could help shed further light on this threat."

"What artifact?"

"A Sleeper from before the Forsaken Ages."

Rami's face pinched with confusion. "What are you—"

A clanging of gongs cut him off. It started abruptly, rising and echoing beyond the balcony. Then, moments later, even louder, coming from within the citadel itself.

Rami stood up, tossing his pipe aside.

Kanthe rose with him. "What is it?"

Rami searched all around. "The Imperial Tocsin." His gaze settled back on Kanthe. "The palace is under attack."

Kanthe swallowed and stared beyond the balcony rail. By now, the imperial warships he had noted in the skies had sailed out of sight. He heard no explosions, no telltale trails of smoke. Kanthe struggled to understand.

*Has my father grown so bold that he would assault the emperor's citadel? Or is it another attack by the* Shayn'ra, *the Fist of God?*

A sudden pounding on the chamber door inside drew their attention around.

After a stunned moment, Rami rushed across the balcony, waving for Kanthe to follow. "That should be the royal Paladins to whisk us to safety."

Kanthe ran after the prince. "If we're under attack, I must get back to Frell."

"Your alchymist will be attended, I promise you."

Rami reached the door and yelled through it, *"Ka ryelyn wu!"* And likely for Kanthe's benefit: "Announce yourself!"

A muffled response followed. Kanthe knew enough Klashean to understand. "It is High Guardsman Typhn! With Chaaen Loryn."

Rami nodded, glancing back to Kanthe as he unlatched the door. "The Paladins, like I said."

As Rami pulled the door open, a cadre of figures in light armor and chain mail veils shoved inside. Their surcoats were emblazoned with the Klashean Arms: a pair of crossed gold swords against a black background.

Rami backed away, making room for them. "We're both safe," he assured the lead guardsmen.

Kanthe grabbed his friend and drew him farther away, knowing that was not true. From his vantage, he had spotted something undeniably wrong. Out in the hall. A figure cloaked in a *byor-ga* robe stood next to the tall, gaunt frame of Loryn. A blade was held at the Chaaen's throat.

*What's happening?*

Before Kanthe or Rami could react further, the swordsmen swept forward and forced them apart. The robed stranger pushed Loryn into the room and passed the Chaaen to Rami. Blades circled them all.

The cloaked man sheathed his dagger and removed the *byor-ga* headgear. Kanthe expected to see dark features with eyes striped in white. But it was not the leader of the *Shayn'ra*. The intruder remained a stranger, someone not of these lands. The man's pale features were sunburned, his hair a shambled mop of graying blond hair. His green eyes swept the room, then settled on Kanthe.

"We must go," he commanded. "Now."

Kanthe stood his ground and forced his voice into some semblance of princely indignation. "Was it King Toranth who hired you brigands?" he asked sourly. "If so, we can pay twice the head price, if not more."

The stranger laughed. "Do you truly think simple brigands could pierce the citadel of Imri-Ka?"

Kanthe frowned. "Then who are you?"

"Ah, of course. We've never met." The man held out his hand. "Symon hy Ralls."

Kanthe blinked a few times, taking an extra breath to place that name. His eyes widened when it came to him. "Graylin warned us about you . . . before we departed for these lands. He said to watch for you. You're part of the Razen Rose."

The man tipped an imaginary hat. "So accused, so I am."

Kanthe shook his head. "I don't understand."

According to rumor, the Razen Rose was a secret confederacy of spies, a group aligned to no kingdom or empire. They were said to be former alchymists and hieromonks who had been stripped of their robes but secretly recruited afterward to use their skills for a greater purpose: to protect and preserve knowledge throughout the rise and fall of realms. Some suspected their true agenda involved steering history, believing the Rose was the hidden hand that moved the gears of the world.

Symon was right about one thing. It would take someone with such deep resources to succeed in piercing through the layers of protections at the palace to reach him.

"But why are you here?" Kanthe pressed.

"The Rose is a prickly master, but we know when our thorns are best put to use. We've been shadowing your efforts here in the city, and though you might not know it, the winds are about to radically shift. Even with the Rose's considerable resources, we barely had time to intercede. If you hope to continue with your mission, you must begone immediately."

Rami had been listening to all of this. "So you attacked our palace to free Prince Kanthe?"

"Attack?" Symon turned to him. "Do you mean that clanging cacophony?" He pressed a palm to his chest. "Not us. We work far more subtly. We found this moment most useful to our own task. To whisk you out of this predicament. Come. We do not have long."

Symon backed away.

Kanthe hesitated, glancing back at Rami. Despite the circumstances, matters hadn't fundamentally changed.

*We still need a strong ally in these lands.*

"Rami . . ." Kanthe lifted a hand. "Come with us."

His friend stared back. He had gone all stone-faced again.

Symon frowned. "We've no need of a hostage."

Kanthe ignored him. "Rami, you know what's at stake. Please trust me."

Rami held his gaze for a long breath, then sighed with a roll of his eyes. "Very well. I was growing bored here anyway."

Chaaen Loryn did not seem happy with this decision. He reached a hand toward Rami but dared not touch him. "My prince . . ."

Rami turned to his counselor and patted him on the shoulder. "You are welcome to join us, Loryn. When it comes to delicate matters, your mentorship is always welcome."

"But—"

Rami gripped Loryn's shoulder and stepped forward, leaving the Chaaen no choice but to follow.

Remembering his own mentor, Kanthe turned to Symon. "Wait. What about Frell and—"

"Your alchymist?" Symon waved them toward the door. "Who do you think roused the entire palace? It's why we had to act quickly. Frell has roiled up a viper's nest, one from which he might not escape."

Kanthe grabbed the spy's arm. "Wait! Can you help him?"

Symon broke free and led them off. "Not us. But there is another who is trying."

# 27

PRATIK KEPT NEXT to Frell, holding his blade high.

Together, they ran up the last turn in the spiral stairs that rose out of the bowels of the Dresh'ri lair. A trail of bodies sprawled across the steps behind them. Some dead, some moaning. Pratik took no pride in his swordsmanship. So far, the Dresh'ri had come at him unarmed. Down here, in a domain ruled by terror and alchymy, the scholars had no need to carry weapons.

Still, the Dresh'ri had cast their lives at Pratik's feet. He understood their sacrifice; it rang clear with every strident strike of the gongs echoing through the cavernous space. Before Pratik and Frell could escape the chamber below, Zeng ri Perrin had fled away and roused the alarm. The other Dresh'ri had sought to delay them, laying their lives down, trying to hold them until the palace guards could sweep down here.

Even a few servitors had struck at them with brooms and mops, only to die just as surely or be driven back. Thankfully, the majority of the baseborn, which vastly outnumbered their masters down here, hung back, adhering to the assigned duties of their respective castes. It was one of the rare times Pratik appreciated his culture's regimented structure and the mantra drilled into him as a boy.

*Each to his own place, each to his own honor.*

To stray from that course brought shame to one's family and clan.

Pratik was long past such conceits. It was what made it all too easy to subdue one of the Dresh'ri, truss him up, steal his outer garb. In a city where one's clothes marked one's caste, none had questioned him.

He had also armed himself.

*And it was providence that I did.*

Earlier, after hearing the details of Zeng ri Perrin's interrogation of Frell, Pratik grew apprehensive, especially with the Dresh'ri leeching blood from his friend. He had decided to disguise himself and learn what more he could. He also kept close watch on the rooms of Frell and Kanthe and luckily spotted the cadre of Dresh'ri heading up there. One had carried a smoking brazier on a chain, and another pair had handheld bellows.

Suspicious at such strangeness, he had trailed them and watched Frell be subdued and carried off. Fearing the worst, Pratik had followed them, keeping his distance until they reached that accursed chamber. It was easy to slip inside and keep his head down. The hardest part was not to gasp in shock at the mutilated sight of the Venin.

As he spied upon the proceedings, he had hoped they would release Frell, that Pratik would never have to reveal his subterfuge, an act punishable by death if exposed. One did not pretend to be a member of another caste, especially a higher one.

Unfortunately, Prya—the god of fate, after whom Pratik was named—was not so cooperative.

"Where now?" Frell asked as they reached the librarie's main chamber. He had to yell to be heard above the echoing gongs. "Do you know another way out of here?"

Pratik shook his head. "I've never set foot down here before."

Frell lifted an arm and pointed between towering shelves. He hugged a crumple of pages to his chest. "Then out the way we came in."

Pratik nodded and headed away. The alchymist teetered on his feet, still addled by the lingering effects of the soporifics that had subdued him. Pratik did his best to steady Frell with his free hand.

In a lull between gong strikes, Pratik heard the scuff of leather sandals on stone behind him. He spun around, brandishing his sword. A servant in a *byor-ga* rushed up from the spiral stairs behind them. A jangle of beads marked her caste as a maid. She froze at the sight of them. Then without a word, she dashed to the side, simply trying to escape.

*Like all of us.*

With his heart pounding, Pratik led Frell onward. The spread of shelves had gone far darker. Only a few lanterns remained lit, and even those were far off. The space looked hastily abandoned. In the distance, a few servitors hid along from their path, crouched low with their lanterns covered, leaking only glowing glimmers.

Otherwise, only the bats stirred above, sweeping the shadows overhead.

Pratik kept a wary watch, while trying to increase their pace. They had no lamps themselves, so their path grew hard to discern. Pratik followed the row of shelves that radiated outward from that central stair. He prayed they were headed toward the lift that led to the gardens.

Frell leaned closer to be heard, giving voice to Pratik's own concern. "Where are the rest of the Dresh'ri?"

Pratik frowned. The attacks had indeed stopped.

Then the answer came from ahead of them.

Down the stretch of shelves, fiery light flowed into the cavern. It looked like a dam had burst, flooding the space with flames. As Pratik's eyes adjusted to the sudden flare, individual lanterns and torches could be discerned. They spread rapidly in either direction.

Pratik knew who had arrived to block their way. "The imperial guard," he warned, and drew them to a stop.

Orders and commands snapped sharply, echoing all around. Deep-throated barks pierced the darkness, accompanied by a rattle of heavy chains. Pratik pictured the massive war dogs of the citadel, dreadful beasts with spiked collars who had been corrupted by alchymies to a fearsome savagery. Only their handlers, bridle-bound to their charges as pups, could control them. It sounded like a full battalion had swept down here.

The spread of lanterns and torches marched inexorably toward them. Howls and barks spread outward, flanking wide.

"What do we do?" Frell asked.

Before he could answer, a new sound intruded. It came from behind them, rising from the well of the spiral stair. Chanting . . . accompanied by a frisson of bridle-humming. The power sizzled through the darkness.

*The Venin . . .*

Pratik searched for them. The mutilated chorus must have collected itself after Pratik's attack, climbing from their lair, likely commanded by Zeng ri Perrin. While a single bridle-singer might not be gifted enough to fully enslave a man, when combined and working in harmony, such a chorus could immobilize, trap its prey in a web of song.

*At least long enough for us to be captured or killed.*

Unfortunately, Pratik and Frell were not the only ones to hear the infernal chorus.

The noise sent the nesting bats into a panicked maelstrom of wings and screeches. The horde descended in a thrashing storm. Tiny bodies dove down, slamming into shelves, striking Pratik and Frell. Tiny claws tore at their clothing, at skin, and tangled in their hair.

The two of them dropped low, slapping and swatting to keep themselves from the worst as the singing grew louder. Pratik pictured the Venin closing upon them through the darkness, a cabal sculpted into vile effigies of the tiny creatures that assaulted them.

Pratik ripped a bat from his cowl.

*Maybe they're even controlling these beasts, like some despoiled version of the Shadow Queen they worship.*

But that was not the only threat.

Swords began to beat on shields. Savage barking echoed to either side. The glow of lanterns and torches grew brighter with every breath.

"What do we do?" Frell asked again.

Pratik answered with the hard truth. "I don't know."

KANTHE FOLLOWED THEIR escort of guards, whose surcoats shone with the Klashean Arms. Another pair trailed behind them.

He gasped to keep up, trying to catch his breath, but not because he was winded. Terror kept him moving, numbing his legs from the exertion. Instead, he tugged at the heavy drape of cloth over his face. Each inhalation sucked the fabric to his lips, trying to suffocate him.

Rami pulled his hand down. "Don't. Baseborn never try to remove their headgear."

Kanthe cursed and let his arm drop.

Before they had left Rami's chambers, Symon had ordered Kanthe to pull a set of *byor-ga* robes over his own clothes. Similarly, Rami had shed his loose robe with no hint of modesty and cloaked his nakedness in the same habiliment. Both Symon and Chaaen Loryn were already clothed, so they only needed to don headgear to hide their features.

The disguised group swept through the vastness of the citadel. Few gave them more than a second glance. Then again, most of the hallways had already emptied out. With the gongs clanging, the entire palace had seemingly retreated to their respective strongholds.

"Where are we going?" Kanthe finally asked.

"If you can't speak Klashean," Symon warned softly, "best keep silent or you'll draw suspicion."

Kanthe stared around at the empty corridor. "From whom?"

By now, they had reached a section of the palace that looked abandoned long ago. Untrampled dust covered the floor, cobwebs draped from the rafters. Even the dark lanterns hanging on rusty hooks looked as if they'd not been used in ages.

Kanthe remembered a similar dereliction out in the city.

*Apparently, that corrupting rot has crept into the palace.*

Rami's feet slowed. Though his face was covered, his head swiveled back and forth. He was clearly taking it all in. He even stumbled a step, as if caught off guard by it all. Kanthe suspected Rami was not aware such places existed inside the sprawling edifice. Then again, the citadel was spread across a hundred towers and a quarter as many levels. As prince of the realm, Rami was likely directed away from such spaces.

They continued in silence, wending down gloomy passageways and up dark staircases. Vermin scattered from the glow of their single lantern.

By now, Kanthe was thoroughly lost.

Maybe Rami, too.

Finally, a door burst open ahead of them. Though it was near to midnight, with the winter sun hovering low, the brightness still stung.

"This way," Symon said, hurrying with their escorts.

Kanthe followed. Once through the doorway, he found himself standing at the bottom of a vast, shadowy well. He shaded his eyes against the glare of the sky far overhead. Windowless walls rose tens of stories to a roofless opening. The stone floor lay cracked and overgrown with thistles and scraggly bushes.

In the center, a small wyndship hovered at the height of his waist. It was tethered in place at four corners, anchored by spikes. Four flashburn forges, two to a side, smoked and steamed, straining those ropes. A few men in light armor patrolled around the craft, testing its lines.

Kanthe gaped at the sight of the ship. He had never seen one in person, only schematics in nautical texts back at Kepenhill.

"A wingketch," he whispered.

It was a unique Klashean design, smaller than a swyftship, but twice that of a hunterskiff. Its draft-iron keel swept into a prominent prow, creating a frozen wave of metal and wood. Curved windows, as tall as Kanthe, flanked each side, looking like the large eyes of an owl. Adding to that image were a pair of folded sailcloth wings, which gave the craft its name. Presently, the sails were reefed and tucked against the hull's flanks.

Such vessels were said to be miraculously agile in the air, but their main purpose was far simpler. Kanthe stared up the throat of the well to the open sky. A wingketch's role was similar to that of sailrafts, which were used to evacuate larger ships in case of emergencies. Only rather than diving downward to safety, wingketches were meant for quick escapes, to blast their passengers skyward and away from any danger below.

*Like now* . . .

Symon pointed toward a dropped door on the starboard side. "Everyone aboard."

Kanthe drew alongside the man. "What about Frell and Pratik?"

Symon grimaced, stared at the moon overhead, then shook his head. "We can give them until the next bell. No more. Then we must begone."

# 28

FRELL SCRAMBLED UP the ladder behind Pratik. They were nearly at the top of a row of shelves. Frell's heart pounded in his ears, but it still didn't silence the insidious chanting of the Venin, a chorus that drew inexorably closer. Already, he felt his will ebbing, his limbs growing leaden. Or maybe it was mere exhaustion.

The only boon was that the Venin's approach had driven off the plague of bats. Frell's skin bled from hundreds of bites and scrapes. But if they didn't find some way out of this trap, they'd suffer a worse fate.

The imperial guards scoured toward them. All around, the slavering howls of war dogs threatened. And somewhere in the dark librarie, the Dresh'ri surely lurked, conjuring other alchymies to confound their escape.

Overhead, Pratik mounted the top of the shelf and rolled out of sight. Frell hurried after him but knew such a ploy would not save them, only buy them additional breaths to figure out what to do.

He reached the last rung and hauled himself up to join Pratik. Though his limbs tremored, the crinkle of parchment under his robes urged him onward. Before mounting the ladder, he had tucked away the pages he had ripped from the ancient tome, stolen from under the baleful eyes of the Shadow Queen sketched on the wall.

*Pray I live long enough to read them.*

Frell sprawled on his back, panting hard.

Pratik was already on his feet and pointed along the top of the shelf toward the only exit. "If we're lucky, we might be able to slip past the encroaching line of guardsmen. Then drop behind them and make for the lift."

"It's surely under guard, too."

"We must try," Pratik insisted.

Frell knew the Chaaen was right. With a moan, he rolled to his stomach and gained his legs. Before he could take a step, a low growl rose directly below them, at the base of the ladder. It escalated into a howl.

Frell cringed.

A war dog.

*Someone must have given the hunters my scent.*

He pictured that damnable Zeng leeching his blood.

Frell stared over at Pratik, both momentarily frozen, likely with the same question in mind.

*Can war dogs climb?*

The answer came quick enough. The ladder shook and rattled. Its length hung from large rings of reinforced steel affixed to a rod at the top, made for sliding the ladder back and forth. There was no way to throw the ladder off and no time to hack through the wood.

"Hurry," Pratik urged, and set off along the shelf.

Frell followed.

The baying of the dog drew the guardsmen toward their location. Victorious shouts and trampling boots aimed their way. Lanterns and torches closed upon them.

Frell ran behind Pratik, trying to keep his feet from pounding on the wood and giving away their position. They had not gotten far when something large leaped to their perch, trembling the wide shelf. Frell turned to see a massive shadow scrabbling for purchase, then regain its footing as claws dug into wood.

The dog shook its spiked collar, hunched its shoulders, then lunged after them.

Frell stood his ground, knowing they could never outrun it. He intended to try his best to knock the beast from this perch, to give Pratik a chance to escape.

"Go!" he ordered the Chaaen. "Get to Kanthe."

Pratik stepped closer. "I won't—"

Then the world exploded.

Fiery maelstroms burst across the librarie with deafening concussions, illuminating the full cavernous breadth of the Codex. Shelves shook; some toppled over in splintering crashes. Their own perch quaked on its footings.

Frell fell to hands and knees. Pratik did the same. Unfortunately for the war dog, the beast had been in midleap when the blasts struck. As it landed, it lost its balance. Its hindquarters slipped sideways off the edge. Claws scrabbled to keep its purchase, digging deep.

Frell knew he had only a moment. He lunged low toward the beast. Once close enough, he spun on his backside and kicked out at the dog's forelegs. Jaws snapped at him, catching the edge of his robe, but not before the strike of a heel dislodged a paw. The dog's bulk slipped crookedly, hanging by the last set of claws—then those too ripped away.

As the beast fell, it kept a stubborn hold on Frell's robe. Its weight yanked him toward the edge. He twisted to his stomach and grabbed for the far side of the shelf. One hand caught; the other missed. He held tight, his fingers straining with the effort.

Then silver flashed past his shoulder.

Pratik swept his sword down and cut through the edge of Frell's robe. With a howl of fury, the beast tumbled away—until a meaty crash silenced it.

Pratik helped him up, but they both stayed crouched.

More bombs continued to explode across the librarie. And not just in the cavern. A series of rumbling blasts echoed up from the lower levels. A spiral of flames shot high out of the central stairwell.

Frell struggled to understand, glancing at Pratik. "Is this your doing?"

In the firelight, the Chaaen's features were aghast at the destruction. "Never."

Frell frowned.

*Then who?*

Across the cavern, the flames spread rapidly, fed by dry parchment and ancient wood. Smoke roiled upward, rapidly filling the dome, stirring the bats. The pall thickened around their high perch.

Frell coughed and his eyes burned.

More shelves crashed and fell as flames ate through their foundations.

"We can't stay up here or we'll suffocate," Pratik warned, and headed toward the ladder. "We must get lower."

As Frell followed, he searched to either side. He spotted no one nearby. The continuing blasts, the spreading flames, must have chased away the guardsmen, silenced the Venin. Both sets of hunters had likely retreated to safety.

Still, he held out little hope that the soldiers would leave the lift unguarded. Most likely, they'd ride the lift up and lock it down from above, trapping their quarry in this fiery oven until the flames subsided—then search for their burned bones.

Pratik mounted the ladder and descended quickly, trying to escape the scorching smoke. Frell followed, nearly sliding down the rungs in his haste. His lungs burned. Tears blurred his vision. Flaming embers stung his cheeks and hands. He was nearly blind by the time Pratik helped him off the ladder.

The Chaaen pointed in the direction of the lift. "We must pray," was all he said, and set off.

They hurried, running low, covering their faces with their sleeves.

They didn't get more than a few steps when someone appeared between the rows of shelves, blocking their way with outstretched arms.

Pratik stopped abruptly. Frell nearly collided with him.

Other figures appeared behind the first. They were all cloaked in *byor-ga* robes, marking them as baseborn servants. Frell was surprised to recognize the one in the lead. It was a woman of small stature. Her robe was adorned with a ring of beads that marked her as a maid. He remembered her bursting out of the spiral stairway, hesitating, then dashing away.

He had thought she was trying to escape. But now he suspected otherwise. He remembered the robed servants he had spotted lurking among the shelves with cloaked lanterns.

*Did they plant all these bombs? If so, why? Was it an act of vandalism or one meant to aid our escape?*

The woman stepped closer, ripping away her headgear. She swept back the sweaty bangs of her close-cropped blond hair. Cold eyes, glinting with copper, glared at them.

Pratik gasped.

Frell took a step back in shock. "Llyra . . . ?"

He struggled to work the gears in his head to accommodate her sudden presence. The last time he had spotted Llyra hy March had been this past summer. She was the guildmaster of a den of thieves out of the city of Anvil in the Guld'guhl territories. She had aided Nyx's cause back then and parted ways afterward. When she left, she aimed to rouse as many of her ilk as possible, to forge a secret army in case they were needed, one that was spread across whorehouses, thieveries, low taverns, and dark dens.

Frell finally found his tongue, still struggling with the impossibility. "How . . . how are you here?"

She scowled. "We can wag tongues later. Let's keep going before all the hairs are burned off your arses."

With fires roaring all around, she turned and headed off with her crew. She set a hard pace, making sudden turns, never slowing. She seemed to know the best route through the flames. Then again, she had planted the bombs. Still, the fires continued to spread rapidly. The heat had become an inferno. Ashes choked the air, making it hard to breathe.

To hold his fear in check, Frell studied the woman. Llyra looked the same as when last he had seen her. Even hidden in the robes, her body remained lithe. Though she bore the short stature of all Guld'guhlians, she had none of their stockiness. She moved like a caged lioness, all power and quickness.

As they continued, more figures folded out of the smoke and shadows and joined them. All wore baseborn robes, though some carried their headgear, revealing hard faces, bearing old scars, whiskey-red noses, and perpetual sneers.

Frell searched around him, then focused back on Llyra. He could not stop from asking again, "How are you all here?"

She huffed with irritation. "Symon thought you all could use my help. We've been working in tandem since you all arrived on these shores."

"Symon?" It took him a full breath to put pieces together. "Symon hy Ralls? With the Razen Rose?"

She shrugged. "We knew you were intent on scouring these stacks. So, while you've been idling up top for months, I used the time to infiltrate down here and plan accordingly, in case something drastic needed to be done." She picked up the edge of her robe. "Easy enough work when you don't have to show your face."

"And no one grew the wiser?"

She scoffed. "Dresh'ri need to eat, have their floors mopped, the cobwebs dusted off their precious books." She eyed Frell up and down. "All you scholars are so full of yourselves. With your noses buried in books, you don't bother to see who's cleaning the privy of your watery shites, which, trust me, *does* stink, as much as you might claim otherwise."

Frell felt his cheeks heat up—not from the inferno growing around them, but from the truth of her words.

Pratik drew alongside them, his gaze searching around. "Where are we going? This can't be the way to the lift."

"That's not the *only* way out." She arched a brow at the Chaaen. "Are you so daft to believe the Dresh'ri would want to share their grandest of entrances with baseborn servants?"

Pratik stared hard at her. "There are other exits?"

"Ten that I know of. Probably more. Some that even the Dresh'ri have likely forgotten about. There are quarters, kitchens, baths, smithies, dungeons that burrow around the librarie and extend in every direction. Many areas are so old they've crumbled into ruin."

Frell had a thousand more questions but remained abashed, even humbled, at how much had escaped him.

Llyra pointed ahead and increased their pace. "Save your breath. We still have a ways to go. And from what little I know of Symon, he'll not wait long."

# 29

KANTHE PACED IN front of the steaming wingketch. The ship's tethers creaked under the strain, matching his own tension. The palace gongs had also fallen ominously silent. He groaned with exasperation.

It didn't help that Symon kept looking at the moon as it drifted across the opening above. The man had given them until the sounding of the next bell before he would force them to depart.

For the thousandth time, Kanthe glanced at the shadowy door into the palace.

*Where are you both?*

Off to the side, Rami stood with his arms crossed, his face turned to stone. Loryn kept near the prince. The Chaaen's expression was far easier to read, shifting between fury and terror.

A trio of swordsmen guarded over the pair; the others had gone aboard to prep for a quick departure. Most of the men had doffed their helmets and veils, revealing faces raw and scarred. They appeared to be a hard lot, showing no humor, only a barely constrained anger.

They likely wanted out of here.

*And I'm holding them back.*

The ringing of the dawn bell made Kanthe jump. It clanged across the palace and extended out into the city. Kanthe turned to Symon, who stared apologetically back at him.

*No . . .*

Rami stiffened, unfolded his arms, and pointed. "Look!"

Kanthe swung around. From the dark doorway, figures spilled into the stone well, rushing headlong. They all wore *byor-ga* robes but quickly stripped off their headgear. Kanthe searched the ash-stained faces until he spotted Frell and Pratik.

He ran over to meet them but stumbled when a small-framed woman shoved to the front, tossing her headgear aside. With a shock, he recognized her.

*Guildmaster Llyra . . .*

Kanthe blinked as he caught his balance. He remembered Symon saying there was someone trying to help Frell. At the time, he had thought the man meant Pratik, but that clearly was not the case.

Llyra noted him, too, and offered a mocking bow. "Prince Kanthe."

She then swept past him, shouting orders to the others.

Kanthe reached Frell and grasped him in a hug. He tried to do the same with Pratik but was gently rebuffed.

"I didn't think you'd make it," Kanthe said.

"We shared that same sentiment," Pratik said.

Together again, they followed the last of Llyra's crew, who had begun shedding their robes. Kanthe collected Rami and Loryn on the way to the ship.

Rami stared back at the discarded *byor-ga* garb. "If I ever become emperor, my first order will be to change the policy of dress. It's clearly a liability."

"Keep moving!" Symon shouted, herding them to the ship. "We can wait no longer."

They obeyed and clambered up the ramp. Symon stopped at its foot and craned his neck, staring skyward, where a column of fresh smoke marred the blue sky. His expression darkened as he backed away from the ramp.

Kanthe called from the hatchway, "Are you not coming with us?"

"No." He waved dismissively. "I have other matters to attend. I'll leave you all to the tender graces of Llyra hy March."

"But—"

"Fear not, young prince. I'm sure our paths will cross again." His eyes glinted with a bit of sly amusement. "No doubt you'll all throw yourselves into a boiling pot before long."

Kanthe couldn't argue with that.

Symon turned and headed away with a pair of companions. They all donned their headgear, ready to vanish into obscurity.

Frell gripped Kanthe's arm and drew him back, allowing a thick-shouldered crewman to winch the ramp up. "The others headed up to the wheelhouse. We should join them."

Kanthe nodded and followed the alchymist through the packed lower hold and over to a flight of narrow stairs that headed up.

From his study of wingketch schematics, he knew the steps led to a narrow tween-deck that contained a few private quarters, a small cookery, and a large bunkroom that filled the stern. But most of that level was consumed by the wheelhouse at the bow. Above all that stretched a flat open deck, shadowed by its tapered balloon.

Eager to see it all himself, he hurried up the steep staircase. At the top, he hauled himself into the bustle of the wheelhouse. Llyra huddled with a group of men. Rami and Loryn stood to the side, under the watchful eye of only a single guard now, who kept a palm resting on the pommel of a sword.

The ship's captain turned from the large wheel as Kanthe joined them.

"Welcome to the *Quisl*." She waved to encompass the ship. "While we stole this ketch for this venture, I've taken it upon myself to give her a name. In Rhysian, it means roughly *Poisoned Dagger*. So best watch your step."

She tempered this veiled threat with a smile. She was a long-legged woman in Klashean black leather, but her features were snowy, nearly silvery, with ice-blue eyes. He suspected she must hail from the far-off Archipelago of Rhys, near the southernmost turn of the Crown. This was further supported by the smooth fall of black hair tied in a long tail and braided through with tiny silver bells. He knew little about the Rhysians, except it was a matriarchal society renowned for its assassins.

Even the crew who flanked her, manning the maneuvering cranks and levers, were all women, as was the ketch's young navigator. They all bore the same complexion and dark hair.

The captain nodded to him, while not ringing a single bell in her braid.

Kanthe suppressed a shiver.

It was said that a Rhysian assassin could move unseen and unheard, even when adorned with those silvery chimes. The only warning of your death was said to be the quiet tinkle of a single bell announcing your end.

Her smile broadened, amused, perhaps sensing his discomfort. "You're the last aboard. Come forward if you like and watch us depart. It's quite the show."

Put at ease by her welcoming manner, Kanthe accepted her offer. He crossed to one of the giant curved windows. The alchymy to craft such large domes of strong glass was a guarded secret among Klasheans. As he drew close, it felt like stepping toward open air. The window curved high to show the sky and low to reveal what lay under the ship's bow. It was unnerving.

He swallowed and backed a step.

The captain bellowed, while leaning over to cast her voice through the highhorn to the rest of the ship, "Hold fast! We're off!"

She pulled a lever, while gripping the wheel with her other hand.

Small pops released the tethers. The ropes fell away from the hull. Free now, the ship shot upward. The four flashburn engines roared in unison, casting flames and smoke below the keel. The ship blasted skyward.

Thrown by the sudden acceleration, Kanthe fell forward, landing his palms against the window. For a terrible moment, he thought he'd fall out, but the glass held. He watched the stone walls blur past the ship's prow.

Then they were out of the shadowy well and into the open air. The brightness blinded. Still, he spotted a column of fiery ash and smoke churning upward from the center of a walled garden. Before he could study it further, wings unfurled on either side of the hull, catching the air. The ship angled away, sweeping quickly over the palace towers.

Other ketches dotted the sky, circling on their wings or whisking away. The earlier gongs must have panicked enough of the *imri,* the richest among them, who sought to escape and seek safer harbors until the danger subsided.

Kanthe smiled, appreciating Symon's plan. The other ships offered the perfect cover for their flight, one ketch among many.

The captain called to him, her voice teasing, "If you get handprints on my glass, you'll be cleaning all my windows."

"Sorry." Kanthe pushed off the glass, collected himself, and retreated toward the others, who were gathered at the back of the wheelhouse.

As he joined them, a noise drew his attention to a closet next to the navigation station where the ship's maps were stored. The others looked that way, too. Something kicked against the door from inside, accompanied by muffled cries.

Llyra squeezed past Kanthe. "Looks like someone is awake."

The guildmaster pulled the door open. A figure was folded on the floor, bound and gagged. Kanthe stepped closer and looked down in horror, recognizing the face, the raw fury.

*Aalia . . .*

"Your betrothed proved to be quite the lioness," Llyra said.

Kanthe swung toward Rami. "I didn't know."

Rami's eyes were huge, his face darkening. His fingers ran to his wrists, likely searching for knives that were missing.

Kanthe remembered Symon's statement from before, when Kanthe had asked Rami to come with them. Symon had claimed they hadn't needed a hostage. Kanthe understood now.

*Because they already had one.*

Llyra waved at Aalia. "Extra insurance. We may need it." She shrugged. "And if not, she'll fetch a generous ransom."

Kanthe breathed hard. He had asked Rami to trust him. He reached for his friend's arm. "I truly didn't know."

Rami backed away, shunning him. "This is a mistake you all will regret."

Kanthe dropped his hand. He could only watch as Aalia was freed. Even with the gag removed, she remained darkly quiet, glaring at him. Her silence was far worse than any curse or slight. She, along with Rami and Loryn, was led out of the wheelhouse to be confined in one of the private quarters.

Frell sighed and patted Kanthe on the shoulder.

Pratik simply looked grim, as if he agreed with Rami's earlier assessment.

Frell turned to Llyra, his voice somber and serious as he moved on to a more pressing matter. "What is the word out of Hálendii?"

Llyra gazed across the wheelhouse toward the open sky. "You're all not as clever as you think," she said. "Not by half."

Frell nodded. "King Toranth clearly knows we're here. And that Kanthe is betrothed to a Klashean princess."

"He certainly does, but that's not *all* he knows."

"What do you mean?"

She turned back to them. "Word is that a Hálendiian battle group was sent off into the Frozen Wastes two months ago."

Kanthe winced, understanding what this meant.

Llyra confirmed it. "The king . . . and worse, that fekking Shrive Wryth . . . must know Nyx is out in the Wastes somewhere."

## 30

STANDING IN A shadowed corner of the tourney yard, Shrive Wryth studied the shining figure of the future king of the Hálendii—and tried to stifle his concerns.

As he pondered his dilemma, he ran a palm over the long silver-white braids tied around his neck like a noose. They marked his status as one of the holy Shriven, as did his gray robe and the tattooed black band over his eyes.

Not that anyone paid him any heed.

Across the yard, a raucous celebration raged.

Ale flowed from a pyramid of tapped barrels. Bards sang of ancient battles and valiant warriors. Minstrels and jesters capered, as drunken as the hundreds of the king's legionnaires who reveled among the scores of bonfires. All had come out to rejoice in the successful assault on the northern coast of the Klashe.

At the center of it all stood the focus of their adoration, the young man who led that attack, his first foray following his graduation from the Legionary school.

Prince Mikaen still wore his full armor. Its sheen reflected the flames, casting the Hálendiian crest on his breastplate into a fiery blaze. The same Massif family sigil—the sun and crown—was also engraved into the silver mask that covered half his face. He made a striking figure and clearly knew it.

He stood amidst a cadre of Vyrllian Guard. They were the legion's most elite fighters, battle-hardened with countenances entirely tattooed in crimson, both to mark their blooded status and to strike fear into their enemies. But the nine who kept closest to Mikaen were his personal protectors, the Silvergard. They had altered their appearances, adding black-ink versions of the Massif sigil to their faces, mimicking and honoring the prince.

Chief among the Silvergard was the mountainous Captain Thoryn, who had rescued Mikaen last summer following a savage ax blow to the prince's face. Despite the best efforts of the kingdom's healers, Mikaen remained disfigured, a hideous scarring that was hidden behind the shining mask.

Wryth knew it was emblematic of the prince's spirit. Mikaen celebrated with those around him, showing his half-smile to all, but that merriment never reached the young man's eyes.

Mikaen remained embittered, which was not unexpected. Yet, that was not all.

There remained an ever-growing darkness, a poison that had seemingly seeped into him from that wound and continued to spread. It was a spiteful mix of fury, pride, and ambition. He had no patience for governance or counsel any longer.

Wryth knew Mikaen would never find peace until his twin brother was dead—and maybe not even then.

Still, the prince's temperament was not what worried Wryth. That slice of an ax had not only scarred the prince, but it had cut the tether that bound the Shrive to the young man. For the entirety of the prince's life, Wryth had been grooming Mikaen to be a king he could control and wield like a sword. But now Wryth had lost his hold on the prince. Mikaen barely spoke to him, ignoring him even here.

*All that effort corrupted by a single blow . . .*

Still, Wryth held out one hope. He watched Mikaen lean toward Thoryn and point toward the gates out of the tourney yard. The prince must have grown tired of feigning jubilance and looked forward to the journey ahead of him. In the morning, he would set off for the rolling plains of the Brauðlands, where his wife's family—the House of Carcassa—kept a sprawling ranchhold. Lady Myella continued to reside there, kept under guard.

Mikaen was anxious to reach there—not so much to bed his beloved wife, but to visit his twins, a boy and a girl, born three weeks ago. The babes squalled out of their mother's womb only seven months after the two were married. Few knew of their birth, which was kept secret to disguise the fact that they were conceived before the royal nuptials. No one wanted to risk muddying the bloodline with a rumor of bastards. In another month, the birth of the twins would be announced amidst stories of an early labor.

Still, if Mikaen had his way, he would have already heralded it.

It was what gave Wryth hope. The prince doted on his boy and girl, all but glowing in their presence, effervescent and happy. Wryth hoped the two babes might be the antidote to the corrupting poison. With their birth, Mikaen had a future to protect.

Wryth prayed it led to a steadier temperament.

*One I can resume molding.*

Wryth contemplated his options and waited until Mikaen left, escorted by his Silvergard. Once they were gone, he turned his back on the festivities and vanished into the darkness.

*I still have one last concern to address.*

DEEP IN THE labyrinthine bowels below the Shrivenkeep, Wryth stopped before a set of ebonwood doors. Still agitated, he needed a moment to center himself before entering the sacred chamber, the very heart of the Iflelen order, a secret buried underground for seven centuries.

He closed his eyes and gripped his priceless Shriven cryst, a leather bandolier that hung across his chest. It was studded in iron and lined by sealed pouches. It was awarded to those holy men who achieved mastery in both alchymy and religious studies.

The pockets of most Shriven crysts held nothing but charms and sentimental detritus, each pouch intended to memorialize one's long path to the holy status of a Shrive.

Not so his own cryst.

His fingertips read the symbols burned into the leather. Each of his bless'd pockets hid dark talismans and tokens of black alchymies. Some hid the powdered bones of ancient beasts. Others held phials of powerful elixirs or ampoules of poisons. But the most treasured of all were the scraps of ancient texts scrolled into the tiny pouches, their faded ink indecipherable but hinting at the lost alchymies of the ancients.

Wryth cared little for the here and now. He sensed this world was but a shadow of an older one, a place of immeasurable power. He intended to gain their secrets. No knowledge would be forbidden to him. No brutality too harsh to acquire it.

*Especially now.*

The Crown was at a pivotal moment, with portents rife and war threatening. In his bones, he knew he was as close as ever to piercing the veil to that ancient font of power. It was why he needed this kingdom—and a prince he could bend to his will.

Otherwise, he held no fealty to Hálendii itself. It was but another realm that would be ground to dust. He had traveled most of the Crown. Born as a slave in the Dominion of Gjoa, hunted across kingdoms and empires, finally schooled on the Island of Tau. His youth was marked by cruelty, abuse, and humiliation.

Even now, after achieving so much, he could still awaken that old pain, to a time when he was at the mercy of so many others. It stoked the cold fire inside him, to never again be under another's thumb. To ensure that, he intended to let nothing and no one stop him from becoming a formidable force, one more potent than any king.

With that goal in mind, he cast a prayer to the Iflelen's dark god—Lord Đreyk—for the providence to succeed. Sixty-three years ago, Wryth had bent a knee and joined this order, one that many considered blasphemous and heretical, but such an uncompromising cabal offered him his best chance to realize his ambitions.

*And now I lead them.*

He opened his eyes and reverently touched the sigil inscribed on the ebon-wood door. It was a curled asp crowned by thorns. The *horn'd snaken* of Lord Đreyk.

More resolute, Wryth pushed open the doors. Before he could cross the threshold, a sharp scream greeted him.

Inside, a gangly-limbed young acolyte—Phenic—struggled with the thin form of a boy enmeshed in a nest of copper tubes and glassine piping. The child was naked, writhing in agony, his chest cleaved open into a window that showed a beating heart and billowing lungs.

The gruff voice of Shrive Keres called out from the center of the chamber. "Wryth! Can you see to that commotion?"

Wryth hurried into the sanctum, a domed chamber carved out of black obsidian.

Ahead, Phenic fought to hold the child in place and looked panicked. "I . . . I don't know what went awry. The boy woke and yanked the tubing from his lips."

Upon reaching them, Wryth slipped a dagger from his belt and slit the child's throat, stopping the plaintive cries.

Once done, Wryth took a step back and scowled at Phenic. "Do you have another bloodbaerne to replace this one?"

"Y . . . Yes." The acolyte waved at the door. "A girl of nine."

Wryth gripped Phenic's shoulder. "Take a breath. Set about preparing the girl, and I'll call for someone to remove the boy. It takes practice to properly seat a bloodbaerne. You'll learn."

Phenic bowed, balanced between relief and terror. "Yes, Shrive Wryth. Thank you."

As the acolyte fled, Wryth crossed to the boy and used his palm to gently close those glassy eyes, offering a silent apology for wasting his life. Another three bloodbaernes continued in the boy's stead, positioned at the other cardinal points of the chamber. The three young children, asleep and nested within their conduits and tubes, lay with their chests squared open. Bellows rhythmically inflated their small lungs. Their tiny hearts pumped life into the great machine in the center of the obsidian cavern.

Wryth took a moment to study the wonder before him.

A convoluted web of copper tubes and blown-glass tanks bubbled and flowed with arcane alchymicals. The apparatus filled the obsidian chamber, stretching from the floor to the arched roof. It huffed, steamed, and thumped like a living beast.

"Come see this!" Keres urged from the heart of the mechanism.

Concerned, Wryth bowed and twisted his way through the gleaming copper web, aiming toward its center—where a talisman of great significance lay hidden and wired in place, fed by the energies of the bloodbaernes.

To the eye, it appeared to be an ordinary bronze bust of a curly-bearded man. But it was so much more. Its bronze skin roiled with the energies suffusing through it. The finest of its curls and strands of hair waved, as if stirred by invisible winds. Crystal eyes of a violet blue glowed dully, blind to all around it.

The artifact had been discovered two millennia ago, but for centuries, no one truly knew what to make of it, only appreciating its beauty and workmanship. It had been studied, dismissed, until it finally made its way to Azantiia.

Over time, following the guidance found in ancient tomes, the Iflelen had learned how to fuel the artifact and stir it back to life. Still, it had taken centuries to wake the talisman from its slumber and glean what little they could. The head had spoken only four times. Each utterance was cryptic, whispered in a language no one understood. Those four messages were inscribed in the Iflelen's most sacred texts, waiting to be deciphered.

Upon further study, their order also discovered that the holy talisman produced a strange emanation, not unlike bridle-song. It was as if it were forever calling out to the world. To monitor this keening, the artifact was surrounded by concentric bronze rings, lined by crystal spheres that contained lodestones suspended in oil, which served like hundreds of tiny weathervanes.

Then, last summer, another artifact was discovered—not just a bust, but an entire bronze figure, one that melted to life. Before they could secure it, the treasure was stolen.

Wryth's hands curled into fists.

*So close . . .*

Still, he refused to give up. It was why he had come down here.

Keres waved him to the side, to where a new addition adorned the web, siphoning off a portion of the apparatus's energy to fuel it. "Something strange is going on. The signal stopped its course and has not moved all day."

"Show me."

Keres made room for Wryth. The other Shrive, two decades younger, bore a matching gray robe and tattooed eyes, but exposure to corruptions long ago had flaked his skin, leaving him hairless, unable to grow the braids of most of their order. Many shunned him, but Wryth valued his brilliance.

Keres pointed to a waist-high dais. "Look for yourself and see."

Atop the table rested a perfect cube of crystal, veined through with copper. At its core, a golden fluid pulsed and undulated. Wires ran from the vast machinery surrounding them to the cube. The artifact had been discovered at the location where the bronze woman had slept, deep in the mines of Chalk.

Another of their cabal—Skerren—a true alchymical genius, had come to believe the cube functioned like a tiny flashburn forge, but one of limitless power. With it, he had engineered a listening device capable of detecting emanations from the stolen bronze woman over a great distance.

Unfortunately, even genius took time.

Above the cube, a crystal sphere hung in a nest of wires that ran down to the pulsing artifact. The sphere was divided into two hemispheres. One had been cast in azure hues, the other in pinkish crimson, representing the Urth's two halves. Between them circled the green band of the Crown.

Keres pointed to a softly glowing yellow blip far out into the Frozen Wastes. It marked the location of the bronze woman's emanations. Sometimes it shone brighter; sometimes it was barely discernible.

This morning it had flared so intensely that it had cracked a web of lines into the crystal. It was what had troubled Wryth all day. He feared the listening device might have been damaged.

Wryth leaned closer, noting that the glow had shifted slightly from where the sphere had cracked—but just barely.

"And it settled there?" he asked. "It's not moved?"

Keres nodded. "Not as of yet."

Wryth frowned, struggling to understand what had happened. Still, he saw an opportunity. "This may serve us."

He reached to the sphere and hovered his fingertip over another glow, reddish in hue. It also shone out in the Wastes, only farther to the east. It marked a fleet of craft—three swyftships and one battle barge—that Wryth had dispatched across the ice. Skerren commanded the barge, wielding an instrument that continually emanated the same bronze signal, one that Wryth could track from here. Skerren also carried a fist-sized sphere of lodestones to locally monitor for the bronze woman's presence—though it could reach only so far.

Months ago, when Skerren had first tested the listening device, it had quickly detected the signal out in the Wastes. The location had made no sense at the time. Even Skerren had thought his calculations might be off. But many lowborn along the Crown's eastern border had been questioned. Gold and torture soon revealed the truth.

The girl Nyx, along with her allies and the bronze woman, had indeed set off into the Wastes. But no amount of gold or torture could reveal *why* they had set off on this course.

Regrettably, the enemy had a month's lead on them. Still, Wryth had the resources of the entire kingdom at hand. Ships had been quickly modified for icy travel and heavily fueled. The hope was to close that distance.

Wryth stared at the glowing yellow blip.

"This may be our best chance to reach them," he whispered hopefully.

He wished he had a way to communicate with the fleet, to share this knowledge. Before leaving, Skerren had devised a clever method to share information, but it was one-way. The fleet could blink their signaling instrument in a code that could be detected here and deciphered. Skerren had already sent back messages, but they were of no significance or import, mostly just mundane updates.

*But now . . .*

Wryth stared at the two blips, growing inexorably closer.

*I should be out there.*

Initially, he had considered leading the fleet, but Skerren was the expert on tracking that signal. If anything went awry, he was the best one to address any problems.

Plus, Wryth was needed here in Hálendii. With war inevitable, he needed to be close by. Confounding matters, there remained the problem of Prince Kanthe. Mikaen's twin brother must have washed ashore in the Southern Klashe for a reason.

*Some other plot is surely afoot.*

Still, Wryth could not look away from the sphere. He glared at the glowing blip in the Frozen Wastes. One quandary above all dominated his thoughts.

*What is happening out there?*

Arkival limne of
the Venin
(of the Abyssal
Codex in Kysalimri)

# SEVEN

# A STORM OF WINGS

*Gard well, peer close, but abandon alle hope*
*For everi moment is an ambush.*

—A couplet from the tragedy
*King Tychan's Folly*

# 31

SPRAWLED ON HER back in the sand, Nyx coughed and gasped. Soaked and dizzy, she fought to her feet. Scores of others moaned and picked themselves up from the street as water sluiced away, returning to the sea.

Moments ago, she had caught a glimpse of the *Sparrowhawk* plummeting out of the mists, riding atop a whirlwind of fire. Standing at the foot of the dais, she had heard its booming crash into the sea. She'd dashed forward to get a better look, only to meet a wall of seawater rushing toward her. The surge carried a tangle of people, a tumbling hide drum. It struck her before she could even turn. The tide spun and cartwheeled her into a confounding blur.

Frantic limbs struck her.

Hands clawed at her.

Salt water burst through her nostrils.

She couldn't stop from being flooded out of the plaza and up a side street. After a seemingly endless time, the surge finally receded. It had tried to drag her back with it, but she had dug her toes into the wet sand to hold herself in place.

On her feet now, she searched for the others, spinning a full circle. The motion set her head to pounding. Her vision squeezed to a tight knot. Everything sounded muffled, even the nearby cries. She squinted at the surrounding faces, but they were all strangers.

*Where is everybody?*

She added her own voice to the chorus of pain and panic. "Jace! Fenn!"

The two had been at her side before the flood.

She scanned the roil of people and hollered again, but she could hardly hear her own voice. Especially as the cacophony suddenly escalated with renewed screams, full of terror. The flow of the wounded and half drowned had been aiming for the plaza, calling for help, for loved ones—only now that tide reversed. People began running in the other direction, knocking her aside.

She flattened against a wall.

*What is happening?*

A hand latched on to her upper arm. She fought the grip. Then a face appeared before her. Ice-blue eyes shone bright with shock. Tight lips were hard with determination.

She stiffened with recognition. "Daal . . ."

*"Krem!"* he yelled. "Come!"

He pulled her away from the wall and into the flow of fleeing people. In his other arm, he carried Henna at his shoulder, hugging her tight. She sobbed and covered her face with her small hands. They stumbled along with the panicked crowd.

Nyx glanced over her shoulder. "What about my friends?"

Daal shook his head, looking as clueless as her. His gaze searched the skies as he ran. "Must go! They come!"

She stumbled along with him. "Who?"

Then she felt it.

A storm brewing above her. Pressure built in her ears. Energy danced across her skin. She knew that malignant touch.

A wave of dark menace swept up from the plaza and down the street. When it struck, it drowned her as surely as the flood had. It sopped through her damp clothes, burned her skin, set her blood to boiling.

Daal gave name to the threat. "Raash'ke . . ."

A dark shadow swept past overhead. The sharper keening struck her, drove her to her knees, addling her senses further. Her limbs grew leaden and heavy. Her breathing strangled.

*No . . .*

She tried to raise her voice against that onslaught, but her throat was salt-scoured, her lungs on fire. She could not even gather a breath.

And she was not the only one afflicted.

Ahead, people staggered or sprawled amidst the floodwater's refuse, succumbing to the malignant bridle-song. Distant screams turned to agonized shrieks. Another shape winged diagonally above the street, sweeping low. A figure writhed in its claws before being whisked skyward, trailing a long wail behind it.

Daal pulled her up, his gaze fixed to the skies. "Need to away. Find *mag'nees* shelter."

Nyx struggled to stand, to clear her thoughts. While being hauled to her feet, she managed a sharper intake of breath. She used the air to weave a weak humming melody, discordant but enough to make her skin glow. The song succeeded in casting back the worst of the bridling malaise.

She leaned on Daal, allowing him to lead her while she gathered her energy. In his arms, Henna hung slack, her form too small, too easily overwhelmed by that dread song.

Daal continued down the curve of the street, climbing through debris, around fallen bodies. They passed many homes, but through a doorway, she spotted figures sprawled inside. The stone walls offered no refuge from that dreadful song.

*Then where is Daal taking us?*

With no way of knowing, she concentrated on collecting herself. As she did, her song grew stronger, but it was still too weak to help others. The glow barely warmed through her wet clothes. She searched around. A few of the afflicted crawled on hands and feet, but only she and Daal were still on their feet and moving.

She frowned at Daal.

*Why hasn't he succumbed? Why is he still standing?*

Then she remembered. Back on the beach, when she had first met him, she had tried to weave her golden strands into him, sensing he carried the gift of bridle-song. She pictured those threads evaporating when they neared his skin, as if innately resisting her.

*If I couldn't reach him, maybe the raash'ke can't either.*

Before she could ponder it further, Daal drew her aside. *"Ree mag'nees fare."*

He led her to a low archway. Beyond it, sandy steps led down to a stone-roofed chamber packed with people huddled shoulder to shoulder. Others fought to get deeper inside, only to be rebuffed by a lone guardsman armed with a spear. Angry shouts echoed out, supporting their warden's stance. It was likely already crushingly tight in there.

Nyx didn't know what was so special about this refuge, but it was clearly important. Those inside had not fallen victim to the bridling menace.

Daal's feet faltered at the sight of the struggle.

"Is there another shelter?" Nyx asked.

He shook his head. "Too far."

Shouts drew Nyx's attention back toward the sea. From this level of the village, she had a partial view of the plaza, where a battle had begun. The village had rallied after the initial shock. Guardsmen had clambered atop rooftops or perched on walls. Two ran past Nyx and Daal with steel-tipped tridents. They were armored in leather and wearing winged helms that bulged at the ears.

Above the streets, barrages of fiery arrows sailed into the sky. A few hit targets, ripping through wings or grazing bodies—but little damage was done. The raash'ke proved to be uncannily swift and agile. Nyx wondered if the bats were using their songs in defense as much as offense. The beasts seemed to anticipate the strikes before they hit, angling away at the last breath.

Her brows bunched. She didn't understand how the guardsmen resisted that malignant bridle-song. They couldn't *all* be like Daal. She wondered if the bulging over their ears somehow protected them, deafened them. She glanced to the shelter behind her. Having lived in the Crèche for millennia, the Pantheans had clearly developed a method of surviving in the shadow of such dread beasts.

Still, the battle remained fraught. Bodies were ripped off the streets. More bats hunted, killing indiscriminately in their fury. They slashed throats, tore off limbs. She watched a bat dig through the reed roof of a home and burrow inside.

Most of the attacks centered on the open plaza, where the creatures' great wings were not impeded by the narrow streets.

Daal drew her toward one of the homes, likely believing any shelter was better than none. She shook free. Anger had warmed away the last of her dismay. Iskar was being attacked because of her group. The *Sparrowhawk* had led the horde down here.

*It's our fault.*

She couldn't just hide and cower.

*"Krem,"* he urged her.

She shook her head. Determined and more clearheaded, she gathered her energies and sang brighter, casting a wider golden shield. Its sudden appearance surprised one of the raash'ke as it dashed past overhead. It shied away with a burst of black wings, like a startled crow.

Daal took a step back, too, his eyes huge upon her.

*So, he* can *see my glow.*

Still, that mystery would have to wait. She pointed to the plaza. "I must help my friends."

She intended to search for the others—Jace, Fenn, Graylin—and, if possible, revive them with her song. She refused to sit idly by when they were at risk, vulnerable to fang and claw.

*That's if they still lived.*

Daal continued to gape at the glow surrounding her—unfortunately, he was not the only one to note it.

Another bat, likely drawn by the shine, dove at them. It screamed, washing its malice over her shield. She fought, trying to bridle it and drive it back. But it was far stronger than she expected, especially for a lone raash'ke. As they battled, she understood why. She sensed a larger malevolence within that body, one she recognized from the attack on the *Sparrowhawk*.

The horde-mind of the raash'ke.

She felt it staring at her, like a massive ice-cold eye, larger than the world. The immensity of that gaze shattered her control. She tried to wrest it back, but the monster was too strong.

With a cry, she fell to a knee.

Daal rushed to her side. "Nyx . . ."

His concern cost him dearly. Free now, the bat swept down upon them—and went for the easiest prey. Claws snatched the limp form of Henna from her brother's arms, snagging the back of her festival dress. She was yanked skyward with a beat of wings.

"Henna!" Daal screamed.

Nyx lunged to her feet.

*No . . .*

GRAYLIN HUDDLED NEAR the threshold of a dark chamber. His heart pounded in his throat. He stared at the carnage outside, at the war being waged across the plaza and in the skies.

On the sands, guardsmen fought with flaming spears and lances, trying to drive off hordes of bats, which fluttered in the air or crawled among the dead. Other men tried to drag bodies to safety, celebrants who had succumbed to the paralyzing bridle-song of the raash'ke.

Atop rooftops, archers swept the skies with fiery volleys of arrows.

Graylin clutched Heartsthorn in his grip, wanting to join the fray and search for Nyx. But he knew he would not make it more than a few steps before falling prey to the malevolent keening of the raash'ke.

He was not the only one frustrated.

"Nyx must be out there somewhere," Jace said at his shoulder. The young scholar clutched his ax in both hands, looking ready to charge out the door.

Fenn, armed with his two half-swords, flanked Jace's other side.

Graylin peered past them into the low-roofed chamber. The Reef Farer and his family crowded near the far wall, guarded over by a pair of men. Earlier, as the raash'ke had attacked, Graylin had wrested Heartsthorn from Berent's numb hands. Graylin's neck still bled from where the man had threatened him.

It was lucky Graylin had gotten hold of his blade. Before the dais could be evacuated, a massive bat had struck the stage, crashing through thrones and chairs. A wing knocked one of the Reef Farer's uncles down to the plaza below. Before more could be harmed, Graylin had dashed forward, coming between Berent's consort and the monster. He speared the beast through the eye, scraping bone to reach its black brain. The bat screamed and flopped away, wings thrashing wildly, until it tumbled off the platform.

Graylin had scooped up Ularia and run with the others down the steps. A handful of guardsmen surrounded them, shielding the Reef Farer and his family.

At the bottom of the stairs, Jace and Fenn rushed over. Both looked like drowned dogs, sodden and dripping. Jace bled from a deep gouge on his forehead. Fenn limped, wincing with every step. Jace stammered out his panic: Nyx had vanished during the surge from the sea.

They had no time to search. Bridle-song had everyone staggering. Graylin could hardly think, his vision blurring. The guardsmen herded them over to a narrow archway off the plaza and down four steps into this dark chamber. Once inside, the miasma slowly lifted. The stone-roofed chamber proved to be a port in this storm. They had no choice but to weather it out in here, impotent and frustrated.

A shattering boom drew Graylin's attention back out. The sound rolled from the sea and echoed off the plaza walls. Graylin leaned farther out, enough that he again felt the frisson of that awful keening.

Out on the water, the *Sparrowhawk* foundered, listing to one side, likely half flooded due to the rent in the hull from the saboteur's bomb. Still, Darant refused to forsake his ship. From atop the forecastle and middeck, the brigand and his remaining crew fired crossbows. Smoke rose from one of the deck cannons. Another blasted with a swirl of fire. A bat was struck, knocked far, before tumbling into the sea.

With the horde's attack focused on the village, the *Sparrowhawk* had been spared enough to rally a defense.

But that would not last.

Graylin drew back into the room, his senses frazzled by the brief brush with that keening outside. He leaned a hand on the wall, waiting for his head to clear.

"What is it about this chamber that protects us?" he mumbled.

The answer came from his other side. Daal's mother and father stood vigil in here, too. Meryk's face was a mask of fear. He clutched his wife under one arm. The two had been drawn in here with them.

"*Mag'nees,*" Meryk said. He touched a black rock imbedded in the sandstone wall. Thousands of the same dotted the space, including the ceiling.

Floraan translated. "You call it *lodestone.*"

Jace gasped in surprise, reaching to the wall on his side. "Such rocks have properties that attract iron, that can align compasses to the Urth's energies. Whatever emanates from those stones must cast a protective pall through this space."

Floraan cupped an ear. "Seashells packed with ground lodestone do the same. Though, the cry of the raash'ke still hurts."

Graylin glanced out to a guardsman running past, flinging a spear, then vanishing out of sight. His leather helm had bulged at the ears.

Meryk frowned. "Over the centuries, we've mined all the mag'nees we can find. There is no more."

Floraan nodded. "Each village only has a few such shelters. Even the number of protective helms is limited. Though, most times it is enough."

Meryk waved toward the cold cliffs. "Our people cut stairs into the ice that lead up. We haul fresh carcasses from the sea and leave them up top for the raash'ke."

Fenn winced. "You feed those monsters?"

"To keep them from feeding on us," Meryk explained.

Floraan sighed. "Occasionally, a few will fly down and grab the unwary. Either for fresh blood or simply for sport. We do what we can, but we remain mostly at the harsh mercy of the raash'ke."

Graylin stared out at the ruins of the plaza, the foundering ship.

*Until we stumbled down here and dragged an entire horde with us.*

Meryk rubbed his chin and lips, plainly anxious, talking to keep himself from rushing out into the village. He scooped his wife closer. Both their gazes never drifted from the doorway.

Graylin knew their concern.

*Nyx isn't the only one missing.*

# 32

NYX LUNGED UP as Henna was snatched from Daal's arms.

"No!" she wailed.

Nyx thrust an arm high. Her fingertips brushed a wingtip as the beast swept upward. But she could do nothing more to stop its escape. She could barely keep her legs, exhausted from her battle with the horde-mind, beaten down and weak.

Next to her, Daal cried out in anguish and panic.

His pain, her guilt, stoked a fury inside her. It steadied her feet, narrowed her vision to a sharp focus. She had suffered so much, an innocent herself. She did not ask for any of this. A litany of misery and pain ramped through her: orphaned and abandoned, tortured and humiliated for being born near blind, seeing her dah and brothers slain—then torn from all she knew and loved, thrust into a role she didn't want, a duty that would only leave a wake of death.

*No . . . no more . . .*

She gathered all that pain as she stared up at Henna's limp form.

Another innocent . . .

*I won't allow it.*

She grabbed Daal's arm, mostly to keep from falling, but down deep, she instinctively knew what she wanted. A part of her knew from the moment she met him. It wafted off of him like his sweaty musk and shone from the ice of his eyes.

With her touch, fire surged into her body.

She gasped at the power, fueled by Daal's panic. Each beat of his heart—sounding like the distant beat of a drum to her roaring ears—filled her with those flames, driving into a dark well that welcomed that energy, sapping it out of him.

She understood what was happening.

*He is flashburn, and I'm the forge.*

Nyx accepted this and stood tall, raising her arm again. She dug the nails of her other hand into the muscle of Daal's arm, drawing blood. She drew and drew upon his fire until she could hold it no longer.

She screamed that energy back out, a dragon's roar of bridle-song. She gloried in that power, ablaze in the energy. It struck like a fiery arrow into the beast.

As it did, for a breath, she saw the creature in its entirety, stripping through shaggy fur, down to bone, blood, and nerve.

The bat writhed in midair, trapped there.

She drove deeper and burned its heart away with a dark satisfaction.

It wailed, flailing wildly, casting smoke from its mouth. Linked by death, she again brushed against the malignancy of the horde-mind. She sensed no fear, no anger, only cold interest, as frigid and immense as the Ice Shield itself.

To it, this death was but a single mote.

She also didn't care.

As the bat died, so did that connection, snuffing out like the life itself. Still, for the briefest flicker, she sensed another lurking in the depths of that malevolence. A spider in the shadows. Thwarted, it slipped deeper into the darkness, turning away, but not before she caught the icy glint of its cold cunning, appraising and adapting even now.

Before she could look closer, it was gone.

*"Fre gah!"* Daal hollered at her, slamming her back into her body.

He ripped his arm free, her nails gouging his flesh. He lunged away, as if scared of her. But that was not it. Instead, he dashed off, arms outstretched. A tumbling figure fell through the air.

Henna . . .

Aghast, Nyx realized she had forgotten about the girl.

Daal had not.

He caught his sister in his arms and rolled to the side. The dead bulk of the bat crashed to the street, shattering wing and limb.

Nyx, emptied and weak, sank to her knees. The surge of fire had hollowed her out. She stared down at her hands, expecting to see through them. She met Daal's gaze over her fingertips. He shifted to his backside, cradling his sister.

She looked at him with hope.

*Is she all right?*

He just stared back. His face strained, his eyes shining with fear—but not for his sister's welfare.

*He's terrified of me.*


DAAL SCOOTED ON his backside away from Nyx. He hugged Henna close to his chest. Cold sweat slicked his body. His arms tremored. His breathing was ragged gasps.

The stench of burnt hair and flesh filled his nostrils, wafting from the broken bulk of the raash'ke. Smoke still steamed from its slack jaws.

*What just happened?*

He swallowed bile. His bones ached. It felt as if the marrow had been scraped from them. His skin prickled painfully, like after carving ice with bare hands. Even his gut had gone cold, his lungs heavy, as if frozen in place.

When Nyx had grabbed him, digging in her nails, he had flashed to another time, deep underwater, when he had been equally cold, his chest weighted down the same. Then, too, blood had been drawn. He pushed that terror away, refusing to let it rise up. Still, he remembered what had been *pushed* into him against his will back then—whereas Nyx had drawn everything *out*.

Both were violations in their own way.

Only Nyx's touch had felt like the most powerful mag'nees stone. *And I was the iron.* The pull had been inescapable. It could not be withstood. In that moment, he had sensed an empty well inside her, a black hole from which nothing could escape. His life was drawn into it, sucking all from him, leaving him cold and numb.

He came close to losing himself then, pulled entirely into that well. But his gaze had remained upward. From down in that well, he had watched Henna being whisked upward. In that moment, even more was ripped from him, all to stoke the power inside Nyx—until finally she cast out that force with a furious scream, burning the beast out of the sky.

As Henna slipped from its claws and plummeted toward the street, panic finally sundered the bond between him and Nyx. He broke free and ran to catch Henna.

He stared down at his sister.

*She's safe.*

His sister's heartbeat fluttered against his chest. She breathed hard, as if somehow sensing her escape.

Tears of relief flowed, melting through the ice inside him. The pounding in his head ebbed. He searched the skies for any other threat. But whatever witchery had ignited here had chased off the bats.

*But for how long?*

His gaze fell back to Nyx. No matter what happened to him, no matter how much it felt like a violation, Nyx had saved Henna. He would give anything to protect his sister. As he accepted this, his terror of Nyx tempered into something like gratefulness.

As Nyx knelt, her shoulders shook with exhaustion. Her eyes shone in a dull glaze, looking forlorn, even frightened. But most of all, she appeared lost.

With a deep breath, she fought to stand. Her legs wobbled. Her first steps stumbled. She cast him a glance, but only from the corner of her eye, as if too ashamed to look at him directly. She headed away, toward the plaza, determined to reach her friends.

Daal groaned and pushed upright, hauling Henna with him. He turned his back on Nyx and staggered to the crowded mag'nees chamber. Those inside had witnessed the felling of the raash'ke. Eyes were huge; whispers murmured among them. He reached the guardsman at the threshold and pushed Henna toward him. As stunned as the rest, the man took her, staring down at her small face, as if she were a miraculous treasure.

*She is.*

"Protect her," Daal told him.

He nodded, withdrawing deeper into the shadows.

Daal swung around. He had his own duty. He stumbled into a run, chasing after Nyx. He paused only long enough to grab an abandoned trident. He intended to pay back the blood-debt he owed for Henna's rescue.

But he knew it was more than that.

*I won't forsake you.*

In her enfeebled state, Nyx had not gotten far. He easily closed the distance and pushed next to her. She shied away, as if not trusting herself.

"Stay back," she warned.

He moved closer and grabbed her hand. She yanked, but he firmed his grip. Her palm and fingers burned his cold skin. With that contact, he again felt that emptiness inside her. Only now, it held no sway over him. She was too weak. He could easily resist that tidal pull.

Still, he knew she needed his strength, the little that remained. He gave it freely. It took no effort. He simply let it flow, like filling a bucket. She gasped quietly, trembling all over. Her legs grew steadier, her breathing less ragged.

She stared up at him, her eyes appreciative but still scared.

As they walked, that essence passed back and forth between them, shared now, not stolen, warm water spilling back and forth. But that was not all that was pooled together.

With each wash into him, he felt her anguish and guilt and a well of heartbreak that was nearly unbearable. Overwhelmed, he almost let go, but he refused and held tighter—even while suspecting she could sense his inner self just as well.

He stared down at their joined hands. He felt her palm in his grip, while also feeling his fingers in hers. It was the strangest sensation, as if they were sharing their bodies, too.

It was an intimacy beyond any kiss.

Together, they continued through the wreckage of the street. While the nearby raash'ke had fled from Nyx's outburst, a battle still raged in the plaza. Agonized screams echoed, along with booming explosions. Flaming arrows traced the sky, illuminating a storm of black wings.

It was certain death to go there.

Still, he tightened his hold on Nyx.

*I won't forsake you.*

# 33

FROM THE TOP step of the lodestone chamber, Graylin stabbed at the face of a massive bat, a male twice the size of an ox. Jaws snapped wildly at his blade, trying to rip it away. Poison slathered those lips and dripped from his sword. Wings beat at the opening. Claws dug with a furious savagery, tearing through the soft sandstone as the beast tried to dig its way inside.

It screamed all the while, determined to drive him into submission. Even with the protection offered here, the bridle-song was a gale in his face. His vision blurred under the assault. His aim wavered.

A shout burst behind him. "Move!"

Exhausted and addled, he fell back. Jace rushed forward and swung his ax with great force. Steel cleaved the air and struck the bat between the eyes. The ax-head cracked deep into its skull. The beast reared back, dragging the weapon and Jace with it.

Fenn rushed up and hugged his friend's legs. The navigator pulled Jace back, forcing him to relinquish his ax. They both tumbled down the steps, tangled together, into the deeper safety of the stone chamber.

Not that *anywhere* was truly safe in this village.

Graylin watched the massive bat flop and writhe in death, the ax still imbedded in its skull—then it lay still, its dreadful keening silenced.

And not just the beast.

Past its bulk, the screams of the dying had ebbed to moans. Only a few stands of guardsmen still fought on the plaza. Bodies sprawled everywhere, soaking the sands black with blood.

Still, a cauldron of bats churned above.

Jace regained his feet and lunged toward the doorway with an arm outstretched, looking ready to rush out and retrieve his precious ax—but that was not his intent.

"Look!" he gasped.

Graylin turned and followed where he pointed. Across the plaza, two small shapes stumbled into view. *Nyx and Daal.* They leaned on each other and waded into the carnage. A bat swept at them. Nyx thrust a hand high and sent it cartwheeling away. Still, she stumbled, weakening. Daal carried her under one arm, a steel trident high in the other.

They would not make it far on their own.

Jace cupped his mouth. "Nyx! Over here!"

His yell was deafened by a cannon blast from the *Sparrowhawk,* where someone was still fighting out on the water.

By now, Meryk and Floraan had spotted their son, too. Their relief was tempered by fear, and not just for Daal.

"Where's Henna?" Floraan whispered, clutching hard to her husband.

Graylin firmed his grip on Heartsthorn, clearheaded enough to know what he had to do. Without a word, he dashed up the stairs and out into the plaza. After only a few steps, that sharp-edged barrage ate into his skull. Wincing against it, refusing to relent, he ran onward. He reached his target—not Nyx, but a fallen guardsman.

Graylin slid on his knees through the bloody sand. He dropped his sword and clawed the helm from the dead man's head. He struggled to don it, his limbs shaking, his vision blurring. He finally yanked it into place. Scrabbling, he palmed the lodestone shells over his ears and pressed them there. The world immediately went muffled.

Still, the keening pierced the helm. It felt like needles digging into his scalp and skull, but it could go no deeper. Graylin hunched over his knees for two breaths to regain his senses.

He heard Jace yell. Graylin could not make out his words, only the urgency and terror. He looked over at Nyx and Daal. The pair had stopped near the center of the plaza, driven also to their knees.

Bats dove at them. Nyx's one arm tremored high, trying to hold them at bay. Two landed in the sand, claws digging, balancing on their wingtips, ready to charge. Daal swept his spear with a flash of steel, trying to guard against both.

Graylin pushed to his feet, grabbed his sword, and sprinted toward them.

Daal stabbed at one of the bats, slicing through an ear, grazing a cut down its neck. The other bat, small and cunning, raced on wingtips and claws, charging low toward them.

Graylin's heart knotted in his throat. He would not make it there in time. He skidded, snatched a bloody spear from the sand with his free hand, and whipped it toward the charging bat.

It struck a wing and tore through it. The blow was not enough to kill it, but it did drive it aside, twisting it around. Black eyes fixed upon its attacker, lips curling from poisoned fangs.

Graylin didn't slow, rushing straight at it.

Still, more bats descended, landing all around. Others beat the air overhead, struggling to get to Nyx, blowing a whirlwind of stinging sand.

Carrying Heartsthorn low and wide, Graylin raced at the beast. As jaws snapped at him, he spun aside and swept his sword high. The blade cleaved through the monster's throat, hewing through bone and sinew. Its head flew and bounced across the sand.

Graylin ducked under a flailing wing to reach Nyx and Daal. His arrival scattered the nearest attackers. They surely scented the fresh kill and were now wary of the newcomer.

Nyx stared wide-eyed at him.

Daal glanced over a shoulder, keeping his trident up.

Graylin pointed toward the shelter, where Jace stood in the doorway. "That way!"

Nyx shook her head, her face pale, running with sweat. She gasped, "Someone's coming . . ."

Graylin didn't understand. He searched around, sweeping his sword.

After the brief hesitation, the horde regathered its nerve. The black storm descended toward them.

Graylin clenched his jaws, ready to defend Nyx with his last breath. From Daal's tight-lipped expression, he was determined to do the same.

Between them, Nyx struggled to her feet and stared toward the sea.

"She's here . . ."

NYX WATCHED A sun rise out of the sea, its golden sheen spreading across the waves. Daal witnessed it, too, gasping in awe. She took his hand and felt the font of his energy stir inside him, responding to the song out there.

Across the sand, Shiya climbed radiant and bright out of the surf and waded to shore. Her face was a mask of fury, her eyes fiery. She sang out like a struck bell, ringing loud and strong.

The bats overhead scattered away.

Those on the ground scrabbled from her path.

She strode swiftly toward Nyx and the others, an unstoppable force.

Moments ago, as soon as Nyx and Daal had entered the plaza, she had sensed Shiya's approach through the sea. Maybe even before that. It had drawn her onward. Through the bloodshed, past the carnage, under those black wings. Nyx didn't know how the bronze woman had come to be here, only that she was. Shiya was a promise of water in a dry desert.

As the bronze woman joined them, Nyx basked in that bridling glow. She let it warm through her, sharing it with Daal via their grasped hands. She closed her eyes, breathing in that power until she found her voice. She opened her throat and heart and added her harmony to Shiya's strength.

The sun around them blasted wider, shining more brilliantly.

The raash'ke screamed and fled from that sudden blaze. It must've been too much, too startling, too frightening. The horde spun and beat and clawed their way into the mists, seeking the blessed darkness of the icy world above. She watched until the skies cleared, and that malignant keening fell mercifully silent.

Only then did Nyx sag again to the sand.

*It's over.*

Still, she stared at the wreckage, the bodies, the ruins around her. She felt no happiness, no glory, only relief.

She could also not shake a deep-seated worry. She remembered the strength of that horde-mind. After her first brush with it during the rescue of Henna, it had never struck at her again with such force. Perhaps it was cautious after her fiery assault. She could still smell the bat's charred heart, feel the flames burning through her. She shied from that memory, ashamed at what she had done to Daal, but also unable to deny a longing ache in her bones to wield that power again.

Yet, that act was likely the only reason she and Daal had made it this far. It had driven the horde-mind into the shadows, leaving the raash'ke with little guidance, allowing her meager reserves of power to forge a path to the plaza.

A voice called to her, full of joy that felt misplaced here. "Nyx!"

She turned to see Jace running toward her, followed by a limping Fenn. As the pair reached her, they drew her into a large embrace. Others began to crawl out of hiding, rising from nooks and cubbies. The town stirred forth all around, recognizing the threat was over.

*At least for now.*

Daal's mother and father rushed to them. Floraan clasped her son's arm. "Henna?"

Daal wiped blood from his brow. "Safe."

Floraan sobbed in relief. Her husband hugged them both tightly.

Graylin kept close. Shiya shadowed their group and continued to glow, though the intensity of her song had ebbed. Still, she maintained a steady hum, like a flashburn forge waiting to be reignited if needed.

Across the square, faces stared toward them, some in horror, others in awe. The Reef Farer and his family gathered at the edge, wary but knowing the newcomers had likely saved Iskar—even if the horde had been lured down here by the crashing of their swyftship.

A harsh shout echoed from the *Sparrowhawk*. She could not make out the words, but she knew who called to them.

Darant had clearly survived, but how many of his crew?

Graylin waved an arm, letting the brigand know they were safe for the moment.

As the townspeople gathered at the fringes of the plaza, Nyx made a silent promise to them.

*We will protect you for as long as we can.*

Still, she pictured her group's ultimate goal—to set the Urth to spinning and melting this world—and added a harsher truth.

*But in the end, we may destroy you.*

# 34

BACK IN DAAL'S home, Nyx sat at the family's stone table. A blanket draped her shoulders, but it failed to truly warm her.

Jace crouched across from her, cradling a hot mug of fish stew in his hands. The fare had been meant for a feast following the festival. But no one was celebrating. Even Daal's parents hovered by a small oven with Henna, clearly relieved but far from joyous.

Mournful bells rang a slow dirge that echoed across Iskar.

A short while ago, back on the plaza, Graylin had collected their group and led them here. The village needed time to gather their dead, to grieve for their loss. He didn't want them in the way, nor did he want that sorrow to have a target. Even the Reef Farer had waved them off, but not before clasping Graylin on the shoulder, silently expressing his thanks.

Still, they all knew such gratefulness could quickly sour.

The next days would be fragile for all.

As testament to the tension and edginess, they all jumped when the drape over the doorway burst open. Jace spilled stew onto his lap and leaped up with a gasp.

But there was no cause for alarm.

Daal shoved inside, breathless and tired. "Neffa is fine," he announced. "She's scared, but I calmed her. A shoalman is gathering the other orksos and moving them to deeper waters, getting them clear of the wreckage. The docks and shoreline are a treacherous ruin of broken boats and cracked piers."

"What about Shiya and Fenn?" Jace asked.

Daal nodded. He had left with those two for the docks. "I found them a boat that was still hale enough to reach your big ship." He shrugged. "I don't know if they can roust enough others to rescue your friends."

Nyx swallowed, worried. Shiya had related her story. Her sailraft had crashed atop a small island. With no way off, the bronze woman had crossed the seabed on foot, drawn by the flames of Iskar. As she neared the shore, she had sensed the bridling threat and rushed to their aid.

*But now Rhaif and the others need her.*

Daal crossed and hugged his mother and nodded to his father. Floraan passed him a bowl of the stew. He joined them at the table, but before he could settle, a spate of shouts and panicked cries erupted in the distance.

Nyx threw off her blanket and stood.

*Are we being attacked again?*

Daal set his bowl down and rushed to the door. Nyx followed, while Jace grabbed his ax from beside the table. Meryk came, too, but Floraan stayed with her daughter.

Daal pulled aside the drape, holding an arm up to keep everyone back. The flow of cries and screams drew closer. A pair of villagers fled past the doorway.

*"Hen wrag?"* Daal called to them.

His inquiry was ignored as the two vanished out of sight.

Daal glanced with confusion at Nyx and the others—then a familiar rumbling growl reached them, underlaid by a threatening chitter.

Relieved, Nyx pushed Daal's arm aside and slipped past him. "That's Kalder."

*No wonder the villagers are panicked.*

Down a curve of the street, Graylin appeared, flanked by the massive vargr and trailed by the mountainous figure of Quartermaster Vikas and the robed shape of Alchymist Krysh. The knight had gone to check on the others, those who had been left hidden in a nest of boulders outside the village. As they approached, Kalder's hackles shivered down his back. His tall ears swiveled in all directions, alert for danger. The others looked equally wary and dour.

But at least they had survived.

Graylin spotted Nyx at the door and waved her back. Once the way was clear, he hurried his group inside. Kalder, too, but the vargr remained at the threshold, padding in a nervous circle near the door.

Daal's parents retreated farther back, guarding over Henna.

The girl assured them, *"Gree Kalder. Nee fayr."*

Nyx noted one member of the group remained missing. Bashaliia. Still, she understood why Graylin had left the Mýr bat behind. After the attack by the raash'ke, it would be a horrible time to introduce Bashaliia, especially considering the villagers' reaction to Kalder stalking through their streets.

Nyx turned to Graylin. "How is Bashaliia faring? Is he all right being left behind?"

Graylin winced, his expression pained. He glanced at Krysh. The alchymist stared down to his toes. Even Quartermaster Vikas would not meet her eye.

Nyx's heart clenched, sensing something was wrong. She took a step forward. "What happened? Is he still alive?"

"As far as we know," Krysh mumbled.

Nyx shook her head, not accepting this answer. She found it hard to catch her breath, to challenge them. "What . . . What do you mean?"

Graylin glared at the alchymist. "Tell her."

Krysh swallowed hard and nodded. "We all heard the attack on Iskar.

The screams, the fighting, that awful keening. Kalder turned savage. Even Bashaliia fought to break free, maybe to aid you all. But I spotted the storm of wings over the village. I knew Bashaliia could not fight so many, especially while still recovering from his wounds. Vikas guarded the exit, refusing to let them leave. All the while, Bashaliia called and called for you, his cries deafening in that small space."

Nyx rubbed her chest, trying to calm her pounding heart. "Then what?"

"It wasn't you that answered. A covey of bats, half a dozen, crashed to the beach. The raash'ke screamed at us, muddling our senses. Bashaliia cast out his bridle-song in a furious wail that freed us. Before we could act, Kalder broke past Vikas and killed one of the raash'ke, ripping out its throat. Bashaliia went to his aid, trying to protect the vargr from the bats' keening—but the pack was too fast, too strong. They surrounded Bashaliia. They pounded him low with their bridling, pinning him to the sand."

Krysh looked with pity at her. "I didn't think he could be brought down like that, not even with five attacking him. It was as if something far stronger was wielding them."

Nyx closed her eyes. Guilt and fear strangled her. She knew the alchymist was right. During the battle, she remembered being relieved when the horde-mind had retreated from the fighting. She had believed her fiery attack upon the bat in the street had unnerved it, made it cautious and wary. She also remembered the dark presence, the spider in the shadows. She had sensed its cunning as it turned away from her—not to escape.

*But toward another target.*

Krysh continued, "None of us could resist the strength of that force. We all staggered, dropping, losing our senses. Before I fully succumbed, I saw those dark bats leap away with a blast of sand."

"And Bashaliia?" Nyx whispered.

Krysh stared at her, his eyes apologetic. "He followed them, haltingly, trying not to go, but unable to stop."

Nyx shook her head and stumbled away from the truth.

*No . . .*

But she could not escape the certainty inside her.

"They bridled him," she gasped out.

Jace joined her. "He'll break free. I know he will. The first chance he gets."

She clutched her throat, remembering the force of that horde-mind, the malevolent intent of the spider. She flashed back to her first brush with that darkness. Up in the *Sparrowhawk*. She pictured the black bat clutching to the ship's window, wings battering against the glass, its gaze fixed on her. Back then, she had felt the horde-mind staring through those eyes, casting out a silent threat.

It echoed in her head even now.

**We will break you.**

She closed her eyes, knowing the truth, knowing why they took Bashaliia.

*They will break him instead.*

# 35

RHAIF SHIVERED ON the floor of the sailraft's hold. His teeth clattered, and his chest heaved up and down. His impaled leg was a fiery torch, but it failed to dispel his feverish chill. Agony flared with each beat of his heart. Cold sweat pebbled his brow. All the while, he quaked and shook under a blanket made of ripped sections of the raft's balloon.

Herl and Perde knelt beside him, ready to pin him down if his shaking grew worse. Their worried glances and pinched brows did not make Rhaif feel confident in his survival following the venomous attack by those sea creatures.

But at least the beasts hadn't returned.

Off by the raft's stern door, Glace stood with Hyck. "We'll have to dig out that hooked barb," she mumbled. "We can't just wait for him to die."

Hyck shook his head. "Doing that might spread the poison faster. Kill him even quicker."

"We must try. Blood keeps boiling out around that thorn. It's not scabbing or clotting. As if the venom is thwarting it from doing so. If we do nothing, he'll bleed his life away while we wring our hands."

Hyck was doing just that and dropped his arms. "How long has Shiya been gone?"

"Over two bells. She should've been back by now."

"You don't know that. None of us saw those torches that drew her into the sea. We can't say how far off they were."

"But we all heard those cannon blasts."

Even Rhaif had. The booms had echoed across the sea like distant thunder.

"Those came from the *Sparrowhawk*," Glace said. "I know the timbre of those cannons as surely as my father's bellow. The ship is battling something out there."

"But we've heard nothing for a spell. Is that good or bad?"

Glace shrugged. "My father is a hard one to kill. Besides, we have our own challenge here."

Their gazes turned to Rhaif.

"What do we do with him?" Hyck said. "Wait for rescue or intercede?"

Rhaif coughed and spoke through his shivering. "Can I have a say in the matter of my own fate?"

They stared, awaiting his verdict.

"Hack my leg off if you have to," he said. "But get this sodding poker out of my thigh."

Perde grunted and stood up. "I'll crack open the last cask of ale. He'll need a cup or two of courage before you get to cuttin' on his leg."

Rhaif twisted to look at the man. "Better bring me the whole cask."

Glace left Hyck to guard the door and drew a dagger from her belt. She set about heating the blade over a flaming tin of flashburn. Perde returned with a cup of ale. Herl helped Rhaif sit up enough to take it with trembling hands. Rhaif downed the cup in one gulp, staring all the while at Glace, knowing what was coming.

"More," Rhaif said, pushing the cup at Perde.

His order was obliged—and thrice more after that.

He suddenly didn't mind warm ale.

Finally, Glace turned and nodded to the twin brothers. "Hold him down."

Rhaif groaned as he was laid flat and rolled on his side. It felt like shifting over a bed of hot coals. As his leg was exposed, he grimaced at the sight of the black barb, the bubbling blood, and the greenish veins driving outward from the wound.

Glace knelt next to him and lifted her fiery-tipped blade.

"Wait!" Rhaif gasped, and held out a shaking arm toward Perde. "One sip more. I'm not feeling quite courageous enough."

The brother indulged, emptying the last of the cask, and handed over the cup.

Herl did not look pleased. "He *did* drain it all."

Rhaif tilted his head and glared over at the man. "You're welcome to take my place."

Herl frowned, not accepting his generous offer.

Rhaif turned back and swallowed the last of the ale. He took a deep, shuddering breath and nodded to Glace. "Do it."

As she shifted closer, Rhaif leaned back. His head spun, but he didn't know if it was from poisonous delirium or drunkenness.

"I'll be quick," Glace promised.

The two brothers closed on him. Large hands pinned his shoulders and ankles.

Rhaif squeezed his eyes shut, readying himself. It didn't help. With his flesh inflamed, the first cut drew an agonized scream from his throat. The second cut was worse. He thrashed and bucked from the planks. Herl and Perde sprawled over him. Glace continued digging, breaking her oath to do this quickly.

She swore and hollered for the brothers to hold him steady.

Rhaif writhed and panted, soon too agonized to do more than mewl in pain. His vision narrowed to a pinch.

Finally, Glace sat back. "Got it."

Rhaif collapsed with relief, shaking and shivering. The cabin continued to spin and wobble. His leg remained a torch.

"Let it bleed," Glace warned. "Best to drain some of the poison before wrapping it."

Herl made his own assessment. "It'll leave quite the scar."

Perde agreed. "Make a right pirate out of ya yet."

Rhaif groaned, still in agony, but with the thorn out of his thigh, he already felt better. He lifted his head, trying to will the world to settle into one place. "You did good. I should be—"

His head lolled back as a dark wave swept over him. His legs stiffened, then began pounding the planks uncontrollably. As his arms followed suit, his spine arched under him. His neck craned to the point of breaking.

"He's seizing!" Glace shouted.

His head started hammering the wood—hard enough to finally pitch him into a feverish blackness.


FOR AN ENDLESS time, Rhaif swam through that darkness, lost in oblivion, rising and falling in a rolling tide. He thought he heard voices, chased after them, only to be drowned away again. He eventually gave up the pursuit. A certain contentedness settled over him, both weighing him down and making him feel lighter.

Then a slight glow shone high above. It caught his fading attention, stirred him from his lassitude. It drew him like a curious trout toward a lure. As he rose toward it, it grew into a golden sun, casting out rays deeper into the blackness. A few streams brushed through him, bringing warmth, along with melodic notes, echoes of his mother's lullaby.

He let those strands draw him higher. His cold heart thawed in that glow, thumping stronger. The spread of heat over his chest coalesced into a palm and fingers.

Words reached him. "I think he's coming round."

The world exploded into brightness. He groaned and tried to shade his eyes.

Someone held his arm down. "Don't move too quickly."

He blinked, recognizing Glace's voice.

But his first sight was that of a goddess, hovering over him. Perfect lips parted, sighing with relief, still laced in a melodic song. Blue eyes, full of concern, shone like a cloudless day. Burnished bronze swam with hues that no word could describe.

"Shiya . . ." he whispered hoarsely.

"I've got you," she shushed back at him. Her palm—still warm, still humming with a soft glow—rested on his bare chest. "Lie still."

Rhaif obeyed, knowing he would do anything she asked. Besides, the world continued to rock around him, dizzying him. He stared up at the misty skies, which rolled back and forth over him. He groaned, either still drunk or still feverish.

"Wh . . . Where are we?"

"In a boat," Shiya said. "Headed to Iskar."

Rhaif waved away her words. They made no sense. He got his elbows under him and pushed slightly up. Glace crouched with Hyck ahead of him. Beyond the two, a stranger stood at the prow of a wide-bellied skiff, his strong legs braced wide. He carried woven reins in his hands. Other tethers ran from cleats out to sea.

Rhaif tilted high enough to follow those leads. He spotted a pair of harnessed creatures cresting the waves. They humped and worked strong tails, showing flashes of wings beneath the water. But strangest of all, they thrust opalescent horns ahead of them.

Rhaif moaned. "Either this is a dream or I'm clearly still delirious."

"They call them orksos," Herl said behind him, confirming their existence.

Perde acknowledged the same. "Ugly beasts."

The dark-haired stranger, bare-chested and wearing snug breeches, scowled back. His blue eyes flashed icily. "Watch your tongue. Noorish or not, I'll dump you back on that island. I don't care if you might be long-lost relations. Maybe you'd rather have another go with those pickkyns again."

Rhaif let the mysteries fall aside. Especially as he remembered a greater concern. He stared down at his leg. His thigh still throbbed and burned.

Shiya must have noticed the worried set to his lips. "Fear not. Shoalman Hess had a remedy to counter the pickkyn's poison."

The boatman heard her. "You don't travel these waters without it, not with those long-necked beasts prowlin' about. Regular skorpans of the sea." He frowned back at Rhaif. "Your mates made a right mess of your leg digging out that spine."

Rhaif parted a flap of his makeshift blanket, enough to reveal a leafy bandage wrapped around his upper thigh. It wafted a sulfuric scent that curled his nose, but he was not about to complain.

"Such foolishness," Hess said. "Just gotta piss on that bastard, a good stream, and the spine will release its hooks. Then she slides out smooth as shite out an orkso's tail."

Rhaif flashed to that torturous extraction and glared at Glace.

Hyck shrugged. "I told ya we shoulda waited."

Hess waved back. "All that trouble on the island, and you left a mountain of meat rotting on that sand. The flanks of pickkyns make good steaks. 'Specially with eel gravy."

Rhaif tried to picture such a meal. It was a mistake. He clutched his belly as the world tipped sideways. *Oh, no . . .* He rolled to the boat's rail and emptied his stomach into the sea, heaving hard, the sour smell reminding him of his last imbibement.

Herl sniffed it out, too. "All that ale wasted."

AFTER A LONG spell, Rhaif squinted as a shoreline came into view through the fog. The village of Iskar glowed with torches, as if welcoming them to its bosom. But the slow ring of bells, mournful and solemn, echoed over the waves.

He lay in Shiya's arms. He still occasionally shivered with chills, but the heat of her bronze kept him warm. He shifted his buttocks as the shoalman Hess blew a curled horn, announcing his homecoming through the mists.

Shiya had already related all that transpired. The attack, the deaths, even the loss of Bashaliia. He could no longer whine about his own struggles. Especially as the aftermath came clearer into view.

Boats lay broken along the beach. Rubble and debris had washed deep into the village. Huge bonfires burned winged shapes, casting up flumes of oily smoke. But worst of all, a long row of draped bodies lined an open square. People knelt beside them, rocking in place or leaning on one another.

Rhaif had to look away.

On the far side of the village, the *Sparrowhawk* had been hauled to shore— maybe by the same horned beasts that pulled the skiff. It lay crooked in the shallows, its bow nosed deep into the sand. The necessity was obvious. Water continued to slosh into and out of the huge rent in its hull.

*But it hadn't sunk.*

Not that it made much difference. Above the ship, only a fraction of its great balloon still fluttered; the rest lay draped over rails and deck. According to Shiya, its flashburn tanks were nearly empty.

Figures scurried about the beached ship, inspecting damage, unloading the hold, stacking crates on the sand. Another craft floated above it all. It was the other sailraft, drifting and occasionally flashing fire from its forges. Its gasbag remained perk and taut.

Rhaif pointed it out to Glace. "Looks like your sister managed *not* to crash her raft."

Glace scowled. "Sard off."

He only meant to tease the woman, but from all the grim expressions, no one was in the mood for any amusement.

They all knew the truth.

*We're trapped here.*

Rhaif sighed loudly. He gazed up at the mists overhead, brightening with every breath, as if marking a new day—the first of the rest of their lives down here.

He shook his head, resigned to this fate, knowing they'd failed in their mission. He pictured the Crown, a home they'd never see again.

*Let's hope Kanthe and the others are faring better than we are.*

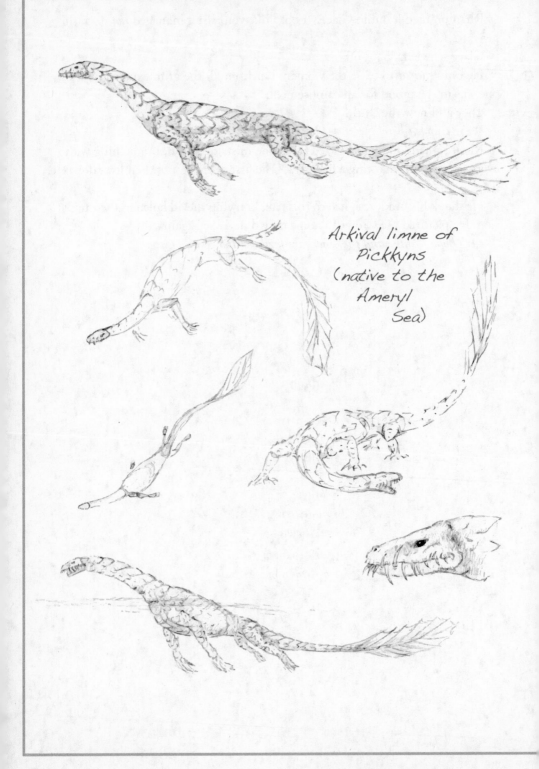

Arkival limne of
Pickkyns
(native to the
Ameryl
Sea)

# EIGHT

# THE DRUMS OF WAR

*Sound the horne & rattle the sweord,*
*Bridle the steed & ripen the wipp,*
*For we be the Anwyn who alle feyr.*

*Poune the shield & reddi the ax,*
*Schyne the armor & sharp'n the spear,*
*For we be the Anwyn who know no feyr.*

*Wenn dawn brayks & blood does flowe*
*Ryse anew, you warriors bolde,*
*For we be the Anywn who kenn næfre die.*

—A battle chant of the ancient
Anwyn Legion

# 36

KANTHE LEANED OVER the rail of the wingketch and studied the sweep of verdant forest far below. It called to him in distant whispers of birdsong and sharper cries of hunters. As the *Quisl* floated over it, scudding through low clouds, he could smell the rich loam and wet leaf.

It was the legendary Myre Drysh, a hunter's dream. Its bower swept in all directions and washed up against the mountains to the east, the towering peaks of the Hyrg Scarp.

He wished he could forsake this journey and vanish into the forests below. He pictured leading the simple role of a tracker, eking out a living under that shadowed bower—and not just because of his love of woodlands and the challenge of a hunt.

*It's so sarding hot up here.*

Sweat dripped from his nose and fell toward the distant canopy. He straightened and scowled at the rise of the Scarp mountains.

For two days, the *Quisl* had been following those peaks, heading due south. The mountains were too high near Kysalimri, the winds too fierce to risk crossing the range in such a small ship. As they trailed along the edge of the Scarp, the craggy peaks had grown steadily smaller. According to the ketch's captain, a Rhysian named Saekl, they would head across those craggy peaks later in the day.

*Not soon enough for my tastes.*

Kanthe glanced back north, wishing the mountains were already between them and Kysalimri—especially considering who was held prisoner on board. He pictured Rami's features, darkened by thunderheads. The Klashean prince still believed Kanthe had betrayed him. And Aalia's disdain only grew worse with each passing league. No doubt the Imri-Ka was already hunting for his son and daughter, in ships far swifter than theirs.

Frustrated at their slow pace, Kanthe tightened his fingers on the rail. A ketch was built for quick launches and winged for agile maneuvering. It wasn't designed for speedy passage over a long distance. The fluttering snap of the *Quisl*'s wings reminded him that they were flying as fast as they dared.

A harsh curse—followed by a sharper squawk of complaint—drew Kanthe's attention to the bow.

Under the draft-iron cables that ran from the curve of the high prow up to the ship's balloon, Llyra knelt with a slim woman named Cassta, one of the Rhysian assassins. She was the youngest of Saekl's crew, maybe a year or two older than Kanthe. Her braid was shorter, holding only four bells, marking her as an acolyte.

Cassta pulled a squirming skrycrow away from Llyra.

"Hold it still," Llyra complained.

"You're too rough," Cassta scolded. She frowned at Llyra. "It's well for you to remember. Nothing is as strong as gentleness."

Kanthe smiled, surprised at such words from an assassin-in-training. Over the past two days, he had often noted Cassta, more often than he should. She moved with a sultry grace that whispered of hidden strength and talents. He caught her occasionally looking his way, too. But she seemed to stare straight through him.

Llyra, though, was not amused. "Let's get this message into the winds and be done with it already."

Cassta held the crow away. "First, take a deep breath."

This suggestion was met by a deep scowl from Llyra.

Kanthe crossed over, drawn for many reasons. "Maybe I can help."

Llyra huffed and stood, clearly done with the whole affair. She thrust a hand at him. Her fingers clutched a curled ribbon of oilskin, sealed with a dab of wax. "This message needs to get to Symon, to let him know we're about to make the crossing toward Malgard. One of his crows arrived earlier, with word that the situation in Kysalimri grows more heated with each passing bell. He wants to know our progress to determine how best to proceed."

Kanthe took the scroll. Skrycrows had been flitting back and forth as they had traveled along the Scarp. Such swift birds flew faster than any ketch, but eventually the distances would be too great, making communication and coordination difficult once they crossed the mountains. If they wanted any further support from Symon and the Razen Rose, they could not delay any longer.

Llyra brusquely waved for Kanthe to take her stead. He suspected some of the guildmaster's frustration was not just due to an obstinate skrycrow. Last night, Llyra had come to Kanthe's cabin, half-drunk, or at least feigning so, and kissed him roughly. She had tried to push him toward his bed, but he had maneuvered her back out before she could do more. Still, his reaction had been more reflex than rejection. Her lips had been soft, her tongue probing. The rise of her breasts pressed against him had not been entirely unwelcome.

Still . . .

*Probably for the best.*

Llyra strode across the deck. Once at the hatch, she swept her half-cloak, as if to brush them both off, and vanished below. While Llyra might have wanted to share Kanthe's bed, he knew another whose ardor had gone ice cold. He regretted the loss of Rami's friendship and still held out hope that it could be rekindled.

With a sigh, he turned and dropped to a knee across from Cassta. The woman's face was stoic, but her eyes glinted with amusement, as if she had been listening in on his private thoughts. And maybe she had. It was said Rhysians were capable of reading another by studying the tiniest movements of eye, mouth, and breath. It's what made them such skilled assassins.

Of course, Kanthe's hot face hid little of his discomfort—both from last night and now.

Cassta smelled of honeywood and leather. Her silver-white complexion set off the rose of her lips. Her ampleness filled her bodice, especially when she leaned over to hold out the skrycrow toward him.

He stared a breath too long.

"Prince Kanthe," she said coldly, stating his title with a hint of disdain.

He tried not to take offense. The Rhysians' matriarchal society notoriously held little regard for hierarchal rule.

He cleared his throat. "Sorry . . . just a lot in my head at the moment."

"No doubt." Cassta's gaze flicked to where Llyra had vanished. "She is quite handsome in her own hard way."

Kanthe's cheeks grew hotter. It was a small ship, making secrets difficult to keep. He lowered his face and concentrated on freeing the capped end on the crow's message tube, which was harnessed to the bird's back and positioned lengthwise between its wings. He struggled to accomplish this simple task. The bird fidgeted, still clearly agitated from Llyra's rough handling.

*Trust me, little bird, I feel the same way.*

Discouraged, Kanthe sat back on his heels. Then he remembered Cassta's instructions. Taking a deep breath, he reached a finger and ruffled the feathered crest along its neck. He shushed softly to the bird. The skrycrow fluttered its wings, then seemed to grow calmer.

"There you go," he whispered.

He uncapped the tube and slid the scroll into place. Once done, he thanked the bird with another ruffle of its crest. The crow twisted its head and rubbed a cheek against a knuckle, raising a smile to Kanthe's lips.

Cassta drew the bird to her bosom and gently smoothed its crest. "As you can see, it's the tenderest touch that warms the heart. But after that—" She shrugged. "A firmer touch is often welcome."

Before he could respond, she stood, crossed to the rail, and freed the crow to the winds. Kanthe watched her—with her arms held high, her back arched—and momentarily forgot how to breathe. Still, he recognized one other detail.

All this time, not a single bell in her braid had tinkled.

It served as a dire reminder that he'd best be cautious with her.

*For that pale rose has thorns.*

SWEATY AND OUT of sorts—and not just from the day's swelter—Kanthe climbed down the ladder into the cooler confines of the ship's tween-deck. He had waited for Cassta to depart first, to leave him a moment to collect himself. She had not said another word, hardly seeming to notice he was still there.

*Then again, she is Rhysian and I'm a man.*

He shook his head, perplexed and unsure. Had she been teasing him, an amusement to idle away the passing leagues? He suspected Llyra's interest in him lay along those same bored lines, only the guildmaster was far more forthright about it all. Kanthe found his confusion dissolving into irritation.

He headed down the passageway toward his cabin.

"Kanthe," a voice called behind him.

He turned to find Frell leaning out the doorway of a cabin he shared with Pratik. The two had been locked in there for most of the voyage. They had been trying to decipher the pages torn from an ancient book discovered at the heart of the Abyssal Codex. The labor had clearly taken its toll. The alchymist's eyes were shadowed by exhaustion, his chin and cheeks stubbled and dark.

Frell waved to him. "We need your help."

"My help?"

"Just get in here." Frell withdrew inside, clearly expecting his former student to obey and follow.

Kanthe shrugged, happy for the distraction. Surely decrypting the inked passages from an ancient tome was easier than understanding the wiles of a woman.

*At least for me.*

He crossed down the passage and entered the cramped cabin.

"Close the door," Frell warned.

The alchymist leaned over a small table. Pratik stood on the other side. A stolen page lay between them. Another two had been tacked to the far wall. A pair of bunked beds stood along one side, looking untouched.

Pratik held a large lens in one hand, peering at one of the many images on the page before him. The tiny icon looked like a cracked golden egg with a serpent crawling out of it. The picture was illuminated in bright colors, though the paint was chipped and pocked by age. The lines of writing that wrapped around the image fared worse. The words were barely legible.

But that wasn't the biggest concern.

"We're making little progress," Frell announced. "Pratik knows some ancient Klashean which offered hints of the context. And the pictures help. But what we've discerned is muddled and in pieces."

"What've you figured out?" Kanthe asked. "Anything more about that dark goddess that the Dresh'ri worship?"

"No. The pages I stole only mention the *Vyk dyre Rha* once."

Kanthe frowned. "And you still think it might be Nyx?"

Frell had shared all that had transpired in the dark heart of the Codex, including his own fears about the identity of the dark rider atop a winged beast.

Then again, Nyx was on all their thoughts, especially after Llyra's disturbing report two days ago. Somehow, Hálendii had learned that Nyx and the others had set off across the Ice Shield. The kingdom had dispatched ships in pursuit. With no way to warn Nyx's group, all they could do was fret.

"I've no further insight about the *Vyk dyre Rha,*" Frell admitted. "But the one mention we found here does tie the Shadow Queen to a concerning image."

Frell shifted to a page on the wall. He pointed to another of the illuminated icons. This one showed a silvery countenance of a full moon, only its lower half lay shattered, with the broken pieces spilling down the page.

"Could be moonfall," Kanthe conceded. He waved to the other pages. "What else is in all these scribbles?"

Pratik shrugged. "Nothing that makes sense. Most of it relates to some great war."

Kanthe pictured the bomb dropped atop Ekau Watch, the smoky flume of that destruction. "Well, a war *is* starting."

Frell shook his head. "The battle described is not a prophecy of a war to come. But more like *history*. Or maybe *legend*."

"Definitely out of the ancient past," Pratik agreed. He drew Kanthe to the other page on the wall and swept a finger across a swath of passages. "This entire section is written in the tongue of the Elders, the language of the old gods. And here it dates that war." Pratik ran a fingertip over a few words. *"Pantha re Gaas . . ."*

"The Forsaken Ages," Frell translated. "The time before history. That's when this war is said to have taken place."

Pratik nodded. "The battle must be important. Why else include it in an ancient book of prophecies?"

Frell planted his fists on his hips. "More importantly, what does any of this have to do with the *Vyk dyre Rha* and the threat of moonfall?" The alchymist turned to Kanthe. "That's why we need you. To help us put it all together."

"Me? I barely speak Klashean, let alone *ancient* Klashean."

"But you know someone who is far more fluent than even Pratik."

Kanthe backed a step.

*Oh, no . . .*

Pratik explained. "Ancient Klashean is said to be the language of our thirty-three gods. Only a handful of scholars at the House of Wisdom are fluent. It is a language reserved for *imri* royalty, so they can commune with the gods during rituals, reciting passages in that language. It's why I know so little."

"But Rami is fluent," Frell stressed pointedly.

"As is his sister," Pratik added. "Despite appearances as a pampered daughter of the Imri-Ka, Aalia is well studied, even brilliant."

Frell faced Kanthe, his eyes desperate. "You must convince them to help us."

# 37

KANTHE PLACED A palm on the prisoners' door, readying himself for the storm to come. So far, he had tried four times to broker peace with Rami, to offer his solemn oath that he did not know Llyra would orchestrate the kidnapping of his sister. But Rami remained deaf and unmovable.

The prince loved his younger sister and would protect her with his life. Whether Kanthe knew of the betrayal or not, it had still happened under the guise of getting them free of the palace. To Rami, it was all bundled together.

Down deep, Kanthe knew the prince was not entirely wrong.

*I do deserve a share of the blame.*

Kanthe suspected part of the reason he needed Rami's forgiveness was to assuage his own guilt. Aalia did not deserve to be dragged—literally—into this situation.

"Are you going in or what?" a guard asked, leaning on a wall and picking at his teeth with a dagger.

With no other choice, Kanthe knocked to announce himself. He had left Frell and Pratik back in their cabin with the infernal pages. The best chance of gaining the others' cooperation was to go in alone.

An inarticulate response came from inside. Kanthe unlatched the door and waited. He refused to barge inside after being scolded soundly before. After three breaths, Loryn opened the door for him. The Chaaen's role aboard the ship had been reduced to a manservant.

Loryn scowled at Kanthe. Likely, he had been expecting a crewman at the door with a midday platter.

"If I may . . ." Kanthe waved to the room.

Loryn turned and inquired in Klashean. Rami's gruff voice responded with irritation. The prince clearly had had enough of Kanthe's prostrations. Still, Loryn stepped back and invited him inside with a wave of an arm, as if he were welcoming a guest into a set of private quarters versus a prison cell.

Kanthe entered, struggling with how to win over their cooperation.

The cabin was identical to the others, with two bunked beds along one wall. A thin mattress had been dragged in for Loryn. The only notable difference to this room was that it was slightly larger and had its own privy closet. Still, it was a far cry from royal quarters.

Rami hopped off the top bunk. The lower had a makeshift drape drawn across it, made from a blanket. It sheltered the Illuminated Rose of the Imri-Ka. Aalia had remained hidden during each of Kanthe's prior visits. He had yet to set eyes upon her after seeing her dragged out of the map closet.

Rami stepped before him, blocking the way into the rest of his cabin. He stood bare-chested, his skin glowing with a sheen of sweat from the stifling heat. He wore a pair of ragged leggings cast off by a crewman.

"What do you want?" he demanded.

"Your help."

Rami cocked an eyebrow high, his face darkly amused. "My help?"

Kanthe waved to the draped bunk. "Both of your help."

That brow dropped and joined the other into a deep furrow. "Truly, this must be some jest."

"I know you're angry. Our trust broken. Again, I'm deeply sorry. But I came here at the request of Alchymist Frell and Chaaen Pratik."

The prince crossed his arms, clearly holding those two equally responsible for the kidnapping of his sister.

"Rami, whether you forgive me or not, you know *why* you agreed to travel with me in the first place. You know what all this effort—and missteps"—he glanced to the blanket curtain—"was meant to prevent."

The answer came from that shrouded bunk. "Moonfall."

Aalia pulled aside the drape and unfolded herself from the bed. She still wore her bedclothes, a silken shift, now belted high at the waist. She stood unabashed, as if she wore the finest gown. Her black eyes shone with fire, hot enough to force Kanthe back a step.

She brushed aside a scatter of loose curls that had escaped her fall of dark braids. Her cheeks were flushed darker. Though not primped, coiffed, and painted, she remained regal, even more beautiful now, a stunning black diamond that had fallen from its gold setting.

She challenged him scornfully. "You truly expect us to believe the moon will crash down and destroy the world?"

Kanthe glanced to Rami for help. He must have shared everything with his sister. She had no doubt demanded an explanation from her brother, for how Rami came to be found among the traitors who had abducted her. Rami simply stared coldly at Kanthe, offering no support.

*Up to me, then.*

Kanthe stared down at Aalia, letting her see his sincerity. "It *will* happen. Unless we act. And soon. I did not wish to burden you with any of this. But there is something vital hidden in the Klashe that we must—"

"A mysterious Sleeper," she spat back.

Kanthe flicked a look at Rami. The prince had clearly held nothing back from his sister. He returned his attention to Aalia, remembering Pratik's assertion that there was more to this woman than the indignant fire of a pampered princess.

"Whether you believe me or not, it is what drives our action," Kanthe said. "Consider us deluded, moon-addled, even ridiculous, but we mean no harm to the Klashe. Or to you and your brother. We wish only to follow the path assigned to us."

"By the feverish dream of a blind girl who regained her sight."

Kanthe sighed.

*Rami had definitely spared nothing.*

"Alchymist Frell also believes her," Kanthe stressed. "And he is not one to adhere to the wisdom of soothers and bone-readers. Before even hearing of Nyx, his own precise studies of the moon had already confirmed such a threat."

Aalia took a deep breath, some of the fire dimming in her eyes. "As I understand, your mentor served as a member of the Council of Eight at Kepenhill. An esteemed position and one of high regard."

"That . . . That's right."

Clearly the Illuminated Rose had done her own inquiries.

"And he truly believes this?" Aalia asked.

Kanthe nodded and motioned to her brother. "When Rami picked the lock and broke into our chambers, he saw the focus of Frell's study. About the moon and prophecies of doom."

Aalia glanced sharply at Rami. "What is this? You broke into the alchymist's chambers?"

Rami's eyes widened. He lifted a palm. Apparently, the prince hadn't been entirely forthright with his recounting of events.

Aalia glared at him. "Does that mean you've been continuing your training with Chaaen Pyke? In the ways of thieves and pilferers? Even after I told you to stop? If Father ever found out . . ."

"He didn't," Rami said. "And wouldn't. He never attends to me. Nor to most of the empire, for that matter. You know this, sister. He's too lost in whispers and omens. While Alchymist Frell might not listen to soothers, our father bends both ears to that accursed Augury in Qazen."

Aalia crossed her arms, looking perturbed—but whether at Rami's low pursuits or her father's neglect, it was unclear.

Kanthe sensed a well of pent-up frustration in both of them.

Aalia faced Kanthe again. "You claim your alchymist is not swayed by auguries of his own. Then why does he go to such efforts to aid that swamp girl, someone who is clearly a charlatan of some sort?"

"First of all, she's not so much a *girl*. She's nearly the same age as you." Kanthe pictured Nyx, fiery in the battle atop the Dalalæða, just coming into her power. "And trust me, Nyx is not one to be trifled with. Even your Dresh'ri fear her. They call her the *Vyk dyre Rha*."

Both Rami and Aalia gasped at the name. Even Loryn retreated a step and pressed a thumb to his lips in a warding against evil.

Rami found his voice first. "Why . . . Why do you say that?"

Bewildered, Kanthe stared across the shocked group. He realized Rami had never heard the rest of the story, what had befallen Frell within the Abyssal Codex. Kanthe set about telling them, leaving out no details, describing everything from the Venin to the winged image shadowing a wall.

Loryn shook his head as Kanthe finished his tale, his voice aghast, dwelling on the least of this story. "The Abyssal Codex . . . it was torched. That was the smoke we saw rising from the Imri-Ka's gardens."

Aalia waved this off. She focused on Kanthe, stepping closer, her eyes shining with interest now. "The pages stolen by your mentor. He still has them?"

Kanthe nodded. "It's why I sought you both out. Most of it is written in ancient Klashean."

Aalia shared a look with her brother. "And you want us to help decipher it? That's why you came here?"

Kanthe hadn't mentioned this, but she had extracted his intent, nonetheless.

Aalia stepped forward, brushing past Kanthe. "Show us."

FRELL HOVERED BEHIND the two Klasheans, his patience wearing thin.

For an entire bell, the pair had crossed back and forth between wall and table, examining all three pages ripped from the ancient tome.

Aalia carried Pratik's reading lens. She peered through it often to better discern the writing. She stopped frequently to whisper with her brother, not that she needed to keep her voice low. The two shared their thoughts with each other in ancient Klashean, keeping cryptic what they were able to discern.

All Frell could do—along with Pratik and Kanthe—was wait them out.

"This is taking forever," Kanthe mumbled.

Frell knew a good portion of the young prince's impatience stemmed from hunger. He kept rubbing his stomach and looking at the door. Pratik concentrated on Rami and Aalia, cocking an ear, trying to eavesdrop, but his fluency in ancient Klashean remained poor. Whenever Frell cast the Chaaen an inquiring look, Pratik would merely shrug.

*So we're at a standstill for now.*

The impasse was finally broken by a knock on the door. Kanthe opened it enough to allow a crewman to pass over a platter of soft cheeses and hard bread, along with a flagon of sweet wine. The server tried to poke his head inside, plainly curious, but Frell closed the door in his face.

"Finally," Kanthe grumbled, and rested the fare on the lower bunk.

Each took a turn gathering a small repast, except for Aalia. She had returned to studying the image of a shattered moon. When she finally faced them, her eyes looked pensive, resigned, as if accepting the truth of moonfall. Earlier, she had engaged Frell in a discussion about the frequency of quakes and wilder tides. She had even tied the latter to the increasing severity of storms that had been plaguing the coasts. Frell had not considered this and was left rubbing his chin.

Clearly, Pratik was correct about the sharp intelligence of the Illuminated Rose.

Aalia crossed back to the table and swept an arm to encompass all of the pages. "Some of this is written in a challenging dialect of ancient Klashean. But it's decipherable enough."

"What does it say?" Frell asked.

Rami stepped forward, but before he could open his mouth, his sister silenced him with a raised hand.

She studied Frell with narrowed eyes. "I will tell you—but not before exacting a promise from you all, a sworn oath."

Frell could guess her intent and stated it. "We will free you and your brother once we have sought out the buried Sleeper. We truly mean you no harm."

"That's well and good, but that's not what I desire."

"Then what?"

She gazed around the group. "I'll leave it unspoken for now. But fear not, it's something easily attainable and will not thwart your efforts."

Pratik frowned. "You want us to swear an oath to perform a future act of unknown consequences?"

She arched a brow. "Do you wish to know what is hidden in these pages?"

Frell took a deep breath before answering. "If we have *your* word that such a boon will truly not damage our cause . . ."

Aalia bowed her head. "It is so given."

Frell checked with Pratik, even Kanthe. The Chaaen nodded solemnly. Kanthe merely shrugged.

Satisfied, Frell pressed a palm over his heart. "It is so sworn."

His companions followed suit.

Aalia stared a moment longer, as if judging their sincerity, then turned to the pages. She motioned Rami to her side, but not to engage him. She merely relieved him of his cup of sweet wine.

She took a sip and waved them over to the page atop the table. "This does describe a great war. One that started during the Forsaken Ages. Before the time of kingdoms and empires. Even before the Crown was fully forged."

Frell stepped closer, remembering what he had learned in the glowing vault beneath the Northern Henge. "According to Shiya, after the world stopped turning on its axis, the Urth's lands remained in chaos for countless millennia."

Aalia nodded. "The pages tell of such a turmoil. People scrabbling to survive. The lands quaking and beset by storms that stripped forests and broke mountains."

"But this war?" Pratik frowned down at the page. "If there were no kingdoms of men, who fought it?"

"I did not say they were *men*," Aalia clarified. "In these pages, they're called *ta'wyn*."

She pointed to a set of illuminated images. They showed tiny battalions of shining knights. Some fought in great forces, crashing against one another. Others focused on smaller skirmishes, even on individuals brawling against one another.

"If not men, who are these *ta'wyn*?" Frell asked.

"I don't know," Aalia admitted.

Rami interceded. "In ancient Klashean, *ta'wyn* means *undying gods*."

Pratik frowned. "Maybe the pages are referring to the Elder gods? The divinities before all others?"

No one had an answer.

Kanthe finally raised a question that had been plaguing Frell. "But what does this clash of gods have to do with moonfall or with the Shadow Queen?"

Aalia rubbed at her chin. "It's unclear. The war ended, but it's prophesied to start again. With the birth of the *Vyk dyre Rha*. Either the *ta'wyn* will hinder or help her. If we had more pages, or the entire book . . ."

She finished with a shrug.

Frell pictured that ancient tome burning in the pyre, along with one of the Dresh'ri. He inwardly cringed at the knowledge lost in those flames.

Kanthe scoffed next to him. "Then these pages don't help us at all."

Frell couldn't disagree. Still, he shifted over and tapped a finger on a stylized picture of a stiff-limbed knight. The figure held an arm high, gripping a jagged bolt of lightning in one hand. The image filled an entire corner of a page, as if threatening all the other combatants in the war.

"This *ta'wyn*," Frell said. "He looks like a leader of some sort."

Aalia joined him. "Yes, but it never describes which faction he commands. Only his name." She pointed to a word in faded ink under the image. "Eligor."

"Which means *Morning Star*," Rami shared.

Aalia frowned at him. "Brother, we spoke at length about this. You can't truly say that with certainty—not when it's merely *written* in ink. If spoken aloud with a stress on the first syllable, you are most correct in that definition. But if you stress the *second* syllable, the meaning changes."

"Into what?" Kanthe asked.

She looked pointedly back at him with a flash of fire in her eyes. "It means *Betrayer*. Something you're well familiar with."

Kanthe lifted both palms. "Again, I'm sorry . . ."

As a dispute ramped up, Frell turned away. He concentrated on the image of Eligor, gilded in gold. He picked up Pratik's lens to examine the figure's features in finer detail. He squinted at the artistry, at the brushwork.

The warrior on the page wore no helm. His hair formed a golden corona around his head. His square chin and hard cheeks were bearded in amber curls. His eyes, tiny dots of blue paint, seemed to stare out of the page, out of the ancient past.

Under the lens, the god's expression was stern, unforgiving. His face was painted in darker shades of gold and shone with a severe majesty.

Frell whispered to him, "Who are you truly?"

# 38

WRYTH STOOD WITHIN the heart of the Iflelen's great instrument and studied the mystery before him, an ancient enigma, untold millennia in age.

The bronze bust glowed with cascades of rippling energy. The golden twine of its hair wafted gently in that breeze, as did the curls of its beard, especially around its lips, as if it were whispering in its sleep. Though its eyes remained closed, he knew the violet-blue glow humming behind those lids.

"What are you?" he whispered for the thousandth time.

The mystery remained silent.

But nothing else in the chamber was quiet.

Around him, the instrument's convoluted web of pipes and tanks burbled and steamed, hummed and pinged. The noise, normally a comfort, stoked his impatience. He started to pace within the tight confines of the cramped space.

As he did, the rhythmical bellows of the bloodbaernes—four once again—matched his steps. He glanced over to the latest addition, a young girl whose tiny heart fluttered like a panicked sparrow within her opened chest, adding her life to their efforts.

A nearby mumbling drew Wryth's attention around. His fellow Iflelen—Shrive Keres—scribbled on a crisp parchment next to the crystal sphere of the listening device.

Exasperated, Wryth snapped at him, "What's taking so long?"

Keres ran a palm over his flaking scalp. "I'm working as swiftly as I can."

A bell ago, Keres had dispatched a messenger to wake Wryth from a troubled slumber. It seemed the signal from the bronze artifact out on the Ice Shield had subtly shifted, while also flaring brighter for a spell.

Days ago, Wryth had instructed Keres to alert him if there were any changes.

*So, I can hardly complain about being woken.*

Though, by the time Wryth got here, circumstances had changed yet again.

As Keres worked, Wryth squinted at the crystal sphere. The yellow glow from the stolen artifact had subsided again to a weak glimmer. Luckily, it continued to remain relatively stationary out on the Shield. Unfortunately, the same was true of the red blip that marked Skerren's pursuit fleet. It had closed the distance considerably, but then it had slowed to a stop, too.

*What is happening out there?*

It was that quandary that Keres was struggling to answer. Just as Wryth had arrived at the sanctum, the red glow had begun to blink out a code, a message from Skerren. It went on for some time. Once it had finished, Keres had set about deciphering it.

Wryth feared there might be some debilitating mishap with the fleet, or perhaps Skerren had decided to forsake the hunt. Wryth could almost understand such a decision. Skerren had flown blind into the unknown. While Wryth had the crystal listening device—powered by the glowing cube and fueled by the chamber's machine—Skerren only had a fist-sized sphere of lodestones, each sliver attuned to the bronze artifact's emanations. Regrettably, it could only pick up those discharges once Skerren was close enough to its source.

Under seventy leagues.

Until then, the fleet had no way of tracking the others.

Back when Skerren had first detected the signal, he and Wryth had tracked the enemy's progress across the Ice Shield, while waiting for the Hálendiian pursuit fleet to be prepared. During that stretch of time, the signal had stuck to the same trajectory, a vector that Skerren now followed. They had no choice but to trust that the enemy would remain on that same course, sticking to the same river of winds.

It was a gamble, but if successful, the reward was worth the risk.

The plan was for Skerren to close the distance until his smaller tool could pick up the enemy's signal, then sweep down upon them. The fleet's considerable arsenal should dispatch the enemy with little trouble. Still, Wryth intended to take no chances. He had dispatched another weapon with those ships, one he had personally devised.

"I have the message," Keres said, drawing back his attention.

Wryth faced the other. "Tell me."

Keres pointed to the red glow on the listening device. "Skerren has reached the mountains of the Dragoncryst. That's why his fleet has slowed. A fierce storm roils there. He had intended to wait it out."

Frustrated, Wryth curled his hands into fists, wanting to throttle Skerren for such caution.

*Especially when you're so close to the enemy.*

Keres noted Wryth's aggravation and lifted a brow. "But then Skerren got a *reading* on his sphere. Just the barest flicker of those tiny lodestones."

"What?" Wryth stiffened. "When?"

"About the time I noted the earlier flare. That's why Skerren dispatched his message." Keres grinned in excitement. "He lost the signal after it faded, but he and the fleet are invigorated and excited. They're readying their ships to brace the storm."

"So, they intend to head onward?"

Keres pointed to the crystal sphere. "They're already on their way."

Wryth stared for a long breath. The red glow of the fleet looked like it hadn't moved, but he trusted Keres's sharper eyes, especially as the man had been monitoring the device from the start.

Wryth leaned closer, his heart pounding, no longer tired. He intended to wait out that coming battle right here.

*After so long . . .*

But it seemed the night of interruptions wasn't over.

A loud bang drew his attention to the chamber's door. Phenic, the gangly-limbed acolyte, burst into the chamber, searched around, and spotted them.

"Shrive Wryth!" he called out, breathless. "I must speak to you!"

Wryth frowned and waved Phenic to join them. "Calm yourself and come over."

Phenic looked aghast at violating the inner sanctum, a sacred place reserved for only a handful of the Iflelen. But he knew better than to disobey Wryth's command. The acolyte squirmed and twisted his way to join them. By the time he reached the heart of the great machine, his face ran with nervous sweat.

"What has you so excited?" Wryth asked.

"Word from the Southern Klashe," Phenic gasped out. "Spies report that the emperor has dispatched two warships, captained by a pair of his sons. They're heading north, aiming for the kingdom."

Wryth scowled. "The imperium is just posturing. After the bombing of Ekau Watch, the emperor must respond in some manner or lose face."

Still, Wryth knew the reason behind the emperor's volatile act. He cursed Prince Mikaen for the hundredth time. Before the prince's warship had left Azantiia, King Toranth had ordered his son to only harangue the outpost, to set fires and leave. Such an attack was meant to voice the king's fury at the empire—not only for sheltering Kanthe, but also for the betrothal to the emperor's daughter.

A message had to be sent to the empire.

*Only Toranth had dispatched the wrong herald.*

Mikaen had taken it upon himself to drop the massive Hadyss Cauldron atop the small outpost, killing everyone below and setting fire to a large swath of Tithyn Woods, which continued to burn. He claimed his ship had been attacked, requiring a violent response. Toranth could hardly scold his son upon his return, especially with the reception Mikaen received by the king's legions, who celebrated his victory.

Of course, now Emperor Makar had to retaliate in kind, sending warships north. Wryth could only hope Makar's sons were more reasonable and even-tempered.

Phenic shifted on his feet, clearly not done with his report.

"Out with it," Wryth ordered.

"Prince Mikaen intends to meet them," Phenic blurted out. "To attempt an ambush within the smoke-choked stretch of the Breath."

"No! The king would never allow it."

Phenic cringed at his outburst. "The entire legion is rallying for action. Stoked by the faction of the Vyrllian knights who support the prince."

"His Silvergard."

Phenic nodded. "A royal warship and others are being readied as we speak. They intend to take flight with the next bell."

Wryth groaned and turned to Keres. "Keep monitoring Skerren. Dispatch a skrycrow if there's any further message."

Keres frowned. "Dispatch a crow *where*? Where are you headed?"

"To that warship. Someone must go with Mikaen and try to keep him from another rash act, one that could set fire to all of the Crown."

Wryth headed away, dragging Phenic with him.

Keres called after him, "Will the prince listen to you?"

Wryth didn't answer for a simple reason.

*I don't know.*

Still, another question plagued him as he left the chamber and rushed upward through the buried levels of the Shrivenkeep. Emperor Makar was a notoriously cautious ruler, one who pondered decisions over lengthy spans of time, seeking counsel from among his thirty-three Chaaens, along with countless soothsayers and bone-readers.

Makar was not one to act recklessly.

So why had the emperor moved so suddenly? Even after the savage bombing, Wryth had expected Makar to be slower in response, to consider and weigh all options before acting.

It made no sense.

*What has changed over there?*

# 39

PRINCE JUBAYR BOWED before the fury of his father. The eldest son of
Emperor Makar ka Haeshan stood in the center of the judgement chamber
atop the Bless'd Tower of Hyka, the ten-eyed god of justice. He kept his gaze
lowered, his sandals square in the middle of the executioner's circle of black
onyx. Blood dripped from the scimitar in his hands.

On the far side of the chamber, his father glowered from his tall seat, its
back rising in sweeps of golden wings. It was a quarter-sized replica of the
imperial Klashean throne, which rose three stories in the main hall's vault.
Behind the chair, situated across three tiers, stood the emperor's thirty-three
Chaaen. Their silver runs of chains cascaded like a bright torrent from those
rows to gather around the foot of the small throne.

Behind Jubayr, more tiers held silent witnesses, both members of the imperial court and those who had an interest in the outcome of certain cases.

The entire room waited for the headless bodies of two guards to be dragged
away. The pair had manned the entrance to the Abyssal Codex and failed to
protect it.

Zeng ri Perrin stood to the left of the throne. His arms were folded into the
sleeves of his white robe, its golden embroidery glowing in the torchlight. Jubayr
was surprised the Dresh'ri hadn't also lost his head to atone for the destruction
of the imperial librarie. His survival was a testament to the man's worth to the
emperor, both as a counselor and as an intermediary to the mystic worlds.

But not all would be so spared.

The door opened behind Jubayr. The next penitent would not beg for his
life like the two guardsmen had. For that Jubayr was grateful. Weighted down
by heavy shackles, the Fist of the Paladins entered the chamber. Tykl pa Ree
oversaw the palace battalion who protected the royal residence. He had failed
and knew the exacting punishment for it.

Jubayr swallowed as the tall man, dressed in light armor, marched into the
room. Even shackled, he carried his helm under one arm. His gray hair and
beard had been freshly oiled, likely by his wife and two daughters. Without
needing to be dragged, Tykl stepped atop the penitent circle of white marble,
though presently it was awash in fresh blood.

Tykl knelt, setting his helm aside. "I accept the judgement of Hyka and the
emperor who embodies His justice."

Makar nodded, sighing away some of his anger. Tykl had served the imperial household for longer than his father had been emperor. None had come to harm under his watchful attention.

Until two days ago.

The emperor stood. "You've served us well, Tykl pa Ree, for that your family will be spared the sword."

Tykl bowed his head in thanks.

"But punishment must be enacted according to Hykan Code."

"I would expect nothing less, Your Illustriousness." Tykl lifted his head, baring his throat. "It has been my honor to serve you as Fist of the Empire."

Makar motioned to his son, clearly wanting to make this quick for all of them. Regret shone in his father's eyes. But even an emperor must adhere to the strict code of justice written four millennia ago. In this regard, his father was as chain-bound as any of them.

Knowing he must show no hesitation, Jubayr turned. He kept his feet within the black circle, where he was protected by Hyka for the life he was about to take. He lifted his sword two-handed. He met Tykl's eyes, something he hadn't done with any of the fourteen men and two women he had slain this long day. Jubayr gritted his teeth. He had known Tykl all his life, often running through the halls when he was a boy, wearing the Fist's oversize helm.

Even now the man sought to help Jubayr.

Tykl gave him a small nod of his chin, acknowledging that he understood and forgave this act.

Jubayr raised his scimitar high, took a deep breath, and swept the blade with all the force of his shoulder and back. He cleaved through throat and spine, angling his wrist at the last moment to send the Fist's head rolling to the foot of the throne. It was not his first execution. He had become adept, serving this role for a decade, since he was nineteen.

Still, this was the most painful cut.

He sagged afterward, almost fell from the black circle. He leaned on the tip of his sword, trying to keep his shoulders from shaking. He cursed those who had taken Rami and Aalia—not just for the abduction of his siblings, but also for the needless death of an honorable man.

He made a solemn oath with Tykl's blood splashed across his face.

*I will make you pay.*

His father stood with a jangle of thirty-three chains. He lifted a palm and spoke solemnly, ending the long proceedings. "It is done. Hyka is slaked and served."

Freed by those words, Jubayr stumbled out of the circle. People filed out of the galleries without a whisper. He passed the ceremonial sword to an armory guard, glad to be rid of the bloody blade. Jubayr intended to head directly to the baths, to seek the hottest water, the coarsest salt, and scrub this day from his body.

But it was not over.

His father held a palm toward him, silently asking him to stay. With no choice, Jubayr stood as each of his father's Chaaen came forward and undid their silver chains from his throne and departed. Three remained afterward, stepping alongside the emperor. They were Makar's most revered councillors.

Jubayr sensed there was something else of import, something that had been kept from him until now.

His father came alongside him. "You did well, my son. I know that was difficult, especially the last."

Jubayr didn't deny it.

"Accompany us to the strategy room. There is a matter you must be informed about."

Makar headed out of the chamber and aimed for the bridge that spanned over to the Blood'd Tower of Kragyn, the god of war. It was the second-highest spire of the citadel, second only to the royal residence. The Blood'd Tower housed the empire's map rooms, war libraries, and all manner of chambers dedicated to tactics, strategies, and weaponry. It also held a battery of nests at the top, where bridle-singers trained and dispatched hundreds of skrycrows each day.

Jubayr followed his father. Makar was resplendent in a traditional *imri* cap and splay-sleeved robe that reached his knees. From the emperor's shoulders, a heavy cape hung. Its gold-and-silver embroidery formed the Haeshan family crest of a mountain hawk in flight, where its eyes were thumb-sized diamonds and its claws were solid gold. He also wore a circlet of dark iron, sculpted from a star fallen from the heavens, adorned with a ring of bright blue sapphires.

Jubayr's habiliment was also finely wrought, only now splashed and soaked in crimson. The blood weighed down his clothes as he walked. He carried each death with him.

Like his emperor, Jubayr had oiled his shoulder-length black hair, which was ironed flat and fixed behind his head by gold pins in the shape of the Haeshan Hawk. He shared his father's complexion and strong lines of jaw and cheek. The only distinguishing feature between the two were Jubayr's violet eyes, courtesy of his mother, dead these past twelve years.

Despite those eyes, many considered Jubayr to be the exact image of the younger Makar, but Jubayr wondered how much was due to shared blood and how much was because he had been groomed for the throne, forged into his father's likeness by duty and responsibility.

Still, he doubted if he could ever accept that mantle. He stared down at the caked blood on his hands, knowing he was better suited to be an executioner than a future emperor.

A HALF-BELL LATER, their party reached the Blood'd Tower and climbed to the topmost chamber, just under the skrycrow nest. Jubayr listened to the cries and squawks of thousands of birds. He caught the whiff of their pungent spoor through the open window slits.

He hid a cringe. The reek always set his teeth on edge, a reminder of the chaos that roiled beyond the rhythm and routine of the Eternal City. He preferred order and the established roles found here, adhering to an adage as old as Kysalimri.

*Each to his own place, each to his own honor.*

But of late, chaos had descended upon the city and palace.

There was no escaping it.

Knowing that, Jubayr followed his father into the strategy room. He discovered the Wing of the imperial fleet and the Shield of the empire's ground forces waiting for them. Each man dropped to a knee and saluted Makar with fists to foreheads.

The emperor waved them up and motioned their group to a massive iron-wood table inscribed with a map of the Southern Klashe. The chamber itself was circular. Hundreds of other maps hung from the walls, forming the entire circlet of the Crown.

The party settled around the table, including Makar's three Chaaen. When it came to strategy, no man was above another. All counsel was valued and welcome. Though, the final decision was ultimately made by the emperor. His father hung his heavy cloak across the back of the tallest chair, lightening his load to accept the burden to come, and sat down.

Makar waved for Jubayr to take the seat next to him. "My son, I'm sorry you must come here while still stained from your prior duty. But matters are changing swiftly."

"I'm yours to command, Father."

Makar patted his hand, then motioned to the wide table. Spread across its surface were thousands of small gold ships and tiny silver squares of horsemen and warriors. They were positioned where each of the imperial force was garrisoned or moored.

The emperor nodded to a tall, stern figure. "Wing Draer, what is the latest message from the north?"

Jubayr squinted as Draer stood and picked up a long wooden stick. The Wing used it to point to a collection of warships and other flotillas that had shifted to the northern border two nights ago, guarding over the ruins of Ekau Watch and patrolling the coastline. Draer shifted two of the largest warships out to sea, stopping halfway to the arc of stylized curls that represented the Breath of the Urth.

"The *Hawk's Talon* and the *Falcon's Wing* should enter the Breath shortly after dawn and reach the southern coast of Hálendii by the first bell of Eventoll."

Jubayr stiffened and glanced at his father. "We're moving against the kingdom? Already? We've barely ascertained what truly transpired two nights ago."

"We've determined enough." Fire returned to his father's eyes. A fist formed on the table. "That bastard Prince Kanthe fooled us all. We believed his claims of being exiled by false accusations. A deception supported by our Eye of the Hidden, who had verified the prince's assertions, convincing us of their veracity."

Jubayr tightened his jaw. He had executed the spymaster earlier in the morning for that exact failure.

Makar continued, "We now know Kanthe must have been working in tandem with his twin brother, Prince Mikaen, who led the attack on Ekau Watch. The bombing was not—as we first surmised—an explosive warning to return the traitor prince to Azantiia, but an elaborate ruse. A distraction for Kanthe to make his move upon us." Makar glared around the table. "Those two dogs made fools of us. Grabbed my youngest son and my only daughter."

Jubayr heard the catch in his father's throat at the mention of Aalia. He found his own hands forming fists.

Makar's voice grew louder. "We've scoured the northern lands and coastlines and failed to spot them. No doubt they've secured the swiftest ship and are already on their way to Azantiia. For any hope of securing their release, our response must be rapid and forceful." He slammed a fist on the table. "Before any lasting harm is committed against Rami and Aalia."

Jubayr stared down at the two ships. "The *Hawk's Talon* and the *Falcon's Wing* are captained by Paktan and Mareesh."

They were Jubayr's two younger brothers. All three of them were only a year apart in age.

Makar nodded. "It was King Toranth's two sons who fooled us. It will be my two sons who will exact our punishment."

Jubayr found this fitting, except for one detail. "I should be there, too, Father."

After the death of their mother, Jubayr had practically raised Rami. He had also doted upon and cherished his youngest sister as much as his father did. Their loss cut him deeply. He could barely dwell on it without despairing. He had to shy from his own heart, or the grief threatened to immobilize him.

Makar shook his head. "Mareesh and Paktan have trained all their lives to be my sword in the clouds. You're needed here, my son."

Jubayr frowned, but he had to acknowledge that his two younger brothers had indeed become valiant wingmen. It was their role in the empire, how they served their father.

Jubayr leaned back, accepting this course.

*What else can we do?*

Unfortunately, his father did have another recourse. "We've been duped and blinded throughout all of this. It is time to further open our eyes. So, to better grasp and understand what's to come, I will leave with the first dawn bell for Qazen, to consult with the Augury."

Jubayr choked down a gasp, beginning to understand why he had been summoned while still soaked in blood.

"For too long," Makar continued, "I've neglected the Augury's counsel and see what that inattention has wrought us."

Jubayr turned to his father, voicing what needed to be spoken, knowing no other would challenge him. "You're leaving now?" He waved to the map. "While we assault Hálendii?"

"It must be done without delay."

A meek voice rose from one of his Chaaen. "Your Majesty, might it not be best to bring the Augury to Kysalimri, rather than traveling to him?"

"No. The Augury must inhale of the fumes of Malgard to properly invoke his visions. Now is not the time for half measures. Not with the drums of war sounding louder with every passing day."

Jubayr knew there was no dissuading the emperor from this course. Makar leaned heavily on the wisdom and visions of the Augury, even during times of peace. With war on the horizon, his father would crawl on his hands and knees to gain that counsel.

Thankfully, his father would seek a speedier method of passage.

"I'll leave in an arrowsprite. Such a ship will have me there and back in two days, three at most." He stood and swept up his cloak from his chair and held it toward Jubayr. "Until then, my son, you will take up my mantle."

Jubayr sat stunned for a breath, then obeyed his father. He stood, pushing back his chair with a loud scrape. His father came around and secured the cloak about his shoulders, though Makar kept the imperial circlet atop his head.

Makar waved to those gathered around the table. "Lean on them, my son, but trust your own heart. I've raised you well. This is a burden you can easily carry until I return."

With the heavy cloak weighting his shoulders, he was not sure that was true. He found it harder to breathe. Still, he reached up and secured the cloak's clasp around his neck.

"I will not fail you, Father."

Final details were discussed around the table. Most fell on Jubayr's deaf ears as he struggled with his new position. Once matters were settled, his father whisked away, striding purposefully, determined to seek the Augury's counsel.

Jubayr stared at those who would serve that role for him. A long stretch of silence settled over the room, as if all were suddenly unsure of their status.

Shield Angelon finally stood, bowing his head, asking permission to speak. The leader of the empire's ground forces, in his fifth decade, was a fourth cousin. His dark features were split by a white scar across his forehead.

Jubayr lifted a hand, having to shake loose a flap of the cloak to do so. "What is it?"

"Draer has already related at length about our readiness to act against the forces beyond the borders. But I think we must now address the threats *within* our own walls. There were two attacks by the *Shayn'ra* this past night. The Fist of God burned a pair of supply wagons headed to a southwest garrison, and another group ambushed guardsmen outside a tavern, stripping them of their gear and carving the *Shayn'ra* symbol of an awakening eye into their chests."

Jubayr's jaw tightened. He had to force words out of his mouth. "And what do you recommend?"

"Emperor Makar has been reluctant to bring the full strength of the Shield upon those rebels, even after the attempted abduction of your sister."

Jubayr nodded, having taken part in those debates. "He fears rousing the baseborn to the *Shayn'ra* if we are too heavy-handed. Especially as the Fist have proven themselves to be mostly nuisances in the past. My father believes they've only grown bolder of late due to the attack on Ekau Watch, taking advantage of our distraction elsewhere."

"That may be true, but they've grown even more emboldened following the abduction of your siblings. Prior to this, the baseborn were already warming to them, swelling their numbers. The Fist achieved this by plying the lower castes with rewards. I wager the grain and meat stolen from those burned supply wagons were distributed at large, buying support by filling bellies."

"So, you would have us act now?"

"And firmly. Especially before they learn that the emperor has vacated the city. I have a proposition, a way to bait a trap. With the Fist of God already growing and spreading like a pestilence—and likely to expand during this crisis—it may be our last chance to rip them out by the roots and secure their leader, Tazar hy Maar, before the *Shayn'ra* grow too strong."

Jubayr searched the faces of the others. Most remained stoic, not willing to commit. But two of his father's Chaaen gave small nods of agreement.

As Jubayr struggled with this decision, he felt the heavy weight of his father's cloak. He knew it was a burden he must eventually shoulder. He stared down at his caked palms, the hands of an executioner.

It was a role he knew well, one from which he could draw strength and honor during this time of chaos. He pictured handing the head of Tazar hy Maar to his father upon his return.

He looked over to the Shield.

"Rally whom you must and make it so."

# 40

TAZAR HY MAAR crouched in the low croft above a saddlery. The sting-ing stench of urine-soaked hides drying in the shop's yard wafted into the cramped space, carried on the slight breeze through the open attic window. He stared from his high vantage across the open market square.

The moon hung at the horizon, heralding the start of a new day in another few bells. This early, the shadowy square lay quiet, with shops boarded shut and the surrounding streets mostly empty. A lone cart wended across the cobbles, drawn by a swaybacked mare, the drover half dozing in his seat. The horse hung its head low, equally dull to the world. The poor beast surely knew its path, having trod it countless times.

The pair were emblematic of the entire city.

*Locked forever to one path, blinkered to all around.*

Tazar intended to change that, to rip off those blinders and end the tyranny of empires. The goal fired his blood, fueled by all he had learned in his two decades in the city.

As a boy, he had studied at the *Bad'i Chaa,* not as a castrated acolyte, but as a baseborn servant at the House of Wisdom. His mother had taught him to read when he was barely a babe, which gave him the keys to the knowledge locked within those dire walls. He had stolen books, eavesdropped on classes as he mopped floors, and found a handful of mentors among the students who took pity on the scullery boy. Later, it required the trading of intimate pleasures to pay for the continuation of his secret schooling.

His education was unique in other ways, too. He had not been restrained by the rigors of that scholarly prison. He had the freedom to study what he wanted, without fear of breaking scholastic dictates or imperial indoctrina-tion. He had read of open societies, with less stringent mores, and desired it for himself, and later for everyone trapped in their baseborn castes, unable to ever rise above their stations.

Over time, his intelligence was noted. He was eventually gifted to the pal-ace to serve in the royal residence. Fury built inside him with each passing year. Cloaked in the anonymity of servants, he observed how the *imri* con-ducted themselves. He noted the bounty of their tables, while others starved. The richness of their garb, while others shivered through a winter's night. Even their laughter and music seemed only to deafen them to the sobbing and misery all around.

They were unendingly cruel, puffed with haughtiness, and firmly entrenched in their own superiority, a birthright of blood and incest.

He had also spied upon the worst of them.

The Illuminated Rose of the Imri-Ka.

Her glares made many a servant soil themselves. Her arrogance was boundless—and it was not entirely unwarranted. She was devious in all ways, her intelligence far surpassing that of her siblings. It was that cunning that exposed him when he was sixteen. He had mistakenly tried to befriend her, like he had those at the school. But she saw through his subterfuge, maybe smelled the rancor rising from his skin.

He had barely escaped into the sprawl of the city, where he eventually found a home among the *Shayn'ra,* who shared his ambitions and stoked it brighter. Only four years later, due to his ruthlessness and cleverness, he rose to lead them.

*And I will succeed where every generation failed before.*

He pictured Aalia's face, gilded and painted, shining with the conceit of all the *imri.* Only days ago, he had been so close to—

A shout rose from the dusty planks next to him. "There!"

He followed where Jamelsh, his third-in-command, pointed to the far side of the square.

Armored horses trotted into view, with riders decked the same. Next came a war wagon bristling with arrows and crossbows. The helms of the dozen guardsmen reflected the low sunlight between the buildings and shone brightly in the shadowy square.

Following them appeared their target: a small cart pulled by four yoked oxen. Though the wagon was tiny, the load aboard needed the strength of so many shoulders and legs due to its sheer weight. Gold was far heavier than grain and oat.

Another war wagon followed behind.

Still, it was a meager escort for a fortune in gold, enough to fund the *Shayn'ra* for a decade, with enough left over to feed hundreds for the same span of time.

Jamelsh lay on his belly and rolled to one side. "I was not wrong. It is as I heard. A shipment of gold. Headed to the port."

Tazar nodded. With war rising, the emperor was dispatching the gold to his sailing fleet in the harbor, where the bounty would be spread across the waves, intended to buy the loyalty of brigands and pirates, to use them as spies and saboteurs.

*But we will find a better use for it.*

Over the past day, the entire city was being roused. Garrisons were on the move. War machines hauled to key positions. Through a farscope, he had witnessed an arrowsprite blasting across the sky in a flume of fire and smoke. Both the Haeshan flag and the Klashean Arms had flown from its stern, confirming the rumors that the emperor was headed to Qazen, to consult his pet oracle. It was accompanied by a small fleet of the same vessels.

Everyone was on the move.

Such chaos served the *Shayn'ra* well.

*Like now.*

Someone must have thought this movement of gold would go unnoticed amidst the ongoing commotion, especially this early, when most of the city slept.

*But not all of us are in our beds.*

Tazar glanced to Jamelsh, who breathed hard, sweat dampening his forehead. His friend flashed a smile, excited for what was about to come. Maybe nervous, too. But they had prepared well.

Tazar slid a covered lantern closer to the window. He waited until the imperial force was in the square—then he slipped the cover from the flame three times, signaling his second-in-command, who was hidden in an attic on the opposite side.

A sharp whistle blew, alerting everyone.

From all the shops surrounding the square, the Fist of God struck at the same time. Arrows rained from on high in a deadly hailstorm. Crossbows spat in coordinated volleys, slicing like a scythe through the square. From every doorway, the *Shayn'ra* boiled forth, wielding curved blades and whipswords. Knives flew from fingertips in flashes of silver.

Horses and guardsmen fell.

Still, the war wagons responded, firing everywhere. Many of the *Shayn'ra* dropped, either writhing or dead. But Tazar had drawn almost the entire Fist to this ambush. Over two hundred men and women. They swarmed like ants over the square. The lives lost would be replaced with their weight in gold.

Still, he would not risk their lives and not his own.

Tazar grabbed a coiled length of rope, tossed it out the window, and leaped out. He slid down the line, landed deftly, and freed his own scimitar.

Jamelsh dropped next to him, wielding two hooked blades. When fighting, he was a blur of steel and skill.

Still, such talent might not be necessary. Already, the imperial forces—outnumbered and unprepared—had succumbed to the fierce and sudden attack.

Both war wagons were overrun, becoming slaughterhouses. A few guardsmen fled on horseback, rattling their armor, announcing their cowardice.

Tazar noted the gold cart's oxen all lay toppled in their traces. One still lived, struggling in its harness, bloody and bellowing. Tazar retrieved a crossbow from the dead hands of one of his warriors. The weapon was still cranked with a bolt in place. He lifted the bow one-armed, aimed, and shot the ox through its eye. It stiffened, neck craning back, then dropped to the cobbles.

Anticipating the cart's draft animals might not survive, Tazar had fresh animals secured in a side street. He turned to Jamelsh. "Go fetch the—"

The man's blade cut a swath across Tazar's eyes. He instinctively ducked back, but the tip sliced the bridge of his nose, striking bone hard enough to dance his vision. Still, he had not survived this long by being slow to react.

He swung the crossbow one-handed and smashed it into Jamelsh's shoulder, driving him back a step—far enough for Tazar to raise his scimitar to the man's chest. Jamelsh's expression was agonized, but not because of the sword-point digging into his skin.

"The Shield has my children," Jamelsh squeaked out. "They handed me the tongue of my youngest son. Either I agreed to help them, or they'd take apart my sons and daughters, piece by piece."

Tazar struggled to understand, but clarity came with a massive explosion behind him. The concussion threw him forward, sending his blade through Jamelsh's chest and striking the stone wall behind him.

Jamelsh slumped, dragging the sword with him. His mouth opened and closed, maybe asking for forgiveness, but only spilling blood. Screams erupted behind Tazar. He spun around, yanking free his blade.

The gold cart had shattered in a fiery blast, casting flaming green oil across the square. Where it landed, it burned through cloth, skin, even bone. He recognized the black alchymy.

*Naphlaneum.*

Figures ran blindly in all directions, their flesh melting before his eyes.

Tazar backed away, knowing there was nothing he could do. There was never any gold here, only flaming death. The shelter of an overhang above the saddlery door had saved his life.

He searched the square. Others had managed to escape by sheer chance. They gathered in confused groups. He spotted Althea, his second-in-command, on the far side of the square. Her hair smoked, but she hollered for everyone to gather to her, to make their escape.

But the battle was not over.

A swyftship swept into view. Then another. Their stern doors lay open. From their holds and decks, shapes bailed out into the air. A half century in number. Wings snapped wide across their backs. Guardsmen kited down through the smoke and screams.

Tazar knew their only hope was to flee, then regather their remaining forces later. He lifted a bone whistle from a cord around his neck, brought it to his lips, and blew a sharp retreat. His piercing signal drew Althea's eyes. She nodded to him and waved at those who had been rallying alongside her to escape into the maze of streets.

Tazar fled in the opposite direction.


AS THE SECOND morning bell echoed through the city, Tazar hurried across a dark alley. It stank of excrement and old piss—and not just from the rats that scurried from his path. Gratefully, he could not smell all that well, with snot running from both nostrils.

He held a rag against the bridge of his nose, trying to stem the flow of blood from Jamelsh's blow. Still, he tasted it on his lips, the iron bitter, a reminder of the betrayal.

He had used the same cloth to wipe away the swath of white paint that had striped his eyes from temple to temple. He had also stolen a *byor-ga* headgear and robe to further hide his features. As he crossed Kysalimri, hunters scoured the streets, some in armor, others moving more stealthily. Even disguised, he had to kill three men to reach this alley.

He rushed to an unmarked door and knocked a pattern.

A knothole opened in the scarred wood and an eye peered through. He pulled aside his draped coif, revealing his face, then heard the scraping of a bar being lifted. The door swung wide enough for him to rush inside. A portly matron in a stained apron with disheveled gray hair scowled at him and led him down a pitch-black hall toward a glimmer of firelight.

Furtive voices reached him until one shushed them all quiet.

He entered and found a dozen figures crowded in a small room. Several warmed their hands around a small hearth, ruddy with coals. All were bruised, bloody, and sour in outlook. One had a horribly burned face, half hidden under a bandage. The tallest of the group broke free and strode swiftly to him.

"Althea . . ." he gasped out.

His second-in-command hugged him. "Thank all the gods," she whispered in his ear before stepping back. She held him at arm's length, squinting at the ruin of his nose. "You'll need a healer."

"That can wait. Even this shelter might not be secure for long."

She frowned. "Why?"

He told her about Jamelsh's attack, about how he had lured them into the ambush with that false promise of gold. Tazar finished with a worry, looking around the room. "We don't know if Jamelsh told the imperium about our series of safe houses."

"We have dozens," Althea said. "It's lucky that we both ended up in *this* one."

He offered her a small smile that pained his nose. "Not so much luck. It was simply the closest."

"True, but if you're right about Jamelsh spilling our secrets, this would be the *first* place the guardsmen would look. As they haven't crashed in here yet, we may be safe."

He clapped Althea on the shoulder, appreciating her practical cleverness.

But she wasn't done, adding with a shrug, "Unless they're waiting for more of us to gather before attacking."

He groaned. Sometimes she was clever to a fault.

A frantic knocking silenced them. It echoed from the door to the alley. The rapped code was the correct one.

*But what if Jamelsh had shared that, too?*

He heard the door open, followed by muffled voices. Hurried footsteps led down the hall. Tazar drew his scimitar, heeding Althea's warning, but it sounded like a lone visitor.

An older boy, too young for even a fuzz of beard, burst into the room. He was flushed and sweating. He hurriedly circled his left eye with a thumb and forefinger in the covert salute of the *Shayn'ra*. He searched the faces in the room.

"Tazar hy Maar?" he asked.

Tazar leaned toward Althea. "Do you know him?" he whispered.

She shook her head.

The burned man hobbled up. "That's Bashaar's son. From the fifth quarter's contingent of the Fist."

The boy bobbed his head, confirming this, while pointing to his own chest. "Illias," he said, offering his name.

Satisfied, Tazar stepped closer. "What do you want, Illias? Why have you come rushing in here?"

The boy held forth a capped tube that dangled a few cords. It was a skry-crow's harness. "I was told to give this to Tazar hy Maar."

"Instructed by whom?" Althea asked.

Illias swallowed. "I don't know. An outlander. He paid me a silver ha'eyrie to deliver it. He claims to be a friend of the Fist. He recovered a skrycrow message, one sent to the Razen Rose. Says Tazar needs to read it."

Suspicious, he held out a palm. "I'm Tazar."

The boy looked dubiously at him.

The burned man growled at Illias, "He's not lying."

Illias refused to step any closer, maybe because Tazar was still holding his scimitar. Still, the boy reached out and tossed the harness into Tazar's palm.

Althea held off Tazar from reading it. "Illias, how did you know to come here? To this shelter?"

The boy shrugged. "The outlander told me that Tazar would be here."

Althea glanced at Tazar with a pinched brow, then returned her attention to the boy. "Illias, what did this man look like?"

"Like most outlanders. Pale skin. But older with an ale-reddened nose." He brushed back a fall of curls from his brow. "His hair was the color of dry straw."

Althea turned to Tazar. "Do you know anyone like that?"

He slowly shook his head. "Still, let's see what this *friend* of the Fist wants to share with us."

Tazar uncapped the tube and shook out a curl of black oilskin. The message had already been read, as the wax seal was sliced open. When he held it back together, it did indeed show the five-petaled bud of the Razen Rose.

He unrolled it, pinching the scroll between his fingers. He read the neat lines of script. As he did, his body grew chilled, his breath catching in his throat.

"What does it say?" Althea asked.

"It . . . It's a note, dated yesterday, sent from those who kidnapped the emperor's son and daughter. It says they'll be crossing the Scarp and heading to Malgard."

"That makes no sense," Althea said. "All rumors say the kidnappers were headed north, rushing for Hálendii."

"But what if they're wrong?"

Althea shook her head. "It must be a ruse, some trick to lure us into another ambush."

Tazar was not so sure. "I saw the emperor's arrowsprite flaming off in that same direction."

"Right, to consult his Augury. The entire city knows that by now."

"But what if that's just an excuse? What if he's headed to meet those kidnappers to retrieve his son and daughter?"

Tazar pictured Aalia, her lips hard with disdain, her eyes flashing with indignant fire. He had failed to secure her days ago, whereas another had been successful. He remembered the Hálendiian prince thwarting the Fist's ambush. He had believed the bastard was defending Aalia, but now it was clear.

The prince was merely protecting his own plot to abduct her later.

A masterful stroke, one deserving of respect.

Still, his fist closed hard on his scimitar's hilt. If Prince Kanthe was truly that clever, was it possible he had *not* gone north as everyone expected—but headed *south* instead?

Tazar knew the answer.

*Of course he would.*

Althea touched his shoulder. "Tazar?"

"Gather all of our forces, those who are still hale enough for fast travel."

"Why?"

"We're heading to Qazen."

"But—"

He lifted his hand, brooking no argument, growing more certain with each beat of his heart. The emperor was there, with only a scant escort. He rubbed his bearded chin, considering his options. Kysalimri had become too dangerous for the Fist. Those that remained would be unable to accomplish anything here.

But if they left for Qazen . . .

*No one would expect the Fist so far from the Eternal City.*

He again pictured the Illuminated Rose of the Imri-Ka. Aalia would be worth more than all the gold they'd lost today.

But his ambitions grew far grander.

Tazar gripped Althea's arm, trying to share his passion. "We can't ignore this opportunity—to exact revenge for those killed this day, to strike a blow against the very heart of the imperium."

Still, he kept silent about one last prospect.

*The chance to destroy that upstart Hálendiian prince.*

# NINE

# DREAMERS OF
# THE DEEP

*We mark oure dedd with inke of the squid*
*—To let the Deep know oure loss*
*—To share a histourie that is end'd*
*We giveth oure bodys to the sea*
*—To nourishe the Deep with blode & bone*
*—To rise agayn in fin & shell*
*We free oure spirits into the salt'd depths*
*—To reach the Dremers, who weighe a lif*
*—To judge if another will be grant'd.*

—A Panthean dirge

# 41

THREE DAYS FOLLOWING the raash'ke attack, Nyx maintained her vigil on the beach. She stared up into the glowing fog as eventide brightened to morning. The fungi, lichens, and mosses bloomed in crimsons, yellows, and emerald greens that matched the sea. She came down to the edge of the village many times each day, pulled by her heart.

"Where are you?" she whispered to the steaming mists.

She prayed for Bashaliia to break the bridling hold that had dragged him from her side. She feared the malevolent horde-mind was already bending and warping him to its will, drawing him fully into their colony until he was lost forever.

Each day, that dread grew.

*I must find a way to reach him.*

In contrast to her mood, a bright humming drew her eye to where Henna dug in the sand, forming sinuous walls and small homes made of cupped sand and roofed in shells. The girl had recovered from the horrors of that night. Fortunately, she had no memory of being whisked aloft by that bat.

*Just as well . . .*

Behind Henna, Vikas stood guard over them with her longsword strapped across her back. After the attack, Graylin was taking no chances with Nyx. Henna had tried to engage the mountainous woman in her sandy construction efforts but was rebuffed with raised palms and some dismissive gesturing.

Nyx had to act as mediator, recognizing Henna's confusion and the quarter-master's frustration.

Vikas had been born mute—due to Gynish blood in her lineage, which accounted for her sheer size. The craggy giants of the northern steppes—the Gyns—had lost the ability to speak in the distant past, possibly due to the per-petual howl of winds across their cold lands, which deafened all. Due to this loss, many considered them dim-witted or dull-minded, but Nyx knew from her studies that couldn't be further from the truth. Their culture was rich, com-plex, and deeply spiritual. Their language of gestures and expressions was as expressive as any other.

Over the half year in the quartermaster's company, Nyx had learned some rudimentary Gynish. Nyx had tried to let Henna know that Vikas could not speak, but it was difficult to communicate as Nyx didn't know Panthean. Still, after much pantomiming among them all, Henna seemed to understand, but it failed to engender any sympathy. The girl's demands to engage Vikas now involved more arm tugging than pleading.

Vikas eventually relented, dropping to a knee and trying to make improvements in Henna's village. Unfortunately, the quartermaster's suggestions were all very practical. Henna preferred a more whimsical approach to construction. The two could never come to any compromise, and Vikas returned to standing sullenly over the pursuit.

Sadly, Henna's village was not the only one struggling to find its footing.

Nyx glanced far to her left.

Iskar was slowly returning to life following the assault. The plaza had been scrubbed, its sands combed anew. Flooded wreckage had been hauled from the streets. Broken boats salvaged or repaired. Even the stone pier had been restacked.

But there was no joy in such accomplishments.

Over thirty bodies lined the water's edge, wrapped in a preserving kelp, waiting for a burial at sea that was to commence midday. Tradition dictated a respectful mourning period. Over the past three days, friends and family had knelt beside those bodies before wrapping them, slowly using squid ink and oil to tattoo their loved one's lives onto the canvas of their cold skin.

Nyx had tried watching, but the act felt too intimate. She had no place being there. Grief and guilt drove her off to the fringes of the town, where she had spent the past days. The others worked farther down the beach, where the *Sparrowhawk* had been beached, trying to determine what to do. She heard their raised voices, arguing, resisting the inevitable.

She had no interest in such struggles, especially as they seemed hopeless. She didn't need anything more to be disheartened about.

She swept her gaze across the skies one last time. Though there had been no sign of Bashaliia, at least the raash'ke hadn't attacked again.

A small sandy hand slipped into hers. Henna stared up at her, leaning against Nyx's hip. "I miss him," she whispered. "I didn't even get a chance to ride him."

She squeezed her hand. "I'm sure Bashaliia would've loved that."

"I know."

Nyx smiled sadly. "We should get ready to head back home. It looks like your brother is done fishing."

A fair distance off the beach, Daal rode out of the waves, seated atop Neffa. As he surfaced next to a small raft, he expelled a blast of air. The orkso did the same, shooting spray from both nostrils. Daal carried a spear high with a silvery fat eel impaled on it. He leaped from Neffa's back and landed deftly on the rocking raft. Once balanced, he shook his latest catch onto the pile already stacked on the deck—then whistled sharply.

Neffa circled behind the raft. Careful not to stab Daal with her horn, she bumped her wide nose into the raft and sped it toward shore, propelled by beats of her tail and sweeps of her wings.

Nyx retreated—and with good measure.

The orkso propelled the raft and beached it high onto the sand. It slid to Nyx's toes. Behind it, Neffa bounced on her winged forelegs in the surf, waving her horn. Nyx felt a surge of affection at the simple joy of the happy creature. It wafted off of Neffa, buoying Nyx's spirits.

Still, it also stirred a bittersweet ache. Neffa reminded her of another great beast. Memory blurred as Nyx stood on the sand. She smelled the belches of old silage, the mold of a thick coat. She heard the grunt of contentment, the huff of irritation.

*Gramblebuck . . .*

She had abandoned her friend, a centuries-old bullock, back in the swamps of Mýr, at the start of this journey. She pictured him turning his shaggy back and vanishing into the bog. She did not know what happened to him. Still, she sent a silent plea to that large heart.

*Please. I've lost too much. You must still be alive.*

"*Henna, greef da nef!*" Daal called from the raft, drawing Nyx back to the present.

Henna ran and scooped a net from the sand, then bounded onto the raft, ready to gather up the morning's catch.

Daal got out of his sister's way, joining Nyx on the beach.

Nyx backed a step, hesitant to touch him after that awful night. Still, she caught the scent of salt off his skin. The sea coursed in shining rivulets down his heaving chest. He was breathless from his exertion. He smiled at her, his blue eyes flashing brightly, then glanced over at his bounty, clearly proud.

"The fishing. Good this morning," he declared.

As he stood on the sand, he shivered in the breeze, raising gooseflesh along his arms. She had to look away, especially as she caught the slight glow emanating from him, as if the fire inside were trying to warm him.

"I wish I could say I had your luck this morning," Nyx mumbled.

Daal winced and looked up at the mists. "What the Mouth swallows, it does not let go."

He stated it like it was an old adage, one taught to him in Noorish. And maybe it was. His people had lived in the Crèche for untold millennia. Over that span, countless numbers had been dragged away by the raash'ke.

And more again three nights ago.

After losing Bashaliia, Nyx had asked *where* the horde might have taken him. The answer had been cryptic: the Mouth of the World. According to the Pantheans, it was where the raash'ke made their home, their roost in these eternally frozen lands.

Nyx edged closer to Daal. "Can you tell me more about this Mouth?"

He shrugged, his expression both regretful and pained. "Nothing to say. No one been there and returned. Only see from far distance. Where the great ice ends, the Mouth of the World begins. A great fiery crack that stretches past the sky."

Nyx crossed her arms, trying to imagine such a landscape.

She pictured her own homeland and the volcanic mountain, The Fist, which rose from the Mýr swamps. It was home to Bashaliia's brethren. The Mouth sounded much the same, only where the Fist climbed high, this chasm delved deep.

Daal must have sensed her consternation. "No way to reach it," he insisted. "Need your great ship. Into the air and across the ice. Trek on foot impossible. The ice full of cracks and crusts that break under you. And the cold. Freeze the marrow in your bones. But worst. The raash'ke hunt that ice."

Nyx glanced over to where the *Sparrowhawk* listed crookedly on the beach. Its prow dug deep into the sands, its stern washed by waves. The ship was going nowhere, certainly not anytime soon.

Henna yelled from the raft, trying to heft up the laden net, *"Wree wan!"*

Daal smiled and crossed over and gathered up the heavy net.

Vikas stepped forward and gestured animatedly.

Nyx translated for Daal. "Vikas says she'll carry the load back for us."

Daal nodded and tossed the net over to the woman. He pressed two fingers to his chin and swiped his hand down in thanks. He had already learned a few snatches of Gynish.

Vikas slung the net over a shoulder, then gestured: "Might as well do something. My talents are wasted here."

Nyx thought the quartermaster was referring to the lack of threat, one that might have required her wielding her longsword. Instead, Vikas glared over at Henna, clearly still perturbed that her earlier suggestions about the sand village had been dismissed.

Oblivious, Henna simply danced away.

Daal waded into the water and retrieved a small saddle from Neffa's back, then waved Nyx toward the village. "Hurry now. Must get fish into ice."

* * *

NYX KEPT HER head down as they crossed through the sandy plaza on the way to Daal's home. It was the shortest path. She would've happily taken a longer route, but there was a bounty of fish to clean and stack into an ice bin.

Her reluctance wasn't entirely due to the memories of that bloody night. Instead, it was the row of covered bodies lining the shore. Several were already being carried to a fleet of skiffs, preparing for the burial at sea. A few were still being inked on the beach, their cold pale skin shining sickly, striped by the messages being written by those who loved them.

She also noted the narrowed eyes glancing her way, heard the soft murmuring. More than a few voices were sharpened by anger.

Vikas kept near her side.

Daal got them moving faster, perhaps sensing the animosity, a sentiment that had been steadily growing. It would not be long before that bitterness and grief turned to violence. The only reason it hadn't already was likely the continuing support of the Reef Farer. That, and the cautious fear of Shiya, who had risen out of the sea like a god and scattered the raash'ke.

*But how much longer would that trepidation hold?*

The Reef Farer had suggested some of their party should accompany the burial fleet out to the island town of Kefta, then on to a section of the sea where the Crèche delivered their dead into the waters. Berent thought such an act—joining the ceremony, sharing their grief—might help Nyx's group bond to the community.

It sounded reasonable.

Still, Nyx stared at the bodies being lowered into the skiffs. She was wracked by guilt and doubt, but certain about one thing.

*It will not be me who goes with them.*

Such a journey would be too painful.

Daal noted the direction of her gaze. He pressed three fingers to his forehead in an act of sorrow. "They go soon to the *Oshkapeers* . . . the Dreamers of the undersea."

Henna touched her brow in the same manner.

Daal's words troubled Nyx. Her feet slowed. Vikas bumped into her, then stepped back. Nyx stared over at Daal. He had spoken something about those Dreamers before, when they had first met. Something tied to Bashaliia.

Daal frowned back at her when he discovered her lagging behind. "Nyx . . . ?"

She squinted, sensing something important. "Daal, you had mentioned those Dreamers before. You said something about how you sensed Bashaliia *dreamed deep,* like them. What did you mean?"

Daal swallowed twice. He looked away. He rubbed at a wrist, raising a red scar. She noted a pale version on his other wrist. His hand rose and absently touched his neck, drawing her attention to another mark there.

"What is it, Daal?" she pressed him.

"It mean nothing," he mumbled.

She took his arm, trying to get his attention. Only her touch sent waves of fire through her. She ripped her fingers away. She backed a step, her chest heaving, as if her body were still trying to inhale that heat from him.

*No . . .*

Still, with that brief contact, she flashed to a deep-seated fear in Daal. She felt herself being dragged into the cold, dark depths of the sea. She caught a glimpse of Neffa's tail, then even briefer, a golden glow shining far below. But the overwhelming sense of it all was pure terror.

She stumbled farther back, trying to escape it. Vikas caught her, kept her on her feet. Nyx shied away from the woman's touch, too. It took her a few breaths to finally collect herself and stare back at Daal, whose eyes were huge.

"Daal, I'm sorry. I know something horrifies you, but I must know. What does dreaming and the Dreamers have to do with Bashaliia?"

He looked down at his toes. Henna hung on his arm, sensing his distress and sticking close. "Bashaliia glows," he mumbled. "I see it, but it goes deep into him."

"Bridle-song?"

*"Nyan."* He shook his head, struggling for the right words. "It is his past. Memory. Down deep there was once *more.* He misses, needs, dreams of it."

Nyx slowly understood. She had sensed it herself at times. Bashaliia had been cut off from his brethren. Out on the Ice Shield, he had traveled beyond their reach, beyond their communal bonding. Yet, he still craved and pined for that larger connection.

*And I took it from him.*

Still, something was missing in Daal's explanation. "But what does Bashaliia's dreaming have to do with *Oshkapeers*?" she asked, struggling with the Panthean word. "Those Dreamers in the sea? What do they dream of?"

Daal glanced across the plaza. They had reached its edge and had stopped. Most of the mourners no longer paid them any heed.

He turned back, his face a mask of pain and fear. "Like Bashaliia. *Oshkapeers.* Dream of past. Memory old. Theirs and ours. All. Our dead feed them. With our flesh." He picked a pinch of his skin to demonstrate. "And with our dreams."

Nyx gaped at him. "How . . . how do you know that?"

"We know. Stories old. But I know more." He stressed the last, his eyes strained with horror. "The *Oshkapeers* know too much. About the Crèche. About raash'ke."

With his words, Nyx felt a flare of hope. She reached for him again, then drew her arm back. "The Dreamers know more about the raash'ke? Like what?"

He shook his head. "It fuddled. Confusing. Not dream enough with them. They touch me." He again fingered those strange marks. "Then throw me away. Not worthy. But I tell no one. Not mother. Not father. Not even Henna."

She frowned. Clearly, he had had some horrifying encounter with those Dreamers, whatever they were. It had left him scarred both inside and out. "Why didn't you tell anyone?"

His voice dropped to a breathless whisper. "Forbidden to go to *Oshkapeers*. Only the dead go. If I tell, village will kill me." He swallowed hard, looking down at Henna. "Maybe all of us."

Nyx struggled to put this together. There was more to this story, but maybe it was best told in private. Still, if Daal was correct, these Dreamers must be imbued with some form of bridle-song. And more importantly, they had greater knowledge concerning the raash'ke.

*If I could reach them with my song, maybe boosted by Shiya, could I learn enough to help Bashaliia?*

Nyx glanced out to the skiffs rocking on the sea, carrying the dead. She turned to Daal. "I must speak with the Reef Farer."

"Why?"

"To convince him to let me go with the mourners, to travel with the dead to the town of Kefta and beyond."

Daal understood her intent. "No. I warn you before. On the beach we first met. No go. Not ever." He gripped the edge of her sleeve, careful not to touch her skin. "It is death."

She pictured Bashaliia, enveloped by his warm wings, the snuffle of his velvet nose. Ages ago, she had abandoned Gramblebuck in the swamps, a friend who deserved more. She would not do that again.

If there was even the slimmest chance of saving Bashaliia, then so be it.

*I'll face death.*

# 42

GRAYLIN STOOD IN the dark hold of the *Sparrowhawk*. The beached ship listed on its starboard side. The cavernous space had been emptied of its storehouse of crates and barrels. Even the hay that lined Kalder's and Bashaliia's former pens had been swept clean. He stood before a lake of seawater that filled the stern half of the hold.

Kalder paced the water's edge. The vargr looked as concerned as Graylin felt.

Not only did they need to repair the hole blasted out of the hull's side, but the ship's keel had shattered when the *Sparrowhawk* crashed into the sea.

A sharp curse burned his ears, echoing his own sour sentiment. He turned to see Darant climb out of a hatch in the decking, rising from the bilge, which was equally swamped down below.

The pirate clambered to the planks and shook himself like a drowned dog. He wore only leggings, but they were soaked. His dark hair was plastered to his scalp. Despite his dousing, his arms were stained with black oil to his elbows, along with swaths across his chest.

"Were you successful in freeing the stern forge from its moorings?" Graylin asked.

Darant scowled and waved to the hatch. "Only because Shiya never has to breathe, lucky her. She was able to crawl underwater, unlock the bolts—with her bare fingers, I tell you." He swiped his brows, plainly impressed and maybe envious. "She dragged the forge clear of the water, where I was able to inspect it for damage."

"And?"

"A broken fuel line, a couple bent rods. I have enough spare bits to fix her up." He glowered at Graylin. "But why waste the sweat?"

Graylin understood his consternation. "How much flashburn do you have left in the extra tanks?"

"Maybe enough to keep Brayl's sailraft aloft for a day or so. Certainly not enough to get the *Hawk* into the air. That's if we even had enough fabric to patch our shredded balloon."

A shout echoed through the empty hold, coming from the top of the spiral stairs that led to the wheelhouse. "Come see this!" Jace called down to them. "Up on the middeck!"

The timbre of his voice rang with excitement and something Graylin had not felt in ages: *hope.*

"What is it?" Darant hollered.

"You have to see it!" Jace vanished away.

Darant shared an exasperated look with Graylin and waved toward the stairs. "If that bastard wants to show us some new bird or sarding fish, I'm gonna stew his bollocks in the last of our flashburn."

Graylin understood. Jace and Krysh had spent the past days exploring the wonders of the Crèche, debating a thousand subjects. Their enthusiastic jabbering wore thin, especially considering the dire straits—and the gloom surrounding all the deaths. The pirate had lost four men during the attack.

Still, something had fired up the young man.

Graylin motioned for Kalder to stay below. The vargr crossed to his freshly swept pen and set about sniffing it, then lifted a leg to reclaim his spot.

Graylin and Darant clambered up into the wheelhouse and out the forecastle door to the open middeck. They had to sidestep past the shredded remains of the giant gasbag. Its fabric had been gathered and folded to the portside and weighted down by thick coils of draft-iron cables. One baffled section of the balloon remained intact, hanging overhead, still swollen by its lifting gasses.

Darant glanced up at it with a sad shake of his head. He didn't need to raise yet another difficulty. Even if they could repair the rest of the balloon, there was no distillery that could refill it with fresh gas.

"Over here!" Jace called to them.

He knelt with Fenn and Krysh, who crowded close. Rhaif shadowed over them, leaning on a crutch, favoring his wounded leg. Even Meryk stood with them, a palm over his mouth.

Rhaif spotted them and waved them closer. "You truly need to see this."

Graylin frowned.

*What is going on?*

He and Darant crossed the planks and joined them. Fenn shifted aside to reveal what had drawn everyone's attention.

Krysh crouched over a pumpkin-sized swell of a tiny balloon, made of sewn bits of fabric. Framing its open mouth, woven threads ran down to a tiny tin cup that danced with flames below it.

Jace spoke rapidly. "I remembered reading the histories of flight in an old book back at the Cloistery. It spoke of such early efforts." He waved to Krysh, who held those tiny threads. "Show them."

The alchymist released his fingers, and the small balloon and its flaming package miraculously rose off the planks. It floated past their shoulders and continued upward.

Graylin backed a step, watching it sail ever higher into the air.

"What alchymy is this?" Darant blurted out.

"Nothing but hot air," Jace explained, clearly enthused. "Hotter than what surrounds it."

Still on a knee, Krysh looked up at them. "It functions like a wyndship's lifting gasses. Maybe we could employ such a method instead. Especially once we clear this warm rift and reenter the frigid dark. The colder the surroundings, the stronger such flame-heated air will lift."

Graylin already identified many problems with such an endeavor.

Darant did, too, and proceeded to list them. "First, we'd need *far* more fabric than we have. We lost swaths of it during that battle."

Krysh acknowledged that and made it more challenging. "If my calculations are correct, the balloon would have to be considerably *larger* than its prior size."

"Unless we lightened the *Hawk*," Jace countered. "Got rid of the cannons, the excess cargo, stripped the ship lean."

But Darant wasn't finished with his objections. "And how do you propose we fuel that warming flame? I assume it will have to burn continuously to keep all that air heated. And right now, we don't have enough flashburn to fire up one forge, let alone warm a massive gasbag." He pointed at the flicker of flames high above. "Knowing that, I should burn your arses for wasting flashburn just now."

"We didn't use flashburn," Jace explained. He craned his neck toward Meryk. "What did you call it?"

*"Whelyn flitch,"* the Panthean said.

Krysh turned to Darant. "It's the waxy fat from some great beast of the sea. You see it filling all their firepots throughout Iskar. The village had great reserves stored in ice caves."

Jace nodded. "We performed some tests. It burns *hotter* than flashburn. And in its semisolid form, it's lighter than the same amount of flashburn, but its flame lasts four times as long."

Despite his own pessimism, a flare of hope warmed through Graylin. He challenged Darant, "Could you—maybe with Jace and Krysh's help—find a way to use this *flitch* to fuel the ship's forges?"

Darant rubbed his scrub of beard. "Maybe," he drawled out. "If that sarding fat could be refined in some way, liquefied even. Or if I tweaked the forges themselves."

Hope brightened in Graylin's chest, only to be quashed by Darant.

"But do I have to remind you of the obvious?" the pirate warned. "We *still* don't have nearly enough wood or fabric to make proper repairs. Even if I scavenged material from both sailrafts, we'd need far more."

THE CRADLE OF ICE

Graylin looked to Jace and Krysh to solve this dilemma, too. But the pair of scholars just glanced to each other, then down to the planked deck.

Another voice spoke up.

"I know where you can find all of that," Meryk said.

A BELL LATER, Graylin crouched in the stern of a flat-bottomed skiff.

Ahead of him, Meryk stood braced at the bow, wielding a set of woven reins that ran out to a pair of orksos who were harnessed and tethered to the boat. The beasts humped through the waves as Meryk guided them along the shoreline.

"Where is he taking us?" Jace whispered, voicing Graylin's nagging question.

The young man sat with Krysh and Darant.

Meryk had refused to tell them where they were headed, only assuring them it was important. Graylin craned back, noting the flames of Iskar in the distance, nearly lost in the mists. They must be over two leagues from the village by now. Worry nagged him. He hated leaving Nyx, but she had Vikas with her. Plus, before departing, he had sent Fenn with Kalder to join her at Meryk's home.

Still, Graylin's patience had worn to a razor's edge. He shifted higher and called to Meryk, "How much farther must we go?"

Meryk glanced back over a shoulder and pointed past the bow. "We are here."

Graylin leaned over the boat's side. The stretch of shoreline ahead looked no different from the leagues they had passed. Then he spotted a tiny canal that cut through the sand and aimed for the ice cliffs. He only noted the waterway because of tiny flickers of flames near the base of the cliffs. He squinted enough to make out the source.

Two tall firepots flanked the canal, as if maintaining an eternal vigil.

Meryk guided the skiff over to the canal and turned into its mouth. It was deep enough to accommodate the orksos and wide enough that two skiffs could have traversed it side by side. Graylin stared into the water, wondering if it had to be dredged regularly to keep it open.

*But why?*

Meryk leaned down to ignite a small pot of *flitch* that rested in a stanchion at the prow. Flames sputtered, then blew brighter.

Jace tilted to get a better view. "There's a cave in the ice ahead."

Graylin had noted it, too, but thought it was a rift in the ice, as if the waterway were a stream melted out of the cliff. As they neared it, the flames of Meryk's firepot revealed that it was indeed the entrance to a colossal cave.

"This is a holy spot for my wife's people," Meryk said. "It might anger many if they know that I brought you here. But you deserve to know the truth about our shared history."

The orksos hauled them past a pair of giant sandstone urns and under the entrance's arch of ice. Beyond it, the flames from the skiff's prow illuminated a yawning space. Firelight reflected off its ice walls, illuminating the treasure within.

Jace gasped.

Darant swore.

A small lake filled the cavern. Beached within it was a huge ship. Its hull dwarfed the *Sparrowhawk*. Its draft-iron prow rose even higher, sculpted into the likeness of a fierce wyrm, whose outspread wings flanked the hull.

"It's the *Fyredragon*," Jace exclaimed, not looking away. "Rega sy Noor's old ship."

GRAYLIN PACED ALONGSIDE Darant as they circled around a cold beach that edged the lake. He carried a small lantern and held it high.

The *Fyredragon* rested crookedly in the water. The apparent majesty of the ship upon first sight had waned. The curve of its hull had caved in on one side. Hoarfrost caked everything, including the stacks of centuries-old fabric atop the deck and the massive curls of draft-iron cables.

"What do you think?" Graylin asked Darant. "Can you scavenge enough from the *Fyredragon* to repair the *Sparrowhawk*?"

"I'll get my crew to scour over her. But after sitting in that dank water for so long and frozen on top, there's no telling how much rot and ice has damaged those planks."

"Still, there's hope, right? Meryk told me that the Noorish have been preserving the vessel as best they could over the two centuries. Oiling its hulls, polishing its steel and draft-iron, chipping off the worst of the ice. All to honor this shrine to their ancestors."

Darant nodded, sizing up the ship. "It's indeed a mountain of wood and acres of fabric. Gotta be enough in there somewhere to mend the *Hawk*'s flanks and get her wings to fluttering again."

"You should see this!" Jace called over.

Around a curve of the beach, he and Krysh searched through a swath of sand strewn with detritus. Crates and barrels lay scattered everywhere, looking as if they had been washed ashore from a shipwreck—which was partially true.

Graylin and Darant crossed toward the clutter.

Once close enough, the pirate swore. "Look at that."

Darant rushed to the side, to where a waist-high forge engine sat in the sand. It must've been dragged from the ship. Darant began examining it, digging through it, likely looking for what could be salvaged from it.

Jace waved Graylin over to Krysh. The alchymist had pried the lid off a barrel. Graylin caught the whiff of a familiar spicy scent as he approached. The barrel was full of a dark emerald gelatinous liquid.

"Is that old *whelyn flitch*?" he asked. He searched back toward the cavern entrance, where Meryk had remained with his skiff and orksos.

"It's old," Krysh admitted, swirling a finger into it, proving it was still thick but not firmly solid. "But I don't think it was *decay* that softened or darkened it. I believe it's been refined into its current state, likely centuries ago."

"By Rega sy Noor?" Graylin asked.

"Or someone in his crew," Jace said. "Remember, Rega's trip was one of exploration. He traveled with a dozen alchymists. There's a table near the far wall, piled with books on chymistry, though they've been molded into slabs by the cavern's dampness. Fortunately, the titles are still legible."

Krysh nodded. "They must have been trying to do exactly what we talked about earlier, experimenting with a new fuel for its forges."

"Were they successful?"

Jace shrugged. "There are scores of barrels on this beach, all smelling of *flitch*."

"And there's possibly more stacked atop the *Fyredragon*'s deck." Krysh pointed to the ship, to rows of barrels sitting there.

Darant had heard their discussion and came over. He scowled at the open barrel and dipped his whole hand in, then lifted it out. He let the viscous *flitch* ooze between his fingers.

"That forge over yonder has been tweaked," Darant informed them. "The fuel lines are fatter, likely to allow this thicker sludge to flow through. And they added a bigger damper in the flame barrel. I reckon to keep the hotter burn of this *flitch* from blowing the whole thing up."

"Do you think they got it to work?" Graylin asked.

"Only one way to find out."

Darant reached again into the barrel, this time with both hands. He scooped up a good amount of *flitch* and carried it over to the forge, losing most of it along the way. Still, he dumped the rest into a fuel feed and waited for it to seep into the forge's heart.

He then took Graylin's lantern.

"Best stay back," the pirate warned. "This lump of cold metal is four times as old as any of us."

They all retreated, but Darant waved them even farther back.

Once satisfied, he opened the lantern and used a sliver of old wood to carry its flame to a fuel tap. He opened the valve enough to let a single drop of green flitch show, then lit it with the taper. As it caught the flame, Darant snugged the valve and dashed backward.

He didn't get far.

The heavy forge bumped hard with an ear-pounding boom, nearly lifting off the sand.

Darant tripped onto his backside.

Ahead of him, flames belched from the forge's baffles—then in another breath, it ignited, roaring like the namesake of Noor's ship. It was so fierce that the engine skidded across the sand, driven by the dragon's fire. It hit the lake, plowed through the shallows, and vanished underwater before coming to a stop.

Beneath the surface, the fires continued to burn.

They all gathered closer. Graylin helped lift Darant, whose face was cracked with a savage smile. They all stared into the water as the flames glowed brightly, boiling the shallows.

"That'll do," Darant said.

For far longer than Graylin would have imagined, the forge continued to burn, fueled by mere dregs of that gelatinous *flitch*.

By now, Meryk had raced along the beach to join them. He arrived breathless and panicked, likely fearing what had befallen them. He gaped at the boiling waters, at the fire down below.

Krysh looked over at the other barrels along the beach. "Rega was successful. But if so, then *why* did he and his crew remain in the Crèche? Surely, with enough time, they could've patched the *Fyredragon*."

Jace tried to answer. "Maybe they didn't think about using hot air to fill their ship's balloon."

Krysh cast him a dubious look.

It was Meryk who offered the more likely answer. "The Noor feared the raash'ke."

Graylin nodded, sympathetic to Rega's dilemma. All the flaming forges and hot air wouldn't help the *Fyredragon* escape the bridling song of that black horde. Or their ripping claws. No matter the number of repairs or the ingenious alchymy, Rega and his crew were trapped in the Crèche.

*Just like us.*

# 43

AT MIDDAY, NYX stood at the end of the stone pier. She watched the last of the flotilla of skiffs head out to sea. Mournful bells rang a slow dirge from those boats. Voices rang in sad accompaniment. She didn't understand the words, but the sentiment was somber, yet tinged with hopefulness.

Standing beside her, Daal must have noted her attention. "A prayer," he whispered. "To the Dreamers."

Nyx looked to him. "What are they asking for?"

"For their cherished to be preserved," he mumbled. "To live forever in the dreams of the *Oshkapeers*."

Daal stared across the waves, his features pale, his eyes lost. She didn't need to touch him, to share that intimacy, to know he was recalling his own experience with the Dreamers. She had tried to pry the story from him, but before she could press the matter, Graylin had rushed in with the others, with word of their discovery of the *Fyredragon* and a rekindled hope that the *Sparrowhawk* could be repaired.

She could hardly get her own voice heard over their excited chatter. When she did finally manage, Graylin had balked at her going on this voyage. But by then, it was too late. She had already informed the Reef Farer of her intention; to refuse at the last moment would risk insulting an ally who remained their strongest advocate. Graylin finally conceded, knowing they would need Iskar's cooperation if they hoped to get the *Sparrowhawk* flying again.

Not that he would allow Nyx to go by herself.

Vikas kept behind her on the pier, her ever-present shadow. Shiya stood alongside her. The bronze woman's strength would be needed if Nyx hoped to use bridle-song to reach those Dreamers deep in the sea.

Still, Graylin wasn't satisfied with just Shiya and Vikas as guardians. The knight was already aboard the Reef Farer's barge, speaking to the Crèche leader and his lissome consort. The pair—Berent and Ularia—had shed out of their festival finery and wore plain white robes, the color of mourning. The only embellishment was the Reef Farer's stone circlet of gemstones and Ularia's diadem that held a single bright emerald.

Meryk stood with Graylin, aiding in communication, though both the Reef Farer and his consort understood a smattering of Noorish.

Everyone else in their group had remained behind in Iskar, to start work on the swyftship. Floraan had promised to rally her fellow Noor in the Crèche—those that weren't joining the flotilla—to aid in the labor. Henna had pleaded to go with her brother, but her mother was not about to let her daughter travel so far from her side.

Graylin nodded to the Reef Farer, then strode across the barge toward Nyx. Once at the rail, he extended a hand toward her. "The Reef Farer is heading out. We should get settled."

Before taking his hand and boarding, Nyx turned to Daal. "I'll see you in Kefta."

Daal nodded, his lips a hard line of worry. He turned and crossed to the other side of the pier, to where his family's skiff was moored. Neffa and another orkso floated in their harnesses, waiting for the voyage to the island town.

Daal would be traveling separately—not only because he was considered unworthy of accompanying the Reef Farer, but because Nyx would need that skiff later. Her group intended to sneak off from Kefta and attempt to contact the *Oshkapeers*.

As Nyx took Graylin's hand and stepped into the barge, she searched the mists overhead, praying they would be successful. With Bashaliia gone, it felt as if a part of her was missing. She wondered if this was how Bashaliia felt, cut off from the melding with his brethren. Though for him, it must be a thousandfold more painful. He had given up so much to come with her.

And look what that sacrifice had wrought.

*I cannot let it stand.*

She joined Graylin on the deck, more determined than ever to discover what the Dreamers knew about the raash'ke.

Once Shiya and Vikas boarded, Graylin drew their group to the stern, collecting Meryk, too. Daal's father seemed to be trying to stare everywhere at once, both nervous and excited to be aboard the Reef Farer's barge.

The wide-bellied craft was sculpted of woven kelp that swept up into waist-high walls, bolstered by a long keel that appeared to be the rib bone of some great sea beast. In the center, a pair of shell-encrusted chairs sat atop a dais, thrones for the Reef Farer and his consort. Elsewhere, benches striped the deck, dotted with those who were closest to the leader.

It was an honor to be allowed to travel with such esteemed company, a respect that the Reef Farer hoped would rub off on Nyx's group, to help assuage the growing tension in the village. Nevertheless, they were relegated to the barge's stern—which was just as well.

Nyx still felt she shouldn't be here.

The rails of the barge were decorated with garlands of a sea plant, blooming with bright white blossoms. Stone bells adorned its length, ringing a mournful note as the barge left the dock, pulled by a shoal of six orksos.

Across the waves, the prayerful dirge continued to echo.

Nyx stared over to where Daal guided his skiff. He met her gaze, then turned away, plainly still unconvinced of this course.

He was not the only one.

Graylin sat heavily beside her. He let out a long breath and leaned over, keeping his voice low. "Is it wise to trespass where it is forbidden? Especially now."

She frowned at him. Everything had happened so quickly that none of them had a proper chance to discuss matters in detail. It had been a hard morning for all of them—and it was only the middle of what would surely be an even longer day.

"We have to risk trespassing," she answered. "Daal believes the *Oshkapeers* know more about the raash'ke. We must find out what that is. There's so much we don't know about them, about their history. Something in the past must have turned that horde more savage."

"Not necessarily," Graylin huffed. "I know the Mýr swamps. Bashaliia's brethren were as much a terror to those living there as the raash'ke are to the Crèche."

"This is different," she mumbled.

"How?"

She simply shook her head. She hadn't told anyone about the shadow she sensed hidden within the malevolence of the horde-mind—unsure if it was even real or born of her own panicky imagination.

Graylin touched her knee, his manner softening. "Nyx, I know you hope that you'll learn something to help Bashaliia, to free him from the enthrallment of the raash'ke. But he's been gone three days. It takes bridle-singers far less time to break wild horses or tame giant sandcrabs."

"Bashaliia is much stronger. He'll fight with all his heart."

"I know, but is he strong *enough*? It took only five of them to bring him down and—"

She pushed Graylin's hand off her knee, refusing to listen, but support came from another source.

"We are also not strong enough," Shiya warned Graylin, and nodded to Nyx. "Even together. We barely survived our first encounter with the raash'ke."

Graylin sighed. Clearly, this worry had not escaped him.

"If we should prove successful in getting the *Sparrowhawk* aloft," Shiya continued, "we will only be brought low again by that horde."

Still, Graylin remained stubborn. "But should our trespass among the

Dreamers be discovered, it will quash any good graces we have with the village. We will never get the *Hawk* repaired without Iskar's help and forbearance."

Vikas had been listening quietly and gestured her own opinion: "Then we must not get caught."

Nyx nodded. "Everyone will be busy at the tribute feast in Kefta following the burial. With care, we should be able to slip away long enough to engage the Dreamers."

Daal had suggested this plan, pushing past his own reluctance to offer it.

Shiya nodded. "We must try, or we will never be able to continue on with our quest."

Outnumbered three to one, Graylin simply sighed, accepting the inevitability of this course.

Nyx settled back, listening to the continuing dirge, the ring of the barge's bells. She caught sight of Ularia staring toward them. The woman's eyes matched the emerald in her diadem, both in color and hardness. Her gaze remained fixed on Nyx, until she finally turned away and whispered in the Reef Farer's ear.

Nyx felt a residual chill from those cold eyes. Ularia could not have overheard them, not with their voices low and the bells echoing around them. Still, Nyx was certain of one thing.

*We must be extra wary from here.*


GRAYLIN DROWSED AS the barge humped through the waves, rocking him gently from side to side. But he had been a knight for most of his life. Even in slumber, his ears were forever alert for the slip of steel from a sheath, the furtive footfall, the whisper of a threat.

So, he stirred and opened his eyes when the mourners' song of lament was finally answered by a heavy tolling of larger bells. He shifted enough to spot the glow of flames through the mists ahead.

"Kefta," Nyx said next to him.

As they watched, a shoreline slowly appeared out of the fog, lit by a hundred flickering firepots and lanterns. The island looked like a collapsed volcanic cone, a sickle of red rock and darker sand. Most of it was sheer cliffs, but one side lay open to the sea, creating a large bay in its caldera. The village hugged those waters and stacked up the inner walls in a series of carved tiers.

Much like Iskar, Kefta was made up of sandstone homes and walls, with roofs woven of dried weed. Similarly, a large square bordered the town's rocky piers. The sheltered bay was packed with boats. A few already headed out to meet the flotilla.

More would soon join them.

Kefta had sent many of their young men and women to the Krystnell festival in Iskar. Tragically, a few were returning wrapped in kelp. The flotilla would tarry in these waters only long enough to collect the town's mourners and give them time to say their goodbyes and to ink their loved ones.

Afterward, the boats would continue to the lair of the *Oshkapeers,* to sink their dead into the embrace of the Dreamers of the Deep. The site was another four leagues farther on, in seas challenged by boiling waters. Once done, all would return to spend the eventide in Kefta, where a tribute feast awaited them, where mourners could drown their misery in wine and ale.

Graylin glanced to Nyx.

*Only then will our true undertaking begin.*

Nyx's gaze remained fixed to the sea, but not toward the village. She stared toward a small skiff that plied the waters nearby. Daal stood balanced at the bow, with reins in hand. His gaze appeared to stretch beyond Kefta, toward those boiling seas and the Dreamers below.

Motion drew Graylin's eye. The Reef Farer and his consort rose from their seats, spoke a few words to those gathered around them, then headed toward the stern. Graylin rose to meet them, bowing respectfully to each.

Meryk joined them.

Berent held up a hand. "We anchor," he said haltingly. "Sail again *aree.*"

"I understand," Graylin said, appreciating the Reef Farer's attempt to speak their language. "Is there anything we can do?"

The Reef Farer motioned to his side. "Ularia. Curious. About . . ." Berent frowned and waved brusquely at Shiya. He leaned toward Meryk. *"Sree nix faryn?"*

Meryk nodded. "The Reef Farer wants to know if Shiya is a true woman."

Graylin knew such a conversation was long overdue. He had tried to keep Shiya away from the villagers. From a distance, she looked like a woman. Her molten bronze could be mistaken for darkly tanned skin. She moved with exceptional grace. Even the soft plait of her hair streamed and curled like those of any other woman. It was only her glassy eyes that gave her away, softly glowing with the energy inside her.

"She's a woman," he answered as truthfully as he could. "Just not one born of seed and flesh."

"How that be?" Berent asked after Meryk shared Graylin's answer.

Graylin took a breath. Honesty was usually the best course, but sometimes a lie served one better. "As you know, we Noorish have considerable talents with metal and sophisticated alchymy. Over the two centuries since the *Fyredragon* crashed here, my people have made great achievements."

Graylin motioned to Shiya.

For their own safety, it had been decided to maintain this conceit. Best to let the villagers believe their group had hidden talents, to engender a respectful fear of their abilities to stave off any violence.

Ularia showed none of that hesitation. She stepped around Berent and eyed Shiya up and down. "I assume she can speak for herself. Is that not so?"

Graylin blinked, surprised at the smooth fluency of this inquiry. Even Meryk's eyes widened. Apparently, Ularia had her own talents that she guarded.

"Of course," Graylin stammered out.

Ularia faced Shiya. "Where are you from? When were you crafted?"

Shiya could lie, but most often she did not. "I would prefer not to tell you," she answered honestly.

"Is that so?" Ularia's eyes narrowed.

"We do protect our knowledge," Graylin interjected. "Maybe with time and trust, that will change."

"Hmm . . ." She cast a discerning glance over their group. "Like the tides, trust must flow both ways."

Graylin kept his face stoic. She gave him a penetrating stare, as if she could peer down to his bones. When she finally turned away, he stifled a sigh of relief.

But she was not done. She glanced back, turning those eyes on Shiya. *"Nenta nell ta'wyn nee nich va?"*

Graylin looked to Meryk for a translation, but Daal's father gave a small shake of his head, his eyes pinched with confusion.

Ularia's gaze stayed on Shiya, whose features remained fixed and unreadable. Still, Graylin noted her bronze fingers curling ever so slightly before relaxing again.

Ularia sniffed, then finally turned away, drawing Berent with her.

Graylin waited until the pair were accosted by others and drawn into new conversations. Only then did he sit down.

Nyx leaned toward Meryk. "What did Ularia say at the end?"

The Panthean shook his head. "It is not in our tongue. It sounded like . . ." He struggled for the word, then found it. "Gibberish."

Graylin turned to Shiya. He didn't have to ask the question.

"I do not know either," she admitted. "But I recognize the tongue. If I hadn't lost so much of my knowledge—of myself—I might understand it fully."

Nyx reached to take her hand, clearly responding to the pain and frustration in Shiya's expression. "It will come," Nyx assured her. "Maybe when we reach the site out in the Frozen Wastes. The city of winged protectors."

Shiya frowned. *"Angels,"* she corrected, using the ancient word for that place.

"Once before, I told you that name was recorded in a language older than your histories, long before the Forsaken Ages."

Shiya shifted her gaze over to Ularia. "The words she spoke just now—though I don't comprehend their meaning—I know they were in that same language."

Graylin stiffened. "How could that be?"

Shiya shook her head.

Meryk offered a possible explanation. "Ularia is a *Nyssian*. One of the most revered of the three. It is why Berent is not married to her. Such a union is forbidden. He loves her, desires her, but he does not carry the proper seed to give her the daughter she needs."

"I don't understand," Nyx said. "What is a *Nyssian*?"

"There is no Noorish word for it," Meryk admitted, scrunching up his face. "Nys Ularia and her sisters are the keepers of our history, preserving our past, all the way back to the first melt that formed the Crèche. They keep it all in their heads, far more than we can record in any of our books."

Nyx looked shocked. "Do you mean they studied and memorized the entire history of the Crèche? All the way to its founding?"

Meryk shrugged. "Some say a *Nyssian* is born with this knowledge."

"That's impossible," Nyx mumbled.

Meryk shrugged again. "All I know is that long ago, there were many sisters. Now only three. The first—Nys Pephia—was said to have been touched by the Dreamers. It is believed they shared a sliver of their godhood to grant her this gift. She was the only one to ever commune with *Oshkapeers*. Not counting our dead, of course. It is why it is forbidden to dive in those waters."

Graylin glanced at Nyx. They had not shared their intention with Meryk to seek out those creatures. Daal had been adamant that his father not be involved, nor any of his family. It would pose too great a threat to them.

Across the barge, Ularia laughed, drawing Graylin's attention, less from the outburst than its inappropriateness. Her eyes found him. The smile faded from her lips, turning harder. He tried to fathom the mystery behind the cold woman. How could she know that ancient tongue? And why did she offer those words to Shiya just now?

*What is your game?*

Ularia turned away, brushing past Berent, drawing the Reef Farer in her wake like some bridled pet. In that moment, Graylin knew the Reef Farer was not the true power in the Crèche. It traipsed at his side. As Graylin tracked her, he felt a familiar tingle along his spine. He had hunted the wilds of the deep Rimewood for nearly two decades. The perils of that icy forest had sharpened his senses. He had learned to recognize when a predator was nearby.

Especially one on his trail.

Certainty grew inside him as he watched Ularia settle to her throne.

That woman . . .

*She's far more dangerous than any shark in these waters.*

# 44

FROM THE DECK of the barge, Nyx watched as the last of the wrapped bodies was lowered over a skiff's rail and dropped gently into the water. Weighted by stones, it sank quickly away. She tried to follow its passage, but the form quickly vanished.

She leaned farther out, searching dark depths below for any sign of the *Oshkapeers,* for any telltale glow of bridle-song or other energy.

*Nothing . . .*

Worried, she forced her fingers to relax their grip on the rail. She gazed out at the steam-fogged waters. The hiss and bubble of boiling seas whispered over the waves. The heat stippled her skin with droplets. The air smelled of sulfurous brimstan, which turned her stomach, adding to her trepidation.

Around her, the lamenting elegy of the mourners had faded to a few voices. It was accompanied by the soft sobbing from the inconsolable. Otherwise, all others had fallen into a somber silence. Even those on the raft clustered in quiet groups, hanging on one another.

During the burial, she had noted the baleful glances cast her way, both from the skiffs and the deck of the barge. It seemed—despite Reef Farer's best intentions—their presence among the bereaved, sharing their grief, was doing little to alleviate the smoldering resentment.

It confirmed Nyx's earlier assessment.

*We don't belong here.*

Still, she knew they would have to return again. She searched past the stern of the barge, toward the fiery glow in the mists that marked the distant town of Kefta. Daal had stayed behind and moored his skiff there, allowing Neffa and his other orkso to rest for a time.

A loud clang of a bell made her jump. She turned to where the Reef Farer stood at the prow before a large stone bell. He struck it again with a small hammer, then a third time. The sound reverberated in her chest. She rubbed her ribs to warm it away.

"It appears we're heading back," Graylin said, stepping closer to her.

He was proven right when their barge slowly swung around, pulled by the six orksos. The other skiffs followed suit, each turning like a needle in a compass.

As the flotilla headed back to Kefta, Graylin kept his gaze on the burial site. The hot mists had dampened his shirt to his chest, wetting his hair to his scalp.

"Did you sense any presence of the Dreamers?" he whispered.

"No, but I dared not probe with bridle-song. Not amidst all the grief."

She had also held off for another reason. Ularia kept looking their way with narrowed eyes, her expression darkly curious. Nyx had sensed that the woman would pounce upon them at any misstep, any show of power.

Graylin turned to Shiya. "Do you sense anything?"

She shook her head. "But water muffles sound. Especially at these depths. It would take great strength for any song to reach the surface."

Graylin glanced at Meryk, who stood off to the side with Vikas, clearly not wanting his words to be heard by Daal's father. "If neither of you senses anything, maybe there's *nothing* down there. We'll risk everything by venturing out here again."

Nyx might have succumbed to such reasoning, except for one detail. *Daal.* He had experienced something in the depths of these waters, something that had scarred and terrified him.

"The Dreamers are down there," Nyx insisted. "I don't know what they are, but they abide below."

*Waiting for us.*

DAAL PACED A small circle at the end of a stone pier. He had wended his skiff through the moored and anchored boats of Kefta's bay and found an open spot to tether up.

Nearby, Neffa and Mattis floated in their harnesses. He had fed them fistfuls of thumb-sized minwins. Still, they remained hungry, slashing the waves with their horns, but he didn't want them to bloat. They had leagues to go before the day was over.

He stopped at the end of the pier and chuffed softly to the two orksos, apologizing for keeping them tied up. Neffa answered with a weary puff of steam from her nostrils.

*It won't be much longer,* he promised her.

He knew the beasts' agitation was not solely due to hunger and impatience. The two sensed his own anxiety. Or maybe Neffa remembered when last they'd plied the deep waters off Kefta's shores.

*Half a year ago.*

The memory overwhelmed him, drawing him back.

He and his father had joined an armada of skiffs headed from Iskar to the seas surrounding the island. They came to hunt the massive keftas, the namesake of the town. Such beasts grew to the size of barges, requiring the coordination of many to secure one.

Even now, he flashed to waves washed red, a kefta fighting hard, speared and thrashing. Its flanks glowed and flickered in stripes of panic. Standing next to his father, he had balked with his own spear, a hesitation that had allowed the kefta to lift its tail and smash their skiff, breaking it apart.

He was thrown far, dumped deep into the sea. When he surfaced, the furious fight had moved on. Panicked, he swam toward the battle, only to be blocked by fins rising around them. A shiver of Kell sharks had been drawn by the blood.

In that moment, he knew his death had come, even accepted it.

Then Neffa burst under him, still tangled in the shreds of the skiff's broken harness. She caught him on her back. He barely had time to snatch hold of the leather yoke before she buried her horn into the waves and dove deep, sweeping tail and wings to escape.

They were chased by the sharks, driven farther from the other skiffs. More hunters closed upon them, attracted to the thrashing. Daal didn't try to guide Neffa, trusting in her instincts. She slashed at any threat, bloodying the waters, leaving a trail.

Finally, Neffa burst high out of the water. Daal lost his grip, too tired to hold on. He tumbled off her back, but his ankle tangled in a loop of leather. As she crashed back into the waves, she dragged him with her, driving ever deeper, into dark waters, where light never reached. Still, the hunters closed upon them.

Despite the pressure stabbing his ears, he heard Neffa's distressed cries calling to other orksos for help. The sound echoed in his skull, shook his ribs. He held out for as long as he could, clamping his lips and trapping his breath.

Then he could last no longer.

He used the last of his air to add his voice to hers, screaming in the darkness for rescue. As his lungs gave out and water flooded into him, something finally answered their call.

*But it was not any orkso.*

The memory darkened his sight even now. He rubbed his eyes, realizing the dimming light had not been conjured by his recollection of that day.

Eventide had fallen.

Overhead, the panoply of hues across the ice had faded to dim swaths of blue. He blinked to readjust his sight. As he did, the distant dark fog brightened over the waters, flickering with flames.

It was the returning flotilla.

Daal took a breath, casting aside the shadows of that terrifying day. At last, his vigil had ended. The waiting was over.

*Now comes the hard part.*


TWO BELLS AFTER arriving at Kefta, Nyx still sat at an open-air stone table. She ignored the long platter at its center, piled high with steamed knots of some starchy tuber, fried fish, boiled eels, and oil-blanched weed.

She had no appetite, anxiety souring her stomach.

Instead, she took in her surroundings. The tribute grounds proved to be an interconnecting warren of wide streets, small squares, and more intimate courtyards. Walls, terraces, and balconies were all strung with the same white-blossoming strands of a sea plant that had adorned the barge's rail. Hundreds of firepots and lanterns held back the gloom of eventide—if not the misery of those around her.

That was better assuaged with the free flow of sweet wine. Casks of ale formed pyramids at every corner. As throats loosened, tales were shared of those who had passed. Music echoed confoundedly throughout the labyrinth, rising from different stands of minstrels and wandering bards. They competed against one another in a discordant din.

Nyx's head throbbed from the clamor and tumult.

Across the table, Daal looked no better. His face remained drained of color. He sipped at a cup of wine, but it was doubtful any passed his lips. It was the same cup his father had forced into his hands at the start of the feast.

Meryk stood across the small square, leaning on Vikas's shoulder, talking into her ear. The quartermaster's assignment was to draw off Daal's father, get him well soused, to keep him distracted enough not to realize they had left. From the way he weaved when he straightened, Vikas had succeeded admirably. From here, she would stay behind with Meryk, making sure he grew none the wiser.

A hand gripped Nyx's shoulder, making her flinch.

"It's time," Graylin said, nodding over to Daal.

She stood and glanced around. "The Reef Farer and his consort?"

Graylin had gone off to spy on them in a neighboring plaza, where dignitaries from each village had gathered. "They are well occupied and deep into their cups. At least, Berent is. Ularia is practically holding him upright in his chair."

Daal came around the table, pulling up the hood of his oilskin slicker. He had supplied the same to all of them. Even Shiya stood in the shadows, decked from head to toe, her cloak masking her features. The bronze woman had donned it by the docks shortly after stepping off the barge, allowing their group to disappear within the throngs crowding the grounds.

"Let's go," Daal said, and led them off.

They hurried down dark alleys and side streets, avoiding the growing exuberance where—at least for this one night—grief was being drowned away. The four of them reached the plaza that fronted the bay. It was mostly empty. A few drunken stragglers wandered the edges, arms around each other's shoulders. Someone heaved in a corner, while two mates laughed bawdily nearby.

"My skiff this way," Daal said, and hurried toward one of the stone piers.

He only got a few steps before figures appeared ahead, shedding from the shadows. Three men blocked their way, another two appeared behind Nyx and the others. The group came armed with cudgels and knives.

Across the plaza, the stragglers noted the confrontation and hurried off. They were apparently sober enough to sense the bloodshed to come and wanted no part of it. Even the sick man had been dragged off by his friends.

With no eyes upon them, the stockiest of the group pushed forward to confront Daal. He slapped a hooked gaff into his calloused palm. He spat as much as spoke, reeking of sour ale. *"Rel'n dar nare Noor?"* He waved his gaff to encompass all of them. *"Nee Noor wrench ka!"*

Daal held up his palms, trying to placate the angry group. *"Bakna, nee wrench pa'kan."*

Clearly, Daal had recognized the Panthean. The group must be fellow villagers from Iskar who had come to seek vengeance, or at least make their group suffer as much as the Crèche had.

Daal spoke rapidly, seeking any means to talk them free.

Before he got far, the hard ring of a bell sounded behind Nyx. She turned to see one of the assailants stumble away from Shiya. Her hood had been knocked askew. A wooden cudgel fell from the man's stunned grip. Shiya lunged out and snatched the assailant's neck. Bronze fingers closed around his throat and lifted him off his feet. He flailed in her grip.

Graylin pulled his sword free, flashing the bright steel.

The show of strength succeeded where Daal's diplomacy had failed. The one called Bakna stepped away, holding his gaff wide, plainly relinquishing the field.

Nyx let out a breath, one she hadn't known she was holding.

But it was not over.

Graylin sprang forward. In a blur of cloak and steel, he slashed Bakna's throat and continued past the man. He stopped between the other two and stabbed his sword into a chest. As he yanked it free, he flipped the sword's hilt in his palm and drove the blade under his own arm to impale the other man.

Before either could more than mewl or gasp, Graylin spun on a toe, with his steel held wide. Both throats were cut deep, silencing any cry.

In that stunned moment, bone crunched behind Nyx. She ducked and turned. Shiya tossed her strangled man aside and closed on the other, who tried to flee. But no one could outrun such a being. Shiya reached him in a breath and snapped the man's neck.

Graylin dropped to a knee before Nyx and Daal. His eyes flashed with the same cold steel of his blade. "We need to make these bodies vanish."

"Wh . . . Why did you . . ." Daal stammered. "Bakna was giving up."

Even Nyx was stunned by the cold-blooded slaughter.

Graylin gripped both their shoulders. "Daal, did you not say it was death to be caught trespassing upon the Dreamers? If so, there can be no witnesses to our departure."

Daal unlocked his neck enough to nod.

Graylin turned to Nyx. "And what we attempt now? Is it worth that price?" He pointed to the bodies.

Nyx swallowed and nodded, too.

Graylin stood, addressing them all. "We can't let word of us leaving Kefta reach the wrong ears." He faced Shiya, who joined them with her two bodies in tow. "Can you ensure no one else saw what happened?"

She searched around. "Some had fled."

Nyx pictured the drunken lot.

"Did any of them linger?" Graylin asked. "Stay to witness what transpired?"

Shiya's lids lowered slightly. A hum built in her throat, warming her neck. She stoked it brighter—then cast out a glowing wave of bridle-song. It swept the plaza and traveled up streets and alleyways and through open windows. Then, in the next breath, it rebounded back to its source.

As it did, Daal ducked from it.

Nyx remembered performing something similar in the hold of the *Sparrowhawk*, using an echo of her bridle-song to strip the shadows and reveal all that was hidden, including life in all its myriad forms.

"No one else is nearby," Shiya confirmed.

Graylin nodded and grabbed the arms of two of the men, but that was all he could manage. "Daal and Nyx, you must take the other."

"Take them where?" Nyx asked with a shudder, still stunned by the sudden brutality, still struggling with the cold necessity of this act.

Yet, she also knew she must eventually grow this callous. From here, the path forward would only grow harder. And beyond any doubt . . .

*More deaths will follow.*

Daal had collected himself enough to point toward the stone pier. "My skiff. Large enough for all. The seas will take the dead, whether inked or not."

Nyx bent down and grabbed a slack arm.

*Let's pray that does not include us.*

# 45

THE DIM BLUE glow of eventide shrank the seas closer to the skiff. The steamy mists hugged tighter around them, as if trying to hide their efforts as they rolled the last body into the waters. Kelp ropes strangled the corpse's pale neck, running down to a net full of stones. The weight dragged their shame away.

Nyx sat in the stern of the rocking skiff. She hugged her arms around her. Despite the oppressive heat, her body still shivered. The reek of brimstan, bubbling up from the molten seabed, fouled the air.

It had taken a full bell to reach the boiling seas that edged the deepwater lair of the Dreamers. The two orksos—Neffa and Mattis—had labored through the waters, fighting the overloaded craft, having to contend with the extra dead weight and Shiya's considerable bulk. Graylin had urged their group to dump the bodies shortly after leaving Kefta's bay, but Daal had refused. He insisted the men—assailants or not—be returned properly to the sea, to the embrace of the Dreamers.

"That's the last of them," Graylin said, wiping his palms on his damp breeches as if that would clean his conscience, too. He looked at their group, his face stern and pitiless.

Still, Nyx had noted his lips moving silently in prayer as the dead were sent to their watery graves. His eyes had looked haunted, while his features remained stoic. It only added to her own guilt. He had committed that cold-hearted act to aid her endeavor.

*But will it all be for naught?*

The seas below the skiff remained dark, lit only by a single firepot stanchioned at the prow. Shiya also sensed nothing, her gaze searching the waters all around. But they had yet to call out to those Dreamers.

"We'd best get about it," Graylin warned. He glanced to a distant glow through the dark mists. "Our return to Kefta will undoubtedly be quicker, but we dare not linger longer than we must."

Nyx nodded and shifted over to Shiya. She took hold of the bronze woman's hand, both their fingers slick with hot droplets. Nyx let her eyelids drift half-closed. She took deep breaths, stoking her bridle-song into a warm glow. Still, she had to struggle for focus. The air filling her lungs was too hot, too foul.

Shiya squeezed her hand, humming softly next to her.

Nyx concentrated as Shiya's humming slipped into a melody, rising and falling with the rocking boat. Nyx's chin began to dip and lift the same, riding that harmony. As she found the proper rhythm, she let her own song escape her lips. She added and bolstered Shiya's refrain. With each breath, the song grew around them, tangled together. It built until there was no restraining it any further.

Without a word, they both cast those golden threads across the dark waters, like a shining net. They continued to sing, driving that glowing tangle deeper, passing through the luminescent waters into the lightless depths. Nyx followed those cords, carried within that net. Schools of speckled fish flashed their scales and dashed away, as if sensing her presence coursing past them.

As they delved deeper, Nyx's breathing grew harder, her throat straining. Shiya's earlier words were proven correct. The pressure of the water, its density, muffled their efforts, trying to thwart them. The golden mesh started to fray, dissolving in those black depths.

She sang louder, growing desperate, flashing to Graylin's blade piercing a chest.

*It can't be for nothing.*

Shiya added her strength, but even her well of energy failed to drive those threads any deeper.

*No . . .*

Nyx refused to give up. Her throat ached, and her chest labored. For a flicker, she saw a distant glow, far deeper than she imagined these waters to be. It shone more silvery than golden, then it vanished. She gasped in frustration and despair, unsure if it was real or merely her desire manifesting itself.

She and Shiya struggled for several long breaths, but it was to no avail. Strain turned their melody discordant. The golden net tattered and was quickly consumed by the black waters.

With a last gasp, Nyx fell back into her body, into the skiff.

Graylin dropped to a knee beside her. He cradled her shoulders. Shiya sat heavily next to her. The shine of her bronze had dulled with exhaustion.

"Did you sense those Dreamers?" Graylin asked.

"No . . . maybe . . . I don't know . . ." Nyx stammered, breathless and hoarse. "Certainly not enough to commune with them, to learn what they might know."

Graylin glanced at Shiya.

Her eyes glowed glassy. "For a moment, I felt . . . something . . . a flash, a glint."

Nyx sat up. "Of what?"

Shiya glanced across them all. "Fury."

FROM THE BOW of the boat, Daal had watched it all transpire. The glow of the two had driven away his terror of these waters. Awe had filled him, leaving little else. The surge had warmed through his body, stirring the fire inside him, like raking coals to a hotter scorch.

But as it ended, collapsing away, the hollowness in its wake filled again with dread. Especially upon hearing Shiya's judgement.

"I warn you before," Daal called over. "Must not trespass."

Graylin shifted to face him. "Daal, what exactly is down there? You've never told us. At least not clearly. What happened to you?"

Nyx sat straighter. Since this morning, she had struggled to get him to explain, to fully share his story. But for him, to speak it was to relive it. He turned away and searched the waters, his gaze settling on Neffa. He drew strength from her bravery, when she had risked her life to save him.

He started slowly, stutteringly. He told them of that journey half a year ago, when he came to these waters to hunt with his father, of the bloody battle with the kefta, and his hesitation that destroyed their old skiff and cast him into the sea. He shared his terror and the frantic pursuit—then being dragged into the depths, his ankle tangled in leather, of drowning in these waters.

Nyx's eyes shone with sympathy. Plainly she had known similar terrors. "What happened then?"

"As my chest filled in those black waters, I saw a shine. Far below."

"A *silvery* shine?" Nyx asked in a whisper.

He nodded and rubbed his sternum, feeling that cold heaviness of water even now. "I see it, and my body burned." He fixed Nyx with his gaze. "Like your touch."

"They must have inflamed your gift," she said. "Sensed your power, shining like a beacon in that blackness."

He shook his head. "I know not."

"Then what happened?" Graylin urged.

Daal faced him. "They came for me."

"Who?" Graylin pressed. "What?"

He opened his mouth to reveal the horror, but his breath was trapped in his chest. His throat closed. It took all his effort to move his suddenly heavy tongue. "I . . . I cannot say."

Graylin shoved closer and took Daal's shoulders, his strong fingers digging deep. "You must."

He tried again, gulping to speak. He lifted a hand to his throat. He could not take in air. It was as if his body had forgotten how to breathe.

Nyx leaned forward and knocked Graylin's arms away. "He truly can't *tell* us," she said.

"He's just panic-stricken."

"No! That's not it. I think he's been enthralled. By the *Oshkapeers*. They will not allow him to share what happened." Nyx gripped Daal, careful not to touch his bare skin. "It's all right. Stop trying to speak."

Daal closed his eyes, letting his story roll from his tongue and be swallowed away. As he did, his throat opened. His chest found its rhythm again, though he was still left gasping.

Nyx squeezed her reassurance into him. "It's all right. Just breathe through it."

He did as she instructed. After a spell, his wheezing settled into normal breaths, though his heart still pounded in his ears.

Graylin motioned to Shiya and Nyx. "Can you break through that bridling that holds him silent? Free his tongue?"

"Possibly," Shiya said. "We can try."

"No," Nyx warned, shielding Daal's body with her own. "It could destroy his mind. Even kill him."

"We don't know that," Graylin argued. "And hard choices must be made."

Daal pictured their group dragging the dead men down the pier. He reached and touched Nyx's back, laying his palm there. "All right. I try."

She glanced back to him, her face stricken. "No, Daal. It's not worth the risk. I . . . I can't bear the weight if anything happens to you. It's too much."

"Then no carry it. It my choice."

He had borne this burden for too long, until it was a stone in his chest. He wanted to let this secret go, no matter the danger.

Nyx must have read his sincerity. Tears welled in her eyes.

Before she could argue further, Graylin came and pulled Nyx away. "Listen to him. It's his decision. Leave it to Shiya to at least try."

Graylin drew her back, allowing room for Shiya to crawl forward. Bronze hands lifted toward Daal's face.

He closed his eyes.

*Let it be over.*


NYX SHOOK FREE of Graylin, but she kept back, respecting Daal's wishes. Still, fury burned inside her—mostly directed at herself.

*I dragged them all here.*

Shiya closed on Daal. As she lifted her hands toward his face, her bronze fingers glowed as a humming rose from her chest. Golden strands wended from her fingertips toward Daal's temples.

All the while, Shiya's face remained stoic, showing no hint of trepidation about the harm she might commit. Nyx remembered back on the plaza, hearing the crack of breaking bone, a snap of another's neck. In many respects, Shiya was as coldhearted as Graylin—if not more so. Despite all that the bronze woman had done, the true humanity she had demonstrated, Nyx sensed a core inside Shiya that remained as unmovable and cold as any metal.

Still, Nyx had forgotten one detail. They all had. But she remembered it now.

*Daal is impregnable.*

As Shiya's golden strands touched Daal's skin, they dissolved away. The same had happened when Nyx had attempted to touch him with her bridle-song. She wondered now if it was a fail-safe instilled into Daal by the *Oshkapeers,* to keep him locked up, to secure their secrets from prying.

Shiya's brow pinched, and her fingertips settled hard on Daal, plainly determined to try again. Nyx winced, expecting some strong reaction from Shiya, from Daal, like whenever Nyx touched the young man's skin. But neither reacted. Shiya waxed her song to a stronger glow, but Daal's body still thwarted her efforts to delve deeper.

"What's wrong?" Graylin asked.

Shiya lowered her hands and twisted around. "I can't reach him. But I will try again."

Another decided that must not happen.

From behind Daal, a flurry of large snakes burst from the water and wrapped around his chest and throat, pinning his arms. They glued to his body with bell-like suckers. Before anyone could move, he was yanked from his seat.

He gasped a breath, screaming out a warning before vanishing beneath the waves. *"Oshkapeers!"*

Nyx lunged toward the bow to go to his aid, but before her backside could leave the bench, water flooded over her. The air writhed as muscular snakes fell about her shoulders and waist. They latched hard with clinging suckers. She had one last thought as she was jerked away from the skiff, watching Graylin futilely try to grab her.

Not snakes—*tentacles.*

# TEN

# THE FUMES
# OF MALGARD

*Prai to Hadyss & Madyss, twinne gods of the Winds. One gusts ici, the other fierie. Neglect nyther in yure worship. For no matter whiches ways thei blow, thei be yure fiercest allies.*

—From the Hálendiian war text
*Lessons of the Air: From Warships to Battle Barges*

# 46

MIKAEN SWEPT THROUGH the fiery skies in a small sailraft, savoring the victory to come. He crouched behind the pilot and gazed out the window. The smoky skies burned in every direction. The flames from a score of Klashean warcraft scorched the Breath of the Urth. Their fires hung in the air or slowly spiraled toward the distant sea.

His heart hammered in his throat at the sight of the destruction. His blood surged, hardening him in all ways. A tight sneer fixed his face, paining the scars hidden under his silver mask.

All around, Hálendiian hunterskiffs and swyftships circled through the dense pall, stirring the smoke and flames as they patrolled the skies.

But the worst was over.

For most of the day and well into the night, Mikaen had waged this war in the shadow of the mountainous Shaar Ga. The volcanic peak glowed in the distance through the dense pall of ash and fumes that had spewed endlessly from its fiery cone. What seemed like ages ago, he had arrived at the smoky wall of the Breath, the leagues-wide band of ash and fumes that divided Hálendii from the Southern Klashe. He had intended to ambush one, if not both, of the giant Klashean warships, to drive them back to their homelands.

Regrettably, the two warships had split off before he could engage. Mikaen was left with only one stubborn target: the *Hawk's Talon*. It was said to be captained by one of the emperor's sons. His opponent proved to be craftier than expected, coming close to escaping Mikaen's ambush—until finally the *Talon* and its escorts had been pinned down and trapped against the fiery flanks of Shaar Ga.

The battle that followed had been fierce, but the end was inevitable.

Mikaen tilted onto his toes to stare below the raft as it circled toward its target.

The *Talon* hung crooked in the skies under them, smoking from countless fires. Its balloon had been shredded by bombs and fiery spears. Only a couple baffles of its gasbag still billowed and rocked, but they were not enough to hold the ship aloft. Its draft-iron prow—sculpted into the crested crown and hooked beak of a mountain hawk—pointed high, as if struggling to hold on to the sky. Its stern lay low, dragging through the pall.

All that was holding the ship in the air were two huge grappling cables that had snagged the *Talon*'s flanks and ran up to Mikaen's warship, proving his *Winged Vengeance* had the sharper claws.

A large hand clapped Mikaen on his shoulder. He glanced back at the crimson countenance of the Vyrllian knight, the captain of his Silvergard. The left side of the man's face bore a tattooed sigil of a sun and crown, a match to what was etched on Mikaen's mask.

"Well fought, sir," Thoryn said. "Your father will be proud."

Mikaen turned away, shaking off the man's large hand. He had not flown out into the darkness of the Breath and fought so tenaciously for mere accolades. That was not what fired his fury, his determination.

Instead, he pictured Othan and Olia, suckling on his wife's breasts. The twins were all that mattered. His chest tightened at the thought of them. Even now, he could taste the sweetness of that milk on his tongue, where he had gently licked the drops from Myella's broad nipples, bonding him closer to his children.

Months ago, he had sworn an oath upon their birth, amidst the blood and squalling.

*No harm or hardship must ever come to them.*

He would die before he let that promise be broken.

"The battle is not over yet," Mikaen growled back at Thoryn.

Below, on the tilted deck of the *Talon,* a ferocious fight continued between the Hálendiian knights and the last of the Klashean guardsmen. The brawl was lit by flames. Bodies lay everywhere.

"Get us down there," Mikaen gritted out, bristling with frustration. He was determined to shine, if only at the end of this battle.

While the *Winged Vengeance* was under Mikaen's captaincy, he had not truly led this campaign. Before the fleet had left Azantiia, the king had foisted the kingdom's new war leader, Liege General Reddak vy Lach—freshly promoted from head of the Vyrllian Guard—upon Mikaen. While the prince's counsel and input had been listened to, often even heeded, it was Reddak who had final say.

Still, over the course of the day, Mikaen had come to respect the stern warrior's knowledge of tactics and strategy—if not his overly cautious nature. Mikaen had been kept back from the worst of the battle. Reddak had circled the *Vengeance* at a safe distance from the fiercest fighting, mainly plying the warship's bulk to keep their prey trapped. Only after the *Talon* had been defanged was the *Vengeance* allowed to swoop in for the kill.

Still, while Reddak had been distracted, Mikaen had gathered his nine Silvergard and abandoned the *Vengeance,* flying off in one of the warship's sailrafts. He was determined to bloody his sword, and more importantly, he must be the one who ultimately secured the *Talon*.

The sailraft made one final circle, then dove under the ruins of *Talon's* massive gasbag. The pilot proved his skill by expertly skidding the raft across the smoky deck and coming to a hard stop.

Mikaen turned toward the back as the stern door crashed to the planks outside.

Thoryn blocked his way with a steel-clad arm. "Stay close to us."

Normally, Mikaen would have rebuffed such an order, but Thoryn had earned his status as captain of the Silvergard. If not for the Vyrllian, Mikaen would have suffered far worse than a scarred face from that ax blow. In respect for that act, Mikaen simply nodded. But there would come a time when Mikaen must step out of the man's considerable shadow, to shine like a silvery sun and herald a new dawn for Hálendii.

Until then . . .

Thoryn barked and tightened the Silvergard around the prince. Together, they pounded out of the raft's stern. The heat struck like a fist, both from the scatter of fiery blast holes in the deck and the scorch of Shaar Ga's smoke. Flaming ash swirled all around. Screams and cries pierced the winds. The strike of steel echoed everywhere.

"This way!" Thoryn called out.

Mikaen followed at his back, using Thoryn's body like a shield. The other Silvergard closed a sharp phalanx around them, forming a deadly arrow. They sped across the deck toward the stubbornest fighting, climbing toward the ship's forecastle.

Upon reaching the snarl of armor and ringing steel, they crashed headlong into the midst. Mikaen did not hold back or shy away. With sword in one hand and a dagger in the other, he let loose his frustrated fury. He had been hard-trained in the Legionary and sparred regularly with Thoryn. He wanted to scream and bellow as he fought, but it was Thoryn who had taught him that the most skilled fighter was the silent one.

With his lips clamped, breathing through his nose, he hewed and stabbed and slashed. Thoryn stayed at his shoulder, adding to his effort but giving Mikaen full rein. The captain only corrected—teaching even now—whenever the prince misstepped.

Together, they forged through the remaining Klashean guards. While Mikaen savored each kill, he knew it was enabled by the trembling exhaustion in this last stand of defenders. It was less a glorious battle than a quick slaughter.

He backhanded a curved sword as it slashed at his face, knocking it out of the guard's hand. He followed with a thrust of his dagger, aiming for the gap in the armor under his opponent's raised arm, to sever the thick arteries, as he had been taught.

But his lessons weren't over.

Thoryn blocked Mikaen's dagger with the hilt of his sword and kicked a steel-heeled boot into the guard's knee. The man gasped and fell to the planks. Thoryn pointed his sword at the guard's face.

"It's Prince Paktan," Thoryn explained. "Third son of Emperor Makar."

Mikaen lowered his own blade, shocked. He had expected the *imri* prince to be cowering in the forecastle, that they'd have to dig his craven arse out of hiding. He gaped as the young man rolled to his knees. Under his helm, sweat and ash plastered the Klashean prince's face. Blood ran through it all from a gash in his forehead. Dark eyes glared at Mikaen and Thoryn.

With the prince at swordpoint, the remaining defenders lowered their weapons.

Mikaen retrieved the curved sword, its hilt shining with black diamonds and thumb-sized rubies, the weapon of a prince. In the heat of the battle, he had failed to spot the opulence of the weapon.

Fortunately, Thoryn had—along with the magnificence of the prince's armor. On its breastplate, the crossed swords of the Klashean Arms were made of pure gold.

Mikaen shifted Thoryn aside, replacing the captain's sword with his own. He stared down at Paktan, recognizing the prince was only five or six years older than him. Paktan spat on the planks, not in insult, but only to clear his mouth of blood.

"Do you submit?" Mikaen asked firmly, letting his voice carry across the deck.

Paktan's eyes narrowed, glanced around the ruins of the ship, then back to Mikaen. "I so swear," he grunted out.

Mikaen sheathed his sword and offered his hand. Paktan reached and took hold of Mikaen's forearm. Mikaen matched his grip and tugged the prince up. As he did, Mikaen swung his other arm and punched a gauntleted fist into the man's nose.

Bone broke under steel.

Mikaen felt its satisfying crunch all the way down to his groin.

He stepped back as the Klashean prince crashed to the planks. With a long breath, Mikaen stared up past the billowing ruins of the balloon, to where the *Vengeance*'s forges flamed the skies, fighting to hold the *Talon* aloft. The roaring filled his ears, his chest.

Paktan groaned, drawing his attention back.

Mikaen looked down, searching inside himself for some surge of victory, but all he felt was disappointment. And he knew why.

*This is not the prince I want bloodied and broken at my feet.*

WRYTH STOOD BESIDE Liege General Reddak on the broad deck of the *Winged Vengeance.* The air burned and choked with smoke, but Wryth knew he had to be present as Prince Paktan, the third son of Emperor Makar, was led across the planks in chains, a prisoner of the realm.

The Klashean prince was flanked by Mikaen and Thoryn, the massive captain of the Silvergard, who gripped the prisoner's arm—not to hold Paktan captive, but to keep him on his feet. The *imri* prince swayed on his legs, dazed, blood flowing from the ruins of his nose.

Wryth tightened his jaw. Earlier in the battle, when the tides had turned their way and the *Hawk's Talon* had been greatly damaged, he had urged Reddak and Mikaen to cordon the Breath and force the Klashean ship to retreat home, humiliated and defeated. Such an act would have been victorious enough without raising tensions. It would have also freed them to pursue and hunt down the other colossal warship, the *Falcon's Wing,* to stem any havoc it might wreak.

Reddak had leaned toward that plan, but Mikaen smelled blood in the water, stirring his lust for a more dramatic victory.

Wryth watched it being marched toward them.

*Maybe I was wrong.*

This capture could serve them well. From Mikaen's hard sneer, even the prince seemed to recognize the significance of his triumph. Mikaen lifted a Klashean scimitar in hand, a gem-encrusted trophy. This earned a resounding cheer from the legion gathered on the deck.

Once close enough, Paktan was thrown at the liege general's feet.

Reddak ignored the prize and glared over at Mikaen and Thoryn. The shaven-headed general stood only a brow shorter than the Silvergard's captain, whom most thought was half Gyn from his boulder-sized shoulders and hulking mass. Reddak came outfitted in only light armor, compared to the heavy battlement of the others. Still, the liege general likely could be naked, baring all his scars, and pose no less of a threat. Even Thoryn respected Reddak's talents in warcraft and his daunting skills with sword, hammer, and ax.

One did not defy such a man lightly.

"I do not recall giving you two permission to leave the ship and sneak off like a pair of thieving whores from a bed."

Mikaen stepped forward, his back stiffening. "I need no such consent. I'm still captain of the—"

Thoryn cut him off, doffing his helm and dropping to a knee. He bowed his head. "We apologize for the affront. And accept any punishment."

Reddak turned his hard eyes on the prince. Mikaen stared back, gripping Paktan's sword as if the trophy insulated him from any reprimand. Still, Mikaen slowly sank and matched Thoryn's pose, bowing his head. Captain or not, prince or not, there was a protocol that must be adhered to.

Wryth appreciated the general's strict fortitude, hoping with time that it would rub off on Mikaen and temper his growing recklessness.

Satisfied at the show of respect, Reddak waved Mikaen and Thoryn up. "We'll discuss such matters in private later. For now, what is to be done with our new guest?"

By now, Paktan had rolled to his own knees. "I've sworn submission," he said formally. "I beseech you take my remaining guardsmen prisoners and into your safe custody."

All eyes turned to the *Vengeance*'s rails. The roar of its dozen forges rumbled across the smoky skies. The two giant grappling bows, one on each side of the ship, vibrated and strained from the cables that ran down to the *Talon*.

Reddak cleared his throat and nodded to Mikaen. "You are indeed captain of the *Vengeance* and took the prisoner's oath. What is your judgement?"

Mikaen narrowed his eyes, possibly wondering if this was some ruse.

"It is your decision," Reddak assured him. "You seem more than willing to make plenty of them whenever I'm *not* looking."

Mikaen nodded and turned. He glanced to the two archers posted beside the iron grappling bows. Their eyes were on him, waiting for his order.

Mikaen stepped back and extolled loudly, "We've carried this burden long enough." He slashed a finger across his throat. "No more."

Upon this command, the two archers pulled tall levers next to their bows. Thunderous *twangs* snapped from both sides of the ship. The grappling cables, now free of their locks, spooled away, vanishing over the edge. The *Vengeance*, unburdened of the *Talon*'s weight, thrust upward. Most everyone on the deck was thrown off balance for a stomach-churning breath before the forges compensated.

On the starboard side, the *Talon* fell into view, plummeting through the smoke toward the distant sea—then vanished into the pall.

By now, Prince Paktan, still on his knees, had also dropped to his hands, his head hanging low.

Mikaen lifted his captured sword again, clearly expecting another enthusiastic response from the legion, but all it engendered was a smattering of claps and a couple of cheers.

Wryth glanced sidelong at Reddak. The only reaction to Mikaen's callous decision was a slight narrowing of one eye. Wryth gave a small shake of his head.

*Only the young believe such an ignoble act is a show of strength.*

Mikaen lowered his arm and turned back. The half of his face in view had hardened to match the silver on the other side. His eyes flashed with anger, maybe some embarrassment.

Reddak waited a breath, then nodded again to Prince Paktan. "As to the prisoner?"

Mikaen stammered, clearly trying to regain his footing. "We'll take him to Azantiia. Present him as a gift to King Toranth."

Reddak dipped his chin in approval.

Wryth spoke up. "Prince Mikaen, you've done the kingdom a great service. The Klashean prisoner will serve us well in prying your traitorous brother out from the imperial palace. I'm sure Emperor Makar will happily trade one prince for another."

For the first time in months, Mikaen met Wryth's gaze and smiled. Blood-lust stoked the prince's eyes even brighter. It was a desire they both shared, one that could potentially repair the bond between them. Wryth recalled his earlier anger upon hearing of Mikaen's plans to ambush the Klasheans. He had wanted to stop the prince from such a hasty path.

*Maybe I was wrong then, too.*

But Paktan proved exactly how wrong he was about everything.

"I do not understand," the prince said, sitting straighter. "Why would you need to barter me for Prince Kanthe? He is the reason we set off for your lands."

Reddak frowned. "What do you mean?"

Paktan looked up with bewilderment. "Prince Kanthe is not at our palace. He abducted my younger brother and sister three days ago and fled. We were told he was returning to Hálendii."

Mikaen stiffened. His lips twisted into a snarl so hard he struggled to speak through it. "What . . . What trickery is this?"

Paktan lifted his chin and turned to Mikaen. "Prince Kanthe is gone."

Mikaen bit off each word as he clutched hard to his stolen sword. "Then you are of no use to us."

Wryth stepped forward, knowing what was going to happen.

*No, no, no . . .*

Mikaen swung the royal scimitar with all the force of his fury and frustration. The blade cleaved under Paktan's raised chin and through his throat. Steel rang off bone—then swept high, trailing an arc of blood.

The prince's head flew even farther.

Wryth stumbled back into the stunned gasps of those around him.

He had to turn away, covering his eyes, not at the horror and brutality, but in despair. With that one act, he knew Mikaen was lost to him forever.

He dropped his hand and accepted this truth. He stared beyond the ship's rail, casting his gaze south, toward another prince whose actions continued to dismay him.

*Kanthe, what have you done?*

# 47

KANTHE STOOD BEFORE the wingketch's large windows and gazed beyond the last of the Scarp's foothills. Ahead, a steamy landscape stretched to the glimmer of a distant sea. Yesterday, after their ship had reached the lower mountains, it had taken them another day to slowly sweep over the jagged range to reach the far side.

As he kept his post by the tall window, the final bell of Eventoll chimed throughout the ship. By now, the never-setting sun had fallen behind the peaks of the Hyrg Scarp. Shadows shrouded the lands of Malgard ahead. The expanse of rolling plains glowed with hot pools and boiling lakes, whose clay shores shone with acidic swirls of yellows, crimsons, and bright blues. Geysers spat in an unending spectacle of scalding water. Ponds exploded with great blasts of steamy air, before settling again.

"These lands are the home of Malkanian," Rami mumbled at Kanthe's shoulder. "The Klashean god of the fiery underworld, He who burns betrayers and traitors in eternal torment."

Rami looked over at Kanthe, making it clear whom this lesson was for.

Kanthe turned away. He stared toward the other window across the wheelhouse. Aalia stood between Frell and Pratik. After the two *imri* had helped with the translation of the stolen prophetic pages, they had all come to a temporary truce, which allowed Rami and his sister more freedom. Still, both were escorted by hard-faced members of Llyra's army.

Though, the risk of the two *imri* escaping was minimal.

*And not just because we're in the air.*

Saekl—the Rhysian captain of the ketch—stood behind the ship's maesterwheel, guiding their descent out of the mountains. Four of her sisterhood, all draped in bell-adorned braids, manned the curved helms on either side, working smaller maneuvering wheels and levers.

Little escaped the attention of these assassins.

Even now.

The youngest Rhysian, Cassta, met his gaze from the neighboring station. Her eyes shone with amusement. She had clearly overheard Rami's brusque lecture on Klashean gods.

Kanthe grimaced and returned his attention to Malgard. The *Quisl* had dropped over the foothills, enough to see the scorching terrain was dotted by dense forests of skeletal trees, covered in thorns and gray-blue needles. Their branches twisted and writhed, as if the trees were trying to claw themselves free of this hostile land.

"What could possibly live down there?" Kanthe mumbled.

"Do not be fooled." Rami's arms were firmly crossed. "It is not just the terrain that is dangerous. Malgard teems with life."

"Then why do any of your people make Malgard their home?"

Rami sighed and unlocked his arms and stepped closer. He pointed to the southeast, toward that distant glimmer of a blue sea. "The city of Qazen sits on the coast, where the land of Malgard fades into the Salted Wastes. A peninsula of alkali marshes and sunbaked flats. So blinding in their brilliance, it's said they reflect the wisdom of the gods. It's why Qazen is considered kissed by the heavens, blessed with seers and prophets."

"And home to the emperor's Augury," Kanthe added.

Rami nodded with a huff. "He heads the city, ensconced in a grand villa at the sea's edge. The Augury is but the latest in a long lineage of oracles, going back to the founding of the Klashe. Under each full moon, the Augury leads the other seers in a gilded caravan, traveling into Malgard to imbue and bathe themselves in its fumes. There, they drift into a fugue, allowing them to commune with the gods and return with great wisdom."

A snort of derision rose behind them. "Charlatans," Llyra stated firmly, puffing on a pipe. "The feckless lot of them. They're far more swindlers and filchers than any thief."

Rami's small nod supported this assessment. Kanthe knew how much the prince and his sister resented the Augury's hold on their father.

Drawn by the conversation, Frell and Pratik crossed to join them, followed by Aalia and her guard.

Frell stared toward the sliver of shining sea in the distance. "Do not be so quick to dismiss Qazen's auguries. In my studies of prophecy, I've read of their revered talent. I combed through thousands of their divinations, going back millennia. Time has proven a vast majority of their predictions to be uncannily accurate. Many so detailed that it defies explanation."

"Unless they're truly touched by the gods," Pratik added.

Aalia rolled her eyes. "Or simply touched."

Frell waved the debate aside. "If circumstances were different, I would have liked to consult the Augury about the prophecy that threatens our world—and about the *Vyk dyre Rha*—but that is not what we came out here to seek."

"The Sleeper," Kanthe said.

Frell shifted toward Saekl. "Any estimation on when we'll reach our goal, the site I marked on your ship's map?"

Saekl leaned forward and cast her gaze to the north, well away from Qazen. "Another bell. Maybe longer. We've got some stiff headwinds to fight."

Frell wrung his hands, clearly anxious. They were close to possibly discovering another of the bronze artifacts. Worry etched the alchymist's face. The questions streaming behind his eyes were easy to read.

*Is the Sleeper still there? Can we wake it? Will it agree to help us? And most importantly, will it have the knowledge to fill the gaps in Shiya's fractured memory?*

Kanthe added his own worries, glancing sidelong at Rami and Aalia.

*Even if we're successful, what then? With all of the Klashe hunting us, what will such a discovery win us? Without the support of the empire, where will we go?*

It was one of the many reasons he had agreed to marry Aalia upon first landing in the Southern Klashe. They needed the cooperation and protection of the empire to be able to take advantage of any discovery out here.

Rami scowled at him. While much of the heat had dissipated from the prince, the two were far from friends. And any chance of regaining the empire's trust and goodwill was even less likely.

A heavy silence fell over the gathering. The *Quisl* trembled as it coursed through the headwinds. The extended wings of the ketch occasionally jerked hard, bobbling the craft as it crossed heated updrafts. Still, they forged ahead. Leagues slowly passed under them. The pounding of Kanthe's heart marked the tense passage of time.

The terrain below grew more inhospitable as they continued north. A huge geyser exploded directly before the large window, sending all of them stumbling back. Scalding water splashed against the glass and thrummed atop the balloon and deck overhead.

Saekl remained calm behind the wheel. "Gain us more air," she ordered sharply to her crew. She looked at Kanthe's group. "Be warned. The lands ahead appear to be more hot-tempered and capricious."

Kanthe regained his footing, surprised to find Rami's hand on his shoulder as his friend caught him. They returned together to the window. Kanthe saw that Saekl's assessment had been too kind.

Shaded by the nearby mountains, the landscape was cloaked in darkness. Boiling pots of clay burped and spat. Rivers bubbled hotly everywhere. Even in the dusk of shadows, the rings of shimmering iridescence that framed each geyser shone brightly. Throughout it all, the dark thorny forests covered vast swaths, so dense it looked as if the woodlands were trying to hide the volatile landscape under their canopy. A few lone trees burned brightly out there, solitary torches in the dark.

Kanthe's gaze followed one as they passed over it. The flames revealed the towering height of the forest. The trees were far taller than he had suspected from the air.

Rami noted his attention. "Naphtha pines."

"Their green-black sap is incendiary," Aalia added. "We use it as the main ingredient in the production of our imperium's naphlaneum."

Kanthe's eyes widened. The entire Crown feared the scourge of the Klashe's fiery gel. The craftsmanship to produce it remained a guarded secret. Naphlaneum's flaming touch could burn through the hardest ironwood. Eat through skin and bone. Even water failed to douse its fire, only inflaming it further.

"How much farther?" Saekl called over to Cassta.

The slender Rhysian had shifted to a tilted table with a map tacked atop it. She clutched a compass in one hand and a pointed tool of measurement in the other. It seemed Cassta also served as the ketch's navigator.

Without glancing away from her chart, she answered the captain. "Best I can tell. Half a league."

"Heard," Saekl responded.

Frell crossed toward Cassta. Kanthe followed, but not entirely due to his interest in navigation. With Cassta's back to him, the leather of her breeches hugged her backside in a most comely manner.

Frell leaned next to her. "Can I see?"

She shifted slightly to the side. The map was marked up with circles, radiating lines, and scribbled notations. "The location you shared was not precise," she explained.

"It leaves a lot of ground to cover. A square league, if my calculations are correct. It will take us some time to search through it all."

Frell nodded. "Hopefully we'll be able to spot some landmark from the air to guide us."

Still, the alchymist didn't sound hopeful.

Kanthe glanced toward the window as another geyser burst high. He certainly didn't want to have to search that hostile terrain on foot.

He stared down at his toes.

*Especially in these new boots.*

They were crafted of the softest doeskin.

He glanced over at Rami.

A gift from a former friend.

ANOTHER BELL PASSED, then another, as the wingketch swept back and forth over the territory squared off on Cassta's chart. With each pass, the terrain looked more tortured. The trees grew taller, the scalding geysers erupted higher, the boiling pots of mud became ponds, even lakes.

Kanthe paced between the windows and the map table.

He remembered Rhaif's tale of the discovery of Shiya deep in the mines of Chalk. According to the former thief, she had been entombed in a copper egg far underground. If the Sleeper of Malgard was similarly buried, digging the bronze artifact free would be next to impossible, especially on their own.

He glanced to Aalia, who kept with her brother by the far window.

From the outset, Kanthe and the others knew their best chance of discovering the Sleeper lay in gaining the empire's support, especially if a deep excavation was necessary.

*That's not happening now.*

Still, Kanthe held out a sliver of hope. Rhaif had also described a great quake in the mine tunnels, as if Shiya's awakening had shaken the area. He believed her copper egg might have been trying to force itself to the surface, but something went awry. Maybe from the corruption of the passing ages or simply the weight of all that stone.

Kanthe shifted closer to the window, studying the landscape below. If the Sleeper of Malgard was interred in a similar manner, perhaps there might be some evidence on the surface of such a forceful awakening deep underground.

As if conjured by this thought, a tall cliff rose ahead. It divided the land in two. The tablelands on top were riven with great cracks and fissures, several of them steaming. Huge boulders and shattered rocks filled the base of the precipice.

Kanthe hurried over to Saekl. "Get us higher."

The captain frowned at him, clearly not one to take orders.

Frell shifted around Saekl. "Why, Kanthe?"

He pointed to the stretch of cliffs. He explained about the quake that had accompanied Shiya's awakening.

"Could that be what we're seeing here?" he pressed. "Signs of the same?"

Frell took a deep breath, squinting below. "Whatever shook this corner of Malgard, it happened ages ago. Century-old trees have rooted over those boulders and dug deep into the cliffs. And look at the white scale caked around the steaming vents on top. It would take many centuries to build to that thickness."

Kanthe couldn't argue but tried anyway. "Maybe this Sleeper tried to wake long ago and got stuck."

Frell cast him a dubious look.

Still, Saekl heeded Kanthe's earlier request and fired up the ship's forges. The *Quisl* lifted its prow, and the ketch crested higher, sailing over the cliffs. She tucked the starboard wing enough to send them into a wide circle.

To better study the tablelands under them, Kanthe rested a palm on the glass and leaned over the curved window.

Saekl continued to wind them higher, opening the view wider.

Frell suddenly flinched and dropped his hand next to Kanthe's. The alchymist leaned on the glass, peering intently below.

"Do you see something?" Kanthe asked.

"Maybe. A pattern."

"Of what?"

Frell tried to point, but his finger hit the glass. "The cracks," he blurted out, both frustrated and excited. "All the rifts and fissures. They radiate out from one section of the cliff over there."

Kanthe scrunched his brows and searched below. Once it was brought to his attention, the pattern was obvious. He followed the spread of cracks to a piece of cliff that had shattered apart, as if the storm god, Tytan, had struck it with His mighty ax.

"You . . . You're right," Kanthe stammered out.

Frell pushed off the glass and rushed to Saekl. He pointed below. "Can you get us down there?"

She frowned at him, plainly insulted that Frell should question her abilities. Still, she turned and barked orders to her crew. The ketch swung around and sailed toward the broken section of the cliff face.

"There's a clearing near its base," Frell gushed. "The ground looks solid enough."

Kanthe stared below. The *clearing* was no more than a small gap between a dense fringe of thorny forest and a series of bubbling clay pots. All around, geysers spat and sprayed to some rhythm known only to the gods. Ponds steamed, and a small lake burped out a bubble the size of their ship.

"Can you land there?" Frell asked the captain.

This time, Saekl didn't frown. The descent would prove challenging. She simply grabbed the wheel and spoke quietly to her crew, perhaps afraid Malgard's resident god—Malkanian—might overhear their plans to trespass. The *Quisl* circled slowly. A geyser burst under the ship, jolting it hard. Saekl ignored it and continued downward. Once near the tree line, she ordered the ketch's two wings to be retracted and reefed.

Tense breaths later, the ship landed with a hard bump.

They were greeted by another belch from the lake.

"Well done," Frell whispered.

Everyone gathered by the windows. They all stared toward the tall cliff. Its face looked fragile, riven by many cracks. Sharp-edged boulders formed a massive rubble pile at its base. Up top, a boiling river spilled over the edge, but its waters turned to steam before ever touching ground.

Still, they all saw it.

Past the boulders and steam, a huge fracture cut into the cliff, its depths vanishing into the darkness.

"You want us to go in there, don't you?" Kanthe asked Frell.

"We must."

Kanthe's gut clenched. "It's already late. Mayhap we should all get a good night's sleep and start out in the morning."

Frell remained silent, clearly considering this option.

Rami dashed it. "We cannot wait. Malgard already knows we're here."

Kanthe glanced back at the prince. Rami's gaze was not on the cliffs, but on the neighboring ponds and lakes. Kanthe swallowed and looked in that direction, too. He saw no threat for several breaths, but when he did, he fell back.

He had first thought they were just pearlescent sprays of water hanging in the air. They had certainly been cast high, forcefully jettisoning from the lakes and ponds by the waters' blasts and burps. Once airborne, the creatures spread wide luminescent bells, which grew ever brighter as they drifted through the air. From the undersides of the bells, long frills of fine hairs draped and waved, stretching longer than Kanthe's arms.

Those bells contracted and expanded, propelling the creatures through the air. They spun and danced, casting their frills wider. With each breath, more and more were expelled from the waters surrounding the ship. Clouds of them soon glowed and swam everywhere. A few landed on the hard clay, pulsing like shimmering iridescent hearts. Their frills floated and trembled higher, forming a shining corona around them.

Despite their seemingly aimless paths, their malignant intent was clear. The glimmering cloud inexorably wafted in the direction of the wingketch.

"What are they?" Kanthe whispered.

"Lycheens," Rami answered.

Aalia explained the danger. "A touch of those threads cuts through skin and burns with a paralytic fire. Too many strikes of those threads can kill."

"What do they want?" he asked, dismayed and appalled.

Her answer did not reassure. "To feast on the iron in our blood."

Kanthe swung toward Frell. "Maybe we should reconsider this path. I mean, do we really *need* this Sleeper of Malgard?"

# 48

JUBAYR WOKE AT the knocking on his bedchamber's door. With a groan, he shifted to an elbow, rolled his legs to the floor, and sat up. He didn't need to toss aside any blanket, as he had dropped fully clothed into bed. He held his head in his hands, trying to summon focus after only two bells' worth of sleep.

He and the inner council had worked long into the night, discussing strategies, both defensive and offensive. Afterward, his fretful dreams had swum with images of tiny golden ships and tinier silver knights shifting across a map of the Southern Klashe. They had moved on their own, marching relentlessly onward until they toppled off the table, hitting the floor in splatters of blood and piles of crushed wooden hulls.

*Even my dreams taunt me with my incompetence.*

Or maybe his restless visions had been stirred by the defeat of the *Hawk's Talon*. For most of the night, as the Hálendiian forces engaged the Klashean warship, flocks of skrycrows had swept into the nest atop the Blood'd Tower. The birds had been dispatched by Paktan's forces during the battle. In a stuttering account—not always in correct order—the battle had been relayed to them. Here, all they could do was wait it out, impotent to do more than unroll small scrolls as they arrived—until the streams of crows stopped.

Once his brother's defeat was assured, Jubayr had retreated to his bed to seek some somber rest, his thoughts plagued with worries.

The destruction of the *Talon* struck especially hard following the day's crowning success in routing the *Shayn'ra*. The Fist of God had been ambushed and burned. And while their leader, Tazar hy Maar, had not yet been captured, a canvass continued throughout the city. Tongues wagged, exposing more of the rebel network. It was being torn down piece by piece.

The only other consolation of the day was that the empire's second warship, the *Falcon's Wing*, had slipped the noose in the Breath and continued northward.

Jubayr shook his head, still resting his face in his palms, struggling to accept the tides of fate.

*The gods give, and they take away.*

The knuckles rapped again, too hard to be the soft hands of one of his sixteen chaaen-bound. There was steel in that knock.

He lifted his head from his hands. "What is it?"

A voice called through. "My prince! I must speak with you."

Jubayr closed his eyes, biting back another groan. "Enter!"

He stood to meet Wing Draer. The master of the empire's airborne forces swept in like a thundercloud. On his heels came Shield Angelon.

Jubayr prepared for the worst.

*They wouldn't have woken me with glad tidings.*

Both men approached and dropped to a knee, fists to forehead, still maintaining the pretense that he was emperor. When Jubayr waved them up, they wore matching expressions of fury.

"What's happened?" Jubayr asked.

The Wing lifted a curled scrap of oilskin in his fist. "Another skrycrow arrived. Sent forth by a spy ensconced within the Hálendiian forces. He confirms the *Talon* was destroyed, and your brother captured."

Jubayr now understood the ferocity in Draer's face. They had all hoped that Paktan might have slipped away at the battle's end. Still, Jubayr knew his younger brother would never forsake the *Talon,* even if it was doomed.

"What do we do?" Jubayr asked. "How do we petition and barter for his—"

Shield Angelon cut him off, something the man would never have done with Emperor Makar. Fire danced in the warrior's eye. "They beheaded him. On the deck of the warship. Your brother in chains. A blade wielded by Prince Mikaen in unprovoked malice."

Jubayr stumbled backward. Each statement landed like blows to his chest, leaving him too stunned to breathe.

The Shield and Wing gave him a moment to absorb the tragedy, to let it settle like a stone in his gut. But he knew they awaited instructions from him.

Jubayr covered his brow with a palm and struggled to find his breath again. It took several deep inhalations to regain his voice. When he did, fire burst from his lips.

"We will make them suffer," he gritted out. "For each drop of my brother's blood, so dishonorably spilled, I will lay waste to a hundred of their people."

Both Shield and Wing bowed before his anger.

"We will not wait," Jubayr warned. "Our vengeance starts now."

Draer dropped again to his knee, only this time his deference felt genuine. "What is your bidding?"

"Dispatch orders to the *Falcon's Wing.* Let its captain—my brother Mareesh—know what has transpired. His assault will no longer be tempered or mitigated as instructed. He will unload the full fury of the empire upon the shores of Hálendii. To lay a swath of fire that will burn for ages, a memorial pyre to Paktan."

Draer rose and nodded crisply.

"And that will only be the beginning of their suffering," Jubayr promised.

Shield Angelon dropped next to a knee. "And what of the emperor? He will need to be informed."

Jubayr took another deep breath. He knew how such a grim dispatch would break his father's heart, but it must be done. "Initiate a relay of crows, the swiftest of wing. Let the emperor know what has befallen his son."

Angelon stood briskly. "It will be done."

Jubayr dismissed them both to their respective duties. "I will join you both atop the Blood'd Tower shortly."

He crossed and gathered up the emperor's embroidered white cloak and draped it over his shoulders. It felt heavier than before, but he knew he could carry it.

*For Paktan.*

He snapped the cloak's clasp at his throat, making another silent promise.

*If I ever find that bastard Kanthe—who set this tragedy in motion—his head will fall next.*

# 49

KANTHE STOOD IN the hold of the *Quisl*. The space was windowless and dark, but Malgard let its presence be known. Its heat had turned the ship into an oven. The sulfurous stench of geysers and bubbling clay fouled the air, its reek underlaid by a coppery, sickening taste that sat on the tongue like a dead toad.

*If inhaling these fumes were necessary to induce visions, then I'd rather be blind.*

Still, at least that was *all* that penetrated the ship. The clouds of *lycheens* remained outside, swirling in the steamy air. Kanthe swore he could hear the soft hissing of their poisonous frills brushing the hull and deck.

He stared across at the others in the group, those who would be venturing out into Malgard. To his left, Frell whispered with Pratik. To his right, Cassta held two dark torches—as they all did. Saekl had insisted one of the Rhysians accompany them, though it was unclear whether Cassta was there to protect them or to have some stake in what might be discovered. Likewise, Llyra had ordered a trio of her men to join them. They did not look happy—then again, her men seldom did.

The last member of the party lit his torch. The sudden brightness was momentarily blinding. Rami stalked along the line, passing his flame to their torches.

"Why two torches each?" Frell asked.

"You'll soon wish it was *three*," Rami answered. Still, the prince demonstrated, swinging one of his torches high, the other low. "Watch not just the skies around you, but also the ground at your feet. It's the *lycheens* perched on rocks or hidden behind boulders that often ambush you."

Kanthe squinted at the flames of his torch. "And the fire will hold them at bay?"

Rami scowled. "Their glowing bells are full of lifting gasses, not unlike what fills our ship's balloon. The gasses inside the *lycheens* are also equally combustible. So, while the creatures thrive in the steamy heat—riding updrafts of hot air or living in scalding water—they fear the touch of a flame."

"You've dealt with them before?" Pratik asked.

"Only once. As a boy, when I accompanied my father to Qazen. And we encountered only a small cloud of them at the edge of Malgard, one easily driven away." Rami waved a torch toward the hold's hatch. "Nothing like what we'll face outside."

It was because of Rami's knowledge and experience that Frell had asked him to come along. There was no telling what other dangers or challenges awaited them, threats that the Klashean prince might best know how to handle. Rami had consulted briefly with his sister before agreeing to join them.

Aalia would remain aboard the ketch with Llyra and her men—both to keep the young woman protected and as hostage to Rami's continued good faith.

With a sour expression, Rami reached up and used a free finger to drop the drape of a *byor-ga* coif over his face. "Stay covered," he warned them. "Though a *lycheen*'s frill can burn through fabric, it takes time. When possible, use your gloved fingers to peel them off. And be quick about it."

"Can their frills damage our balloon?" Cassta asked, looking up.

"Possibly, but the *lycheens* notoriously avoid a ship's gasbag. It's believed they can smell and recognize the balloon's lifting gasses. It's theorized that they mistake our gasbags to be one of their own kind."

"A gargantuan one," Kanthe muttered. "No wonder they stay back."

Rami cast him a withering look. "Enough questions. We go now or not at all."

They all quickly covered their faces and slung dark lanterns across their backs.

The prince went down the line one last time, checking that leggings were tucked into boots and shirts under belts. Finally, he nodded. "Let's proceed."

They all crossed to a side hatch, where a thick-shouldered ruffian stood beside a steel crank. Another man held two torches of his own. At their approach, the one beside the crank grunted and started wheeling the door outward.

As soon as the hatch cracked open, a fringe of probing frills wafted and wormed inside. Rami and the other torchbearer waved flames across them and drove them back, burning several frills into charred curls.

"Be quick!" the man at the wheel hollered, cranking even faster. "I'm not holding this open longer than I have to."

The hatch dropped quickly toward the ground. Even before it was halfway open, the group pounded across its planks, led by Rami. They waved torches overhead and jumped off the end of the door to the rocky clay.

As they crossed toward the cliffs, Kanthe breathed heavily, sucking the coif's fabric into his mouth and spitting it out again. The air burned with each breath. The oppressive heat tried to hammer him to his knees. The stench cloyed and gagged his throat.

Kanthe held his torch aloft.

*Lycheens* fled from their combined flames, tucking in their frills.

Steps ahead, Frell stabbed his fiery brand into the air. One of the creatures had dropped toward his head, spinning its drape of poisonous threads. His torch struck the underside of its undulating bell.

The reaction was immediate and dramatic.

The *lycheen* caught the flames in its gullet, flashed brighter, then exploded.

Fiery bits flew everywhere. A few struck Kanthe. Gasping, he swatted and used the stump of his torch to knock the pieces off of him. A burn ignited at his shoulder, near his neck. He twisted, trying to identify the source.

"Hold still!" Cassta yelled. "I've got you."

She rushed to his side, lifted a torch, and plucked a long frill from under the edge of his headgear and tossed it away.

Rami scolded Frell, "Be careful! Attempt to ward them off but not ignite them!"

*Now he tells us.*

As they forged ahead, Kanthe wondered if they shouldn't have asked a few more questions before leaving the ship.

Or at least paid Rami more heed.

One of Llyra's men, Rikard, flanked alongside on the left. He rounded a boulder, paying more attention to the skies than his feet. He ran into a *lycheen* sprawled behind the rock.

Frills exploded around him, enshrouding the man to the height of his shoulders. Tendrils smoked and writhed, burning through fabric. A few must have slithered up a trouser leg, where a hem had slipped free from its boot. Rikard bellowed in pain, flailing wildly. He dropped his torch. It landed atop the *lycheen* at his feet.

The creature blasted apart under him, throwing Rikard back. His clothes caught the erupting flames. Panicked, he rolled to smother them. Or maybe he was trying to escape the pain. He lost his other torch. His headgear got knocked loose.

Kanthe struggled to rush toward him, his feet slipping on the steam-slick clay.

Cassta tossed aside one of her torches and lunged at Kanthe. She grabbed his arm and yanked him back. "Too late."

A score of *lycheens* fell out of the sky, dropping like a glimmering shroud over Rikard. One landed on his exposed face, muffling his scream. His body bucked and writhed within the frills' fiery embrace.

Cassta drew Kanthe away. "We must keep going."

The others realized the same and set off for the cliffs, chased by Rikard's stifled cries. Kanthe kept close to Cassta, who hooked her arm around his waist, defending him with her one torch, while he waved his two.

Kanthe recognized the truth in Rami's earlier words.

*Three* torches were far better than two.

As they ran, the clouds of *lycheens* fell back, either drawn by the prey behind them or simply deterred by their collection of flames. The waning threat allowed Kanthe and the others to reach the pile of boulders at the foot of the cliff.

Still, they didn't slow. They squeezed and climbed their way through the rubble and reached the fractured fissure that cut into the cliff. They rushed into its welcoming darkness, shining their torches all about, pushing back the shadows, searching for any new threat. They clambered deeper until their desperate panting subsided enough for them to catch their breath.

"Hold here!" Rami called out, drawing them to a stop. "The *lycheens* won't pursue us. They shun the darkness, preferring their watery lairs or open air."

The group obeyed him.

"Smother your torches, too," he ordered. "Leave them here. We need to conserve their fuel for the return to the ketch. We'll continue onward with our lanterns."

Kanthe rolled the end of his torch in the tunnel's silt to douse its flame. The others followed suit and stacked the brands against one wall. They all pulled aside their *byor-ga* coifs but kept their headgear in place.

Once everyone had unslung their lanterns, Rami used his torch to light them. Afterward, he kept his torch lit and in hand.

Frell noted this with a raised brow.

"Just in case," Rami said.

Kanthe lifted his lantern and searched down the throat of the tunnel. Cassta did the same. Sadly, she no longer needed to hook her arm around his waist. He rubbed where her hand had rested.

The remaining two of Llyra's men stared the other way, toward the entrance. In unison, they lifted two fingers to their lips, then pointed them high, a salute to their fallen friend. The two brothers were Jester and Mead, neither of which could possibly be their given names, only monikers they had somehow earned.

"Where now?" Rami asked.

Pratik motioned ahead. "We'll see where this leads. And pray the life we lost was not for naught."

With those grim words, they set off into the dark depths.


AN INTERMINABLE TIME later, Frell struggled to solve the dilemma before them. They had clambered, climbed, crawled, and waded their way through the fissure, delving ever deeper—only to reach a difficult crossroad.

Frell lifted his lantern higher, as if that would offer better clarity.

Two tunnels forked ahead. They both dove downward, offering no clue to which way—if either—might lead to their buried Sleeper.

"Perhaps we should split our forces," Pratik suggested.

"Feck that," Mead grumbled, swiping his wet brow. He looked to his brother for agreement. "Right?"

The two were Guld'guhlian—like Llyra—only this pair had the more typical stocky bowleggedness of their people. Their noses were matching knobs of gristle from old breaks.

Jester considered his brother's question and merely shrugged.

Kanthe, though, bolstered Mead's position with far more vigor. "We stick together. We must."

Frell weighed their options. *Haste or caution?* The wiser path forward was to proceed slowly, exploring each tunnel painstakingly and mapping their path along. Or there was Pratik's option. Splitting up and exploring both simultaneously. It would expedite their search, but it would be riskier.

He looked around the group. They stood in torn, silt-caked clothes, all soaked to their waists. Their bodies were scraped, bruised, and bloodied. Their faces streamed with sweat. Their breath panted in the foul air.

The one who seemed least affected stepped forward.

Cassta lifted a palm. Her skin shone with perspiration, and a gash in her brow wept blood into an eye, which she wiped away with the heel of her other hand. "Hold here. Let me assess something first."

She set off for one of the tunnels. Kanthe followed, but she waved him off. "Prince Kanthe, you reek far too much to be close to me."

Crestfallen, Kanthe retreated to the group, sniffing at his clothes.

Frell watched her cross a fair way down one tunnel—then she stopped and raised her lantern. Basked in its glow, she lifted her face. With her eyes closed, she turned four slow circles. Afterward, she returned and did the same pirouette down the other tunnel.

When she joined them again, her face was thoughtful, her head cocked to one side. She pointed to the left tunnel. "We should go that way."

"Why?" Kanthe asked.

"I've noted a slight whiff in the air. Not of damp rock or wet silt. And certainly not the ubiquitous sulfur. It has a bitter quality to it, like burnt oil. Or maybe the taint of a strange alchymical." She gave a small shake of her head. "No matter, it strikes me as unnatural to this place."

Frell lifted his nose, inhaling deeply. The others did the same. They shared looks, but from their confused expressions, no one else sensed the same.

"Are you sure, lass?" Jester asked. "You might just be smelling my brother. His gaseous emissions are just as unnatural to this world."

Mead jabbed an elbow into his brother's ribs. "Like you cast roses out your arse."

Frell nodded to Cassta. "With no way of evaluating otherwise, we might as well follow your lead."

"Or her nose, to be more precise," Kanthe muttered, sniffing again at his body.

As they set off, Frell realized why Cassta—with the sharper senses of a Rhysian—had asked Kanthe to keep away from her. "You do smell ripe," Frell told the prince as he passed.

Rami agreed. "Like a dead boar that's been rotting in the sun."

Kanthe shook his head and followed. "Like you all smell any better."

As they forged ahead, the path grew ever more treacherous. The walls squeezed closer. The roof dropped in jagged shards. One tunnel was so flooded that it required swimming through it, holding their lanterns high.

Along the way, more paths diverged, requiring Cassta's keen senses to guide them onward. Still, after a time, even Frell could smell that bitterness in the air. He also noted that the tunnels had gotten progressively colder, as if they were leaving the volatile lands of Malgard behind and entering an older, more stable region.

Pratik shivered next to him. "We can't continue forever. Not without proper provisions and gear."

Frell could not disagree. They had been traveling for over two bells now—though the passage of time was difficult to judge down here.

*And we still must climb back out, too.*

Even if they turned around now, it would be near to morning when they reached the surface.

This worry weighed on his shoulders. He wondered if they should head back up and come down better prepared. Then a shout rose from where Cassta had taken the lead, flanked by Rami and Kanthe. The three had kept moving steadily, fueled by the bottomless well of strength that only the young possessed.

"Come up here!" Kanthe called back.

Frell and Pratik headed his way, trailed by the Guld'guhlian brothers. Kanthe and the others had stopped at the top of a steep rise in the tunnel. Frell climbed up, sometimes dropping to a hand to keep going. When he reached the top, he was wheezing hard. He straightened with a sharp twinge in his lower back.

Past the rise, the tunnel dropped into a large cavern. The bottom held a small lake, which reflected their light like a mirror. As they all stared down, those waters below began to tremble, then the ground underfoot. A low rumble spread, as if a great beast were warning them away—but it was no subterranean dragon.

"Quake," Frell gasped out as the small tremblor subsided.

They all shared worried looks. Not just about the threat of moonfall. They were all buried far underground. If any of the tunnels should collapse, they'd be lost forever.

"We should not stay down here any longer than necessary," Frell warned, and turned to Kanthe. "What had you so excited a moment ago?"

Kanthe frowned, searching below. "With everyone gathered now, there's too much light. We need to shutter our lanterns."

Curious, Frell pulled the dampers over his light. The others did the same, even Rami doused his torch. As darkness collapsed upon their group, Frell blinked several times, trying to get his eyes to adjust, but he remained blind.

"I still don't understand," Frell said.

"Look beyond the lake," Kanthe whispered. "On the other side of the cave."

He squinted—then saw it, too. A vague blue glow winked out in the darkness, waxing and waning. The light washed in waves over the still waters below.

"Something's definitely over there," Pratik said.

Kanthe nodded. "Must be the Sleeper."

"Or some other threat. We'd best proceed with caution." Frell lifted the shutters from his lantern. Despite his urging of restraint, excitement and anticipation pushed back his weariness and concern. He headed down into the cavern, leading the way. "Watch your footing. The slope is slick."

He picked his way down, only to have Kanthe, Cassta, and Rami go sliding past him, their arms out for balance, skating smoothly down the wet rock. They reached the bottom while Frell was barely a quarter of the way down.

"Wait there!" he called to them.

Frell and Pratik took care, while the Guld'guhlian brothers slid on their backsides to join Kanthe's group. Once together again, they rounded the edge of the lake and closed in on the area of the glow.

As they neared it, the source became clear. A huge copper egg lay half imbedded in the wall. Two curved doors were parted and lifted high, like a pair of metal wings. The light came from inside, pulsing with the regularity of a heartbeat. The bitter tang in the air grew strong, nearly stinging.

They all drew to a stop.

"It's just like Rhaif described," Kanthe extolled with awe.

"Not entirely," Frell said. "According to his story of Shiya's discovery, her copper shell had appeared to be torn open. Ruptured and burnt at the edges. As if something had gone awry with her awakening, possibly damaging her in the process. Whereas this looks intact."

Kanthe started forward.

"Proceed with caution," Frell warned everyone. "We don't know what to expect if we try to waken the Sleeper buried here."

They moved together, shoulder to shoulder. The glow grew brighter as they reached the winged doorway. Frell had to shade his eyes when that light waxed to its fullest.

Kanthe shifted ahead, reaching the threshold first—then stumbled back with a gasp. He grabbed Frell's arm, frantic, too shocked to speak.

Worried, Frell broke free of his grasp and pushed forward. The others crowded at his shoulders. He stared at what that blue glow illuminated.

"It can't be . . ." Frell moaned.

Pratik shook his head in disbelief.

The brothers swore loudly.

Ahead of them, the inside of the egg was in ruins. Glass piping had been shattered into shards across the floor, stuck in pools of dried alchymicals. Copper tanks had been dented to scrap. Even the shell's inner walls hung crookedly.

At the back, a tall crystal cradle—like the crib where Rhaif had first spotted Shiya—lay sideways across the far wall, its lower half crushed to pieces.

But that wasn't the worst of it.

The damaged cradle was *empty*—and the reason lay at their feet.

Sprawled amidst the wreckage was a charred bronze body. That of a man. His head had been caved in, his limbs torn from his torso. Even his chest had been hammered deep in several spots.

"The Sleeper . . ." Frell gasped out with despair. "It's been destroyed."

# 50

KANTHE STEPPED GINGERLY into the copper egg. He kept his shoulders hunched, as if fearful of being attacked by the Sleeper's ghost for his trespass. Still, each time he placed a boot down, glass crunched loudly. He winced at the noise but kept going.

"What are you doing?" Frell called from the entrance.

Kanthe reached his goal. He pointed at the source of the blue glow. A crystal box, cornered in copper, hung crookedly from a conduit bent off the wall. From inside, the pulsing luminosity continued to dim and brighten, as if eternally signaling for help.

*And that's the problem.*

He turned to Frell. "The hue and tinge of this light. Doesn't it remind you of something?"

The alchymist frowned his frustration.

"Shiya's crystal globe of the world," Kanthe explained. "We were guided here because of a glowing blue marker on her sphere, shining deep in the Southern Klashe. A *blue* that matches this glow."

Pratik nodded. "He's right. I'd swear to it."

"Such a light was supposed to indicate where a Sleeper remained intact." Kanthe pointed to the bronze figure. "Does that look undamaged to you?"

"What's your point?" Frell asked.

Kanthe looked up at the crystal cube. "It must be a beacon. One that was never destroyed by whatever force struck here. That's why it's still sending out a signal—a *false* signal." He turned to the others. "Before we leave, we need to destroy it. It's the only good we can make of this entire disaster."

"Why?" Frell asked.

Kanthe exhaled his frustration, trying to explain. "If we extinguish the signal, Shiya's crystal globe should note the change. Like it had with all the other dead Sleepers. If nothing else, it's a way we can signal Nyx and the others that we got here. They may not know we *failed* in securing the Sleeper, but by dousing this light, we can let them know we got this far."

Frell rubbed his chin. "That's true. I'm not sure of the benefit, but it's better than doing nothing."

"We came all this way," Kanthe said. "The least we can do is turn off the light on our way out, ending this farce."

Pratik shook his head. "We shouldn't destroy it."

Kanthe frowned at him. "But—"

Pratik ducked into the egg, too. "You're right that we need to switch it off. But we should find a way to take it with us afterward. Undamaged, if possible. Down the line, with further study, perhaps we can find a way to use it as a means of communication with Shiya."

Cassta glanced at Kanthe, a twinkle in her eyes. "That's an even better idea with a greater possible outcome."

Kanthe felt his cheeks growing flush.

*Why didn't I think of that?*

"Don't look so perturbed," Cassta scolded. "Chaaen Pratik would never have come up with that notion if *you* hadn't made this connection."

"That's right," Pratik agreed.

Cassta kept her gaze on Kanthe. "Remember. True ingenuity seldom comes from one set of lips, but many," she said. "Even lips as pretty as yours."

Kanthe's face grew hotter, and he had to look elsewhere. He waved at the crystal cube overhead. "We should see about getting this down."

"To that end . . ." Jester yanked a hand-ax from a hook on his belt. "I've got some true ingenuity right here."

It ended up not being that simple, but working together, they managed to safely decouple the crystal cube from its mounts and cut it free. As they did, the light flared to a blinding brilliance, then went dark.

"What about the remains of the Sleeper?" Pratik asked.

Frell shook his head. "He's too heavy to haul out on our own. Best to let him rest in his grave for now."

With nothing more they could do, the group prepared for the long journey back to sunlight. Mead picked up the dark cube and hefted it over his shoulder, carrying it in a makeshift sling. Exhausted and still despondent, no one spoke as they set off.

As they climbed out of the cavern, Rami drew alongside Kanthe. The Klashean prince had never said a word upon the discovery of the copper egg. His eyes had remained shadowed the entire time, his brow crossed by deep lines.

Rami stepped closer. He reached a hand toward Kanthe, then dropped it.

"What's wrong?" Kanthe asked—which, considering all that had transpired over the past few days, felt like a stupid question.

Rami frowned. "In truth, I must admit that a part of me still bore doubts about your group's endeavors. But what I saw back there—" He glanced across the cavern. "It challenges all I know of our world."

"I don't blame you. I didn't handle it much better when I was first dragged into it all." He offered Rami a small smile. "Even now, it's sometimes too much for my ale-shrunken brain to fathom."

Rami matched his grin. "Maybe together we can make sense of it."

"I . . . I'd like to try."

Kanthe choked with relief. He hadn't realized how much he had valued their friendship until it was gone. While growing up, he had always had a boon companion at his side: a twin brother with whom he had shared a womb. After his falling-out with Mikaen, Kanthe remained wary of others. He kept everyone at a distance. If the deep bond of twins could be so readily broken, what hope was there for any other close relationships? While Kanthe had found a deep friendship with Jace, such rapport remained rare for him.

Kanthe glanced sidelong at Rami, hoping all could be mended between them. He missed a brother he could call a friend.

Rami caught him looking and must have read his thoughts. "This doesn't mean I'm still not mad at you."

"I get it."

"Though, I may have to declare my anger more obdurately when I'm around Aalia. She'll expect no less."

"I wouldn't have it any other way."

Rami nodded. With the matter settled, the prince raised another, cocking a brow toward Kanthe. "So, what is going on between you and Cassta?"

"Nothing," he blurted out, caught off guard. He then lowered his voice. "She barely knows I exist."

Rami made a noncommittal grunt. "Too bad. I was imagining both of you sharing my bed. I wonder if I proposed such a—"

Kanthe grabbed his arm. "Please don't. I've seen her practicing with her knives. Neither of us would survive."

"If one had to die, I can think of worse ways."

Kanthe looked aghast at him.

Rami elbowed him. "Or it could just be *us* in bed. That's perfectly fine, too."

Kanthe sighed and shook his head, beginning to wonder if friendships were truly worth all the trouble.

The group continued the long trek back through the maze. If anything, the return was more strenuous, as the route climbed ever upward. Still, they made better progress. The path back home had been marked. There was no longer any second-guessing at crossroads. But more importantly, there were no more quakes.

After an interminable time, the distant glow of sunlight flowed around a jagged corner. Kanthe gasped in relief. *Finally.* As he made that turn with the others, the character of the light grew clearer. It flickered and danced along the tunnel walls.

"Is that smoke?" Frell asked, crinkling his nose.

Kanthe smelled it, too. It cut through the ubiquitous stench of sulfur. It smelled like a fiery hearth, only with an acidic tang to it.

Fearing the worst, they all rushed forward.

The smoke thickened as they crossed the last of the tunnel. A dull roaring echoed to them. Desperate for an answer, fearing for the *Quisl* and its crew, they hurried even faster.

But Rami blocked them from leaving. "Grab your torches first and be ready."

Kanthe had nearly forgotten about the clouds of *lycheens* outside. He grabbed two brands and followed the others. The smoke now choked and stung his eyes. The roaring ahead snapped and spat angrily. Still, no one slowed.

They reached the mouth of the tunnel and clambered atop a flat-topped boulder to get a better view. Kanthe gasped as the sight opened. The neighboring forest of Naphtha pines had been set on fire. Flames swirled high, churning smoke far into the sky. Trees exploded with loud blasts as their combustible sap ignited.

"Where's the wingketch?" Pratik yelled over the fire's roar.

Kanthe had already noted the ship was gone. "They must have fled from the fire."

"But what happened?" Jester asked, resting a palm atop his head. "Where's our sodding ride out of this boiling piss pot?"

As if hearing him, a large shadow swept over the cliff and into view overhead. They all looked up. The ship was bathed in smoke. The ketch must have been circling, keeping clear of the flames, waiting for their return. But if nothing else, at least the fires had chased the clouds of *lycheens* from the area.

Kanthe waved his two torches, trying to signal the ketch.

Cassta yanked his arms down. "It's not the *Quisl*."

"What?"

As the smoke wafted clearer for a breath, revealing more of the wyndship, he saw she was right. Its keel was twice as long, its hull three times as wide. Flames blasted from its many forges. As it swept fully over the cliff's edge, its flat stern displayed a prominent pair of gold crossed swords, the Klashean Arms.

"It's an imperial battle barge," Rami said with a note of terror.

Something *twanged* from the boulders ahead of them, sharp enough to pierce the fire's roar. Jester grunted and dropped to a knee. He touched the feathered end of an arrow sticking out of his thigh. Another bolt sliced through his left ear in a spray of blood, sending him toppling over with a grunt of pain.

Rami waved them all back. "Down! On your bellies," he yelled, not in anger but in fear.

Kanthe threw himself flat, knocking the air from his lungs.

Once the others obeyed, too, Rami stepped forward, raising his arms and hollering loudly to the sky, "I am Prince Rami im Haeshan! Fourth son of His Illustriousness, Emperor Makar ka Haeshan. My captors have submitted!" Kanthe lifted his head to peer around.

Shadows stirred from among the boulders and to either side. Overhead, warriors leaped from the ship's deck. Wings snapped wide across their backs. They swept downward, rushing to secure the prince of the realm.

Kanthe looked toward where the *Quisl* had been moored.

*Where did the ketch go? And how did the imperial forces find them?*

He feared the worst.

*Either Llyra betrayed us—or there was a spy with us all along.*

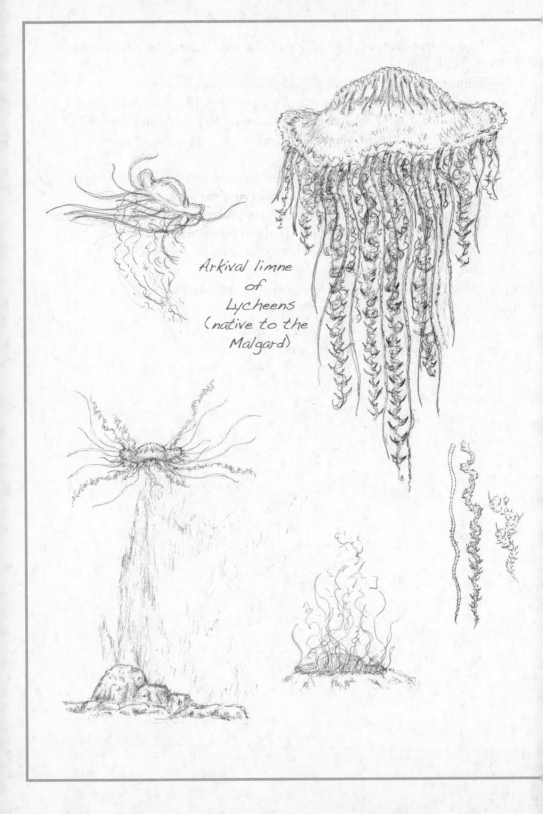

*Arkival limne*
*of*
*Lycheens*
*(native to the*
*Malgard)*

# ELEVEN

# THE TIDES OF
# AGES PAST

*The lifes of the ded onli ende when thei are forgoten. It is the memori of the livyng, pass'd from one age to the necst, that is the onli tru font of immortality. May your well næfre go dri.*

—From the prelude to *The Histories of Lost Heroes*

# 51

DESPERATE, HEART POUNDING, Graylin dashed from one side of the skiff to the other. He searched the dark waters. But there was no sign of Nyx or Daal. The image of Marayn's daughter being dragged off the boat, tangled in clinging tentacles, seared his mind. Though it had only been breaths ago, he knew he had to do something.

He pulled his sword, prepared to dive into the sea, to drown if he must.

*I lost her once in the swamps of Mýr. I won't lose her again.*

"Someone comes," Shiya warned from the stern.

Graylin leaned farther over the waves, looking to see what had alerted the bronze woman.

"Not that way." Shiya pointed toward the distant glow of Kefta.

He didn't see anything—until a closer flicker of flames glimmered through the fog. Voices echoed eerily, calling toward them. Though the words were in Panthean, the threat and anger were clear. From the mists, the outline of the Reef Farer's barge slowly appeared, lit by its firepots. It was flanked by smaller boats.

*They've found us. Somehow learned we were out here.*

Graylin knew the edict for disturbing the Dreamers. While simply being in these waters was dangerous enough, any attempt to reach the *Oshkapeers* below was punishable by death.

Graylin shoved over to Shiya. "Get overboard. Into the waters. Find Nyx and Daal."

Shiya didn't acknowledge his command. She simply stepped over the side and dropped away, vanishing like a bronze anchor into the dark depths. He hoped she could hunt below and somehow find and free Nyx and Daal.

But would that be enough?

As he watched the barge approach through the mists, he found himself holding his breath. How long could Nyx do the same? He finally gasped for air, knowing that answer.

Still, he refused to give up hope.

As the barge drew abreast of him, the other skiffs circled wider, searching the mists. On the deck of the barge, the Reef Farer's consort, Ularia, stepped to the bow, looming over Graylin. Her emerald eyes sparked with a furious fire.

Behind her, ten men stood in leather armor, threatening with silver-tipped tridents.

Graylin realized he still had his sword in hand and quickly sheathed it. He sought for an explanation as to why he was alone in these waters and latched on to the first that made any sense.

"Why do you disturb my prayers?" he stammered out. He silently added an actual entreaty to the gods, fearing Ularia might have witnessed Shiya stepping overboard.

The woman frowned, her narrowed gaze casting over the waters. "Where are the others?"

"What do you mean? I left everyone back in Kefta." He let his panic shine through. "Has something befallen them?"

"A party of your people were spotted from the cliffs above Kefta. Aboard a skiff. Headed in this direction." Ularia glanced back toward the glow of the town. "I had my personal guard sweep the tribute grounds. None of your other companions could be found."

Graylin shook his head. "I can't explain that. Maybe they sought a quiet place to rest. It's been a long day. I came here for some solitary reflection after so much death. This place felt sacred and holy."

"You shouldn't be here," Ularia warned. "This is *our* hallowed sea."

Graylin took a deep breath, trying not to stare into those waters, his heart still in his throat. He remembered how Meryk had explained that the Reef Farer's consort was one of three *Nyssians,* those with the gift for preserving the history of the Crèche and its people. A talent, it was said, that was gained by the first of their sisterhood communing with the Dreamers.

*No wonder she is so furious at this trespass.*

"I meant no disrespect," he pleaded. "Only quiet reflection and prayer."

She looked only slightly mollified.

He couldn't stop himself from searching the waves. He prayed for Nyx to be safe, but he also willed her to stay below. For violating those depths, she would die above as surely as she would from drowning below.

"With your permission," he said, "I'd like to spend more time here. I've not finished my prayers or absolutions."

"I don't care about your Noorish ways," she said with acid on her tongue. "You'll return with us."

Ularia waved to her men. They quickly tethered his skiff and its two orksos to the barge and forced Graylin aboard at the point of a spear. With no way of arguing otherwise, Graylin could only watch as the barge swept around, drawing the other skiffs in its wake.

As they set off for Kefta, he stared past the stern to the quiet waves, hoping against hope.

*Please be alive, Nyx.*

# 52

NYX DROWNED IN darkness.

After being yanked out of the skiff, she had struggled to hold her breath, fighting the clinging arms that held her in their constricting embrace. She lost both battles. The tentacles writhed and tightened, as if anticipating her every move. Suckers clung and shifted, cupping her everywhere.

All she managed was a brief glimpse over her shoulder. The creature— whether one of the Dreamers or its defenders—hovered at her back. A ring of fist-sized black eyes circled a bulbous, nearly billowing mass. It looked more like a spill of oil in the water. Crowning it, as if trying to hold that oil in place, was a spiked carapace or shell.

Those black eyes stared back at her, unblinking. A tracery of lights streaked through its dark mass. They flickered, blinked, and streamed in some myste- rious endless pattern as she was pulled deeper.

She noted the same lights coursing through the water, marking the unseen passage of more of the beasts. A thrashing in the distance, illuminated briefly by another's shine, revealed she wasn't the only one fighting in these waters.

*Daal . . .*

In that moment, misery weakened her. Too weak and despondent, she could no longer hold the sea at bay. The last of her breath burst from her lips. Salty water flooded into her mouth, down her throat, into her lungs. She gasped, her chest heaving, instinctively still searching for air. Her vision constricted toward a point. Her body grew heavier and lighter at the same time.

Next came the pain.

She writhed in that embrace, still unable to move. Where suckers stran- gled her neck and latched on to her wrist, something pierced her flesh. The same stabbed her inner thighs, gouging through clothes and skin. From those wounds, something pushed into her. She felt them. Tendrils far smaller than the tentacles. They wormed through her veins, rooting deep and everywhere, until she was as much part of the beast riding her as she was her own self.

As this happened, a strange sense of tranquility swelled, slowly dampen- ing the pain in her limbs and throat until she felt only numbness. Even her chest stopped fighting the seas, the water weighing heavily in her lungs. She expected death to come, but it was held at bay. Her vision cleared—though there was little to see but the zip and spin of those strange blinking lights. Her head also lightened as a slow realization grew.

*I'm not drowning.*

Whatever had writhed through her body was sharing its air. She had been taught that sea creatures could draw life from the waters around them—through gills or thin skin. The beast that held her must be doing the same, only passing some of that sustaining life into her.

Amazement and terror warred within her.

She remembered seeing the scars on Daal's neck and wrists.

*This is what caused them.*

She stopped her fighting as she was drawn ever deeper. The pressure pained her ears, coursing down the back of her throat. As if sensing this, suckers shifted to the sides of her head and cupped over her ears. They sealed tight and pinched back, withdrawing the pressure from her ears. The pain faded quickly.

As she fell downward, she felt as if she were floating in the dark depths of the void between stars. Blackness surrounded her. Lights burst and dashed all about, marking the passage of these strange creatures.

*Are these the* Oshkapeers?

She remembered Daal declaring as much when he was yanked from the skiff.

After an interminable time, light bloomed under her, vague and illusory at first, then clearer, illuminating a seabed. The glow etched a convoluted labyrinth across the sandy bottom. Past it, the waters boiled fiercely. It steamed from tall rocky cylinders, casting up black smoke, as if the Urth were burning below in an unending furnace.

As she was towed to the bottom, her toes were left hovering above the sand. The source of the glow became clear. It rose from a maze of tall reefs, climbing in rocky ramparts four times her height. The ridges were phosphorescent and luminous, like the icy roof of the Crèche, only shining in hues innumerable and unnameable.

Strewn across it all, large skeletal growths sprouted everywhere, forming fantastical horns and branching fans. Softer creatures—blurring the line between plant and animal—waved bulbous limbs or shivered with delicate fronds. No matter where she turned, life stirred, swam, and flickered.

But most of what thrummed throughout the reefs were the glowing *Oshkapeers,* crowned by their whorled and spiked carapaces. There were hundreds scouring the reefs, dashing about or hovering in place, their tentacles stirring in the currents. They varied in size—from ones no bigger than a melon to giants that would dwarf a bullock.

Certainty grew in her.

*These must be the Dreamers.*

She barely had time to absorb all of this when another tentacle-shrouded figure dropped next to her. Daal lay cradled and trapped in another *Oshkapeer's* embrace. Like her, he no longer fought, accepting his fate. But his expression was horrified.

She looked where he was staring, wide-eyed and open-mouthed. A dark leafy hump lay in the white sand. One of the *Oshkapeers* crawled over it, using its tentacles to gently pull aside those leaves. A pale arm fell loose, its length inscribed with tiny whorls of ink.

Nyx spasmed with recognition and shock.

*One of the dead from Iskar.*

The creature shifted over to the arm and lowered a beaklike mouth and began slashing through the tissue, stripping flesh from bone. The *Oshkapeer* sucked in great curls of meat, while inhaling the smoke of dark blood.

Nyx wanted to cover her mouth in horror, but her arms were trapped. Only now did she spot the other mounds scattered all around. More of the *Oshkapeers* feasted on the dead, ripping and tearing. As her eyes adjusted to this appalling reality, she recognized that the rocks and lumps in the sand were *bones.* Even the reefs, while mostly coral and rock, still showed layers of ancient skulls, crushed rib cages, and the knobbed ends of long femurs.

All around, the gorging continued, a macabre counterpoint to the tribute feast in Kefta. With that memory, she struggled to balance the gentle care of the loved ones above with the savagery below.

Nyx had to turn away.

As she did, a late arrival crashed into the reef. Bronze flashed and reflected the glow as Shiya tumbled down the side of a steep ridge, gouging a path of destruction in her wake. Nyx pictured the bronze woman diving from the skiff, coming to their rescue.

Shiya rolled off the reef's bottom and skidded through sand and bones.

Life fled in all directions with flips of tails and squirts of ink. Even the *Oshkapeers* leaped off their dinners, swirling away from the intruder. The one holding Nyx drew her to the side, toward Daal, as if trying to protect her.

But that defensive posturing lasted only a heartbeat or two. Responding to some unknown signal, the beasts swarmed back in, ready to defend their reef from this strange trespasser. They struck Shiya from all sides, tangling around her limbs, pulling her off her feet, denying her any traction in the battle. Still, Shiya was incredibly strong. She freed an arm and began ripping other tentacles loose—until a bullock-sized *Oshkapeer* shot over the edge of the reef and struck her broadside. Its arms were twice as thick as Shiya's thighs. They wrapped her completely, leaving only her head exposed.

With its prey captured, the giant pulsed its way back over the ridge.

Nyx realized the direction it was headed.

*The boiling seas . . .*

According to Shiya's tale of her trek across the seabed to reach Iskar, even her strong form would succumb to that molten heat.

Panicked, Nyx elbowed an arm free. As she thrust her limb out, she caught sight of the tendrils running from her wrist over to the sucker that had been fixed there. Curls of blood wafted from the penetrating wound. She ignored it and reached to Daal, grabbing his bare shoulder.

On contact, her fingertips ignited with fire. Daal arched back within his embrace of his *Oshkapeer*. His body glowed. The tentacles briefly loosened their grip, as if sensing the flare of energy inside him. Daal hung there, threads running into his neck, wrists, and thighs—then the tentacles closed back tight.

Daal's flames filled her, drawn by her fear for Shiya. Though she had no air to sing, she let her body burn in the water, burnishing a glow from her skin. She willed a single word, staring at Shiya being dragged away.

It burst from her in clear command.

**No.**

The strength of it momentarily unnerved her. Her control tremored. Her glow faded. But she drew more from Daal, trusting he could handle it. She steadied both her will and her power.

Still, she had been heard.

The giant *Oshkapeer* who clutched Shiya had come to a stop, hovering at the reef's ridgeline. It turned in a slow circle, staring back at her with its ring of black eyes.

She didn't know what to do or what to expect.

She simply tightened her grip on Daal, readying herself. But it did no good.

Nothing could prepare her for what came next.

IF NYX HAD the capacity to hold her breath, she would have, but her lungs were full of water. A long impasse stretched. The giant *Oshkapeer* still held Shiya trapped atop the reef, but it looked ready to jet away toward those boiling seas at any moment.

Movement, closer at hand, drew her eye.

The ridgeline before her shivered and glowed brighter. From every crevice and pock in the rock, around every shard of bone, small tendrils boiled forth. They wafted long and high, so thick in number that they obscured the reef. They looked like the threads that burrowed into her veins, but these shone with all the colors of the reef.

The storm of glowing tendrils crossed over and fell atop Nyx and Daal, as if trying to smother the fire they shared. She cringed, expecting the threads to dig into her skin, but they only lightly landed, dabbing everywhere, settling like snowflakes across her body. A few drifted up her nostrils, so thin and gentle that she barely felt them.

What she did feel was an overwhelming sense of peace. Her head lolled back. She sensed an inquiry forming like mist inside her head. Her eyes, unbidden, rolled to stare at Shiya. Curiosity piqued through her, but it was not born of her own inquisitiveness. Something wanted to know more about Shiya. A dark undercurrent of dread and fear underlay that interest.

Nyx sought a way to share what she knew. Though her eyelids remained open, she let her mind drift through her experiences with the bronze woman. All of them. From when they first met in the woodland town of Havensfayre—when Shiya had helped Nyx ward off a pair of steel-helmed scythers—to Shiya's defense of Iskar, rising like a bright sun from the sea. But memory was a fickle master. Nyx also flashed to Shiya snapping the assailant's neck on Kefta.

Still, Nyx felt sharing this was right, both the good and the bad.

Curiosity dissolved inside her. She felt a gentle probing, a sifting through all of her memories. She pictured the *Oshkapeer* peeling the leaves of kelp around the dead body to expose the richness within. This felt like that. She wanted to fight such a violation, but the gentleness and tenderness stemmed her apprehension. She let it be done, exposing herself fully.

Her eyes fell upon Daal. He met her gaze.

*Is the same happening to him?*

With that passing thought, gazing upon each other, enmeshed together in that glowing web of tendrils, she suddenly found herself staring out his eyes. She saw herself in the embrace of the *Oshkapeer.*

As that happened, Daal's memories flooded through her. She had experienced a fleeting sense of this before, but now it was a torrent, filling every space and sense. She was Daal, experiencing flashes of his life.

—*learning how to repair a net, sitting on the knee of his father, the salt bright on a breeze off the sea.*

—*shivering in his mother's embrace as a lone raash'ke screamed over the village.*

—*feeling the tiny fingers of Henna wrapping around his thumb, her giggling breath smelling of milk, and the ache of love in his heart for his sister.*

—*fumbling in the dark with a woman's bare breasts, then a moment later, a streak of humiliation, a shame buried deep.*

—*seeing Nyx on the beach for the first time, watching her come toward him, her hands up to reassure him. Awe and fear tremble through him.*

The images began to quicken, flowing ever faster, backward and forward through his life. Eventually it trimmed down to just snippets of emotion or sensation. Still, it all blurred into one overwhelming sense: of Daal's warm-heartedness and honorable spirit.

Finally, it all faded away. She was allowed to settle back into her own skin. She couldn't tell if a day had passed or a heartbeat. She let her fingers fall from Daal's shoulder, but her gaze never left him, seeing him in a whole new light.

*Yet not truly.*

Down deep, she had already known who he was.

As Daal stared at her, his eyes looked as huge as hers felt. Had he also experienced the same shuffling and sharing of memories?

She finally had to look away, feeling naked, but also not regretting any of it. She focused instead on *why* she had traveled down here and risked so much. She closed her eyelids and pictured Daal on Iskar's plaza. She heard his words again, about how the Dreamers knew more about the history of the Crèche, and more importantly about the raash'ke. She also relived Daal's shame, remembering his description of his first encounter with the Dreamers.

*They touch me. Then throw me away. Not worthy.*

Maybe it was his acute pain that pierced through to the *Oshkapeers* the strongest. To address it, to explain it, images flowed into her from many eyes. She briefly became a multitude.

*—she thrashes her mighty body amidst bloody waves, her body pierced by scores of spears.*

*—she swims, flicking fin and tail, driven by an unslakable bloodlust toward a figure struggling in the dark, dragged deeper by an orkso.*

*—she continues following the hunt, hopping from one body to another.*

Nyx knew what this was.

A recounting of Daal's chase from six months ago.

But similar to sensing the entirety of the young man next to her, she divined a meaning behind the blur of energy and purpose. She felt the huge kefta being lured into the deepwater seas near the Dreamers, driven to strike a tail across a certain skiff. She saw how the sharks were equally drawn, like pieces on a board of Knights n' Knaves.

A dawning realization grew. It wasn't an *accident* that Daal had ended up with the Dreamers. *They had herded him here.*

A question coalesced inside her.

*Why?*

Though unspoken, it was answered.

An image filled her head from Daal's past, from his first encounter with the Dreamers. He again hung in the embrace of an *Oshkapeer*, shrouded in tendrils.

While still imbued with those foreign senses, Nyx watched that glow inside him be changed. Tendrils cast weaves of silvery energy into him, molding his fire, enriching it brighter, tamping it into his bones and blood. It turned him into a great storehouse, far stronger than before.

She struggled to accept what she was being shown, both awed and horrified.

*They had drawn Daal down here to fortify his gift, forging him like hot steel, hardening him into a sword.*

She flashed to a moment ago, when she had gripped Daal's shoulder, drawing his fire into her. Certainty firmed in her. She suddenly understood *why* the Dreamers had changed him into a great font of power.

*To ready him—for me.*

# 53

DAAL STRUGGLED TO anchor himself in his body. Moments ago, he had been washed through Nyx's life. It came in waves, unfettered by time and jumbled. He experienced her life as a young girl, where the world was just a blur of light and shadows. He joined her as she trekked through dark swamps atop the broad back of a great beast. He climbed the steps of a school alongside her and joined her at the supper table, surrounded by the love of her dah and two brothers.

Yet, two details struck him the hardest.

He flashed again to those school's steps. He stared up at the endless blue skies and the miracle of a fiery sun. His heart welled at such a bright and sunlit world.

But even that brilliant memory was shadowed by what came next: the deaths, the bloodshed and terror, being driven from her home and all she had ever known.

Even now, Daal grieved for her, but in the salty sea, he could not tell if he shed any tears.

Still, like Nyx, he found one sustaining comfort, a love that was boundless and pure. He again felt the warmth of wings enfolded around him, the gentle nuzzle of a soft nose, the quiet pining of a song shared together, merging two hearts into one.

Daal stared over at Nyx. She was locked in a tight embrace, but he knew that was not who she wished were holding her now.

*No wonder you risked so much to come here . . .*

Over the past days, he had repeatedly warned her away from these seas, but now he understood. Not only about her winged brother, but also about his own first journey to the Dreamers.

While they were bonded together, Daal had experienced the wordless communication between Nyx and the Dreamers. While he hadn't followed everything, he still understood enough to know he had been changed down deep, as if the *Oshkapeers* had known he would be needed to help Nyx.

*And maybe they had.*

Like all Pantheans, Daal had been taught the sacred scriptures, which claimed the *Oshkapeers* were unmoored by time, drifting on the tides between ages past and what was yet to be.

For now, he pushed down his misgivings about his transformation. Especially as Nyx started to pressure the Dreamers for more knowledge about the raash'ke. The pain of her loss still ached his heart and must have reached the *Oshkapeers,* too.

The Dreamers responded. It felt like a dam breaking, as if they had been waiting to share what they knew. Images flooded into him—into both of them. It came swiftly and in a deluge that could not be stopped. He struggled against that surge. It was too much, filling him to bursting.

He gasped water from his lungs. He writhed in the tentacles. Still, he could not escape the history of the Crèche pouring into him. It was delivered through millions of eyes and as many lives. It was confusing, with no linearity to it.

Nyx struggled the same. Together, they were tossed and rolled wildly across the stormy passage of time. Still, moments struck clearer, images that burned brighter, possibly stoked by Nyx's yearning, focusing on what she wanted to know.

—*Daal flies high through the air, under the icy arch of the Crèche. He stares down at his mount, at the spread of wide wings to either side. He is saddled atop a raash'ke!*

Shock threw him back into the tumult of history, until he dropped into another scene.

—*he hikes toward a village. Overhead, more raash'ke ply the skies. Others hop along streets or perch on walls. Children play among them, especially with the smallest of the beasts.*

Time slipped, falling backward now. Daal sensed the passage of eons. A new image spun into focus.

—*he sees his hands, tapping blood from a leathery wing.*

Time snapped forward again.

—*he stares down at a tentacled beast on a table, its arms writhing, suckers trying to grab at his fingers. He plunges blood through a sharp needle into the creature.*

Daal fell briefly back into himself, as if allowed to come up for air. Though he didn't understand fully, he knew he had been shown the birth of the *Oshkapeers.* The Dreamers had been forged in the past as surely as they had done to him—transformed by the potent blood of the raash'ke.

Then he was dragged back down into the roiling flood. He became a stone, skipping across water, traveling forward in time again.

—*he lies on his back and lifts a broken hand, the same hand as before, only far older and covered in blood. He heaves through his last breaths. A shadow looms behind him. Terror etches through him.*

The horror of that moment, of that death, shoved Daal away. The next images flashed through him quickly, only glimpses of a past, jumping ever forward.

—*a clutch of raash'ke bursting away in a panic of wings.*

—*another fighting in the air, as if trapped by an unseen net.*

—*he's a girl, fleeing down a street, a winged silhouette pursuing her.*

—*he's a Reef Farer, wearing a heavy stone circlet, staring across the ruins of a village, his feet standing in a pool of blood.*

Daal returned to his body again, his chest heaving, but only pumping water. He remembered flying atop a raash'ke, full of exhilaration and joy. His fingers curled in the water, as if still trying to reach for those ancient reins again.

With a jolt of recognition, he realized that Neffa's saddle matched the one mounted atop the raash'ke.

*Is that where the gear came from, adapted from a past when the raash'ke were our allies?*

Even living through those brief moments, he had trouble imagining such a time. Still, it was clear something had corrupted the raash'ke, turning them into winged monsters. The Dreamers seemed to hint at the source. Throughout the last images, he had sensed a shadow looming over all those glimpses. It was the same shadow—underlaid by the same terror—from earlier, when a man had died on his back.

Daal cringed in the embrace of the tentacles.

*Who or what cast that shadow?*

The answer didn't come from the Dreamers. Though Nyx couldn't speak, he shared her memories. He flashed to when she had fought off the bat that had grabbed Henna. Through her senses, he felt the dark presence lurking behind the greater mind of the raash'ke horde. She had even given it a name.

*The spider.*

Nyx glowed brighter next to him, fury stoking her fire. Whoever or whatever that spider was, it had stolen Bashaliia from her.

She cast out a single word, a fiery demand.

**Who?**

The question seemed to quake through the Dreamers. The mesh of glowing threads shivered over his body. For a moment, it felt as if the tendrils were about to withdraw, that the *Oshkapeers* would refuse to answer.

But the threads settled again.

An image swirled and formed inside his skull. It was the same memory from before, as if the Dreamers were repeating themselves.

—*Daal lies on his back again, lifting a bloody hand, knobbed and thinned by age. With his final gasps of life, he senses another's approach. A shadow looms over him, sparking terror.*

Only this time, Daal was not allowed to escape. He was held there for that last breath of the dying man.

*—his arm drops as death envelops him. The world darkens to its end—then brightens for just a moment. A blurry torch of reflected light passes over his face, coming from the shadow behind him. It coalesces into five fingers and a hand.*

Daal thrashed with recognition, tearing himself out of the past. Still, the last image persisted, burning across his brain, branding it there forever.

*The hand was made of shining bronze.*

# 54

WHILE THE WATERS remained warm, Nyx's body had gone cold. The glow from her skin dimmed as she stared over at Shiya. Her bronze body was still wrapped in powerful tentacles.

Nyx knew it wasn't Shiya's hand that had formed over the dead man's face. The palm had been far broader, the fingers more thickly knuckled. It was the hand of a man.

Still, there was no mistaking the truth.

*The spider was another Sleeper.*

She tried to fathom his existence, how he came to be in the Crèche. A thousand questions filled her. He clearly had arrived countless millennia ago and corrupted the raash'ke. But the ancient alchymist who had died had kept a secret, burying it deep under dark waters.

She stared through the mesh of glowing tendrils to the spread of reefs, to the teeming life, to the hundreds of Dreamers skimming these waters, creatures who shared a lineage with the raash'ke, but who diverged along a different path.

She pictured the blood being infused into the specimen on the table.

*Was the alchymist's creation of the* Oshkapeers *happenstance, or had he known what was coming?*

She had no way of knowing. She doubted even the Dreamers could answer it—but there was one question they could. She gathered the last of Daal's fire and cast it out in a fiery plea.

**Where is he?**

She waited, bracing herself for another rush of preserved memories. But nothing happened. She didn't know if the *Oshkapeers* were holding back or if she was wrong about them knowing the answer. Trapped underwater, they were likely limited in their reach.

Finally, a memory formed, freshened by cold winds and lit by stars.

*—atop a raash'ke, she flies high above an ice cliff. She follows her mate, who wings ahead of her. Below, sections of the cliff had calved away long ago, crashing down to a plain of cold and barren rock. In the distance, she spies a massive crack across that endless slab of stone, splitting and dividing as it spreads outward from the cliffs of ice. From its depths, a fiery glow lights the landscape, ruddy and threatening. She shies away.*

Time flitted forward.

*—she glides over a glittering desert of fallen stars.*

*—she fights winds that howl through peaks as jagged as shark's teeth.*

*—she watches her mate head on foot across a shattered landscape, leaving a crumple of broken wings behind him. Her heart aches. Her mate waves for her to abandon him and return to the Crèche. She knows she must. As she turns away, far in the distance, something glitters under the icy shine of a full moon.*

Before Nyx could spy more, she was jolted back into her body, but it was not of her own volition. Her return felt like dismissal. Or maybe prohibition. The underlying sentiment was one of warning, of overwhelming danger.

The message was clear.

*Never go there.*

For now, Nyx let this slip behind her. Instead, she focused on the worry closer at hand, one nearer to her heart. She pictured the massive fiery crack in the stony landscape. It had to be the Mouth of the World. According to Daal, it was where the raash'ke roosted.

*And where Bashaliia must have been taken.*

Her fear for him was bright enough that she needed no flames to convey her need to know more, to discover a way to reach him.

The Dreamers responded, pulling her into a flurry of memories, a cascade of horrific deaths. But they all started the same way, at the same spot:

*—she stands at the prow of a skiff pulled by orksos. The green seas ahead crash against a wall of broken ice, marking the farthest western edge of the Ameryl Sea. The cliff is pocked with fissures and caves. She heads for the largest opening.*

From there, time lines and lives diverged into a chaos of misadventures, tragedies, and death. They all marked hundreds of attempts to navigate beyond the Crèche, to travel under the ice to reach the Mouth. Explorers were boiled in water, frozen under a crush of ice, tumbled over bottomless falls, or sucked down endless chutes. Others drowned or starved or took their own lives while lost forever in the labyrinth of ice tunnels.

Nyx experienced them all.

Still, the multitude of deaths and stories blurred together, slowly forming a map, outlining a path through that maze, until finally . . .

*—she rides an orkso down a tunnel whose walls are lit by a fiery light. She hangs over the saddle, barely able to lift her head. An arm drags through the water next to her, leaving a trail of blood. She is near to death. The faithful orkso under her struggles with a torn wing. She had lost her skiff, both brothers, and the other three orksos. With no other choice, no way back, she lets the orkso pull her the last of the way. The walls of ice fall to either side. The roof vanishes above. She glides out of*

*the tunnel into a river that rides over rapids into a great ravine. She stares up as her life fades out. Far above, distant stars shine and glitter like ice. She finds little satisfaction, only tired relief as she dies.*

Nyx returned to her body. A map—the only path through the labyrinth—burned in her mind. Its route seared into place, never to be forgotten. Still, she wanted to know more. She struggled to impassion her need, her plea.

But it did no good.

The lattice of glowing tendrils withdrew from her skin, her body. They wound back to the reef, reeling back into the heart of it. As much as she wanted to continue the communion, she knew why it had abruptly ended. The Dreamers had instilled one last sense. It burned inside her: an urgency, a heavy press of time, underpinned by a well of grief, of love lost.

She understood the *Oshkapeers'* last warning.

*I must hurry or lose Bashaliia forever.*

She turned to the side. The shroud of tendrils had shed from Daal, too. He stared over at her. She swore that she could feel the pound of his heart in her own chest. He had also sensed that urgency.

*We must go.*

The Dreamers gleaned her desire. Tentacles tightened around her, and with a strung pulse of its body, her *Oshkapeer* surged upward. She tilted her chin down, searching below. Daal followed, safely ensconced in tentacles.

Still, she looked until she spotted Shiya. She worried the Dreamers—considering their animosity toward figures of bronze—might drag her to a molten death. But the giant *Oshkapeer* swirled up after them, hauling Shiya's heavy body in their wake.

Relieved, Nyx turned away—until movement along the seafloor drew her eye back again. From this height, the full expanse of the reef glowed below. As she watched, the entire labyrinth lifted and shifted huge branches across the sand. The largest mass of reef rolled enough to expose a huge black eye, staring up at her, shining with silvery fire, watching her depart.

Then the eye sank away under a brow of rock and bone. The rest of its limbs, covered in coral, settled back to the sand.

She gaped at the vast spread of the reef, recognizing it now for what it really was: one ancient and massive *Oshkapeer.* The queen of them all. Maybe the very first. She pictured the ancient alchymist infusing raash'ke blood into a small tentacled beast.

*Was this that same creature?*

Either way, she understood why this *Oshkapeer* had been forged.

*To be an undying sentinel against the darkness.*

Nyx warmed her body and cast down one last message, imbuing it with all her gratitude, knowing the long vigil that this Dreamer had kept for ages on end.

*Thank you . . .*

# 55

DAAL KNEW SOMETHING was wrong when they reached the brighter water. Rather than being drawn to the surface and returned to the skiff, he and the others continued coursing through the seas, staying deep. The Dreamer that gripped Daal spun as it traveled, twirling all its black eyes, likely searching for threats.

Daal's head swirled dizzily.

Still, he appreciated such caution when he caught a glimpse of a pod of pickkyns sweeping below him, undulating their long bodies. Thankfully, the large shadows vanished away.

The three of them sped onward, clutched by their caretakers.

Daal searched around.

*Where are they taking us?*

He imagined Graylin must be panicked, certain they were dead. But there was nothing Daal could do to rectify the matter. They were all at the mercy of the *Oshkapeers*.

Daal could not even fathom how long he and Nyx had been down here. It felt like a thousand lifetimes. He expected to find Iskar fallen into dusty ruins by the time they surfaced.

As they traveled, his head still throbbed, blurring all that had been shown him. So much history, so many lives. Most of it was already fading, like waking from a dream. He would try to grasp a piece only to have it dissolve away.

*Maybe that's for the best.*

He could not possibly hold that entire history in his head without going mad. Still, the most important stories remained, etched deep into his bones. He knew the raash'ke had once been companions, working in harmony with the people of the Crèche. Until they were corrupted by a figure of bronze.

He twisted enough to see Shiya being hauled by a giant *Oshkapeer*.

*Can she truly be trusted?*

With no way of knowing, he turned back to the sweep of the seas. He caught sight of Nyx coursing on his left. He knew what preoccupied her mind and heart. While much had faded, he could still touch the love she felt for Bashaliia. It ached through him. He knew where she intended to go next.

It burned in his mind, a fiery map of a labyrinth that led to the Mouth of the World. That path was scorched in place, never to be forgotten. It felt so branded into him that he suspected even his children would know it.

This last thought crinkled his brow.

He wondered if that was what had happened to the first *Nyssian*—when Nys Pephia communed with the Dreamers centuries ago. While Daal felt all that history slipping away, perhaps Pephia was able to retain it. He didn't know how that could be. Perhaps she was uniquely talented. Or maybe the Dreamers had changed her, like they had him, sculpting Pephia's mind to be able to hold the entire history of the Crèche, to even pass it to future generations. The *Nyssians* certainly had the innate ability to sense those men who had the proper seed for their future daughters.

Daal shook his head, resigned that he would never know. It was all beyond him. Besides, he had enough to worry about. Most importantly—

*Where are we being taken?*

The answer came as they reached shallower water. The sandy seabed rose under them, forcing them to the surface.

Daal broke through the waves. Though blinded by the spray, he caught glimpses of high red cliffs and a white stretch of beach. Through his waterlogged ears, he heard distant music, even fainter laughter.

It was the island of Kefta.

The *Oshkapeer* did not slow, riding the surf, jetting him toward the shore. Its spiked shell led the way, like the prow of a sea god's boat. Once the *Oshkapeer* was close enough, Daal was whipped around and tossed toward the beach. He rolled and tumbled out of the water and across the sand.

He lay stunned for a moment on his back.

From the corner of his eye, he saw Nyx discharged just as roughly.

Then his body spasmed violently. He remembered this from his first communing with the Dreamers. He rolled onto his side—and just in time. His body wracked hard, gushing seawater out of his mouth. Still unable to breathe, he got on his hands and knees and continued to heave, pouring a river from his lips and nostrils. His lungs and throat were on fire, scoured by the salt, by the violence of the expulsion. He kept gagging and hacking until finally he was able to catch a clean breath.

He wanted to remain where he was, but he crawled over to Nyx, who was similarly afflicted. She was hunched over her knees. Her spine was an arch of agony. Water streamed and coughed and choked out of her. Tears washed the salt from her eyes. Eventually she sagged, gasping, able to breathe. But she trembled all over.

He drew her into his arms and pulled her onto his lap. She stiffened, possibly fearing his touch. He gathered her closer, passing some of his fire into her, letting it warm through her.

"Wait it out," Daal said. "It'll end."

She hung in his arms, still occasionally coughing, spilling more seawater. He rocked her gently, like he did with Henna whenever she was overwrought or scared.

Splashing drew his attention to the sea. Shiya waded out. Clearly her *Oshkapeer* was too large to get close to the beach and had dumped her farther out to sea. Not that it mattered to the bronze woman. She did not need to breathe, nor did she have lungs to clear.

She strode over to them. Her glassy eyes shone with concern. Her words were tender and quiet. "Will she be all right?"

He nodded. "Give her a few more breaths."

Daal forced his arms to relax, realizing they had tightened at Shiya's approach. The Dreamers' terror of such figures still echoed inside him.

Nyx finally sat up on her own. She stared down at her wrists. The bleeding had already stopped, as he knew it would. Some property of the *Oshkapeers'* sting encouraged clotting and healing.

He fingered the soft scabs on his neck, knowing he would need to hide them, like he had before. Not that such marks had any meaning, as no one living had communed with the Dreamers since Nys Pephia. Still, their matching wounds would be hard to explain.

He glanced down the empty beach. A shoulder of the headlands separated them from Kefta's bay. They would have to hike and circle around it to reach town. But at least they were alone for now, able to collect themselves.

After a time, as they rested, the mists overhead bloomed from pale blue to bright spatters of crimson, yellows, and greens, marking the start of a new day.

Daal stirred. "We should get going."

Nyx nodded. "I must find Graylin. I don't know if he's still out at sea or if he gave up and returned to town."

Shiya stood nearby, a bronze sentinel in the sand. She frowned at them, tilting her head slightly.

Nyx must have noted her expression. "Shiya, what's wrong?" she asked.

The woman's gaze swept between the two of them. "Just now, you were both speaking Panthean. I could not follow what you said."

Nyx frowned, touching her lips.

Daal backed a step, glancing over at Nyx. He switched to Noorish, a tongue that he normally found challenging, but now it felt as if he had been born to it. "Shiya is right. I had been speaking Panthean. So were you. How could that be?"

"When we were communing, joined together with the Dreamers . . ." Nyx stared hard at him. "We shared our lives."

He winced, knowing how much he had learned about her. She'd surely gained as much knowledge about him.

He switched to Panthean again, certain she would understand. "Clearly, we shared *more* than just our lives."

Nyx kept alongside Daal as they circled around the headlands. The town's large bay opened before them, crowded with boats of all sizes. A few strands of music still flowed from the festival, greeting the new day, but even those sounded defeated and tired.

She understood that sentiment. Her legs remained weak and wobbly. Even the short hike strained the little reserves she had left. Her chest continued to burn. Her throat had closed tight, rasping her breath.

With Shiya guarding them, they followed the beach that bordered the dock. They tried to stick to the deepest shadows cast by the neighboring cliffs. The intent was to find Daal's father and Quartermaster Vikas, who had been left behind at the festival.

Despite her exhaustion, anxiety kept her edgy. She stared sidelong at Daal, picturing the *Oshkapeer* changing his gift.

*Altering him for me.*

According to Daal, that had happened six months ago, about the same time she had experienced her poison-induced vision, when her whole world changed. Had the Dreamers felt that awakening inside her? Was that why they had forged Daal, knowing she must eventually travel this way to reach whatever was hidden out in the Wastes?

She also considered Ularia, one of a long sisterhood of *Nyssians*. Ages ago, the first of them had been altered and forged to hold all the Crèche's history and memories, not unlike what she and Daal had experienced. Was the sisterhood's creation an early attempt by the Dreamers to do what had been done to her and Daal—before the Noor came and added their blood to these people, blood rich in bridle-song? According to Meryk, the *Nyssian* sisterhood had been fading in number over the past couple of centuries. Was that because the *Oshkapeers* had found a better method when the Noorish people arrived, a people imbued with a similar gift to their own? So they let the *Nyssian* sisterhood fade away.

She shook her head.

It was all too much to grasp, to even ponder.

Still, one impression of the Dreamers' communion weighed on her the most. The overwhelming sense of urgency and warning. Bashaliia was in danger, and the longer they waited, the greater the risk that she would lose him forever.

Daal stiffened next to her and stumbled a step.

"What?" she asked.

He swallowed and pointed toward the spread of boats and piers. "That's our skiff," he said. "Tied up next to the Reef Farer's barge."

"Are you sure?"

"I see Neffa. I could spot her horn from a league off."

Nyx hurried toward the town. "If your skiff and Neffa are here, Graylin must be somewhere, too."

They sped past the last of the docks and reached the open plaza. As they marched across it, Nyx searched the packed sands, especially where last night's slaughter had taken place. Before leaving Kefta, they had done their best to scuff away the blood, but a few patches of ground were clearly darker. She hoped it wasn't enough to draw anyone's attention.

Daal dashed to the side and returned with two mismatched cloaks, abandoned by some drunken partyers. They were stained and fouled, but Daal passed her one. He threw his over his shoulders. She did the same. Hers stank of either sour ale or maybe piss, not that the two smells were all that different.

Daal inspected her, pulling his cloak's collar higher. He then reached toward her face. She leaned back, but he simply untucked a few damp locks of dark hair from behind her ears and let them drape to her neck.

"You'll want to keep those fresh scabs on your throat covered," he warned. "And hide your wrists under the edges of your cloak. I don't think anyone will notice the cuts in your leggings."

She stared down at the holes, edged by dried blood, in her pants.

A loud bark made her jump. "Hold there!"

She twisted around. A cadre of guardsmen in leather armor appeared from a side street. They marched toward them, carrying spears and tridents. Nyx wanted to back away, but Daal steadied her with a hand.

Behind the men, a clutch of familiar figures appeared, led by the lithe form of Ularia. She wore a deep frown of annoyance.

Nyx barely noted her, spotting Graylin behind the woman. The relief shining on his face came close to breaking her. His normally stony countenance crumbled. His eyes welled with tears. He rushed toward her. One of the guardsmen tried to stop him, but Graylin knocked him aside with an elbow.

While still harboring a knot of resentment toward the man, Nyx stumbled to meet him. The night had been too long and too full of terrors. He reached her and hugged her to his chest, squeezing out what little breath she had left. She didn't fight his embrace. Instead, she sank gratefully into his feverish warmth, a heat likely stoked by his terror for her. She drew strength from his hard arms, even as they trembled.

"Are you all right?" he whispered in her ear.

She could only nod, suddenly choked by tears.

He held her until they both stopped shaking.

Daal was greeted by his father. But Meryk, oblivious to all that had transpired, gave his son a short hug, then a scolding frown. "Where have you all been?"

"I would like to know that, too," Ularia demanded in Noorish. She drew up to them, flanked by the armed men. "We spent half the night turning this town over."

Before Nyx could respond, Graylin took a step back and grabbed Nyx by the shoulders. His eyes were wider than normal. "I went out to sea for a time of *reflection*." He stressed the last word, clearly emphasizing a story he had fabricated. "Only to learn you had all vanished while I was gone. I told you to stay close to Vikas until I got back."

He glanced over to the quartermaster, who stood nearby. Vikas silently gestured in Gynish to Nyx: "Take great caution with this woman."

Nyx gave a small nod while clearing her throat. On the way here, she and Daal had come up with their own story. She looked down at her toes. "I . . . I'm sorry. We partook of too much ale. More than I could handle."

Daal stepped forward. "Don't blame her. It's my fault. I challenged her more than I should have. When she started to get sick—"

"I didn't want to embarrass you," she told Graylin.

Daal pointed to the corner of the bay. "I took her past the headlands. Away from everyone. Shiya came as our guard. It proved to be a long eventide for us. Still, as ale-sick as we were, our bellies fed many fishes. But I think Nyx is feeling better now."

Nyx realized Daal was speaking Noorish far too smoothly. No one commented on it. Though Meryk was looking at his son with a pinched brow.

Before his father could say anything, Nyx offered a sheepish look to Graylin. "I'm sorry we scared everyone. That was not our intent."

Graylin pulled her into a stiff hug. "That's all right. We've all overindulged from time to time."

Meryk snorted his agreement. "I think that applies to the Reef Farer, too."

Ularia only scowled deeper, then dismissed them with a wave of an arm. "Then prepare for our return to Iskar. We've wasted enough time on such foolishness."

As she stalked past Nyx, Ularia whispered to one of her guardsmen, likely the leader of the group. She spoke in Panthean, likely believing that Nyx wouldn't understand.

Nyx did—though the woman's words were disturbing.

"I don't trust any of them," Ularia hissed. "When we get back to Iskar, you and your men keep close watch on them. Don't let them out of your sight."

# 56

~❦~

RHAIF KEPT TO the beach as Kalder stalked back and forth across the shallow waters. His large paws splashed heavily with each pace, as if demonstrating the vargr's frustration. The beast's gaze remained fixed out to sea, waiting for his master's return.

Rhaif maintained this vigil, too, leaning on his crutch. He remembered Shiya wading into the sea off that sandbar island. His heart had ached to see her go back then, as it did yesterday when she left with the others. He had expected them to be back before now.

He stared up at the brighter glow of mists overhead. It was midmorning already. Nearly an entire day had passed.

*Where are you all?*

Loud hammering and louder curses echoed to his right, coming from the bulk of the *Sparrowhawk*. After the others had left for Kefta, Darant and his remaining crew had set about repairing the swyftship. They were aided by a score of Noorish locals whom Daal's mother had rousted up to assist them. Fleets of skiffs flowed in an endless procession, traveling from the wreck of the *Fyredragon* to this beach and back again. High stacks of wood and hillocks of old gasbag fabric dotted the sands around the bow of the *Sparrowhawk*.

Rhaif had gone himself to see Rega sy Noor's old ship. He was astounded to find the exploratory barge still intact. When he had arrived, men and women were scouring over it, like ants on a dead moth. Darant oversaw it all, inspecting sections, calling out orders, while Glace coordinated the shipments as they arrived at the beach. Brayl used her sailraft to ferry heavier supplies.

Jace and Krysh were there, too, encamped on the beach circling the cavern lake, doing arcane tests on barrels of green oil.

All in all, the amount of progress made in such a short time was impressive. Then again, pirates—as a necessity of their trade—were likely accustomed to swift repairs under daunting conditions.

From the busy work site, two figures crossed the sand toward him. The smaller of the two dashed forward, legs flying, arms waving.

*"Slan wee, Henna!"* Floraan called after her daughter, clearly scolding her haste.

Rhaif smiled at the girl's enthusiasm, but it wasn't to reach him.

*"Kalder!"* Henna hollered. *"Nee vish'na, kee norn vargr!"*

She shot past him, nearly knocking Rhaif's crutch out from under him. She splashed through the waves and leaped high at Kalder, hugging her arms around the vargr's shaggy neck.

The beast lifted his head, pulling a giggling Henna off her feet. Kalder then turned and carried her to shore. He shook the freeloader off, dropping Henna on her backside, which only triggered more laughter. When Henna tried to get up, Kalder nosed her back down with a warning growl, as if reprimanding a pup.

Floraan joined them. "Sorry," she said in Noorish to Rhaif. "She's been pestering me all morning to come see Kalder. In apology for our intrusion, I brought this."

She lifted a basket, stuffed with bread, cheese, and, most welcome of all, a stone bottle of sweet wine.

He took the fare in hand. "Thank you."

Floraan inhaled a deep breath, staring out to sea. The lines of worry on her face were easy to read.

"Shouldn't they have returned by now?" he asked.

The woman shrugged, glancing at him with a small smile. "Depends on when they ran out of ale . . . and how long it takes them to get their legs back under them afterward."

Henna chattered animatedly at Kalder, which made her mother's smile broaden. He lifted a brow for a translation.

Floraan shook her head, clearly amused. "She's telling him that she never got a chance to ride Bashaliia, but that we have saddles that might fit Kalder."

Rhaif grinned. "Oh, I'd love her to try. Be worth aggravating Kalder just to see Graylin's expression when he gets back."

Floraan pointed out to sea. "Unfortunately, it looks like Henna won't have the time to saddle Kalder."

Rhaif turned to see a group of boats appear out of the mists. It was the returning funeral fleet—though it looked smaller than when it had departed these shores. Clearly, some of the mourners hadn't regained their sea legs yet.

The Reef Farer's large barge led the boats, aglow with firepots and lanterns. Shiya's bronze form, reflecting all that flickering light, was easy to spot.

Rhaif sighed loudly. The knot of tension in his chest finally relaxed.

"If we hurry back to town," Floraan noted, "we should reach the docks about the same time as they do."

Rhaif appreciated this plan. "You are a wise woman."

He shifted on his crutch to head in that direction. Floraan retrieved the food basket to unburden him, but before she could turn away, he plucked out the bottle of sweet wine.

He hiked it high. "To celebrate their return."

"Ah, I see you are just as wise as me."

Floraan called over in Panthean for Henna to join them. Her daughter balked, until Rhaif heard Daal's name mentioned. Henna's eyes widened, and she leaped to her feet, excited to greet her returning brother.

Rhaif whistled sharply to Kalder and used a hand signal that Graylin had taught him. But the vargr needed no encouragement to follow. Kalder had also noted the approach of the boats. The beast had stuck his nose high, testing the sea breeze, confirming what his heart had hoped. His tail gave one wag, then Kalder swung around and headed down the beach.

"Wait for us!" Rhaif called, and whistled again. He feared how a charging vargr would be welcomed at the Iskar docks.

They all hurried after Kalder.

As they ran—and in his case, *hobbled*—Rhaif caught a glimpse of movement in the mists overhead. He slowed, squinting, allowing the others to leave him farther behind. He shaded his eyes against the glare of the shining fog.

For a breath, he thought he spotted a dark shadow sweeping high above, swirling through the mists, but it never revealed itself. He swore another two followed in its wake. His heart clenched in his throat, remembering the description of the attack by the raash'ke. But as he blinked, the shadows dissolved away—if they were there at all. He rubbed his eyes and kept staring. The mists stirred and glowed, but no other shadows revealed themselves.

A burst of laughter from Henna got him moving faster again. He periodically glanced high, searching, but still saw nothing. He slowly released his breath.

Maybe it was a trick of light in this strange place. Or maybe a small patrol of raash'ke had swept in, drawn by the noisy commotion—then fled back home.

Still, Rhaif could not shake a feeling of foreboding.

He glanced behind him, to where the hammering and shouting continued.

*Best get that bird into the air as soon as possible.*

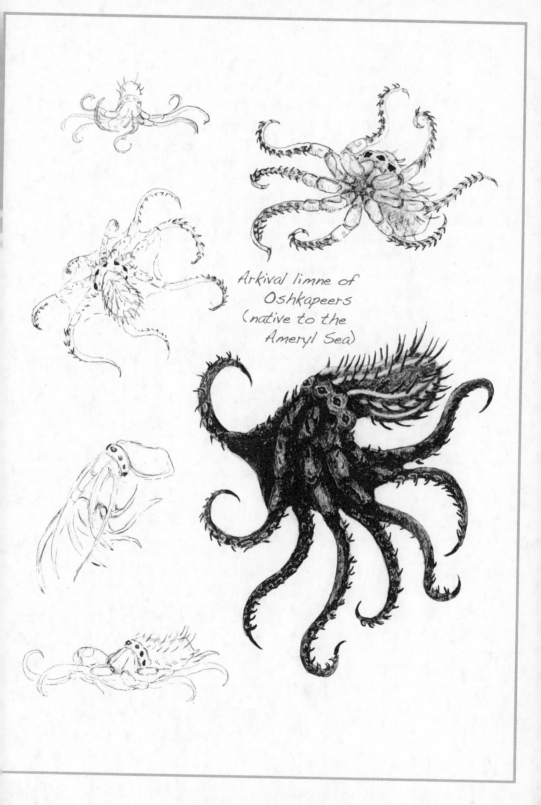

Arkival limne of
Oshkapeers
(native to the
Ameryl Sea)

# TWELVE

# THE AUGURY
# OF QAZEN

*Of alle the Orakles, I am the wizest. For I will spaek the grettest trueth. One that alle men should hede & accept. That, in the ende, we knoew naught about oure faate.*

*For that, be joiful.*

—Kastal au Tellilas, the Blasphemer of Kaant

# 57

*I **AM DOOMED** never to sleep.*

Like two days ago—which felt like a lifetime ago—Wryth was pulled from his bed far too early. Exhausted and defeated after yesterday's battle in the Breath, he found himself again standing within the heart of the Iflelen's great instrument, facing down the bronze bust while he waited for Shrive Keres to decipher another message from Skerren.

His heart pounded, and his hands were clamped into fists at his waist.

Skerren's last message, sent via code from his battle barge, had his forces approaching a storm over the mountains of the Dragoncryst. Skerren had picked up a weak signal from the bronze artifact. With their target located, his barge and its three swyftships had headed off into the storm.

And since then, nothing had been heard from Skerren.

Until two bells ago.

The message had come in slowly, in blinks and long glows, taking a chunk of the morning just to be transmitted. Now came an even longer wait as the lengthy code was laboriously deciphered. It was nearing midday, and Wryth was losing patience.

Wryth glanced over to the crystal sphere of their listening device. The yellow blip marked the location of the bronze artifact. It still hadn't moved, as if lodged in place. The red glow of Skerren's fleet had closed upon it, was almost on top of it.

Then his ships had stopped, hovering so tantalizingly close to the target.

*What is happening out there?*

Keres finally straightened from his crouch over a stained and scribbled parchment. His brow sweated from his concentrated effort to work through Skerren's new message. His eyes remained squinted, as if he were still struggling with the code.

"Strange . . ." Keres muttered.

Wryth exhaled hard. "In Đreyk's blasted name, what does it say?"

Keres cringed from the sharp curse.

"Out with it," Wryth demanded.

Keres nodded. "Skerren reports that he's reached the western slopes of the Dragoncryst. While crossing over, he lost one of his swyftships in the ice storm. He's still not entirely sure what had happened to it."

Wryth waved away this loss. "It doesn't matter. What else?"

"During his passage across the mountains, Skerren kept getting flickers from his detecting device. He followed it cautiously as the signal came and went. But when he reached the far side of the Dragoncryst, the location became clearer—but also made no sense."

"What do you mean?"

Keres licked his lips. "The signal seemed to be coming from deep *under* the Ice Shield."

"Under it?" Wryth stiffened, picturing his bronze treasure buried beyond their reach.

Keres explained. "After losing one of his ships, Skerren held back his barge and his remaining two ships. He feared triggering whatever disaster took down the enemy. Especially when they were so close. To investigate further, he dispatched a bevy of small slipfoils—ten of them—to furtively skim down the mountainside and hug the ice."

Wryth nodded. He pictured the stealthy one-man crafts. The slipfoils were little more than shells with wings, mounted by sleek balloons and a single flashburn maneuvering forge. They were perfect for covert scouting.

"What did Skerren learn?"

"Unfortunately, only a trio of foils came back. The rest were lost. The returning pilots claimed to have discovered a massive, heated rift in the ice. When they descended into its steamy depths . . . they found another *world*."

"What are you talking about?"

"They discovered a great hot sea. Under the ice. While exploring, the slipfoils kept to the mists under its glowing roof. Spying from on high, they spotted a village, with people—people of the Ice Shield—and boats. But most importantly . . ." Keres's eyes had gotten huge by now. "They identified the wreckage of a Hálendiian swyftship on its shore."

Wryth had a thousand more questions, but he focused on the most important.

"The enemy must've crashed down there. No wonder they haven't moved." Wryth clutched Keres's arm. "What about the bronze artifact?"

"It must be down there, but Skerren kept getting varying, sometimes contradictory, signals, as if there were other sources emitting a similar vibration."

"What are Skerren's plans from here?"

"He remains cautious, especially after most of the slipfoils vanished. Still, he intends to invade that world with his two remaining swyftships. To ambush that village, secure the wreckage, and establish a literal beachhead."

Wryth nodded at all of this.

Keres wasn't finished. "For now, Skerren will hold back his barge until everything is secure, then he'll descend for the final hunt."

Wryth closed his eyes.

*At long last.*

One question still shone above all the rest.

"When?" he asked.

"Skerren is finalizing elements, and he wants to—"

Wryth's voice sharpened into a dagger. *"When?"*

Keres cleared his throat. "By nightfall."

# 58

MIKAEN STOOD BEFORE the storm of his father's wrath. Shortly after midday, he had been summoned to the council chamber by the king's chamberlain, a tall, skeletal man with a hooked nose, whose sepulchral nature had always unnerved Mikaen as a boy. And it still did, especially as the chamberlain had barged unbidden into his private bath. Mikaen, naked and unmasked, had felt unduly exposed.

Few saw the ruins of his face hidden under the silver plate. The scrabble of scars twisted a corner of his lips into a perpetual leer and knotted his cheek. Half his nose was gone, turned into a piggish hole. A jagged, cratered line stitched his face from brow to jaw.

He kept such horrors away from his beloved Myella, only letting her see him when he was masked, including when he bedded her. The only time he ever removed it was when he took her from behind, her face pushed into a pillow. Even then, he had been too conscious of his mutilation and could hardly perform.

Certainly, he never let his son or daughter see his true face.

Thus, his mood was already foul as he climbed the steps behind the throne room and entered the stone-walled council chamber. Overhead, huge beams held up the roof, while underfoot, centuries-old rugs covered the floor. A fire in the room's hearth had burned to coals, smoldering as red as his father's face.

King Toranth ry Massif, the Crown'd Lord of Hálendii, sat at the end of the long ironwood table. He had shed his cloak, exposing an embroidered velvet doublet with a ruffled silken collar. Fury had sharpened his features, softened only by a halo of blond-white curls that had been oiled flat across his brow. A scowl etched his lips. He remained silent, just glaring across the table.

Mikaen waited for his father to speak first. There was no need to goad him further. A bead of sweat trickled down the back of Mikaen's neck, but he dared not wipe it away.

Finally, his father shoved up, pushing his heavy chair back with a resounding scrape. The fire in the king's eyes almost drove Mikaen back a step, but the captain of his Silvergard stood behind him, blocking any retreat. He and Thoryn both wore light armor, polished to a sheen for this audience with the king.

Toranth motioned to Liege General Reddak vy Lach, who was seated to his right. "Share with the crown'd prince what a gale of skrycrows carried to us. The dispatches from our southern coast."

Mikaen stiffened his spine. He and Reddak had returned to Azantiia this morning, just as the dawn bells were ringing over the city, as if celebrating the victorious arrival of the *Winged Vengeance*. But word of all that had transgressed in the smoky Breath of the Urth had reached the castle of Highmount ahead of them. The warship's decks had been scrubbed of royal blood, a body and head secured in a wood coffin.

Still, his rash act could not be so easily hidden.

Unlike the fete following his bombing of Ekau Watch, there was no cheering, or pounding of swords on shields, or flow of ale, or endless recitations in praise of his bold action. The atmosphere had been grim. All knew that the Southern Klashe must eventually react.

Last night, aware of this threat, Reddak had ordered the *Vengeance* home. Before leaving the Breath, the liege general had sent forth all the remaining ships to scour the smoky pall for the *Falcon's Wing*, the other Klashean warship, which had escaped their ambush and vanished.

Reddak stood. He glanced around at the handful of the king's council in attendance. They were his father's inner circle, his most trusted advisers, which included the provost marshal of the crown, the grand treasurer of the territories, the mayor of Azantiia, and the high seat of Kepenhill's Council of Eight. The only other attendee stood behind the king's left shoulder: the dourfaced Chamberlain Mallock.

Reddak cleared his throat, but before he could speak, a latecomer rushed in, passing around Mikaen and Thoryn. With swift strides, Shrive Wryth swept to a bow before the king, then rose to take his position behind Toranth's other shoulder.

"Apologies, sire," Wryth whispered, breathless and flushed. "It's a long climb from the depths of the Shrivenkeep."

Mikaen's father waved away this excuse and nodded to Reddak. "Go on."

The liege general skipped any preamble. "The Shield Islands have been attacked," Reddak declared flatly. "Brought to ruin."

Treasurer Hesst, a crow of a man with graying black hair, shifted straighter. "The Shields?" He glanced to the king. "Those islands supply a majority of the rare minerals we need for procuring our ship's lifting gasses." He turned his pinched, dark eyes back on Reddak. "How many towns and refineries did they bomb?"

"They didn't just *bomb* the Shields," Reddak clarified. "They laid waste to them. The main island of Helios is a fiery cauldron, choked in smoke, flames still burning. All that is visible are the giant stones of the Southern Henge that crown the island's highest hill. A half dozen smaller outer islands also burn."

"How?" Provost Balyn struggled to stand, but his rotund belly dragged him down. "How is that possible?"

"Naphlaneum," Reddak answered. "Reports describe the Klashean warship, the *Falcon's Wing,* raining fire across the island in a continual flaming storm. A few islanders made it to the boats, but thousands died. The fires will burn for months, if not years. And even after that, Helios will be a dead burnt rock in those seas. Nothing will grow there for centuries."

Mikaen had read of the horrors of naphlaneum. The Klashe rarely deployed such a devastating weapon, reserving it only for the direst circumstances. And even then, it was usually a tool employed for a more precise strike, not wholesale slaughter.

Torusk, the mayor of Azantiia, shook his head. "But why? Why such fury?"

Before Reddak could answer, King Toranth pointed an arm at his son. "There stands the reason."

Mikaen clenched his molars, refusing to balk as all eyes turned his way.

"Word must have reached Kysalimri," the king continued, "about the cold-blooded execution of Emperor Makar's son by my son."

Mayor Torusk's mouth dropped. He clearly had not been informed about Prince Paktan's death.

"And I wager both my bollocks," Toranth said, "that such an attack is only the start. There will be no negotiation or recompense that will assuage Makar's loss. Only blood and ruin."

"What of the *Falcon's Wing* now?" Wryth asked softly, plainly cautious not to draw the king's ire his way. "Prince Mareesh's warship?"

Reddak answered. "After dumping its vast hold of naphlaneum, it was last seen vanishing back into the Breath, likely returning to the Klashe to replenish its armaments."

Wryth nodded. "Then perhaps we can anticipate a short reprieve before further attacks commence. We must be ready."

Mikaen's gaze narrowed on the Shrive. Wryth had shown no reaction to Reddak's report. He had likely heard about it already from his network of eyes and ears throughout Highmount.

Still, Mikaen studied the man. Wryth stood with his arms folded into the wide sleeves of his gray robe. His eyes, banded in a black tattoo, shone darkly.

*Those eyes . . .*

They gave Wryth away. It wasn't only the lack of surprise. Wryth was *excited.* But not about what had transpired at the Shield Islands. Something else, something that made him late, which even now sought to pull him away.

Wryth caught him staring.

Mikaen kept his face stoic. He had known Wryth since he was a boy. The Shrive had been as much Mikaen's shadow as the king's. Only of late, Mikaen had begun to rankle at the man's presence, cringing at his whispers. It had grown to where he could hardly stand to look at him anymore. Mikaen also knew Wryth was dangerous, full of secrets and hidden ambitions—but for now, also useful.

"But how are we to get ready?" Marshal Balyn asked the table. "What manner of strike from the Southern Klashe can we anticipate next?"

The king answered, returning to his seat. "If the Klasheans ever catch Kanthe, there's no doubt they'll be sending me his head."

Mikaen hid a sneer.

*As if we'd be so lucky.*

The mere mention of his brother's name set his heart to pounding and rushed fire throughout his body, paining the scars under his mask, a permanent reminder of a traitorous attack.

"What is going on with your other son?" Treasurer Hesst asked. "Has he truly absconded with two of the emperor's children? If so, why? And where has he gone?"

Toranth sighed, some of his storm abating. "Maybe he seeks to return to Hálendii, to use the ransom of Makar's son and daughter to buy his way back into my good graces."

Mikaen clenched both fists, frustrated and furious. His father forever sought ways to forgive Kanthe, to excuse his failings, to believe the best of him. It had been no different in the past. Kanthe was always failing in his studies, often found more drunk than sober. Yet, the king still held out hope.

*Even now.*

But for Mikaen, no fault could be overlooked, only punished. Mikaen was held out as the silver son, whose glorious shine must never be blemished. As a boy, he had been cast into the Legionary, to be hardened further, tempered to a strong steel. Still, every slip required castigation and humiliation.

Like now, with the death of an enemy prince.

Toranth continued, still holding out hope. "Kanthe was clever enough to abscond with his two *imri* captives. It was clearly an attack directed at the heart of the empire. Even Makar believes my son was in league with us. And maybe, in his own way, he was."

Mikaen could stand it no longer. He took a furious step forward, driven by the fire inside him, by the pain hidden under silver.

"Feck that!" he blurted out.

All eyes turned on him, accompanied by a range of shocked expressions.

He ignored them all. "It's been *four* days since the supposed abductions. Where is my brother? Why hasn't he come on bended knee to us all? Either he plots with another realm, or the empire is lying and making fools of us all. There can be no other reason."

Mikaen clenched his fists, drawing blood from his palms, trembling with frustration, impotent to get his father to face reality. He knew of only one way to make his point, to leave no doubt.

He grabbed his mask and ripped it away, exposing the ruin beneath.

Gasps rose all around.

"Does *this* look like the act of a peacemaker or a clever scoundrel?" he demanded, fury flecking his lips. "Or is it the mark of a traitor?"

Thoryn came up and placed a hand on his shoulder. Mikaen shook, tears welling. He turned toward the silver of his captain, both to hide his tears and fumble to fix his mask in place.

Thoryn helped him. "I've got it."

Mikaen let him, a whisper spilling from his lips. "Why can't he see me?"

Still, except for Thoryn, there was no sympathy to be found in this chamber.

His outburst only inflamed his father. King Toranth was back on his feet, ready to punish as always. He struck Mikaen where he knew it would hurt the worst.

"Maybe I made the wrong *choice* when I picked a firstborn," Toranth growled, raising a specter that had haunted Mikaen all his life.

The room went dead quiet. Everyone here had heard the whispers, the rumors, the sleights, the innuendos. Mikaen and Kanthe had been born twins, which was not unusual. The royal families of Azantiia had a long history of twin births, some born with the same face, others with different appearances. And in the tumult of those births, sometimes the order got blurred, the bloody babes mixed.

Still, *one* would have to be declared the firstborn to firm a lineage.

Especially that of a king.

It was whispered that Toranth had purposefully disordered their births, to lift higher the son who looked more like him, with blond curls and a matching pale complexion. Whereas Kanthe took after their mother, with his coppery dark skin and coal-black hair.

Mikaen wondered if such rumors were the first wedge driven between the two brothers. Even now, deeper down than he would care to admit, a part of him believed this story. Such doubts seeded a measure of insecurity in him and an animosity toward Kanthe.

Still, when it came to the official lineage, none dared say otherwise. Even the midwives and healers had all died under strange circumstances—or so it was said, but those stories could be fabrications to embellish those rumors and prop up such gossip.

Not even their mother could attest to the truth.

After a hard pregnancy and harder birth, she waned, plagued by a ceaseless melancholia. She slowly wound down, refusing to eat and wasting away. Some said she took her own life, others that she expired on her own. But no one disputed how she doted on her two boys, cherishing them equally.

Such was not the same with their father.

He had loved their mother with all his heart, never taking another wife afterward, especially as there was no need to sire any more sons. He took what little relief he needed at his palacio of pleasure serfs. Perhaps it was why the king forever sought to cast Kanthe in a better light, seeing in his dark son the shadow of the woman he once loved.

Still, it had left little room for another son in his heart.

Toranth amply demonstrated it now, red-faced and seething. "You're lucky you have children. Especially a boy. At least, one *sword* of yours hasn't shamed me. We can only pray that your son proves to have a better temperament than his father."

Mikaen withstood this beratement. The mention of his son, Othan, poured steel down his spine. He intended to be a far better father to his son than the king had ever been. He added this oath to the many he had made concerning his children's welfare. Knowing this, he easily withstood the fury in Toranth's face.

Still, Mikaen breathed heavily. Thoryn kept a steady hand on his shoulder, but there was no need for such support. Mikaen refused to debase himself any further after exposing himself so starkly. He reached up and shifted the mask more firmly into place.

Movement past the king's shoulder drew his eye.

Wryth shifted and whispered in Toranth's ear. His father leaned closer, ever bending to the Shrive's counsel. Toranth gave a small nod, sagging away some of his anger, clearly appeased by his words.

All the while, the Shrive's gaze never left Mikaen. Only now those eyes were shrouded, impossible to read. Wryth was hiding something.

*But what?*

Finally, his father straightened and waved Mikaen off. "Begone. Leave it to the rest of us to discuss how to amend your mistake. Before it brings down the kingdom."

Mikaen gave a curt bow, though it strained the steel that had hardened his back. He turned on a heel and strode brusquely away with Thoryn in tow.

Behind him, he heard the king ask Reddak, "Is there any way of discerning

Kanthe's plot? If his actions were indeed in service to the kingdom—as Emperor Makar believes—is there some way we can support him?"

Mikaen took a deep breath and continued through the door. He would be goaded no longer. He didn't care what Kanthe was plotting.

*Only that I be the one that ends it.*

# 59

KANTHE SWEATED AND burned at the bottom of a glass well. He stared up at the midday sun as it hung in the open sky above. He had read about the prison of Qazen, but he had never thought he'd experience its cruel design firsthand.

"Stay out of the sun," Pratik warned. The Chaaen demonstrated this by flattening his body along the only section of the well still in shadows.

Frell helped Mead shift his injured brother to the same spot. Jester's leg and the side of his head were bandaged. After being ambushed out in Malgard, healers had attended to the man's arrow wounds. Apparently, their captors wanted their deaths to be harsher and slower.

*But thankfully it's only the five of us.*

Back at the entrance to the fissure, Rami had been separated from them. The Klashean prince had promised that he would do his best to get his father to understand—about the circumstances of the abductions and about the danger of moonfall. Afterward, the five of them had been hauled aboard the imperial barge and swept to Qazen, where they were thrown into this honeycomb of a strange prison.

It was designed not only to hold prisoners, but to punish and torture them, too.

Kanthe joined the others in the small curve of shadows. The circular pit—like all the cells here—climbed three stories to the open sky, tantalizing prisoners with the freedom so close. But the walls and floor were sheer black glass, fused from the surrounding sand by alchymies lost to time.

There would be no scaling these walls to escape.

And that was not the worst of it.

Though the sun of the Crown never set, over the course of the year it would make a slow circle in the sky, marking the passage of time. The ancient builders of this spread of pits angled each well in such a precise manner that the circling passage of the sun was mimicked below. The face of the Father Above would wax and wane, heating the pits to searing temperatures, then backing away and letting shadows slightly cool the space. It meant prisoners had to shift with those shadows or risk burning atop the glass floor.

At midwinter, like now, that edge of shadows was razor thin, requiring them to perch on its edge, pressed against the wall. With the five of them in this one cell, there was barely enough room.

Kanthe stood on the tips of his toes to keep them from the sunlight. The glare off the walls seared through his closed lids. Directly across from them, bars squeezed off the tiny door into the pit. A pair of imperial guards watched their struggles to keep from burning with clear amusement.

"Maybe they'd like to cool off," one said—a Klashean with the tiny black eyes of a sand snake. "We can always crank open the sea valve and give them all a nice bath. If nothing else, it would wash the stink off of 'em."

The other, who looked more like a lizard with a bulbous nose, laughed.

Kanthe was not amused at the reminder of the other fail-safe for this prison. The entire complex of pits was interconnected by underground tunnels. Pipes led out to the neighboring sea. When their valves were opened, the entire prison could be swamped and drowned. It led to an especially cruel death, leaving prisoners swimming in circles until exhaustion drowned them.

"Serve 'em right," said the Lizard. "Trying to abduct the emperor's son and daughter."

"Too bad we couldn't nab the lot of 'em," Snake Eyes groaned.

"Still, thank the merciful gods that Rami and Aalia were safely recovered."

"True," the other agreed, touching three fingers to his forehead in gratitude to the heavens.

Kanthe sighed.

The escape of the wingketch had been the only fair tidings of this disastrous morning. While flying to Qazen earlier, Kanthe had eavesdropped on the chatter among their captors and learned what had happened. Saekl must have spotted the approach of the imperial ships and blasted skyward with the renowned speed of the ketches. Still, she took two precautions. She swept low over the neighboring Naphtha pine forest, setting it ablaze, then took advantage of the smoke to cover her escape. She also left behind a treasure that would attract the imperial forces away from their escape.

The Illuminated Rose of the Imri-Ka.

Aalia had been abandoned outside. The furious fires of the ketch's forges, followed by the torching of the forest, had driven away the clouds of *lycheens*.

The move forced the imperial soldiers to rescue Aalia, allowing the others time to vanish into the steamy landscape.

"At least we know that Llyra didn't betray us," Kanthe said, gasping in the heat.

"That's not necessarily true," Frell whispered. "She still could've given up our plans, but not informed the ketch's captain."

"Or there could be another spy, as you suggested," Pratik added, his face streaming with sweat.

Kanthe pushed higher on his toes. "Either way, we're stuck here."

While perched in place, he clung to a sliver of hope. He prayed for Rami to be successful in his attempt to explain the events of that harrowing night: the burning of the librarie, the escape to the skies, the misguided taking of a hostage. Still, the prospects of success were as slim as the curve of shadows under his feet.

Especially after the guards' next exchange.

"I heard Emperor Makar is in a frenzy at the Augury's villa," the Lizard said with a bit too much glee at the emperor's distress. "All but pulling his hair out with grief."

"I don't blame him. If my son had his head cleaved off by that Hálendiian prince, they'd have to weigh me down in irons to keep me from getting revenge."

Frell glanced at Kanthe, both brows raised.

Pratik called to the guards, "What happened to one of Emperor Makar's sons?"

Snake Eyes spat into the cell, his spittle sizzling on the hot glass. "As if you don't know!"

The Lizard glared at them. "Prince Paktan did not deserve such an ignoble death. Beheaded in chains." He pointed his curved sword through the bars at Kanthe. "By your fekkin' brother."

Stunned, Kanthe slid down the wall. His toes breached the shadows and burned in the sunlight. He hardly felt it.

*What did Mikaen do?*

Snake Eyes pressed his face to the bars. "No doubt, your head will fall next. Sent to your father before the day's last bell."

Kanthe touched his neck.

A commotion sounded down the hall. The pounding of many boots approached with a scatter of shouts. Snake Eyes stepped away to meet them. Kanthe overheard an order for the prisoners to be hauled to the Augury's villa.

The Lizard lingered at the door and leered in at them. "Seems it might not take until the last bell before that gift is prepared for your king."

FROM A HIGH window in Qazen, Tazar watched an imperial procession of guards ride into town on horses and wagons. They entered via the sea road, coming from the distant prison grounds. In the midst of them, a caged cart held five chained captives.

A short time ago, when the second midday bells had chimed, one of Tazar's men had rushed off the streets with a report that the Hálendiian prince and his cohorts were being transferred to the Augury's palacio.

Tazar had climbed up to the second story of a small villa to confirm the same. He stared off toward the Augury's palacio, a grand estate that sat atop a bluff overlooking the ocean. Like most of the town, its walls were salt-encrusted bricks, the crystals reflecting the sunlight into the sparkle of diamonds. The many roofs of the sprawling estate were covered in white slate to keep the worst of the sun's heat away. The shadowed grounds danced with fountains and sheltered flowering gardens, all dotted with blue pools and tall stands of green palms.

Most dramatic of all, set amidst the gardens, stood the ancient Giants of Qazen. The seven priceless sculptures were made of black glass, forged by lost alchymies. The figures stood taller than the villa's walls. They depicted stylized giants, adorned with matching seamless helms. Their features were crude and sharp-edged, with eyes depicted by concentric circles. The warriors struck threatening poses: a fist raised, a spear lofted, a bow poised. Age had damaged most. A swordsman carried a broken shield. A boxer only had a stump for an arm. An archer stood posed with half his head gone.

Still, the Giants loomed tall, undisputably intimidating, as if forever guarding this coastline—not that these statues had come from these shores. The collection was said to have been dug up during the excavations of a necropolis far out into the blasted wastelands, beyond the Crown's edge, where the sun beat down in an endless, merciless fire.

The clatter of hooves and the creak of wheels drew Tazar's attention back to the road below him. The prison caravan slowly worked through the crowded streets. Vendors and shopkeepers hawked their wares. Soothsayers and seers begged for patrons to visit them, assuring the most accurate guidance and prophecies. All were ignored as the cage trundled through the press of people. The crowd hid mostly under *byor-ga* robes. A few barefaced *imri* were scattered among them.

Still, when it came to the prisoners, all divisions of caste broke down. People crowded close, trying to spit through the bars, throwing rotted refuse. Curses flew in even greater numbers.

The guardsmen did little to stem this barrage, only keeping the prisoners from any true harm. That privilege belonged solely to the emperor.

Tazar's jaw tightened as the cart passed under his post and continued toward the palacio. His fist tightened on the dagger at his belt. His eyes narrowed on the dark figure behind the bars.

Cool fingers touched Tazar's hand. "We must conserve our forces," Althea reminded him. "We dare not waste it on him."

Tazar let his grip drop from his dagger, acknowledging the wisdom of his second-in-command. He glanced back at the two dozen or so *Shayn'ra* who spread across this wing's interconnecting rooms. More crowded below. The rest of the Fist of God's army gathered in outlying buildings or plied the streets.

Tazar had arrived before dawn with all he could muster from Kysalimri after the fiery ambush there. He spread a call throughout Qazen, gathering those who were either of the *Shayn'ra* or its devoted allies. Still, their numbers were not what Tazar had hoped for when he set off from Kysalimri.

Especially as circumstances had rapidly changed and were escalating with each ring of the day's bells.

He had learned of the capture of Prince Kanthe and the death of another: the emperor's son Prince Paktan. The extent of Emperor Makar's grief and fury could be measured by the flurry of forces that descended onto Qazen. Guardsmen and warriors surrounded the Augury's palacio and patrolled the streets with the fierce determination to protect the emperor and his two re-covered offspring.

Makar was taking no chances.

"Perhaps we should return to Kysalimri," Althea suggested. "Attempting to reach the emperor now will surely fail and only waste lives. Best we regroup and firm our position back at the Eternal City."

Tazar could not discount the wisdom of such a plan. The situation was dire enough and was only getting worse the longer they waited. He blamed the Hálendiian prince for all of this. Even captured and defeated, Kanthe contin-ued to thwart his plans.

Tazar tightened a fist as he watched the barred cage vanish around a corner, chased by a litany of curses.

More than any moment in the past, he envied Emperor Makar.

*You will get to take that traitorous bastard's head—not me.*

Sharp shouting and startled yelps drew his attention from the window. Beyond the door, a clamor erupted. The sharp strike of steel rang out. A body could be heard crashing down the steps.

Althea signaled, and men swept over to guard the entry. The door crashed open, and a trio of figures barged in, cloaked in *byor-ga* robes. Similarly shrouded figures guarded their backs.

Tazar had his sword bared. Althea carried long daggers in both hands. No one spoke, all frozen in place.

Then Tazar heard the strange tinkle of a bell behind his shoulder. The tip of a blade pressed against the side of his throat. Though keen-eared and tense, he had not heard anyone approach.

"A *quisl*," the wielder whispered, turning the edge of the blade. "Poisoned."

Althea noted the threat. She pointed one of her knives at Tazar's captor and the other toward the intruders.

One of the three stepped forward and stripped off the *byor-ga* headgear, exposing the stony face of a hard woman. She glared at him. From her size and features, she appeared to be Guld'guhlian.

"Everyone stand down and back a step!" she boomed, letting her voice echo in all directions. She followed her own example and sheathed her two half-swords and held up her palms. "We only came to talk."

Althea looked to Tazar. He nodded his acquiescence, careful not to cut himself on that poisoned blade.

Its wielder retreated, shaking back a hood, revealing silvery-white features and a long black braid. She could be no more than seventeen or eighteen. She must have come up behind him from one of the connecting rooms. He stared down at the small knife in her hand. He blinked, and it vanished, though he swore she never moved.

He took a step back from her, his heart pounding harder. He turned to the Guld'guhlian. "What do you want?"

By now, the intruder's companions had shed their headgear, too. Their features matched those of the young woman with the knife, but they were older and looked even more deadly.

"To parley," the short woman said. "I'm Llyra hy March, guildmaster of Anvil. And I think you might recognize the others as Rhysians of a distinguished sisterhood."

"Why should I care?" Tazar asked, regaining his composure and most of his anger.

Llyra explained. "At the moment, we share a common foe. Yet, neither of us has the wherewithal or numbers to combat it. So I suggest we combine our forces."

Althea frowned, her eyes narrowing warily. "You mean to strike for the emperor."

Llyra shrugged. "I suspect some of our aims have crossed purposes, but yes, ultimately, we mean to raid the Augury's palacio and secure the premises. At least for as long as possible. Hopefully, long enough to satisfy both of our goals."

"And what about those *crossed purposes*?" Tazar asked.

Another shrug answered him. "Best we accomplish one goal before worrying about the next."

Althea scowled at the trio and glared at the young Rhysian at Tazar's side. "I hardly think you have the numbers to help us."

"I'll let you be the judge." Llyra stepped forward, her palms up. She headed to the window. "Not all armies wear armor or stripe their faces with white paint."

Tazar joined her at the window. He stared out at the crowded street, which looked the same, only more settled after the passage of the prisoner convoy. Hawkers yelled. Seers begged. People milled about between the two.

Llyra waved below. "I've been rousing an army more skillful than most. From whorehouses, smoky taverns, dark dens, and thieveries of every ilk. We are everywhere and nowhere. Even here in Qazen. I rallied them days ago when I knew our paths would cross here. Just in case."

Tazar frowned, staring below. "What army?"

Answering his question, responding to some hidden signal, half the churning crowd stopped all at once. Hundreds of faces turned and stared up at the window.

"That's only a fraction of 'em," Llyra commented.

Behind Tazar's shoulder, Althea whistled softly, appreciatively.

On the street, moving again in unison, the faces dropped, and the figures folded back into the crowd, vanishing away.

Tazar glanced at Althea, lifting a brow. "Well?"

"Maybe we don't need to return to Kysalimri quite so soon," she answered.

Tazar held a hand toward Llyra. "Done."

She shook on their pact, her palm dry and firm. "Best we hurry before more of the imperium crashes down upon this town."

Tazar nodded, agreeing at the need for haste. Still, a worry gnawed at him, centered on two words.

*Crossed purposes.*

# 60

KANTHE HOBBLED UNDER the cold gaze of a giant glass swordsman who protected the grounds of the Augury's palacio. There was no sneaking past this sentinel. The prisoners clanked and rattled their way along. The heavy iron chains cut into Kanthe's wrists and ankles. He reminded himself never to complain about the thin silvery links that joined the *imri* to their chaaen-bound.

As they crossed through a garden, escorted by a cordon of guardsmen, Kanthe appreciated the cool breezes off the sea. The winds swept up the bluff in fierce gusts but were tamed by the surrounding walls. The scent of lily-wraiths and poppies carried to him. Fountains burbled and gold-scaled karp flashed through still ponds. He would've liked to tarry longer, to spend a leisurely day within this lush oasis, but that was not to be.

He and the others were marched quickly, and if they slowed, the poke of a spear encouraged them to move faster. Jester bore the worst of those assaults, doing his best to hop along on his good leg, leaning on his brother for support.

They reached the Augury's main villa. It rose three times the height of any of the other structures and wings. The sun glared from the salt crystals of its upper levels and blinded off the white slate roof. Its tall double doors, gilded in gold, stood open to the gardens. Soft music lilted gently out to them, the harmony promising tranquility and peace, replete with the promise of the wisdom of the gods.

It all fell on Kanthe's deaf ears.

Beyond the threshold, marble floors stretched across a vast atrium. Even here, orchids draped from the ceiling in long falls of bright blossoms, as if the gardens had swept inside on petaled wings. Lanterns shone in a thousand colors, casting their glows through tinted glass. Golden urns burbled with more fountains.

Kanthe searched around.

*If I were a god, I would happily make this my home.*

Jester made a drier assessment. "Plainly, soothsaying sucks a lot of coin out of purses."

This earned the man another poke of a spear.

Guardsmen drove them through the atrium to another set of gilded doors that were etched with the thirty-three Klashean gods. Apparently, there was no getting away from the lot of them. Kanthe flashed to the pleasure barge drifting across the Bay of the Blessed, sailing among this same pantheon. Now that felt like another's life, not his own.

The doors opened ahead of them without anyone knocking. Either everyone in the palacio was prescient or the rattle of chains had announced their approach. They were pushed through the doors and into the Augury's grand audience chamber.

The same marble stretched ahead. Only the lanterns here glowed more dimly, all shining in a single dark color. The lenses appeared to be made of the same glass that sculpted the Giants outside—or the walls of their prison. The dim lighting cast pools of shadows along the walls to either side, likely to enhance the feeling of the chamber's sanctity.

For Kanthe, it only felt threatening. Then again, maybe that was the intent, too—to unnerve supplicants who dared approach the Augury.

*It's certainly working.*

To either side, high up the walls, small clerestory windows flowed with light, which made the upper arch of the room glow as if the gods were hovering above.

On the chamber's far side, two lower windows illuminated a golden dais, its shine beckoning them forward. Not that Kanthe felt like drawing any nearer, especially considering who awaited them there.

The emperor, crowned by a circlet of gems that reflected the light, sat atop a throne. Even from across the long hall, Makar's eyes flashed with black fury. He came regally dressed in embroidered white, a counterpoint to the figure who towered at his right shoulder.

That had to be the illustrious Augury, displaced from his usual seat by Emperor Makar. The oracle was dressed more somberly in shades of black, from his polished boots to the small cap atop his head. His clothing looked to be a single cloth wrapped around his tall form and belted in gold. The only adornments were his boot's gold toes, crafted into two all-seeing eyes.

*Perfect for peering up a woman's skirt,* Kanthe imagined sourly.

Still, the Augury captured Kanthe's attention. There was something about the man. His features, a rich ebony of the Klasheans, were undeniably striking, as regal as any king or emperor. But it was his eyes that captivated. By now, Kanthe knew violet was considered rare and valued among the people here. Only the Augury's eyes were so rich in hue that they looked like pools of indigo.

No wonder the Augury commanded such attention and respect.

*Even I'd believe anything that man said.*

The five of them were forced at spearpoint to the foot of the dais and driven to their knees. On the other side of the emperor, two figures stood side by side. They were both as resplendent in white. Rami wore loose pants topped by a surcoat embroidered with the swords of the Klashean Arms at its center. Aalia wore a matching gown, with a light veil, woven with diamonds, over the fall of her dark hair.

Kanthe caught Rami's eyes, searching for any indication that the prince was able to sway his father to their well-intentioned, but misguided, efforts.

Rami gave the smallest shake of his head, confirming the worst. Not that the chains weren't answer enough already.

As to Aalia, she refused to look Kanthe's way, her gaze disdainfully up. She must be furious after she was unceremoniously dumped out of the wingketch. Kanthe could only imagine her terror, considering what floated out there in Malgard's steamy air.

Rami turned to the emperor. "Father, I beseech you. At least, hear them out. Despite all that has happened, Prince Kanthe meant no harm. A great doom approaches, and they only seek a means to thwart it."

The prince glanced to his sister for support, but Aalia refused to look her brother's way or acknowledge his words.

The same could not be said of their father. Though furious, Emperor Makar tempered his words. "Son, you are young. Easily duped by such trickery. They've abused your good graces to malicious ends. That alone warrants a harsh punishment."

"Please, listen to what they know about the moon—"

Rami was cut off as the Augury cleared his throat. The oracle stepped forward, his head bowing ever so slightly in apology. "Prince Rami, I've communed countless times with Fryth, the goddess of the silvery moon. If there were any danger, She would have told me."

Makar motioned a palm in the Augury's direction. "See? Do we need any further guidance than that, my son? It is such wisdom you should be heeding, not the treacherous tongues of these Hálendiians."

Rami took a step forward.

This earned a hard scowl and a flash of fire from his father, driving Rami back to his proper place next to Aalia. The only reaction from his sister was the slight narrowing of her eyes.

Makar motioned again to the Augury. "If it wasn't for his godly sight, we would never have recovered you both. I sought his esteemed counsel after coming here, entreating him to beg the gods for their wisdom. He graciously obliged. He inhaled Malgard's fumes, swooned into the gods' embrace, and woke with your location, marking it on a map."

Kanthe glanced at Frell. *Could that be true?* Kanthe remembered how Frell had studied centuries of Qazen prophecies. The alchymist claimed to have found them strangely accurate, down to exacting detail in many cases.

"Upon the Augury's urging, I quickly dispatched a barge to Malgard," Makar continued, his voice growing with exaltation. He pressed three fingers to his forehead. "Where, thank all the gods, you were found."

The Augury bowed deeply. "It is not I who saved them. The gods forever smile upon the Haeshan dynasty. This we all know."

Kanthe fought not to scowl, to raise the obvious.

*Apparently, those smiles never reached Prince Paktan.*

Rami tried one last time to help them. "Father, all I ask is that you listen to them. After that—"

"Enough!" Makar boomed, making everyone jump—except the Augury, who must have been forewarned about this outburst. "I will hear no more. I have a son to mourn." He twisted hard to Rami and Aalia. "And you, a dear brother. We will head for Kysalimri before the day's end."

The emperor faced the five thrown in front of him and lifted an arm. "But first, there is a matter to settle."

Upon his signal, a towering figure stepped from a doorway to the right of the dais. Kanthe gaped at the man's sheer size: his thick thighs, the breadth of his chest, the hillocks of bulging muscle. Black leather strained to hold it all in. It was as if that glass Giant out front had come to life. And like that ancient statue, the hulking figure hauled a curved sword with him. It stretched longer than Kanthe's height.

To the left, another giant appeared. In his gloved fists, he carried a glowing iron cauldron, from which an iron brand poked out. His ebony features shone with a sheen of sweat, reflecting the ruddy light of the coals.

Makar leaned forward from his seat. "Before we pay in kind the damage done to my family, we'll let Prince Kanthe watch the others fall first. But their deaths will not be quick. Limb by limb, we'll take them apart before his eyes. Burning each stump to stave off the end for as long as possible. The screams will stretch all the way to Hálendii. King Toranth will know the grief he has sowed, and the punishment it has wrought."

Rami closed his eyes, his shoulders sagging in defeat.

Mead leaned toward his brother. "Those sodding *lycheens* out in Malgard don't seem so bad now, do they?"

# 61

TAZAR RUSHED DOWN the street, sticking to the deeper shadows. Althea paced him on the left and the guildmaster of Anvil on his right. More of the *Shayn'ra*—accompanied by a mix of ruffians and cutthroats—swept through neighboring alleyways and narrow lanes. They all closed upon the walls of the Augury's palacio.

Tazar passed two guardsmen sprawled on the ground, their blood still spreading across the cobbles. In a few more steps, another appeared, slumped against a wall, clutching his sliced throat, trying to keep his life from spilling away. They had already passed a dozen such victims, marking the handiwork of Llyra's secret army as they silently dispatched patrols along the way.

While they crossed the town, shutters were clamped over windows and doors slammed. The denizens of Qazen wanted no part in the bloodshed to come.

"Slow," Llyra hissed as they came within sight of the salt-encrusted walls of the palacio.

Blocks and blocks of imperial soldiers filled the square, guarding the gates into the palacio. They were easily two centuries in number. In addition, a large barge plied the winds above the villa.

"More than we anticipated," Althea noted as they drew to a stop. "Even with the strength of surprise, we face a hard battle."

Tazar conceded this point; still, his blood thrummed with excitement. "We can't balk now."

*Especially when we're this close to achieving the impossible.*

They all waited for the signal before attacking. Llyra breathed heavily next to him. A tall Rhysian—an assassin named Saekl—shadowed her.

"We've already delayed too long," Llyra said. "My spies inside the palacio report that everyone has gathered inside the Augury's audience chamber. We must strike swiftly to keep them pinned there. We don't want to risk—"

A muffled scream pierced the breeze off the ocean, coming from beyond the tall walls ahead.

Llyra scowled, looking ready to rush forward on her own, but Saekl held her back.

"Wait for the signal," the assassin warned.

Then it came—the first of the latterday bells echoed across the town.

* * *

**KANTHE HAD REFUSED** to look away as the sword fell hard upon Jester's arrow-bit leg. The blade cleaved through the Guld'guhlian's shin, just below his knee. The severed limb skittered over the marble as the man cried out, thrashing in the grip of two guardsmen. His scream echoed in the small space, as if a hundred men were being tortured.

Blood spurted far, all the way to the dais. Droplets spattered the hem of Aalia's gown. Still, she didn't back away.

Jester's cries devolved into heaving curses, especially as the other giant dropped to a knee next to him. He swung around an ax that had been burning in the cauldron's coal. Its iron shone ruddy. The giant pressed the hot blade against the stump. Flesh seared and smoked. Jester jolted, his back arching with pain, his breath trapped in his chest.

When it finally burst loose, his scream deafened the ringing of the town's bells. After an interminable time, Jester sagged, snot running from his nose, tears from his eyes.

His brother, Mead, clenched both fists to his chest. Frell had gone pale. Pratik's lips moved in a silent prayer.

In the quiet that followed, a horn blared outside. Before it faded, another answered, then another. A strident chorus soon rose all around.

Everyone in the room stared in different directions.

Kanthe glanced at Frell and Pratik, but he found no answer in their confused expressions. Next came shouting and the sharp blasts of bombs. Then screams, both furious and pained.

From the doors to either side of the dais, a score of guardsmen in shining armor—imperial Paladins—swept to encircle the emperor and his family.

Their leader offered a bow to Makar. "Hold fast, Your Illustriousness. A scrabble of baseborn dare to attack. Accompanied by the *Shayn'ra*. But they dash themselves against our forces. None will breach these walls."

The emperor was on his feet. He did not look scared or worried, only angry at the interruption. He cast a hard glance at the Augury, as if he had expected the oracle to have anticipated this assault.

"We will prove victorious," the Paladin promised.

**WE CANNOT WIN** *this battle.*

From the edge of the square, Tazar despaired. Moments ago, their two armies—his and Llyra's—had crashed against the imperial forces. Even caught off guard, the two centuries of guardsmen formed a silver cliff that looked impregnable. Furious fighting continued along its edge, but little progress was made.

Frustrated and angry, Tazar could no longer stand by and watch.

*If this is our end, I will die with my sword bloodied.*

Althea grabbed his shoulder. "We cannot lose you, too. You are the foundation on which a new Fist can grow."

Tazar ground his teeth. He glared over at Llyra, wondering if this were all some ruse, another trap set up by the imperium. True or not, he knew he was ultimately to blame, letting ambition overrule restraint.

*I should have heeded Althea's caution from the start.*

Still, his fingers clutched as he stared over at the Guld'guhlian, wanting to strangle her for luring him to this bloody defeat. She ignored him, looking unfazed. Her gaze was not even on the fighting, but toward the sky. He glanced in that same direction.

The imperial barge swept outward from its hover over the gardens, coming to put a resounding end to the battle.

Llyra spoke firmly to Tazar. "Sound a retreat."

"What?"

"Now!" she yelled.

Before Tazar could fumble for his bone whistle, Althea blew hers, heeding the woman. His second-in-command must have been awaiting such an order, knowing they were doomed. Her blasts pierced the clamor of battle. She blew four more times, making sure all heard her strident command to pull back.

Tazar glowered at Llyra, but the woman's gaze remained on the skies. The barge reached the battle as their two forces fled from under the ship's shadows. Out of the corner of Tazar's eye, he caught Llyra give a small nod.

As if heeding this signal, a barrage of flaming spears shot from rooftops around the square. They *twanged* from longbows hidden until now, requiring two men to draw them. The spear's passages left trails of emerald fire and smoke.

Tazar gasped, all too familiar with the eerie cast to those flames.

*Naphlaneum.*

The spears struck the barge's balloon in several spots. The ship shuddered as if anticipating what was going to happen next. Then the gasbag ignited in one blinding burst. Tazar shielded his face, feeling the heat on the ground. The barge plummeted, its forges flaming under it, futilely struggling to hold it aloft.

The barge crashed into the centuries of guardsmen below, shattering into them, casting a wall of fire wider. The concussion blasted open the wall's gates.

Llyra turned to Tazar. "Into the breach we go!"

Tazar stood, stunned, but Althea switched her whistle and blew for their forces to regroup and charge ahead. Llyra set off with her assassin shadow. Tazar got pulled in their wake and sped up alongside the Guld'guhlian.

"This was your plan all along!" he hollered at Llyra. "Why didn't you tell us?"

"Couldn't risk our forces hanging back. The battle had to be fierce and bloody."

Althea understood. "To lure the barge overhead."

Then they were into the fighting, dancing through flames and carnage.

KANTHE PICKED HIMSELF up off the floor and rolled back to his knees. The blast had blown out the windows across one side of the chamber. Glass still danced and skittered on the marble. Lanterns swung wildly overhead. The clash of steel and screams reached them.

Ahead, the cordon of Paladins closed tightly around the imperial family. They looked ready to rush them off, but for the moment, no one seemed to know where safety lay.

Still, Emperor Makar remained focused, but not on escape. He pointed at the five in chains. "Dispatch them! Now!"

The two black-clad giants closed on their group, hefting ax and sword. The guards behind them pinned Kanthe and the others on the floor. The Paladins ushered their *imri* charges in the other direction.

The hulking swordsman stepped in front of Kanthe, blocking his view to the dais. He swung his curved blade high—then cringed. His other hand slapped his cheek, then his neck. A tickle of feathers fell, spinning to the floor, pulled down by a black barb.

Then the giant swooned, toppling backward. He crashed to the hard marble. The other took a step toward his felled partner, only to sway and stumble, falling headlong, smashing his face onto the stone floor.

The guards behind them fled in panic, but it was too late. Before they got far, feathered darts struck them. They dropped within steps. One toppled onto his own sword, carving the edge of his blade through his throat.

The threat finally revealed itself.

From the gloom along the walls, shadows broke free. They looked like dark sparrows, flitting and spinning into and out of the room's dark edges, vanishing and reappearing. They held long pipes pinched between their lips. But their music was deadly.

Barbs flew from those pipes.

Knives flashed out of shadows.

With elegant efficiency, the Paladins were stripped from the emperor. Bodies fell everywhere.

It would have been beautiful if it weren't so terrifying.

Emperor Makar, along with Rami and Aalia, were forced back to the dais by this storm of shadows. The Augury huddled with them. The oracle brushed a feathered barb that had lodged at his collar, just missing his throat. They all gathered near the dais's tall throne.

Then, as if they were never there, the sparrows vanished.

On this cue, the main doors crashed open behind Kanthe. Men poured into the room, pursued by the strident clash of a continuing battle. In the lead rushed a familiar figure. The stripe of white paint across his eyes did nothing to hide his identity. Kanthe flashed to the streets of Kysalimri, the bloody ambush.

Here came the leader of the *Shayn'ra*.

Behind him, an impossibility strode in his wake, clearly supporting this assault by the Fist of God. Llyra stalked across the marble. Her eyes were as steely as the two half-swords in her hands. One blade was broken near its hilt. Her face was steeped in blood.

Saekl swept alongside her—though the tall woman looked hardly mussed. Only a single drop of blood marred her pale cheek.

Kanthe struggled to understand.

Unfortunately, the leader of the *Shayn'ra* was not so confused. Clearly focused on one goal, he swept straight to Kanthe and grabbed a fistful of the prince's hair. Shackled and chained, Kanthe could not defend himself. His head was yanked back, baring his throat. A sword flashed high.

Before it fell, a shout thundered across the chamber. *"Don't!"*

The blade froze in place.

The command had not come from Llyra or Saekl. Not even from Kanthe's stalwart friend, Rami.

Aalia strode down the steps and whisked in her gown toward them.

Behind her, Makar and Rami looked as stunned as Kanthe felt.

She reached up and pulled the sword down. "No. There's much you still don't understand, Tazar."

His captor released Kanthe's hair and used that arm to scoop Aalia into his embrace. "All I understand is that you're safe."

He kissed her deeply, bending her back with his passion.

Kanthe met Rami's eyes, as stunned as his friend.

From the floor, Jester voiced all their concerns. "What in Hadyss's blistered, fiery arse is going on?"

# 62

TAZAR SAVORED HIS victory—but no more so than the sweet taste of Aalia's lips. It had been far too long. She finally drew back, but she kept her arm possessively around him as she faced her father and brother.

"What is this?" Makar asked, his gaze flickering through hurt, confusion, and fury.

Rami settled on anger. "Sister, you've been aligned with the *Shayn'ra* all this time?"

Aalia firmed her hold on Tazar. "More than *aligned*. I've supported their efforts for the past five years. The empire has been in decline for *ages,* stagnant and calcified. Only freedom can reverse that course. We must break down the stultifying caste system that has chained the baseborn in place. Rami, you and I have spent months of late on this very subject."

Rami waved at Kanthe. "I thought it was because you didn't want to marry him."

"True. That was problematic. Such an unfortunate arrangement *did* require me to act sooner than I wanted, forcing me to orchestrate my own abduction. Which unfortunately failed. And with far more bloodshed than I intended."

Tazar watched Rami struggle to realign events in his head.

"But why?" her brother asked. "How?"

Tazar knew the answer.

Years ago, after Aalia had exposed Tazar in the palace for his duplicitous attempt to co-opt her, he had fled to the streets. He had found himself drawn into the *Shayn'ra*, stoked by his anger at *imri* class. Only afterward was he shocked to discover a covert benefactor to their cause. Someone who secretly supplied the Fist with aid, support, and intelligence from within the palace, allowing their order to flourish. Someone who wanted to tear down the order in Kysalimri as fervently as he did.

Aalia, of course, had recognized him right away. She immediately disparaged him, believing he remained as disingenuous as ever. Still, he eventually convinced her, which sharpened her guilt at nearly having him killed back at the palace. Time and purpose drove them closer together, until they could no longer deny their attraction for one another, their affection. She admitted she had been drawn to him from the beginning, when he was a servant in the palace. It was one of the reasons she had exposed him back then. She had been young, fearful of herself, of that first yearning. She needed him gone.

*But no longer.*

He pulled her closer and pointed his sword at Kanthe. "What of this Hálendiian prince, your former betrothed?"

Llyra stepped in front of Kanthe. "He is with us. None will harm him."

Tazar winced.

So here were those *crossed purposes* she had mentioned before.

Llyra was backed up by Saekl. From the shadows, other Rhysians appeared in black leather. Dark cloths wrapped their faces, leaving only their silver-blue eyes exposed. One shed her covering. It was the young woman who had accosted him. She once again held her small *quisl,* flipping the poisoned dagger between her fingertips.

Tazar lifted a palm. He was not about to challenge any of them.

Aalia supported this decision. "Though the prince is not the brightest, he's not the enemy."

Kanthe frowned at the insult but knew better than to protest.

"There is much we must talk about," Aalia continued. "Concerning a danger larger than any empire or kingdom."

Kanthe sat straighter. "So we convinced you about moonfall after all?"

She waved disdainfully to another chained man. "Your alchymist did."

Rami crossed to join them. "I will help. As best I can." He glanced Tazar up and down, then faced Aalia. "But we *will* talk later, sister."

The alchymist interrupted, struggling to stand in his chains. "If we're going, we should hurry."

Tazar nodded. "He's right."

Outside, the sounds of battle had abated, but Tazar knew it could not hold. Reinforcements from the mooring fields would fall upon them before long.

Even Emperor Makar felt confident enough in this fact to glare across the room. "This will not stand!" he threatened.

Before anyone could respond, the Augury slipped past the emperor, running a finger across Makar's cheek. "Hush."

The emperor stiffened at this touch and stumbled back. He trembled for a breath, his eyes rolling white—then he slumped to his knees, where he stayed. His eyes returned to normal, but as he gazed around, his face was a mask of confusion.

"What did you do?" Rami blurted out.

*     *     *

As RAMI RUSHED toward his father, Kanthe was content to remain on his knees. The continuing whirl of events dizzied him. His neck hurt from the strain of trying to look everywhere at once.

The Augury glanced at Rami. "No harm's been done, I assure you—well, no *lasting* harm."

Rami reached his father, but Makar shied away from him, as if not recognizing his own son.

The Augury crossed to stand before the rest of them. "As your alchymist has warned, we don't have much time. I've gone to great efforts to get you all in one place. And we dare not waste it."

Frell rattled to his feet. "You gathered us here? How?"

"It would've been easier if you all didn't keep thwarting me at every turn." He pointed at Kanthe and Aalia. "All you two had to do was get married as planned and come here for a postnuptial divination. Would that have been so hard?"

Kanthe, flummoxed and confused, looked at Aalia.

"I had to act quickly." The Augury waved across the chained group. "I risked much exposing your location in Malgard. To ensure that the emperor brought you all to my palacio."

Pratik gained his feet, too. "But how did you know where we—"

The oracle ignored him and pointed to Tazar. "And you! I had to contact the Razen Rose. To arrange for Symon to pass you an old skrycrow message, letting you know your beloved Aalia was coming to Malgard."

Kanthe's head spun, struggling to understand this puppeteer. "You're part of the Razen Rose?"

"No. Though I've worked with them in the past. They often serve as my eyes and ears from afar. Together we've accomplished much."

"Then who are you?" Frell asked.

The Augury rested a hand on his chest. "You can call me Tykhan."

Kanthe challenged him, wanting a clear answer. "A name alone doesn't truly explain *who* you are."

"I suppose that's true. Perhaps it's best if we follow the example of the *Shayn'ra* and throw away our masks."

"What mask?" Kanthe asked.

The Augury lifted an arm. Bending it, he used the crook of his elbow to rub his face from brow to chin. As he did, the rich Klashean ebony wiped away—revealing the bright sheen of bronze beneath.

"I'm who you all came to find," the Augury explained. "The Sleeper of Malgard."

# THIRTEEN

# THE FANGS OF
# THE CRÈCHE

*To reach the worldes Mouthe, yu must fyrst survive its*
*Fanges. Lette that be warn'n enough.*

—An old Panthean adage,
from the 22nd Nyssian Cycle

# 63

NYX STOOD AGAINST the gale and bluster of those packed inside the *Sparrow-hawk*'s wheelhouse. Her concentration was thrown off by the muffled shouting from outside and the loud hammering in the ship's hold. It all sharpened the ache behind her eyes. She squinted against it, determined not to relent.

"Your plan is pure madness," Graylin insisted as he paced in front of the ship's maesterwheel.

Others murmured or grunted their agreement. To the side, Darant leaned on a console, shaking his head. His two daughters looked dour. Jace hugged his chest, his eyes huge. Krysh crouched over a map table, tacked with a hand-drawn chart of the Ameryl Sea. Fenn leaned near the alchymist, peering over Krysh's shoulder.

Nyx ignored them all. "I'm going. Nothing will stop me."

She pictured her destination. Across the inside of her skull, a map blazed, fiery and insistent. Urgency pounded in her heart, fueled both by her own fear and by what the Dreamers had instilled in her.

She voiced it now. "I will lose Bashaliia if I wait even another day," she pressed. "I know it. I must go now."

Krysh glanced over his shoulder at her. "Nyx, why must you risk so much for the Mýr bat? I know he's your bonded brother and you bear great affection, but there are far higher stakes, as you know, as you've seen in your vision."

Nyx had difficulty putting into words what burned in her heart. She had already explained in private what had befallen her and Daal, about their communing with the Dreamers, what they shared, even about the threat of another like Shiya.

Nyx looked at the bronze woman, who stood next to Rhaif. Even now, Nyx could stir up the *Oshkapeers'* terror of such inhuman figures. Yet, she also sensed the Dreamers' compulsion for Nyx to rescue Bashaliia. Daal had described the *Oshkapeers* as *unmoored by time*, with the ability to ride the tides forward. Had they foreseen a time when Bashaliia would be needed, for him to be at her side?

*Or is what I'm sensing just a reflection of my own heart's desire?*

She could not discount that possibility.

Still, she continued. "Krysh, you mentioned my vision from last summer. Mind you all, Bashaliia was *in* that dream of mine."

She could easily dredge up that nightmare. It had become ingrained in her as firmly as the Dreamers' fiery map. She pictured it now.

—*she flees up a shadowy mountain and skids to a stop at its summit. She is older, scarred, missing a finger on her left hand. Ahead, a cluster of figures in blood-soaked robes circle an altar where a huge shadow-creature thrashes and bucks, its wings nailed to the stone with iron.*

—*she swings her arms high and claps her palms together as words, foreign to her, burst from her lips, ending in a name. "Bashaliia!"*

—*her skull releases the fiery storm held inside. It blasts outward with enough force to shatter the altar stone. Iron stakes break from black granite. The shadow-beast leaps free.*

—*one figure runs toward her, a blade held high, a curse on his lips. Wasted and empty, she can only fall to her knees and lift her face to the smoke-shrouded skies, to the full face of the moon.*

—*as she watches, time both slows and stretches. The moon grows ever larger. The ground quakes under her knees. And still the moon fills more and more of the sky, its edges on fire now, darkening all the world around it.*

—*she knows what's coming: moonfall.*

—*then a dagger plunges into her chest—piercing her heart with the awful truth: I've failed . . . I've failed us all.*

Nyx found herself trembling as she returned to the present. Though shaken, she clung to the memory of this vision to firm her resolve.

"If Bashaliia was *there* on that fiery mountaintop," she insisted, "then I'm *destined* to rescue him. Is that not so?"

A heavy silence fell over the room—until a dissent rose from where she least expected it.

"That's not necessarily true," Jace said, stepping closer, his eyes pained. "Your vision . . . you can't place such weight on every detail of it."

Wounded by his words and doubts, she stared over at her friend. Over the past half year, everyone had pored over every snippet of her vision, seeking additional insight.

Jace held up his hand and splayed it wide. "For instance, you still have all your fingers. In your dream, your left hand was maimed."

"But I was also older," she reminded him. "That fate may yet befall me."

He sighed and looked to Graylin for help, but the knight nodded for Jace to continue, likely happy to let another take the reins in this attempt to draw her from the plan to cross under the ice to reach the fiery Mouth.

"But, Nyx . . ." Jace's voice fell to an apologetic whisper. "The end of that dream. You died. And so did the world. By your own words, you *failed.*"

Nyx felt punched in the chest, bruising her heart.

Jace did not let up. "If every detail of your vision was true, then we might as well all go home and live our best lives until the end, especially if we're *destined* to fail." He waved across the room. "But we're here, supporting you."

She struggled to speak but managed to get out one word that contained many questions. "Why?"

*Why do you have such faith in me? Why is Bashaliia in my vision? Why does this all fall on my shoulders—to end the world in order to save it?*

Jace answered them all. "Nyx, you were born with an innate gift for bridle-song, but for the first six months of your life, you were raised in the fold of the Mýr colony. Back then, your mind was soft clay, still pliable, far from fully formed. Your brain grew while under a constant barrage of the bats' silent cries. Under such persistent exposure, your mind and gift may have been for-ever altered by their keening, as a tree is gnarled by winds. It changed you."

Nyx remembered Frell making a similar claim. She also pictured the glow-ing tendrils of the *Oshkapeers* manipulating and altering Daal's gift.

Jace continued, plainly having pondered all of this, maybe with Frell's and Krysh's help. "Years later, it was that lingering change that made you suscep-tible to the warning of the Mýr bats. As nocturnal sentinels from an ancient age, they must have sensed the changes in the moon. They were possibly engi-neered for that very purpose. Once alerted, they sought out the only one who could understand them, who could carry their warning to the world."

"Me . . ."

Jace nodded and waved to Shiya. "And possibly those like her. Sleepers who needed to be woken by their keening. Those ageless beings who could stop moonfall if it ever threatened."

"Unfortunately," Krysh added, "while they are ageless, the ravages of time still destroyed many of the Sleepers and damaged others."

Nyx glanced to Shiya. She pictured that spider hidden behind the shad-owy wings of the raash'ke. There was clearly more to the story of these bronze figures, but it would have to wait.

Especially as Jace wasn't done.

"I think the vision that the bats instilled in you—it was a general warning, a cry for help. They likely cobbled their own memories, along with your fears, and maybe some elements that were a mix of prophecy or simply extrapola-tions of what might happen next. The great mind of the Mýr bats had lived for countless millennia at the fringes of man, watching kingdoms rise and fall. It would not be hard for them to calculate what a future might look like if moonfall should threaten."

Jace ticked them off on his fingers. "A great war due to the ensuing panic. Dark forces trying to stop you. How the struggle could cost you greatly in mind and body. A promise from the Mýr bats, in the form of those shadowy wings on the altar, to be your staunch ally during the strife to come. And ultimately at the end, a warning about what would happen if we all fail."

Nyx's eyes had grown wider with each statement. She sensed the truth behind this interpretation of her dream. Still . . .

"I accept what you're saying, Jace. I do. But despite all you've argued, I *know* Bashaliia is supposed to be at my side. That he's important to all of this. The Dreamers—like the great mind of the Mýr bats—have hinted as much, instilling an inescapable drive in me to rescue Bashaliia. Trust me on this."

Nyx kept her expression imperative, tamping down her doubts, knowing what she just said might not be entirely true. But one detail was:

"I must go," she said. "Daal is already on his way to the western edge of this sea, waiting for me."

She pictured him aboard his skiff, tethered to his two orksos, Neffa and Mattis. This morning, after overhearing Ularia speaking to a guard about watching them closely, the pair had decided that Daal should stay behind. He wasn't allowed aboard the Reef Farer's barge anyway, so no one would miss his lone skiff if it didn't return with the other boats. Once everyone had left Kefta, Daal had headed out in the opposite direction.

"Daal's probably already at the wall of ice that closes off the western side of the sea," Nyx said.

"The Pantheans call those cliffs the Fangs," Krysh noted, pointing to the map of the Ameryl Sea. "It's a great icefall, pocked and riddled with caves and tunnels. According to a brief talk I had with Meryk, there is no way through there to reach the Mouth of the World."

Nyx knew that wasn't true. Still, she winced, but for another reason. She turned to the alchymist. "You didn't tell Daal's father or mother what we're planning?"

"Of course not. I couched my inquiry as an interest in cartography, nothing more."

Nyx relaxed.

Due to the prohibition against disturbing the Dreamers, they had kept Meryk and Floraan in the dark. Nyx had told them that Daal had remained behind at Kefta to do some fishing before returning. Guilt had panged her at this lie, especially with the way Nyx now felt about his mother and father. After she had shared Daal's memories, her heart ached with the love he had for them.

While much of that commingling of their lives had faded, her edges still blurred with his. Her memories of him were *more* than just if Daal had sat down and told her his life's story, but *less* than if she had lived all his days in his skin.

She could still remember what that intimacy had felt like. As that connection now waned, its absence only made her crave it more. She felt far emptier as Daal's memories dissipated. She longed to return to Daal's side, as if only his presence could fill that growing void in her.

And it wasn't just the hole created by the loss of his memories.

There was a hungrier abyss, too.

She remembered a moment with the Dreamers—when she had grabbed Daal's shoulder. She pictured his fire flowing into her, drawn into a bottomless black maelstrom at the core of her being.

She shuddered even now.

Graylin shifted toward the *Sparrowhawk*'s portside window, staring across the sea to the west. "If we should head to the Fangs," he said, "how do you propose to get there? Ularia has rallied the Reef Farer's warriors to guard us close. They're posted all over the beach. Any move and she'll learn of your plan. I suspect she wouldn't approve of this scheme any more than I do. If we do reach the Mouth, we risk stirring up the raash'ke into another attack on the Crèche. For that reason alone, she and the Reef Farer would prohibit us from going."

"True. That's why they must *never* know we left."

Graylin frowned. "How are we accomplishing that?"

Nyx noted that Graylin had stopped fighting against her going and now struggled with the groundwork to make it happen.

Luckily, she and Daal had already discussed this hurdle, too.

# 64

Through the small windows of the sailraft, Graylin watched the deck of the *Sparrowhawk* fall away under him.

Despite his trepidation, it was not a bad plan.

Next to him, Brayl sat behind the wheel, her feet manipulating the pedals, firing the small forge sparingly. She guided them away from the neighboring cliff of ice and out to sea. She barely seemed to pay attention, concentrating more on a pipe the size of his thumb.

"This dried weed that the Pantheans smoke is shite compared to Klashean tabak," she commented. "Though it does make your tongue pleasantly tingle."

"Mind the skies," Graylin rumbled.

She cast him a sidelong glance and spooled a dismissive curl of smoke his way. "Do you know how many times I've made this trek?" She glanced to a small hashing of marks on a paper pinned next to the wheel. "Twenty-three times. Nope, missed one. Twenty-four times if you tally this one, which might not count as we're straying from my usual route."

Graylin knew she flew regularly to the *Fyredragon,* to aid in ferrying heavier supplies from Noor's old ship to the *Sparrowhawk.*

*It's that routine that we're all counting on.*

The small group accompanying Nyx had snuck aboard the raft after it landed briefly on the *Hawk*'s deck. To stay out of sight, they kept the bulk of the ship between them and the guards on the beach below. The plan was to make off into the mists overhead, pretending to be on another supply run to the *Fyredragon*—then, once lost in the mists, they'd set off for the western Fangs.

Graylin looked over his shoulder and studied their small group.

Jace sat on a thin bench, balancing his Guld'guhlian ax across his knees. He had insisted on coming along, maybe to make up for his failed attempt to sway Nyx from this course, but more likely simply because he feared for her safety. His white-knuckled grip on the ax was testament to that determination, and maybe some measure of fear.

Besides Nyx, two others were aboard.

Quartermaster Vikas would be continuing her duty as Nyx's guardian. The woman was so tall, she had to keep her head ducked from the raft's low roof, even while seated. She massed twice Graylin's weight, all of it muscle encased in leather. Graylin planned on leaning on every stone of that bulk and every fiber of that strength to keep Nyx safe.

The last member of their group, Shiya, stood at the back, anchoring all that bronze to keep the raft's flight even. She would not only act as a defender during this trek, using her speed and considerable power, but she would also work in tandem with Nyx to bolster her bridle-song.

Still, Graylin wished their numbers were far greater.

Nyx must have read this desire as he sized up each member of the party. "We must trust we're enough," she said. "We dared not take any more with us, or Ularia might note we're missing. It's risky enough with the five of us leaving. Plus, once we get to the Fangs, Daal's skiff can only hold a few people. Especially with Shiya aboard. And we'll still need room for Bashaliia when we sail back."

Graylin frowned at her optimism. For him, their best hope was to reach the Mouth, for Nyx to recognize the futility of a rescue, then quickly duck back into the icy labyrinth of the Fangs before the raash'ke were any the wiser. Still, he had to begrudgingly concede that a smaller, less conspicuous party offered the best chance for that outcome.

Brayl also supported their fewer numbers, but for a more practical reason. "Nyx is right. I'm not sure this sailraft could handle any more weight. We're low on flashburn as it is. My father hasn't gotten around to tinkering with my raft's little forge. He's been focusing on the *Sparrowhawk*'s big engines, retooling them to handle that Panthean *flitch*. I heard the forges are already provin' more powerful. Can't wait to try 'em out."

Graylin noted her spark of envious excitement.

"I also heard they'll be testing the new balloon in a bit," she added. "Seeing if hot air alone will lift the *Hawk*. I hope I'm back in time to watch."

Graylin doubted it. Once Brayl dropped them off, she would sail straight to the *Fyredragon* before returning to the beached swyftship. She had to maintain their story that this was just another supply run.

Everyone back at the beach would also cover for the missing members: diverting any inquiries, muddying and misdirecting, anything to keep their disappearance from Ularia and the Reef Farer.

As the raft reached the mists, the sea below vanished. Nyx rose from her bench and crossed over to the window opposite Brayl. Her gaze remained fixed ahead, likely picturing the young man waiting for her.

Silence settled over the raft, all lost in their own thoughts and worries. Traveling through the mists, it was difficult to judge the distance they'd crossed. Brayl kept her focus between a compass and the skies, watching for any threats. Though she looked calm, sweat pebbled her brow. Still, she kept puffing on her pipe and sailed them onward, only firing the forges periodically, mostly letting them drift.

Slowly, the mists grew brighter ahead of them.

"The island of Kefta," Nyx whispered, as if fearing the townspeople below might hear her.

Graylin touched Brayl's shoulder. "Best circle clear. We don't want the flash of our forge to be seen by anyone down there."

Brayl didn't acknowledge him, but the raft tilted and angled away, giving that patch of glowing mists a wide berth.

Once past it, they continued their quiet passage across the Crèche. Time stretched. Graylin's eyes strained from staring into the featureless fog. Overhead, the radiant glow of the day dimmed to the eerie pale blue of eventide. With less light, the mists drew closer.

Brayl swore and jerked hard on the wheel. She pounded a pedal. The small forge roared, turning the mists fiery behind them. The raft heaved high to the starboard side.

Only then did Graylin spot the danger.

Ahead, a spear of ice cut through the mists.

The raft rolled to the side of it. But just barely. Their gasbag bumped against the frozen lance. A loud scraping trembled the hull on that side. A thunderous snap of ice reverberated through the hold. Graylin pictured that spear breaking away and slicing through the mists to stab the sea.

Everyone held their breath. The only signal that they were truly safe was a spool of smoke from Brayl's sigh of relief.

"I'd say that's enough of this soupy clag," Brayl muttered. "We should be beyond any prying eyes by now. I'm taking us down."

As she lowered the raft, Jace came up to join them. His face looked paler after the collision. He likely intended to help watch for any additional threats.

Once they dropped out of the mists, the dark green of the sea appeared under them. It was far closer than anyone expected, suggesting that the roof overhead had been slowly lowering the farther west they traveled. Below, they could discern the stripes of whitecapped swells. Something large humped through the waves, showing a flash of a wide tail before vanishing deep.

"A kefta," Nyx mumbled.

Graylin frowned, not understanding.

She motioned to the sea. "The island town is named after those massive beasts."

Jace searched where she pointed. "How did you recognize it?"

"Daal . . . I remembered when . . ." She gave a small shake of her head, as if trying to dislodge a memory. "Never mind."

Graylin's frown deepened. She had told them—though her account was sketchy—how she had briefly shared some of Daal's life while merged with the Dreamers. He suspected her recognition of the kefta came from a memory that was not her own. But he didn't press her on it.

"We're getting pinched," Brayl warned.

Graylin's attention returned to the window. The seas kept rising under them as the bank of mists above forced them downward.

"The cavern roof keeps dropping on us," Jace said, craning his neck to look up. "We must be nearing the western edge of the sea."

"Not *nearing* it," Nyx declared. "We've reached it. Look ahead!"

The end of the world pushed out of the fog. A jagged ice cliff cut across their path. It climbed from the sea to the mists. Cascades of luminous growth spilled down its side in shining blue cataracts. The glow revealed deep fissures and hollow-mouthed cavern openings. Shallow grottoes shone with brighter hues of crimson and yellow, as if eventide had not yet reached this western edge.

Across the breadth of it, one detail was prominent.

The cracks and broken slabs of ice did indeed look like the fangs of a monstrous beast—a giant leviathan rising out of the sea, waiting to devour them.

"There!" Nyx yelled, startling them all, pointing near the base of the cliffs.

Graylin searched for a breath, then spotted a spat of flame floating in the seas off that jagged coast. A tiny skiff bobbed in the dark water. It looked like a flake of fiery ash drifting before an icy colossus.

He glanced over to Nyx, picturing that tiny skiff sailing into those towering Fangs.

*I should've tried harder to dissuade her.*

Still, he saw how bright her eyes shone as she stared down at the skiff, at Daal and his two orksos. But he knew there was *another* who drew her even more.

Graylin had to accept the inevitable.

*I could never have stopped her.*


NYX CLIMBED FROM the stern of the hovering sailraft to the bobbling skiff. Daal helped her down, grabbing her hand. Upon his touch, she felt a flash of his inner fire, a lash of power that drew a sharp breath from her.

"I've got you," Daal said in Panthean, but she understood him. That piece of his memory remained with her.

Once she gained her balance aboard the skiff, she forced herself to let go of Daal and shift to the bow where Jace waited. He sat to the right of where

Daal's reins were draped across the curve of the prow. She took a seat on the left. In the waters ahead, the horns of Neffa and Mattis pierced the waves, knocking playfully against one another. Nyx knew from Daal's memories that Mattis was Neffa's father. Their loving antics drew a small smile, helping to calm her, to stifle some of her anxiety.

Behind her, Graylin and Vikas dropped into the skiff, swaying the boat. When Shiya followed next, the stern dipped deep under her weight. Water washed over the rails before the skiff settled into a rocky bobbing.

Daal expertly crossed the deck toward the prow, balancing with little effort, and took up the skiff's reins.

Shiya remained standing at the back. Overhead, the open door of the skiff hung near her head. Brayl crouched there and passed down additional supplies. They all had their own packs, but with so much unknown ahead, everyone else had contributed as best they could.

"Careful," Brayl warned as she handed down a large basket. "Rhaif packed enough tack to last you all a good week. Plus, four bottles of sweet wine and a tiny cask of ale to wash it all down. Clearly, he had his own idea about *essentials.*"

Shiya took the basket and stored it in a small fish pen at the stern.

Brayl lowered more satchels and tools. Krysh had sent an oilskin-wrapped parcel of ink, pens, and parchment, to help them chart their route. The *Hawk*'s engineer, Hyck, shared a small farscope to help them survey the Mouth's ravine, should they ever reach it.

"Fenn sent this for you!" Brayl called out, and heaved a pack at Jace, who fumbled but caught it. "There's a compass, star charts, and a sextant. And other navigational tools that he thought you'd know how to use."

Jace secured the satchel under his bench. "Once clear of the ice, we should get our first look at the open skies again."

Last, Brayl rolled away and returned with a big crate. Straining, she held it toward Shiya. "Careful with this one. My father scavenged through the *Hawk*'s dwindling armaments. It's packed full of our last hand-bombs and two folded crossbows and a score of bolts."

Shiya added the weapons to the fish pen.

In their own way, everyone had contributed something. While they couldn't be here, they intended to be a part of this expedition in spirit. Their generosity warmed Nyx. Still, as she watched Shiya settle the large crate of bombs into the stern, a twinge of unease trickled through her.

*What are we about to face?*

She turned to the towering cliffs.

From this vantage, the Fangs looked as if they climbed forever. The seas washed against their flanks with a shushing that felt like a warning. Caves looked like dark dens. The glowing blue drapes of foliage cast the ice in an eerie sheen. Breezes flowed in and out of those fissures and grottoes, carrying with them the scent of damp mold, stagnant algae, and salt-encrusted ice.

She stared up at the frozen titan before her.

*What will we find in there—and beyond it?*

Daal shook his reins and whistled to his two orksos. The beasts humped higher in their harnesses, then dove their horns deep. The skiff pulled forward, sliding from under the shadow of the sailraft. The raft was already skimming higher as Brayl headed back.

The blast of its forge made Nyx cringe. The flash of its flames turned the ice cliffs fiery for a breath—then went dark.

Daal drove them toward a wide crack in the ice, one among many. But he knew where to go, which path to take. He had the same map blazing inside his skull and had already searched the Fangs while waiting for them to arrive.

"Nyx . . ." Graylin whispered behind her, offering her one last chance to change her mind.

She simply shook her head as the skiff was swallowed by the icy Fangs.

*There's no turning back now.*

# 65

THOUGH A FIERY map glowed behind his eyes, Daal felt deeply lost. He could have never imagined such a strange, unsettling landscape.

Every turn brought new wonders and horrors. They had passed channels that roared with rushing waters. Others billowed forth with clouds of steam, burning skin and searing lungs, reeking of sulfur. They had hurried past those, chased by the torrid bubbling of boiling water. Some sections were so cold it frosted their breath and chattered their teeth.

As they continued onward, they crossed through routes that required ducking their heads from low ice-blue roofs. Another had them sailing across a great cavern, so vast and tall that the small flame from his lone firepot could not reach the roof or the walls. It was as if they had discovered another sea.

On and on they traveled, guided only by the map in his head.

By now, they must have traveled deep into eventide—though he couldn't say for sure. The timelessness of the endless tunnels challenged his senses.

Behind him, the others occasionally whispered, mostly generated by the nervousness of Jace, who likely staved off his terror by commenting or questioning every new discovery. Daal tried his best to ignore them, to let that chatter fall from his ears. He concentrated on the winding, tortuous path ahead of them. His memories overlapped with the journeys of the many explorers, shown to him by the *Oshkapeers*.

*Hundreds of deaths, even more despair.*

As the skiff coursed through the ice, the past and present overlapped. He heard the ghostly screams of the many who had lost their lives down here, while also noting the grunts and whistling exhalations of Neffa and Mattis. The orksos were nervous, too, chuffing and rubbing against one another, though it was mostly a father comforting a daughter.

He hummed to them often, reassuring them with his voice, his presence. As he did, he noted the slight glow from his skin in the darkness. But he didn't know if he was seeing it with his own eyes or if Nyx's memories were blurring with his.

After communing with the Dreamers, he better understood what he had been doing innately all his life. He even had a name for it now: *bridle-song*. It was likely a gift passed to him from his Noorish ancestors, a talent further strengthened and molded by the Dreamers. Knowing all of this, he now found this ability unnerving, whereas before he had given it no thought. A part of him wished he had remained oblivious.

Still, his efforts helped settle the two orksos—if not his own trepidation.

"Look!" Jace called out, while trying to stay hushed.

He pointed to a shelf of ice protruding into the tunnel. It looked like a frozen beachhead covered in scores of white rocks. Then, as if hearing Jace, large black eyes popped open—disturbingly only *one* per rock. Legs unfolded and the creatures hopped with great bounds into the water.

"Steer clear of them," Graylin warned.

Daal followed this instruction. He had never seen such creatures, but when it came to these waters, it was best to be cautious. As they slipped past the icy shelf, a lone beast crouched by a clawed hole. A clutch of crimson eggs filled it. It hissed as they glided by, showing rows of needlelike teeth.

Such strangeness was not the first. Even in this inhospitable and changeable world, life had taken a foothold. Earlier, they had crossed a domed cavern draped with glowing fronds. The foliage waved and shone. But it was not because of the constant breezes. As they skimmed under it, long tendrils unfurled, lined by thorns. Graylin had used his sword to part them aside so the skiff could pass through. As they skimmed under the weedy growth, Daal had noted hundreds of fish skeletons clutched in curls of those spikes above their heads. A few carcasses had scraps of flesh and scale, and one karp still thrashed in that deadly embrace.

They had hurried past, but life was everywhere. Flitting, crawling, scrabbling, splashing. One passage was overrun by thumb-sized spiders that fled from their path, even skirting atop the water's surface to escape. Luckily, that horde appeared to be as scared of them as they were of the spiders.

Some sights, though, were stunningly beautiful, haunting even.

A short time ago, a huge ray had glided under the skiff, four times the breadth of their boat. Its skin had shimmered and flashed, reminding him of the *Oshkapeers*. But this giant left behind a glowing trail in its wake. It shone long after the ray had fled.

Graylin shifted closer behind Daal, eyeing Nyx, too. "Do either of you have any idea how much farther we must go?"

Daal glanced at Nyx.

She answered, "We're about halfway."

Daal nodded, knowing she was right, picturing the fiery path ahead.

Graylin's brows lowered sternly at this report, but Daal didn't know if his grimness was due to how *far* they still had to travel or about how *close* they were to getting there.

Daal still had trouble reading the knight, especially when clouded by Nyx's

conflicting feelings for a man who could be her father, a man who had abandoned her in a swamp. Daal could touch Nyx's prickly irritation for the man,
but also a deeper warmth that had been growing steadily—which oddly only
stoked Nyx's exasperation, as if she were angry at herself for any tenderness
toward the knight.

Daal gave a shake of his head. It was all too confusing, but the heart was
never a seat of sensibility and prudence. He knew that all too well.

He shifted his gaze to the others, where there was less conflict. Nyx's love
for Jace was rooted deep. Her appreciation shone for Vikas's steadfastness.
Even Nyx's wariness of Shiya jangled through him—though some of the latter might have been inspired by the Dreamers.

Somewhere far away, a great beast rumbled.

Daal stiffened as the threat echoed to them. He tried to picture the monster
that made that noise. He prayed it kept away from them—but his plea was
ignored.

The rumbling swept closer, growing into a shuddering roar, coming from
all around. The waters surrounding the boat trembled, then shook into a boil.
The walls cracked with thunderous snaps.

"A quake!" Graylin warned.

They all clutched the skiff's rails. Daal ducked low. He lifted an arm and
held his palm over the water, trying to calm the panic of the orksos. They
thrashed in their harnesses, tossing the boat about in their terror.

Then Nyx was there.

She grabbed his forearm, her fingers clutching hard. She drew some of his
fire and cast it forth with a burst of brilliant song. He watched its melodic
chords cast over the seas like a glowing net. It settled over the two orksos. He
felt the calmness and comfort suffuse into those boiling waters, steeping the
beasts with reassurance and encouragement. A chorus echoed to the orksos—
through him, from her.

*All is safe . . . all is safe . . .*

Neffa, then Mattis, slowly quieted within the embrace of that song.

Nyx nodded to him and let his arm go. Still, her palm lingered over his
skin for a tentative breath. He watched his fire snuffing from beneath her fingertips. She almost followed those last flames back to his arm, but she pulled
her hand away.

Around them, the quaking continued, rumbling and shaking.

It seemed to go on forever, but it finally ended with a resounding crash ahead
of them. A huge swell of water rushed around a turn in the tunnel and shoved
the skiff high.

Daal lifted a palm protectively over his head. His hand struck the smooth cold roof. Then the boat fell under them as the wave departed. He was lifted from his feet for a breathless moment, then crashed with the others to the deck. They all lay flat as the skiff was tossed to and fro until the waters calmed to an uneasy rocking.

But at least the quake had ended.

They all regained their seats, breathing hard. Except for Shiya, who looked unfazed by it all.

Jace's voice still held a tremble from all the shaking. "Let . . . Let's hope that doesn't happen again." He searched behind them, then to the front. "Before we left the Crown, Frell had suggested such violence might be a sign of moonfall's approach."

All eyes fell upon Nyx, as if she were to blame.

Graylin finally waved ahead. "Keep going."

They set off again, wending down the tunnel. The smoothness of the blue walls hinted that this was not the first time that warm waters had flooded through these tunnels, melting the ice to the slickness of an orkso's flank.

*Could this be evidence of prior quakes?*

Over his life, Daal had felt them periodically in Iskar. And they did seem to be coming more often, causing great slabs of ice to calve from the cliffs that bordered the beach.

Nyx gasped and stiffened.

Her shock drew his attention forward. Ahead, tunnels, fissures, and chasms coursed away in different directions, which was not unusual in this icy labyrinth.

Then he recognized what had shaken Nyx.

In his mind's eye, the fiery path stretched forward—only to hit a massive slab of ice that had crashed down, surrounded by a floating blue raft of shards and pieces. The quake had collapsed a large section of the roof, closing off multiple tunnels.

Including the one marked in Daal's head.

He fought against the sight, but there was no denying the truth.

*We'll never reach the Mouth now.*

# 66

As Nyx gaped at the wall of broken ice, she battled between fury and despair. They had risked so much to get here. She had argued so forcibly to rescue Bashaliia, only to be stopped by fate—and, if Jace and Frell were correct, by the damnable moon itself.

*Maybe the world was never meant to be saved. Maybe my vision of defeat and failure was as prophetic as moonfall itself.*

"What can we do?" Jace asked.

"We must go back," Graylin stated firmly. "I'm sorry, Nyx. Once we return to Iskar, we can try reaching the Mouth once the *Sparrowhawk* is repaired. Darant is making swift progress. If Bashaliia can hold out until then—"

"He won't," she said darkly.

Shiya spoke from the stern. "The path you were shown," she said with cold authority. "How much farther past this blockage does it continue? Can you see that far?"

Nyx let her eyelids drift closed, shoving aside her anger. The route through the Fangs glowed there. It laid a fiery line from their location all the way through to the Mouth. She could not tell how much of the tunnel had collapsed, but farther along it, she saw where the path widened into a huge void under the ice.

"There is a massive chasm," she mumbled, still focusing, following that path. "Two, maybe three, leagues away. Even bigger than the one we sailed through before. The blocked tunnel leads there after several switchbacks and turns. Even if the tunnel has collapsed its entire length, that chasm must still be open. Even the quake couldn't have closed it down."

Daal nodded. "It's huge."

Nyx faced the others. "The mapped trail continues onward from there. If we could reach the chasm, we'd regain that path."

"But how?" Jace asked. "How do we reach it? You said hundreds of explorers had died wandering blindly through the Fangs. If we leave the known path, we risk meeting the same end."

Vikas shifted forward and waved at the other tunnels and fissures that remained open. She then gestured in Gynish: "Do you have any idea where these lead? Can you discern a path from here to the chasm?"

To try to answer her, Nyx closed her eyes. The *Oshkapeers* had burned the route into her skull, but they'd never given her a complete map of the Fangs' surrounding landscape. They likely didn't think it was necessary, as they had supplied her with a secure path, one that avoided the worst dangers.

Still, while communing with them, she had experienced the hundreds of tragic deaths of failed explorers. Those stories had faded in detail, but if she could conjure them up again, they might reveal a side route to resecure their path.

*It's our only hope.*

She swallowed hard and gathered all the fading threads of those stories and concentrated on the fiery map. She tried to stoke those flames brighter, to push its shine farther to the left and right. She sought to illuminate all the side tunnels, fissures, cracks along the route's edges, the parts of the maps where previous explorers had wandered to their deaths.

"Anything?" Jace whispered.

She sighed her exasperation. For just a breath, she managed to melt some of the gray ice that obscured the surrounding edges of the fiery path. "I can almost see it, but it's like trying to grasp mist."

Daal shifted to her side. "Take my hand."

She knew what he was offering—not just his strength, but also the pieces of those tragic memories that he still retained.

She took a deep breath and accepted his help. As their palms locked, fire burst into her, more than she intended to take. But her frustration demanded it. Daal gasped next to her. As his fire flowed into her, so did he. She again felt that strange sensation of floating between two bodies, sharing senses and memories.

She tightened her fingers, feeling both his hand in hers and hers in his.

She closed her eyes again. She knew she would have only one chance to flame those fading memories back to life, to reveal more of the surrounding landscape.

She focused on the map, poured Daal's fire into it. The path ignited blindingly bright. The gray ice to either side melted into mist, then it burned away, too. The tunnels and fissures, hidden before, appeared. She scanned through them as swiftly as she could, working through the many paths, searching for a route from their skiff to that chasm.

Her fingers clutched harder to Daal.

She could almost hear his voice.

*I see it, too.*

Unable to sustain it any longer, she let the fire collapse. The gray ice refroze along the path again. Breathless with relief, she let go of Daal's hand, nearly throwing it down to force her grip to release.

She opened her eyes to find everyone staring at her expectantly.

"There's a way through," she confirmed, excited and hopeful again.

Daal added a measure of caution, dampening her enthusiasm. "But we don't know if it's *safe*. The path we were shown and conjured briefly to life came from old explorers who *died*. If we travel that way, we must proceed with great care."

Graylin looked ready to argue against going.

Nyx cut him off. "We must attempt it."

She stared the knight down until he finally gave a small sigh of defeat.

With the matter settled, they set off again.

Nyx glanced back to Vikas and pressed two fingers under her chin and swiped it down, silently thanking the quartermaster for this suggestion. Vikas nodded back.

Nyx settled back to the bench next to Daal. It wasn't just Vikas who helped guide them past this obstruction. She stared up as Daal guided them onward.

*Without you, we would've had no hope.*


DAAL FOLLOWED ALONG the darker path, one that didn't burn as bright in his head. He had done his best to memorize the route to the chasm, but his insecurity mounted. He checked often with Nyx to confirm each new turn or tunnel to take.

His heart thudded in his ears, drumming with warning. He had to keep wiping sweat from his eyes. The tension only further confounded the passage of time. Memories blurred, especially along this new route. The ghostly screams of dead explorers grew louder, more insistent.

"It can't be much farther," Nyx whispered.

He sensed the same, but he didn't know for sure.

All around them, the ice creaked and groaned, stressed by the recent quake, trying to resettle after the jolt. Occasional distant booms made him wince.

Behind him, Graylin cursed under his breath.

Jace's knee kept bobbing up and down.

Vikas breathed hard through her nose.

Only Shiya remained quiet and unmoving, a statue of bronze at the stern.

"There's a light up ahead," Jace said, his voice wavering between hope and terror.

Daal saw he was correct. The flame from his firepot had masked the glow from the next passageway. Seated farther back, Jace had spotted it first.

"What is it?" Nyx asked.

Daal shook his head, not so much to indicate his ignorance, but to shake the ghostly cry of agony that filled his left ear. He glanced to Nyx, but she didn't seem to hear it.

"Something's there," Daal said. "Something we need to be wary of."

"How do you know?" Graylin asked.

"I just do."

The scream slowly faded, but not his trepidation. Still, he urged Neffa and Mattis ahead.

As the skiff glided forward, the glow revealed a cavernous grotto ahead, a wide swelling of the tunnel walls. The roof twinkled and shone with an ameryl gleam, iridescent and radiant. The flat waters beneath mirrored that starry roof, creating a shimmering oasis.

"It's beautiful," Jace said.

Graylin lifted out of his seat to search ahead. "But what's giving off that glow?"

As the prow of the boat pushed into the grotto, Daal felt something sticky swipe his cheek, accompanied by a tiny *ping*. Then another struck on his bare arm, snapping away. He ducked and waved a hand ahead of him. He saw nothing, but his fingers and palms broke through more strands.

The others suffered the same, jerking and wiping as they were equally assaulted.

"It's webbing," Graylin said.

With a shudder, Daal remembered the rampage of spiders in that other tunnel. He searched up at the glow. It took him an extra breath to recognize what hid up there, what was stirred and alerted by their passage through its web.

Overhead, radiantly glowing worms writhed on thin, jeweled threads. They descended swiftly along those cords or simply dropped headlong.

One struck his upturned face. His cheek ignited with fire, as if lanced by a flaming brand. He hollered and picked the burning worm off his blistered skin and tossed it into the water. The splash rippled away the mirrored illusion. The offending worm still shone as it wriggled into the depths. Bones lay strewn along the bottom. A hollow-eyed skull stared up at him, its jaw forever open.

His left ear again erupted with that agonized scream.

He now knew *where* that cry had risen from.

In less than a breath, a furious cascade of the worms fell upon the boat, squirming through the air or swinging on those sticky, dew-dropped threads. Screams and bellows erupted from the others. He tried to protect Nyx with his own body. But the worms were everywhere, an inescapable storm of fire.

Even the water offered no refuge.

Neffa and Mattis dove deep with the first stinging burn, but the worms pursued them even in the depths, their touch still as agonizing. Maddened by the pain, the orksos fled in different directions. Neffa tried to retreat to the safety behind them. Mattis fought to drive ahead. The skiff spun in the middle of this tussle, keeping everyone trapped under the fiery assault.

Shiya boomed, "Overboard! In the water!"

Daal didn't understand, knowing there was no escape that way. Still, as others rolled over the rails, he followed, hoping the water would cool his score of burns.

It did not—if anything, it inflamed those spots.

"Stay together!" Shiya yelled as she splashed in with them.

As she did, she sank quickly until her feet struck bones. Only her forearms and hands were above water. She crossed to the skiff and lifted it higher, demonstrating her considerable strength. As she did, she kept it balanced evenly.

Graylin was the first to understand the bronze woman's intent. "Get under its keel!" he bellowed.

Daal kicked and paddled through the fire until he was able to duck beneath the makeshift shield. Everyone crowded close. Even Neffa and Mattis. Daal rubbed a palm along the orksos' flanks and shifted their horns to keep them from impaling anyone.

Once everyone was sheltered, Shiya set off across the grotto. They followed with her, staying under that shield. Worms still struck the skiff, but they found no more flesh to burn.

After a time, the glowing lair faded behind them. Soon, the only light came from the firepot up top. In the dark, the worms abandoned the skiff in droves, rolling and squirming to escape. Once in the water, they wiggled a glowing path back toward their grotto.

Daal and the others waited until they were gone, then clambered back into the skiff. They were blistered and in agony, but before attending to their injuries, they shifted the skiff over to a shelf of ice that allowed Shiya to climb up and rejoin them.

"Thanks," Graylin said to her as she settled into the stern.

Shiya simply nodded.

Vikas slipped out a healer's satchel from her gear. She rummaged through it and removed a small jar. Her strong hands broke the wax seal and opened the lid. A sweet scent wafted off a thick ointment inside. She lifted it and motioned with flicks of her wrists and long fingers.

"Almskald," Nyx said, interpreting the gestures for Daal. "It should cool the burn and settle the blistering."

The jar was passed around. Daal dabbed the ointment on his fiery cheek.

He exhaled as the balm doused the worst of the heat. He attended to his many other blistered spots, as did the others. He even called Neffa and Mattis closer and slathered the thick gel over their wounds. Neffa's flanks shivered with relief. She tossed her horn high in gratitude and bumped her father, regaining some of her happy composure.

As Daal settled back, taking up the skiff's reins, he saw Nyx staring at a deeply blistered spot on the back of her hand. It looked to be the worst of her wounds. Her expression was pensive and worried. And he knew why. He recognized the scar it would leave.

He had seen it already.

While communed together, he had shared her vision of moonfall in all its bloody terror. He could picture her hand lifted, missing a finger. She had carried many scars to that mountaintop; one of them lay at that exact same spot on her hand. It was as if her prophetic dream were slowly and inexorably coming to life, marking her body as it did so, bringing her a step closer to the doom forecast in that vision.

Once everyone had dealt with their burns, Graylin pointed ahead. "We should keep going."

Nyx lowered her hand and nodded, as if acknowledging the necessity of this journey—and the greater one ahead of her.

Daal got the orksos situated in their harnesses and set off along the remainder of this side route. No one spoke, too daunted and tired. In the silence, a new noise slowly rose ahead of them. It started as a distant whistling, a haunting, continual note. Then as they swept forward, it grew into a perpetual howling.

"It sounds like the wind," Graylin noted.

He was proven right a short time later when the skiff slid out of the tunnel and into a vast, empty void. The world vanished ahead of them. The tiny firepot revealed only a stretch of dark sea, spreading endlessly beyond the prow.

But this chasm wasn't a cavern.

"I see stars," Jace said.

Daal craned his neck. Far above, there was no roof. Winds whipped across a distant opening, creating that howl. They had sailed into another rift in the Ice Shield, like the giant fissure that opened into the Crèche.

Still, that's not what drew a gasp from Daal.

Far above, bright gems twinkled.

*Stars . . .*

All his life, he had never been allowed to travel with the village men as they hauled carcasses to the top of the ice as an offering to the raash'ke. So, he'd never witnessed the open sky before. While some of Nyx's memories had revealed such a glittering wonder, it was nothing like seeing it firsthand.

"They're amazing," he whispered.

The sight of that shining splendor stirred hope inside him.

*If such beauty exists, anything is possible.*

Still, he could not forget how a nest of worms had almost ended their journey. And far worse lay ahead of them.

Then, as if to further dim any optimism, a low roar cut through the wail of the winds. The seas shook again. Distant ice cracked.

Another quake.

Daal held his breath, but it ended quickly and with far less violence.

*Just a warning from the gods to hurry.*

As he exhaled his relief, he stared past the stern, praying that the path home would remain open long enough for them to return.

Next to him, Nyx stared forward, focused ahead, not behind.

Still, Daal pictured who lay behind them: his mother and father, his sister, Henna, even Nyx's companions, who were closer to his heart after his sharing of Nyx's life.

With all the quakes and terrors along this journey, he cast out a brief prayer back home.

*Please be safe.*

# 67

RHAIF WAITED FOR the sands to stop dancing across the beach. As he held his breath, he balanced on his crutch, riding out the minor quake—praying for it to stay *minor*. It was the second tremblor since the violent shake that had toppled walls and collapsed homes in Iskar. To make matters worse, that big quake had sent a huge swell across the town, wreaking more damage to a village that had sustained so much misery already.

*At least, this time it wasn't our fault.*

The sands finally settled around him. He looked to Kalder for confirmation. The vargr had stiffened a moment ago, as if sensing what was coming. Prior to the massive quake, Kalder had howled in warning—not that anyone understood him until the ground began to heave and roll.

Steps away, the vargr paced a few wary circles, but his hackles slowly smoothed across his back.

Rhaif called over to Floraan and Henna. "Kalder says it's over."

"At least for now," Fenn added from Rhaif's other side. The navigator glared at the sea, as if daring it to surge toward him.

"Let's pray that's the end of it," Floraan said.

Henna still clung to her mother's arm, hugging tight to her leg.

The four of them—and Kalder—had been headed from the *Sparrowhawk* back to Floraan's home, to fetch a late repast for those working around the ship. It was well into the night, but teams continued to labor in shifts on the repairs. Prior to the big quake, the crews had been enthused and reinvigorated by an earlier triumph.

Rhaif glanced behind at that *success.*

Down the beach, the ship hovered to the height of two men over the shallows. Atop its deck, a row of six large firepots blazed beneath the open mouth of a massive balloon. Those pots, even the gasbag full of hot air, glowed in the dimness of eventide. It made for a striking sight. The height had also kept the ship safely above the sea's surge during the big quake.

Throughout the night, tests and inspections had continued. One of the balloon's baffles had busted open a poorly sewn seal. Draft-iron cables had to be repositioned to better balance the ship's load.

Limned against the firelight, Krysh shouted to be heard above the flames' roaring. The alchymist had been overseeing and orchestrating this miracle. Meryk was up there with him, helping where he could.

While all that was happening atop the deck, Darant worked below with more of his crew and Noorish laborers. With the ship lifted, the broken keel could be addressed, along with patching the last of the holes in the lower hull. Repairs continued steadily, proving the old adage: *Many hands make for short work.*

Not that Rhaif adhered to such a philosophy. He had kept to the periphery of the efforts, leaning more heavily on his crutch whenever anyone looked his way for help. His attention was focused more on the seas, worried about Shiya and the others.

Even Floraan looked that way now. Her brows were knit with worry. She pulled Henna closer, but Rhaif knew that she wished she could safely clutch another.

"Where's Daal?" she muttered. "He should've been home by now."

"Maybe the fishing is good," Rhaif offered lamely, feeling guilty for supporting the lie.

"With those quakes," Floraan said, "you'd think he would head straight home. If only to check on us. This is not like Daal."

Rhaif winced at Fenn, who looked equally uncomfortable. But if they told her where Daal had gone, it would only compound her fear and risk exposing the others. So far, Ularia and the Reef Farer did not suspect anything was amiss, especially as the two had enough to deal with after that quake.

"I'm sure he's fine," Fenn said. "Daal knows these waters."

"Better than most," Floraan admitted, sighing out her anxiety.

Rhaif nodded. "He's probably on his way back and will be home by morning."

"He'd better be."

Rhaif glanced toward the sea.

*I hope so, too.*

As a group, they headed toward the village. They only made it halfway when a loud roar made them all jump and turn. But it wasn't another quake. Down the beach, one of the *Sparrowhawk*'s maneuvering forges cast out a huge swirl of flames. Apparently Darant wanted to test another of the *Hawk*'s new features, especially after it had regained its wings.

The force of the *flitch*-fueled forge whipped the ship around, proving far stronger than Darant could have expected. The balloon shook from the sudden turn and the flames danced under it. The forge quickly snuffed out before anyone was thrown from the deck or damage was done.

A stunned moment of silence followed—then a great cheer rose from the ship and echoed across the beach.

Rhaif smiled at yet another success.

*We may be flying out of here sooner than anyone had hoped.*

Still, Rhaif knew why Darant rushed through his repairs and performed such risky tests. It had been half a day since the others had departed for the Mouth. The captain had promised Graylin that he would do his best to head out there as soon as possible—that is, if the others hadn't returned by then.

Rhaif hoped such a trip wouldn't prove necessary. But if so, Darant had shown himself to be a man of his word. The *Hawk* could be airborne within the next day or two. Rhaif stared back at the glowing ship, praying that was true.

Unfortunately, the gods ignored him.

Henna pulled away from her mother and pointed up at the mists. *"Sen fa gen thah?"*

Rhaif didn't understand her words, but he heard the confusion laced with fear. He stared up as the dark blue of eventide flushed brighter, turning fiery.

Fenn swore next to him.

From the mists, a large ship dropped into view, falling fast, forges blazing. To its right, a matching craft appeared.

"Swyftships," Fenn gasped out.

Rhaif struggled to understand how that could be. Questions spun in his head: *Who are they? Where did they come from?*

Still, one thing was clear.

*They're a threat.*

Kalder lifted his nose and growled, confirming the same.

Out of the mists, the two ships separated and dove toward their targets. One aimed for Iskar's glow of firepots and lanterns. The other dropped toward the enfeebled *Hawk.*

Rhaif's group was stuck between the two—and exposed on the open beach. He spun on his crutch and faced Floraan. "Is there a place to hide? Away from both village and ship?"

She dragged her gaze away from the blazing skies, clearly struggling. She pulled Henna back to her side. Her eyes looked everywhere at once.

Rhaif pressed her again. "Floraan . . ."

She slowly nodded, then more firmly. "An ice pen. A large cave that we use for the cold storage of larger catches."

"Can you take us there?"

"Yes, but—" She stared out at the sea, clearly still worried about Daal, then back to the *Hawk,* where her husband worked with Krysh.

"We can't help anyone if we're dead," Rhaif said bluntly. He pressed on a more immediate concern. "We need to get Henna to safety."

Ever a mother, she reacted to Rhaif's warning and swung toward the towering ice cliffs. "This way."

As they fled, a swyftship reached Iskar, sweeping over it. From its open stern, large black barrels rolled forth. They plummeted toward the village, toppling through the air. As they hit, explosions thundered, pounding Rhaif's ears and chest. Flame and smoke cast up burning sections of roofs and shattered stones.

Before the enemy craft turned to survey the damage, a trio of small sailrafts blasted out its back. They shot high, their balloons popping open. They swept over the village, scouting low, then circling outward toward the beach.

"Go!" Rhaif hollered. "Make for the cliffs!"

# 68

❧

**THIS IS TAKING** *us far too long.*

Rhaif scrabbled through a shattered landscape of broken ice. Tall, frosty sickles, sharp-edged wedges, and huge ice blocks towered all around him. He cursed the treacherous maze.

Earlier, the big quake had cracked massive slabs off the wall. They had slammed like icy hammers onto the beach. Apparently, such icefalls were a constant danger in the Crèche. It was why their villages had been built close to the sea and away from those treacherous cliffs.

Still, the route to Iskar's ice pen crossed through one of those fallen slabs. By now, his armpit was on fire, rubbed raw by his crutch. His breath came in ragged gulps.

Ahead, Floraan picked her way forward with Henna in hand, flanked by Kalder.

More explosions echoed as the bombardment continued. Screaming chased them, echoing all around. Groups of villagers fled across the sand or sailed out to sea.

"Everyone down!" Fenn warned.

They all ducked for cover, except for Kalder. Floraan had to push his bulk under an icy overhang. A small arrow-shaped craft with tiny wings and a tapered balloon shot past overhead, its stern forge flashing with blue-orange flames.

"Slipfoil," Fenn said as the navigator crowded next to him.

Rhaif followed its passage. It swept and dove over the beach, where it unloaded a small black cylinder toward a clutch of evacuees. The explosion sent them all flying, gouging a deep crater in the sand. A couple of figures regained their feet and kept running. But the rest remained down, scattered like broken dolls.

"Keep going," Rhaif said.

As they fought through the ice, he no longer complained about the broken terrain. The towering labyrinth offered some measure of protection. It also helped that the eventide gloom deepened the shadows surrounding them.

A sharper boom, followed by another, drew his attention behind him. These blasts sounded different, more insistent. Far down the beach, the *Shadowhawk* continued to be harried by the other swyftship—not that the crippled *Hawk* could offer any true resistance. Another of those booms echoed, revealing a curling blast of smoke from the deck of the enemy ship.

*Cannon fire.*

The first two blasts must have missed the ship, as it appeared undamaged. The third pierced a section of its gasbag, sending it fluttering and sagging. The rest of the balloon, baffled into sections, still held the ship up.

Rhaif realized the first two cannon blasts were likely meant as warning shots and the third underlined the enemy's intent.

They wanted the *Hawk* grounded.

Darant got the message. The firepots atop the deck snuffed out. Slowly, the *Hawk* sank back as the air cooled within the remaining baffles of its gasbag. Its broken keel settled back in the water and its stern came to rest on the beach.

But the damage could have been far worse.

Rhaif pinched his eyes, suspecting *why* the *Hawk* had been spared. The enemy wanted to capture and interrogate those aboard, which could only mean one thing.

*They want something from us.*

He pictured Nyx.

"Why have you slowed?" Fenn hissed at Rhaif. "They're swarming all over now."

Rhaif tore his gaze away and followed Fenn, hopping on his crutch. The swyftship that had grounded the *Hawk* had discharged its trio of sailrafts, like the other swyftship had done earlier. Of the six rafts, half had landed, unloading foot soldiers in light armor, even several knights atop horses.

They were all clearly Hálendiian.

Somehow the king's forces had found their group.

As he fled, Rhaif caught glimpses and snatches of the war.

The ground forces swept the beach, cordoning off Darant's ship and blockading the village. Overhead, more slipfoils patrolled, sweeping back and forth, casting down fire from on high.

Explosions still burst, but they had dwindled in number as this corner of the Crèche was quickly subdued. Boats now burned out on the water. Blast craters blackened the sand. Bodies sprawled everywhere.

The Pantheans had been ambushed and outgunned. It had been no battle, only slaughter.

Rhaif despaired, knowing the doom they had brought to the Crèche.

*First the raash'ke, now these Hálendiian butchers.*

"Over here!" Floraan called to Rhaif and Fenn.

They hurried to join her.

From the shelter of the labyrinth's edge, she clutched Henna close and pointed down the stretch of wall to the right. "The entrance to the ice pen is right there. It delves deep into the cliff."

Rhaif looked aghast at the woman. The giant doors into the ice cave gapped open, as if welcoming them. But to reach it, they would have to abandon the broken ice and flee a quarter league across open sand.

"We must try for it," Fenn said.

Rhaif glared at him. "Are you the one on a crutch?"

Fenn pointed behind them, where voices echoed eerily through the ice, accompanied by the stomp and nicker of a horse. "A patrol is hunting through here. We go now or get caught."

Rhaif considered his options.

*If I'm going to die, I'd rather be fighting for my life than huddling in a corner.*

Rhaif scowled, knowing what he'd rather do.

*Not die at all.*

Rhaif waved them on. "Then go already."

With a deep pained breath, he followed behind the others. Kalder kept close to Floraan and Henna, as if instinctively protecting the youngest among them. Fenn wavered between keeping up with them and trying to help him.

Rhaif waved an arm.

*Better one of us dying than all of us.*

They continued along the wall. Ahead and to the right, Iskar burned, cloaked in smoke, ruddy with fires. Some of the pall was blown by the sea breeze and piled against the ice cliffs, offering some cover.

Rhaif heaved and huffed after the others. It felt as if his crutch were about to rip his shoulder out of its socket. With each step, he cursed everything around him. The crutch. The gods. The pickkyn that had hobbled him. His own stupidity. He saved his last and most heartfelt curse for the moon.

*You couldn't stay up there a little longer? Until I lived a long and uneventful life?*

Still, somebody took pity on him. The others safely reached the door. He hobbled after them as they ducked inside. Kalder had the courtesy to wait, though it might be because the vargr was not keen on close spaces.

Either way, Rhaif huffed to the great beast, "Good boy."

Then Fenn came retreating back out, followed quickly by Floraan and Henna.

Rhaif reached them as they all stumbled to a stop. The door swept wider. A cadre of warriors armed with tridents guarded the threshold. Behind them, he spotted Ularia and Berent. The Reef Farer's face was one of confusion and anger. Ularia had decided on just fury. This group must have fled here, too, seeking refuge.

Ularia pointed at them. "You did this! You brought this ruin upon us!"

Rhaif couldn't argue. She was right.

Fenn tried to placate her. "We only seek shelter. This enemy is as much yours as ours. We can help."

She looked aghast, incredulous, her anger flaring even brighter. "The only way you can help is by dying." She waved to the guardsmen. "Kill them. Maybe their bodies will appease those who came to hunt them."

Rhaif waved for the others to back away.

The warriors hesitated.

Ularia growled her frustration. She clearly would not tolerate any such insolence. Not now, likely not ever. The arrival of their entire group days ago had upset a precarious balance of power. Her ambitions were shaken by all that had happened. She intended to regain her authority by any means necessary.

She shoved one of the warriors forward, to get them all moving. "Kill them! Or I'll have your heads, too!"

The men strode after Rhaif and the others. They all frantically backpedaled. Henna tripped, sprawling on her side. Floraan lost her grip and fell, too. A warrior rushed forward, trident high—that was a mistake.

The child had a guardian.

Kalder lunged with a swiftness that the vargr seldom demonstrated. His speed was unnerving, reserved for hunting the deep Rimewood, for bringing down a fleet-footed buck. The vargr struck the man a glancing blow, ripping away his arm as he passed. The trident flew from the severed limb and impaled into the sand.

No warrior of the Crèche was prepared for a vargr, especially one fully unleashed and feral. Here was the heart of the beast that no one had ever tamed. Not Graylin, not Nyx. Kalder was a blur of savagery, a shadow with teeth. He crashed into the clutch of warriors before they could react. Throats were ripped, skulls crushed in jaws that broke the bones of bears, chests torn open by huge, hooked claws.

Two warriors made it back into the ice pen. The door slammed behind them. The scrape of a heavy bar could be heard over the screams of the dying. One last man survived. He threw aside his weapon and lifted his hands, begging in Panthean, dropping to his knees.

"Enough, Kalder!" Rhaif called to the vargr.

It was a wasted breath. Bloodlust deafened the beast. A reminder that Kalder truly heeded no man, just his nature.

The vargr leaped, fangs bared, and grabbed the warrior's throat. He shook the man's body wildly, wrenching it back and forth until the limbs went slack.

Only then did he throw the dead weight against the door, letting all within know who the victor was.

Kalder turned to them with a snarl, his muzzle steeped in blood.

They backed away, giving the vargr space for that fire to ebb from his eyes.

"What do we do?" Floraan asked, gathering Henna.

The girl's face ran with tears, her eyes wide with terror at Kalder. She would not be trying to put a saddle on him anytime soon. She hugged tight to her mother.

Fenn pointed back to the broken ice field. "We could try to hide back there. If we're lucky—"

Before he could finish, a handful of men appeared out of the jumble of ice, followed by two knights atop armored horses.

Rhaif turned the other direction, toward the thicker smoke hugging the ruins of Iskar. "Make for the village!"

It was their only hope.

As they ran, Rhaif tossed aside his crutch. At this point, it was more of an anchor than an aid. Each step flared with pain, but the agony only urged him faster. Kalder followed, sticking to his pack.

The smoke thickened around them, but there was little breath left to smother. Still, the patrol and horsemen vanished into the pall behind them. It stirred some hope that Rhaif and the others might reach the village.

"No . . ." Fenn moaned, glancing behind him.

Rhaif cringed and looked back, expecting to find the patrol closing in on them. But it wasn't a soldier or a knight. Overhead, a slipfoil sped through the pall, sweeping like a winged shark at them.

They could never outrun it.

Even if they could, it was backed by a sailraft diving at them, intending to close off any escape ahead. Rhaif slowed, accepting defeat.

*Might as well not die so winded.*

The sailraft fired its forge, blazing fire through the smoke. But the raft's pilot made an error in his haste to catch its prey. It got too close to the slipfoil. Its keel hit the slim ship's balloon. The forge's flames burned through the fabric and ignited the slipfoil's gasbag. It exploded into a huge fireball that rolled high, just missing the raft.

The slipfoil swept past overhead, spinning its wings in an uncontrolled roll. It sailed far, then struck the sand, cartwheeling end over end until its flashburn tank exploded, blasting the foil apart.

The sailraft followed the same trajectory, passing over Rhaif's group as they stumbled forward, less with any hope of escape and more on momentum alone.

Ahead of them, the raft skimmed the beach. Its stern door dropped open, its far end dragging across the sand.

Brayl glared at them from beside the door. "Run, you idiots!"

She dashed back to her controls.

Rhaif sprinted, forgetting his pain, buoyed by hope.

*Or maybe I'm dead and just imagining this.*

Still, they all reached the bouncing door and flung themselves into the hold. Kalder leaped in after them. Rhaif rolled around enough to see a pair of horsemen come galloping out of the gloom.

Rhaif thrust his arm up in a rude gesture.

*Too late, you bastards.*

Brayl fired the forge and shot the raft higher. The beach fell away under them. The horsemen vanished again into the smoke rolling off the flaming ruins of Iskar. All around, enemy ships dashed and floated. But for now, no one suspected this lone sailraft wasn't one of their own.

"Someone get that door!" Brayl called.

Fenn rushed and cranked the stern closed, sealing them in.

Rhaif knelt up. "How did you . . . where did you . . . ?"

"I was just returning from the *Fyredragon,*" Brayl shouted back. "Saw the battle. Snuck in when I saw the other rafts. Blended in as best I could, sticking to the thickest smoke. Lucky I did, or I wouldn't have spotted you. Then again, a fleeing vargr . . . that's hard to miss."

To the side, Floraan hugged Henna in her lap. The girl sobbed and shook. Kalder paced in a tight circle, still snarling, hackles held high.

*"Nee . . . faza ja . . . Kalder,"* Henna got out between her gulping breaths. *"Wall thah."*

Floraan whispered reassurance in her daughter's ear. Henna gave a tiny nod and settled deeper into the lap, already calmer.

Rhaif cast her mother a questioning look.

"I told her Kalder is not a monster. That he just got scared. And was only trying to protect her from the bad men."

"I think everything you said was true—except maybe for the *scared* part."

Fenn crossed between them to join Brayl. "What do we do from here? Where do we go?"

Brayl pointed at Floraan. "I was hoping she would know."

"What about making for Kefta?" Rhaif suggested. "Get the sea between us and them?"

"Not enough flashburn in my tanks to reach there. I'm running on dregs as it is." She glanced back at Floraan. "Is there a village close by—"

Rhaif stiffened and jerked back as something flew past the window behind her.

Noting his reaction, Brayl swung around. "What?"

"It's gone," Rhaif said.

"What was it?"

He shook his head.

Overhead, something suddenly tore into the balloon, shaking the entire raft. Past the window, a black silhouette cut through the mists. It dove past the bow. Then another. And another.

"Raash'ke," Floraan moaned.

All the explosions and screams must have lured the beasts back into the Crèche.

The raft whipped hard as the last of the raft's balloon was ripped away. Rhaif caught a brief glimpse of a wing and a tattered flap of fabric.

Then the ship plummeted.

Brayl cursed and pressed both pedals flat to the floor. The forge roared under them. Its flames fought to slow their fall, braking their descent, but not by much. As the raft spun, Rhaif caught snippets of a beach, the sea, the cliff wall.

Which of them would they strike first?

Brayl struggled to get them over water. But she had little control over the raft. Most of the forge's force was directed downward, trying to curb their speed.

But even that quickly proved useless.

The forge's flames sputtered with its last gasps of flashburn.

Once, twice—then died.

The forge fell silent, leaving only the winds shrieking outside.

No one bothered to add to that screaming.

They rode the spinning raft down—heading for a splintering crash.

# 69

Nyx did not need the fiery map burning inside her skull to know they neared the end of the Fangs. For that last half league, the tunnel had widened, its walls flowing with bright meltwater, reflecting the skiff's firepot. The roof arched higher, dripping heavily atop them.

The channel flowed more swiftly beneath them, requiring little effort from Neffa and Mattis. The two orksos merely floated ahead of the prow, resting in the current, letting it propel them along.

"We must be almost through," Daal said as he held his slack reins.

Nyx glanced around the boat. Across from her, Jace clutched his Guld'guhlian ax. Graylin and Vikas shifted the hilts of their weapons closer. Shiya manned the stern, near the fish pen that held their crate of armaments.

Except for the bronze woman, everyone's expression was a mix of wariness and trepidation—along with some relief. They had all had enough of this confounding and threatening labyrinth.

As they continued, the tide under them flushed steadily faster, worrisomely so. The meltwater above grew into a winter's storm of pelting drops. Yet, as chilling as that icy rain was, the heat in the air grew hotter. The ever-present whiff of sulfur now stifled. The chattering of drops soon deafened. It became difficult to see farther than an outstretched arm.

Daal had pulled a small shield over his firepot to protect its flame and hovered over it, trying to peer ahead. They couldn't risk the current tossing them down a wrong turn.

Nyx drew to Daal's shoulder, overlaying her fiery map across the storm that lashed and propelled them. "We're not far," she yelled in his ear.

He nodded.

A low roaring pushed through the meltwater tempest. Nyx had no time to question its source when they were suddenly in it. The pelting storm became a pounding deluge. Nyx was knocked flat, nearly tumbling over the side, but Daal caught her, yanking her beneath him. She only knew it was him because of the fire of his skin.

Then they were through it.

The skiff sailed out of a ragged cliff face that was both ice and rock. A meltwater cataract swept across the tunnel mouth behind them. Ahead, a wide river cascaded into a huge starlit chasm that cut deep into the Urth's crust.

The moon shone far above. The crystalline rock reflected its stark shine. Elsewhere, ruddy glows and brighter molten fires dotted the darkness. It was a terrifying landscape, a volcanic ruin, a jagged scar across the Urth.

Unable to thwart the river's current, the skiff and its soaked occupants were swept along, dragging the orksos with them. To either side, the walls looked even higher than the ice cliffs that led down into the Crèche. But they were not sheer. Fissures and cracks splintered off in countless directions. More streams flowed out of those canyons, joining the river. Other rifts glowed ruddily deep down their throats, breathing fire at them as they passed.

As the current drove them deeper into the maze of chasms and ravines, the air grew steamier, near to blistering. The sulfur burned eyes and throats. The water under them remained cold, still retaining some of its ice. They splashed their faces to cool the heat.

"We can't go much farther," Graylin called out.

While the urgency to protect Bashaliia still clenched Nyx's heart, she knew Graylin was right. Still, the river had its own will. The torrent rose into swells to either side as more streams joined this one. At the edges, rocks and boulders churned with whitewater.

Daal rode at the prow, balancing deftly on his legs, reins in hand. He had cajoled and whistled Neffa and Mattis ahead of them again. He expertly used the two, either together or at cross-purposes, to keep the skiff in the smoothest stretches of water—but even those were becoming rare.

"Hold tight!" Daal called out, spotting something from his standing height.

Nyx gripped the rail and leaned out. Ahead, the river dropped down a dark raging cataract, a roil of foam and spray. It looked like a toppled and broken slope of whitewater. It roared at them, as if trying to threaten them away.

They did not heed that warning.

Daal crouched, bracing his legs, his calves bunching into hard stones. As he sized up the challenge, he reset his grips on the reins, loosening one with a flip of his wrist and tightening his fingers on the other. Nyx could nearly follow his intentions, due to some vague recollection of instinct and memory from their past communing. She found her own hands mimicking his and had to force her fingers to latch hard to the rail, relinquishing control.

*He's got this.*

Then they hit the rapids, and her confidence fled with the first hard leap and turn of the skiff. She lost one grip, clutched harder with the other, then regained a hold with both. They were tossed, rocked, thrust up, then down. At one point, the portside lifted so high that Jace hung above her, casting a terrified look down at her—then his side dropped away again. Several gasping breaths later, they were shot out of the torrent and across flat black water again.

Daal glanced back, likely making sure they were all still in the boat. He wore a huge grin, as if he were ready to do it again.

Graylin sat straighter, his face ashen. "Get us to shore!"

Nyx nodded in rare agreement with the knight.

"Now!" Shiya intoned from the stern, but there was no fear in her voice, only urgent command.

Nyx glanced back. The bronze woman stood at the stern. Her gaze, though, was cast far ahead. Nyx turned to look in that direction. All she saw was the tortured run of the river, churning back and forth through a broken fiery tumble of canyons, rifts, and defiles.

With the roar of the cataracts fading behind them, a new rumble grew, coming from ahead. It was heard less with the ears than with the gut. It grew quickly louder, filling all the gorges ahead of them.

Daal heeded both Shiya's warning and the ominous timbre of that rumble. He whistled and nickered his two orksos toward an eddying pool along the right riverbank. The current tried to thwart him, but he mastered its riptide and plunged them into that calmer bay.

Once there, he drove them into a hard turn, sliding the skiff sideways up the shore's slope of rock. He beached them there and loosened his orksos' tethers to give them greater range of movement in the pool, but they were still safely tied to the skiff.

"Not too loose," Graylin warned as he scanned ahead. "We may need to ship off quickly."

Daal nodded and pulled back on the tethers to secure Neffa and Mattis closer. He apologized by tossing them fistfuls of small fish and a few eels from an ice storage in the pen alongside their gear. The orksos honked and exhaled their pleasure through their twin nostrils, riding their wings, knocking their horns against one another like two playful knights expelling nervous energy.

By now, Shiya had climbed a riverside boulder the size of Daal's home. Limned against the starlight, she stared off across the breadth of the fiery Mouth. They all clawed and gripped their way to join her.

Under Nyx's palms, the stone was unsettlingly hot to the touch. Graylin pulled her up the last vault. Together, they crossed to Shiya and flanked to either side of the bronze statue. Once the view opened, Nyx wanted to take a step away, as if that would help her escape the sight in the distance.

"We're lucky we got off the river when we did," Jace muttered.

Vikas turned to Daal, pressing two fingers to her chin and flicking them down in thanks for his skill, for keeping them from the danger ahead.

Nyx agreed with both of them.

Off in the distance, the river coursed another half league, then dumped into a large black lake. But its surface was not the placidly eddying pool behind them. The huge basin spun and whirled into a great threatening gyrus, rumbling its danger at them. From its center, a steamy swirl of mists climbed into the sky, matching the churn of that lake.

Nyx noted a berg of ice floating down there. It shone under the moonlight like a diamond imbedded in that black water. It spun a course several times around, sweeping faster and faster around the fierce eddy at the center—then vanished down its gullet.

"If this is the Mouth," Jace said, "I think we've found its sodding Throat."

Nyx searched beyond the ravenous monster, knowing it wasn't this beast she had come to find.

She cast her gaze past the lake. The cracks and chasms of the Mouth spread forever outward. Some passages were shadowed, others lit by moonlight. Most glowed from the ruddy heat of hidden molten pools.

It all looked barren and lifeless.

Still, as her eyes adjusted, she spotted skeletal outcroppings, all branched and stemmed. They were pale white, like the ghosts of long-dead trees. She didn't know if they were truly living or some sculptural mineral deposits. A few cliffs shone with lichens or molds, softly suffusing in the dark shadows.

Beyond the deathly rumble of the swirling morass, all that could be heard was the howl of high winds and a low grumble of the land. Otherwise, the Mouth remained silent, refusing to reveal its secrets.

Nyx voiced the biggest of them all. "Where are all the raash'ke?"

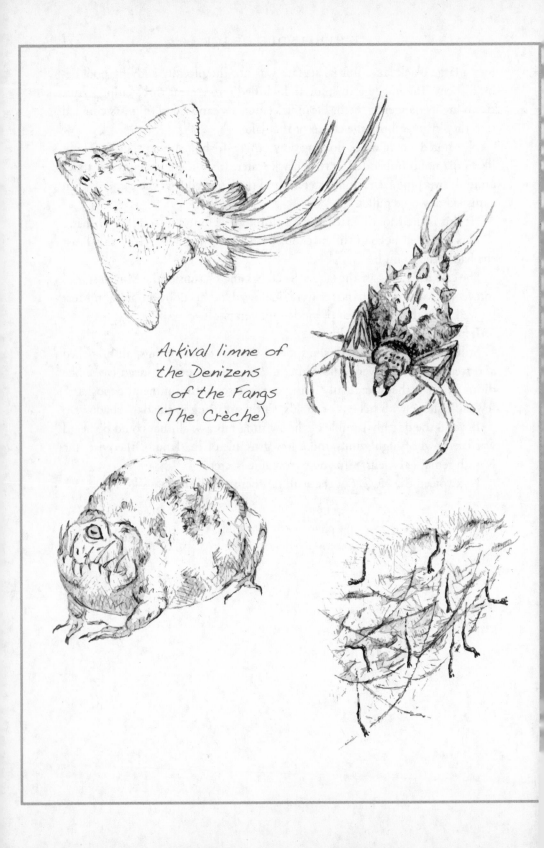

Arkival limne of
the Denizens
of the Fangs
(The Crèche)

# FOURTEEN

# A MYSTERY
# IN BRONZE

*Alle rivers flowyng forward ryse from the hedwateres bi-
hind them. The same is true for propheci. It is but a pre-
dictioun of the future rysnge from the lessons of the past.*

—A quote from Welt ry Torn,
the philosopher-king from the
seventeenth dynasty of Bhestya

# 70

WRYTH DESCENDED DOWN the stairs toward the kingdom's war room. The cavernous chamber lay four levels beneath the castle. It was more of a bunker than a council chamber. He passed sentries at each level, heavily armed.

None tried to stop him, backing from his sweep of gray robes.

Wryth had been summoned a short time ago. Dawn was still a few bells off, but Wryth had not slept all night. He doubted he could sleep even if he tried—and not just due to the stimulant elixirs he had imbibed to sharpen his attention.

Despite the early summons, excitement thrummed through him. Prior to the king's bidding, he had been shoulder to shoulder with Shrive Keres at the heart of the Iflelen's great instrument. Together, they had monitored a series of messages from Skerren. Earlier in the night, Skerren had dispatched his two swyftships into the massive rift in the Ice Shield. They brutally subdued a village and the enemy's ship. By the time Wryth had been called away, Skerren's forces were still locking things down along the shore of that hidden sea.

Still, a major problem had presented itself. The prize they sought to capture—the bronze artifact—was not found in that village or aboard the captured ship. Skerren, who remained in his battle barge above the rift in the ice, claimed his monitoring device was registering her location much farther *west*, somewhere across the rift's steamy sea. Most disconcerting, though, was that her signal kept blipping off and on, as if something were blocking or confounding the tracking of her.

To investigate this mystery, Skerren had unleashed Marshal Ghryss upon that hidden world, to interrogate and torture answers out of the enemy. The marshal was notorious for his clever tactics and coldhearted brutality. It was no wonder he so quickly quashed any resistance below. Before leaving for the Wastes, Ghryss had been slated to be the kingdom's next liege general. Wryth had stymied that promotion by co-opting him for the hunt across the ice. The marshal had been furious at the assignment, but the king had ordered him to go.

*Hopefully that anger will drive the man to pry out the location of the bronze artifact.*

Still, as of yet, Wryth did not know if Ghryss had been successful. After that last message, Skerren had fallen silent. Prior to that, the updates had been coming with a fair regularity—then nothing for a long spell.

While Wryth had been waiting for more, he had received the king's summons to the war room. It had been poor timing, but there was nothing to be done about it.

He crossed toward the tall, iron-strapped doors of the war room. The two guards who flanked it opened the way ahead of him. He swept across the threshold and down the three steps.

The war room had been excavated out of the bedrock beneath the castle's foundations. It was a stark and austere place, where battles were plotted and the fates of armies decided. No comfort was to be found here. The surrounding stone was heavy with iron, creating an impregnable chamber, one capable of surviving the devastating blast of a Hadyss Cauldron—not that anyone had tested that theory.

*At least, not yet.*

Wryth still didn't know why he had been called to the war room versus the council chamber. Something must have changed beyond their borders. His heart pounded harder at this thought. After the attack on the Shield Islands, he had believed there would be a short reprieve from the fighting, long enough for him to confirm the acquisition of the bronze artifact, a device that could turn the tides of war, especially if Wryth could fathom how to replicate such a wonder.

*And what other knowledge might I obtain from it?*

Desire burned through him with an avaricious fire.

*I must have it.*

While Wryth held no love for king or kingdom, Hálendii's stability and resources offered him the best chance to achieve his goal of piercing the veils of the past to uncover the lost knowledge of the ancients.

*Knowledge likely preserved in bronze.*

All he needed was for the kingdom's constancy to be sustained. The ravages of war threatened all that Wryth had built, especially with the king's heir proving to be so rash and reckless, unpredictable in his tantrums.

As he entered, he spotted Prince Mikaen standing to the side of the room's stone table. The captain of his Silvergard listened with his head bent as the prince whispered in his ear. Thoryn slowly nodded.

Mikaen noted his arrival, turning his cold mask and colder gaze his way. For the thousandth time, Wryth wished he had wrested control over the young prince, but events this past summer—the maiming, the humiliation by his brother—had ruined all of that. Mikaen had found succor, instead, among harder men whose lust for glory and battle spoke best to the prince's vengeful heart.

Wryth turned away.

King Toranth had yet to come, but around the edges of the room, lieutenants and captains from the kingdom's legions gathered in clusters. The only ones standing at the table were members of the king's council: Treasurer Hesst, Provost Balyn, and Mayor Torusk. Nobody would take a seat until the king entered.

Wryth stepped to the opposite side of the table. Its stone surface had been carved into a map of Hálendii and its outer territories of Guld'guhl and Aglerolarpok.

As he crossed down the table's left side, he ran a hand along the western edge of their territories, riding his fingertips over the sharp range of mountains that marked the border between the Crown and the Frozen Wastes. A razor edge of a peak sliced through his skin, welling blood that dribbled down the mountain's slope. He ignored the cut and tucked his hand into the sleeve of his robe. He pictured the glowing sphere buried under the Shrivenkeep and the glow of the treasure far out across the Wastes' Ice Shield.

*I must have it. If I could—*

A burst of a horn cut off this reverie, drawing his attention to the far side of the room. Doors swept open. The king entered with a brush of a dark blue cloak that draped from shoulder to ankle. His face was flushed, but it was hard to say if the heat came from anger or eagerness.

Behind him, Liege General Reddak followed, flanked by the heads of the kingdom's ground and wind forces. Bows and salutes greeted Toranth. The king barely noted them. He quickly took his seat at the end of the table and waved everyone to sit or gather closer.

"A flurry of skrycrows arrived in the last bell," Toranth announced, staring hard down the table. "From the Southern Klashe. We've learned Emperor Makar had fled to Qazen to consult with his oracle."

Wryth had heard stories of the Augury of Qazen, the illustrious seer who clutched hard to the emperor's ear. Wryth felt a flicker of envy. While he had the king's attention, plying and manipulating him with hints of prophecies and hidden knowledge, Wryth did not have as firm a hold on Toranth.

"What counsel did the emperor gain from the Augury?" Hesst asked.

"From what we've been able to gather—" Toranth's eyes shone brightly. "Makar was informed of the location of Kanthe and his abducted children. Some cavern system in Malgard, I understand."

Wryth frowned. *What was Kanthe doing there?*

Toranth continued. "Imperial forces secured them. Took them to Qazen."

Mikaen stirred. "So the traitor is in Qazen?"

"No," Toranth corrected. "The latest message spoke of an attempt on the emperor's life. By a rabble of lowborn and rebels. The uprising was crushed, but Makar was injured. Though the nature of his wounds remains unclear. He was last reported to have boarded an imperial arrowsprite headed north. Accompanied by his son and daughter, along with the Augury himself. They have Prince Kanthe with them—not as prisoner, but ally."

Mikaen stood, leaning a fist atop the table. "Then it is as I warned you all. He has been plotting with the imperium all along."

Toranth frowned Mikaen back into his seat. "We know little more than what I told you. For now, it seems Kysalimri remains equally confused."

Wryth stared at those gathered around the table. If they had all been summoned to the war room, the king must intend to take advantage of this moment of perplexity and disorder in the Klashe.

"What would you have us do?" Wryth asked.

"This is a chance to strike a resounding blow. After the execution of Prince Paktan, we know the Klashe will attack again." His gaze flicked angrily at Mikaen, but the king pressed on. "Makar will undoubtedly demand more blood. But he is wounded and said to be addled. His son Jubayr rules in his stead—a young prince no more fit to command than my own son."

Though Mikaen was masked, Wryth saw the prince's jaw clench.

Toranth continued. "We must use this rare moment to quash Makar's desire for further revenge. We must show the imperium the cost of vengeance."

"What action do you propose?" Provost Balyn asked. "Do we attack their coast, like they did ours?"

Toranth's eyes gleamed. "This is not a moment for half measures."

Balyn sat straighter. "Then what—?"

"We will bomb Kysalimri itself."

A stunned silence followed.

"We can't hope to take the city," Toranth admitted. "But if we move swiftly enough, we can wreak a path of destruction that will scar Kysalimri for centuries."

Reddak glanced to the king, who nodded for the liege general to speak. "Tomorrow morning," Reddak said, "we'll be taking three warships, led by our newest flagship, the *Hyperium*. Each ship will carry a Hadyss Cauldron— while the majestic *Hyperium* will wield the latest of our Cauldrons—a Madyss Hammer."

Gasps rose from around the table. Even Wryth flinched. A Madyss Hammer had never been dropped. It was said to be an alchymical storm trapped in metal. Once unleashed, it created a cascading wave of destruction that would lay waste for leagues in all directions.

Mikaen ignored all of this and shifted higher. "But what of my brother? What of Kanthe?"

Toranth cast a scolding frown toward the prince. "Wherever he is, he is of no consequence."

Mikaen huffed, his deep glower suggesting otherwise.

Wryth knew all the fiery Cauldrons in the world wouldn't satisfy Mikaen's lust for revenge. Still, the prince wisely settled back to his seat.

Thoryn rested a palm on Mikaen's shoulder, as if ensuring that the prince remained there.

Wryth wished that hand were his own, that it was *his* will that reined in and wielded the future heir. But even under Thoryn's steadying palm, Mikaen remained obstinate, his face growing redder. Atop the table, the prince formed a hard fist. Mikaen didn't even bother to hide it.

In that moment, Wryth accepted a darker truth.

No one truly ruled this prince.

## 71

AALIA WAITED WITH ink in hand. A long, blank strip of parchment lay on the table in front of her. She watched the black ink in the crystal well roll back and forth with the motion of the imperial arrowsprite as it fled through the clouds. Out the tiny window near her elbow, she tried to judge the landscape passing below.

Green forest stretched in all directions, marking the woodlands of Myre Drysh. Directly ahead, a silvery waterway split the forest into two halves.

*The river Styma . . .*

She frowned. From the width of the river, she calculated they were much farther west of Styma's headwaters than she had expected. If their destination was Kysalimri, it made no sense to be this far off course.

Where was the Augury—*Tykhan,* she corrected—taking them?

Aalia struggled with the many mysteries of the past day, determined to discover a path through them. She refused to stay idle and passive, something she had always fought against.

As the Illuminated Rose of the Imri-Ka, Aalia had been forever confined and restricted in her movements. It was a cage of perfumed oils, pampering, and idle days. She chafed at all of it, especially watching the freedoms allotted to her older brothers. Before her mother passed away, she had instilled and encouraged an active imagination, an insatiable curiosity, and a sharp mind.

*A woman's greatest weapon is her wits,* her mother had once told her. *Keep them as keen as any dagger.*

Aalia lived by that philosophy, especially after her mother died. She had studied with private tutors in every discipline, only releasing her tutors when she could surpass them. With every passing year, she honed that dagger. All the while, she allowed herself to be primped and paraded, keeping secret what was in her heart. Once older, with the help of a maid, she often snuck away to explore the city, to learn more, to cultivate interests wider than the walls of the palace citadel. It was such study and explorations that slowly revealed the rot and decay and stagnancy of an empire in decline.

She had read of other kingdoms, of other dominions, of other beliefs.

Interest grew into discontent.

Discontent led to rebellion.

Rebellion brought her to the *Shayn'ra*.

Still, in one day, all she'd known about the world had been upended.

Irritated more than scared, she faced the ship's long hold. The arrowsprite was designed for swift passage, little more. Certainly not privacy. A small wheelhouse closed off the bow. At the stern, a single cabin was reserved for the emperor. Between the two stretched an open hold. It was divvied into clusters of chairs and couches.

Near the back, Kanthe huddled with Frell and Pratik, surely discussing the mystery in bronze that was Tykhan. Ahead of her, Tazar and Althea whispered quietly, as if still trying to keep their secrets. Between them, the black clutch of Rhysians were playing a game that involved flipping daggers—possibly poisoned—and landing them between the fingers of an opponent. It was unnerving to watch.

The only others aboard were a pair of Guld'guhlian ruffians whom Llyra watched over. The guildmaster stood with her arms crossed, her features tight with anger. The Guld'guhlian who had lost part of his leg drowsed under a heavy draught of poppy's milk. His stump had been bandaged and attended to earlier. His brother sat next to him, resting a palm on the other's forehead.

Aalia stifled a flare of guilt at the sight of the wounded man, even though she had not ordered him maimed. She stared past Kanthe to the closed cabin door. Rami was in there with their father, who remained addled by some witchery of Tykhan. Despite her own frustrations with her father and the empire, fury at such a violation burned through her.

Still, there was little any of them could do. After the battle in Qazen, their group—some disguised under *byor-ga* robes—had fled through town to the mooring fields. They met little resistance, especially with the emperor in tow. Tykhan continued to exert some strange control over their father. He was able to get Makar to blurt out commands or offer reassurances. The emperor's words, though, came out stuttering, accompanied by odd tics and mannerisms.

The Augury—who had refixed the oils over his face—had told anyone who showed concern that the emperor had been afflicted by enemy forces, likely poisoned, but Makar was mending and under the Augury's auspicious care.

Eventually, they had reached one of the imperial arrowsprites and commandeered it. They replaced its wheelhouse crew with the leader of the Rhysians and a young cohort. The two managed to expertly guide the sleek ship away from the mooring fields, racing off with the excuse that Emperor Makar needed prompt care.

Before leaving, Tykhan had asked Llyra and Tazar to dispatch messages to their respective forces, to have them abandon Qazen and return to Kysalimri.

Those that returned were to rouse as many of the *Shayn'ra* and Llyra's low army as possible in the city and to be ready for further instructions.

Still, Aalia was at a loss. About nearly everything. She felt as manipulated as her father was, pulled by the invisible strings wielded by Tykhan. Everything was moving far too swiftly. Even now, she could not decide whether to fully trust the Augury or not. Still, in the haste of events, she had little choice but to be swept along his path.

*At least for now.*

As if summoned by this reverie, the door to the wheelhouse opened, and Tykhan reappeared. Aalia stiffened at the sight of him, at his startling transformation. Gasps rose from Tazar and Althea, who both retreated away. Tazar drew protectively closer to Aalia. She took the hand he offered, drawing strength from him.

Those behind her showed milder reactions, more curious than shocked.

Then again, the others had all witnessed such a miraculous creature before.

Though still wearing his black robes, Tykhan had washed off the black stain that had hid his true features. The hard planes of his face now swirled in mesmerizing hues of bronze and copper. Even the curls of his hair shone brightly, forming a sun's corona around his head. But it was his eyes. They had always been a stunning dark indigo. Only now, his eyes glowed an azure blue, as if lit from within.

Frell drew Kanthe and Pratik closer to Tykhan. "You truly are a Sleeper, a being like Shiya."

"We are alike," he admitted. "You call her Shiya, but only because she's forgotten her true name—along with most of the knowledge she needs as an Axis."

Kanthe frowned. "What's an Axis?"

"A long story," Tykhan said. "And even I don't know all of it. I'm just a Root, a lower caste of the *ta'wyn.* Little is shared with us."

Aalia shifted to face Frell and Pratik. "*Ta'wyn?* We read that word in those ancient pages. *Ta'wyn.* The *undying gods.*" She turned to Tykhan. "That's you."

"*Ta'wyn* actually means *defender,* but storytellers love to sensationalize and embellish."

Frell frowned. "In those pages, it also spoke of a great war among the *ta'wyn.* Was that an embellishment, too?"

"Sadly, no. But as a Root, I was not privy to the full scope of events. Roots serve at a lower level. Construction, mining, and other scut work. All I know is that during or following the cataclysm, the *ta'wyn* were created to build great machines that would set the world to turning again if it ever became necessary. Once done, we were to bury ourselves deep and wait to be woken."

"Sleepers," Pratik said.

"Our creators also engineered living sentinels to monitor from the surface and wake us if any apocalyptic threat arose."

Kanthe nodded. "Like the Mýr bats."

"And others." Tykhan stared around. "But I know little about those details."

"What of the war?" Aalia pressed, curiosity piquing through her.

"Yes, a shameful time. When the world stopped turning, the *ta'wyn* observed the great floods, the world-shaking quakes, the devastation that brought down mountains, the burning of seas to salt. Throughout it all, we watched those who still lived brutally trying to survive, clinging desperately to whatever foothold they could manage. The cruelty, the savagery of that time . . . it was beyond any imagining."

"You're speaking about the Forsaken Ages," Pratik whispered.

Tykhan nodded, looking haunted. "And those barbaric and brutal people were once our *creators*. It was hard to watch. It broke many. In great dismay, a faction of the *ta'wyn* deemed you all unworthy of our further protection. They believed that the Urth should be cleansed of your stain, to make room for the reign of its new masters."

Frell looked appalled. "The *ta'wyn*."

Tykhan sighed, acknowledging this. "But most of us adhered to the original definition of the name given to us. *Defenders.* War ensued. It lasted for a full millennium, long before the Crown ever formed. The defenders came close to losing, especially as one of our Krysts betrayed us."

"Krysts?" Aalia asked.

Tykhan lowered a palm to his waist. "I'm a Root." He lifted his hand to his shoulder. "The one you call Shiya is an Axis, a *ta'wyn* of higher status and knowledge. But a Kryst—" He shoved his arm as high as he could reach. "They truly are *undying gods*."

Aalia shivered, trying to contemplate such a being.

"It took every defender to finally defeat Eligor. He was as monstrous as any infernal god in the Klashean pantheon."

Aalia shared a look with Frell and Pratik. "We saw that name in those pages, too."

She pictured the looming figure of a man, holding aloft a thunderbolt. *Eligor.*

"Though he was defeated," Tykhan said, "some of his surviving members absconded with his broken body. They fled to distant corners of the world, still wreaking havoc. Before leaving, they damaged or destroyed many of our buried libraries of knowledge."

Frell flinched. "I think we saw such vandalism. In a crystal librarie beneath the stones of the Northern Henge."

Tykhan looked grim. "Such knowledge is needed by an Axis. They are the only ones who can ignite the massive forges and set the world to turning again. Without it, the Axis rise as newborns. They are driven by an insatiable desire to seek out that knowledge in order to fully restore themselves."

"I believe we've witnessed that compulsion, too," Pratik added. "With Shiya."

"Unfortunately, continents and landmasses shifted and reconfigured during the long sleep, often separating an Axis from its librarie."

Frell frowned, clearly frustrated. "Why didn't your creators just steep that knowledge into an Axis from the beginning? Why bother with a separate librarie?"

"Our brains are not like yours. They are resilient, pliant, able to hold vast amounts, but the problem with such flexibility is that our means of storing knowledge is corruptible by time. The crystal *arkada* that you saw down in the vandalized librarie . . . if left intact, such volumes can retain their knowledge until the universe goes cold. Knowing that, our creators only instilled a *core* base of knowledge into us. Even I was greatly confused when I first woke in my *eyran*."

"*Eyran?*" Kanthe asked. "Do you mean that copper egg?"

Tykhan scrunched his brow. "I supposed that's an apt enough description. When I was attacked there, I only survived due to a baseline of self-preservation. That and a Root's inherent strength and fluidity of form. It allowed me to tear apart my attacker."

"We saw a body in your copper egg," Kanthe whispered.

"One of the enemy. Besides destroying libraries, they also tried to kill Sleepers. It was why I woke up so early. With my *eyran* destroyed, I could not return to my slumber. So I traveled down a longer path, one never attempted by a Root."

"And what was that?" Aalia asked.

Tykhan looked at all of them, as if the answer were obvious. "Like any Sleeper, I waited through the passing millennia until I was needed. Though awake this entire time, my core directive remained the same."

Aalia frowned. "Which is what?"

"I'm a *ta'wyn,* which means my primary goal is to defend."

This answer was unsatisfactory to another. Her brother Rami had quietly stepped through the doorway of the stern cabin. He pointed back inside, his voice furious. "Is that what you call *defending?* What you did to my father?"

Tykhan lifted a palm. "I said it was my *primary* directive. Around that, I'm allowed a fair amount of latitude and flexibility. Even for a menial Root. I found the role of Augury useful in manipulating and guiding this quarter of the Crown. All to prepare for the war to come."

"With Hálendii?" Aalia asked.

"No, the greater war that is on the horizon." Tykhan nodded to Kanthe. "Your seer has already dreamed of it."

"Nyx?"

"Yes. But I wonder . . . is what she saw a *prophecy* or simply an *inevitability* due to your natures?" He shrugged. "I don't know. But I do know that as moonfall approaches, war will come. So, I became the Augury. To try to steer the path as best I could."

Rami stepped forward, challenging him. "So, to accomplish that, you killed the prior Augury and usurped his position?"

Tykhan frowned with disdain. "There has only been *one* Augury in Qazen since it was founded. Well, mostly one. As a *ta'wyn,* I'm untouched by time. I changed faces, voices, attitudes. I skipped a generation now and then to wander the breadth of the Crown, but ultimately, I've been the Augury of Qazen for over four millennia."

Stunned silence met this announcement.

"How is that possible?" Aalia finally blurted out. "In all this time, no one discovered this ruse?"

Her words seemed to confuse him, then his eyes widened. "Ah, when I said I changed faces, that's exactly what I meant. One feature unique to all Roots—due to the many tasks required of us—is fluidity of form, to change bodily shape to match our varying needs."

Aalia remembered him saying something like this when he mentioned the assassin who tried to kill him. "What does that mean?"

"This." He tilted his head slightly and the bronze of his face melted and flowed, remodeling and settling into new features, still coldly handsome but very different. "There are limits to such an ability, but it has sufficed to maintain my secret."

His features slurred again, returning to the face first presented to them.

No one spoke for a long time.

Tykhan used this moment to turn to Aalia and point at the blank strip of parchment and inkwell on the table. "I see you've readied yourself as I requested?"

She struggled for composure after this shock. Before disappearing into the wheelhouse, he had asked her to prepare a message, a note that a skrycrow would deliver to Kysalimri.

"What am I intended to write?" she asked.

Tykhan's eyes shone brighter. "Only the most important note you've ever written. One that could save the world."

"And say what?"

"To declare yourself empress of the imperium."

# 72

"HAS AALIA GONE mad?" Prince Mareesh asked. "Or is she as addled as our father is said to be?"

Jubayr shook his head, struggling to keep abreast of the rapidly changing events of the past night. He listened as the dawn bells rang over the city, using the moment to compose himself, to try to fathom the intent and meaning in the skrycrow message sent by Aalia a short time ago.

He sat at the head of the table in the strategy room, a seat normally reserved for his father. The table and room were packed. All eyes stared toward Jubayr: Shield Angelon, Wing Draer, Sail Garryn, a dozen lesser-ranked leaders of the imperial forces, and half of his father's chaaen-bound and three of his own.

They all waited for some guidance from Jubayr.

But it was his brother's eyes that burned the hottest. Prince Mareesh sat across the table, seated in Jubayr's former seat. Mareesh had returned yesterday aboard the *Falcon's Wing*, victorious in his destruction of the Shield Islands. But there had been no celebration, not with a brother to mourn.

*And now this.*

Sail Garryn, the commander of the imperial naval fleet, cleared his throat. "Could your sister have also been tainted by the Hálendiian poison that debilitated Emperor Makar? Could it have addled her, too?"

"Something must have," Angelon agreed firmly. "There has not been an empress of the Klashe in over seven centuries."

"But prior to that, it had not been so rare," Chaaen Hrash added. As the oldest of those bound to the emperor and the closest of his father's advisers, Hrash was highly respected and his counsel was welcomed by all. "As to her being addled or tainted, I know the curve of her ink. It was steady, her wording cogent, and in Aalia's distinct tone. To me, she seemed of sound mind, and I know Emperor Makar held his daughter in high regard, not only for her poise and beauty, but also for her intelligence."

Jubayr stared down at the curled messages in his hands. The skrycrows atop the tower continued to scream and caw, as if mocking his indecision. The crows had been arriving all night, building the story of what had happened in Qazen. The council had heard it all. Of the safe recovery of Aalia and Rami and the capture of the traitor Prince Kanthe. Of the attack by rebels and baseborn. Aalia's note reported a gaseous bomb had struck near Emperor Makar, killing his Paladin guards. While their father had survived, the exposure had left lasting damage.

In the end, *nothing* of the past days was as it seemed. Aalia's note described an entirely different stream of events. With the aid of Prince Kanthe, Rami and Aalia had uncovered a plot against the empire, one based in Qazen. Initially, they didn't know whom to trust, so they fled south under the cover of night to investigate. They could tell no one, fearing members of the emperor's inner circle were aligned with the enemy. In truth, there had never been any kidnapping. Even the immolation of the Dresh'ri librarie was part of this same nefarious plot in some way.

And in the end, Aalia and Rami were proven right about a threat in Qazen, but not in time to stem the attack. She and the others had barely escaped Qazen with the emperor. They had fled hastily, avoiding even the remaining imperial guard, fearing who among them might be part of this plot. The Augury and his healers had attended to their father, pulling him back from the edge of oblivion. The esteemed oracle traveled with them. His presence alone added much weight and validity to this story, along with accounts of guardsmen back at the mooring fields who attested to the addled state of Emperor Makar.

But it was what Aalia wrote at the end of her message that had shocked everyone in this chamber. Though for Jubayr, he could not discount a measure of relief. It had sounded true to his ear and heart.

Before succumbing to the worst of the poison, knowing he might die or be debilitated for years, Emperor Makar had passed his circlet to Aalia, declaring her empress of the imperium in his stead. She had refused, denying a request that could be their father's last. But Makar had explained his reasoning, telling her that Jubayr was a wonderful son, gifted in many ways. But he was more fit as a temporary leader, not for the long term. In this time of war and strife, the Southern Klashe needed someone of brilliance, grace, and wisdom to lead them forward—that figurehead could only be the Illuminated Rose, a personage that all of the Klashe adored and revered.

Still, his sister had refused their father.

Until the Augury further bolstered Makar's words, declaring the gods had shown him the next century of the Klashe—with Aalia crowned and leading it to greater glory.

Only then had she reluctantly accepted the circlet, but she had refused to don it. Not until she sought out the wisdom of the imperial counsel. If they deemed her unworthy or decided to castigate her as a usurper, she would gladly accept any punishment. She truly did not want the crown and would gladly pass it to another.

Jubayr understood that last sentiment all too well.

*And maybe that humbleness makes her worthier than any of us.*

Wing Draer pressed for an answer. "What do you propose we do? How do we respond?"

Jubayr stood, drawing up the imperial cloak with him. As he did, the clasp choked his neck, but he kept it in place, asserting the authority given to him by his father before he left. He intended to wield it for the betterment of the empire.

"My sister has proffered to meet as many of the counsel as would like to attend her in the coastal town of X'or. It is there—among the sanctuary's healing baths—that the Augury believes my father has the best chance of recovery. Aalia also comes with no army, leaving herself defenseless to our will and decision. I say we take up the mantle she had laid at our feet. To go meet with her, to see firsthand how the emperor fares. Then decide the future of the imperium."

His judgement was not met with any resounding agreement, only murmurs and whispers. His face heated, wondering if he had made the wrong decision.

Still, Chaaen Hrash drew closer and gave him a small nod. Jubayr gratefully accepted this small amount of praise.

Across the table, Mareesh kept his own thoughts guarded. His eyes remained fiery, but they had tamped down to embers—for now.

His younger brother had always been hot-tempered. His grief at the loss of Paktan had only stoked that volatility. The two had been closer than brothers, both warriors in the clouds. It was a bond that Jubayr had always envied.

Mareesh also placed great stock in routine and order. He always had. Even as a child, Mareesh had kept his room meticulously neat. Everything had to be in its proper place. He would cry if it wasn't. Perhaps such fastidiousness was why he excelled within the regimentation of the imperial forces.

So, this sudden upending of the hierarchy did not sit well with Mareesh.

Whereas Jubayr—confined mostly to the citadel alongside his father—had seen Aalia blossom into the Rose she was now. Mareesh had not witnessed her transformation from child to a brilliant woman. Instead, he had flown off into the clouds with Paktan, leaving his other two brothers grounded here.

Jubayr kept his focus on Mareesh. "We will leave at midday. And judge all for ourselves. Is that understood?"

The murmurs of agreement strengthened around the room, growing stronger as they spread. Jubayr waited for one other.

After a long breath, Mareesh slowly nodded—though it looked as if it broke his neck to do so.

Jubayr straightened his spine, the clasp of the heavy cloak choking him harder.

"It is decided," he declared. "We head to X'or."

# 73

KANTHE WATCHED THE last of the misty forest of the Myre Drysh vanish under the arrowsprite. He remembered longing to vanish under its dark canopy, to set aside his responsibilities and live the simple life of a tracker. It was not to be. Those woodlands and hopes faded behind him.

As the ship sped onward, a vast patchwork of green fields, pastures, farms, vineyards, and orchards spread before him. The open lands ran to all the horizons, looking endless. Canals crisscrossed and sectioned off vast tracts. Their waters reflected the low light of dawn, turning them into runs of silver.

"The M'venlands," Rami said. He was seated across from Kanthe, sharing the window. His voice was sullen. "Its bounty fills the troughs of the Eternal City's boundless hunger."

Kanthe's somber mood matched the prince's. "This is not exactly how you wished to show me these lands."

What seemed like ages ago, atop Rami's balcony, his friend had expressed a desire to take Kanthe into the M'venlands, to share with him the blooming fields of tabak.

*Now everything has changed.*

He glanced over to Aalia. She lounged next to Tazar, leaning her head against his shoulder. He held an arm around her, as if trying to protect her from the storm of events.

"Aalia would make a great empress," Rami said. "If allowed."

"Still, she did not look happy at Tykhan's offer of the crown. As I recall, she and Tazar had ambitions to end the hardfisted tyranny of emperors—only now she must take on that role herself."

"The circlet may chafe, but she'll be able to make changes, to break chains, to try to stem the decline of a stagnant empire."

Kanthe nodded. "I don't doubt her good intentions. But it is easier to wish for such a goal, even to fight for it, but once the reins are handed to you, lofty dreams become weighted by stony reality."

"Like facing my brothers and the imperial council."

Kanthe read the worry in Rami's face. "How will your brothers take such a claim?"

"I cannot truly say. The Augury's ploy may end up getting us all killed.

That's if we can even trust him? He is weighted down by secrets as much as all that bronze."

Kanthe slowly nodded and stared toward the wheelhouse door. Tykhan had vanished inside after Aalia finished her long missive. It had required multiple strips of parchment to lay out her case. But Kanthe doubted all the parchment in the world could truly accomplish that. Any success depended on the addled emperor and the puppeteer who pulled his strings.

Tykhan had taken Aalia's curled and sealed message into the wheelhouse, where he had affixed it to a skrycrow and sent it winging out a window toward Kysalimri. Afterward, Tykhan had remained inside there, leaving many questions on this side of the door.

Behind Kanthe, Frell and Pratik debated and pondered a hundred subjects concerning the Sleeper of Malgard. For Kanthe, their chatter had faded into a drone. At one point, they had tried to pull him into their discussions, but he had waved them off. To him, it was all spent breaths and suppositions. Any true answers were locked in bronze up front.

He preferred the patient attitude of Llyra, who picked at a fingernail with a tip of a dagger. Jester and Mead drowsed nearby. Elsewhere, the Rhysians had also given up their game of daggers and sat quietly, looking meditative.

"How is your father doing?" Kanthe asked Rami, wincing a bit, knowing this was a sore matter for the prince.

Rami craned back to look at the stern cabin. "When I left him, he had fallen asleep. But I should—"

The door back there banged open. Emperor Makar burst out, wild-eyed and disheveled. From the dampness at his crotch, he had soiled himself. He rushed out with a shout of fury. He tripped over a table in his haste and sprawled headlong to a crash.

Rami rushed toward him. "Father!"

Makar rolled away, lifting his arms. "Who are you all? Where am I?"

He clearly remained confused, but his words were ripe with command, firm with the authority he once wielded.

"It's Rami . . . your son."

His sister hurried over, drawing Tazar, too. "Father, it's Aalia. I'm here, too."

Makar shook his head, breathing hard, struggling to recognize them.

The wheelhouse door slammed open behind Kanthe. Before he could turn, Tykhan blurred across the space, demonstrating the speed of a *ta'wyn*. He brushed through the others.

"Let me," he said as he drew to a stop, dropping to a knee next to Makar.

Bronze fingers brushed across the emperor's brow. Upon their touch, Makar slumped to the deck, accompanied by a small sigh of relief.

"I'm sorry," Tykhan said as he stood and faced them, lifting an arm. "I've been distracted."

They all backed away, fearing that same touch.

Tykhan lowered his arm. "I had needed a quiet moment to ruminate on the variables that lay ahead of us. So much has changed of late, and I wanted to ensure my calculations and suppositions hadn't been skewed off course."

Rami remained at his father's side. "What did you do to him?"

Aalia nodded. "You owe us some explanation."

Kanthe agreed, focusing on a more immediate concern. "Can you do that to any of us?"

Tykhan shook his head. "No. It has taken me five decades of slow manipulation to achieve this with the emperor. Closing a pathway in his mind. Opening another. Moving a few others. A million tiny changes to be able to enthrall him."

"Like bridling?" Frell asked.

Tykhan lifted his bronze fingers. "Such gifts are weak in a Root. They're stronger in an Axis. And in a Krysh, they're frightening. Each caste is imbued with unique gifts, to suit our needs in the collective. While Shiya is stronger in bridle-song, she cannot melt her form like I can."

"'Each to his own place, each to his own honor,'" Aalia said, quoting an old Klashean adage about their strict caste system. "The *ta'wyn* are not unalike in this manner."

"I suppose we are," Tykhan admitted. "While my communication skills are robust, my *synmeld*—my bridle-song, as you call it—is weak. I can barely cast a glow past my fingertips. As such, it has taken me these fifty years to be able to achieve a weak form of bridling over Makar."

"But why do this?" Kanthe asked.

"I foresaw a future where to wield an emperor would serve my cause."

"So you truly are *prophetic*," Aalia said, her brows pinched.

"Not at all."

"Then I don't understand." Aalia folded her arms, clearly not happy to be in the dark, not in this matter, and likely not any other.

Tykhan stated matter-of-factly, "I don't believe in prophecy."

Such words from an augury stunned everyone, especially as they all were placing their faith in his guidance.

Tykhan continued, "The fumes I pretended to inhale are mildly hallucinogenic—not that they have any effect on me. But I've learned that the fumes make others swoon with a thrill of exaltation, as if the very gods were smiling upon them. It was not hard to suggest that such feelings were indeed visitations by the deities, who sought to share their divine wisdom. Time and belief took care of the rest. I built a temple, then a village, and now a town around such claims."

Frell stepped forward. "But I reviewed centuries of Qazen's prophetic statements—*your* words—and they've shown to be uncannily accurate."

Kanthe nodded, remembering Frell claiming as much before.

Tykhan sighed. "It was not hard. I've lived in the Crown long before I took up the shawl of an oracle. I've watched history write itself. I've observed the lives of untold millions. I retain it all. While I might not be able to predict the outcome of the fall of a single coin, I know after thousands of tosses that the two sides must eventually fall an equal number of times. Time is like that on a grander scale. There are tides that flow, where the accumulation of past trends points to future events. I merely have to recite what history seems to forecast."

"But some details of your prophecies are so exacting," Frell challenged him. "About personal lives, about what's in another's heart."

"Ah, that's even easier. I have eyes and ears everywhere who help me. Oftentimes, my revelations are just recitations of what's been told to me. Plus, after so many millennia, I can read the subtlest of expressions and interpret the responses that are secretly desired. A wife who suspects a husband of adultery and seeks a reason to poison him. Someone who believes a rival is corrupt and looks to me to justify discrediting and ruining them."

He shrugged. "More often than not, *prophecy* is just me telling someone what they want to hear. And other *predictions* are simple obfuscation, couching my words in such vague ways that they fit nearly any situation."

Pratik looked crestfallen, barely able to speak. "So *nothing* you've said was gifted by the gods. It's all trickery or extrapolation."

Tykhan didn't bother to answer.

"Then why are we following you?" Rami exclaimed. "We're risking everything on the words of a charlatan."

Tykhan showed no offense. "A very *ancient* charlatan. I've been following variables and trends, going back millennia, pointing to the certainty of a war to come. With enough knowledge, I can predict likely outcomes. It's allowed me to rule empires and bring down kingdoms, all leading to this moment. To ready the Crown as best I can for the tumult to come. If you follow history in all its telling detail, prophecy is simply inevitability."

Kanthe remembered Tykhan using similar words in describing Nyx's vision.

"It is a dangerous game you're playing," Rami said darkly as he collected his father under an arm. "With all our lives."

\* \* \*

AFTER HELPING RAMI carry Emperor Makar back into the cabin, Kanthe stayed there. He needed time to ponder all that had been shared. He also helped Rami gently clean his father, a difficult task for any son. Rami said little as they worked, but he gave Kanthe a brief and sincere hug of gratitude afterward.

Once done, Kanthe left Rami with his father and returned to the arrow-sprite's main hold. He now felt more settled, especially as he had dug out the thorn that had been troubling him about Tykhan's story. A detail had been brushed over, one that still nagged at him.

Steps away, Frell and Pratik had cornered Tykhan, likely trying to pry more information out of that bronze lockbox, but from their looks of frustration, they were making no headway. Aalia had also returned to her couch with Tazar and Althea, their heads bowed together.

Kanthe crossed to Tykhan, interrupting some inquiry from Frell about the *arkada,* the crystal books found shattered in the storehouse beneath the Northern Henge.

"A question," Kanthe interjected without any preamble, confronting Tykhan. "You stated earlier that your bridle-song was weak, but your communication skills were *robust.* That was the word you used. What did you mean by that?"

Tykhan looked mildly peeved, as if this were a line of inquiry that he'd rather not talk about. Still, he relented. "The *ta'wyn,* even a Root like myself, have the ability to speak to one another from afar. A necessary skill to coordinate and facilitate our work."

Frell quickly understood the goal of this line of questioning. "Does that mean you can communicate to Shiya?"

"I can," Tykhan admitted.

Frell, Pratik, and Kanthe shared hopeful glances.

Tykhan dashed them. "But I won't."

"Why?" Kanthe pleaded.

"As I said, we can communicate, but if I do, it will expose my location to all *ta'wyn.* They might not be able to discern the content of such a discourse, but they will know where it came from."

"So, it would expose you to the enemy," Pratik said.

Tykhan nodded. "They're still out there, hidden and in unknown numbers. I survived their first attack, but I would not likely do so again. Since leaving my *eyran,* I've stifled any emanations of mine to remain concealed. Even my *synmeld* is too weak for anyone to register unless they were in the same room."

Kanthe's stomach clenched with a frightening realization. He pictured Shiya and Nyx casting forth with bridle-song.

Frell realized the danger, too. "Shiya . . . she's not been silent."

"She has not. After emerging from her *eyran,* she was basically a newborn. And it's not just her *synmeld* that can be detected. A part of her is constantly calling out. She moves through the Crown like a leaking sieve. I've listened to her cross the Crown and out into the Wastes. She leaves a glowing trail in her wake. It's how the Hálendii forces are tracking your friends." His bronze brows wrinkled. "Though I don't know precisely *how* they're accomplishing such a feat. It's worrisome and centers on something I've feared for centuries."

Kanthe sensed Tykhan was skirting off the subject, but Kanthe was not ready to let it go.

"If Shiya is leaking and you've been tracking her, where is she? Did she and the others reach the site in the Wastes?"

Tykhan paused as if questioning whether to reveal something.

"What is it?" Frell asked.

"Where they're headed," he eventually said, "I know what's out there."

"What?" Kanthe asked.

"One of our creators' great machines, what the *ta'wyn* built for them."

Frell nodded, as if this made sense to him. "But what exactly is it?"

Tykhan shook his head. "I don't know. That knowledge was either taken from me, or as a Root, I wasn't high enough in status to be privy to it."

Kanthe returned to his earlier question. "Did Shiya and the others reach there?"

"They are close—but where they've settled at the moment is confusing. There's much interference. Something strange is happening there."

"If so, then that's all the more reason to reach out to them." Kanthe looked to Frell and Pratik for support. They both nodded in agreement. "If Shiya has been leaking all this time and drawn no enemies, then surely a brief message to her is a small risk for a great reward."

"I have to concur," Frell said.

Tykhan shrugged. "I won't do it."

Kanthe formed a fist, but he knew if he punched that mass of bronze, he'd only bruise his knuckles. "I don't understand why—"

"There is too much at stake in the days ahead," Tykhan snapped. "Not only can't I risk alerting any of Eligor's cohorts, but I told you about how Hálendii has discovered a way to track a *ta'wyn*. If I attempted even a brief communication, the kingdom would know another Sleeper is awake. Such a new variable would take a hammer to all my plans. All the trends and forecasts that led to this one moment could be dashed. Nothing would be predictable afterward."

Frell nodded. "He's right. If Shrive Wryth suspects there is another Sleeper here, he'll direct all of Hálendii's forces toward us."

Tykhan nodded. "For now, the situation remains too fragile. We've cast our lot. There's no taking it back."

Kanthe growled his frustration.

Tykhan tried to soothe him. "Once we've secured the imperium and if the others successfully reach the great machine, then I will break my silence." He stared hard at Kanthe. "But only briefly."

Kanthe frowned.

*That's a lot of ifs.*

But he would have to settle for it.

Frell used the lull in the conversation to broach a concern that had been troubling him since he was dragged into the librarie of the Abyssal Codex. "You stated that you don't believe in prophecy, but what of the *Vyk dyre Rha?* The foretold rise of such a dark figure seems tied to the *ta'wyn.*"

"Certainly, I recognize such a name. Over the millennia, I've heard whispers and rumors. But I don't know if such stories are myths, legends, prophecies, or simply a daemon created out of necessity. Another inevitability."

"What do you mean?" Pratik asked.

"Every culture has a dark corner of their pantheon. Hálendii has Hadyss. The Iflelen have Đreyk. The Southern Klashe—never one to limit their gods— have four of their own. Maybe it speaks to a frailty in all of us, a need to put a name to the darkness in our natures, a way to cast blame for our worst aspects, rather than accepting and addressing it."

Kanthe swallowed.

"And maybe we *ta'wyn* are no better. Perhaps we, too, needed a dark god to blame."

Kanthe shared a worried look with Frell and Pratik.

Tykhan finally shrugged. "Again, as a Root, I can't offer more on this sub-ject. Perhaps there was once a *ta'wyn*—someone far more skilled than I—who foresaw the rise of such a creature. Only time will reveal the truth."

Kanthe had his fill of such mysteries. They made his head throb. With an exasperated sigh, he headed to his seat and fell heavily into it.

Out the window, the arrowsprite had finally crossed the vast breadth of the M'venlands and reached the southern shore of the Bay of the Blessed. To the east, the sprawl of Kysalimri rose in blazing white tiers, climbing in stacks of walls, each more ancient than the last, leading to the towering citadel, the crown of the Eternal City.

The arrowsprite angled away from it.

That was not their destination.

*Not yet.*

Tykhan believed it would be too sudden to dive upon Kysalimri with a new empress aboard. Change came slowly to the Eternal City, and they needed to take that into account. To that end, the Augury had settled on the town of X'or along the bay's northern coast. It was a sanctuary of healing, renowned across the Crown for its hundreds of cascading baths, all bubbling with elixirs, oils, and tonic.

There, the fate of an empire would be decided.

Kanthe sighed, picturing a long, hot soak.

*If nothing else, at least our bodies will be clean when they kill us.*

# FIFTEEN

# THE MOUTH OF THE MAELSTROM

KALENDA: *I aske you. Whenne it comms to betrayal, which'es easier to forgive—frend or enemi?*
MARCELUS: *I saye enemi, for it is a wound expect'd.*
KALENDA: *I say neither. For in both, it is youre innocens that bears the grettest gylt & is the hard'st to absolve.*

—From the second act of *The Vale of Treason*
by Sensaoria of Hyparia

# 74

RHAIF WOKE INTO chaos. His head throbbed with each strained blink as he fought to keep his lids open. One eye went blind. He swiped at it in a panic, only to smear away blood and clear his vision—which still swam wildly.

The world was muffled, as if he were hearing everything underwater. He jerked higher, thinking he was drowning, only to realize his head had been half-submerged. He splashed up with a gasp. The muting cleared from his ears, replaced with a cacophony of screams, crying, howling, and a frantic pleading for help.

The world continued to spin, flaring brighter, then dimming. Shapes danced in and out of focus. Then hands grabbed him and yanked him higher.

*"Hala nee ya nestala wenn!"* was shouted into his ear.

He blinked a few more times, trying to force the world back into its proper place, tasting blood on his tongue. "Wha . . . What . . . ?" A familiar face swam into focus. "Floraan . . ."

She leaned closer, searching his face as if she were reading a book. She seemed satisfied with the content and drew back, pulling him with her.

"You must help us," she gasped. "Now!"

He swallowed down more blood, wiped his eye, took another breath to search around him. Then he remembered.

*The crash . . .*

He let Floraan lift him half up, then managed the rest himself. Sloshing for balance, he surveyed the wreck of the sailraft. Water climbed to his knees. Underfoot was a hazard of broken boards. The roof had crushed lower. The stern door had torn away, replaced with the bulk of the stern forge that had shoved up from below. Seawater steamed and hissed from its overheated bulk. Beyond, shreds of the gasbag floated in the lapping tide.

Floraan had hold of Rhaif's hand and tugged him the other way, toward the bow. He turned and stumbled after her.

Kalder hulked to one side, one ear hanging low, ripped by something sharp. The vargr growled, still protecting the youngest of them. Henna clung to his ruff with both fists. Her eyes were huge, but her fear of his savagery had been replaced with a need for the same fierceness. She must have innately sensed that place of security.

"Before we crashed," Floraan wheezed out as she pushed past the vargr, "Kalder shoved me, wrapped around Henna. Saved her."

Only now did Rhaif notice the woman was cradling a limb close to her belly, her forearm crooked.

He tried to get her to stop. "You're hurt . . ."

"It can wait." She continued to the bow. "This can't."

Rhaif followed her to the front. As she stepped aside, it took Rhaif a moment to make sense of the sight. Then his heart pounded.

Fenn sat waist-deep in the water. His brow had been sliced open, showing bone through the flow of blood. But he was not the one imperiled. His right shoulder held Brayl's head and upper body out of the water.

"Help us," the navigator rasped.

Even in the shadows, Brayl's face was a ghastly white, her eyes tight with pain. Her breathing panted through strained, bloodless lips. She could not move. A spar of draft-iron from the balloon rigging pierced her chest, pinning her in place.

"I can't get it to move," Fenn said, both hands tight to the bar. "Not on my own."

Rhaif hurried over. He braced a leg to either side of Brayl's submerged waist and grabbed hold of the draft-iron bar above Fenn's hands. "You push. I'll pull."

Together they fought the spar, straining and cursing. They changed their grip, wrestled it all directions, but to no avail. The spear of iron—thick as his wrist—would not budge. It was lodged up top by the crush of the roof and impaled below, maybe as far down as the seabed.

Floraan recognized the truth. "We need more men. And tools."

Rhaif backed a step, breathing hard. "Where?"

Floraan looked out the stern, to where a war was being waged, but it was no longer just the Hálendiian butchers. The sharp cries of the raash'ke cut through the bellows and screams, undercut by the low booms of cannons. The battle sounded distant, down the beach to the left, centered around one target.

"Iskar," Rhaif said.

Floraan looked at him, clearly knowing what she had to ask but afraid to voice it.

"Someone needs to go over there and fetch help," he finished for her.

Rhaif turned with a wince toward Brayl. Agony pinched her eyes. Fresh crimson flecked the corners of her lips. More blood stained the waters dark, spreading wider with each hard breath. Brayl glared through her pain and shook her head, but she didn't have the breath to curse, to tell him not to bother. She was a pirate's daughter. She knew death was near.

"Where would I even look for help in Iskar?" Rhaif asked.

"If there are any survivors, they'll be holed up in one of our mag'nees shelters, protecting themselves from the raash'ke's cries. I can tell you where to find such places."

He had heard the stories of the attack a few days ago. He had inspected a few of those lodestone chambers himself.

For this very reason—in case there was another attack.

"I can find them," he said.

"Go first to our house," Floraan warned. She cupped a hand over an ear. "I have two shield-helms in a cupboard. I gathered them after the last time. From the dead who no longer had use of them."

Clearly, she had taken extra precautions, too.

Fenn shifted higher. "If there are *two* helms, then I should go with Rhaif."

Rhaif wanted to refuse. Prior to all of this, he had been a thief in Llyra's guild. He knew how to skulk and move unseen. But any good thief could always use another set of eyes, especially with dangers on the ground *and* in the air.

"Henna and I can see to Brayl," Floraan said. "And considering the dangers out there, take Kalder, too."

Rhaif pictured the vargr tearing into the guardsmen. Still, he balked at leaving two women and a girl unprotected in a crashed sailraft. "There are dangers in these waters, too."

"Nothing I can't handle in these shallows. All the noise will keep the worst away. Even the raash'ke are unlikely to bother us this far out." She waved Fenn up, ready to take his place. "All of you, go."

Rhaif took a breath and nodded. He glanced at Brayl one last time. She still glared but managed a hoarse curse. He took it as a thank-you. He headed for the broken stern and the cooling ruins of the forge. He collected Kalder on the way out—or tried to. The vargr was reluctant to leave Henna's side, and for the girl, that feeling was clearly mutual.

Floraan helped by calling Henna to her side. She then addressed Kalder with the scolding voice of a mother toward a recalcitrant child. *"Tak ga, Kalder. Tak ga nya."*

The vargr curled a lip at her, then hung his head and swung to follow Rhaif.

Fenn waded after them, binding his gashed forehead with a scrap of gasbag sailcloth.

Floraan called after them. She had briefly inspected Brayl as she took Fenn's place. "Wait! In that same cupboard, there's a healer's satchel. I have elixirs to stem bleeding and pain. If you can, bring that back, too."

Rhaif turned to her. "While we're at it, how about a couple bottles of sweet wine?"

She smiled at him. "If it's not too much of a bother."

He grinned back at her, then skirted around the forge. He led the others to the stern but held them at the threshold. The sailraft had crashed into waist-high shallows. Using every bit of skill and luck she could muster, Brayl had gotten them over the sea, instead of hitting the beach. Even this meager cushion of water likely saved their lives.

Rhaif glanced at Fenn, who nodded.

*We owe it to her to take this risk.*

Still . . .

The beach ahead was cloaked in smoke from the blasts and fires. The heavy pall had blown against the towering ice cliffs and rolled to either side. It had also swallowed Iskar. The village was only a brighter glow within the dark fog.

Screams and cannon fire echoed out. Near Iskar's docks, one of the enemy swyftships had lowered in front of the village's plaza. Its forges steamed but it had gone dark, as if trying to hide from the horde in the skies.

And with good reason.

A slipfoil sped over that smoke bank, wobbling uncontrolled, pursued by a winged shadow. The tiny ship slammed into the cliff, crushing its narrowed nose, then exploding into a fireball. Dark wings swept away the wreckage.

Lower down, a small bonfire lit the edge of the beach between them and the village. It marked another crashed sailraft, one that hadn't had Brayl manning its wheel and hadn't emptied its flashburn tanks. Bodies washed back and forth in the surf.

*That could've been us.*

Honoring the debt owed, Rhaif headed out. He waded through the shallows, hopping with his bad leg. He kept low and aimed for the cover of the smoke-shrouded beach. Fenn flanked one side. Kalder splashed along the other.

Rhaif watched the skies. No other sailrafts or slipfoils plied the mists or sped overhead with flaming forges.

The air had become the dominion of the raash'ke.

Off in the distance, one last vessel challenged that authority. The second enemy swyftship fired its cannons at the flock of raash'ke haranguing it. But the shot was wild, desperate. Its gasbag had been shredded down to a few baffles. It hung crooked in the sky. Dark shadows fluttered across its deck. Screams and cries echoed eerily over the water.

More raash'ke dove toward it, drawn by this sole torch in the sky.

Tinier black specks tried to wing away, abandoning the foundering ship. *Skrycrows . . .*

But the raash'ke sped through them, nabbing them up. It seemed nothing was allowed passage through their skies.

Then—as if letting out one last gasp—one of the ship's forges exploded, bumping the stern high. The fireball chased the raash'ke back for a hot breath, but as the blast rolled away skyward, the horde fell heavily back upon the ship. The last of the balloon was shredded. The back quarter of the ship was on fire. It spun a final wild turn, then crashed toward the sea, waving the shreds of its balloon in a trail of flames.

It hit hard, shattering across the water.

Still, the wreckage continued to burn, becoming a floating pyre to the dead.

Rhaif reached the shore and hurried into the smoke, followed by Fenn and Kalder. They ducked into the pall—and not a moment too soon. With the skies cleared of targets, the horde swept the mists and circled toward the glow of Iskar.

Rhaif cast one last glance at the ruins of their raft. It sat dark in the waters, just another shoal in this sea. He prayed it remained hidden and ignored.

"Let's go," Rhaif urged the others—and himself.

*Before it's too late.*

RHAIF HOBBLED AND limped the last of the way, staying low in the smoky pall. His leg was on fire, his head pounded, and his lungs burned. He clutched a wet scrap of sailcloth over his mouth and nose, courtesy of the resourceful Fenn, who had gathered the bits before abandoning the sailraft and soaked them in the sea.

Rhaif wanted to curse the choking smoke, but it had kept them well covered. The only sign of the raash'ke was the occasional stirring of the black pall as their wings swept overhead. For now, the horde concentrated on the village, blanketing over the top, becoming a swirling black tempest lit from below. Even at a distance, their screams ate at his ears. Their louder bursts dizzied him.

Still, they'd made it—many others had not. While trekking across the beach, they had skirted around broken bodies, both villagers and Hálendiians. They also took a wide berth past the burning pyre of the crashed sailraft at the edge of the sea. Its flames briefly revealed a horrific sight. A raash'ke scrabbled out of its hold, dragging a screaming body, a survivor. Even still, the man tried to claw his way back into the flames, determined to burn to death versus being eaten alive. He lost that battle. The slavering crunch of bones chased their group farther into the smoke.

Rhaif slowed as they neared Iskar, wary, inspecting the way ahead. The village glowed fiery through the smoke. Its walls and outermost homes could be discerned through the haze. Firepots still flickered throughout.

He waved toward the Noorish corner of the village, where there were fewer flames—and hopefully fewer eyes. Fenn kept close as they skirted into the village's outskirts. Kalder panted heavily, slinking low.

Occasional screams burst across its streets. Small hand-bombs exploded with sharp blasts. A bevy of crossbows twanged somewhere. Still, the raash'ke continued their piercing cries that ate through skulls and swooned the senses. Rhaif winced as they edged along the periphery of that strident dissonance. His feet wobbled, and his vision pinched from the noise. He rounded the last curve of the street, dragging a hand along a wall to keep upright.

Fenn gasped next to him and pointed. "There . . ."

Rhaif spotted the twin firepots that flanked a familiar doorway. The flames danced merrily, as if welcoming them back. But Floraan's home—like all of Iskar—had not been spared. Its reed roof smoldered with embers and danced with flames. Still, they stumbled inside. Smoke filled the rafters. The heat was a stone oven.

Rhaif rushed to the cupboard near the home's hearth. He yanked open the doors and rummaged through its contents. He quickly found the shield-helms with their lodestone-filled earpieces. He shoved one at Fenn's chest. The navigator donned it, his eyes closing with relief. Rhaif did the same. The world mercifully muffled. His head cleared of its dizzying haze in a few breaths, though he could still feel those cries itching across his scalp.

Rhaif searched and found a satchel that clinked with small jars and bottles. This had to be the healer's bag that Floraan had mentioned. He passed it to Fenn, who clutched it to his belly. The navigator's face was pallid—at least what could be seen of it. Blood covered most of his face, running from under the binding across his gashed brow.

Kalder panted heavily, hoarsely. There had been no damp covering for his nose and mouth. The vargr's eyes squinted against those awful cries.

Rhaif had already made a decision while crossing the beach. He voiced it now. "Fenn, get that satchel to Floraan. It's Brayl's best chance. I'll look for some men and come as quickly as I can."

"But—"

"No. You're in no shape. Neither is Kalder. Take him with you. I must head deeper into the village. He'll do me no good slumped and passed out from those cries. He can at least help protect you on the way back."

Fenn looked ready to argue, but the navigator was no fool. He exhaled hard and nodded.

They set off again, ready to separate. Back on the street, Kalder tried to follow Rhaif, but he shouldered the vargr toward Fenn. "You go with him, you big oaf."

Kalder glared at Fenn, then rumbled back at Rhaif, showing a glint of teeth. The vargr's eyes glowed fiery. Rhaif didn't know if Kalder wanted to keep close out of loyalty or to stay in the village and search for his missing pack members, Graylin and Nyx.

*Or maybe he just doesn't like Fenn.*

Still, Rhaif knew someone the vargr *did* like.

"Henna needs you, Kalder." He pointed in the direction of the abandoned raft. "Go to Henna."

Those fiery eyes narrowed, then looked off into the smoke.

"That's right. Go to Henna."

With a sharper growl, Kalder turned toward Fenn.

"I'll get him there," Fenn promised, hugging the satchel. "But make haste yourself."

Rhaif pictured the blood pooling through the water around Brayl. "I will do my best."

Fenn nodded and took off, drawing Kalder with him.

As they vanished around a corner, Rhaif headed the other way. He seated the helm's earpieces more firmly in place. Ahead, a firepot lay on its side, spilling a river of flaming *flitch.* He leaped over it and ducked into the smoky pall.

Time to be a thief in the dark.

A LIFETIME LATER—or it felt that way—Rhaif climbed out of the depths of another empty mag'nees shelter. He had already inspected two others.

*Where is everyone?*

By now, the village had gone ominously silent. Even the raash'ke had stopped their dreadful keening and had begun a silent hunt. All that remained in the streets were bodies, intact or torn. Occasional shouts or screams echoed, but they were so rare that they made him flinch each time.

Off by the water, a bomb blasted, followed by angry bellows.

Rhaif winced.

*Someone's still fighting.*

He inspected the street outside and slipped into the smokiest shadows along one side. He edged down the wall. He had covered his face and arms with oily ash to hide any shine from his skin. He carried a bag over a shoulder, holding all that he had managed to pilfer from homes and structures.

Along his route, he had taken advantage of every bit of cover, ducking into doorways and out back windows, avoiding the open streets as much as possible. He gathered what he needed along the way, fabricating on the fly.

Llyra had drilled into all of her thieves the cornerstones of their vocation: *flexibility, ingenuity, resourcefulness*. Few schemes ever went as planned. One had to be prepared for the unexpected.

Still, above and beyond all that was one foundational imperative.

*Don't get caught.*

To that end, Rhaif aimed for a sprawling dark villa. He felt too exposed on the street. He rushed toward its door, only to have its roof, two stories above, explode forth with a sweep of huge black wings. He backpedaled as a massive raash'ke burst from its roost inside the home. A scream trailed in its wake.

Rhaif gaped as an armored stallion was ripped out of its hiding place. Its broken neck jostled loosely as the raash'ke swung away with its prize. But it wasn't just the horse. From the saddle's stirrup, a knight hung, flailing his arms, his steel-clad ankle twisted in the leather. He wailed and thrashed to no avail. As the raash'ke flew off, bits of loose armor rained down in its wake, leaving a trail of ghastly clanging.

The doleful ringing only reinforced Llyra's dictate.

*Don't get caught.*

Rhaif hurried through the empty streets, ducking away where he could. Even muffled by the helm, his ears remained sharp. So, he heard the voices as he neared a last corner. He stopped and peeked around the bend into the sprawl of Iskar's open plaza.

Rhaif had hoped he would not have to come here. But he knew of no other lodestone shelters.

Just this last one.

Still, he hadn't been the only one to seek out this spot. He heard an angry outburst, explosively loud in the quiet. He recognized the timbre of that outrage.

*Darant . . .*

The pirate cursed hotly.

Rhaif wanted to rush over and dive into the shelter. But the plaza was too exposed. Raash'ke swirled and spun high above. They were mostly fixated on the enemy's beached swyftship. Its balloon had been ripped down. Fabric draped over its deck and one side of the hull. With its forges cold and the ship grounded, the horde held back, more guarding it than threatening it.

For now, the bats ignored those gathered in the shelter, likely having recognized the futility of reaching the prey inside. Outside the chamber, the bomb-blasted bodies and broken wings of three raash'ke gave testament to that pointlessness.

Rhaif shifted back, taking a deep breath, knowing he had to get closer, but he knew the risk of such an endeavor, especially with the thieves' maxim burning in his head.

*Don't get caught.*

As he stepped back, his heel hit a large rock, kicking it away. But it was no stone. A head, torn from its body, rolled twice, then stopped, dead eyes staring up. A circlet dislodged from its crown and spun farther, bumping across its imbedded gemstones, then toppling sideways.

Rhaif cringed, horror-struck, recognizing what lay at his toes.

The head of the Reef Farer.

He gulped down his panic and peered around the corner. He pictured Berent and his consort, Ularia. The last time he had seen their faces was back at the ice cave. When the raash'ke attacked, they must have fled for better protection.

*One of them didn't make it.*

A sharp voice cracked through his shock.

"He knows where the others went," Ularia snapped darkly. "His companions wouldn't have left without letting this one know. Kill another of his crew and his tongue will loosen."

"Who next?" a gruff voice demanded, the accent Hálendiian. "Who should we choose?"

Rhaif formed a fist, knowing what he had to do. With a grimace, he dashed low around the corner. He needed a clear view into the room without anyone seeing him.

Llyra's voice filled his head, warning him to be cautious—and *resourceful*.

He reached the edge of one of the blasted raash'ke carcasses. He lifted its slack wing and crawled beneath it, ducking out of view. The space reeked of sulfur, moldy fur, and shite. Still, he dropped lower and squirmed under the span of bone and leather. He reached its far side and used the back of his hand to raise the fringe enough to peer out.

The entrance to the mag'nees chamber lay directly ahead.

Inside, torches and lanterns glowed, revealing the truth. It was no longer a shelter, but a torture room. Four bodies lay on the floor, rolled haphazardly to the side. He recognized all of them, including Herl. His ale-loving friend's throat had been slit ear to ear.

Rhaif spotted his brother, Perde, on his knees in there. Both eyes swollen shut, holding a broken arm to his chest, his wrists in chains. More of the crew suffered similar abuse. They were all surrounded by Hálendiians in armor.

Held at the front, on his knees, Darant glared up. He spat through the ruins of his mouth. "I'm not telling you nothing. You can go fekk yourself, Ghryss."

The gruff leader leaned his nose close. The man was clad in armor, too, along with the cape of his command. From his scarred and ruddy features, he was a hard man that few dared to defy.

Ghryss snarled darkly, "We shall see." He waved to his men, who dragged up another prisoner. He turned to Ularia. "You had better be right about this one, or your pointy-eared head may be joining the others we removed."

Ularia kept her back straight, refusing to bend at these threats.

Ghryss scowled. "You're lucky you bought your life with knowledge of this shelter. But such goodwill could end if you're wrong."

Rhaif ground his teeth. The *Nyssian* had clearly sold out the others, even the Reef Farer, all to spare her own skin, aligning herself with these Hálendiian butchers.

"I'm not wrong," she answered coldly as she stepped aside for the new prisoner.

The captive was thrown down hard.

Still, Glace rose to her knees, a hard sneer to her face. Her hair and head were yanked back and a dagger thrust to her throat.

Rhaif's leg flared with pain as he remembered that—like Brayl—this sister had also saved his life at the site of a crashed sailraft.

"Tell us where the others are hiding," Ghryss hissed at Darant. "Or we'll carve this one down piece by piece."

Rhaif closed his eyes with despair. He had come here to save *one* of Darant's daughters—now the pirate might lose *both*.

# 75

FROM HIS PERCH atop a boulder, Graylin clutched a farscope to his eye. The tool had been a gift from the *Sparrowhawk*'s engineer, Hyck—one that proved constructively useful now.

*If only to convince Nyx of the folly of this venture.*

He scanned the distant cliffs. Most of them remained dark under the stars, unreadable, but several glowed with hidden molten fire. In his ears, the rumble of the nearby watery maelstrom echoed in his chest, full of warning and threat. With each breath, the burn of sulfur flamed his lungs and stoked his fears. They could not stay out here forever.

"Do you see anything?" Nyx asked. "Any sign of the raash'ke?"

"Not yet," Graylin answered honestly. "But it is a labyrinth of broken rock, wide chasms, and narrow defiles. And much of it is too dark to discern any detail. But I'll keep trying."

He continued his search, being as meticulous as possible, while also anxious to give it up. Once he admitted defeat, they could head back to the Crèche.

"Where could they be?" Jace asked behind him.

Daal answered, "The Mouth spreads for great distances across this rock. Hundreds of leagues, it is said. The nest of the raash'ke could be anywhere."

Jace didn't agree. "They would need fresh water, and it looks like it gets hotter the farther out you go. For those reasons alone, they'd likely roost close to the Ice Shield."

"I agree," Nyx said.

Graylin suspected her reasoning had less to do with the beasts' need for resources and more about her heart's desire. Even Nyx knew that they could not search this blasted landscape on foot. She needed the raash'ke—and Bashaliia—to be close by.

He swept his view down another canyon. It barely glowed. Whatever fires lit it were far down its throat. With a twist of the farscope's tube, he focused in and out. He almost missed it. A white gleam against the dark rock. It could easily be a vein of chalk or another bright mineral. He shifted and sharpened his view.

The mouth of a large cave cut into the rock. He had seen many like it. Only this one's threshold and the cliff below it was caked with aggregations and streams of a white blemish. It was too messy and haphazard to be a mineral extrusion. He knew what it was.

"Guano," he mumbled.

Nyx heard him. "What?"

"Hold," he warned. "Don't nudge me."

Even speaking jostled his scope's focus.

He scanned the rest of the gorge, shifting through it methodically, painstakingly. He spied other befouled holes and cracks. He cast his view lower. The bottom edges of those cliffs were piled with deadfalls of broken bones. He shifted higher again, searching the glow itself. He held there, letting his vision adjust to that suffusing haze.

Slowly, he was able to perceive tiny silhouettes dashing throughout, winging wildly. They looked like tiny sparrows, but considering the distance, they must be the size of winter geese. He kept watching, waiting, then finally lowered the scope.

Expectant faces stared his way.

Except for Shiya, who merely continued gazing across the broken lands.

Vikas signaled impatiently in Gynish: "Well, what do you see?"

Graylin read the anxiety and hope in Nyx's face. "They're out there."

Nyx sagged with relief, clutching Jace's shoulder.

"But not close," Graylin warned. "They're tens of leagues away. Impossible to cross on foot. And I didn't spot any full-grown raash'ke. Only small ones." He held forth a spread of his hands. "No bigger than when Bashaliia first revealed himself to you."

As Nyx swallowed hard, he immediately regretted his choice of description, recognizing the pain that memory triggered.

"But where could the others be?" Jace asked again.

Graylin shrugged. "All I saw were young ones. Maybe the larger ones are resting somewhere within the rock."

Daal offered a more ominous option. "Or they're off hunting."

"Could they have returned to the Crèche?" Nyx asked.

Daal stepped back, his eyes wider, looking worried.

"I'm sorry," Nyx whispered, clearly regretting her words, too.

Graylin folded his scope and pocketed it. "If they did return to the Crèche, then it's all the more reason to head back. If Bashaliia is here and not already bridled into submission, we can't reach him. We can do no good here."

"How do we get back?" Jace asked. He turned and stared at the rise of ice behind him.

"It'll be hard," Graylin admitted. "We'll have to strip the skiff down to the barest bones. Carry it back up these cataracts with Shiya's help." He turned to Daal. "Once near the tunnel into the Fangs, can your orksos drag us against that current until we can reach calmer waters? Shiya could cross along the riverbed to lighten our load. Can they handle that?"

"Neffa and Mattis. Together. Yes. They will not fail us."

Graylin nodded, appreciating Daal's firm confidence. "Then we should set off."

Nyx had kept next to Shiya, both staring out into the Mouth.

"Not yet," Nyx warned.

PLEASE LET THIS *work* . . .

Nyx nodded to Shiya. The bronze woman bowed her head, then lifted her face to the sky. A hum flowed from her throat, warming her bronze. Shiya sustained that note and layered others on top, building toward a chorus. Still, she kept it bottled tight inside her, refusing to release it.

*Not yet,* Nyx willed to her.

Shiya had done something similar to this back in Kefta, when she had cast out a golden surge that swept in all directions, searching for any hidden threats in the surrounding streets. Nyx intended to attempt the same here. But the distances before them were far too great for Shiya alone.

Nyx let her eyelids close, shutting off the world. She added her voice to Shiya's, humming along with her. She sensed the glow of bronze next to her, a ghostly companion. Together, they built that song toward a crescendo but still kept it trapped.

*Not yet* . . .

Nyx blindly reached out an arm—not toward the glowing phantom next to her, but to another.

Daal took her hand. As their palms touched, fire ignited between them, but it was not the explosive force to break a grip. It was the flame of a forge, melding two metals into one. She flowed into Daal and he into her.

They grasped each other tightly.

She drew upon the font of his fuel, struggling to control that flow. Her anxiety and fear demanded more, but she tamped it down. She took Daal's flame and stoked her song, burning it brighter. Through the air, wafting on golden threads of power, she shared the power with Shiya. Together, they let that song grow, stoking its fire to a blaze.

Daal gasped next to her. For a breath, she saw through his eyes. Shiya glowed like a torch next to her, nearly blinding to the eye. Nyx shone nearly as bright. Then the vision quashed out. Still, the sight remained burned into the backs of her eyes.

She continued to let the fire pass through all three of them.

From Daal, to Nyx, to Shiya.

Like the bellows of a forge, each breath blew it brighter. Each heartbeat pumped more power. She waited until she could hold it in no longer. She let Shiya and Daal know.

**Now.**

The command's strength startled her, but she did not relent or falter. She opened her throat and heart and cast out a golden wave. Shiya did the same.

As their waves undulated across the Mouth, rising and falling, the two found their rhythm together. Shiya filled Nyx's valley with her song; Nyx did the same to hers. The ripples of their casting flattened into a tremendous golden tide, a merging of both their songs into a single unbreachable harmony.

Nyx was swept with the surge, riding along within it, spread throughout all of it.

She aimed for the section of chasms that Graylin had pointed out. The wave struck there, washing down the canyons, spreading through other tributaries, flooding down cave mouths.

As it did, nothing was hidden from her.

Those ghostly trees she had spotted earlier were life, blurring the line between stone and flesh, not unlike coral. She sensed the colonies of tiny, frilled animals encased in rocky skeletons, fed by molten minerals and the sulfur in the air.

Then she was swept into the skies, into the flurry of tiny bats. They were indeed reminiscent of a young Bashaliia, as Graylin had said. Nyx studied them, allowing her energies to penetrate past fur. As she did, she perceived their hollow bones, their tiny panicked hearts. She read the map of their veins, the billows of their lungs.

Being creatures of bridle-song themselves, they fled from the flood, sensing the surge of power. They dashed and cartwheeled away. They sped into shadows that could not hide them. They dove down holes that she could easily follow. She flowed everywhere in all directions.

Still, her drive was singular.

To search for one.

She poured herself into every cranny, surged into every vast space hidden in the canyon walls. She made herself into a torrent.

Then at last . . .

A lone heart thumped out in the darkness, pained and struggling.

Once, twice, and again.

She knew the song of that heartbeat as surely as her own. She swept upon it, coming from everywhere, closing in all directions. That song was a beacon of hope, of love, of need.

She reached a chamber deep in the rock.

Bashaliia huddled on the floor, head tucked low, wings wrapped tight. He glowed in the darkness with the purest golden light. She saw him in his entirety. His thrumming blood, his panting lungs. The fiery contours of his brain glowed with bridle-song, fighting the assault.

Around him, five raash'ke lurked in lairs up the walls, hunched with concentration, their eyes shining with sickly fire. All focused on Bashaliia. Their coppery threads of power—tarnished with an emerald corruption—lashed at him, seeking a way through his purity.

Bashaliia was clearly exhausted, nearly spent. Several of those malignant strands had found purchase, worming deep and spreading smaller tendrils, like the roots of a cancerous tree.

She swept to him.

*I am here.*

He sensed her, his wings stirring. He keened tentative notes, hopeful but still wary. Distracted, he lost some of his focus, his fighting wavered. The raash'ke saw this and attacked more furiously. The chamber filled with a storm of their emerald malignancy.

*No.*

Bashaliia's glow collapsed under the assault.

Leagues away, she tightened her hand, as if trying to break bones. But that was not her desire. She extracted what she needed. She felt Daal fall to his knees, then to one hand.

Flames coursed through her body, through the tide. When it struck her out in the canyon, she repeated her repudiation, only with far more force.

**No.**

She dove down to Bashaliia, into his fading glow. Once there, she opened her heart and let her fury explode. The emerald threads imbedded in Bashaliia were burned away. The malignant storm in the cavern got crushed against the rock wall.

Still, she was not sated.

She followed those threads to their sources, to the five raash'ke. She did not stop there. She traced those tendrils even deeper. She burned her way through fur, skin, bone. She reached stony hearts and fiery skulls.

She repeated her command again, scolding and warning.

**No.**

She branded that threat in place, burning five hearts, five skulls, upon the pyre of her being. Only then did she relinquish the fire inside her.

Far away, her knees struck stone.

The tide receded, taking her with it.

Before it did, she called to Bashaliia, clawing to hold her place.

*Run, Bashaliia. Fly. With me.*

He heard her and scrabbed up to his legs. His wings spread wide.

*Forever with me,* she sang to him, urging him to follow.

She flowed backward with the ebbing surge, out tunnels, through a cavern mouth, and into the open air. As the tide receded across the Mouth, she stared back, anxious.

Then Bashaliia burst out of a cave and swept high.

*Always and forever,* she promised him.

He chased her across the sky as she flew backward, guiding him home.

Unfortunately, that was not all that she had drawn out of the fiery Mouth.

Behind Bashaliia, rising from chasms all around, great wings unfolded, spreading wider and wider with each terrified breath. Seven in all. The monstrous bats dwarfed Bashaliia. He was a gnat before eagles.

Nyx flashed to the *Oshkapeer* queen stirring an entire reef, a creature of untold age and power. Here was the same, only sevenfold. Each must be centuries, if not millennia, in age. She knew what came, what she had stirred forth by her trespass. Here was the horde-mind of the raash'ke, manifested in ancient flesh and bone. They were the seven massive roots from which the entire colony grew.

With each beat of those mighty wings, a dark storm of power grew around them. With every league crossed, the thunderhead stacked higher. Energy built in the air, burning the sulfur brighter. Crackles of energy—shining a malignant emerald—speared jagged bolts through those black clouds.

Storm and beast rolled toward them.

All lured by the tiny flight of a determined bat.

*Hurry,* Nyx urged Bashaliia.

Once her essence reached the boulder, she crashed back into her own body. Already on her knees, she fell to her hands. She pushed higher, staring across the Mouth.

Bashaliia struggled to reach her, his small wings beating hard.

Behind him, a dark wave crested, climbing higher and higher, propelled by the tempest of those massive wings. As she stared into the abyss of dark power and green fire, she felt another's gaze staring out, through seven pairs of eyes.

But only one source.

The spider in the shadows.

# 76

RHAIF CROUCHED UNDER the heavy wing of the dead raash'ke. His bag lay open on the sand. He worked swiftly, picturing Glace's darkly sneering face and Darant's terror at his daughter's demise. A sharp cry of pain goaded him to work more quickly.

He remembered the ox-faced man's threat to take Glace apart piece by piece. *Has that started?* Darant's curses and rattle of chains answered that.

"I will rip your bollocks off with my bare hands," Darant gasped out. "And stuff them down your throat."

The Hálendiian leader was unfazed by this threat. "Talk, or I'll take her entire hand next."

Panicked, Rhaif fumbled with a tiny pot of embers. On his route through the village, he had collected burning shards from a section of flaming roof. He had stored them in a lidded pot that he'd stolen from another house.

He blew the embers inside back to a flicker of flame.

Between his knees, two hollow sea-gourds rested in the sand. Small wicks dangled from them, stuffed past a ticking of cloth from his own shirt. Inside, he had created his own concoction based on *flitch*.

Over the past days, he had found plenty of idle time to ask questions and wander the village. He hung with Krysh and Jace, looking over their shoulders, both at the *Fyredragon* and aboard the *Sparrowhawk*. He followed Glace and Brayl around like a sad cur, as they inventoried supplies. Floraan showed him these very gourds, said they were dried from some bulbous kelp.

When it came to thievery, one never stopped observing. One never knew when a coin purse might be unattended, when a window might be left ajar, when an unexpected opportunity might arise. Llyra's main tenets remained in place at all times, even between assignments.

*Flexibility, ingenuity, resourcefulness.*

Days ago, after the first raash'ke attack, the worry of another assault weighed heavily. It was why he had mapped out the location of a few lodestone chambers. One never knew what fate would throw at you. Likewise, from watching, listening, and some background in pyro-alchymy, a skill most thieves honed, Rhaif had come up with a fiery concoction of his own, merging Panthean and Hálendiian know-how.

*Just hope it doesn't blow up in my face.*

He used the flaming ember to light both wicks, which he had trimmed to two lengths, short and long. He waited a breath until the *flitch*-soaked wicks flamed brightly—then he crawled on his elbows back to the fringe of the wing. He used his head to nudge the edge up.

He had to act quickly. The gourds' flickering flames risked drawing the eyes of the enemy inside. He lifted the wing higher. As the view opened, it appeared everyone inside was focused on Glace, their backs to the door. A large ax was raised above her wrist. Her arm was pinned to the sand. From her trapped hand, blood poured out of a finger's stump.

*Bastards...*

"Tell us where the others took that bronze woman," Ghryss demanded. "Last chance."

The only one looking out the door was Glace. Her pained eyes went huge. He could only imagine what she was thinking, seeing him rise on his knees under the wing of a dead raash'ke.

*But surely not this.*

Rhaif tossed both gourds toward the door.

"Bomb!" he screamed.

One of the gourds made it across the threshold, bouncing down the steps. Its flaming wick spun wildly, sizzling even brighter as it did. The other fell short of the doorway and landed in the sand out front.

This second one had the shorter wick.

Rhaif dropped flat and pulled the wing over his head.

The explosion shocked even him. Flames blasted searingly bright, revealing the shadowy bones through the leather over his head. The concussion flapped the wing, too, as if the dead raash'ke were trying to take flight.

As the ringing in his ears died, he heard panicked shouts, the rush of footfalls out the chamber.

"Get clear!" Ghryss hollered as he fled the bomb inside. "Make for the *Drakyl!*"

As Rhaif had hoped, the fiery blast and the threat of the other bomb had chased the Hálendiians out of the enclosed room. It also drew the raash'ke upon the fleeing men. Their savage cries deafened him. The bridling tried to eat through Rhaif's lodestone earpieces but failed. Still, it felt like his skull was being ripped apart.

Grimacing, Rhaif waited until the last boot pounded past him. Then he shoved out from under the wing and dove across the threshold. He rolled down the steps into the chamber.

Glace stumbled back from his sudden arrival, clutching the wrist of her maimed hand.

Darant swore.

Chains rattled as other members of the crew fled to the side. Perde lay on his stomach, trying to smother the second gourd.

Rhaif waved him off. "Don't burn yourself. It's only a little firepot I made."

Perde rolled away and patted the scorch across his shirt, glaring at Rhaif.

"What was in that other?" Darant asked as he headed to the door.

Rhaif followed him, ticking off the ingredients. "Three parts refined *flitch* from the new forges, a fistful of powder from a hand-bomb, and just a dash of flashburn."

"Write that down for me," Darant said.

Glace joined them. "Good one on that ruse. Always knew you were a sneaky sod."

"Thieving never leaves your blood," he mumbled. "Even when you're trying to save the world."

Outside, the raash'ke had already laid into the fleeing Hálendiian forces. Several men thrashed under the throes of beating wings. Rhaif spotted the armored hulk of Ghryss pounding toward the dropped ramp of his swyftship.

One of his men turned and fired a crossbow. The bolt struck a small bat diving at them. It pierced a shoulder, sending the beast into a rolling crash into the sand. The archer fled away, rejoining Ghryss. Both were unaffected by the debilitating cries of the raash'ke—due to shield-helms protecting their ears.

Rhaif could guess where they had learned about such gear. Out on the plaza, Ghryss hauled Ularia along with him.

"Grab that ax," Perde hollered to another of the crew. "Break these sodding chains."

Rhaif glanced back. Perde stood over his dead brother, his face hard with fury. Rhaif made a silent promise to share a cask of ale with Perde, in honor of his fallen brother.

"Serves him right," Darant mumbled.

Rhaif glanced back outside again. Ghryss had reached the bottom of the ramp into his ship. The bat with the wounded shoulder had righted itself and sped on wingtips and legs, running like a feral dog across the sand, racing with shocking swiftness toward the ramp.

Ghryss bellowed and sprinted up the ramp, but the raash'ke took flight, barreling through the air straight at him. The Hálendiian used his only weapon. He flung Ularia, still clutched by the arm, and tossed her at the beast. She flew high, arms pinwheeling, and struck the bat.

They both splashed down into the shallows.

Knocked free, Ularia sputtered up. She scrabbled on hands and knees back to the sand. The bat lunged out, snagging fangs into the back of her thigh. She screamed, then louder as jaws snapped bones and her leg was ripped off. She fell flat, but she still tried to claw away, trailing blood.

The bat leaped high and landed on her back. Claws snagged into ribs. It flapped off the sand, carrying her with it. It must have forgotten its injured shoulder and slammed back down, crushing Ularia. It tried again with the same result.

Ularia mewled and weakly squirmed.

Rhaif had to turn away. "Even she didn't deserve that."

Darant disagreed. "She sold out her own men. Got them killed. Left them as carrion, taking only their bulky helms." He thumbed to a pile at the back. "She merits no pity."

A loud boom drew their attention. From the stern of the *Drakyl,* a sailraft blasted out. Its keel skidded the waves, then its gasbag burst taut above it. Its forge ignited with a blast of flames, casting the raft high, propelling it swiftly across the sea.

"Bastard had a fourth sailraft," Rhaif muttered.

Darant glowered. "A personal escape ship."

Over the plaza, a flock of wings gave chase, but Ghryss had a good head start.

"What now?" Perde asked.

Rhaif stiffened and grabbed Darant's arm. "Brayl . . ."

"What about my daughter?"

Rhaif gave a short account and pointed beyond the village. "We must get to her." He turned to Perde. "And bring that ax."

Glace stepped forward, tying off her hand with the sleeve of a dead man's shirt. "I need a couple of the crew."

"Why?" Darant asked.

"I overheard the Hálendiians. They left bombs aboard the *Hawk,* along with a few of their men. Someone needs to check on her."

Darant nodded, his face tight with worry. "Krysh and Meryk are over there, too. Before the bats attacked, the Hálendiians wanted information about our new *flitch* and modified forges."

"Then let's go," Rhaif said.

To get everyone moving, he passed around helms, while the axes freed chains from wrists.

By the time they were done, the plaza had emptied of the raash'ke. Some had flown off with their prey. A larger portion had fled after the fiery star of the fleeing sailraft.

This moment of reprieve offered their best chance.

Rhaif pointed to the left. "Darant, I can lead you and a couple men through the village, backtracking the way I got here. But we should hurry."

Glace pointed her thumb in the other direction. "I mapped a route of these lodestone rooms. Should be able to hop our way across, then stick to the beach's smoke to reach the *Hawk*."

Rhaif was impressed. Apparently, pirates were as good as thieves when it came to preplanning for disaster. Then again, there was some overlap in their vocations.

With matters settled, they all slipped out of safety and back into danger.

Rhaif set off with Darant, but his mind kept snagging on Ghryss's question, the one that the Hálendiian had been willing to torture and kill to get the answer to.

Rhaif wanted to know, too.

*Where are the others?*

## 77

EXHAUSTED AND ON her knees, Nyx stared out across the Mouth. She willed Bashaliia more speed. The small Mýr bat fought through the hot air, his wings striking hard, his body pumping for every bit of swiftness. She knew how exhausted he must be.

Behind him, a roiling storm gave chase. Unlike the golden shine of pure bridle-song, the power that surged in that storm churned with darkness, jagged with green fire, boiling with the scorch of molten rock. It filled the breadth of the Mouth ahead of her.

Buried at the heart, seven great beasts—winged daemons—rode that storm, pursuing Bashaliia.

Beside her, Graylin lowered his farscope, no longer needing it. "We can't fight those giants. And more raash'ke follow in their wake. Scores and scores."

Nyx couldn't see through the black storm to confirm his words.

"What's that haze surrounding them?" Jace asked.

She glanced over, shocked—then back out again. Even Jace could vaguely perceive what was coming, some innate sense of the approaching danger. The beasts were that strong.

*How can we hope to defeat them?*

Even if she tapped Daal's full strength, it would be like tossing a bucket of water at a raging forest fire. Worse, she had already depleted Daal to free Bashaliia. He was on his knees next to her. His face ran with sweat, his breath ragged. Still, he reached to her, offering his hand.

She took it, not to draw upon his fire, simply for his reassurance and comfort.

His fingers squeezed, igniting the fire between them, melding two into one for a few brief breaths. In that moment, she felt how much he also craved this union. But he meant more with this touch.

His voice was a hoarse whisper. "They're not corrupt . . ."

She didn't understand. She gaped out at the dark storm and the bright speck fleeing from it. Bashaliia was almost back, crossing over the insatiable maw of the river's swirling vortex. The stormy manifestation of the horde-mind was as black and unappeasable as that watery maelstrom below it.

"Not *corrupt*," Daal repeated, insistent. "*Corrupted.*"

She shook her head, still not understanding.

He squeezed her fingers. "Remember."

Locked with Daal, she felt his memories became hers. He showed her what had already been revealed to her before—by the *Oshkapeers*.

In a heartbeat, she fell into the past.

*—she hikes toward a village. Overhead, more raash'ke ply the skies. Others hop along streets or perch on walls. Children play among them, especially with the smallest of the beasts.*

Nyx dropped back to the present with her next breath, bringing with it an understanding. The raash'ke had once been as dear to the Pantheans as Neffa and Mattis were to Daal. He was right to remind her. The raash'ke had not always been corrupt.

"I remember now," she whispered.

Daal let his arm drop. "Make *them* remember, too."

"How?"

Daal pointed to the sky. "Show them."

Close now, Bashaliia struggled over the last distance to reach her. His wings faltered, his movement frantic. Once near the boulder, he fell, more than dove, toward her. He didn't have the strength to slow.

"Get out of the way!" Graylin lunged at her.

*Never.*

She held her ground and cast a silent thread to Shiya. The bronze woman stopped Graylin, grabbing Jace, too. Vikas retreated on her own.

Nyx stood up as Bashaliia struck the boulder, wings wide. His claws scraped across the rock, gouging deep tracks. She lifted her arms, trusting him, knowing his heart. He struck her, but she caught his neck and let herself be carried with him to a stop. He leaned his soft cheek to hers, velvet rubbing her ear. His wings wrapped around her. His body was a furnace, but she clung tightly, happy to burn there forever.

"I've got you," she whispered.

He shivered and mewled, panicked and scared.

She sang to him, softly and calmly, both a lullaby and a promise. She heard her dah's voice joining her in chorus, alive again in her memory, where death holds no sway. She let the old refrain repeat over and over again:

> *I am here, right beside you.*
> *So, close your eyes and know it true.*
> *I am here, right beside you . . .*

Bashaliia's breathing slowed and his shaking trembled away.

"I've got you always," she promised aloud, while never losing her song.

With golden threads, she wrapped past and present. She folded in every moment of their lives together, from warm milk shared under safe wings to this reunion now. She spared nothing: the terror, the hardship, the sting of a merciful knife, the joy amidst the terror. Through it all, there was one constant.

There were no words for it, not in any tongue or gesture. Love was a pale utterance, a placeholder for something far grander. It could only be felt, experienced, endured, even lost. Though there was no true word for it, she placed all of her faith in it.

The closest way to express it was in the purity of song, starting with a chorus of two beating hearts, of breaths sighing in harmony. From there, it continued in a symphony of joys shared, of lives entwined, of sorrows endured, until two became one.

She let that all glow forth, wordless and bright, forming a corona around them.

She sang out to the storm as it descended upon them.

*You once had this, shared this.*

Still, she knew it wasn't enough. She reached into her memories and stirred them brighter, bringing back to life a span of centuries, when the raash'ke had lived in harmony with the people of the Crèche. She added this chorus to her glow, filling it with thousands of memories, of generations sharing this indescribable feeling.

She cast that corona wider, turning this past into golden light.

*Remember . . .*

Most of the raash'ke were too young to have been alive back then—but these seven giants were not. They knew a time when the Crèche had lived in harmony. Somewhere in the shadows of the horde-mind that memory, that brightness, still existed.

As if sensing the danger of reviving a past long forgotten, the storm swirled. Seven shadows beat the air, holding the sky. Smaller raash'ke swirled farther out.

*You must remember . . .*

It wasn't a demand, only a hope.

The stalemate held for several more breaths. Exhausted and drained, she felt her legs faltering. She hung from Bashaliia's neck. Then a warm hand touched her shoulder, fire burning through to her skin.

*Daal . . .*

Next, fingers of cold bronze gripped her other shoulder.

*Shiya . . .*

Daal poured his last flames into her, allowing her song to shine brighter. With that energy came a flood of additional memories from the *Oshkapeers,* thousands that had faded from Nyx but that Daal had still retained. She fed those into the glow, too, making the past an inescapable trap.

*You will remember.*

This time, it came with a lilt of command.

On Nyx's other side, Shiya added her voice, easily finding Nyx's harmony. Like before, they stoked it into a storm and held it trapped, letting it build into a massive tide, damming it behind walls. Only this time, the dam didn't have to be so tall. Their target was right here, all around them. So far, both storm and giant wings skirted the threat of those shining memories, as if wary of them.

Still, Nyx felt that impasse would not last.

A nidus of hard darkness lurked within the shadows.

*The spider . . .*

From its hiding place, it lashed out with whips of emerald fire and lances of jagged spears, demanding for the storm to crush them.

In that moment, she recognized that malevolence, that corrupting force.

Nyx flashed to six months ago, when she had knelt atop the Shrouds. Shrive Vythaas had wielded a small metal box that sparked and keened with this same malignant fire, coursing to copper needles driven into the skulls of Nyx's two beloved brothers, Ablen and Bastan.

This was much the same, a corruption of control, only she sensed this spider was much farther away.

She had no more time to ponder it further. The massive golden tide could no longer be held back. Nyx opened her throat and broke the dam inside her with a single word.

**Remember.**

It was no request this time, but a demand.

The golden corona surrounding her burst into a sun, blasting upward in every direction. It struck the storm and the seven winged giants. The ancient darkness shattered wide for a few moments—but it quickly smothered down, trying to quash that fire, to erase a past.

Still, a few rays of that new sun broke through the shadows, reached the tiniest bits of brightness buried in the storm. With a touch, those beams ignited what had been protected and preserved long ago but nearly forgotten—the memory of harmony, when two lived as one, when hearts beat together.

That bit of brightness exploded, eclipsing even her sun.

Nyx gasped.

The storm broke around her.

As it did, she caught a glimpse of the spider.

A bronze figure stood within a crystalline vault, crouched in a web of copper tubing, glass pipes, and bubbling tanks of a golden elixir. A malignant green fire sizzled and sparked across this glistening web, reflecting off the spider's bronze with a pestilent sheen.

The figure was clearly a man, but he carried none of Shiya's majesty of form. He looked more toadish, his bronze a melted slag, as if denying any commonality with humanity.

His eyes stared out at her. The hatred and enmity shining there drove her back a step. Then that gaze shifted to Nyx's left, to where Shiya stood, her bronze hand on Nyx's shoulder.

The spider flinched away, his eyes flaring with shock. One word hissed out, reaching across that vast distance. *"Axis."*

A bronze arm swept across the web, snuffing the emerald fire. Nyx sensed the permanence of that act. The spider was terrified of Shiya, relinquishing the battlefield, too fearful to ever return, recognizing the Crèche had a new bronze guardian.

The view into that crystalline vault vanished.

Still, before the connection severed, Nyx sensed a greater threat. It was unspoken, but the impression was conveyed through the momentary fusion of bridle-song and corruption. The spider had a way to thwart them, something that terrified even him. But the sight of Shiya had burned away any trepidation, leaving only necessity. He dared not hesitate.

As the view vanished, Nyx was left with a sense of urgency.

It could not be denied.

*Time is running out.*


"WHAT IS HAPPENING?" Jace asked.

The panic in his voice drew Nyx back to the boulder, to this moment. She shoved aside the terror and strangeness. She cast her gaze outward, both with her eyes and with her bridle senses.

The dark storm had broken, but now, stripped of that emerald hold, it had turned turbulent and chaotic. No longer anchored by that dark nidus, the horde-mind frayed, tearing itself apart. Its sense of self was lost between the shining golden past and the dark, savage centuries that followed.

The seven giants thrashed and writhed in the air, as if burning in that storm. Other raash'ke dashed in panicked flights in all directions. One great beast crinkled its huge wing, neck twisted, squeezing out a cry of anguish, of guilt, of horror—knowing all the misery the raash'ke had inflicted. It could not hold that much grief. It tumbled through the air, struck the churning lake, and was swept down into the maelstrom's darkness.

"Help them," Daal begged.

Nyx swallowed, at a loss. Bashaliia trembled before the desolation and panic raging above him.

Daal drew next to her. "They are rudderless and lost. I can feel it. Madness threatens."

She nodded. "They need a new anchor."

She stared up, knowing what she must do.

*I must be their new spider.*

At least for now.

She turned to Daal and Shiya. "I will need everything."

Daal held out a hand, so did Shiya.

Nyx took them both.

"We will need to create a beacon of pure bridle-song," she said. "One strong enough to draw the tattering flock and its shredded mind together, to anchor them until they can find their center again."

Daal gripped her hand. "Take what you need."

She nodded and drew his fire. She knew if she took too much it would kill him—and he did not have much left. He was still weak, his flames more smoldering than blazing.

With the two merged together, she let Daal see her fear, his danger.

He stared into her eyes, his words filling her without speaking.

*Take* all *of it.*

She knew there was no other choice. She opened herself fully, no longer denying the dark well at her core. She used its hunger as a force, pulling every-thing from Daal.

He cried out.

With the two of them merged together, it felt as if she weren't just sucking the marrow out of him, but his bones, too. He slumped to his knees, but he still gripped her hand. She felt the pound of his heartbeat as if it were her own. Its rhythm grew erratic, his energy too weak to work that fist of muscle in his chest.

*I can't do this to you.*

His answer was weak, one word, shining with the hope for that harmony to be restored—between his people and the panicked and grief-stricken above.

*Must.*

His grip slipped from hers. She tightened her fingers to hold him, while knowing it would kill him. The last of his energy swept into her, swirling down the dark well inside her, joining all the fire she had already drawn.

She pictured the watery churn of the nearby lake—and despaired.

*I am that maelstrom.*

Shiya shifted in her other grip. "Share this burden."

Nyx knew, to create a strong enough beacon, the bronze woman would need Daal's fire, too. She passed a stream of power through her palm to Shiya.

As Nyx gazed into that well inside her, watching the swirl of flames—spinning around and around—she realized a new truth, a possible hope.

For all of them.

*We don't need a* beacon *in the sky—we need a* maelstrom.

And she knew how to create it.

Shiya's earlier words inspired it.

*Share this burden.*

Nyx pulled the bronze woman closer. "Grab Daal's hand, too. Like you're holding mine."

Shiya cocked a brow, curious, but she reached down to Daal's slack arm and took his hand. He did not respond. His head hung low. His breathing was spasms.

With them all linked together, Nyx turned the sucking force of her dark well into an untapped power source. As Daal's flame spun inside that vortex, she used that speed to cast fire into Shiya. Still, Nyx refused to let it linger there. She forced the fire through all that bronze and back to Daal's other hand, returning it to him, enough to sustain him.

Around and around, Nyx flung that fire, whipping it faster, creating a maelstrom. She added her voice, humming it all stronger. Shiya carried it higher, stoking it with each pass. All their lifeforces and bridling energy swirled through all three of them.

Daal lifted his face, breathing stronger, his heart finding its rhythm again.

Still, Nyx drove that song, that energy, that force, until it could no longer be contained. She thrust it high, her voice sending it up, bolstered by Shiya. The golden, fiery maelstrom whipped into the sky. The strength of its pull was undeniable, powered by the gravity of that dark well inside her.

From across the skies, the insatiable pull of the maelstrom drew the shreds of the dark storm, gathering them back into some semblance of a whole. The maelstrom's golden brilliance shed light into those desolate shadows.

Below, Nyx sang a promise to the sky—that grief could be healed, that horrors could be forgiven, that blame was not theirs.

She repeated Daal's earlier words.

*You are not corrupt.*

She filled the skies with the memories of a harmonious past, showing them again, over and over, whipping it through the maelstrom, refusing to let them look away.

Throughout it all, she made another promise, knowing that the raash'ke would need more than memories of the past. They needed an anchor, something to hold them together long enough for that healing to happen. She sang that assurance into the sky, merging her voice with her dah's once again.

*I am here, right beside you.*
*So, close your eyes and know it true.*
*I am here, right beside you . . .*

She let them know that they were not alone. She did not intend to control them, to wield them, only to *be* there for them.

Overhead, the dark storm calmed, clearing somewhat, revealing the spatter of stars, twinkling bright. Still, the view was marred by shreds of tortured clouds. It was not over. True healing, true forgiveness, would take time.

This was only the start.

Six giant wings circled high, silhouetted against the spangle of stars. Smaller raash'ke made wider orbits.

Nyx cast herself into the fiery maelstrom and spread herself out to them, offering herself, singing softly of harmony. As she did, her view splintered, seeing the landscape below through scores of eyes. She remembered this from before, back with the Mýr bats of Bashaliia's colony.

In turn, she was watched. She felt the weight and ancientness of that horde-mind staring at her, wary, suspicious, wounded—but also hopeful.

For a moment, her gaze flickered, catching fractured glimpses through eyes far off. She saw the Crèche. Iskar glowed fiery through smoke. A wreckage of a large ship burned on the water. Another sat in the shallows of the village. Other pyres lit the beach. And bodies. So many bodies.

Panic jarred her. She dropped swiftly, shedding free of those eyes, and fell back into her body.

She gasped as she did so.

Daal was still on his knees, but he stared up at her.

"What's wrong?" he asked hoarsely.

"The Crèche . . . it's under attack."

She turned to Graylin, knowing where those ships must have come from. She told him, told them all.

"The kingdom has found us."

# 78

DAAL STRUGGLED OFF the boulder, still weak, feeling a century older. He was the last to get down, but Shiya waited below and helped him. To the side, Nyx spoke animatedly with Graylin and Vikas.

Despite his exhaustion, fear pounded his heart.

Moments ago, he had shared some of Nyx's journey among the raash'ke, but he had faded in and out, spent and drained. He had caught only glimpses through those other eyes, but he had been too weak to follow her all the way to the Crèche.

Still, Nyx had been clear about the threat. They all knew the urgency, the imperative.

*We must get home.*

He stared up at the sky, where giant wings still circled, gliding under those sparkling stars. Clusters of smaller raash'ke sped in ragged groups, still agitated, expressing their edginess. Nyx had warned them how fragile they were and would likely remain so for some time.

As he gazed above, he wondered if *this* was the Dreamers' purpose in sharing the Crèche's memories, why they had instilled that harmonious past into the two of them.

*Was this the Oshkapeers' intent all along? To preserve those memories until a time when they could be used to break the raash'ke free?*

Daal had no way of knowing.

Jace called out, "I'll start unloading the skiff."

Daal returned his attention to the others as Jace headed down the rocky slope toward the river. It reminded Daal of who else was down there.

He followed Jace, anxious to check on Neffa and Mattis. The two orksos had a hard haul back to the Crèche. He wanted to check their harnesses for chafing and examine their burns from those fiery worms. But more than anything, he wanted to comfort them.

From the top of the slope, he recognized their nervousness. They had noted the circling raash'ke, too. The pair kept close to the shelter of the skiff, father and daughter, their horns knocking together, reassuring each other.

He glanced to the skiff's fish pen and its icy storage of eels and minwins. A small meal would help return the orksos' good natures. But he knew he shouldn't overfeed them before—

"What's that?" Jace asked, stopping ahead.

The thunderous blast threw Jace into Daal. They both rolled in a tangle. A flash of flames and a wave of blistering heat swept over them. Then parts of the skiff rained and crashed all around them.

Daal shoved away from Jace, panic returning his strength.

*No, no . . .*

He crawled through the burning wreckage, over broken crates. Once close enough, he denied what his eyes were seeing. He shook his head, trying to wish it away.

Mattis lay on the rocky slope, thrown out of the river by the blast. One wing fluttered. His horn had snapped off near its base. Blood pooled under his bulk.

Deafened by the blast, choked by his heart, Daal slid down the slope to reach the orkso. He ran a palm over his slick flank. Mattis's nostrils heaved with misty exhalation. An eye swiveled to look at Daal, then over to the river, expressing his worry.

*Neffa . . .*

Daal scooted through the blood. Out in the water, Neffa rolled amidst the wreckage, piping in distress for her father. She struggled to claw and hump her way onto shore. The water around her was dark with the blood flowing into it.

Daal slid into the river, shying past her horn.

"I've got you," he said, reaching for her.

She rolled, showing him why she struggled, why she couldn't reach her father. Blood sprayed from where her foreleg and wing had been ripped away. Each beat of her huge hearts pumped the life out of her.

*No, no, no . . .*

He cried out in a wracking sob and hugged her huge head. Still, she beat her tail, fighting to push out of the river, to get to her father.

The others crowded behind him, unsure what to do, but Daal knew there was nothing. Her wound was fatal. From the bank, Mattis tried to lift his head with a whistling wail, calling to his daughter.

Daal recognized the one thing he could do.

He shoved out of the water and crawled, stumbling and shaking, up to Mattis. "Help me," he cried out.

He shifted to Mattis's head and tried to shoulder the orkso's bulk back into the river, to his dying daughter. The others closed to help. They would've failed if not for Shiya's strength. They slid Mattis through his own blood and into the river.

Daal slipped in with them, between them, hugging both. Neffa rubbed her father, nuzzled Daal, whistling as she bled away, flowing her life down the river. Mattis rolled and lifted a comforting wing over his daughter's flank, but Mattis was weakening, too.

Daal sat waist-deep in the cold water. He sobbed and leaned his brow to each, inhaling their fishy musk, the salt of their last exhalation. Their piping and whistling faded into the air. He didn't know who died first, but he stayed with them both to the end and beyond.

He hung over them, running a palm along the spiral of Neffa's horn. The others tried to coax him out of the river, but he refused.

Nyx whispered to Graylin, "What happened?"

His answer was dull with despair. "The crate of armaments in the stern. One of the hand-bombs must have exploded."

Vikas stepped into view, looking out at the wreckage, gesturing in her language.

Nyx's reaction was sharp. "Sabotage? Like back on the *Hawk*? Why?"

Daal tried to block them out, closing his eyes.

"They wanted to make sure we never returned," Graylin said dourly. "They must have used a long-wicked stykler. Like the one planted in the *Hawk*'s forge. Delayed to explode until we were far enough away, leaving us dead or stranded."

"Who put it there?" Nyx asked.

Jace spoke up, his voice small and shocked. "The bomb. It wasn't in the armament crate at the stern. When I was headed back to the skiff, I saw a curl of smoke rising at the *bow*, from under the bench. Where I was seated."

"What was under there?" Graylin asked.

Jace gulped, trying to get his next words out. "It was Fenn's pack, the one with the compass and the navigational tools."

Despite Daal's grief, he turned to face Jace. His voice was hoarse, fueled by fury. "Are you certain?"

Jace backed a step from whatever showed on Daal's face. "Y . . . Yes."

Daal shoved around, slid deeper into the water, and rounded the bulk of Neffa.

"What are you doing?" Nyx asked softly.

Through clenched jaws, he answered, "We need to get back to the Crèche."

Nyx stepped closer. "How—?"

"You know as well as I do. We've done it before."

Daal removed Neffa's harness—and freed the saddle from her back.

## 79

Nyx watched Daal undo Neffa's rigging with great tenderness. His shoulders shook, but she didn't know if it was from grief or fury.

He climbed out of the water and handed her the saddle. It was draped by a tangle of cinches. It looked complicated, but she knew each piece, drawing the knowledge from a blur of memories—both Daal's and those of the ancient riders of the raash'ke.

The two saddles were not dissimilar.

Daal collected a second one from Mattis, then joined her.

His eyes were pained, pleading. "Ask them."

She wanted to argue, but she knew there was no other way for them to return to the Crèche. And Daal was right about one thing.

*We have done this before.*

The knowledge of those ancient riders was buried inside her, inside Daal.

Graylin suspected what Daal was requesting her to do. "You mean to attempt to saddle and mount a pair of raash'ke? To fly back to the Crèche?"

"We must get back somehow. The blistering heat, the lack of fresh water, the sulfur in the air. We won't last more than a day or two."

"There could be a chance. Darant had promised to search for us with the *Sparrowhawk* if we didn't return."

Nyx shook her head, remembering her fiery view of the Crèche. "It may already be too late for the *Sparrowhawk.*"

Vikas gestured her mute support, "While we're stuck here, we might as well attempt it."

Jace stood with his arms crossed. "There are only two saddles." He unfolded his arms and waved to the others. "What about us?"

Daal answered. "The raash'ke are very good at carrying live prey back to their roosts."

His words did not sit well with Jace—not Daal's choice of description, not what he was suggesting.

Graylin looked undecided, but it was not his choice.

Nyx turned to Shiya. "Can you help me reach out to them?"

The bronze woman nodded.

Before joining her, Nyx ran a palm over Bashaliia's crown. Her fingers brushed his ear, his soft cheek, borrowing some of his warmth, his love, knowing she would need both.

Once done, she stepped alongside Shiya. "I'm ready."

Together, they stoked up a glow, letting it warm over skin and bronze. Nyx started first with a quiet melody, infused with the memories of raash'ke sharing the air with their bonded riders. She folded in a harmony of her own hopes, refining each note to make her need clear, her desire.

She let those golden threads rise out of her—from both lips and heart. She reached to Shiya, who was ready for her. The bronze woman sang brightly, the music heartbreaking, expressing what was lost, what was longed to be regained.

Nyx knew Shiya had no memory of those past flights, those ancient bonds between riders and winged companions. Still, each note rang poignant and true, rising out of Shiya's own loss. Her loneliness and need for connection flowed through Nyx's threads, adding a depth of pathos that could not be ignored.

The threads and tendrils rose high, like golden smoke from an ancient fire.

One of the giants wafted down. Its wingspan was so wide that there was no need for them to flap. Movement and guidance were but ripples in those great sails. It soared high, still hanging back, but it brushed through those golden threads.

As it did, Nyx felt the immensity of its intelligence. It wasn't just this lone raash'ke, but all of them. Nyx shivered with awe, a mote before a god. It then glided off, riding in a slow spiral up a column of hot air.

There was no answer, no response.

She knew she could do no more and let her song fade. Above, the golden threads dissolved into a sparkle that scattered off, like embers from a dying fire.

"What happened?" Jace asked as she stepped away from Shiya.

"I don't know." She shrugged. "We wait, I guess."

She had barely taken a few steps, lost in contemplation, when Graylin grabbed her arm, his grip like iron. Vikas stared up with an exhalation of surprise. Jace drew closer to them all.

Daal nodded, satisfied. "They come."

From the skies, six raash'ke separated from the others. Each was only a tenth the size of the giants, but they were still huge. They swept up the river, one leading, then another. They were followed by a clutch of smaller wings, forming an escort.

The six broke off and crossed low over their group with a rush of hot air. They alighted on rocks and boulders. Dark eyes shone down from those perches. The beasts' tiny ears pricked tall. Large flaps opened and closed over slitted nostrils.

They panted in the heat, showing a hint of fangs. Their wings remained high, ready at a moment to fly away.

Bashaliia warily hopped back, likely remembering his last encounter with a group of raash'ke. But he was not the only one dismayed.

"You're going to saddle those?" Graylin asked dourly.

"And just look at those claws," Jace mumbled, focusing on his own means of transport.

"Let me go first," Daal said.

Nyx stepped next to him. "We'll do it together."

She offered her hand.

He took it.

As their palms touched and fingers folded, a familiar fire flared. It felt like coming home. Daal didn't have much reserve left, so she borrowed only a trickle, enough to cast out a flush of reassurance, of memory again, showing the raash'ke what she and Daal wanted to do. It was the first tentative step to renew an ancient bond.

They headed over.

Three shied away immediately, still wary, hissing in warning. A fourth lost its nerve, too, but a pair remained. Their claws dug into stone. Their brows lowered, studying the strangers with one eye, then the other.

Still awash in that glow, she and Daal approached with great care.

From Daal, a memory was shared with her. She passed it to this pair. It showed a rider securing a saddle, of cinches hitched. It was suffused with the excitement and joy of both rider and mount, along with a deep-seated affection.

*This can be yours, too.*

One head, then the other, slowly bowed, willing to try. It was far from confirmation, but it was a start. Without saying a word, Nyx and Daal separated, proceeding to their respective mounts. She chose a male, the most like Bashaliia. She let her love for her winged brother shine.

Daal's mount was a shy female, much like Neffa. Knowing this, Nyx stirred up a memory from Daal that was still inside her—from when he had first trained Neffa. A time of abundant joy, many mistakes, and even more laughter, but underlying it all was a sustained affection and warmth.

She shared it with the raash'ke.

Working in tandem, she and Daal fixed their saddles. They relied on memory, instinct, ingenuity, and some gentle irritated nudges from the raash'ke. She compared her rigging to Daal's and Daal's to hers. It took some additional improvisation, but Daal finally nodded his satisfaction.

Nyx wasn't as sure, but she turned to the others. "Ready?"

They were not—but how could they be?

She crossed around her mount, running a palm over him, never breaking her touch. She lifted a foot into what passed for a stirrup: a small pouch of sharkskin that barely fit her toes, especially in boots. She snugged a purchase, then pushed up. Her knee came to rest in a pocket in a leather side flap. She leaned and lifted her leg over his back.

An orkso saddle—now a *raash'ke* saddle—sat higher than on a horse. It rested on the withers, near the base of the neck. And rather than dangling her limbs to either side, she bent her legs and balanced more on her knees and toes, keeping out of the way of the wings' movement.

As she settled her weight, the raash'ke shifted—not to throw her off, but to balance her better. She ran her fingers through the thick fur of his neck.

"You remember this, too," she whispered, knowing all the raash'ke shared one mind, one memory.

*We've all done this before.*

She crouched low and glanced over at Daal.

He balanced on his knees, clearly more comfortable than her after his years of riding orksos. Maybe he thought the same thing. His gaze swept over to the river, to the bodies resting together. The waters ran clean again, as the orksos' blood, like their lives, had washed away.

Daal lowered his gaze, his hands coming to rest on the two leather grips at the front edge of the saddle. There were no reins, as there had been for guiding the orksos. Control was all balance, knee pressure, and instinct between rider and mount.

Daal's knuckles whitened as fury hardened through him. His raash'ke sensed his anger and shivered with a flap of wings.

Nyx knew they needed to keep moving or that anger would loosen Daal's control, panic the mounts. She lifted higher in her saddle.

"We're leaving," she called to the others. "Try not to move. Arms out."

She took a breath and sent shining tendrils wafting through the air to the other raash'ke. She reinforced what she had already shared with the giant beasts, with the horde-mind. In the past, the raash'ke had ferried Pantheans, latched in claws, tucked close to the heat of their furry bodies.

The four skittish raash'ke accepted this accommodation. They were familiar with hauling captured prey between the Crèche and the Mouth. Only here the route would be reversed—with no feeding allowed.

The four raash'ke leaped off their perches. They swept low and snatched up those gathered along the river's shore. The plucking was not gentle. The four were snapped off the rock. The one who tried to lift Shiya nearly crashed.

It bobbled, fought, and finally found its rhythm, dragging its bronze anchor skyward.

Before Nyx could wish it or say it aloud, her mount burst upward. Caught off guard, she slid in the saddle. Her rump caught the lip at the back, keeping her in place. Her hands, as white-knuckled now as Daal's, latched hard to the grips. Her stomach sank deep in her gut.

She glanced in time to see Daal's raash'ke take flight, too.

Bashaliia leaped after them.

She swung back around, balancing between terror and joy. Other smaller raash'ke were swept up in their wake, giving chase, following them, forming an escort.

She hunkered low, struggling to find her seat, her balance. Then after a time, without needing to think about it, she found a hand tightening at the exact right moment. Her knee shifted on its own as the raash'ke made a turn. She settled lower, letting the wind whip through her hair. She kept her face down, protecting her eyes, searching ahead with just the peripheral sight past her brows.

It all felt . . . *right*.

She recognized what was happening. It was an awakening of old memories, blurring instincts and reflexes of the past with hers now.

And it wasn't just her.

The raash'ke under her slowly responded, too, remembering, falling into a familiar rhythm of balance between rider and mount. They circled a wide path out of the Mouth, using the rising hot air as much as the strength of wings. A peek back under her elbow showed the fiery spread of chasms and fissures.

They climbed away from it and swung toward a broken cliff of ice, the westernmost edge of the Shield. The air quickly cooled, and the world darkened, lit only by the stars, the moon, and the reflection of both off the ice.

She leaned harder, staying closer to the hearth under her. She didn't need to tell her mount where to go. That had already been shared.

The raash'ke swept higher, fighting to crest over the ice cliff. For a breath, Nyx believed they wouldn't make it. She prepared for a crash—but at the last moment, with a hard beat of wings, they cleared the edge. It was so close she swore she could reach down and brush her fingers over the ice.

As they continued, her mount skimmed across the Shield, rising and falling with its contours. Stars glinted overhead like broken shards of ice. The air grew colder, frosting her back, her hair. She hugged tighter.

Ahead, she spotted the other four, clutched tight to warm bellies. Far to the side, she caught a glimpse of Daal, curled close to his saddle. On her other side, Bashaliia sped with her, occasionally rolling through the air with unbridled joy.

Nyx risked letting one hand free. She ran her fingers through the cold edge of her mount's shaggy fur to the hot warmth beneath. She sang softly, only because it felt right. She suffused her appreciation, shared her exhilaration. She bared her heart, her gratitude for her mount's bravery.

Slowly, he sang back, echoing the same. This wasn't the horde-mind, just her mount, a lone raash'ke discovering a miracle. Still, she sensed that greater presence watching her from the shadows, silent and immense.

Finally—too soon—the world ahead vanished into a wall of steam, marking the rift into the Crèche. She let her song sink to a whisper. She was not ready to return to screams, terrors, and fires.

*Let's just keep flying forever.*

Still, she knew that could not be. Ahead, the others—one by one—vanished into the steam. Then she was in it, too.

The sudden warmth took her breath. The steam blinded her, stinging with sulfurous brimstan. She squeezed her eyelids against that pain. She felt her mount shift into a shallow dive. As he did, he keened sharply, casting forth ripples of sound and bridle-song. Even with her eyes closed, she felt those golden waves wash back to her, returning with contours and shapes, delineating the steamy world.

She could pick out the others spiraling below.

They wound around and around. Just when she thought it would never end, they shot out of the mists and into open air. The emerald sea spread below them. The ice cliff climbed to the right. Between them ran the stretch of beach.

It was not hard to discern Iskar's location. A dark pall of smoke cloaked a swath of sand and sea. As if sensing her desire—or reading it in the whispers of the song she maintained—her mount swung lower, heading toward the smoky scar.

Closest to Iskar, the pall had spread far out to sea. She could no longer tell if the Hálendiian ship was still blockading the village's docks. Even the *Sparrowhawk* had been swallowed away, hiding its fate.

Ahead of her, other raash'ke spun a circle, swinging Nyx's friends under them, waiting for guidance. Above, an escort of smaller bats shot out of the mists like dark arrows. The air filled with wings.

Daal appeared farther out, circling wide.

She could only imagine how he took in that view, of Iskar burning, the wreckage in the sea, the bodies along the beaches.

Still, she could guess where he focused his fury.

## 80

RHAIF LABORED DOWN the beach, limping through the smoke, using a stout reed as a cane. It didn't work as well as his old crutch, but his bruised underarm was happy to let his bad leg carry some of the load.

"Can't you go any faster?" Darant scolded him.

"Unless you want to carry me, no."

Darant scowled and looked Rhaif up and down, plainly considering it. Rhaif hurried faster before he made up his mind.

Earlier, he had led Darant and three crewmen through the ruins of Iskar. They had to proceed slowly, wary of the raash'ke and any other lingering patrols of Hálendiians. Strangely, the only visible threat—though it wasn't much of one—was a lone figure in armor, peeking out from around the drape of a doorway, then ducking away.

Still, other figures had scurried furtively through the village, just hazy shapes in the smoke. The shadows were likely Pantheans who were taking advantage of the lull in the fighting.

Otherwise, Iskar had gone eerily quiet.

Far down the beach now, Rhaif glanced back. Off in the distance, he could barely make out the village. Besides falling quieter, it had also gone darker. The flames had burned through their fuel of reed roofs. A few firepots still flickered, but the worst of the blaze had died to smolders. Even the smoke had lessened.

But not by much.

Rhaif tried not to rub at his sore eyes, as it only worsened the burn. His lungs felt heavy with ash. They all struggled not to cough, lest it lure any hunters in the sky.

"How much farther?" Darant asked, his voice tight with worry for his daughter. He also kept looking back, concerned for Glace, too.

The smoke hid the world around them, but Rhaif had used the crashed Hálendiian sailraft near the beach as a marker. It had still been smoldering as they passed it.

"We should be—"

A coughing chuff cut him off, but it also answered Darant's question. A vargr had keener eyes than any of them. Kalder came barreling through the pall, looking as if he coalesced out of the smoke. He sniffed a fast circle, confirming who they were—then leaped away, vanishing in a breath.

They headed after him.

With the destination at hand, Darant abandoned Rhaif, no longer needing a guide. His trio of crewmen rushed after their captain, axes in hand, ready to free Brayl.

One of them hung back for a few extra breaths. Perde's broken arm had been hastily splinted, but he refused to stay behind. He carried an ax over a shoulder. "Quit draggin' your arse."

Perde turned and sped after the others.

Rhaif frowned at the general lack of gratitude by pirates. Still, he tossed aside his cane and hurried as best he could after them. He feared what they all would find inside the sailraft. It had been a hard day for everyone.

*To lose Brayl, too . . .*

Rhaif cleared the edge of the smoke, and the green sea opened before him. The crashed sailraft lay dark and silent. Darant and the others waded toward it. Kalder splashed ahead, leading them.

A short distance from the raft's open stern, Fenn waved an arm. The navigator tossed something aside with his other hand.

Rhaif followed the others through the shallows. As he did, he searched the glowing mists overhead. A few wings cut across the sky. And it looked like more stirred higher.

Fenn waited for Rhaif, noting where he was looking. "They've been circling, stirring about, but I've not seen them approach any closer. Maybe they've eaten their fill."

"Then let's hope they don't get a sudden craving." Rhaif shifted to a topic that Fenn seemed to be avoiding. "How's Brayl?"

Fenn's lips drew into hard, pained lines. "Floraan attended to her. She was relieved to get that satchel. If you hadn't sent me back, she might not have lasted this long." He gave a sad shake of his head. "She's lost a lot of blood."

With a grimace, Rhaif headed over, if only to say good-bye. He was glad she lasted long enough until her father returned.

As he crossed the last of the way, Kalder nosed at something small and dark bobbing in the waves.

"What's that?" Rhaif asked.

Fenn waved a hand dismissively. "A dead skrycrow. I saw it out here when Kalder ran off and fetched you. I was hoping it might still have its message. Get some idea of what's going on with the Hálendiians."

"Did you find anything?"

"No. The crow's harness must've fallen loose or washed off."

Rhaif frowned. Those harnesses were difficult to dislodge. They had to be. The birds made long flights, often through foul weather.

"Too bad," Rhaif muttered, picturing that ox-faced Ghryss blasting away in his sailraft.

Together, Rhaif and Fenn reached the broken stern and climbed past the cold wreckage of the forge. Ahead, Darant knelt in the water next to his daughter. Brayl nodded, offering a weak smile. She looked like a ghost already.

Rhaif held back, not wanting to intrude. Floraan stood to the side, having done all she could. She held Henna close with one arm, as if that grip alone could keep Floraan from ever suffering the same fate.

To have to say farewell to a child.

Rhaif saw that Floraan had also managed to rummage a crude splint together for her arm. A very resourceful woman.

*She'd make a good thief.*

Rhaif caught Floraan's eye and nodded toward Brayl.

The woman simply shook her head.

Rhaif winced—then a loud crack of boards overhead made him jump. Henna cringed low. Kalder growled outside. Footsteps pounded up top, accompanied by muffled voices. Darant's men had climbed to the roof, to inspect the lodged spar.

An ax struck hard overhead. Boards splintered. More hacking followed. Rhaif grimaced. Especially as Brayl's eyes pinched with each strike, clearly feeling the impacts reverberating down the impaled spar.

Then the chopping stopped, followed by three loud splashes.

Darant's men came clambering inside.

Perde called over in a hushed voice, "Sodding bastards are coming."

No one had to ask who.

The cries of the raash'ke filled the skies all around them. The bats, with their keen hearing, must have been drawn down by the chopping.

Rhaif hated to abandon Brayl, but he shifted to Floraan and Henna. "Make for the smoke. It's our only hope."

But it was already too late.

Dark shapes crashed into the shallows all around the raft, trapping them inside.

Then something explosive struck right at the stern, sending them all scurrying back. Water splashed high. As it washed down, it revealed a figure of shining bronze down on one knee.

"Shiya . . . ?"

It looked as if she had fallen out of the sky.

More large shapes swept down.

Huge wings flared past Shiya's shoulder. A massive raash'ke landed in the shallows. It tucked its wings and bowed a furry head.

From the arch of its back, a figure straightened in a saddle. Her dark hair, flung high by the descent, settled to her shoulders, shining with strands of gold that scintillated with bridle-song. Her eyes glowed with the same fire as she stared fiercely into the hold.

Rhaif recognized her, but he still stepped away.

"Nyx?"

# 81

EXHILARATED, STILL FLUSHED from the cold, Nyx shook ice crystals from her hair. Ahead, Shiya stalked into the sailraft to make sure everyone was safe.

Nyx twisted in her saddle, checking how everyone had fared from the flight. Graylin and Vikas shook free of the claws above and dropped into the shallows with loud splashes. The raash'ke who had ferried them swept high.

Jace waited until his boots dragged the water before shoving free. He scurried out from under the huge wings. He got nearly flattened as those sails of leather beat higher and away.

Bashaliia spiraled toward her, keening, elated to have been able to share the skies with her, even if it wasn't atop him. Once above the shallows, he snapped his wings wide and landed with the lightest of splashes. There, he rocked on his legs, clearly still full of joy, hardly able to contain himself.

Moments ago, as Nyx had swept toward Iskar, a sharp noise had cut through the wind. Flashes of steel drew her eye below. She made out figures hammering or chopping atop a broken sailraft. It made no sense to her. Then she spotted the whitewater splashing of a large shadow. She recognized that dark silhouette against green water.

Kalder.

Anxious and confused, she had sharpened her bridle-song with both demand and hope. The horde-mind had heard it, too, and shared it with the others. They all descended to surround the raft, wanting answers.

For everything.

To her side, Graylin and Vikas waded swiftly toward the sailraft. Graylin frowned at Nyx, not in anger, but silent inquiry. *Are you all right?*

She nodded back, still speechless, a part of her still in the air. All those memories of prior flights were nothing to experiencing it herself.

Still, those memories had gotten her here.

*And one other.*

A huge sail of wings swept over the raft. As they passed above her, she smelled salty ice and a sulfurous musk. Small frozen crystals shed from its fur, showering her.

The large raash'ke landed near the beach, its claws splashing up water and sand. It stretched its neck into a long keening cry, as if voicing the fury of its rider.

Daal slipped off the saddle and ran a hand along his mount's neck in gratitude. Contrasting that gentleness, Daal's face reddened with fury. He held a
fist hard to his waist. His blue eyes shone with a fiery rage. The wonder and
exhilaration of the flight had not dimmed his anger; if anything, it had sharpened it, especially with the focus of his fury so close at hand.

Nyx had already spotted Fenn inside.

So had Graylin and Vikas.

Before Daal reached her, Nyx slid off her mount. She tried to block Daal
with her palms raised.

"Leave it to Graylin and the others," she pleaded. "Please."

"What if it had been Bashaliia?" he asked coldly, and splashed past her. A
hand settled to the dagger at his belt. "What would you do then?"

Nyx flinched at his words, both at his fury and recognizing he was not
wrong. She glanced at her winged brother. Daal had risked much to save
Bashaliia.

*How can I fault Daal's fury now?*

Still, she swung after Daal, wading quickly to join him. She struggled to
find the words to temper his anger, but she knew there were none.

Ahead, Jace stood with Rhaif, trying to explain what happened. Kalder
crouched near them, his legs braced, growling at the spread of raash'ke.

Before she and Daal could reach the raft's open stern, Floraan came rushing out with Henna under one arm.

Rhaif noted her panicked haste. "What's wrong?"

Before Floraan could answer, fierce shouting rose from inside the raft, then
a loud scuffle of heavy bodies. Nyx heard Fenn call out, his voice panicked,
"What are you doing?"

Nyx and Daal rushed toward the hold.

With a look of shock, Floraan tried to stop her son. "Daal, where have
you—?"

He ignored her, brushed past, and continued inside. Even his mother could
not stem his fury or sway his singular focus. Daal had heard Fenn's voice, too,
and nothing would stop him from exacting his revenge.

Nyx cast Floraan an apologetic look and hurried after Daal.

Inside was chaos.

Nyx tried to take in everything at once. Darant knelt at the front. More of
his men jostled in the cramped hold, trying to pull Graylin off of Fenn. The
knight had the navigator lifted by his throat and pressed against the wall. Vikas helped hold Darant's men off. But the two were outnumbered, and neither
Vikas nor Graylin wanted to hurt anyone—and Darant's men had axes.

One of them clubbed Graylin hard, knocking him aside.

Fenn slumped down the wall, grasping his neck. A bandage had been knocked loose, showing a deep gash across his brow.

Darant shifted around and bellowed, deafening the cramped space, "Stop this shite now! Or I'll skin the lot of ya!"

His face was stricken, his eyes shining with misery. Only then did Nyx see whom Darant had been kneeling over. His daughter lay in water, her torso propped up. Her skin pallid and bloodless. Her lips drawn and thin. An iron bar impaled her chest.

Nyx gasped. "Brayl . . ."

Distracted, she could not stop Daal in time. He dashed through the others, fury fueling his speed. He hit Fenn in the chest with his knees and drove the navigator farther down the wall. Daal kept him pinned under his weight, a dagger at Fenn's throat.

"You killed Neffa and Mattis," Daal hissed, rage frothing his lips.

Fenn stammered, "I didn't . . . what are you . . . who . . ."

Daal pressed the edge of his blade, hard enough to draw a bloody line across Fenn's throat. Still, Daal's hand shook. Then his shoulders. He fought with himself, with his heart, with his need for vengeance.

"They . . . they suffered so . . ." Daal gasped out, sorrow and fury straining his voice. "They didn't deserve that. They had such love . . . for everything, for me. They trusted me. To keep them safe."

Daal kept his dagger pressed to Fenn's throat.

Darant's men looked ready to rush him, but Graylin and Vikas guarded Daal's back.

Nyx passed through them all and knelt next to Daal. She sensed the truer target of his wrath. Daal was angry at Fenn, but more furious at himself.

Nyx recognized that shame and misery. She had felt it often enough. "Don't do this," she whispered. "He'll get his justice. Don't stain your hands over this traitor."

"I have to," Daal said. "For them."

He shifted higher, leaning into the dagger.

"Stop," a weak voice whispered hoarsely.

The softness and pleading, more than the word itself, made everyone halt. Nyx shifted back to see Brayl struggle to sit up. She had to reach her hand and grasp the bar to do so, but it clearly agonized her. Blood rushed around her wound.

"Leave him be." She slid back down. "I'm the saboteur. Not him."

In that stunned silence, no one moved.

Daal finally fell away from Fenn, staring down at the dagger in disbelief.

Darant sank back on his heels, his eyes huge and glassy. "What . . . ?"

Nyx pictured Brayl passing down gear from her sailraft into their skiff. There had been plenty of opportunity for Brayl to plant something in Fenn's pack—maybe she intended to frame him if anything went awry. Only now, with death pending, did she feel the need to be honest.

Nyx stared at Darant's daughter and recalled the first attempt at sabotaging their group's efforts.

*If anyone would know how to cripple the* Sparrowhawk*'s portside forge without blowing up the ship, it's her. She must've hoped the damage would have forced them to limp back home. And when that failed, she had sought out another means to the same end.*

Graylin asked the question for all of them. "But why? Were you bought off by the Hálendiians?"

Brayl's breath rasped out a dismissive huff. "Fekk that. No gold or coercion swayed me." Blood dribbled from her lips. "My choice. My doing alone."

Darant shifted away, shaking his head, still refusing to believe.

"Then why?" Nyx asked.

Brayl's gaze rolled toward her. "Because . . . of you."

Nyx cringed.

Brayl lifted an arm, only to have it slap in the water. Her voice drifted to a tired whisper. "All the sodding prophecies, visions of doom, what-ifs . . . fekkin' shite, the lot of it. I was raised a pirate's daughter."

She leaned her head toward her father, but he would not meet her eye, so she closed hers. "We believe what we can grasp. Right? Not this shite . . . Someone had to right this ship before we hit the rocks. Meant stopping *you*. Without killing the lot of us . . ."

Brayl tried to lift her arm again, reaching for Darant. "Then we could've all gone sodding home . . ."

Her arm dropped, and she slumped backward. Her face slid underwater.

No one moved to help her.

Not even her father.

# SIXTEEN

# THE BLOOD BATHS OF X'OR

*Long ere the Stone Gods were carv'd, the steemyng springs
& bubblen pools of X'or were bless'd by the Graces obove.
If yoeu wyssh a miracle, yoeu wil find it here.*

—A promise from an old touting card found in
a dead man's pocket (writer unknown)

# 82

KANTHE STROLLED THROUGH the gardens and pools of X'or. A soft morning breeze off the Bay of the Blessed stirred the flowering trees, disturbing pink and white petals. They floated in the air all around him. Small crystal chimes, hanging from those same branches, rang in notes so quiet it felt like a lover's whisper in the ear.

"It's all so beautiful," Frell noted.

The governess of these baths, Abbess Shayr, smiled and offered a small nod of thanks. Of the *imri* class, she wore a handsome white robe, but there was no embellishment. Still, the purity of that whiteness was as resplendent as the finest gown. The only blemishes were the few pink petals clinging to it, which added a humble charm.

Her features were unlined, but her hair, bound in braids about her head, was as white as her robe. She looked ageless, as if she had always been here.

She lifted an arm to encompass the grove. "The baths of X'or have been a place of healing and succor for over two millennia. The Talniss trees around us were here long before the town was ever established."

Kanthe gaped at the bower overhead as it dappled the sunlight. The overlapping layers of canopies looked as if they never stopped climbing into the sky. Easily, it would take ten men with outstretched arms to encircle a single Talniss trunk.

Rami strode beside him. Like the three of them, he wore sandals and a simple gray shift that fell to the knees and was belted in crimson. "It's said the very air of X'or has curative properties."

Kanthe inhaled deeply, appreciating the spicy fragrance from the trees.

Curative or not, he did feel far calmer, especially after the days of terror and bloodshed. They had arrived in the arrowsprite from Qazen yesterday as the last of the latterday bells were ringing. Aalia had received word from the council that they would be arriving this morning to visit the emperor and to discuss her claim as future empress. They had wanted to come last night, but she had told them that her father was exhausted and needed to rest.

Still, after the attack in Qazen, the council had dispatched two centuries of guardsmen to secure the emperor's private palacio. Overhead, a dozen swyftships patrolled the skies. And X'or itself was insulated and well protected. The impenetrable Nysee Bog, with its sucking mud and viper-infested waters, spread to the north, while the rest of the shoreline was tall unscalable cliffs.

In some ways, Kanthe and the others had delivered themselves into a sweet-scented prison.

As if highlighting this fact, Abbess Shayr led them past a seaside overlook. The land fell away in a scrabble of high cliffs. The view opened across the bay to the towering spread of the Stone Gods. The tiny islands, carved into all thirty-three of the Klashean deities, marched off across the waters. The sails of a few ships and pleasure barges wended their way through that pantheon.

Kanthe remembered his own journey among them.

*It's like I've come full circle from where I started.*

Rami pointed to one of the sculpted atolls. It was a robed woman whose arms lofted high a stone bowl, holding it toward shore. Rainwater glinted from its basin, as if it were another bath.

"The Goddess X'or," Rami introduced, confirming a connection between the goddess and this town. "She who heals the sick and comforts those heavy of heart."

The group continued onward, climbing over an arched stone bridge, one of dozens. It forded a silvery brook that spilled over the cliff's edge in a long water-fall. A glance upstream revealed a chain of pools, some bubbling and steaming, which climbed in a series of cascades throughout X'or.

The nearest pool showed a half dozen bathers. From the frolicking and moans and unabashed flashes of skin, apparently there were all definitions of *healing* and *succor* to be found among these baths.

He turned away, but Rami nudged him with an elbow and nodded with a raised brow toward the pool.

Kanthe pointed ahead and reminded his friend, "We came to see how *others* are healing."

Rami shrugged, glancing back. "We should take time to do some exploring together."

Kanthe imagined he wasn't just talking about testing the variety of baths.

Ahead of them, Abbess Shayr motioned to the next bridge. "The blood baths are up ahead."

They followed her to a stream that ran crimson. She diverted them away from the cliffs and up a path that led through the trees and followed those dark waters. As they traveled, the trees grew ever larger.

"This is the most ancient of our Talniss groves," Abbess Shayr informed them. "It protects our sacred baths."

A short distance later, the stream split off in seven directions to wide black pools steaming with crimson waters, the famous wellsprings of the blood baths. A few were open to the bower, their surfaces covered in petals. Others were enclosed and hidden within marble temples, from simple to ornate.

Abbess Shayr led them to a temple that was just slabs of marble, crusted with layers of moss and lichen. It looked to be the oldest of them all.

She ducked under the lintel of the doorway. The three of them followed. It was steamy and warm inside, but the air felt oddly light versus moist and heavy. The spicy perfume in the air was sharper, strong enough to be tasted on the tongue.

The pool inside was shored in marble, dropping in steps into the dark waters, where a lone supplicant of the Goddess X'or soaked. Another visitor was already in attendance, seated at the edge, feet dangling in the water.

"Ack!" Mead gulped and slid his nakedness into the water. "Give some warnin' when a lady's comin' in."

In the bath, Jester grinned, though it looked strained. "Don't mind 'im. My brother was hopin' for some young lass to traipse in and catch him perched there, showing off his wares like a shopkeep."

Mead sank farther, looking willing to drown.

"How's the leg?" Kanthe asked.

"See for yourself."

Jester lifted his stump. The end was covered with some sort of fine net. A wiggling leech, striped black and crimson, dropped back into the water.

"Keep your limb submerged," Abbess Shayr warned with a scolding frown. "Let the *vulnus* do their work."

"If I soak my arse cheeks much longer, they'll be as wrinkled as two hairy—"

"Four more days," the woman said firmly. "If you want to keep the rest of your leg attached to that arse."

Jester grumbled but dropped his limb back down.

The abbess turned to them. "As you can see, one of our patients is irritable but faring well. The *vulnus* and these waters will help him heal cleanly. It shortens the mending of such wounds in half."

"Amazing," Frell said. "How does that work?"

"Only the goddess knows. The *vulnus* and these waters have been here longer than the Klashe. But alchymists have studied both. The *vulnus* remove vulgar tissue, hence their name, allowing healthy growth. It's believed the waters and secretions of the leeches further encourage tissues to mend."

"And what of my father?" Rami asked, his earlier airy tone now weighted with worry.

Abbess Shayr took a deep breath. "Some wounds even the *vulnus* can't reach and our waters can't heal. I will take you to him."

She led them back out. Kanthe shared a worried look with Frell. Tykhan had tried to assure Rami that Makar's bridling would leave no lasting damage. Still, the Klashean prince was not willing to take Tykhan's word, especially from a figure that had fabricated his presence for centuries.

Even Kanthe had his doubts.

The abbess took them along another path to the most ornate of the temples. It was sculpted with gods and goddesses, adorned with crowns of gold. The marble had been scrubbed to a pristine sheen. In the shadows of the ancient grove, it nearly glowed.

The paths and surrounding woods also shone with the armor of scores of imperial patrols. Accompanied by Prince Rami, their group was allowed to pass unchallenged.

They crossed to tall gold doors where two Paladins opened the way before them.

Kanthe kept his face lowered, picturing the fate of the royal Paladins at the Augury's villa.

Abbess Shayr bowed them inside, allowing Rami privacy with his father.

Frell returned that bow. "Thank you, Abbess. We should be able to return to the emperor's palacio on our own." He nodded to the guards. "As it is, we have plenty of escorts."

She smiled, though it turned a touch sad as she glanced inside. "I wish we could do more."

Guilt flared through Kanthe. The abbess and her sisters had been nothing but kind, and their group had returned such compassion with lies.

Kanthe hurried after Frell and Rami.

The chamber inside was gilded and pristine. Lanterns glowed along the walls. The emperor sat waist-deep in the crimson basin. His remaining nakedness was hidden under a cloak that draped into the water and across the neighboring marble. Still, it failed to add any majesty to the patient. Makar's chin rested on his collarbone. Twin ropes of drool ran from his lips. His hair was soaked by the steam and clung to his skull.

A single nonne—the sister assigned to the emperor—knelt beside the crimson basin. She waved a small silver thurible, in the shape of a tiny boat, smoking with a curative incense.

Kanthe knew her efforts would prove futile. The source of the emperor's malaise stood behind Makar. Tykhan kept vigil, tweaking his bridling as needed to keep the emperor subdued and under his crude control. Tykhan nodded to them as they entered.

Pratik stood next to him, looking grim.

Rami crossed and dropped to his knees. He wet his hand and gently cleaned the drapes of saliva from his father's lips.

Tykhan whispered solemnly to the nonne, "Sister Lassan, if you could give Rami some privacy. I will let you know if we need your assistance."

She rose with her thurible, bowed to the prince, and quietly left the temple, closing the heavy doors behind her.

Once alone, Rami scowled at Tykhan. "How much longer must we maintain this ruse? You said yourself that it took five decades to achieve this bridling. You can't possibly know with any certainty what damage it is causing or what possible ramifications might follow from such abuse."

Frell scowled—but not at Rami's accusation. "The walls are thick marble, and this pool drains deep before joining the stream outside, but we should keep our voices *low*."

Tykhan, his eyes wounded, addressed Rami. "Your father is not the first that I've bridled. I promise, despite how it appears, I've been as gentle as possible. Still, I cannot fully discount your words. Bridling always carries some risk. I'm sorry."

Rami closed his eyes, clearly struggling to accept the necessity of this act.

Tykhan moved on from this tender subject. "We have a hard path ahead of us. It is not only the emperor who risks suffering. For any hope to mitigate the war to come—to keep the Crown from tearing itself apart—we must return to the path that my calculations originally pointed to that offered the best possible outcome."

"Which is what?" Kanthe asked. "We're trying to get Aalia seated on the imperial throne. What more can we do?"

"That wasn't my full plan," Tykhan snapped, clearly still irked that his carefully orchestrated manipulations had gone awry due to a certain Prince in the Cupboard.

"Then what was?" Frell pressed him.

Tykhan looked at Kanthe. "As I tried to arrange before, Empress Aalia and Prince Kanthe *must* be married."

Kanthe shook his head. "But why? Why is that so important?"

"The kingdom and empire must be united, or all may come to ruin. All forecasts dictate this is the only path forward."

"Then imbibe more of those Malgardian fumes," Kanthe said. "I can't see how that's important or why my marriage to Aalia would make any difference."

"It will." Tykhan's eyes glowed through the lenses that had turned his eyes to a rich indigo. "You are critical to *all* of it."

The third bell of the morning rang out, heard only as distant muffled chiming through the thick marble.

Frell frowned. "Talk of such unions can wait. We must get Emperor Makar ready for the visit by the imperial council. We fail with them, and none of this matters."

Tykhan nodded. "Fear not, with time, all will become clear."

Kanthe frowned at those words, spoken with the vague execrable mystery of all oracles. Still, one thing remained clear.

*It's too late to turn back now.*

# 83

AALIA WAITED FOR the morning's third bell to finish ringing across X'or. The small gold bell in the steeple topping the emperor's palacio made her teeth ache. When it finally ended, she sighed with relief.

"We're running out of time," she said, rolling to her side under a tangle of sheets. "I must be ready to receive the council in another bell."

Tazar pushed up to an elbow, his hair rumpled, his lips slightly bruised. He reached to her breast and gently rolled a thumb around her nipple, urging it harder. "I can accomplish a lot in less than a bell."

She pushed him away, stronger than she intended to, but anxiety kept her tense. He had snuck into her bedchamber last night, cloaked under a *byor-ga* robe. Not that any subterfuge was truly necessary. Aalia's servants knew of his presence, as did most of the guards by now. No one could fault the Illuminated Rose for needing companionship, especially now. Often enough in the past, she had shared her bed with both men and women. While she had to preserve her maidenhood, which was examined regularly, she was left with abundant latitude for other explorations and enjoyments.

"I need to bathe and prepare," Aalia said. "The council will fault even a hair out of place in an effort to deny my claim."

Tazar slid a palm down her leg, settling his fingers in a manner meant to encourage her to relent. "There are some areas they won't inspect."

With a great deal of regret, she pushed his hand away. "I wouldn't be so certain of that."

He smiled in defeat and rolled away. He crossed to his pile of clothes, turning enough to show the firmness of his disappointment—which was prominent in its statement. He donned his robes, hiding the run of hard muscles and downy glisten of his skin.

She slid out of bed as he finished. She crossed to join him as he pulled the *byor-ga* headwear in place. She lifted to her toes and kissed him deeply, bruising those lips more, leaving her mark on him.

She settled back to her soles with a sigh. "If all goes well, I'll see you in Kysalimri by the end of the day."

"I will do my best to be ready by then."

She reached down and grabbed him. "You seem ready enough to me."

He groaned. "You'll make for a wicked empress."

She let him go and drew the coif of his headgear over his handsome features. "Do well in rousing the *Shayn'ra,* and I will show you how *wicked* I can be. But for now, go. Llyra is surely pacing a hole through the deck of the arrowsprite."

"Very true."

Once in Kysalimri, Tazar and Llyra had work of their own to do. The guild-master would rouse the low army that she recruited from the city's thieveries, taverns, and dark dens over the past year, while Tazar gathered his *Shayn'ra* into a larger, harder Fist.

Much depended on the days ahead.

Knowing this, Tazar turned and headed toward a balcony door. He gave a final glance back, then leaped over the rail outside and vanished. The drama of his exit was more artifice than stealth. One had to go through the motions of secrecy to maintain some semblance of decorum when it came to such dalliances.

But for what must be accomplished in the next bell, such feigned pretense would not suffice.

Aalia stared into the mirror leaning on a wall. Naked and unabashed, she straightened her shoulders and stood taller.

*I must* be *the empress.*

JUBAYR SETTLED WITH the others in the small dining hall in the emperor's palacio. He had visited here often enough to tell the room had been prepared for this tense gathering.

The large table had been shifted to face the balcony that overlooked the villa's grounds and out to the Bay of the Blessed. The Stone Gods stood tall, casting their august shadows across the water. Five seats had been positioned along one side, facing that view.

Clearly the staff had been alerted to the number of councillors who would be attending. There was also a sixth member. Chaaen Hrash. But the man was not officially a part of the imperial council, so he would remain standing. Still, Jubayr had asked Hrash to come with them. If anyone knew Emperor Makar the best, it was his father's most adored and esteemed friend and adviser. If they were to evaluate the emperor's temperament and fitness of mind, Hrash's insight would be useful.

As they waited for Aalia, Jubayr did his best to judge the mood in the room.

Wing Draer and Mareesh, both of the aerial fleet, stood with arms crossed, wearing matching frowns. They seemed equally set against Aalia, refusing to even unbend those stubborn limbs to accept a dram of wine or a crumpet of brined eel on toast.

On the other side, Shield Angelon had his head bowed with Sail Garryn, in midargument with each other, weighing or dismissing the merits of such a radical course. Angelon leaned away and Garryn toward Aalia. Still, like any sail in a tempest, their positions tipped in all directions.

The only neutral party seemed to be Chaaen Hrash, who looked pensive and worried—not about the decision to be weighed this morning, but about an emperor whom he loved dearly.

Finally, a small horn sounded. The master of the palacio—a spindle of a man in an ankle-length gray shift and crimson belt—requested they all take their seats. As they did, a flurry of servants swept in and cleared the table of plates, platters, and other detritus of the small morning repast that had welcomed them. Every crumb and droplet of spilled wine was wiped away, leaving the table as pristine as it was priceless.

Its timber had been hewn from the rare fall of a dead branch from the Talniss groves of X'or. Its surface was as black as ebony and grained in bright silver. The wood was so dark that it looked like the table had been sculpted out of those shining filaments. Talniss wood was prized above all, valued a hundred times its weight in gold. The table alone would finance an entire warship.

Jubayr ran his palm over its surface as he crossed to his seat. Once there, he kept the imperial cloak clasped about his neck, but he tossed its length over the low back of his chair. The embroidered Haeshan Hawk with its diamond eyes and gold claws glinted brightly, as if trying to compete with the rich table.

The others settled to either side. The Wing and Mareesh to his left and the Shield and Sail to his right. Hrash stood behind Jubayr's shoulder, ready to offer support. Still, seated at the table's center, Jubayr felt the weight of this responsibility. His father had left him this cloak and the leadership of the imperium while he was gone. Jubayr would honor that blessing by not relinquishing it without cause.

The horn sounded again.

An expectant silence settled over the room.

Footsteps could be heard approaching down the marble hall. All eyes turned. As Aalia stepped into the room, a few gasps greeted her. One of them might have been from Jubayr, but he was too shocked to know for sure.

Aalia stepped into the room naked, her skin oiled to a dark ebony, nearly the same hue as the table. Enhancing this effect was the tracery of silver lines that wrapped her skin. Across her belly, they formed a shining hawk, the Haeshan crest. Her long hair had been unbraided and ironed into a fall of shadows.

In her hands, she carried a silver platter. Atop it rested the imperial circlet of dark iron. Its bright blue sapphires matched the waters of the bay behind her. As she crossed, the Stone Gods towered behind her shoulders.

Two princes flanked her, Rami on her left, Kanthe on her right. They stopped halfway and let Aalia continue forward on her own, bared to all. She kept her gaze forward, humble but unbowed.

She stepped to the table and placed the circlet and platter down before Jubayr.

"No hand has touched this since my father forced it upon me. I now lay it before you all."

She retreated four steps, while the two princes came forward, flourishing a grand cloak between them. It was a silken gold on the inside and layered on the outside with petals of every hue of red. They placed it across her shoulders and drew it over her nakedness, transforming her in a sweep into the Illuminated Rose of the Imperium.

She took one step forward again, asserting her space. "I have no desire to be empress. I only come to repeat and share my father's wishes before delirium fully consumed him. I leave it to you all to decide to set it aside or honor it."

Jubayr realized he had been holding his breath. He let it out slowly, glancing to his right and left. No one had the wind to speak, still stunned. Mareesh barely noted Aalia. His gaze was fixed to the circlet. He looked ready to lunge over and grab it, and he might have, if not for the presence of Shield, Wing, and Sail. To ever hope to wear that crown, one would need the approval of all three.

Jubayr glanced to the circlet, too. Unlike Mareesh, he had hardly looked at it. If anything, he felt a trickle of fear at the sight of it—whether due to the hard man who once wore it or his own reluctance to ever carry its weight.

The first person to speak did not come from the table but from behind Jubayr's shoulder. "And what of Emperor Makar?" Chaaen Hrash asked. "How does he fare?"

Aalia closed her eyes, her chin dropping. "See for yourself."

Upon her words, another trio entered. This time, everyone truly did gasp.

Jubayr stood up, choking himself with his cloak. "Father . . ."

Emperor Makar hobbled in, leaning heavily on the arm of the Augury of Qazen. At his father's other side came Abbess Shayr, governess of X'or and one of the most esteemed healers of the Klashe. The emperor was dressed as resplendently as always in a stark white *gerygoud* habiliment, complete with polished snakeskin boots and gold cap. Only the rich attire seemed to mock the man wearing it. His father looked everywhere and nowhere. Spittle flecked his lips. His right cheek twitched with every step.

Chaaen Hrash rushed around the table. "Makar," he blurted out, shocked into forgetting any proper title or honorific. Only when he reached the emperor's side did he finally collect himself. "Your Illustriousness, it is I . . . Chaaen Hrash."

Makar looked at his closest friend, but clearly there was no recollection. Still, the emperor tried, as if Hrash's heartbreak more than his words had worn past the haze that overtook the emperor's senses. A single tear rolled down his father's face.

Jubayr noted Rami wringing his hands as he watched this greeting, his face furious and frustrated.

*I feel the same, dear brother.*

"What has caused this affliction?" Hrash asked.

The Augury nodded to the abbess to answer.

"As well as we can discern, from the muscular tics and waves of lucidity, we suspect a poison of Quelch Bonnet. A venom from an asp that resides in the Shrouds of Dalalæða."

"In other words," Shield Angelon sneered out, casting Prince Kanthe an accusatory glare, "from the highlands of Hálendii."

KANTHE FOUGHT TO keep his face stoic as guilt etched through him. What afflicted the emperor wasn't a Hálendiian poison, but Kanthe and the others were still to blame.

Aalia spoke up in his defense. "If it wasn't for a plot uncovered by Prince Kanthe, a most loyal friend, Prince Rami and I would not have been able to save my father. I wish we had only known sooner and whom to trust. We still remain leery and don't know fully whom we can depend upon." She turned to the figure on her right. "Except for the Augury, who pulled my father from the brink of death and who offered us great counsel throughout our ensuing ordeal."

"If I may speak?" Tykhan asked with a bow of his head.

Jubayr sank back to his seat and waved permission.

"While the state of His Illustriousness may look distressing, there is hope. He does have moments of clarity. Like when he urged for his daughter to accept the heavy mantle of the imperium."

Kanthe noted he directed his words at Prince Jubayr, who fingered the clasp at his neck.

"In truth, I was not surprised by this offer. I have often had visions of the imperial throne with a woman sitting atop it. But she was much older, wiser, and greatly revered by her children and the imperium at large. It was only upon Emperor Makar's supplication to his daughter that I realized *who* that revered woman was." He motioned to Aalia. "There she stands."

Murmurs spread across the table.

Mareesh spoke up sharply, with a slightly mocking tone. "So you say, Augury. But it remains your word and my sister's. Perhaps you both have much to gain by such assertions. Like the imperium itself."

Wing Draer muttered a half-hearted agreement.

Tykhan touched his lips, feigning deep consideration of these words. "As I said before, Emperor Makar does have moments of lucidity. He seems especially roused by the circlet itself. Perhaps due to some property of the meteoric iron or simply how adamant he is about who should wear it. We've kept it from his sight, as it does agitate him and afterward sets him back for a spell. But if you wish, you may see how he reacts. Somewhere deep inside, he likely does recognize everyone here. I saw the tear on the emperor's cheek when Chaaen Hrash approached in such a heartfelt manner."

Jubayr gave a small nod.

"So with all of his dearest councillors and advisers present, perhaps we can elicit some lucidity and guidance from Emperor Makar. If Prince Jubayr could bring the circlet forward, then—"

Mareesh reached over and snatched it from the tray. "I'll do it."

He stood and stalked around the table, carrying the circlet as if it were a child's toy. He approached his father. Only when he was a few steps away did his confidence falter. Kanthe had no doubt Makar ruled his sons with a hard hand. Mareesh slowed, his shoulders bowing slightly. He held forth the circlet with more reverence now, recognizing the prominence of the one who once wore it.

"Father," he asked softly, "what would you have us do?"

Tykhan urged the emperor forward, gently brushing the back of the man's head as he let him go. Makar stumbled, arms out. He took the circlet from his son's hands and tilted it right and left, the sapphires glinting in the light. He then held it out, as if offering it to Mareesh. His son reached to accept it, but Makar stumbled past him, shouldering the prince aside. He crossed to Aalia, toppled to his knees, and held the circlet up toward her.

One word was forced through his lips. "P . . . P . . . Please . . ."

Kanthe suspected this plea had nothing to do with the circlet, and everything to do with the emperor begging to be released from his bridling. Aalia took it, her face stricken with a sadness that was not feigned. Tears welled. Rami could stand it no more and turned away.

Tykhan and the abbess collected Makar, who swooned and nearly fell. He could barely keep his legs now.

Tykhan looked apologetically toward the table. "As I warned, these moments of clarity are rare but also debilitating." He turned to the abbess. "Would you take him back to his room to rest? I'll check on him when we're done."

She nodded.

"And could you ask Novitiate Liss to bring in Sister Amis?" Tykhan added.

"Of course."

As the abbess guided Makar out, Kanthe looked at Aalia and Rami, who appeared to be just as mystified as Kanthe about this next visitor.

Chaaen Hrash watched Makar depart the room. "How long will the emperor be afflicted?"

Tykhan sighed. "Years certainly, maybe longer, maybe forever."

Sail Garryn spoke up into the silence that followed. "Considering this verdict, we must consider the good of the imperium. Word of the emperor's affliction will surely spread. Both within our borders and without. The people will look to us for guidance. We must not look indecisive."

Shield Angelon nodded. "I agree. During this time of strife, we must quickly shore up the people's morale." His next words were spoken begrudgingly. "To that end, no one is held in higher esteem than the emperor's daughter. People will rally around her."

Kanthe had expected such a judgement would wound Prince Jubayr, the eldest son, but the man simply ran a palm over the table's surface, as if inspecting it for flaws. Next to him, Prince Mareesh had recovered enough to stare with narrowed eyes as the circlet was returned to the table.

Off to the side, footsteps approached the room. A young woman entered with an elderly sister on her arm. They were both dressed in gray, but the younger woman was darkly complected, clearly Klashean. The older one was nearly as gray as her robe, both her braided hair and her skin.

Everyone glanced around, waiting for an explanation.

Tykhan nodded to the pair, then turned to the table. "I told you of my vision of the imperium's glorious future, with a beloved empress on the throne, but I held off mentioning who sat beside her, father to her children. He was older, too, but he was wearing a crown."

Murmurs whispered in confusion.

Kanthe was not mystified at all.

"He was wearing a Hálendiian crown," Tykhan explained, turning to Kanthe. "You all knew of Emperor Makar's desire to have Prince Kanthe marry his daughter on the winter's solstice."

Kanthe tried not to groan.

*I truly have come full circle.*

Aalia looked no happier, but she did not appear surprised. Tykhan must have already informed her, possibly with the promise that this would be a marriage in name only.

But Tykhan was not done. "What the emperor did not share at large but what he has known for over a decade—" He pointed at Kanthe. "There stands the true heir to the Hálendiian crown—not his twin brother, the heinous executioner of our beloved Prince Paktan."

Mareesh jerked to his feet. "What new trickery is this?"

Kanthe stammered, agreeing with the prince, "That's . . . It's preposterous."

Mareesh waved at Kanthe as if to say, *See, not even this miscreant agrees with you.*

Shield Angelon looked just as dubious. "We've all heard the whispers and rumors. It happens with every twin birth."

Tykhan turned to the old woman. "Sister Amis came to X'or fourteen years ago, after years of hiding, seeking refuge and finding it under the gentle wings of Abbess Shayr. She had another name prior to the one she has now." He stared across the faces. "Fay hy Persha, royal Hálendiian midwife of the Massif clan."

Mareesh sank down.

Kanthe's stomach did the same.

"Please tell us what you told the abbess and what she shared with the emperor."

The woman nodded, looking relieved and casting Kanthe a sad look. "On the night of the twins' birth, amid the blood and panic, I was between the queen's legs. I saw who first squalled at the world. It wasn't a bright child with curled locks, but a quieter babe with shadowy hair and skin like warm toffye."

Kanthe swallowed, his legs weakening.

Surely this couldn't be true. It had to be another ruse by the duplicitous Augury of Qazen, a man of a thousand faces. Kanthe stared around at the others, looking to them to refute this claim.

Aalia and Rami appeared equally stunned.

Tykhan gave the smallest nod toward the old sister. "Show him."

With the novitiate's help, Sister Amis crossed to Kanthe. From a pocket, the old woman removed a folded piece of silk. She unwrapped it to reveal a gold signet ring set with a crimson garnet. Inscribed into the gem was a winged horse, sigil of the House of Hyparia.

"It was your mother's ring," Sister Amis confirmed. "After learning that you were pushed aside as firstborn, the queen rightly feared your father would silence anyone who knew the truth. So she gave me her ring to buy passage away. But I could not part with it, as I loved your mother with all my heart. I kept the ring, hoping one day"—she took another step forward and offered it to Kanthe—"to hand it to the rightful heir."

Kanthe accepted the ring, too stunned to do otherwise. He stared down at the garnet, at the symbol. He barely remembered his mother, just hazy glimpses, all full of warmth. He felt tears rising unbidden.

*This is a piece of my mother.*

"It has been authenticated," Tykhan said. "While some may still dismiss it, we all here know the truth, as did Emperor Makar. Prince Kanthe, sworn to the Illuminated Rose, is indeed the true firstborn son of King Toranth."

Kanthe found it harder to breathe, his world upended, both believing and disbelieving, both hoping and fearing. He shook his head. Rami came to him, hugged him, as if sensing his distress.

"I will be a truer brother than you've ever known," he whispered in his ear. "This I swear."

Kanthe hugged him back, hanging on him, rudderless for a moment.

A sharp clatter of boots rattled down the hall, drawing them all straighter. A shining Paladin burst into the room. He stared around at the assemblage, unsure of his footing or even where to look.

Aalia asserted her first dominance as future empress. "Out with it," she snapped. "Why do you disturb us?"

While still breathless, he stiffened straighter at her command. "Word from Kysalimri," he said, gulping twice more. "Hálendii is moving once again. Warships are being readied. Including their flagship."

Kanthe knew of the *Hyperium*. Half a year ago, before he was deemed a traitor to the crown, the ship was still being finished. He remembered viewing its skeleton of beams and draft-iron. It was easily three times the size of a regular Hálendiian warship and twice that of the largest of the Klashean fleet.

Upon this announcement, chaos briefly broke out as everyone tried to speak at once. Aalia silenced it with a word. "Enough!"

All eyes turned to her.

She stared them down, unbending. "The imperium will not survive a thousand voices squabbling, nor even the five here. One must lead. Will you honor my father or dismiss him? I will abide by your decision but will not tolerate waffling. Either you all agree or none."

Sail Garryn did not hesitate, responding to the firmness in her voice, looking relieved to hear it. He bowed his head, raising fist to forehead. "Empress."

Shield Angelon waited a breath, looking briefly at Prince Jubayr. The hesitation he saw there bowed the Shield's head and raised his fist.

The Wing followed suit, though it looked like he was bending iron to do it.

Jubayr stood and reached to undo the clasp of his cloak.

"No," Aalia said, striding forward. She refastened the clasp in place. "Our father gave you his cloak. I will respect that. You have spent your life under his tutelage. I will always seek your counsel. You will forever be at my side."

She turned to Mareesh. "I know you do not agree, dear brother. You were never one to hide your heart, and I've loved you for that passion." She placed her hand atop the circlet. "In respect for your doubt, I will not don this. Not until the empire is safe. But for now, can you . . . *will* you be my warrior in the clouds until such a time comes?"

Mareesh stared at the circlet, then at his sister. The Wing put a hand on his shoulder. He nodded and placed his fist to his brow. "I agree. As you say, for now."

"Thank you, Mareesh."

She turned to the room. "I will head to Kysalimri with the council. Prince Kanthe, I'll ask for you and your alchymist to remain here. Animosities toward Hálendiians are already running high. Best you stay here until these storm clouds clear."

Kanthe bowed his head and placed a fist to his forehead. He clutched the signet ring in that same hand. He couldn't argue with her.

*It's stormy enough right here.*

# 84

MIKAEN STRODE THROUGH the legion's mooring fields toward the majesty of the *Hyperium*. It was a sight to behold, to stir hearts in wonder and inspire terror in an enemy.

It had taken two decades to build the ship. Entire forests had been cleared to shore its hull and build its decks. Hundreds of seamstresses had worn fingers to the bone sewing and waxing the fabric of its gargantuan gasbags. Unlike other warships, three large balloons pulled overhead, straining their draft-iron cables, each the thickness of a century-old tree trunk. Three rows of cannons poked from its sides; triple rows of ballistas lined its middeck, stacked one atop the other. The open deck itself spread to twice the size of a tourney field.

Mikaen's heart stirred at the sight of it. His pace increased. He was anxious to be aboard and to assume the captaincy of the mighty flagship. Thoryn kept to his side, trailed by a phalanx of his Silvergard. They all wore heavy armor, which glinted in the morning sun. They were the shining arrow of the kingdom, ready to pierce the heart of the imperium.

For once, his father had shown the true steel of a king. There would be no mercy for the torching of the Shield Islands, for the thousands killed, for turning those islands into scorched rocks, where nothing would grow.

Mikaen approved this course of action. He stared at the *Hyperium*'s massive hold, picturing the giant steel drum hidden inside, twice the size of any Cauldron. He hardened and stirred at just the thought of the Madyss Hammer and the destruction it would wield.

*Its thundering quake will make the imperium tremble.*

He headed to the large ramp that led into the lower bowels of the ship. He ached to place his palms against the Hammer's steel flanks. Ahead, at the foot of the ramp, King Toranth waited with Liege General Reddak. As with the prior mission, Mikaen would have someone watching over his shoulder, questioning and judging his every decision. Still, he would tolerate such a position for the chance to captain the *Hyperium* on its first voyage.

He swept up to King Toranth and Reddak. Mikaen gave a swift bow to his father and a curt salute to the general. "I'm ready to carry out your will, Father. We will knock the imperium to its knees and keep them there."

Toranth nodded his agreement. "We all know this undertaking is critical in asserting our dominance. A sixth of the legion's winged force will be sailing forth. There can be no mistakes or mishaps that make us look weak."

Mikaen placed a fist to his breastplate in acknowledgment of these words.

"For that reason," Toranth said, "I'm assigning the captaincy of the *Hyperium* to Liege General Reddak, along with full command of this mission."

Mikaen fell back a step, no less shocked than if his father had slapped him hard in front of the entire legion—which, in truth, he had.

"No hesitancy in command will be tolerated," Toranth finished. "Nor will any rash or imprudent choices be allowed."

His father stepped forward and clapped Mikaen on the shoulder. It took all of Mikaen's effort not to knock the arm away. "I know this wounds you, my son. But you're still young. You have much to learn from Reddak. Use this opportunity. Bring glory to the kingdom, and nothing will ever be held back from you again."

The king shifted his hand to cup Mikaen's neck. His voice lowered to a sincere pitch. "I'm hard on you because I have faith in you. You will bring great honor to the Massif name. In this, I have no doubt. You just need to tame that fire inside you. The flame that best serves the kingdom should be that of a forge, one that tempers steel, not a wildfire of destruction."

"I understand, Your Majesty," Mikaen said stiffly.

His father patted his neck. "I knew you would."

The king dismissed Mikaen so he could board. He did so quickly, pounding up the ramp with his Silvergard in tow. He entered the hold and climbed the dozen levels to the top of the forecastle. He no longer had any interest in paying homage to the Madyss Hammer in the hold. Instead, he headed to a door marked with a golden sun and crown, sigil of the Massif clan, the cabin of the ship's captain.

He stopped before it, trembling, humiliated.

Thoryn drew closer but knew better than to touch him.

"Hide your fury and bide your time, my prince," the Silvergard warned. "Do not let them know your pain. Become as hard as the mask you wear, that we've marked upon our faces to match. All will come in due time. This, I swear to you."

Mikaen nodded. He made sure no one was in the hall and spit a heavy gobbet onto that symbol. He watched it dribble off the gold and down the planks. Only then did he turn away and head off toward the open deck. He would glory in their departure and, as Thoryn wisely recommended—

*I'll bide my time.*

For now.

He hurried through the forecastle and shoved out onto the open deck.

Winds cooled the heat from his face. The massive gasbags shadowed his angry countenance. He crossed to the starboard rail, passing between the tiers of giant ballistas.

As the knights guarded his back, he stared across the fields to the distant rise of Highmount. The castle walls towered over the city of Azantiia, forming the six-pointed sun of the Massif clan. His family had ruled the kingdom for centuries, eighteen generations had claimed its throne.

*I will be the nineteenth.*

Mikaen pictured the faces of his son and daughter. He gripped the rail harder, determined and assured of one certainty, a destiny that would not be denied.

*My son, Othan, will be the twentieth.*

A stirring drew his attention away. A black-cloaked figure passed through the wall of silver. The man dropped to a knee before him.

"My prince," he said, "we've confirmed the location of your brother."

Mikaen stepped forward. "Keep your voice low. The very winds up here have ears."

The man bowed his head. "Prince Kanthe remains in the Southern Klashe as all have suspected. But he does not reside in Kysalimri."

"Then where?" Mikaen asked sharply, defying his own dictate from a moment ago.

"He abides in X'or."

Mikaen glanced to Thoryn. The Vyrllian knight's crimson-tattooed face remained stony, leaving this decision to him.

*As it should be.*

Mikaen faced the spy. "Alert your brothers. They know what must be done."

The man bowed again and swiftly departed to carry out Mikaen's order.

Mikaen gazed out across the deck as it bustled in preparation for the inaugural launch of the *Hyperium* and the glorious mission ahead. No longer in command, he cared nothing about the success or failure of this venture.

*Before this day is over, I will have my own victory.*


WRYTH SUFFERED THROUGH a defeat that stung all the way down to the bowels of the Shrivenkeep. He had tried to persuade passage onto the *Hyperium*. Not only to keep close to Prince Mikaen in what would likely prove to be another vain attempt to warm the bond between the two, but as the first voyage of the kingdom's flagship, Wryth should be there.

The lack of an Iflelen—or any Shrive—damaged their order's standing. His absence would be noted by many, and the slight taken as a falling from royal grace—which it was. Wryth had not even bothered approaching Mikaen or his crimson-faced lapdogs. But both King Toranth and Liege General Reddak had asked him to step aside. After failing to rein in Mikaen during his last outing, Wryth was being punished.

Angry and perturbed, he shoved into the Iflelen's inner sanctum, needing a moment to firm his composure. He was already calculating ways to polish this affront with face-saving measures. As he stepped inside, a loud shout made him trip a step, indicating how out of sorts he was.

"Phenic finally found you!" Keres yelled to him.

Wryth took a deep breath and called across the obsidian dome to the heart of the Iflelen's great instrument, "What do you mean, Keres? I've not seen Phenic."

Keres shouted back, not looking up, concentrating as he worked, "Another message from Skerren! It's still being sent."

Wryth's heart pounded harder, surging with hope that this day could yet be saved. If he could bring word to the king of the recovery of the bronze artifact, he would shine far brighter than any victory in the Southern Klashe. The last message from Skerren had his forces locking down the hidden sea out there.

Holding his breath in anticipation, Wryth wiggled and ducked his way through the instrument, chased by the hissing sighs of the four bloodbaernes' bellows. He reached Keres and hovered over the man's shoulder. Wryth kept a silent, anxious vigil, watching the glowing red blip that marked Skerren's battle barge blink in stops and starts in a complicated code. Keres recorded it diligently until the glow returned to a solid, fixed shine as the message ended.

Wryth folded his arms into his sleeves as he waited for Keres to decipher Skerren's words. Wryth grabbed his elbows, gripping them hard. He tried to pace away his anxiety and excitement, but it was to no avail.

"What did he say?" Wryth finally demanded.

The grim expression on Keres's face did not bode well. He continued to work while explaining. "Skerren lost both swyftships."

"What?"

"And nearly all the forces he sent down into that steamy sea."

"How is that possible?"

Keres paused his work to turn to him. "Commander Ghryss returned to the battle barge with the last of his men. He barely escaped."

"From what?"

"I deciphered it twice, though it makes no sense."

"What?" Wryth pressed him.

"From *bats*. Ice bats. They attacked both his men and the village. It was chaos and slaughter down there."

Wryth shook his head, trying to dismiss Skerren's claim. It sounded out-landish. Still, none of that mattered. "What about the bronze artifact? Did he ever discern its location?"

"I need a moment more to finish decrypting the rest."

Wryth returned to his pacing, even more impatient and anxious. He stared over at the bronze bust that softly glowed, slumbering in peace. Wryth wanted to wrench it out of the instrument's heart and throw it across the room.

Keres finally cleared his throat, his eyes wider, shining with hope. "The artifact is not lost. He says a swyftship rose out of the mist, ablaze with flames, and sped off to the west. It was the enemy."

"They're on the run again?"

"Skerren doesn't say, but they must have finally fixed their ship enough to escape the bats and flee. Maybe they were chased off by those infernal crea-tures, flushed out by them."

"And Skerren?"

"He's in pursuit. He's following at a distance, trying to keep his presence hidden for as long as possible."

"What's his plan?"

"The enemy is clearly headed somewhere. Fast. He intends to follow them, not only to chase down the artifact, but to determine what had driven them on such a strange course."

Wryth nodded, just as curious.

Keres continued, "Once they slow or reach their destination, Skerren says he'll not hold back. He'll release, as he states here, *the weapon you sent.*"

Keres glanced over, looking for some explanation. Not even Keres knew of this weapon. Only a handful in the Shrivenkeep had been informed of Wryth's project, an undertaking of the darkest alchymies.

"Go on," Wryth urged. "What else did he say?"

Keres frowned at Skerren's message. "All it says is that he's 'readied the formidable Kalyx.'"

Wryth shook his head, not in disbelief but certainty.

*No one is ready for Kalyx.*

# SEVENTEEN

# THE BRACKENLANDS

*To stryve & fail is far bett'r thenne to turn awei in defeat. Ev'n the reward of deth from effort is bett'r thenne a punishement of liffe in regret.*

—From the eulogy of Gharan sy Wren,
a knight who stood his ground against
the ravening Hrakken Horde

# 85

SADDLED ATOP HER raash'ke, Nyx circled wide around the *Sparrowhawk*. The ship blazed across the eternal night of the Wastes. Off to the east, the fiery glow of the Mouth warmed the horizon. Below, a desert glinted like broken glass, reflecting starlight and the moon's sheen.

According to Daal, the spread of crystal-rich sands was called the Fated Desert. Nyx twisted in her saddle and peered to the west. A row of peaks cut a jagged line across the sky.

*The Desolate Range.*

She pictured the broken plains beyond those mountains, what Daal aptly called the Brackenlands. All those names came from the distant past. For countless generations, no Panthean had traveled beyond the Ice Shield. But Nyx knew, further in the past, Daal's ancestors had made such journeys. She could still draw up a memory—gifted by the *Oshkapeers*—of two ancient riders flying across this desert and over those mountains. She conjured up the last snippet, as the two riders reached the Brackenlands.

*—she watches her mate head on foot across a shattered landscape, leaving a crumple of broken wings behind him. Her heart aches. Her mate waves for her to abandon him and return to the Crèche. She knows she must. As she turns away, far in the distance, something glitters under the icy shine of a full moon.*

Only one of the riders had returned from that journey. The other had headed toward the distant glittering shine. She sensed that was where they were headed now, the site marked with an emerald glow on Shiya's crystal sphere of the world.

The *Oshkapeers* had warned her against trespassing there, tying that fear to the bronze spider who corrupted the raash'ke.

Without being told, Nyx knew that was where he made his lair.

Another raash'ke swept the stars, careening over the *Sparrowhawk*'s huge balloon, drawing her attention back. Daal tipped his mount's wings up and down, signaling it was time to return to the ship.

She did not resist this summons. Her limbs had started to shiver, and ice frosted over her jacket and hood. She leaned closer to the saddle, into the warmth of her mount. She sang her thanks and used her knees to guide the raash'ke back to the ship.

As they glided toward the firelit deck, she took stock of the *Hawk*.

Yesterday, in great haste, they had fled the Crèche around midday, shortly after she had discovered the others in the crashed sailraft. It had not taken their group long to discover that the *Sparrowhawk* had been spared any significant damage by the hostile raash'ke. By the time the bats had attacked, the ship had been beached away from the village and mostly swallowed by smoke. The *Hawk*'s cooling balloon had also sagged low after its *flitch*-fueled firepots had been snuffed out.

Yet, in the end, it had been Glace who truly saved the ship, raiding it and dispatching a straggling crew of Hálendiians. She had also safely rescued Krysh and Meryk.

Still, their group knew the battle wasn't over. They all knew another warcraft of the kingdom was likely lurking outside the Crèche. Especially with the enemy dispatching skrycrows toward the mists.

Something was up there still.

Fearing another attack, their group had quickly readied the *Sparrowhawk* and fled the Crèche.

Unfortunately, their swyftship was far from fully repaired. Holes still marred its lower hull, and its broken keel looked like a crooked beak. But the *Hawk* could still fly. Between its heated balloon and its remaining two forges already retooled, they decided to risk leaving. Darant had wanted to replace the portside forge that Brayl had sabotaged, but they didn't have the time.

As Nyx flew toward the *Sparrowhawk,* she noted the rich emerald of the forges' powerful new flames. She could feel their heat as she approached. Once close enough, she urged her mount into a harrowingly steep dive.

This was her third sojourn off the ship since they had departed, so she felt slightly more confident—but only slightly. The descent was both exhilarating and terrifying. At the last breath, her raash'ke crossed under the balloon and snapped its wings wide, cupping the air to bring them to a sudden, but manageable, skate across the planks.

As they came to a stop, Daal swooped in next to her.

A flurry of other raash'ke fled to either side. Before leaving, Nyx had sent out a request to the horde-mind of the raash'ke, asking for a handful of the flock to accompany them on this journey. Besides wanting their strength of force, Nyx had hoped their presence would help sustain her connection to the horde-mind. With so much unknown and a possible enemy both ahead of them and behind, she wanted all the allies she could muster.

As Daal dismounted ahead of her, he wore a huge grin. He shook ice from his hair and patted his raash'ke.

"Thank you, Nyfka."

Their two mounts were the same pair who had carried them out of the

Mouth yesterday. Since then, Daal had made modifications to their saddles, relying on his knowledge and that of his ancestors. Already she had noted the improvements. Even the raash'ke seemed to appreciate them. The saddles sat more firmly and seemed to chafe their mounts less.

"How did Metyl fare?" Daal asked as he joined her.

She smiled. Daal had chosen the names in honor of Mattis and Neffa. He hadn't wanted to use their exact names, as he thought it marred their memory. So he had modified them enough to be unique but still pay tribute to the brave orksos.

"He did well," Nyx answered. "I think we're both finding our rhythm. It helps that the horde-mind retains memories from when the raash'ke lived in harmony with your people."

"Can you still sense the horde-mind's presence this far away from the Mouth?"

She nodded. "So far, but it grows fainter."

Nyx and Daal jostled through the raash'ke on the deck to reach the warmth of the firepots blazing under the open gullet of the hot balloon.

In addition to the raash'ke here, there were more in the empty hold below. Darant's crew had cleared the space out days ago while repairs were underway, and no one had a chance to restock it. This allowed room for a few more raash'ke aboard the *Hawk*.

Someone nudged her from behind.

She turned to find Bashaliia standing there, rocking on his legs, casting her a scolding pout. She gave him a firm hug and a whisper of an apologetic song.

"Don't be jealous. You'll always be first in my heart."

He nuzzled his forgiveness into her ear, raising a warm smile.

Earlier, to his great disappointment, she hadn't allowed him to come on this flight. He was still young, prone to distractions, and attracted by curiosities. If he had wandered off too far, the ship could have traveled beyond his range to return.

The *Sparrowhawk*'s new engines proved to be monsters. After a slow, cautious start, they were now sweeping three or four times faster than any swyftship. A trip that would've taken a week now would take under two days. At those speeds, Bashaliia might not be able to catch up. Only larger ships with bigger forges could hope to maintain this pace—and even then, it would be a challenge.

Reminded of that concern, she gave Bashaliia another hug and a scratch behind his ears and turned to Daal. She nodded her head toward the doors into the forecastle.

"I'm sure someone is impatient for our report."

* * *

GRAYLIN PACED THE wheelhouse, nearly tripping over Kalder as he made a turn and swept the other way. The vargr kept close, unnerved by the number of raash'ke aboard the *Hawk*. His hackles would raise with every hiss or sharp cry from them.

*I get it.*

The noise was unnerving, especially with the backdrop of the ship's continual howl, created by the winds sweeping over the holes in the hull and across the drag of the broken keel.

Graylin headed to the navigation station, where Fenn worked with Jace and Krysh, laboring over star charts and hand-drawn maps. "How much longer until we reach the site that Shiya gave us?"

Jace answered, "Hard to tell with any precision. According to Fenn's sextant readings, we're moving swiftly. So rapidly that he wanted to check again to make sure his calculations were correct. We should have an updated consensus in a moment."

Glace overheard this from her station next to the maesterwheel. "If the *Hawk* didn't have gaping holes and a broken keel, we could go even faster."

"We're flying fast enough," Darant warned. "Don't want to rip her apart. Even at these speeds, best pray she stays in one piece."

"If that's a concern, should we slow down?" Graylin asked.

Darant glanced back. "Right now, we don't know who or what might be following us, so I say we let the *Hawk* fly as fast as she wants."

The brigand's mood continued to remain sullen and short-tempered. Not that anyone faulted his sourness. Between the loss of his daughter and the betrayal behind it, Darant was still struggling to come to some degree of acceptance, if not understanding. Though the latter might never be possible.

Everyone expected a betrayal of trust to be born of larger ambitions or grander schemes or greater umbrages. Sometimes it was just a tired daughter wanting to go home.

The door slammed open behind him, pushed by the winds sweeping through the ship. Nyx ducked in with a bodily shiver, while Daal shouldered the door shut.

"It's colder down here than up on the deck," Nyx said.

Kalder trotted over to her, sniffed her legs, then curled his nose in distaste, smelling the musk of the raash'ke on her. He returned to Graylin with his tail dragging lower.

Likewise, Fenn scowled at Daal. Across the navigator's neck, a scabbed line marred his throat. Daal noted the hard look and glanced away, sheepish and ashamed. His anger had nearly killed Fenn. While Brayl had deceived Daal, Fenn thought he had earned enough trust by now to have had his protests of innocence listened to and not summarily and bloodily dismissed.

Daal headed to the far side of the wheelhouse, where Rhaif stood with Shiya. Vikas was there, too. She had taken over Brayl's place at the arc of smaller wheels and levers on that side. Of Darant's original crew, Vikas and Glace were the only two women remaining. By now, half his crew had been lost, leaving barely enough to keep the *Hawk* manned.

Before leaving, Daal had tried to recruit some additional hands from his Noorish people. But in their group's haste to depart, his request had fallen on deaf ears. Daal barely had time to explain to his mother and father all that had befallen him. They had been furious, scared, and appalled in equal measures. Still, they had understood enough to allow Daal to come with them.

Graylin turned to Nyx as she joined him. "When you were out there, did you see any sign of us being followed?"

Nyx shook her head. "No. Nothing moving against the stars. Nor any flashing forges. If someone is behind us, they're traveling dark." She stared toward the approach of the tall mountains. "And they're not the *only* enemy we need to worry about."

She had already related her encounter with the spider, a bronze figure like Shiya. Only this one was misshapen and hostile. Nyx believed the spider had corrupted the raash'ke as a means of protecting his lair, a living wall of defense.

Darant looked back at them. "We're almost to those mountains. But we still have a way to go. So, I suggest you all get as much rest as possible."

"He's right," Fenn said. "It'll take us another half day to reach that site in the Brackenlands."

Darant nodded grimly. "Let's hope the *Hawk* doesn't lose her wings before then. Even if we're successful, we still need to get back to the Crèche."

Considering the dangers ahead, that was a very big *if.*

Graylin crossed closer to the windows and watched the peaks cut higher, rising more jagged, as if warning them all back.

*Maybe we should heed their advice.*


NYX WOKE OUT of a vague dream of being lost in a labyrinth of dark caves. She had been pursuing the glowing wisp of a Liar's Lure. The willowy gasses plied the dark bowers of her home back in the Mýr swamps, enticing the unwary to chase the wisps to their doom in the trackless bogs.

She groaned softly, having no difficulty imagining where such a dream had come from.

"I see you're up," Jace said from a table next to her bed.

"What time is it?" she asked blearily, pushing higher on the small cot.

"Two bells before midnight."

"I'm surprised I fell asleep. And for so long."

"I'm not. I was reading you a passage from *Aerodesign in Cold Climes*. A text I borrowed from Krysh's small librarie. Put you right to sleep." He gave her a small smile. "Even I find it boring."

She rolled to a seat. She had dropped fully clothed into bed. "Somehow, I doubt that. It was you and Krysh—and I'm wagering mostly *you*—who suggested replacing the lifting gasses in our balloon with hot air."

He shrugged, blushing around his collar. "I may have come up with the concept, but the execution was all Alchymist Krysh."

"Really?" she asked doubtfully, then covered an ear-popping yawn with a fist.

He lifted a brow. "You need more rest. You've tapped yourself dry over the past two days. After you fell asleep, I had to fend off people trying to disturb you. I hope it's all right that I stayed here to do some reading."

The two of them had been talking for some time before she fell asleep. It was comforting to be cubbied up with Jace, her old tutor and friend from school. Talking about nothing, skewing off into odd tangents. It felt warm and familiar, as if she had fallen back to simpler times. Being alone with him now, having this respite from responsibilities and questions, had rested her more than a quarter day of troubled sleep.

She forced herself to stand and take a few wobbly steps to gain her legs. "Thanks for serving guard duty." She leaned on his shoulder as she slipped past the table. "And for being my friend."

As she pulled her hand away, she felt a wave of misgiving. She rubbed her palm on her other sleeve, trying to erase the momentary flare of anxiety.

"Nyx?"

She shook her head as the feeling passed, recognizing it had likely come from the same well of anxiety that had fueled her dream. "Sorry. Just jittery. Need to move, I guess, shed some of this nervousness. I'm going to head to the wheelhouse and check on our progress."

"I'll come with. Fenn was working on some intriguing calculations. On projected paths back to the Crown."

She nodded, hoping they'd be able to use them.

They headed out of the cabin and into the tight passageway that ran from bow to stern. She led the way forward. The winds passing through the damaged ship howled and chilled the air. To escape their icy grip, she hurried quicker and pushed through the door at the end.

The wheelhouse was warmer but nearly deserted. Darant still stood before the maesterwheel. She doubted he'd slept at all since his daughter's death. Another crewman had replaced Glace and Vikas, manning both secondary control benches by himself. The only others awake were Fenn, who still looked hard at work, and Shiya, who never slept.

As Nyx headed toward Darant, she spotted Graylin hidden to the side, seated on the floor in a back corner, his chin to his chest. Kalder lay curled at his feet, one hindlimb thrumming in some dream, maybe chasing a Liar's Lure, too.

She also noted Krysh snoring in the small map room off the navigation station.

She joined Darant and stared out the window in front of her. When she had retired to her cabin, they had just reached the mountains, a forbidding, lifeless scarp of frost-scarred black rock. She had been happy to turn her back on it.

The view now was even more desolate, beaten flat and cracked. The plains stretched in all directions. The nearly featureless landscape looked like a pan of black mud that had been left too long in the sun, drying cracked and brittle. Only it wasn't mud, but the outer crust of this terrain.

"The Brackenlands," Nyx muttered.

Darant grunted his assent.

"How long have we been crossing it?"

"Near on three bells."

The barren, eerie landscape cast a melancholy pall, as if they were the only ones alive in all the world. But she knew that they were likely not alone out here.

"Any sign of another ship behind us?" she asked.

Darant shook his head. "Fenn's been checking with the ship's farscope, scanning all the way back to the mountains. But the moon has set, and it's gone dead dark. Even the stars are hazed over by some dust blowing off those dry mountains, dimming the view. If someone is riding the wind's current without burning forges, they'd be hard to spot."

"I can take Metyl up and do a quick pass around."

"No, lass. Not by yourself. And Daal is bedded down somewhere and needs to rest. If there's anyone out there, there's naught we can do about it now."

Fenn called over from his station, "We can't be far off from Shiya's marker."

As if stirred by her name, Shiya spoke up, lifting an arm and pointing to the south of their path. "Something shines there."

Darant left his post and followed with Nyx to join the woman.

"I don't see anything but the same sodding hardpan," Darant said.

Still, Shiya's glassy blue eyes were sharper than any of theirs. Knowing that, Nyx kept staring until she saw the shine, too. As she did, past and present momentarily overlapped. The memory from the *Oshkapeers* returned again.

*—as she turns away, far in the distance, something glitters under the icy shine of a full moon.*

"It's there," Nyx confirmed. "Just at the horizon. Darant, can you angle us slightly to the south?"

"Aye." He headed back to the wheel, calling orders to the crewman posted at the secondary controls. By the time the brigand got his hands back on the wheel, he spotted it, too. "You two were right."

Their commotion drew a growl from Kalder, and a moment later, a matching one from Graylin. They both climbed to their legs and came over.

"What is it?" Graylin asked, rubbing an eye.

Nyx and Shiya both pointed.

At the swift speed of the *Sparrowhawk,* the shine had grown quickly, reflecting ever brighter, even more than could be attributed to starlight alone.

*Strange . . .*

Ahead, a shape rose out of the landscape, looking distinctly metallic in sheen, like a hot coppery boil bursting out of the cold flat terrain.

Darant got on the ship's highhorn and roused his crew. Soon the wheelhouse grew crowded. Daal spotted Nyx and joined her by the window.

"What is it?" Daal asked.

Nyx shook her head.

With every passing league, the structure climbed higher and spread wider. At the same time, it looked as if it were floating away, warily keeping back. But the effect was just an illusion due to its massive size.

Finally, it gave up fleeing them and revealed itself fully. For a moment, Nyx flashed to the ancient *Oshkapeer* queen, with her giant tenacles draped across the sand around her bulbous head. The structure before them glowed with a familiar coppery gleam. They had all seen such metal, forged by the ancients.

The center of the complex was a dome that could have sheltered the nine massive tiers of her former school, the Cloistery of Brayk. Spreading outward in sweeps and turns were seven massive extensions, winding across the Brackenlands for tens of leagues in all directions. The entire complex looked seamless and free of rivets, as smooth as the skin of an orkso.

It looked uncannily natural, almost like something living had crawled out of the neighboring ocean. And that frozen sea behind the structure itself was a sight to behold. It had broken into huge shattered plates that rode up on one another, stacking easily half a league in height along the shoreline. The edges looked razor sharp, defying the scour of the winds. The ice captured every glint of starshine and glowed a phosphorescent blue in the dark.

"The Shattered Sea," Daal said, staring past the copper structure.

"But what's on its shore?" Rhaif pressed them all.

"It must be what we came to seek." Nyx turned to Shiya for guidance.

The bronze woman gave a tiny shake of her head. "If I was supposed to have knowledge of such a place, I do not have it now."

"We'll have to explore," Graylin said, and turned to Darant. "Can you do a slow pass over it? Look for an entrance?"

Nyx saw the challenge facing them. The macabre source of the structure's glow came from a crevice that outlined the entire complex, cutting around its dome and along those sinuous legs. The moat looked a quarter-league wide and glowed with molten rock down deep. A pass over the complex failed to reveal any bridge over that fiery gap.

"Can you get us lower?" Nyx suggested. "Search the dome itself."

Darant complied, dropping the *Hawk* close to the curved walls of the dome. This near, the sheer size of the structure was frightening.

They circled it twice before Nyx saw it. "Wait! Swing us back around."

Darant fired those powerful forges and got them headed back. He returned to what had caught her eye.

Barely discernible along the top arc of the dome was an inscribed circle, large enough for the *Hawk* to lower through it, though it would be a tight fit. Even fainter within the circle were seven arched lines that met in the middle, forming a petal-like engraving.

She turned to the others. "We've seen such round copper doorways before. Only much smaller. Under the Oldenmast in Havensfayre and over at the Northern Henge. This must be a way in."

"But if it's a door," Daal asked, "how do we open it?"

Nyx turned to Shiya. "Bridle-song. Like before. Only it took both of us—and a Kethra'kai elder named Xan to do it."

"My great-grandmother," Rhaif noted.

Nyx faced Daal. "Maybe if you took Xan's place, we could open this door together."

He nodded, willing to try.

She turned to Darant. "How close can you get us to that doorway?"

"Close enough to kiss it, if you think that'll help us get inside."

"It might."

Darant spoke swiftly to Glace and Vikas, who had resumed their positions at the secondary stations. With great care, fighting the winds curving around the dome, he lowered the *Hawk* until the engraved circle filled the window.

The copper looked close enough to touch.

Nyx reached and took Daal's hand, feeling a familiar flash of fire. She hardly had to hum to raise a glow to her lips. Shiya did the same.

As Shiya and Nyx built their song, layering on harmonies and melodies, Daal fueled their efforts. Nyx remembered how stubborn those doors had been in the past, with locks that only bridle-song could pick. She readied herself for a battle. She sent out tentative golden strands of song to test the copper.

As soon as her first thread touched the surface, a spiky coruscation of emerald fire danced over the copper and burned her thread to ash. Shocked, Nyx faltered and her song collapsed. Shiya grimaced, too, sensing the enmity in that fire.

They all knew the source of that energy.

And so did others.

Throughout the ship, the raash'ke screamed and keened, a fiery chorus of fear and fury. They, too, recognized what hid in this coppery lair.

The spider who had enslaved them.

# 86

KANTHE LOUNGED IN a steaming bath within the grounds of the emperor's palacio. A spring bubbled into the pool. The bath was a natural pond whose rock had been polished and smoothed into seats. With his eyes closed, he listened as the fifth bell of Eventoll rang across X'or.

When it finally ended, Kanthe sighed and wiggled, struggling to find some relief from his tension. Relegated to the mercies of the sisters, he felt abandoned and left trapped in this gilded and fragrant prison. Aalia and Rami had been ferried to Kysalimri, taking Pratik with them. The sense of being jailed here was enhanced by the high walls of the palacio—and the scores of Paladins and imperial guards who patrolled the surrounding woods and hallways.

Kanthe had discovered this small oasis, a tiny garden in a quiet corner of the grounds. The bubbling pool was canopied by a marble pergola, which kept the petals of the surrounding Talniss trees from sullying the shadowed waters. Though, a few floated past Kanthe's fingers. The petals had been blown in by breezes that also tinkled hundreds of chimes.

Nearby, a lone, caged songbird twittered mournfully into the last of the night.

*I know how you feel.*

But it wasn't just being abandoned that made him tense and out of sorts. He lifted his hands and spun a gold ring around his smallest finger. It was the only digit whose knuckles accommodated its slim width. He imagined his mother wearing it, seeking a connection with her. It stirred up hazy memories, but they were not warm enough to dismiss his trepidation.

*Firstborn . . .*

It still seemed impossible to contemplate fully. His second-born status had been ingrained deeply into him, by nearly two decades of slights, abuses, and beatings. His bones and flesh were steeped in the certainty of it. He could not so easily dispel it, especially not with the trifling heft of this ring and an old garnet stone inscribed with a winged horse.

He pushed both hands back underwater, hiding them away. He sank deeper with them. The shadowy garden matched his mood. Midnight was only a couple of bells off. The high walls hid the low sun, casting this oasis into a deeper gloom.

Unfortunately, this oasis was not impregnable.

A door opened across the garden. He stirred higher as Frell approached through the manicured hedges and tall pots of flowers and simpering tiny fountains.

Without any preface, except for a scowl, Frell updated Kanthe. "Pratik sent word. Aalia has successfully roused the Klashean fleet. After the battle in the Breath, the northern coast of the Klashe had been left meagerly protected. It hadn't been reinforced by Prince Jubayr. A mistake by a prince who should have been counseled better. He had been assured that King Toranth would not act so soon."

"I can see where the imperial council might have that impression. My father was always more bluster than action. But torching the Shield Islands had clearly lit a fire under him. It was a step too far, too fast, even as punishment for Mikaen's execution of Prince Paktan. My father can only be goaded so far before he explodes. Prince Mareesh should have held back his worst."

"It was as much Jubayr's fault. He had removed the reins from his brother, allowing the devastation to happen. Again, his council should have encouraged restraint on the part of both the princes."

"And Aalia?"

"From what I've heard, she listens to the council but leans upon her own astuteness. She was swift in getting the fleet—which had been listless for too long—into the air. She has them moving north in great force. But her armada won't reach the northern coast before the ships of the royal fleet breach our shores. The hope is to hold the three warships and the *Hyperium* at a battle line over Tithyn Woods, to keep them from reaching Kysalimri."

"And what are the chances of that happening?"

Frell frowned. "Prince Jubayr had been lax in his stewardship. Reacting rather than acting. He's left Aalia in a poor situation. It will be a hard battle."

"And here we sit, being fed dainties and encouraged to enjoy the luxuries of the baths."

Frell waved at him. "Which I see you're taking advantage of."

"It would be rude not to."

Frell rolled his eyes. "I'm off to update Tykhan over in the blood baths."

Kanthe nodded. Like all of them, Tykhan had clearly wanted to go with the others to Kysalimri, but he still needed to stay close to Makar, to keep the emperor under his thumb.

Kanthe made a half-hearted effort to stand. "Do you want me to go with you?"

Frell scowled again. "That's not necessary. And clearly, you're much too busy contemplating the status of your navel."

Kanthe sank back down. "True. I have a navel that requires considerable introspection."

Frell huffed his derision and set off across the gardens, slamming the door on his way out, punctuating his scorn.

Kanthe smiled, feeling incrementally better.

He lounged back, letting his eyes drift closed, listening to the caged bird's soliloquy to the night. Through a slight gap under his relaxed lids, he caught sight of a dappled shift of shadows.

He tilted to the side to peek past the marble columns of the pergola. Something ticked off the stone next to him. A glance up revealed a black-cloaked figure, with features hidden behind shadowy wraps, rushing at him. Other shadows swept in behind the first.

*What are the Rhysians doing here?*

Fearing something was amiss, he sat up. Fiery stings struck his chest and neck. Flinching, he brushed aside a tiny puff of feathers. As he did, the world spun and grew hazy—then he slumped face-first into the water.

AALIA STOOD ON the private balcony outside of the emperor's spread of rooms. She preferred the open air. Inside, she still felt like a trespasser. Her father's presence was everywhere. From the grand treasures he had collected adorning the walls to more personal items: small notions, oddments, trinkets that marked a man's more private life. But what had struck Aalia the hardest was the discovery of a jeweled comb that once belonged to her mother. It rested at her father's bedside, as if he were still waiting for her to return. It was an intimacy of heart that her father rarely shared.

It broke Aalia into pieces, knowing what had been done to him.

The smell of him also filled the spaces, as if even in his absence, his grandness refused to be ignored. Standing at the rail, she took deep breaths, trying to gather her thoughts before she returned to the Blood'd Tower, where a war was about to be waged from afar.

"Are you all right, sister?" Rami asked.

Her brother had accompanied her here, as much a Paladin to her as the warriors in silver outside the door.

"What have we done?" she whispered.

She hated to show weakness. All her life, she had hardened herself. A Rose that could never be bruised. Only with Tazar had she let her softness show, but even with him, there was a core she kept hidden, walled off and protected.

Rami crossed to her and drew her into his arms. She hugged him back, needing this brother who was the closest to her heart. She hung there, letting his arms pull her back together when she could not do so herself. She sobbed for several breaths, but she allowed herself no more.

She finally broke free and turned back to the rail. Off in the distance, a storm of fire rolled north. Hundreds of forges blazed the sky, marking the passage of the imperial armada.

She gazed out at their flight.

"How will we survive this?" she whispered.

She wasn't just talking about the battle to come.

Rami took her hand and answered.

"Together, sister." He squeezed her fingers with that promise. "Together."

WITH A FARSCOPE fixed to his eye, Mikaen stood at the prow of the *Hyperium* as the mighty ship crested out of the smoky Breath. Fires burned behind the ship, marking the end of a brief skirmish against meager Klashean forces.

As expected, the Klashe had luxuriated in victory following the razing of the Shield Islands. They had not reinforced the coast after the *Falcon's Wing* had returned to roost in Kysalimri. It was further proof that his father and the king's council—including Reddak—had correctly surmised that Prince Jubayr was weak, swayed by those around him, listening rather than leading, tossed about by the council as they debated and argued and delayed.

At this moment, the Klashe was truly leaderless. With the iron fist of Makar loosened by madness, the empire remained rudderless.

Mikaen smiled at the destruction to come. As the *Hyperium* cleared the Breath's pall, the coastline of the Klashe rose in the distance. It was a bright green line rising from the blue waters, marking the northern edge of the Tithyn Woods. Far to the west, a huge column of smoke marred the shores, marking where he had dropped a Hadyss Cauldron atop Ekau Watch. The forest there continued to burn.

*Unlike Prince Jubayr, I do not hesitate.*

He shifted his farscope's view to the trio of warships leading them, escorting the *Hyperium* to the coast. One of them was the *Winged Vengeance,* the ship he had once captained, the wood of its deck still infused with Prince Paktan's blood. A new Cauldron also filled its hold, to replace the one he had dropped.

Mikaen felt no affection for his former ship. From his current perch, the *Vengeance* seemed so small. It was a poor stage for a prince who intended to shine the brightest, whose light would sweep through the centuries ahead, establishing a line of radiant sun-kings—starting with his son, who would follow Mikaen to the throne.

Mikaen lowered his farscope and turned to take in the breadth of the *Hyperium*. This made for a far better stage to launch that future lineage.

*And what a stage it will be shortly.*

As Mikaen pondered the centuries ahead, he noted Reddak, looking agitated, on the opposite side of the flagship's prow. The liege general crossed to the rail and disappeared into a glare reflecting off the magnificent figurehead that adorned the ship's bow.

Sunlight flashed blindingly off the draft-iron sculpture of a rearing stallion. It bore wings that swept to either side of the bow. It was dramatic and inspiring. The flagship had been christened as a memorial to his mother by King Toranth, who still held the former queen in great regard. Mikaen's mother had come from an illustrious family, the House of Hyparia, which gave rise to the naming of the great ship. Even the figurehead represented the Hyparian sigil of a winged stallion.

While Mikaen loved his mother, he considered such dedication to be oversentimental, a weakness that his father always possessed.

Finally, Reddak reappeared out of the blinding glare, coming straight toward Mikaen and Thoryn. Clearly something was amiss. Mikaen narrowed his eyes, wondering if this should concern him or if it was something he could take advantage of.

Reddak joined them, nodding respectfully to Thoryn, then addressed Mikaen. "A large line of Klashean ships just crested the horizon."

Mikaen stiffened. "What?"

Reddak waved to the farscope in Mikaen's hand. "See for yourself."

Mikaen returned to the rail and lifted the instrument to his eye. He focused back on the green spread of Tithyn Woods, which had already grown wider and taller as they swept closer to the coast. He shifted his view higher.

A line of fire blazed across the horizon.

"What does this mean?" Mikaen asked.

"It means we have underestimated Prince Jubayr's competence and grit. Or Emperor Makar has regained his senses. Either way, someone was able to shut down dissent, rally their forces with astounding speed, and send forth a considerable number of warships and hunterskiffs. More ships are likely already locking down Kysalimri."

Mikaen savored the frustrated fury in Reddak's voice.

Any failure would be laid at the liege general's feet.

Behind Mikaen, Thoryn addressed Reddak. "What is our course from here?"

"We forge on. We may lose a warship, maybe two, but we'll still break through and reach Kysalimri and pound them flat with our Hammer."

Mikaen had to respect the liege general's courage.

Still, no matter the outcome—barring his death—Mikaen would still win. Either he would return in glory and share in the triumph, or he could place the blame for any failure on Reddak's shoulders. Either outcome would suit him.

Furthermore, Mikaen didn't intend to return without his own victory.

He lowered his farscope and swept his gaze to a lone figure in black across the deck, a dark sparrow who had been waiting for a crow.

The figure noted Mikaen's attention and gave a crisp nod, signaling that the skrycrow had indeed arrived—and the message was good.

Mikaen shifted focus and studied the *Hyperium*'s open deck.

*Yes, this will make for the perfect stage.*

HIDDEN UNDER A *byor-ga* robe, Pratik followed his quarry. The white-cloaked Dresh'ri moved across the imperial gardens of the palace. It was the fifth scholar he had tracked since arriving in Kysalimri. Pratik had lost a few of his targets due to being overly cautious; others had ended up somewhere innocuous.

*One of them must lead me to Zeng ri Perrin.*

The head of the Dresh'ri remained an unknown variable to their plans in the Eternal City. Zeng had not attended the gathering in X'or—though he was a member of the king's council.

Over the course of the day, Pratik had made discreet inquiries, but with little result. Shortly after the incineration of the Abyssal Codex, Zeng had faded away. Many believed he had fled due to his fear that eventually the emperor's mercurial wrath would turn his direction. But now with a new empress on the horizon, Zeng must know his position was even more precarious.

Pratik feared what that might portend. So, he went hunting through the palace and all the usual haunts of the Dresh'ri. Llyra had mapped out the many entrances she knew—both into the Codex itself and into the more extensive lair of the Dresh'ri's subterranean quarters. Blind searches through that labyrinth would take years. And Zeng might not even be down there. Still, the possibility that he fled the city was too much to hope for.

*You're around here somewhere.*

Pratik finally abandoned his inquiries after noting the occasional Dresh'ri poking a head aboveground. If Zeng wanted to know more about what was happening in the palace, he would send only someone he trusted, one of his own, one of his inner cabal. Knowing that, Pratik had begun his hunt, tracking whom he could.

But as midnight beckoned, he might have to abandon the search. A battle was about to be waged to the north and would likely sweep to the walls of Kysalimri. He would need to return to the Blood'd Tower by then. In preparation for the worst, the entire sprawling edifice would be locked down, especially the war-tower. He dared not risk being trapped outside.

As the last bell of the night rang out, he followed the pale shape of the Dresh'ri through the darkest shadows cast by the tall garden walls. His quarry strolled with a casual determination, flanked by a pair of *byor-ga* servants, who carried books and other boxes. This Dresh'ri seemed no different from the other four Pratik had followed. The man was likely returning to his subterranean quarters after gathering books to read, which were certainly in short supply below.

Pratik was ready to give up his futile search. Then one of the servants stumbled over a loose stone and toppled crookedly to the ground, catching himself from a bad fall on an arm. The servant's headgear was jarred askew by the impact, but it was quickly reseated.

Shocked, Pratik tripped, too, but collected himself before anyone noticed.

Across the way, in that stumbled moment, a single ear of the servant had been revealed. The sharp point of it was unmistakable.

*A Venin . . .*

Pratik pictured the mutilated bridle-singers, with their flailed noses and eyes sewn shut. Though blind, the Venin had shown an ability to cast their gift around, allowing them to navigate. But a loose rock was missed and betrayed the creature's footing.

Pratik followed through the garden, continuing his disguise of being a servant.

*I'm not the only one.*

He eyed the second *byor-ga* servant following behind the white-cloaked Dresh'ri. Pratik knew who must be hidden under the second robe, a figure who moved with far more dexterity.

It was not another Venin.

*Zeng . . .*

The Dresh'ri leader must have taken a lesson from their group's prior attack, choosing to hide in plain sight. Such a course made sense. Zeng wouldn't trust another's eyes to canvass the palace and assess the situation. Zeng would only trust himself.

*But where are you going now?*

Despite time running short, Pratik continued his pursuit, paralleling his quarry through the shadowy gardens. The trio ended up at the ruins of the main entrance to the Codex. A haze of smoke still seeped from below, rising through the collapsed walls and jumble of stone that had once marked the librarie's water-powered lift.

The three met with a cloaked figure hiding in the smoke-fogged rubble. Zeng shifted forward, casting aside his submissive role. He exchanged words with the other. The cloaked man nodded and took hold of Zeng's upper arm in a congratulatory manner.

Zeng slipped back. As he did, more robed and hooded figures parted out of the rubble, gathering to Zeng's side. Pale faces shone in the darkness like macabre lanterns.

The remaining Venin.

The other cloaked figure stepped to the side and lifted a flash of silver to his lips. A whistle blew in three sharp notes. Before the last note faded, it was picked up by another whistle, then a horn, then more horns.

From archways on the far side, armored figures rushed into the garden, sweeping across it at a dead run. On the other side, Paladins posted at the palace doors fell forward, their throats slashed. New Paladins took their places—or at least men wearing such armor.

Pratik retreated out of the way, dropping to his knees in passive submission.

Legs swept past him. Boots crushed gravel. Swords slid from sheaths.

He kept his head bowed until the wave passed and flooded into the palace.

He lifted his face and spotted forges firing across the sky. Ships had vacated the blockade around the palace walls and drove toward the main edifice—all seeming to aim for the Blood'd Tower.

A flash of silver drew his gaze back to the garden.

A cloak was thrown aside, revealing the bright armor beneath. Pratik easily recognized the face, the stance, the imperial manner. Apparently, someone had changed allegiance since the meeting in X'or, deciding on another path to secure the imperium after Makar's debilitation.

Prince Mareesh pulled free his sword and headed toward the palace.


FRELL PACED THE edge of the crimson bath. Tykhan knelt beside the emperor, who continued to soak in the water. Tykhan gently rubbed Makar's shoulders—though Frell was unsure if this was to comfort the afflicted man or to firm up the emperor's enthrallment.

Frell looked toward the door. Abbess Shayr had suggested four immersions a day. Sister Lassan—the nonne dedicated to the emperor—would be returning momentarily to collect Makar and return him to his garden palacio.

"What do you make of Aalia's efforts so far?" Frell asked. "Is it enough to stop the kingdom's assault?"

Tykhan continued his massage. "Are you asking me as a strategist or as an oracle?"

"Are you not a little of both?"

"Perhaps, but during times of conflict this unpredictable and chaotic, I am neither. Even I can't track so many variables, trends, and potential outcomes. I can forecast a collision but not necessarily how the rubble will land. That's where we're at now. In the flux of possibility."

Frell frowned at this answer.

Tykhan stood up and turned to the door. "This is one example, I fear."

Distracted, Frell had missed the muffle of voices, but as they grew more heated, even he could not miss it.

The gold door swung open, and two dark-cloaked figures rushed in. They came so swiftly that Frell backed away and nearly fell into the bath.

The two Paladins posted outside pounded in after the intruders.

It took an extra breath for Frell to identify the two Rhysians, Cassta and Saekl. The two women skidded to smooth stops. The two Paladins closed on them, but Tykhan cut them off with a raised hand and a voice booming with authority.

"Fear not, Paladins! All is secure. These two are known to us and welcome. Their arrival is as predicted!"

The Paladins stumbled to a stop, looking confused, but they mumbled apologies, respecting the seer's abilities. The pair retreated to the door, closing it on their way out at an urging from Tykhan.

"What's wrong?" Frell asked, recognizing the Rhysians' restrained panic.

"Prince Kanthe is gone," Saekl said. "Taken."

Frell stammered through all of his questions at once. "When . . . how . . . who?"

Cassta stepped forward and opened her palm, revealing a single black barb with a tuft of dark feathers. "We found this floating in his bath after one of our sisters caught a glimpse of shadows where they shouldn't be."

Frell pinched his eyes in suspicion. "That looks like a dart from one of your pipes. Was he attacked by one of your sisters?"

Both Saekl and Cassta looked aghast at this suggestion.

"Then who?" Frell pressed them.

Cassta tossed the feathered barb aside. "Such craftsmanship is distinct from our own, but also well-known. It's the handiwork of the Brotherhood of Asgia."

Frell knew that name and their connection to the Archipelago of Rhys.

The Brotherhood was the dark mirror to the Rhysian sisterhood. Their group splintered away long ago, even before the matriarchy had been established across the Archipelago. It had less to do with an issue of gender and more to do with philosophy.

Both sold their talents, but Rhysians tempered their choices with consideration and a sense of justice. The Brotherhood operated with no such restraint. Purely mercenary, brutal, and cruel, they were as feared and as efficient as the two women standing before them.

"Someone must've paid them to grab Kanthe," Frell said. "But who?"

Tykhan frowned at him, clearly disappointed. "Surely you can guess." He shook his head sadly. "As predictable as he is, I thought we had more time. Still, it cannot be allowed to stand. It will mark the end of everything."

"Then what should we do?" Cassta asked.

"I chose X'or for more reasons than just its luxurious baths." Tykhan turned to Saekl. "So far, you've proven yourself adept with both wingketch and arrowsprite. How would you like a greater challenge, one with considerable risk?"

Saekl's eyes gleamed, reflecting the blood-red waters.

"Then we must hurry. A collision is about to happen, and I have no idea how it will end—or the rubble it will leave behind."

# 87

RHAIF QUAKED AND shivered in the bone-numbing cold. The *Sparrow-hawk's* hold was dark, lit by a handful of firepots that cast little light and only deepened the shadows—and hid the monsters down here.

All around him, wings flapped and brushed against one another, sounding like corpses rubbing their leathery hands together. Sudden hisses and sharper keens spat through the howl of the winds. Worst of all were the flashes of bright fangs reflecting the firelight. They flickered in the dark, poisonous and deadly.

*I've had nightmares tamer than this.*

So far, the raash'ke had kept to the depths of the hold as Rhaif and Graylin rolled the barrel toward the winds screaming across a rent in the hold. Perde followed them with his broken arm slung across his belly and a lantern raised in his other hand.

Rhaif truly wished he hadn't suggested this plan.

Even Graylin rumbled under his breath, "This is madness."

"I never said it weren't," Rhaif answered.

"Are you sure you mixed it right?"

"Taste it and find out."

Rhaif stared down at the large barrel, strapped in iron, with a *flitch*-soaked twist of cloth sticking out of its corked bunghole. He had spent a half-bell mixing together the refined *flitch,* a full cask of cannon powder, and a bucket of their remaining flashburn. It was the same recipe he had used to make the bomb that had chased the Hálendiians out of Iskar's lodestone chamber. Only this was on a far grander scale.

They finally reached the hole torn through the hull. The winds pelted them, the air felt like ice, even when sucked through the scarves wrapped around their faces. The thick gloves and fur-lined coats did little to hold back the cold, which cut to the bone. He swore his eyeballs would freeze solid before they were done with this task.

Graylin abandoned him with the barrel and slipped around it to the ragged hole in the hull and peeked out. He glanced for less than a breath. When he turned back, ice had crusted his scarf, turning it into a solid mask.

Graylin hurried back and yelled in Rhaif's ears, "The door is right below us!"

Rhaif nodded, his teeth chattering—and not just from the cold.

Graylin crossed to Perde and collected the lantern. "Let Darant know we're ready and to call down when the others are."

Perde slipped into the darkness, his shape becoming a slightly blacker shadow. The big man crossed to a highhorn tube and pressed his lips to it. He called up its baffling to let the captain know they were in position.

Perde then returned.

By now, Graylin had the lantern open and protected its flame from the winds by crouching on the leeward side of the barrel, right next to the fuel-soaked twist of cloth.

Rhaif and Perde joined him.

"Maybe the bomb will blast open the door all by itself," Perde suggested.

"I've seen the thickness of the smaller copper doors," Rhaif answered. "This monster? It'll be like a kitten swiping at a milk wagon and expecting it to tip over."

"What if it were a really strong kitten?" Perde challenged him. "Or it were really hungry, say?"

Rhaif gave up. "You make solid points."

Darant finally called down, his voice echoing through the highhorn. "On my mark!"

The captain counted down from five.

On *three,* Graylin lit the cloth, brightening the space with a flare of flames. Rhaif winced at the glare.

On *two,* they got the barrel rolling toward the hole; even Perde helped by kicking at it, maybe demonstrating how a kitten might knock over a milk wagon.

But that was not their goal.

While Rhaif was weak in bridle-song, he had noted the flashes of malevolent green fire burning away any of Nyx's attempts to unlock the copper door. Even with Shiya's and Daal's support, the trio failed each time and were only exhausting their energy.

So Rhaif had suggested this plan.

On *one,* they tipped the barrel through the hole and watched it tumble through the air toward the curve of door under them—then ran.

On *zero,* the blast deafened. The *Hawk* jolted hard as a fiery sun exploded under them. Rhaif and the others got tossed off the floor planks and crashed down. A spate of flames washed through the hole behind them.

Raash'ke panicked, flying throughout the hold, beating at their group with their wings.

Rhaif covered his head.

*I've rung its bell, Nyx—now it's your turn.*

* * *

EVEN THOUGH SHE was prepared for the blast, the concussion and hard shake of the ship nearly loosened the song trapped in Nyx's throat, chest, and heart.

She clutched to Shiya for the anchor of her bronze and to Daal for his font of power. Before signaling Rhaif below, the three of them—all on their knees—had built a golden pyre of bridle-song. They stoked it and threw more fuel atop it, until Nyx could see its glow through her closed eyelids.

Only then had she nodded to Darant.

They had one chance to make this work—if it worked at all.

Prior to this, their repeated attempts to reach the door were thwarted and blocked by the unnatural emerald energy from the hidden spider. As frustration grew and they became tired, Rhaif had wondered if the spider was suffering the same, spending all his energy concentrating on the door. Rhaif had suggested dropping a bomb atop it, ringing the dome below like a struck bell. If the spider was down there, the sound inside would be a thousandfold worse than outside, hopefully startling the spider and breaking its concentration long enough so they could do this.

Nyx released her flood of song, fueled by Daal and focused through Shiya. Nyx followed down with it. As it struck the dome, she continued into the door itself. Despite outward appearances, the copper—like all metals—was mostly empty space, just billions of motes of hard matter, each surrounded and held apart by twirls of energy. She easily slipped between those gaps and through the copper.

Within the metal, she read the map of the lock. Once the pattern shone in her mind's eye, her bridle-song picked it open.

At the last moment, emerald fire lashed out from below, trying to burn away what she had done, but it was too late. A great rumble rose around the ship, trembling it. Below them, the seven petals of the door peeled open, sliding into the surrounding dome wall.

Warm air burst upward, instantly turning to mist in the cold and swamping around the *Sparrowhawk*. Blinded, Darant backed them out of that thermal chimney. The sudden warmth also challenged the lift of their balloon's hot air. They momentarily dropped until they reached the frigid cold, then lifted higher again.

Jace and Krysh helped them stand. Shiya managed on her own.

"What if the spider closes it again?" Jace asked.

Nyx knew the answer, but Shiya voiced it.

"I locked it open," the bronze woman intoned.

Nyx nodded. At that last moment, as the spider recovered from the deafening blast, Nyx had felt the shift in the copper. Those hard bits of matter had realigned, wrecking the pattern. Like jamming an iron bar into a forge.

"How did you know how to do that?" Nyx asked Shiya.

She gave a confused look. "I . . . I just did."

Nyx remembered when she had flown her raash'ke for the first time. Certain buried reflexes had risen without thought, from memories instilled into her. Had Shiya experienced something like that? In the past, Shiya had demonstrated some knowledge of these doorways and their locks. Though Shiya's memories were corrupted or missing, some deep corner of her awareness still reacted instinctively when the spider had lashed out, thwarting him.

Graylin and Rhaif came rushing in, looking frozen.

"Did it work?" Rhaif gasped out through chattering teeth.

As answer, Nyx pointed to the misty column of warm air rising out of the open dome.

"What now?" Jace asked. "Do we drop the *Sparrowhawk* through there?"

Darant spoke from the wheel. "That hot air will make it treacherous. And as it is, it's a tight fit through that hole. We lose the *Hawk,* and none of us are leaving."

"Then how're we getting down?" Rhaif asked.

"You know as well as I do," Nyx said, repeating Daal's words from two days ago. "We've done it before."

Jace closed his eyes and groaned.

ATOP NYFKA, DAAL swept a circle around the *Sparrowhawk,* waiting for the others. The cold was brutal. It felt as if the air had turned brittle, too hard to even inhale. He didn't know if it was due to their flight deeper into the Wastes or some strange property of the massive copper *Oshkapeer* below, as if the structure were sucking heat from the air around it, maybe from the Urth itself.

He skimmed high above one of those fiery chasms that lined the copper's edges. The rift glowed from molten rock hidden in its depths. But what wasn't hidden, but still far down, was a massive tangle of heavy, twisted metal beams— not copper, maybe iron or steel, but clearly ancient, older than the complex above, marking the skeletal ruins of another age buried under this one.

Nyx had told Daal about the site they sought in the Brackenlands. She described it as a large village, what she called a *city,* but nothing lay out in these barren lands except the copper structure. Was the wreckage below the remains of a lost city? Was the copper *Oshkapeer* its grave marker?

He shuddered and turned away. He scanned the skies to the east, searching for any sign of the enemy who had attacked the Crèche. But the fires of the *Sparrowhawk* and the reflected fiery glow of the copper only made the surrounding Brackenlands darker. The warm mists still rising through the open door further hazed the view.

Still, he searched for several more breaths. With no danger in sight, he swung back to the ship and waggled his wingtips, letting the others know that all looked clear for now.

On his signal, Nyx took flight. She burst low under the ship's balloon, then swept high. Behind the pair, more wings spread into the sky. Tiny figures dangled under them before being drawn closer to keep warm.

Daal leaned over his saddle and tucked his knees tighter, signaling Nyfka, but his mount seemed to know his intent and dove. He remembered a similar harmony whenever he rode Neffa, those moments when two became one. He knew now such a deep bond was due to his innate bridle-song. Though he couldn't bridge to another heart as intimately as Nyx could, he still felt that gifted connection, that bond between rider and mount. In moments like this, he felt closer to Neffa, as if she rode these skies with him; his memories of hunting with her had helped forge his bond with Nyfka, as if the orkso had been preparing him for this all along.

*Thank you, Neffa.*

Daal swept down to the others and drew alongside Nyx, riding wingtip to wingtip. Hugging her saddle, she glanced across to him. She glowed with bridle-song, trailing wisps of golden fire in her wake. Her eyes shone with the same blaze.

The sight of her stole his breath—then they were into the warm mists.

After the frigid cold, the warm air scorched. He gasped at the sudden heat. But after a few breaths, the burn tempered to a steamy balminess. He dove steeper, taking the lead, protecting Nyx.

Once through the huge doorway, the air cleared. The shock of the sight below and around him bobbled his flight. He clutched harder to his saddle and urged his mount into a smoother arc across the interior of the dome. The vast space looked even bigger from the inside.

Nyx drew alongside again.

She nodded to him, broke away, and guided the others toward the copper floor.

He let her go, making a final sweep above them.

*What wonders have we opened to the world?*

* * *

NYX SPIRALED TOWARD the dome's floor, her gaze sweeping dizzily in all directions. The copper of the inner walls was coated by a dense labyrinth of crystalline tubing, steel joinery, and great windowed tanks bubbling with golden potions. It all glowed softly, with occasional brighter energies coursing over sections, like tamed lightning.

She had to blink away some of the sharper dazzles as she wound cautiously below. Seven huge tunnels led off down those tentacles. From them, giant rubbery cables—as tall as lumbering martoks—snaked out and dove under the copper floor, vanishing away. But Nyx knew where all seven were headed, what they were meant to power.

Before landing, she circled the wonder at the center of the dome.

Cradled in bronze and suspended by a rigging of archways was a perfect sphere of crystal. It was the size of a warship and felt as threatening. The upper hemisphere rose above the floor, while its lower half hung over a huge hole, wider by half than the orb itself.

The crystal's surface was circumscribed by crisscrossing bands of bright copper, while smaller wires etched a complicated pattern between them, like the arcane scribblings of a mad alchymist.

Still, none of it hid what lay at the heart of the crystal.

A huge pool of golden fluid pulsed and writhed, churning and swirling.

Though awed and terrified, Nyx recognized its character, if not its massive scale. She tore her gaze away and stared at the shine of Shiya's bronze form. When the miraculous woman had climbed out of the mines of Chalk, it took the power of the sun to keep her moving. She had to constantly draw energy from the fires of the Father Above. Only later, she had recovered a crystalline cube, swirling with the same golden elixir. Once implanted into her, it had granted her continual power thereafter and sustained her still.

Nyx turned back toward the golden sea shining at the center of the sphere and cowered at the thought of all that energy. She finally had to look away, shying from the enormity of it all.

As she turned and swept away from the sphere, she caught a glimpse down the massive hole along the orb's edge. She expected to see molten fire glowing below, but the sight was worse. The shaft fell away into a darkness that felt bottomless. She imagined the shaft drilling to the core of the planet. What little could be seen of the upper reaches was a complex of ladders set amidst shelves of scaffolding, all descending into that eternal blackness.

She shivered at the sight of that abyss and continued around the sphere to descend to the floor. She landed first, her mount's claws skidding with a bone-chilling screech across the copper. The others were lowered or dropped by the raash'ke.

Staying seated in her saddle, she surveyed her group. Their faces shone from a spectrum of wonder and awe to horror and disbelief.

Overwhelmed, Jace sank to his knees. Krysh stumbled over to his side, having to lean on his young friend. Nyx didn't know if the alchymist was stunned by the flight down from the ship or from the astonishing sights around him—likely a combination of both.

Graylin stared back at her, focusing on her, ignoring the rest.

Past his shoulder, Shiya helped Rhaif to his feet. He hung on to her like a drowning man on a bit of floating flotsam.

A shout drew her attention to the side, where Darant gathered Vikas and two more of his men, one of them with a broken arm in a sling. Darant stared up at the fiery glow of the *Sparrowhawk* through the chimney of mists. His face was pained but determined. He had hated to abandon the ship, but they needed as much force down here as possible and Glace had proven herself fully capable of defending the *Hawk,* though she had been left with only the barest skeleton of a crew.

The last member of their group still swept high, on patrol. Daal watched for any sign of that molten shape of the spider. But after being thwarted, the bronze spider must have scurried off down one of those seven tunnels, hiding in the shadows.

Daal was not alone up there. The flock of raash'ke, who had ferried the party down, now winged through the air, adding to the patrol, ready to defend them. Nyx reached up with a thrum of song, thanking them for their diligence and help. As she did, she felt a faint presence of the raash'ke horde-mind. It watched with the cold immensity of its ancient eye, still weakly linked by its brethren circling above.

Nyx finally slid from her saddle, running a glowing palm over Metyl's damp flank, whispering her thanks to him. He stirred and reached back, rubbing a cheek against her chest, a rare sign of true affection. She scratched his small ear, earning a rumble back.

Rhaif called over, a note of panic in his voice. "Help me!"

Nyx hurried over with the others.

Rhaif stood before Shiya, his palms on her chest, his feet being pushed across the copper, unable to find a foothold on the seamless surface, not that it would've helped against Shiya's immense strength.

"What're you doing?" Darant asked.

"What does it look like?" Rhaif's face purpled with the strain, hopping a bit on his bad leg. "Trying to stop her."

They all crowded to his side, ready to help.

Rhaif explained. "She barely got her footing when she suddenly stiffened.

Her eyes went dark. She started marching away without a word, deaf to my questions. Something's got ahold of her."

Nyx noted the copper under Shiya's feet vaguely glowed, casting out ripples with each step, as if she were marching across a still pond.

"Let her go," Nyx warned, moving closer.

Graylin tried to stop Nyx, but she shook off his arm.

She pushed Rhaif aside.

"We've all witnessed such dogged compulsion by Shiya," Nyx explained. "Back when she led us to the Shrouds. Some buried part of her is reacting to this place. This is where she was meant to be. Trust her."

Nyx remembered Shiya reflexively locking the dome open. Whatever was driving her must come from the same core of her being.

Rhaif backed away. They all followed in Shiya's wake as she strode with swift steps, still rippling that glowing pond under her. She crossed around the circumference of the massive sphere that towered high, churning with its golden sea.

Shiya drew no closer to it, wending wider, heading to the dome's wall.

Her goal came into view.

Imbedded deep into the crystalline web that bubbled and shone throughout the dome's interior stood a tall shield of copper. It looked molded out of the back wall itself. Nyx stared up and around, sensing the vast spread of the glowing maze led here, to this one spot.

*Shiya is meant to be here. She is the key to this place.*

The bronze woman marched inexorably toward her destiny. Once close, she shed out of her shift, baring her nakedness. She mounted a short ramp up to the copper shield.

Rhaif no longer tried to stop her. Like Nyx, he had seen such a cocoon of metal and crystal. "It's like back at the Shrouds," he mumbled. "Or inside the egg where I first found her."

Shiya turned her back to the shield and pressed herself against it. As contact was made, the floor jolted under them. The dome rang like a bell. The noise deafened and drove them to their knees.

Shiya stiffened, her head thrown back.

*We have witnessed this before, too.*

*But not this powerful.*

The crystal that cupped around the copper shield grew brighter and spread outward in dazzling waves of energy. The rhythmic sweeps of fire sailed outward, swirled wide, then rushed back, crashing like a wave against a cliff.

With each strike, Shiya's back arched off the copper, her mouth open in a silent cry that looked rapturous.

Rhaif took a step forward, but Graylin held him back—not that Rhaif could have reached her.

Thick curves of glass swept out of the walls to either side and closed over Shiya, encapsulating her, becoming a true chrysalis.

Nyx knew this felt right, where Shiya's long journey was meant to end.

She was wrong.

From the edges of the cocoon, jagged coruscations of green fire burst forth, wrapping around the crystal. More flames shot across the inside of the dome. The energies out there still swirled but only seemed to fuel the green fire with every crashing wave. The emerald flames became an inferno across the chrysalis.

Shiya vanished behind the blaze, but not before Nyx saw her bronze form thrashing and convulsing inside. Her silent scream was no longer rapturous—only tortured.

Nyx and the others backed away, recognizing the truth.

This wasn't Shiya's destiny.

It was a trap.

# 88

Aalia rushed alongside Rami through the cavernous throne room. They were surrounded by a cadre of forty Paladins. The clatter of their escort's steel-shod boots on hard marble echoed throughout the great hall, sounding like a stampede of panicked horses.

Her heart pounded in tempo with them.

They sped around the huge pillars that held up the roof, past the arcades to either side that would seat the thousands who would gather for great events. They aimed for the two gold thrones atop the dais at the far end. One was slightly less prominent than the other. Sheltering both were two huge wings, spreading high, climbing toward the rafters. Two giant obsidian swords curved in front of those wings, standing out against the gold feathers, merging the sigils of the Haeshan Hawk and the Klashean Arms.

Between those wings rose a huge rosette of stained glass. The low winter sun shone through its center, creating a shining bloom that blessed those seated below. It was the glorious Illuminated Rose—a namesake that her father had gifted to Aalia.

As she fled toward the thrones, she wondered if the violence committed upon the emperor had cursed her.

Still, she ran, refusing to relent.

A short time ago, she and Rami, along with a small cadre of Paladins, had been on their way to the Blood'd Tower, to ready for the battle over Tithyn Woods. Then horns had sounded everywhere, echoing from within and without the palace. Screams soon followed and the strident clash of steel.

Aalia had urged her Paladins to reach the Blood'd Tower. Along the way, they had gathered more royal defenders. As they fled, they caught flashes of fighting in the surrounding halls. Bombs blasted in the distance.

Now their goal was in sight.

The archway into the Blood'd Tower stood to the right of the throne dais. They rushed toward it, only to meet another force flooding out. The Paladins closed tight around Aalia and Rami. Through their barricade, she spotted Shield Angelon as he came pounding out the archway with a rush of guardsmen. He had Prince Jubayr under his wing.

Both sides froze, not sure who was enemy and who was friend.

Aalia shouldered through her Paladins. "Shield Angelon!" she called over, testing the mettle of the matter.

The relief that crashed over the man's face was answer enough. He turned and shouted orders. Their two forces merged.

Angelon pushed Jubayr over to her and Rami. "The Blood'd Tower is compromised. A warship poured forces and fire from on top, forcing us to flee."

Aalia heard fighting and explosions. "The Sail and the Wing?"

Angelon nodded. "Garryn and Draer are trying to hold them off with a handful of forces." He pointed to the entrance into the throne room. "We must go."

They all turned, but before they could cross more than a few steps, the battle broke into the hall, both at the far end and through side galleries. It was not the start of the fight, but the end. The last remaining defenders fell. The bloodied attackers swept together and rushed toward them.

"Back!" Angelon urged.

He tried to retreat to the archway of the Blood'd Tower, only to have Sail Garryn come running out with a handful of wounded men. The Sail wiped blood from his eyes and shook his head.

"Lost," Garryn wheezed as he stumbled to join them.

"Wing Draer?" Aalia asked.

Garryn placed a fist to his forehead, both in greeting to his empress and as a salute. "Fallen."

Their group was forced to the pair of thrones and pinned down in the open. There was not even any shelter behind the chairs. Still, Angelon was determined to die serving out his title, to act as her personal shield.

He pushed Aalia between the thrones, standing before her. Jubayr took a post on the other side of one seat, Rami across the other—the emperor's throne.

*My throne,* she reminded herself.

Though it might not be for long.

The Paladins and guardsmen closed tight ranks before the dais, forming seven rows, the last walls of the imperium.

The attackers—both in armor and without—rushed to crash against those walls.

Then a piercing whistle cut through the hall, seeming to get louder with every echo. The tide slowed, and a voice called out.

"Hold!"

At the rear, a figure in shining armor appeared, lofting a pair of swords high, crossing them over his head, forming a defiant Klashean Arms.

"Yield and live!" Prince Mareesh shouted, his gaze burning across the tide of silver to the golden thrones—to Aalia.

"I have no wish to shed my siblings' blood!" Mareesh called to them. "You have been deceived into a traitorous act, so I won't demand your heads. But fight and I will have no choice!"

Shield Angelon turned to Aalia.

Fury fired her. She shoved the large man aside and strode forward to stand before the two thrones. She glared across at her brother. She noted shadows skulking behind him—and the white robes of the Dresh'ri. It was that bastard Zeng ri Perrin. She didn't know how much of a hand the man had in swaying Mareesh to this act of betrayal, to break his oath to her. Still, it didn't matter. She knew it would not have taken much to move her brother to act.

Aalia addressed the greater traitor here.

"Dearest brother," she shouted over with a mocking tone, "did you fall off the *Falcon's Wing*? Or did you abandon your ship and desert the imperial forces to commit this act of betrayal?"

"Fear not, sister! The *Falcon's Wing* is already on its way here. Leading others of the Wing who will not stand by this treason within our walls."

Aalia fought against cringing. How many had been swayed to Mareesh's side? How many more would? She knew that if this overthrow proved successful, none would support her after this.

"And what of the battle over Tithyn?" she challenged him. "You would weaken us when we need to be strongest. Is that an act of an emperor or a coward?"

A murmur rose among Mareesh's ranks.

He was not cowed in the least. "We can always defeat the Hálendiians!" he boomed. "They are but ants under our heels. Are they not?"

Cheers of assent greeted those words, drowning out those first tentative murmurs.

"The greater peril to the imperium is in this room." Mareesh pointed at her. "Standing right there!"

Aalia knew her brother would never back down.

*Nor in the end, will he let me live.*

He would have to condemn her. She coldly recognized that and accepted it. But she knew Mareesh. If she submitted, he would spare her two brothers.

She turned to Jubayr. He must have read the question in her eye. He stiffened his shoulders and gave a small shake of his head. He touched the clasp at his throat. He refused to hand this cloak over to his faithless brother. Their father had given it to him, and he would not part with it to appease a traitor, not even if it meant his life.

Aalia turned to Rami on her other side.

His exaggerated wounded expression drew a small smile from her. His silent scold was clear. *Must you even ask, dear sister?*

She nodded and took a step forward and matched the thunder of her brother. "We do not yield! Not for you! Not for anyone." She lifted a fist high. "Long live the imperium!"

A roar broke across her ranks.

She stepped back, knowing she had sentenced them all to death.

Rami leaned over her throne. "What about Tazar?"

She shook her head, knowing he was outside the palace, with no way to reach them. Still, she remained resolute, content with one small bit of grace.

*He will not have to watch me die.*

TAZAR FOLLOWED BEHIND Pratik through the dark tunnels beneath the palace. He prayed the Chaaen knew his way. Tazar searched right and left and ahead, thoroughly lost in this Dresh'ri labyrinth. Behind him, they were followed by a force of *Shayn'ra* a hundred strong.

Three times along the way, Pratik had Tazar stop and dispatch a smaller group of the Fist out other exits. His second-in-command, Althea, had taken the last group. All were under orders to strike for the Blood'd Tower, where the new empress was supposed to be orchestrating the battle to the north. Worry for Aalia narrowed his vision to a sharply focused point. His heart choked his throat.

A short time ago, Pratik had rushed headlong into the *Shayn'ra* refuge near the outer walls of the palace, where Tazar was continuing to organize his army. By then, Tazar had already heard the blasts, witnessed the fiery explosions beyond the walls.

Then Pratik had arrived, breathless and with a plan. He clutched a map drawn by Llyra days ago. They had all known that eventually Aalia might need to be defended against those who would oppose her rise. Tykhan's plan had been to ready an army among the baseborn and lower folk, to be ready to bolster her ascendancy.

No one expected anyone to make a move against Aalia so soon, not while the Hálendiians threatened. Especially with the oaths taken in X'or.

But someone had.

*That bastard Mareesh.*

It was a cowardly act, to strike while another's back was turned—especially if that back was his own sister's.

Fury burned through Tazar's anxiety. His forces were not prepared. Worse, Llyra was still out in the city, trying to rally and forge her own army to be ready down the line. He had sent a dozen couriers out into Kysalimri to let her know, but no one truly knew where she sheltered. Still, no matter where she hid, she could not have missed the explosions at the palace. He could only hope she understood the threat and would reach here in time with her rabble.

"This way," Pratik said, raising his lantern toward a narrow stair that spiraled up. "It should take us close to the base of the Blood'd Tower."

Tazar nodded, waving the Chaaen to lead, praying that Pratik had not confused his way in this subterranean warren. He pictured Althea and his other splintered forces, all aiming for the Blood'd Tower from different directions. He feared they were too few against a palace in revolt. Even any allies up there might misconstrue their arrival. Tazar could end up fighting *both* sides before he could reach Aalia.

Tazar followed Pratik's lantern around and around. He grew dizzy from the ascent. Fearful panic shortened his breath. He had not realized how deep they had traveled. Or maybe his worry only made it seem so.

Pratik finally stopped at a door and pressed his ear against it.

Tazar saw little reason for caution or stealth at this point. He moved the Chaaen aside and pulled a lever. A section of wall swung open. He peeked out into a root cellar stocked with crates of potatoes, onions, and tubers of every ilk. A moldy cloy filled his nose, slightly assuaged by the aromatics of drying herbs hanging from the low roof.

He crossed the cellar to steps on the far side. They led up to a door. Behind him, Pratik ushered in as many of the *Shayn'ra* into the cellar as he could fit. More still waited below.

Despite his earlier impatience, Tazar climbed to the cellar door and put his ear against it. According to Pratik, they had entered under the kitchens off the throne room where banquets were prepared for grand celebrations, and where apparently a few hungry Dresh'ri occasionally snuck up to pilfer food.

As he listened, he fingered the whistle around his neck, hoping he would get to use it to rally his other splinters. For now, all sounded quiet in the neighboring kitchens. He was about to turn with final instructions when a sharp voice cut through to him.

*"Long live the imperium!"*

His heart clenched.

*Aalia.*

He grabbed the hilt of his sword and shoved the door open. "With me!" he ordered, and rushed headlong into the long hall of a kitchen. A fire still roared in a hearth, bubbling a pot of stew. The space was a wreckage of pots and pans. A few scullery maids and kitchen boys hid in corners, waiting for the fighting to end, indifferent to who sat on the throne, only that they lived.

Tazar had once been one of those boys.

No longer.

He *did* care who sat on the throne. He cared deeply.

He hurried his forces down a pinched tunnel that led toward the throne room. He didn't need a map any longer. The clash and screams drew him forward. He reached the end and drew the others to stop behind him. Pratik squeezed up next to him.

The tunnel exited at a shadowy back corner of the throne room. No grand entrance was needed for menial servitors or drudges. Out in the cavernous hall, Tazar watched two forces crash into one another. The din was deafening, echoing across the space. In that moment, several despairing realizations struck him.

—He and the Fist were vastly outnumbered.

—He could never reach Aalia in time.

—There was no evidence that any of the other *Shayn'ra* splinters had made it this far.

And his last realization was the grimmest.

—*We cannot prevail.*

As if highlighting this assessment, a huge explosion lit the rosette window behind the thrones, so thunderous that it cracked the stained glass, fracturing the Illuminated Rose. The fighting paused at the strength of the blast.

Behind the window, the silhouette of a large ship fell across the glass. Its fiery prow swung and shattered the rest of the window, raining glass across the dais below. Flames raged through the opening, roaring like a dragon into the throne room.

Tazar smiled, hope surging.

Those flames were the emerald of naphlaneum. He flashed to another ship brought down by such fire, off in Qazen, a battle barge smashing down before the gates of the Augury's villa.

"Llyra's here," he whispered into the chaos—and watched it get worse.

Men and women poured in from all sides, shedding *byor-ga* robes or wiping ash from faces. More explosions echoed from outside. Another spear flamed the skies, trailing naphlaneum flames.

Of course, Llyra would not have set up camp *out* in Kysalimri, not when the clever guildmaster of thieves could build her low army right here in the palace.

Tazar lifted his whistle and blew with all the strength of his lungs and heart—less to draw his allies and more to alert someone that he was here.

He rushed with the others into the fray.

*Aalia, I'm coming for you.*

\* \* \*

PRESSED AGAINST THE tunnel wall, Pratik let Tazar's *Shayn'ra* sweep past him. With his cheek tight to the wall, he spotted Tazar's second-in-command rush out of an arcade on the far side. Althea had responded to Tazar's signal, drawing her men with her.

Elsewhere and around, Llyra's forces continued to flow into the throne room, but their numbers were already dwindling. Like Tazar, she must have been caught off guard by the unexpected attack. It must have taken her until now to organize her forces and get her weaponry into position.

The battle remained far from over.

To the side, off in a back corner, Prince Mareesh huddled with a hard group, all surrounded by a barricade of guardsmen and archers. More supporters to his cause flooded through the main doors, drawn by the fighting, summoned from their posts.

As the battle worsened, Pratik focused his attention closer at hand.

Not far from Mareesh, keeping from the edge of the fighting, the white robe of Zeng ri Perrin glowed like a lantern. An arc of nine Venin protected him from the room. But those mutilated creatures were doing more than just protecting. Their arms were lifted outward, toward the battle.

When any of the throne's defenders brushed too near, they fell into a swooning malaise, allowing Mareesh's men to slaughter them. Zeng slowly backed from the fighting, clearly willing to slip away if the tide should turn against him.

Pratik was unsure what to do. He dreaded to watch the malevolent scholar escape yet again, but Pratik was no warrior.

As he hesitated, movement drew his attention back to the fighting. A familiar figure had been driven back by a fierce brawl. Althea drifted too close to the arc of Venin. Her legs wobbled and her sword arm fell.

*No . . .*

She stumbled—but mercifully *forward*. She fell out of the malaise and regained her footing. An ax swung at her chest, but her sword burst up and blocked it. Still, she was held at bay, fighting at the edge of the Venin's oblivion.

Unable to watch her die while standing in shadows, Pratik covered his face with the drape of his *byor-ga* coif and slipped out of hiding. He crossed to the back of the throne room and hurried along the wall, feigning a fearful baseborn trying to escape the fighting.

Pratik clutched a knife, keeping it hidden in a fold of his robe.

Once he got close to Zeng's position, a body slammed in front of Pratik, hitting the wall and sliding down. It was a Paladin with a spiked mace cracked into his skull. Pratik did not need to feign crippling terror. He skirted over those legs and crossed toward Zeng's back, lifting his blade.

It was not a noble act, but sometimes even an ignoble one was necessary.

He stabbed down hard—only to have Zeng spin around before him and thrust a dagger into Pratik's throat.

The Dresh'ri hissed at Pratik, "Do not think you can fool me twice."


TAZAR FOUGHT SAVAGELY toward the dais. Paladins still protected Aalia, but with each step that he carved across the room, another defender fell.

*Hold out until I can get to you.*

Atop the dais, Shield Angelon still guarded over Aalia, but even the huge man was faltering. His face bled heavily, gashed by fallen glass from the shattered window. He had protected Aalia with his body. Impaled shards still poked from his back, turning any movement into a wrench of agony. Still, determination etched his face.

To the side, Sail Garryn protected Jubayr. Tazar lost sight of Rami, but the chaotic battle had allowed for only quick glances toward the dais.

A loud shout drew his attention over his shoulder.

"Archers! Hie!"

Tazar caught a slash of an arm by Mareesh.

From the traitorous prince's position, bowmen fired a volley of arrows, so dense that it dimmed the lanterns overhead. The barrage arced through the air and fell toward the thrones.

*No . . .*

Mareesh must have held off such a brutal attack until now, perhaps willing to spare his brothers. Or more likely—simply waiting for enough archers to gather and get into position.

Tazar turned to the dais, praying for Angelon to protect Aalia one last time.

As the Shield stared at the doom sweeping down, he swung around to do just that—only to have an armored soldier break through the line of Paladins and heave a heavy ax at the Shield's back. Steel imbedded deep. Like a hooked fish, the attacker threw Angelon off the dais.

Before the bastard could do more harm, Sail Garryn tackled into him, and the two rolled down the steps into the fray.

Tazar could only watch as arrows rained down upon the dais.


ON HER KNEES between the two thrones, Aalia prepared for her death. There was nowhere to hide. Then a shadow swept over her with the wings of a hawk. She flinched down as Jubayr sprawled over her, spread across the two thrones, balanced on the armrests to either side.

His heavy cloak draped over her.

"Jubayr . . ."

With his cheek pressed to the crook of his elbow, he stared down. "Sister, no one will ever harm you while I have breath."

Then the volley struck.

Trapped under the tent of his cloak, the arch of his body, she watched the arrows shatter off marble and gold. They hit Jubayr with impacts that shuddered his body. Arrowheads burst through his chest and neck. His blood rained down on her. Still, he held his perch, proving himself stronger than the fiercest Haeshan hawk.

His eyes never left hers, pinched with pain, shining with love.

He did as he had promised.

Only with his last breath did he lose his perch and fall atop her. She caught him in her lap, cut and sliced by those arrowheads, but she only hugged him tighter.

She sobbed and rocked. She didn't know how long she held him, but finally he was gently lifted. Tazar was there by some miracle. He pulled her hard to his chest, to his heart. She allowed herself two breaths and pushed away.

The fighting still raged.

Tazar guarded her with sword and dagger. More of his men defended the dais. White-striped *Shayn'ra* stood shoulder to shoulder with Paladins and guardsmen.

Aalia searched around her, realizing she had lost more than one brother.

She clutched Tazar's arm. "Where's Rami?"

---

"Do not think you can fool me twice."

Pratik flinched as Zeng's dagger struck, expecting death. But both had forgotten that Pratik was chaaen-bound. The blade struck the iron collar fixed around Pratik's throat. The knife's edge still sliced a fiery line across the side of his neck, just under his ear.

The impact and surprise knocked the dagger from Zeng's grip.

Pratik dropped, grabbed its hilt with both fists, and thrust up with all the strength in his legs. He jammed the blade's point under Zeng's jaw.

"How's this for one last trick?" Pratik gasped out.

The blow lifted the Dresh'ri off his toes. The bastard dangled there, writhing on that point—then the dagger slipped farther through bone and drove deeper into his skull.

Only then did Pratik throw Zeng's body aside, but he kept the dagger.

Venin turned toward him with a hiss. Shocked by their master's death, they lost hold of the insidious song that had been their only weapon.

Pratik lunged forward while calling to Althea for help. Responding to his panic, she swung to the horror behind her. Together, they dispatched the creatures.

Once done, Pratik ripped away his headgear.

"What were those beasts?" Althea panted out.

"Not our problem any longer. That's what they are."

A bellow caught their attention and turned them around.

*Now what?*


AALIA HEARD AN angry bark echo over the throne room. She knew that voice, that mocking fury.

"Dearest brother!" Rami shouted from halfway across the hall.

Aalia shifted higher to get a better view. Rami shed a cloak from his shoulders, revealing himself fully. She inhaled sharply, shocked to see him so far from the dais. She struggled to understand how he had managed to get there unobserved and unnoticed—then she remembered that Rami had been trained in more than knife play. One of his chaaen-bound had come from a long line of thieves and had skilled her brother in the art of subterfuge and misdirection.

It seemed such training had proven useful.

And not just the trickery of disguise and slippery-footedness.

Also in the art of pilfering.

"I brought you a gift!" Rami shouted. "Two, in fact, as a token of my generosity!"

He threw both arms high, casting a pair of hand-bombs into the air. Their flaming wicks spun as they flew.

Mareesh turned to run, his men closing tight behind him.

The bombs struck at their heels, exploding with a concussive blast and a wash of fire. Armored men were bowled over. Flames swept through them. Mareesh had been knocked to a knee, insulated from the worst of the bombs' pounding—but not their blaze.

The tabard over Mareesh's armor caught fire, burning up to his oiled hair. Then his head became a torch. One of his men smothered the flames as best he could. Another helped drag Mareesh away, hauling him out of the throne room.

Abandoned by their leader, his conspirators faltered, their will and spirit quickly snuffed. The fighting in the throne room continued for a short spell as a few of Mareesh's men struggled to keep the imperial forces from pursuing their prince.

Another prince found his way back to the dais. Rami's face was grim at the sight of so many dead around the thrones. Especially one. Rami closed his eyes and sank to his knees in the blood of his brother.

A commotion drew Aalia's attention around.

Llyra pounded over from the archway into the Blood'd Tower. She was covered in sweat and ash. She stank of naphlaneum. She surveyed the carnage without any expression. That was not her concern.

"What is it?" Aalia asked.

Llyra frowned. "If we were attacked here . . ." She glanced toward the throne room doors. "What about Kanthe?"

# 89

KANTHE WOKE WITH a pounding headache that lanced across his eyes and throbbed his molars. But worse was the foggy confusion. He struggled to figure out where his body ended and the world started.

"He's stirring," a harsh voice grumbled.

Something foul was shoved under his nose. It stung his sinuses, as if a *ly-cheen*'s fiery frill had been jammed up there. He gasped and choked. Bile rose up his throat, then burned its way back down to his stomach.

He sat up as the world snapped sharply into focus, but it did nothing to dispel his confusion. He reached to wipe the snot running from both nostrils, but he discovered both his arms were bound behind him. His legs were also weighted by chains.

*What the—*

He glanced to his right and left, discovering black-cloaked figures seated to either side. Their wraps had been pulled to their necks, revealing silvery pale skin and ice-blue eyes. *Rhysians?* But these faces were *men*. Their black hair had been sheared to a stubble that formed a tight V over their brows.

Kanthe cringed inwardly, suddenly knowing what group had kidnapped him.

*The Brotherhood of Asgia.*

Kanthe flashed to the garden bath, the feathered barbs. His chest and neck still burned from those impacts. He silently apologized for thinking it was Cassta and her sisters who had attacked him.

*Where am I?*

From the motion of the cabin and the low roar of a forge, he knew he was in a small ship, though he could not discern the design or type. The lack of windows only added to his confusion. He heard booming outside.

Sadly, *that* he recognized.

Cannon fire.

He feared the worst, and as a door opened in front of him, it was confirmed. Beyond a man's shoulders, Kanthe spied a bulbous window that looked out over the ship's pointy prow. The small vessel sped low over treetops. High above, a battle raged as ships bearing the Klashean Arms fought others waving the Hálendiian flag.

Smoke filled the air. Grappling chains linked ships that spun together in some deadly dance. Fighting swept decks. Bombs burst in the air. A misfire arced low and detonated in a blinding flash to their portside. The wheelman at the front cursed and rolled them away, tipping the ship nearly sideways.

The cloaked Brother who had opened the doorway clung to its frame. "*Hyperium* ahead! Make ready to board!"

As they turned, a floating island of wood and draft-iron filled the skies ahead and swiftly grew larger. The sounds of battle faded behind them as their craft slipped past the fighting and approached the flagship.

The *Hyperium* loomed over the war, ready to engage the enemy or pick over the spoils. Sunlight flared from the ship's sculpted prow. A draft-iron stallion reared its head high, with wings flaring to either side.

Kanthe fingered the gold signet ring with a sigil that matched the ship's figurehead. He had no doubt who orchestrated his kidnapping.

Their vessel dove steeply and sped under the monstrous keel. The *Hyperium*'s hull now roofed the world. A score of forges flamed the skies, their roar vibrating through their tiny craft. More ominous still were the huge doors overhead. If they were open, a regular-sized warship could rise into the *Hyperium*'s hold. But Kanthe knew the purpose of those doors wasn't for something to *enter*, but for something to be *dropped* out.

He had heard the rumors, the claims, even the name of *Hyperium*'s notorious cargo.

A Madyss Hammer.

Kanthe was glad when they finally cleared those massive doors. The skies opened again, and their craft shoved its pointy nose up into a steep climb. Just when he thought the vessel would roll backward, it tipped sideways, twisting as it fell.

Kanthe groaned, bile rising again.

Then the world righted itself as the little craft caught air, straightened, and now faced the *Hyperium*'s stern. The massive wooden cliff was sealed tight, except for one bay.

"That had better be a blast hold," the Brotherhood leader warned.

"We'll find out."

The wheelman hunched low, made tiny tweaks to their trajectory, and shot them toward the opening. It looked too small for even their tiny ship. But it was all a matter of perspective, which was thrown off by the *Hyperium*'s size.

As they raced toward the stern, the bay and its hold grew until it dwarfed their ship. He expected them to slow, but they maintained their speed.

Kanthe cringed as the small craft dove into the shadowy hole. He braced for a crash—then fire burst ahead of them. Flames shot out the pointy prow, illuminating walls lined by draft-iron. It was clearly a hold designed for such fiery vessels.

The flaming forge braked them swiftly, throwing Kanthe forward. The Brothers to either side must have expected this maneuver and caught his shoulders and pulled him back.

The tiny ship came to a swinging stop and lowered swiftly to the hold's deck with a small bump. "Out in five!" the lead Brother shouted.

Kanthe searched around but saw no door.

Then the entire starboard half of the vessel fell open. The curved hull dropped toward the deck but stopped with a slight bounce, suspended by draft-iron cables. Kanthe had no time to gape. His body was unceremoniously hauled by the two Brothers and tossed out of the ship. He rolled across the deck and struck the armored legs of a knight.

"Get clear!" the lead Brother shouted as the ship resealed.

Kanthe was dragged away by his collar.

Ahead of him, the forge at the prow fired, and the small craft shot backward out of the *Hyperium*.

Kanthe winced at the surge of heat from its passage.

*I don't think that was even a count of five.*

Kanthe was hauled to his feet by two knights, their faces stained crimson, marking them as Vyrllian knights. But these two had additional markings. Black tattoos stenciled one side of their faces, forming the Hálendiian sun and crown.

*Strange.*

But he had no time to question it. The knights manhandled him out of the hold and up a confounding maze of stairs and walkways. Crewmen gawked as they passed or simply went about their duties.

Finally, a hatch opened ahead, and sunlight blinded him. He winced at the glare and at the louder sounds of battle. The two knights dragged him from the stifling interior and out onto the *Hyperium*'s main deck. The fresh air helped clear his head, but only stoked his fear. He had expected to be secured in some dark cell, waiting to be hauled back to Azantiia to face his father's wrath.

But it was not King Toranth that he should have been worried about.

"Hello, brother!" Prince Mikaen called over. "Well met!"

FRELL WANTED TO look everywhere at once as they flew through the shadowy forest. Their vessel—which Tykhan called a *lampree*—was unlike any design he had ever seen or read about. Outwardly, it looked like a flat-bellied beetle with a domed top and two tapered balloons, like the wings of the same insect. Beneath it, and curled tight to its flat keel, were six jointed draft-iron legs.

The interior, though, was far more astounding. It was one undivided hold, nearly as wide as it was long. It easily held the four Rhysians, including Cassta, who was strapped down next to him. Saekl and Tykhan manned the two seats in front. The Rhysian captain gripped the wheel, while Tykhan assisted with secondary controls, trying to explain some of the arcane mechanics.

"I have the feel for it well enough," Saekl scolded. "Let me focus before I slam us into a tree."

"Don't forget to keep the level—"

Saekl's scowl shut him up.

Frell stared at the apparatus that surrounded the wheel. It was a convoluted network of copper tubing and crystal tanks, bubbling with a golden elixir. Tykhan twisted a metal valve overhead that triggered a harsh hissing and one of the tiny tanks along the roof emptied with a furious swirling.

Frell stared overhead, picturing those gasbags. He had thought the slim pair were too small to lift the squat beetle, but they had—proving that whatever alchymy fueled this strange craft must produce a far stronger lifting gas.

Tykhan noted his attention. "*Ta'wyn* ingenuity paired with Klashean design," he explained. "Like the other two ships I crafted."

Frell pictured their trek through the treacherous Nysee Bog north of X'or. Tykhan had led their party via a tortuous route through the deadly and poisonous fenland, all steeped in thick mists. Their guide had cleared the path ahead of them, casting aside vipers with his impervious bronze hands or warning them where to set foot to avoid sinking sands or mud that could trap a leg. They finally reached a nest of chokevines that climbed twice his height and had thorns longer than Frell's forearm. In the center, hidden by the mists and protected all around, three ships rested, each stranger than the next.

Tykhan had directed them to one—the lampree—explaining the three ships' origins as he inflated the twin gasbags. Over the passing millennia, Tykhan had constructed fourteen of these wyndships, all of varying designs, and hidden them throughout the Klashe and elsewhere.

*Built for emergency,* he had told them. *And somewhat out of boredom.*

According to Tykhan, a Root's primary imperative was to construct. Apparently, even Tykhan could not resist the urge to tinker, fabricate, and assemble, especially over such a long span of endless years. He even admitted to sharing some of his creations with the Crown, stirring advancements along the way.

"Hold tight!" Saekl called from the front.

Frell shifted as the Rhysian captain goosed the forge to a louder roar. The lampree rolled through the air, while dodging around trees and crashing through bushes. Frell clutched his seat, understanding now why they had been told to strap tight. Their dizzying path finally leveled out.

Tykhan had suggested this route—to travel *through* Tithyn Woods rather than *over* it. They could not risk being seen. The echoes of cannon fire and sharper blasts reminded them of the danger above. Not that his path was much safer.

"Grab tight again!" Saekl warned.

Despite the wonders within, Frell squeezed his eyes closed.

*Let's hope we're not too late.*

DESPITE THE SHIPBOARD welcome, it took Kanthe an extra breath to identify the silver-masked figure striding toward him as his twin brother.

Still, Mikaen struck a shining figure, a prince sculpted of sunlight.

As his brother approached, he shed his heavy armor, piece by piece, helped by an escort of the same tattooed Vyrllian knights. Apparently, they must be a personal guard to the prince. Kanthe now recognized where the idea for those black tattoos had come from. They mirrored the sigil of Mikaen's mask.

By the time Mikaen reached him, the only armor remaining on his body was that mask. His brother stood only in his leathers now. His lips—at least the halves that were visible—twisted into a sneer, one hard enough to draw forth some of the scarring hidden behind the silver.

"This reunion is long overdue," Mikaen said.

By now, his crimson-faced guardsmen had closed around them, forming an armored wall. One of them sliced Kanthe's wrists free and removed the chains from his ankles. Another broke ranks and stepped forward, carrying a broadsword across his gloved palms.

Kanthe recognized the hulking man from half a year ago, from the Shrouds of Dalalæða. *Captain Thoryn.* Kanthe pictured the roof atop a cluster of stone homes, where he had been ambushed by Mikaen and this giant knight.

More of the crew gathered closer from across the wide deck.

"What is all of this?" Kanthe asked.

"Besides our reunion being belated, so is the sparring match that we left unfinished. When we were so callously interrupted." Mikaen touched his mask and nodded to Thoryn. "Now we may carry on where we left off."

The huge knight brought the sword in hand and held it out toward Kanthe.

He balked, stepping back, but a hard palm blocked him from behind.

Thoryn came forward, with a glint of pity in his eyes. His voice, though, remained firm. "You must take it, Prince Kanthe. If you must die, better with a sword in hand than on your knees."

Kanthe respected this ruthless assessment and took hold of the sword's hilt. He stepped back, unsheathing the blade from the knight's palms. Thoryn nodded his head and returned to a post behind Mikaen, joining his fellow guardsmen.

Kanthe lifted the ponderous broadsword. It was unwieldly and heavy. He brought his other hand around to steady it.

Across the circle, Mikaen drew the same weapon from a sheath at his waist, but he was able to lift it with one arm.

"Shall we begin?" his brother asked.

Before either could move, a booming shout echoed across the deck. A tall figure strode through the clusters of crewmen—who quickly scattered back to their posts. Kanthe didn't know the man, but from the laurels engraved on his breastplate, he was a liege general.

"What is the meaning of this, Prince Mikaen?" he shouted as he approached. "We're about to engage in battle!"

The explosions had grown louder. Ahead, the wall of smoke rolled toward them. Distant screams and shouts could be heard.

For once in his life, Kanthe prayed for war.

As the liege general reached them, he finally noticed the other prince aboard the *Hyperium*. While Kanthe might not recognize the man, the liege general had no difficulty identifying him. Shocked and startled, the man tripped a step. Clearly, he had no idea of Mikaen's plot and the successful abduction of the traitorous prince.

"This is between brothers, Liege General!" Mikaen shouted back, fury sharpening his voice. "It does not concern you. My father has made it clear that I'm not captain or commander here. The battle ahead is yours to wage. I will address my own fight here, rather than sit idly by. And we'll see who brings home the greater glory to Hálendii."

The liege general glowered, his face going dark under his helm. Still, he stared between the two brothers, trying to judge whether to intervene. After a long, tense pause, he gave a small shake of his head, settling on neutrality as the best course. If there would be any punishment for what happened next, it would be meted upon Prince Mikaen.

To further settle matters, a hunterskiff shot high across the *Hyperium*'s bow, flashing the Klashean Arms. It looked to be a scout, surveying the approaching behemoth. As the enemy ship turned and rocketed away, the liege general followed after it, pounding across the planks, bellowing orders.

"Now where were we?" Mikaen asked, lifting his sword higher.

Kanthe guarded himself, knowing there was nothing he could say to dissuade his brother. Still, he tried. "It's not too late, Mikaen. Together, the two of us have a rare chance to broker peace between Hálendii and the Southern Klashe, to bring greater glory to both."

"Whoever said I desired *peace*?" Mikaen stepped forward with a flourish of his sword. "And when I bring your head back to Azantiia, I will garner plenty of *glory*."

Mikaen lunged at him, his sword driving low for his belly. Kanthe side-stepped and parried with the flat of his blade. Steel rang loudly. The impact stung his palms, but he gripped harder.

Still, there was no pause to savor or sulk. Mikaen spun off his parry and swung his sword high, while Kanthe's sword hung near his waist.

Kanthe ducked, hearing steel sing over his head. He twisted to the side. Mikaen came again and again. Kanthe matched him—two-handed to Mikaen's one, but still holding his own. Kanthe found a rhythm.

Mikaen's first attacks had been taunting, nearly mocking, wanting Kanthe to look foolish. But soon their fighting grew earnest. They circled, clashed across one another, rebounded to new positions.

Kanthe still played a defensive role, which he knew was foolish. He would tire out quickly. Still, he couldn't bring himself to go for a mortal blow. It was less a conscious decision than it was reflexive. He could still hear Mikaen's childish laughter as the two fled through the halls in some grand adventure of play. This battle had also come too suddenly. To kill a brother took time to digest, to let sit in the gut and weigh, before committing to such an act.

Mikaen hissed and came at him again.

Plainly, his brother had found that time.

Distracted by these thoughts, Kanthe missed a feint. The edge of Mikaen's sword sliced along his ribs, down to bone. He fell back with a gasp.

Mikaen retreated rather than going for a killing blow. But it wasn't a hesitancy against a mortal strike. His brother wanted to relish first blood.

"You've vastly improved," Mikaen commended him.

"I've had good teachers." Kanthe leaned a hand on a knee, resting his sword tip on the planks. He pictured sparring with Jace, being taught balance and technique from Darant and Graylin. "It's a shame our father refused to let me train with the legion."

"Our father made many mistakes," Mikaen answered, his voice tightening with anger—but not toward Kanthe. "I will not make the same mistakes with my son."

Kanthe straightened, paining his wound. "You have a son?" He had not heard. "With Lady Myella?"

Mikaen glanced sidelong; clearly few others had known about this. Kanthe had no difficulty doing some swift calculations and realized *why* no one knew.

To be born this early meant they were conceived before marriage. Mikaen looked ready to refute this, but his face strained to hold the secret. In the end, he couldn't deny them.

"And a daughter," Mikaen hissed low, so only his immediate guardsmen could hear—who likely already knew.

"Twins?" Kanthe dropped his voice accordingly, both to avoid goading Mikaen and to protect those children from the scandal that such a revelation would cause. The twins—his niece and nephew—were innocent of all this strife. He would not sully their births.

Mikaen nodded, his face breaking with pride, a flash of the sun through clouds. "Both of them—Othan and Olia—beautiful and healthy."

Kanthe offered a tired smile. "I'm happy for you. I truly am."

Mikaen winced warily at his words.

Kanthe left his sword tip on the boards and leaned out his other hand. "Congratulations, my brother. No matter the future, I hope they live long and happy lives."

Mikaen acknowledged this with a nod. He took a step forward to meet him and clasped his hand. "Thank you, brother."

Kanthe squeezed, trying to remember the last time he had grasped his brother in any measure of true warmth.

Mikaen stared at their clasped hands, too. Then his grip tightened, spasming hard. "What is this?" he gasped out.

Kanthe looked down as Mikaen turned their hands, further exposing the gold ring on Kanthe's finger. The crimson garnet caught the sunlight, revealing the winged stallion engraved on it, a match to the ship's draft-iron figurehead.

"One of Mother's signet rings," Mikaen said, calculating in his own head. Like Kanthe, his brother had lived with the same rumors and whispers of a twin birth. Mikaen glared at him. "That's why you sided with the Klashe! To challenge our bloodline!"

"No, I never—"

His voice swelled into a murderous roar. "To challenge the birthright of my son, my daughter!" He lifted his sword high, clamping hard to Kanthe's hand. "Never!"

The blade fell with the fury of a father protecting his children. The sword cleaved through Kanthe's arm, severing it below the elbow.

Kanthe fell back in disbelief, dropping his sword.

Mikaen stumbled the other way, still clasping Kanthe's hand—and the remains of his arm. He finally threw them aside, along with the ring on a finger.

Kanthe collapsed to his knees. Blood poured and pumped across the planks. Mikaen shouted to Thoryn, but Kanthe's ears rang with shock. Then the pain doubled him over. He swooned and fell to his side, his blood pouring over him now.

The world narrowed.

Shadows swam in and out.

Then he felt his body clasped, the stump of his arm raised.

Mikaen leaned his face close, his voice acid. "You're not escaping that easily, brother."

The agony in his arm flared—with the sizzle and smoke of searing flesh.

# EIGHTEEN

# THE ROOT OF ALL PAIN

*Agoni kenn be the grettest teacher & payne the very fonte of wisdoum. But ferst yoeu must survive. No lessons are learn'd bi the ded.*

—From *The Rue of the Penitent*
by Anagorac hy Damoa

## 90

NYX AND THE others gathered around the chrysalis. Emerald fire raged across the inside of the dome. Nyx hummed under her breath and cast forth a few glowing strands, testing the energy, searching for a way through the flames to reach Shiya.

Overhead, the raash'ke screamed and battered the air with their wings, terrified, skimming away from the coruscations and waves of the emerald fire that had enslaved them. Daal swept among them, doing his best to calm and reassure them. He was slowly having some success, relying on his own innate ability to commune with others, to sympathize and soothe.

Nyx had her own challenge before her.

She waited for one of the waves of fire to pass, then darted her thread to the cocoon's glass. She managed to touch it for less than a heartbeat. A glimpse of Shiya reached her. Not an image seen with the eye. Shiya was a golden corona of bridle-song, whipped and lashed by malignant fire. It was like with Bashaliia back at the Mouth. The spider fought to break her, to bridle her with his false, corrupted song. Nyx could sense not only the enemy's fury, but also its terror of Shiya.

Nyx urged the bronze woman to hold out. While Shiya was far stronger than Bashaliia, the spider was wielding the full power of this entire dome against her.

*Shiya will break.*

Then a snap of fire cracked into Nyx's strand. The recoil struck her hard enough to knock her back a few steps. The strength was unnerving, formidable. She rubbed the fiery sting in the middle of her chest.

"What do we do?" Rhaif pleaded. "We can't leave her in there."

"She's strong," Graylin said.

Nyx shook her head, firm about what she had sensed. "Not strong enough."

"What about Daal?" Rhaif pleaded. "Maybe with his added power you could break through."

Nyx stared up. Daal continued to sweep arcs through the raash'ke. She also noted her mount, Metyl, who remained on the floor. He was at the edge of panic, too, ducking his head low whenever a tide of green fire swept overhead, keening his distress.

"No," she answered Rhaif. "The raash'ke need Daal. If we lose those wings, we'll never leave here. And even with Daal's strength added to mine, I don't think it would help, not against the full power of this dome."

"What about brute force, then?" Jace asked, hefting his Guld'guhlian ax.

Darant and his men nodded at the wisdom of such a course.

Vikas looked skeptical, and rightly so.

Nyx stared at the chrysalis, catching glimpses of Shiya convulsing within. "Not yet. That cocoon is the lock, and Shiya the key to whatever it is we're supposed to do here. Damage either and we've lost already."

Krysh spoke off to the side, where he had been studying the giant crystal sphere hanging over the bottomless hole. "Something's happening here."

They all turned.

Up until now, the sphere had seemed unaffected by the fiery storm around the dome. It remained latched and suspended in bronze, resting silently in its cradle, a crystal eye staring back at them with a pupil of pulsing gold.

But now the crystal shook. It was just a small vibration, but in an object that massive, it was disconcerting enough. The golden sea inside sloshed, lashed by an unseen tempest. The bronze cradle groaned. The rigged archways that suspended it creaked with the strain of holding that trembling sphere.

"What's causing it?" Jace asked.

Nyx looked back at the chrysalis. She pictured the bronze woman quaking in her prison. "It's Shiya. The sphere is responding to her assault."

"Then we must break her loose," Jace warned. "Take the chance."

All eyes turned to Nyx—but the answer came from elsewhere.

"It is too late," a voice called over in a sibilant, grating voice, as if it were the speaker's first attempt to communicate aloud. There was no amusement, no satisfaction, just a cold statement of fact. "It is done and cannot be reversed."

They all swung to a curve of the dome a short way off. A bronze figure stepped out from the depths of one of the massive sinuous extensions. It was the spider, come out of hiding.

He rounded past the giant cable that dove under the floor and continued toward the sphere. As with the quality of his speech, there was no hostility or threat in the spider's approach, more a vague indifference, maybe a touch of curiosity.

She had glimpsed his monstrous form back in the Mouth, but that view had been for less than a breath. Revealed now, his form churned the stomach. His bronze had melted into slag and had only the barest resemblance to a man. He walked on two legs, had two arms, and a head. But that was the only similarity. His mouth was a straight slit and looked newly formed. The metal lips appeared smoother and newer, as if freshly smelted and only formed to speak to these trespassers.

His eyes, though—a glassy blue—matched Shiya's.

It was in those eyes that the creature showed any reaction to their trespass. Fire shone behind the glass, but it was the burn of frost. The glow was cold and cunning, nearly as inimical as his form. It was as if the spider sought to strip away any residual humanity—both in form and spirit.

As the creature drew nearer, the others backed warily with weapons raised. They all knew Shiya's strength and speed.

Nyx stood her ground.

As the spider noted her stance, his animosity flared brighter, showing enough humanity to hate. Even his bronze warmed with the restrained fury. "*You* are the one who broke my hold over the raash'ke, who carried an Axis to my territory."

Nyx absorbed his words, hearing again that strange term. "Axis? What is that? What did I bring?"

He glanced to Shiya. "As a Root, I held out little hope to capture and imprison a *ta'wyn* as powerful as her." A trickle of emotion seeped into him, one of cold satisfaction. "It is a worthy reward for ending the world."

Nyx stiffened. "What do you mean?"

He motioned to the sphere. Its cradle quaked more violently now, shaking the ground underfoot. His next words were terrifyingly matter-of-fact, spoken with unshakable certainty. "The *turubya* will tear the world in half."

The spider tried to smile with its slit of a mouth, as if a rock had discovered amusement. "The irony is that an *Axis* will do it. I don't even have to break her to my will. I just needed *her*."

Nyx stared over to Shiya in the chrysalis. "You needed a *key*."

He considered her words, then nodded. "I could never have accomplished it on my own. Not as a Root. I needed an Axis. And you brought her to me."

Nyx resisted the guilt that tried to rise, refusing to let it numb her.

"It must be done," he intoned gravely. "The *turubya* is anathema to anyone but the *Rab'almat*. No one else can wield it. Not you, not your Axis. It *is* done."

A measure of exhalation had entered his voice, a glorious terror.

Nyx watched his bronze flow and churn across his body. His mouth dissolved and re-formed, only to fade again. Nostrils drilled into a skull and swept away. She backed from the horror of it all.

"Can this sphere truly break the world?" Graylin whispered to her.

Krysh answered, "We came here to seek a way to set the world to turning. If such power exists in the Wastes and is now corrupted, I would believe him."

"Then how do we stop him?" Jace said. "Back at the Crèche, Shiya mentioned that her form could be melted in the molten seas. Could we get one of the raash'ke to carry this monster out the dome and drop him into one of those fiery canyons outside? Maybe if he's destroyed, it'll release Shiya."

Krysh nodded. "It's worth trying."

Unfortunately, the plan was heard, and a mouth re-formed. "Such a destruction would result in the immediate and catastrophic failure of the *turubya*."

Again, this statement was spoken with an icy certitude, with no sense of dissemblance or lie.

Rhaif grimaced. "We probably don't want that to happen."

Nyx turned to the spider—or the *Root,* as he called himself. "When?" she pressed him. "Without interference, when will the *turubya* trigger this cataclysm?"

The Root melted his bronze enough to turn his face toward the rise of the sphere. His gaze ticked to the arc of the trembling crystal, to the vibration of the bronze suspensions, to the rocking of the thick cradle. His legs absorbed the floor's tremoring, which rippled up through his bronze. He turned his eyes on her, cold with certainty.

"In less than a quarter day," he said.

Nyx went cold.

*We don't have even until morning.*

She moved closer to him, seeking words to dissuade him.

"It *is* done," the Root declared with finality. "No force can alter this course. Only an Axis has the knowledge to deactivate me and stop the inevitable, but that threat has been eliminated."

Nyx glanced to Shiya.

*And we let her walk straight into that trap.*

Despairing, Nyx turned again to the Root. His eyes remained fixed on the crystal orb of the *turubya,* no longer evaluating, simply waiting. This sense was firmed as the ends of his legs spread tendrils of bronze across the copper, as if becoming his namesake, rooting himself in place until the world's end.

She backed away, and Jace drew alongside her.

"If the end is *inevitable,*" Jace said, "then maybe you should wield your bridle-song against him. You thwarted him before, back in the Mouth. Maybe you'll discover . . . I don't know, *something.*"

All eyes turned to her.

She glanced at the shaking sphere, felt the trembling underfoot.

*Jace is right.*

She swallowed down her trepidation and nodded. She backed from the group and signaled for Daal to come down. By now, he had somewhat calmed the raash'ke—though they kept a wary distance from the molten spider, circling near the edge of the dome.

Daal acknowledged her signal and swept in a low arc. She followed his trajectory. He was going to land Nyfka near Metyl. He likely wanted to keep the two raash'ke close, to support each other during this storm.

She crossed to meet him.

As she did, she glanced back to the molten bronze of the Root. She was nagged by one detail. The creature could have stayed hidden. He did not have to reveal himself. His actions made no sense.

*Did he come out to gloat? To exact revenge? To watch us struggle at the end?*

She frowned, knowing she had sensed no such pettiness.

She glanced over to Shiya, who—while often cold and distant—had shown moments of tenderness, compassion, even humor.

If this Root was of the same ilk, then somewhere down deep, no matter how much he tried to melt it, a core of humanity must still exist. She had witnessed inklings of it when they spoke—not that those traces were enough to sway him away from his exalted plan.

*He's too far gone for that.*

Still, this insight might explain *why* he had come out of hiding. She looked across at their group, bonded to a cause, supportive of one another. She stared at the sweep of wings overhead. She remembered what she had shared with the horde-mind. She had shown them what they had lost, that nearly indescribable, wordless sense of connection, of a wholeness that could only be found in another heart, that commonality that went beyond love to something even deeper and more meaningful.

*We all seek that,* she thought. *From those around us, from the bonds we form, from the lives we share. It's the core of our humanity.*

She returned to looking at the Root.

*You can't melt that away completely.*

Perhaps it was this need that drove the Root—alone for millennia—to maintain his stubborn enslavement of the raash'ke. It wasn't just for the *protection* of his lair. Deep down, he must have desired some measure of *connection* to another, corrupted though it may be.

She stared back at him with narrowed eyes. After she had severed his connection to the raash'ke, he had been left isolated again. And now, knowing the finality of death was coming, maybe he didn't want to be alone, not at the end.

She felt a flare of sorrow for this lonely sentinel, abandoned for ages to guard this spot. Still, such pity would not stop her from seeking a way to stop him.

Ahead, Daal landed with a sweep of wings. She hurried to him, knowing she would need his font of power. The two of them dared not hold back.

For any chance of success, it was *all or nothing*.


DAAL CROSSED ALONGSIDE Nyx toward the melted figure of a bronze man. The glassy eyes remained eerily open, unblinking, yet shining with awareness. Nyx had briefly told him what had happened and the doom that threatened.

"This *Root*," he whispered as they reached the bronze figure, fearful it was listening even though it had no ears. "He says only Shiya can stop him. Even with bridle-song, how will we get him to obey *us*? He's surely too strong to bend to your bridling, even *with* my power."

"I don't know. But the Root must have expended considerable energy in preparing and executing this trap. It had to tax him."

Daal glanced to the others, who all gathered behind them, their faces tense. Ahead, the Root was a statue fastened to the copper. Beyond the creature's shoulder, Shiya remained locked in a cocoon of crystal and fire. She quaked inside, somehow transferring that violence to the *turubya*'s orb in the dome's center.

Nyx stepped next to him.

"What do you want me to do?" he whispered.

She held out her hand. "What you've always done. You be my flashburn, I'll be your forge."

He closed his eyes and clasped her hand. As their palms touched, fire ignited with a furious heat. He melted into her. It no longer felt unnatural, but welcoming. His flames flowed out of him, pumped by his own heart, flaring hotter with each breath.

He felt his skin chill, but he held firm.

He was rewarded as Nyx sang softly next to him, a wordless melody, fed by his flames. He felt the vibrations of her throat as if it were his own. Her song grew, washing between them. She drew more and more, eventually drawing gasps out of him.

The song now flooded, filling both, until there was no more space. He remembered drowning in the Dreamers' sea, alive but with his lungs weighed down by water, a heaviness without panic.

This was like that.

And still the song grew.

As Nyx drew more fire, the cold in him deepened to numbness. He felt the surrounding world fade. Still, as before, *her* desire was *his*. He felt her ache, her longing for more. She was the black abyss that could never be satiated.

Still, he gave himself fully to her.

Why hold back if it was the end of the world?

*If I must die, let me die within you.*

She heard him. Melded together, they could keep no secrets. She spoke in threads of light and song.

*Stay with me . . .*

He wanted to refuse, to give her all of him, but those strands of song wrapped to him, holding him closer. He threw her words back from a moment ago, words that still resounded inside her and he could read.

*All or nothing.*

They dared not hold back.

But she refused to accept those extremes, offering an alternative.

*All* yet *nothing.*

He didn't understand.

*Stay with me . . .*

She bridled him to her, using his own energy to hold him. He read the reasons. A mix of fear, loneliness, need, even desire.

He stopped fighting and released himself to her.


WITH DAAL'S CONSENT, along with his trust, Nyx let her song burst from her heart and throat. A golden torrent flooded out of her, fueled by Daal's flashburn and shaped by her forge—but she aimed her power where no one expected.

*One chance . . .*

She emptied her tide *down,* into the copper floor. She followed that rush, bound with Daal. She was too terrified to try this alone, to risk the impossible by herself. She needed his anchor.

*I need you.*

She felt his gaze sharing hers, his hand in hers, his memories with hers.

As with the dome's door, she struck the copper—and dove into its emptiness.

Daal gasped *in* her ear, maybe *using* her chest. They were both too confounded together to tell one from the other.

She flooded through those empty spaces, around those hardened motes spinning with energy. She showed him the duality that still defied her understanding.

The *all* of solid copper, yet the *nothing* within.

*All yet nothing.*

She swept along the floor until she sensed the shadow entrenched above.

The darkness of bronze. She dove deeper into the copper, ducking under the Root's position.

She shared with Daal the memory of the copper floor vibrating and rippling up the Root's legs. She showed him the tendrils of bronze draping across the copper, spreading his base thinner.

Once under that shadow, she gathered her light and Daal's fire. She took both and forged a golden spear and shot upward, traveling with it. She pierced through the thin bronze at the Root's base—and burst into his core.

The emptiness of bronze exploded into liquid fire and impossible energies. Suns were born and died around her. Or so it seemed, so it felt. She clung to Daal, torn and ripped by forces and dynamisms she had no words for. She became both fleeting storm and ageless rock. Madness threatened in a breath.

Then she spotted it—or willed into being because she knew it must be here. Above her hung a perfect cube of crystal, pulsing with golden fire.

Like the sphere.

Like in Shiya.

She drove toward it, then hovered. She dared not crush it or it might end the world. She hung there in the wildstorm at the Root's core, struggling how to smother the cube's fire, to deactivate without destroying.

She cast a few questing tendrils.

*Can I pick this lock like I did the dome's door?*

She touched the cube, and in a heartbeat, she knew the truth.

*I can do this.*

But that single beat took too long.

The world burst around her with an explosive boom.

She was thrown far, out of the storm, out of bronze, and into her own body. She slammed hard, toppling backward to the copper floor. A wave of emerald fire blasted over her and away.

She struggled to breathe, to remember how. She finally gasped once, coughed, and breathed again. She sat up into chaos. Her vision swam; her ears rang hollowly and muffled. Sights became snatches of confusion.

Another thunderous boom made her flinch.

Before her, the Root had reared up, hardening all of his surfaces. He fled to the dome wall, a blur of metal. He shoved a hand into the labyrinth of crystal and pipes, melting his fingers deeper. Jagged bolts of green fire spat and chained over the arc of the dome and blazed down to his arm, sweeping over his body, turning his bronze into a lightning rod for those infernal energies.

Nyx despaired, knowing the Root was impenetrable now.

Next to her, Daal struggled to rise to an elbow, drained and shivering, pale nearly unto death.

Then Krysh and Graylin crashed upon them and struggled to drag them up. The world spun worse. The alchymist shouted something to Graylin, but the ringing in her ears deafened his words. Still, he pointed to the side.

Her head swung in that direction, responding to Krysh's terror.

Across the way, the *turubya*'s orb rattled hard in its bronze cradle. Metal twisted and screeched loud enough to pierce her ears. The golden sea inside the crystal roiled and thrashed. Underfoot, the copper floor violently quaked.

She realized what was going on.

Her trespass had not only failed—but it had brought doom to their threshold. They no longer had a quarter day. Likely only moments now.

Another boom shook the room, ringing the walls.

Crystal cracked across the dome's inner surfaces, raining down in a glittering cascade.

Nyx gaped all around.

*What is happening?*

GRAYLIN PULLED NYX under his arm. He felt the panic trembling through her, the terror and confusion strangling her breath. He hugged her closer, trying to squeeze his strength into her. To the side, Krysh struggled with Daal, who hung in the alchymist's arms.

Glass showered over all of them. Graylin drew them to the far wall, avoiding the green torch of the Root's imbedded form. He aimed away from the rattling orb as it threatened to tear loose from its cradle. He sought the only shelter—one of the yawning tunnels that led down the coppery limbs of the complex.

Another boom deafened and drove him protectively low over Nyx. Krysh dropped Daal, as the alchymist focused back over his shoulder, craning up at the source of the blasts.

Moments ago, the first explosion seemed to wake the Root. Emerald fire had flashed across his bronze—then Nyx and Daal had been thrown back into their bodies. Still, some damage was done in the process, jolting the massive crystal *turubya*, rocking it to the brink of destruction.

But at the moment, none of that was important.

Graylin helped Krysh get Daal up and moving again.

He stared as another blast of cannon fire punched a hole through the *Sparrowhawk*'s hull. Fiery boards rained through the warm mists over the dome's doorway. The ship could take no more damage. Glace had bought them as much time as she could, guarding the entrance with the bulk of the *Hawk*—but there was too little of the brave ship left.

Its powerful forges ignited as the *Hawk* slipped sideways, skating its keel along the dome's exterior, then blasting off into the icy night. Smaller ships gave chase with tails of flames. In the *Sparrowhawk*'s place, a ship three times its size drew its shadow across the doorway.

A Hálendiian battle barge.

Before the massive craft sealed them in, six sailrafts dove under its bulk and shot into the dome, circling wide. They were followed by a bevy of one-manned slipfoils. Past them all, the battle barge fired its cannons overhead, shooting off into the night, discouraging the *Sparrowhawk* from returning, loudly claiming this space for king and kingdom.

Below, Darant had collected his men. Vikas had grabbed Jace by the scruff. They hurried toward the same towering tunnel into the coppery extension. They were all too out in the open, too exposed. Not that their small party had any hope of challenging the invading Hálendiian raiders.

But Graylin wasn't counting on their group alone.

They had allies—in the sky.

The raash'ke roiled throughout the dome. A storm of black wings. When the *Sparrowhawk* had been attacked, the remaining few raash'ke aboard the ship had flooded through the doorway, seeking shelter within.

Angry and fearful, the raash'ke descended upon the entering ships. Claws ripped into balloons. Wings dove and smashed into slipfoils, cracking hulls and sending the tiny vessels cartwheeling away.

"Run!" Graylin shouted to the others as ships fell out of the air.

Splintering crashes struck all around. Fireballs burst as forges exploded on impact. Smoke blasted high. A slipfoil rolled wildly past them with flames spiraling behind it. It struck the dome wall and blasted a crown of shattered crystal around it.

Unfortunately, the Hálendiian forces had dealt with the raash'ke before and had readied themselves. The pilots seemed immune to the beasts' insidious keening, which in the dome already frazzled Graylin's senses. That bastard Commander Ghryss must have returned to the battle barge with knowledge of the protective property of lodestones.

Worse, from the open sterns of the sailrafts, jets of flames waved out, burning wings. Hand-bombs were tossed. One struck a raash'ke and blasted a hole in its chest with a rain of bone and blood.

"No!" Daal moaned, as if sensing the flock's pain and terror. His anguish drove him out of Krysh's arms.

Before the alchymist could stop him, Daal fled away, heading toward the pair of raash'ke huddled on the floor, burrowed tight to one another. He refused to abandon the two mounts. As he ran, Daal glared up. It looked like he intended to take the fight himself to the air, to rally the raash'ke into a more deliberate offense instead of the panicked chaos.

And not just him.

Nyx broke away from Graylin and chased after Daal. Graylin bolted after her, but she shouted over her shoulder, reminding him that the Hálendiians were the least of their problems, "Guard Shiya! Help Rhaif!"

Graylin skidded and turned, realizing in his haste he had forgotten about the pair. He turned and saw Rhaif crouched near Shiya's chrysalis, refusing to forsake the bronze woman. Graylin knew Nyx was right.

Nothing mattered if they lost Shiya. She remained the *key* to everything.

Still, he called in desperation to Nyx, "What are you—?"

She shouted without turning, "Going for help!"

# 91

NYX FLED THROUGH the pall of smoke cast by the wreckage of a flaming sailraft. Bodies lay broken and burning all around it. She shied away and chased after the darker shadow of Daal.

She didn't know how he was still on his feet after being so drained.

Ahead, Daal reached their two mounts first. They hissed and reared from him, blinded by panic, deafened by the blasts. Daal bowed low, arms raised, palms toward them. She heard him sing to them, like she had heard him do with Neffa. While there was a trickle of bridle-song there—all he had left—he didn't need more. His compassion and concern welled out of him brighter than any song.

That was his truest gift.

Nyfka mewled and trilled her fear toward him, responding first. Metyl was slower, but Nyx shouldered behind Daal, adding her harmony, a blend of song and residual fire.

The two beasts calmed enough to accept their greeting, to allow fingers to be run along their necks to saddles. Nyx kept hold of the edge of her song, letting them know what they needed, to be brave one more time.

Daal nodded to her as he hooked a toe into a stirrup pocket, innately sensing what needed to be done. The two were still connected without any magic. He would rally the raash'ke, turning panic into purpose, both to defend and attack.

Nyx climbed atop Metyl but stayed low in the saddle. With both hands, she pushed fingers into the heat of her mount. She let her song shine brighter, burning through the last of Daal's fire. She needed to be this close to one of the raash'ke to make the connection.

They needed help.

Daal could not do it alone.

She closed her eyes and cast out for one last ally, one that could truly calm and direct the raash'ke, to focus the few here into a strong army. Shiya needed to be protected—not just on the ground, but in the air. While Daal waged his war across the dome, Nyx would guard over Shiya.

To do that, she needed another's strength and cast out a plea to the horde-mind of the raash'ke.

*Help us.*

To reach the distant horde-mind, she had expected it would take great effort. But as soon as she extended herself, it was there, waiting and expectant.

Nyx gasped at its enormity, its ancientness bared so nakedly to her. It was no longer a cold, eternal presence. It was a black wall of wrath, a towering wave of fury and vengeance.

In that moment, Nyx saw that it needed her, too. The distances were too great for the horde-mind alone. It had needed Nyx to reach out, to bridge the gap, so it could channel through her to reach the dome.

Its intent filled Nyx, wordless but clear in her head.

**I see him.**

That dark wave broke over and through her, flattening her to the saddle. Without Nyx's bidding, her mount shoved off the copper floor. Its huge wings buffeted smoke and fanned flames higher.

Gasping, Nyx clutched fistfuls of Metyl's fur to keep to her saddle. She sang to her mount, but he was gone, washed into the horde-mind, absorbed there. What she rode now was not a single raash'ke—but all of them.

To the side, Daal burst out of the smoke atop Nyfka. Unaware of what was happening, he turned and headed off into the fray.

The horde-mind drew her the other direction, toward the curve of the wall, following the tracery of green fire to its source. From the back of Metyl, she saw the Root imbedded in the crystalline matrix, still a torch of emerald flames, as impregnable as ever.

On her other side, she spotted Graylin and the others below, guarding before Shiya. One or two sailrafts must have landed safely and unloaded forces. Dark shadows, flashing with brighter sparks of armor, closed upon them through the smoke, all aiming toward the chrysalis, as if somehow sensing Shiya's presence and being drawn there like iron to lodestone.

Behind her, raash'ke screamed with renewed determination as Daal rallied them, intent to let no other invaders breach his defense.

But neither battle was hers.

The horde-mind filled her with its vengeance, setting her jaw tight. Metyl drove down toward the imbedded Root. The creature had tortured and enslaved the raash'ke for millennia, forced them to commit atrocities and brutalities that scarred them deep, down to their core. It was a wounding that would never heal, an abuse that could never be assuaged, a guilt that would never end. The raash'ke could never return to their innocence, to who they once were. The Root had stripped that from them forever, leaving only one last path open.

Retribution.

As Metyl drove toward the Root, the horde-mind gathered all its pain and fury and guilt. It bound it with bridle-song. But as with Nyx's mount, it was not one song, but a multitude, all the raash'ke who had ever lived, all those tortured over the millennia.

It finally released it in a raging song of fury. Its power blasted through the channel that Nyx had opened. It filled Nyx and Metyl, but neither had any hope of holding it.

Her mount roared.

She screamed.

The song tore out of both, ripping Nyx with it. The force struck the Root. It must have sensed the torrent coming and hardened its bronze and flared a shield of emerald fire, intent to remain an unbreakable stone in a tide even this powerful.

Nyx feared they would fail, remembering the Root's adamant claim that only an Axis could unlock him. Moments ago, Nyx had almost succeeded, striking when he left himself momentarily vulnerable, but the Root had learned and forged himself into a bronze fortress around his core.

The flood struck him with such force that it cracked the crystal around him. She cringed as she rode that tide, expecting to crash against the Root's impregnable fortress.

Instead, his bronze blasted away, torn and ripped by the force of that torrent. Molten metal splattered in all directions, splashing across the floor and up the wall, exposing his blinding heart.

He stood there, pinned to the wall, unable to move.

Nyx saw the confusion and terror in the ruins of his face. She read the question glowing in his eyes. Nyx was just as bewildered.

*How? How was this done?*

In a heartbeat, the horde-mind told her.

**I see him.**

In another beat, it showed her. A cascade of ages swept through her, an endless stream of brutality. But through it all, a cold eternal eye had stared back at its tormentor. Nyx had experienced the same after freeing the raash'ke, fixed by the ancient gaze, watched from the fringes. It was no different for the Root.

The horde-mind had bided the turning of ages, silently watching, observing, just as the ancients had forged it to do. To be an eternal sentinel. The horde-mind had focused its discerning eye upon its nemesis. Over the passing millennia, it had studied and analyzed, stripping secrets one grain at a time, made all the easier with the two bonded together by the intimacy of bridle-song—even as corrupted as it was.

Nyx understood.

The horde-mind had watched the Root all this time, gaining knowledge of him, possibly more than even an Axis possessed. Over millennia, the Root's secrets were laid bare—as surely as his heart was now.

The horde-mind formed a fiery fist of bridle-song, intending to crush the cube of crystal with its pulsing golden glow.

Nyx rushed in ahead, casting out a warning and demand.

**No.**

It was firm enough to force the horde-mind to pause, but she knew it would only last a moment. She surged ahead of the flood and cast forth a tangle of shining tendrils of song. She had already studied this cube, learned its lock. So, this time, she did not stop—not even for a heartbeat, knowing such hesitation had betrayed her before.

With golden fire, she quickly picked the crystal lock and held her breath.

The cube flicked, flashed brighter—then fell dark.

She waited, hoping, praying.

The glow died in the Root's eyes, looking almost like relief. The remains of his body slowly sagged down the wall, drawing the emerald fire with it, flushing the corruption off the walls above. Over the crumple of its ruins, a green pyre burned for another breath—then snuffed out.

As it did, a loud crystalline bell rang off to the side. A glance that way revealed Shiya collapsing out of the chrysalis, falling into the arms of Rhaif and the others.

*But were we in time?*

Still saddled atop her mount, Nyx twisted around and saw the huge sphere violently rattling, only a moment from being torn loose. Her heart clenched. She didn't know if Shiya had the strength to stop what the Root had started— then a scream rose above and behind her.

Nyx ducked from it, shivered from its timbre. It was a cry rife with madness and power and fury. She knew it came from no raash'ke.

She turned as a huge shadow swept down through the dome's opening. Black wings spread wide, brushing the copper to either side. It was all darkness and hatred. A steel helm mounted its skull. Jagged bolts of fire drove it down into the dome, coming from the barge overhead. The energy struck that steel helm and frazzled across the hundreds of copper needles drilled into bone and brain, creating a crown of emerald fire.

As the monster swept lower, it drew the residual green fire still skimming across the dome's inner walls. Energy arced through the air from all directions, drawn to the helm, further fueling its fire.

The winged beast screamed as it hung in the air.

Framed in fire and crowned in inimical glory.

In that savage cry, the horde-mind discovered a name buried deep and shouted it out in warning to all.

**Kalyx.**


RHAIF CRINGED NEXT to Shiya as the monstrous bat screamed overhead. The nearby clash of steel in the smoke fell silent as combatants retreated apart, likely all gazing up.

Rhaif never lifted his face. He cradled Shiya's upper torso across his lap. Her bronze crushed his knees, squeezed fire from his stabbed thigh. Still, he held her as her body quaked and shivered. She seemed unable to fully escape the tortured horrors of the chrysalis. He clutched her hand, sensing no warmth, only frigid metal. Her eyes were open but looked cold.

Krysh crouched on her other side. "We must get her back into the cocoon."

The alchymist stared with concern at the giant crystal *turubya*. While Shiya's tremoring had calmed, the orb's rattling had worsened. Rhaif felt the shaking in the floor, in his bones, all the way to his skull.

He understood the urgency.

"Even if we wanted to," Rhaif said, "she's too heavy to move ourselves."

Krysh shifted to the smoky fighting as it resumed once again. Graylin, along with Vikas and the other men, continued to guard the chrysalis. They had used the smoke and feints to lure the Hálendiians aside. They now fought a fierce battle at the mouth of a nearby tunnel. But none of it would matter if Shiya failed to stop whatever dire machinations the Root had set in motion.

Krysh grabbed Shiya's shoulder and struggled to lift her torso, but it would not budge.

Rhaif pushed him away. "That's not going to work. A lady should be treated with respect."

Despite his flippant tone, his heart knotted in his chest. He feared what he must do next—not that it was any risk to her. If he failed, it would only confirm what he secretly feared. That Shiya had no real connection to him, that whatever sense he had that she cared for him was not real, just his desires reflecting off her bronze.

*If I must die, leave me at least this illusion.*

Still, he'd rather not die.

So, he lifted his hands and rested his palms atop her naked chest, between the swell of her bosom, where he imagined her heart would be, where he wished it to be.

Rhaif was far from gifted in bridle-song, but there was one melody that the two had shared in the past. He started it as a whisper, nearly breathless with fear. With each few words, he let his voice grow stronger, lifting his mother's lullaby out of the past and offering it to Shiya. It was a song of comfort and assurance, of a love that would never fade.

*Hear me, Shiya . . .*

He had done something like this half a year ago, coming upon her broken and dying in the Cloudreach forest. It had taken the strength of Xan—his great-grandmother—and four other Kethra'kai to revive her back then. He had joined them, too, offering what little help he could.

*But now it's just me, Shiya.*

His hands glowed faintly, a few tendrils wafting forth, stirred by the lullaby. He let them settle and warm this most tender of spots.

Back in Cloudreach, he had hardly known her. They had barely met. Since then, they had spent a half year together, most of it confined aboard the *Sparrowhawk.* He had found comfort in her company: in quiet talks, in silent meals, in touches that were perhaps more meaningful to him. Still, she had seemed to find some measure of contentment with him. Her smiles deepening, her touches more lingering. She often sought him out first, rather than the other way around, as if she needed him, too.

*But was it just me, Shiya? Was I fooling myself?*

He continued to sing, his hands glowing a richer golden as he remembered those moments. He stared into her eyes and offered the only gift left to him.

*Just me . . .*

His palms grew warmer, drawing his gaze. From her chest, golden tendrils rose, frilling into a mist. It settled over his hands, holding him a moment. Her song flowed up to him, reassuring, sharing what she thought of him.

*You're always enough . . .*

Her bronze warmed outward from his palms, from the well of power he had stirred. Her tremors and shakes smoothed to calm bronze. Fire restoked her eyes to an azure fire.

"We must hurry," Krysh urged.

Shiya sat up, first tentatively, then more swiftly. She cast her gaze about: at the smoky fighting, at the war of wings, at the violence of a storm trapped in crystal.

She stood and turned to the copper shield, to the crystal cocoon. She took a step, then another, no longer driven by the compulsion from earlier, only the necessity of this moment. Still, she hesitated before the last step. He read the map of apprehension in the slight squint of her eyes, the thinning of her lips.

It was not the fear of torture that held her trapped, but the same dread that had frozen him a moment ago. He answered it by taking her hand and reassuring her.

"You're always enough, too."


DAAL SWEPT UNDER the winged daemon in the sky. It screamed with a furious madness, entrapped in a net of emerald fire. The bat writhed and flapped and tore the air with its thrashing. Silver glinted from its skull, flashing with a dread warning.

He knew such restraint wouldn't hold.

The bat would break free, made stronger by the wildfire.

He took stock around him. The raash'ke had fled lower, circling warily. At least the dome's skies were otherwise empty of ships, except for the hulking lurker above the door. The other rafts and foils had either crashed or landed.

He searched below and spotted Shiya stepping into the cocoon, the chrysalis closing behind her. To the side, a battle raged near the mouth of a black tunnel, nearly lost in the smoke but revealed in flashes of steel. With his breath tight, Daal scanned until he spotted Nyx sweeping wide and saddled low. Her face was a mask of terror. Her gaze was fixed above.

He understood her worry. It pounded his heart, too. But while the monster was alarming, nearly half again the size of their mounts, it was outnumbered. A dozen raash'ke plied the air.

Still, Nyx swooped along the circling raash'ke. She lifted an arm and swept it down, over and over again, as if trying to get them to retreat from the beast above. He didn't know why she wasn't using the horde-mind to get them to obey.

Worried and confused, he shifted his weight and applied pressure with a knee, guiding Nyfka toward Nyx. She spotted him diving toward her and tried to wave him off, motioning frantically.

*What is wrong?*

Then the dome erupted with a scream that ate through his skull. He wanted to cover his ears, but he needed both hands to hold on to the saddle. The noise narrowed his vision, pounded his ears.

He recognized what he was hearing. It was similar to but different from the paralyzing keen of the raash'ke. Only this was a terror meant to stop a heart. He fought to raise his shoulders to his ears—but he was not the intended target. He was not what the monster above had been designed to attack.

It was a prey with far more sensitive ears.

*Oh, no . . .*

He urged Nyfka toward the floor, diving her steeply. He understood now, why Nyx wanted them all out of the air.

Under him, Nyfka stiffened, her neck writhing to escape that cry, but it was everywhere, rebounding off the walls and echoing from all sides. With a final strained cry of agony, she went limp under him.

Daal clutched hard to his saddle, knowing there was no waking his mount—if Nyfka wasn't dead already. With her wings still out, fluttered up by the wind of their descent, Nyfka spiraled in a steep dive toward the floor.

Daal leaned tight, struggling to understand.

*Where was the horde-mind during all of this?*

NYX FOUGHT A hundred battles—and lost all of them.

With the first scream of the monster, she knew all was doomed. Linked with the horde-mind, she felt that cry of madness tear into the ancientness that she carried with her. It shattered the horde-mind. Fragile after being freed and weakened by its attack on the Root, it had been left vulnerable. And even if not, the horde-mind might not have withstood this fierce assault.

The force felt designed for this purpose, a flaming spear whetted and fueled for one end: to destroy a horde-mind.

She stared up, recognizing that this monster—Kalyx—was not raash'ke. From its tall ears, sleek fur, and long tail, she knew what it was.

A Mýr bat, one of monstrous size.

Even more terrifying, she recognized its steel helm and those copper needles. She flashed to her two brothers, similarly outfitted and tortured, equally enslaved to do their master's bidding.

She stared higher. The jagged bolts striking the steel and copper led up to the Hálendiian battle barge. The master of the weapon hid up there—though she wagered its creator did not. The monster had to have been forged by the Iflelen, by the depravities of Shrive Wryth. She knew this in her heart. Before their group departed the Crown, Wryth had still been in Azantiia, where he surely remained. The cunning bastard would never abandon his stronghold and risk the Wastes.

So, he sent someone else to do his bidding.

Sending a weapon with them.

One meant to thwart her.

A poison for her garden.

She understood *all* of this before Kalyx's first scream ended—after that, it was a battle to hold the raash'ke horde-mind together. It had splintered into hundreds of flailing pieces. She fought to weave and hold them together with her bridle-song, to be a beacon in the madness.

She managed to hold a fraction together, a fifth at most. She lost hundreds of those battles, seeing memory and mind dissolve in front of her. Or worse, to see fiery madness rush through them, delivered by the poison of the attack. Those scraps spread flames to others, burning away swaths, leaving a wordless bleakness or an empty dissonant tone in their wake.

She saved what she could but lost more with each wail of the huge bat.

Unfortunately, it wasn't just the horde-mind that she had needed to protect.

With Kalyx's first maddening scream, she had severed the connections of the raash'ke inside the dome to the horde-mind, trying to protect them. But she had known it wouldn't last. Fearing the worst, she had wanted them grounded somewhere safe before their minds were attacked, too.

She stared around, knowing she had failed here, too.

Bodies plummeted all around the dome, swinging wildly on wingtips or crumpling into hard crashes.

Under her, Metyl fought, sustained for now by a shield of bridle-song. She watched Daal lose Nyfka, saw him spiraling steeply. She risked all to save him, urging her mount to dive after him, to try to grab Daal from Nyfka's back.

But the *screams* were not Kalyx's sole weapon.

A sweep of shadow was the only warning. Kalyx dove upon the only threat still in the air. Nyx responded instinctively, kneeing Metyl into a hard turn. But she failed yet again.

Claws hooked her mount's upper wing and thrashed his body hard, ripping leather and breaking bone. Nyx was tossed from her saddle. She tumbled through the air. Her vision reduced to flashes: the spread of a smoky floor, the shatter of crystal, the curve of quaking bronze. She caught sight of Metyl cartwheeling down, blood spraying from him. Then she spun toward a shield of curved crystal, inscribed with arcane copper.

*No, no, no . . .*

She struck the side of the *turubya*'s orb and skated down on her belly. Her fingers clawed but found no purchase. She slid off the curve and back into the air. One of the bronze suspension arches rose before her. She flung her arms high, struggling to catch herself.

And lost that battle, too.

She plummeted down the center of the shaft beneath the sphere.

And fell forever into darkness.

# 92

KANTHE WOKE INTO a blinding brightness. He sputtered from the splash of frigid water. Acid again burned under his nose. He coughed and thrashed his head, struggling for the comforting oblivion of darkness.

Loud booms, one after the other, shook through him.

"Get him up," a harsh voice demanded. "He's slept long enough."

Another dunk of cold water shook him the rest of the way. He sat on the planks of a ship—the *Hyperium*. He blinked his memory and vision back into focus. A growing pain sharpened his awareness, but he could not shake the fogginess in his head. His tongue felt thick and slow.

"How much poppy's milk did you give him?"

"You wanted him up enough to move, Lord Prince. I did apply a numbing balm, so as not to have to use a heavier draught. His head and senses should clear soon."

"It had better. We have only a short reprieve before we attack Kysalimri."

Kanthe blinked his brother into focus.

*I thought I'd dreamed this.*

He gazed past Mikaen's shoulder. The skies were heavy with smoke. Fires hung in the air like lanterns, marking the flaming wreckage of warcraft of every size. One fell past his view, trailing flames, going slow, as if to reveal the fiery destruction in all its glory. He saw the Klashean flag draped behind it as it sank out of view.

*Am I still dreaming?*

The booming grew louder with his awareness, thudding his chest. Cannon fire. And close. He turned his eyes and spotted the distant sprawl of the Eternal City of Kysalimri, climbing out of the Bay of the Blessed. A defensive cordon of Klashean ships still plied the skies over there, forges blazing through the haze, as thick as a swarm of fireflits.

Closer at hand, two Hálendiian warships floated, one farther out than the other, looking like grim twins.

Kanthe's twin leaned closer to his face. "Get up," Mikaen ordered, giving his cheek a stinging slap. "You're awake enough."

Hands hauled him to his feet. Someone grabbed him by his left arm, flaring a lance of pain. He shifted away and stared down at the offending arm—only it wasn't there.

Or at least, *half* wasn't.

He backed again, not from pain, but from the impossibility. It felt as if his limb were still intact. It ached like it was there. The shock woke him the rest of the way. Memory tumbled together, first in disorder, then into some semblance of sense.

*The abduction, the fight, the brutal conclusion . . .*

His stump had been seared just below the elbow. It was swollen and blackened, bruised to his shoulder. Blood seeped in slow drops.

He took another step back—into the hulk of Captain Thoryn. The Vyrllian knight took hold of his good arm, squeezing hard.

He leaned to Kanthe's ear and whispered with an exhausted sadness, "Brave face, Lord Prince. It will be over soon. You will not wake when he takes your other arm. This I swear. Too much milk of the poppy and you will find your peace."

Thoryn pushed a long-hafted ax into Kanthe's numb fingers and guided him forward to stand again within a circle of crimson-faced guardsmen. Thoryn gave a final squeeze, cementing that promise of release.

Across the way, Mikaen pushed through his guards. He hefted a matching ax and lifted it higher. "Fitting that our second sparring should be with such a weapon. One that stole my face due to a cowardly act. Let us see how a fair fight ends."

Dazed and addled, his missing arm throbbing, Kanthe mocked such a word. "*Fair?* This? Who is the coward now?"

Mikaen motioned with his ax to the bay. "We strike for Kysalimri with the next bell. I want to watch our Hammer fall and crush the city. To watch it burn like our Shield Islands. And we'll follow that with the drop of *two* Cauldrons to further pound them flat."

Kanthe stared past the wall of crimson and silver surrounding him. In the distance, the white-marble towers of Kysalimri shone brightly through the smoke, clear enough to spot a darker pall shading the tallest spires, those of the imperial palace.

He frowned, picturing Aalia and Rami.

*Did some Hálendiian ship break through the blockade earlier?*

He also noted Mikaen had mentioned only *two* Cauldrons. Kanthe knew from reports that the king's forces had left with *three*. The Klashean Wing must have destroyed one of them. Still, these other two warships had cleared Tithyn Woods to reach the Bay of the Blessed, opening the way for the *Hyperium*.

Before his abduction, Aalia had felt confident about the Klashe's chances to keep the battle to the woods. Kanthe stared at the curl of smoke from the palace towers, at the ships over the Bay of the Blessed.

*Something has gone wrong—but what?*

Mikaen pointed his ax at Kanthe. "Next time we wake you, you'll be able to see the devastation we've wrought and know the cost of treason." Mikaen lowered his brow. "Then we'll play again."

To the side, Thoryn loomed, his face grave and grim.

Kanthe lifted his ax, but it slipped from his grip and clattered to the deck.

Mikaen laughed, as if this were the finest of jests.

No one else did.

Another of the crimson-faced Vyrllian knights stepped out of line and recovered the ax. The man leaned close, hopefully to offer another path to a quick death. It was good to have options.

"You look recovered enough to me," the stranger growled.

Kanthe frowned.

"So be ready to run."

As Kanthe stared in confusion, the man's face melted into a new countenance. Still painted red, but familiar.

*Tykhan . . .*

The Sleeper of Malgard rushed with astounding speed. One hand sharpened into claws and ripped out a throat. The other hand's fingers melded into a long dagger, which was jammed into an eye. Tykhan danced across the ring of guards, delivering death quicker than an eye could follow.

Kanthe stumbled away from the carnage.

Another knight stabbed at Tykhan only to have his blade slide off metal. Bronze fingers caught the steel, snapped it in half, and stabbed the end through the shocked, open mouth of his attacker.

Still, bronze had limits.

Someone lobbed a hand-bomb that exploded at Tykhan's chest, throwing him far in a concussive blast of flames. Two more men ran forward with hand-bombs lifted.

Kanthe took a step forward—only to have a hand grab his good shoulder and spin him around. A black-cloaked figure stepped in front of him, a pipe at her lips. Though the face was wrapped, he knew who it was.

*Cassta . . .*

She fired two hard puffs. The men with the bombs took another two steps, then fell. One hand-bomb blew, tossing their bodies high.

Tykhan gained his feet as Cassta pushed Kanthe toward an open doorway. The Sleeper closed on them by the time they reached that doorway.

Kanthe glanced back across the deck. Thoryn had retreated halfway across the ship, pushing Mikaen behind him. Kanthe met Thoryn's eyes and nodded his thanks, but confirming that this was not over.

The captain dipped a chin in acknowledgment of both.

Cassta tugged Kanthe through the doorway and down steep steps.

Tykhan took the lead, scolding Cassta as he passed, "What're you doing up here? You're supposed to be down with the others."

Her answer was calm, as if they were on a stroll. "As a Rhysian, I've found it useful to be where I'm not expected."

Tykhan rubbed the scorched dent in his breastplate. "That is a wisdom I can appreciate."

FRELL HELD THE tiny version of the lampree in his hand. The beetle-shaped tool was the size of his fist. The other three sisters carried the same—though they had vanished out of sight, crossing to the cardinal points of the massive drum. He gaped at the sheer height and breadth of the Madyss Hammer. Constructed of ironwood and plated in steel, it rose seven stories and was half as wide.

Sweat slickened his palms as he worked.

Perched on a scaffolding halfway up its side, he placed his palm against the weapon's flank, imagining the infernal black alchymies inside it, the secrets of which were guarded over by a cadre of Shriven deep beneath Highmount. All Frell knew was that the materials were distilled using methods obtained from ancient tomes that dated to the Forsaken Ages.

He hated when knowledge was used to dark ends, but curiosity piqued inside him nonetheless. Of course, that would not stop him from destroying it.

He checked the compass supplied to him by Tykhan and placed the little steel beetle against the side of the tank and pressed a button on its back. Its six little draft-iron legs peeled from beneath it and jammed against the steel. Caustic alchymies leaked from their tips, melting through the metal and allowing the jointed legs to slip through and latch deep into the ironwood and thick plating.

Frell stepped away.

Small wings opened on the beetle's back, revealing a crystal core that swirled with a mix of oil so black it looked like a pinch of the void between stars and a silver so bright it stung to look at. With each revolution of that mixture, the black grew and the silver faded. Tykhan had told him that when it turned solid black, it would explode with the force of a dozen cannons. This beetle and the other three—coordinating in some arcane fashion—would create a simultaneous blast, with enough force to ignite the Hammer.

Frell leaned closer, trying to understand this *ta'wyn* implement—another bit of craftsmanship from Tykhan's past, from the Forsaken Ages. Frell stared up at the drum, remembering how the Madyss Hammer had its roots in that same age.

*Why did history only preserve that which was most destructive?*

"You!" a voice barked behind him. "What are you doing down here?"

Startled, Frell spun around. The Rhysians were supposed to have cleared this hold. A crewman—a ship's drudge, from his oil-stained bibs and ashy face—came forward with a huge iron turnscrew in hand, a tool made for tightening the large bolts of the gasbag riggings.

Frell straightened. "Ship's alchymist second order. Completing a final inspection. Why?"

"Ah, that's all right then, innit?"

Frell nodded, waiting for the man to pass.

He pointed his nose high. "Heard half a bell ago they lopped that traitor prince's arm right off."

Frell flinched. "What?"

"You never heard?" He pantomimed with his turnscrew with a feigned strike to his left arm. "Burnt it black af'erwards. Serves the sodder right. That's what I say."

Frell stared up fearfully, taking a step forward. "Is he still alive?"

The crewman shrugged, then tipped sideways, looking past Frell. "Say, what's that there?"

Still worried for Kanthe, he stepped to block the drudge's growing curiosity. He heard the whisper of soft sandals on wood as the other Rhysians returned. He pushed the crewman back, fearing the others would kill this simple, innocent man—not that the drudge wouldn't die if they were successful here, along with so many others. Still, maybe it helped assuage Frell's guilt if he could spare this man a bit more life.

"This is black alchymies," Frell warned direly. "You should not be here. That's why the hold is empty."

"Ack." He looked around worriedly. "Then I best be off."

Frell guided him away, back toward a shadowed doorway. The man disappeared as the three sisters returned.

"Who were you talking to?" one of them asked.

"No one," Frell fumbled. "Just warning off a drudge before he got any closer."

The sister looked suspicious, stepping toward the door, but another waved her off as a ship's bell sounded the lateness of the night. "Tykhan should be headed back to the lampree. We have no time to spare."

The sister nodded her grudging agreement.

They set off for their ship.

Frell glanced at the levels of scaffolding below, down to the curve of the hull's bottom. "Were you able to jam those doors?" he asked.

One of the sisters gave him a scolding look for questioning their competence.

Frell cast his gaze higher, picturing the many hundreds who made this floating city their home. Still, he understood the necessity.

*Better these hundreds should die than the thousands if this bomb reaches Kysalimri.*

They hurried out of the cavernous hold and down to an abandoned section of bilge. Saekl stepped into view at the sound of their approach. She uncovered a lantern to guide them the last of the way to the small hole cut through the hull by the lampree's ring of jagged teeth. Those sharp edges protruded into bilge, as did the hooked legs that latched the ship to the lower hull.

"Inside," Saekl hissed, responding to the sound of boots pounding from the other direction.

Frell ducked and squirmed through a hole the size of a wine barrel's lid. His robe's edge caught on one of those sharp teeth. He pictured the ring of them spinning and burring this hole and yanked himself free.

The sisters entered with far more grace and alacrity.

Saekl greeted the others arriving outside. "Hurry."

"Help us get him inside," Tykhan said.

Kanthe's head and torso wiggled through the hole. His face was pained, feverish, his dark hair plastered to his pale skin. The sisters helped him, as did Cassta, who climbed in after him. Tykhan and Saekl followed and shifted to the seats at the front. One of the sisters pulled a hinged door over the hole.

"Get ready!" Saekl called back.

Beyond the window, another fiery ship fell past the *Hyperium*'s bow.

Kanthe groaned as he was strapped into one of the seats. Frell winced at the savage wound, blistered and blackened, seeping blood. The drudge had not been mistaken about the cruel damage done to the prince.

Kanthe blearily noted Frell's attention. "Seems my brother and I are determined to whittle each other down piece by piece." He let his head fall back to the seat. "I took his face, and he took my arm. Not sure who got the worst of it so far."

Then they were off.

The lampree's legs retracted and the tiny craft fell away from the lower hull. A moment later, the forge ignited, and they blasted away from the *Hyperium*. Saekl aimed them toward the northern forests of Tithyn Woods. The path to Kysalimri remained too dangerous, guarded over by two Hálendiian warships and, farther ahead, the Klashean blockade.

They sped as fast as their little craft could manage.

"Get us as far away as possible," Tykhan warned. "No one's witnessed the force of a Madyss Hammer that size. When the *Hyperium* blows, we don't want to be anywhere near here."

Kanthe lifted his head, his eyes pinched with confusion and concern. "What . . . the ship's going to explode?"

Frell explained, "We lit the fuse on the Hammer and locked it in its hold."

"What?" Kanthe twisted, staring out the tiny window at the back. "But my brother . . ."

Frell saw the pain squeeze Kanthe's face. Even after all of this, the prince still could not let go of some hope for Mikaen, some future redemption where amends could be made and a brotherhood regained.

"I'm sorry," Frell said. "It's either him . . . or lose most of Kysalimri."

MIKAEN RAGED ACROSS the wide deck, ignoring the seven bodies of his Silvergard, all torn by some daemon or witchery tied to his brother. Terror still fired through him, which only made him more furious.

Thoryn paced with him as he circled the carnage.

Liege General Reddak stood in the midst of the bodies. He had been drawn from the *Hyperium*'s wheelhouse, come to see if what had been told to him was true. "Where have they gone?" he challenged his second-in-command.

"We're still searching," Master Ketill answered crisply. "Someone spotted a strange craft jettisoning away from our starboard flank. It vanished into the smoke. It could've been them."

Mikaen lunged closer. "Then we must go after them."

Reddak ignored him, turning a shoulder and continuing to address his second-in-command. "No matter, Master Ketill. We stay the course. Alert the *Vengeance* and the *Wraith* to forge ahead. We'll break through the Klashean cordon and exact our revenge upon their shores." He set off across the deck. "Then we'll head home."

Mikaen pursued him, shaking off a restraining hand from Thoryn. "Lend me a ship, and I'll go after my brother."

"A fool's errand," Reddak scolded. "We don't know if Prince Kanthe was even aboard that craft. And even if so, they're already well lost. I've allowed you your petty, malicious fun, but no more. We have a battle to finish."

Mikaen clenched his fists, ready to argue.

Before he could, a trio of crewmen came running up with wild eyes and flushed faces.

"What is it?" Master Ketill asked curtly.

Panic stammered them until one caught his voice. "A drudge, sir. Showed the armory brigade. Some strange alchymy clamped to the Hammer. Four of 'em, all glowing and vile."

Master Ketill turned to Reddak. "Sabotage?"

"It means to blow the Hammer," another stated. "That's what the lead armorist says. Can't remove 'em or smash 'em. Or it'll blow right away."

Another nodded frantically. "Bay doors jammed up, too. To trap the Hammer with us. The brigade has ordered axes to the door."

Mikaen cringed back, bumping into Thoryn.

Without hesitating, Reddak turned to his second. "Master Ketill, to the wheelhouse. Get all our forges firing. Send us straight up."

"What are you—?"

Reddak pushed one of the crewmen ahead. "Take me down there." He pointed to the other two. "Rally everyone with an ax and send them running."

Thoryn pulled Mikaen back. "We must find a ship."

Mikaen stared across the deck, picturing the daemon possessing one of his Silvergard and slaughtering the others around it. He sensed the truth and muttered it aloud.

"There's no time."

KANTHE HUNG IN his straps, chin to his chest. His left arm—both what was there and wasn't—throbbed with lances of pain. Apparently, the poppy's milk and the numbing balm had begun to wear off.

Their small ship had reached the northern coast of the bay and now crested low over the treetops of Tithyn Woods.

Frell stirred in his seat. "Something's happening with the *Hyperium*."

Kanthe turned to the scallop of a rear window.

Smoke masked most of the view across the water, but the *Hyperium* blazed inside the gloom, a bright sun in the pall—and that sun was rising.

Its scores of massive forges raged, creating a fiery gale beneath the royal flagship, driving it upward. The smoke parted enough to reveal the full majesty of its blazing glory: the triple billow of its three gasbags, the sweep of its hull, the glint of cannons and ballistas. The sculpted stallion at the prow kicked its draft-iron legs high as if trying to escape the waters, with its wings spread wide.

None of the other Hálendiian ships followed their flagship, remaining close to the bay. A flutter of movement drew Kanthe's attention back to the *Hyperium,* to the ship's keel.

"I think they got the bay doors open," Frell said.

This was made clear when the massive flagship shat out a huge drum. The flames of the *Hyperium*'s forges reflected off the tank's steel flanks, lighting its fall from that great height. It tumbled and rolled through the air.

Tykhan called from the front, noting it, too. "Someone over there's more resourceful than I thought."

The tank struck the bay, casting up a massive crown of water. Far above, the *Hyperium* continued to climb. Kanthe winced, expecting the Hammer to blow. But the bay's watery crown crashed down, and the sea swelled back over the hole of the drum's impact.

Frell frowned. "Were they able to disarm it after—"

The Bay of the Blessed lit up like a brilliant lantern, so bright it stung the eyes. Then the water welled high, as if a great sea beast were rising from the deep. The blast that followed was the thunder of all the gods' wrath into one mighty boom. The brilliance flashed brighter as the bay emptied in all directions, hollowing out in the center, down to the rock and sand of the seabed. A massive tide surged outward into a huge wave that grew higher and higher— taller than the cliffs, taller than the trees here on top, taller than the height of their tiny ship.

Saekl saw what was coming and turned their vessel's nose straight up, balancing on the flames of their forge. "Hold tight."

She shot them upward as the force of the blast struck. The ship was hit hard, as if kicked by those same thunderous gods. It spun and toppled end over end.

Kanthe caught glimpses around him.

Below, the wave churned through the forest, ripping out roots, breaking trunks, pushing a gnashing froth of timber and rock ahead of it.

Their craft spun again to show the Stone Gods being smashed off their pedestals, toppling and drowning in the sea.

Another swing revealed a huge Hálendiian warship getting struck in the stern. It slammed into the twin ahead of it. The first crushed its bow, ripping free of its draft-iron cables and tearing its balloon. It fell into the wake of the wave, caught an edge of the tide, and was ripped out of the sky by the force of the water.

The other warship fell to the front of the wave and rode it toward Kysalimri for a stretch, then toppled sideways and was spun around and around, its gasbag flailing and beaten flat.

Ahead, the Klashean ships fled out of the way, given enough warning and buffeted higher by the blast.

Another spin and he caught a glimpse of the *Hyperium* high above, rocked by the force of the detonation under it. It tipped along the edge of that concussive wave and slid north, heading for Hálendii.

A new explosion shuddered their ship and brightened the skies.

A final flip revealed its source. The wave-swept warship had struck the docks. The impact must have ignited its Cauldron. Fire and rocks and sections of pier with boats still tethered to them blasted high—then the rest of the wave drowned it all away. The surge rode up into the city but was thwarted by the first tall wall. It crashed against it and washed back.

Saekl finally got their little leaf of a ship back under control, leveling their flight. She turned them around to witness the aftermath as the wave receded back to its source.

The bay washed back and forth several more times as Saekl aimed them toward Kysalimri, passing over the wreckage of the Hammer's fall.

Kanthe despaired at the lives lost, but he knew if the Hammer had fallen upon the Eternal City that the devastation would have been a thousandfold worse. While the water of the bay had turned deadly, it had also helped insulate the blast.

A small blessing.

*I'll take even that.*


AALIA STOOD AT the window of the strategy room of the Blood'd Tower.

The spire had earned its name this night.

After surviving Mareesh's attack—a betrayal that still wounded—she had gathered all she could. With the imperium still threatened, she had no time to mourn her brother Jubayr. She would bury him with their father's cloak. It was all she could decide this night.

She had lost her Wing and her Shield—two more men she must mourn. The only respite from this misery was that Sail Garryn had survived. She had leaned heavily on him this long night. Along with Tazar, Llyra, Rami, and all others willing to offer counsel. She heeded everyone, knowing only by working together could they survive.

Their forces had managed to destroy one of the Hálendiian warships earlier in the night, but Mareesh's betrayal and his swaying of a section of the Wing to his side had weakened their line. Two more Hálendiian warships had made it through Tithyn Woods, along with the kingdom's flagship.

Still, determined to fight, she had set a hard line before the city.

Then something had happened—both miraculous and tragic.

She stared down at the ruins of the lowermost tier of the city. The bay still rocked, washing even now into the city's edge, but the worst was over.

From this window, she had watched the massive bomb drop into the bay.

She didn't understand why the *Hyperium* had discharged its weapon like that.

*Had it been a mishap? A bit of providence from a god?*

The flagship had fled afterward, leaving its shameful devastation behind. A warship's Cauldron had also exploded at the bayside piers. Yet, as devastating as that blast had been, the massive wave had dealt a far deadlier blow. The Cauldron's blast did little more than disturb what had already been destroyed.

She stared down at the wreckage.

She tried to find her fury, but all she felt was sorrow.

*Anger will come later.*

She closed her eyes, but she knew she could delay it no longer. She took a deep breath and cast her gaze farther across the bay. Half, if not more, of the Stone Gods lay toppled and broken. She spotted the raised arm of one, thrust crookedly out of the water, as if drowning and begging for help.

With a wince, she moved her attention to the north, to the town of X'or. The wave had swept as high as those cliffs and washed across the top, but not as fiercely. Lanterns still shone from those heights, sparking some hope of survivors. She had dispatched skrycrows there before the first wave had fully receded.

A commotion drew her attention back to the room. It was in a shambles after the long night. Sail Garryn stood, leaning on the table, his head hanging low. Tazar stood to the side, giving her this moment alone, respecting her enough not to intrude. Others murmured in groups, still struggling with the aftermath.

Rami burst into the room with Llyra. His eyes shone brightly, his breathing hard from more than just the climb. "Word from the Paladins, from the high mooring of the palace."

Aalia clutched hard to her hope.

"Prince Kanthe and the Augury . . . they've arrived just now."

She let out her breath and smiled, though it felt strained. She gazed out the window again, wondering if the two had an explanation for what had happened out there.

She was relieved they were both safe, but that was not the hope she held closest to her heart. Footsteps rose from the other side, tentative, as if unsure to intrude.

She turned to find Chaaen Hrash standing in the doorway that led up to the skrycrow's nest above them. The shoulders of his robe were speckled with droppings. He carried a missive in hand, tight to his chest.

He read the question burning in Aalia's face. "From Abbess Shayr," he confirmed.

"So she lives." Aalia gripped her hands together. "What of my father?"

Hrash looked down. "He was being moved from the baths to the pala-cio . . . when . . . when . . ." The Chaaen lifted his face.

His tears finished the message for her.

She turned away, stepped back to the window, and let go of her last hope.

# NINETEEN

# KALYX ASCENDANT

*Nothynge ends that kenn not be reborne, iffe onli in one's heart.*

—Proverb from *The Book of El*

# 93

Nyx toppled through darkness. As she spun, she saw the sphere falling away above her and the blackness of the abyss rising toward her. The clash of steel and the scream of Kalyx chased her down. Her heart choked her throat. The plummet ripped at her breath.

She had defeated the Root and freed Shiya, only to be rewarded with the arrival of Kalyx, a beast crafted in the dark lair of the Ifelen. It had shredded the horde-mind and ripped the raash'ke out of the skies.

As if lured by this thought, a shadow swept under her, appearing out of the darkness. Wings spread wide, lit from the wan light.

Kalyx had found her.

There was no escaping it.

She hit the body under her, instinctively clutching to it. Her fingers scrabbled into fur, for anything tangible in the plunging darkness. Her chest struck a warm back, earning a panicked keening under her. She knew that song anywhere.

It wasn't Kalyx.

*Bashaliia . . .*

She clutched harder as he fought to slow her fall, his wings striking hard, battering wildly. But he was far too small to carry her weight, let alone fly her out. Still, he slowed her dive, braking slightly, pushing her more firmly into him.

As he trilled his distress, his bridle-song reverberated off the walls and back to her, revealing what the darkness hid. She caught flashes of the rushing walls and understood his intent.

*No, Bashaliia, no . . .*

The walls of the pit were covered in a scaffolding of ladders and wider footways. Bashaliia fought her weight and wafted side to side, beating his wings hard to slow her down even more. But he reached his limit, incapable of braking any further.

He angled to the wall and swept toward the only perch.

Together, they struck one of the platforms. The impact tossed her hard, slamming her hip and skull into the wall. She heard bones break. She slid down to the footway, tangled with Bashaliia. He flapped and keened, trilling in pain.

She crawled off him, climbing blindly past his head. Only a trickle of light reached this far. The huge opening far overhead was no larger than her palm. As she cleared him, she sprawled across the platform. Her left leg was a lance of fire. She felt down its length to the jabbing knot and flare of pain in her shinbone.

Broken.

But it wasn't only her bone that had fractured. Even in the feeble light, she could tell Bashaliia's wing had crumpled upon impact. It lay crushed under him. His hollow bones were even more fragile than hers.

"Bashaliia, you shouldn't have come."

He mewled and nudged her with his nose, burrowing under her hand, needing her comfort. She could never refuse him. She rubbed his ear, softly singing her reassurance, though she could not put much heart into it. Still, slowly, the worst of his crying subsided—due less to her gift and more to her touch.

"Why did you come?" she whispered.

Still, she took comfort from his presence.

*At least we're together.*

She left her other question unvoiced.

*How did you get here?*

She knew he must have fled the *Sparrowhawk* when it was attacked, coming down with the last of the raash'ke. But she struggled to understand *how* he was still in the air, able to fly, to even attempt this futile rescue.

She pictured the raash'ke falling out of the sky.

Then she understood.

*Because you're not raash'ke.*

Bashaliia had never been part of the horde-mind. Even now, she could feel the remains of that ancient presence at the back of her awareness, as fractured and wounded as they were. Whatever vibration that Kalyx had divined from ripping into the horde-mind had been unique to raash'ke, drawn from their commonality—a commonality not shared with Nyx's little brother.

Bashaliia was a Mýr bat, and in the dome's storm of wings, Kalyx must have missed his presence within the greater flock.

Still, such providence had proven little good. It left both Nyx and Bashaliia broken and stranded. Even if she had both legs, she could never climb out of this pit, not in time to stop what was coming.

*I would need wings myself.*

Then she knew the answer.

*   *   *

GRAYLIN FOUGHT TO drag Daal's body to the shelter of the tunnel.

"Grab his legs," he urged Jace.

Shouldering his ax, Jace swung around and grabbed Daal's ankles.

Together, they worked through the smoke, sticking to the densest cover. Daal had struck his head hard, knocking himself limp, but his limbs moved weakly, and he still breathed.

*When he should be dead.*

There was only one reason he wasn't.

Graylin stared through the smoke, toward the remains of Daal's mount. Whether due to the vagaries of the winds—or some protective sense still buried deep in Nyfka—the raash'ke had shoved higher at the last moment, blunting the steep dive and cushioning the impact with her own body. Nyfka had saved Daal's life.

Graylin would always believe that.

And it wasn't just her death that helped them.

As the raash'ke had plummeted out of the sky, two had crashed into the party of Hálendiian raiders who had been hounding Graylin's group. He and the others were close to being overwhelmed. Darant had lost one of his men during the last skirmish. They were all bloodied and could barely lift their weapons. Then death rained out of the sky. Sheltered in the tunnel's mouth, his group was spared. The Hálendiians—just outside the threshold—were crushed under bone and leather. Those that weren't killed scattered. A handful had run off into the smoke. The wisest among them—fearing further rain might fall—had fought past Graylin's group and fled down the tunnel, led by Commander Ghryss.

Darant, Perde, and Vikas had chased after them.

At that same time, Graylin had seen Daal crash, but he had lost sight of Nyx. Dreading the worst, he had grabbed Jace to help rescue Daal and search for any sign of Nyx. He succeeded with the first, but not the latter. He could only pray that Daal knew where she might have fallen.

They reached the tunnel and moved down it, but Graylin refused to go too far, knowing Nyx must be out there somewhere.

Jace knelt next to Daal, who was propped up against the wall. Daal murmured and swiped his arms, slowly coming around.

Jace looked out into the dome. "What about Krysh and Rhaif?"

"I spotted them huddled by Shiya's cocoon."

Jace stared with concern, plainly worried, too—and not just for Nyx. "I caught a few glimpses of the huge sphere. It's still quaking, but not any worse. Maybe Shiya is making headway at reining in the damage."

Graylin nodded. "We can only hope."

Daal finally stirred enough to grow panicked. He battered wildly while Jace tried to console and calm him. Finally, he shoved Jace away.

"I'm all right." His gaze swept between the two of them. "Where's Nyx?"

"We hoped you knew," Graylin answered with a sinking sense of defeat.

Daal shook his head, his eyes widening with fear.

Before Graylin could question him further, an agonized scream rose from deeper down the tunnel, rife with pain and terror, echoing louder as it reached them.

They all looked at each other, but they were not the only ones to hear that cry.

It drew down a monster.

Winds slammed into them as a huge shadow swept to the threshold, landing outside the tunnel. With black wings held wide and head low, the bat screamed at the three inside—then stalked toward them.

NYX CLUTCHED HER belt knife in both hands. She leaned her head against the wall and stared up at the distant light. She prayed to all the gods. She squeezed her heart, trying to find the will.

*Don't make me do this.*

She closed her eyes and gathered all the strength that was in her. She stared down into the black abyss inside her, trying to hold the gaze of that cold, implacable eye. She would need to be that steely.

*Don't make me do this.*

She drew all the fire that Daal had left her, meager though it was. She drew it to her heart, sang it brighter.

*Don't make me do this.*

She reached out to the frayed remains of the horde-mind and shared what she knew, what she remembered. It needed to understand. Part of her wished it would not, but it did. The raash'ke and Mýr had diverged down different paths, but at their core, they were much the same, communal and eternal. She asked the horde-mind to help her, to show her what she needed to do. She wanted it to refuse. It did not.

*Don't make me do this.*

She huddled over Daal's fire and stirred it with as much song as she could muster. Bashaliia tried to join her, keening in harmony, but she closed him off. This was a song he could not share—not if her efforts had any chance of working.

*Don't make me do this.*

The horde-mind watched with the immensity of ages, waiting, ready.

*Don't make me do this.*

But she had done it before.

Before she could balk, she swung to the side, rolled Bashaliia's head over, and plunged her knife deep into his throat. This was not the merciful sting of before, where she had cradled the small spark of Bashaliia and delivered him to the greater Mýr.

This was a merciless slaughter.

She dug deep with her blade and tore through tissue. Hot blood washed over her hands. Bashaliia cried and mewled, wings battered weakly, wanting to escape but still not wanting to leave her side. She clung all the harder. His whimpers begged for forgiveness, not understanding.

She could not comfort him with song, to blur her edges with him. For this to work, he must be isolated, to remain his pure self.

She sobbed and rocked but drove her knife deeper. She sought the coldness of bronze that could snap a neck, the stoniness of a warrior that could slay the innocent.

Finally, soaked in his blood, shaking all over, she felt his fighting stop. His wings sank down. His keening for forgiveness faded to a plaintive whisper—then went silent.

She reached a palm over his heart, as pure as it had ever been.

Then it stopped.

She leaned back and screamed her song at the world. She wound a bright net and cast it over Bashaliia's body. It covered every sweet bit of him. She drew it tighter as she sang her pain, collecting all that was Bashaliia within those golden strands.

She kept tightening and tightening it, gathering all of him: his love, his innocence, his irritability, his hunger, his fears, his habits, his dreams, every mote of his vital essence.

As she did, the spark of Bashaliia grew into the golden blaze of a summer sun. Still, she closed her net tighter, straining with song and fire to hold him close. The sun became a hard star, ageless and perfect. She wanted to gaze upon it forever—but inside, she handed it to another.

An act every bit as hard as the slaughter.

To let him go, to trust in another.

The horde-mind drew that star into its black ancientness, covering him completely, eclipsing his beauty. Being raash'ke, it could not merge its consciousness with Bashaliia. It was why Nyx had to pull Bashaliia out, pure and unadulterated, separate from herself, untouched even by the bridle-song they shared.

But while that ancientness couldn't *absorb* Bashaliia, it could *hold* him.

She whispered to that eternal spirit, knowing what she was asking of it.

It did not deny her.

*Take me.*


DAAL STRUGGLED TO help, but Jace pushed him back behind his shoulders.

Ahead, the huge bat shoved into the tunnel, screaming in defiant madness. Emerald fire danced and spat through bright copper imbedded in steel and skull. Fangs slashed the air, flinging saliva and poison. It hissed and slavered. Its eyes were pools of fire.

The sight of that emerald fire sickened Daal's stomach. It was corruption and rot and pestilence. It was depravity and enslavement, too. It was everything vile in the world turned to fire.

Impossibly, Graylin stood against it, perhaps only seeing the beast and not the perversion that fueled it. The knight raised his sword, its length etched in vines that ran with blood. He stabbed and slashed, fighting hard. His blade rang off the beast's steel helm.

The monster snapped and spat and screamed.

Graylin retreated, but exhaustion tripped his feet. He landed hard, hit his elbow. His hilt knocked from his grip, skittering and bouncing between the wingtips of the monster.

The bat lunged at its stubborn prey.

Then stopped—so close that its huffed breath blew back Graylin's hair.

The monster looked over its shoulder toward the dome, as if hearing the whistle of its master. The bat turned and screamed out into it.

Under the cover of that cry, Graylin scooted on his bottom, sliding between those wings. He snatched up his blade. The monster's chest loomed high. Grayling grabbed the hilt with both hands and braced a leg under him, ready to thrust for the bat's heart.

"Finally," Jace gasped.

Daal wanted satisfaction, too, picturing the raash'ke plummeting through the air. While he knew the bat was enslaved, it was better to end its misery. Daal glared at the corrupting fire—only to have the helm's fiery crown flicker, going golden for a breath.

Still, for that moment, he heard a distant chime of song.

But it was enough.

He lunged past Jace and leaped through the air as Graylin thrust for a heart, one that still had hope.


* * *

AFTER ABANDONING HER body in the darkness below, Nyx rode the corona of energy surrounding the raash'ke horde-mind. It was a golden fire around a black sun. And even deeper, hidden in that darkness, a brilliant white star shone.

The horde-mind carried her out of the endless pit and across the dome. Ahead, Kalyx crouched, half tucked into a tunnel. Emerald fire lashed and crackled across its body and wings. Its steel helm shone with a malevolent pyre.

She balked at the sight. It looked far more menacing in this ethereal plane. Still, she urged the horde-mind closer. As they flew toward the bat, Nyx drew that corona of fire to her, lifting it about her body, exposing the ancient blackness below, a lure for a daemon that had not yet been sated.

Kalyx swung his head around, drawn by the rawness of the horde-mind, sensing all that had escaped it before. A savage scream burst from its throat. The power behind it was a menacing gale.

Before, Nyx had used her bridle-song to protect the horde-mind. But she did not now. Instead, she held that corona of fire to herself, a power that was not even her own. It came from the ancient darkness under her. The horde-mind had left itself defenseless, offering one last sacrifice, to atone for the millennia of horror and terror it had afflicted.

Kalyx's scream struck the horde-mind hard, peeling it away, burning memory and guilt and joy into nothingness. Nyx pictured the Root being stripped of its bronze, revealing its shining heart.

This was the same.

As the horde-mind let itself be consumed, a white star was revealed. Focused fully on destruction, enslaved to one purpose, Kalyx failed to react to something so pure—or perhaps some buried part of it remembered this shining piece of itself, a brother from the Mýr.

Either way, Nyx only needed this moment of distraction.

She gathered all the power given to her by the horde-mind and dove upon that white star. She lifted it and carried it along with her tide. She used every scintillation of strength to push under Kalyx's steel helm. She drove hard into a skull full of madness and emerald fire and planted a white star at its heart.

Once there, she sang a single small thread, as thin as a hope, and touched that star.

Her song was a simple plea.

*Come back to me.*

The star exploded, releasing Bashaliia in all his beauty and purity. Nyx was thrown back in a wash of golden fire. Emerald flames were snuffed against bone. As she fell away, she watched Kalyx be burned out of his skull, released at last from his torture, leaving an empty shell behind for Bashaliia to fill.

Nyx dropped again into a bottomless well of blackness.

But she felt no despair this time.

Only hope.

*Come back to me.*

GRAYLIN STABBED UPWARD with all the force of his legs. The steel of Hearts-thorn sliced high. Its tip pierced through the fur and skin—then Graylin was struck from behind. He sprawled flat, striking his chin hard. His sword flew even farther.

He elbowed hard and rolled upon his attacker.

Daal gasped under him. "Don't."

Jace came running up, his Guld'guhlian ax raised high, a bellow on his lips. He swung for the neck of the monster.

Graylin saw something in Daal's eyes, an urgency, a hope.

With a curse, Graylin shoved up and tackled Jace in the midsection, driving them both back. Jace gasped, the wind knocked out of him. Graylin held him by the shoulders. He stared back, praying he hadn't misplaced his trust.

Daal still lay under the beast.

Drops of blood from the sword wound spattered Daal's face in a macabre baptism. Then the monster leaped with a great beat of its wings and sailed low across the dome. They all followed it out.

"Why?" Graylin asked Daal, with many questions buried in that one word.

Daal didn't answer.

The bat flew high, turned on a wing, and dove down. It looked like it was going to smash into the huge sphere, but it skirted to the side and vanished down the hole under it.

Graylin turned to Daal and repeated the question silently.

Daal answered this time.

"Hope."

NYX FELL BACK into her own body and hugged herself. She was soaked in blood. Her broken shin throbbed with every inhale. She stared over at Bashaliia's body, still warm but silent forever.

She reached to him anyway. She ran a fingertip down the bristly pinna of his ear, remembering all the whispers she had shared. She rubbed the velvet around his nose, fixing all the soft comfort it had given her. She slid a palm over his heart and rested it there.

Though Bashaliia was not here, this body was a map of her memories. She wanted to read it for as long as she could.

But another demanded her attention.

She still retained a small pyre of golden fire, all that was left of the life and verve of the raash'ke past. Yet, that was not all. Over that fire, a shred of blackness fluttered, the smoke from the ancient past—but it was fading fast.

She sang to it, sensing it fought to remain for a moment longer. She wove golden strands and brushed them gently against that shred of ancientness. She expressed her thanks. The mind answered with a gratefulness of its own. For this release. For allowing some measure of atonement and grace.

She also sensed a promise. That this wasn't truly the *end*.

For the past, yes.

But not the future.

The ancientness stirred a memory out of her, one given to her by the *Osh-kapeers.*

*—overhead, more raash'ke ply the skies. Others hop along streets or perch on walls. Children play among them, especially with the smallest of the beasts.*

She understood. The raash'ke could build a *new* horde-mind, one free of stain and guilt, to be pure again. To return to what they once were, what they were always meant to be.

She hoped that would come to pass, but she feared it would not. How could it? As always, that awful vision of a mountaintop rose up. She tried to force it away. She didn't mean to taint this last moment, this final farewell.

The smoke of ancientness—just a haze now—heard her fear of what was to come. From that smoke, she felt pity and sorrow, yet still an underlying grate-fulness. Then just as the smoke dissolved to nothingness—a final surge passed through her. She gasped, recognizing the bright burn of it. From her time with the Dreamers. It was a branding, an ingraining into her as firmly as the fiery map of the Fangs.

It was also a terror.

She recognized what had been burned into her.

As that ancientness released fully, it left behind a single word, a correction, firm and assured.

**Gift.**

Then it was gone forever.

Nyx sat quietly, trembling in the darkness, still fearful of that final gift.

Before she could find some peace with it, an urgent keening reached her.

Hope surged through her.

With her good leg, she pushed her back up the wall and balanced there.

Above, a huge shadow swept back and forth across the distant moon of the crystal orb. Wings swept wide, slightly unsteady as Bashaliia struggled with his new form. He trilled his confusion and disorientation.

She lifted her arms and cast out ribbons of golden song, reassuring and welcoming. She repeated her last words to him, both in melody and voice.

"Come back to me."

He swept to her level, overshot, then with a single beat of his wings pulled abreast of her. He tried to join her on the footpath, but there was barely room. She hopped to the side, buffeted by his wings. She grabbed the rung of a ladder to hold herself steady.

Bashaliia fought to perch next to her, but he struggled to get his claws in place. Then a talon reached, snagged his old body, and rolled it off the footway to make room. She gasped and reached for it, but then pulled back. She had said as much of a good-bye as she could.

She stared up at Bashaliia as he finally landed and folded his wings. He rocked in place, like he always did when happy or nervous or both. It was still Bashaliia in there. She suspected she would have to keep reminding herself of that.

Before, the top of his head had barely reached her nose. Now that steel-helmed crown was so high. She would have to reach her arm up to scratch his chin. He cocked his head, as if testing the weight of that steel. He keened in distress.

She reached a hand to his heart, then shifted her palm higher.

*He is so much taller.*

She sang a promise, adding words to cement it. "We'll get that off you."

*And those copper needles out of you.*

He rocked on his legs, this time clearly nervous. He stared with one eye, then the other, down at the blood, at the knife still on the platform. He whined in his throat, a note of apology, asking even now for forgiveness, believing he had done something wrong.

"No, my sweet boy." She reached to him, still balancing on one leg, hiding the wince of pain so as not to scare him. "You are perfect."

He leaned his head down. She hooked her arms around his neck and pressed into him. He smelled rank from his abuse, a reek of excrement from a poorly kept pen, the burn of punishment. She felt the scars around his neck from chains and steel collars. She felt the reflexive tremor from a body that had seen too much torture.

*I'm sorry this is the body I had to give you.*

He pushed into her, needing more reassurance, nearly knocking her off the platform with his strength. She clung tighter. She closed her eyes and sang to him. She used the fire left inside her to warm a glow. She let it suffuse into his frightened heart, to let him know he was loved. He slowly joined her, a soft keening, rocking again, but more with contentment. She layered on harmonies that were both memories and promises. She infused her sorrow and shame for what she had done to him, asking for his forgiveness.

He keened back his trust.

She pressed her brow to his chest.

"Thank you . . ."

She straightened and rubbed ears that were too tall. She felt the snuffle of velvet at her neck. Such touches, more than their shared glow, drew them closer. They sang together until his heart lost its panic, allowing him to start to find his center again in this new body.

Then lightning struck them both.

Bonded in that moment, she felt the rip of emerald fire. Flames burned the inside of his skull, seeking to dominate and enslave. Madness frilled the edges, ready to rip away sanity, leaving only mindless control.

Nyx gasped and stared up.

*No.*

Jagged bolts of energy chased down the pit, striking walls and ricocheting off them. They struck the steel helm and frazzled across the top, demanding submission.

Bashaliia screamed, toppling off the platform.

She leaped out and onto his back. She snagged fistfuls of scruff at the base of his neck and clung there as he fluttered and fought to regain himself. She never let her song drop, protecting Bashaliia, refusing to let him go.

She drove her fire into his skull. He remained too fragile to fight on his own, to resist the torture that demanded obedience. Instead, she siphoned that pain and madness into herself, stripping it from her winged brother.

Bashaliia recovered enough to draw level, to catch her under him.

She stared up, full of rage, edged by madness, rife with fire both golden and emerald. She took a breath and screamed one word, one command, one promise.

**Never.**

DAAL CRINGED AS a new storm erupted inside the dome. It came from the enemy barge above. Lightning cascaded through the dome's door, dazzling with its malignancy. It chained and laddered across the crystal walls. It sparked with furious emerald flashes. It balled into malevolent shimmering fogs that shot wildly.

Still, Daal could read the pattern.

"It's searching," he whispered.

A scatter of bolts spun and danced over the sphere, then chased down the hole.

Where the beast had vanished.

Graylin stood next to him, Jace on his other side.

"Searching for what?" Jace asked. "For Nyx?"

Daal shook his head. "I think for the winged monster."

As if called forth by his words, a huge shadow burst from beyond the orb. Black wings tipped and swept a wide arc through the dome. Drawn by its passage through the air, fire and lightning lashed out at the bat, striking from every direction. The fires became so fierce that the beast was lost in those flames.

Then it burst free again, trailing fire.

Daal squinted, expecting that energy to be focused on the bat's steel helm, forming a fiery crown. While a few sparks still danced there, most of the bolts glanced off the helm and hit the figure clinging on its back, ducked close. It was as if the rider were drawing that inimical energy, bearing the brunt of the assault.

In all the dazzle and distance, Daal could not discern who rode that monster, but he knew who it was. The slight golden glow about her shoulders left no doubt.

Terror and worry flared through him.

No one could withstand such an attack.

Not even Nyx.

RIDING ON A column of fire, Nyx clawed her fingers into Bashaliia's fur. She twisted both wrists, wrapping harder. She clung with her knees as best she could. Her broken shin shot lances of pain into her hip, but she burned away the worst of the pain.

As she shot across the dome, emerald energies filled the air, swelled her lungs, and traveled over her skin. The dark abyss inside her howled at that power. She denied it, refusing its demand, intending to hold out for as long as possible.

Instead, she focused on the two golden reins of bridle-song, shimmering cords that ran from her shoulders to the steel helm. She tied the ends to the copper needles, securing them there.

With each strike to that steel, she siphoned fire away from Bashaliia. While she could not keep all that dread energy from him, hopefully it was enough. Ducked low into his warmth, merged into his glow, she willed him confidence and infused into him the memory of ancient raash'ke riders to help him carry her, but mostly she just kept him protected.

All the while, a scream built silently inside her.

It, too, was a *song*.

She built that new melody, a darker, scathing ballad of madness and power. She fed it that emerald fire, to keep it from the dark abyss, to keep her sanity.

She rode up that fiery green tide, higher and higher, the scream of madness building with every beat of Bashaliia's wings. They reached the top and shot out of the dome's door. Bashaliia banked away from the keel of the barge and swung wide. They left the warm chimney of air and sped out into the frigid, endless night.

The air was ice, each breath a labor, but she burned with inner fire. She rode out until frost and ice coated her and the emerald flames could no longer reach her. Only then did she swing around. High above the barge, she hung with Bashaliia in the air, free and raging with power.

The barge faced them, its windows glinting. Its forges burned in the darkness but drew no closer.

Nyx gathered that scream of madness, scintillating with emerald fire. She used the cold and ice to help her temper those flames. But it was like taming a wildfire. She felt those corrupting flames burning her edges, eating into her.

Bashaliia was also not unscathed or untouched. Bonded with her brother, she felt a savagery that was never a part of him. He shivered with rage under her.

She knew she could not hold this scream in any longer or she would risk them both. She tightened her knees and shifted her weight forward. Bashaliia responded and tipped into a steep dive. She let him fly, not guiding any longer, only riding.

She needed all her concentration to bind that scream, to forge it into a weapon. The sigil of a bright brand burned in the back of her mind, gifted to her by the horde-mind. It was as much a map as the path through the icy Fangs—but this chart was one of ancient fire and control. She wanted to deny it, to will it away, knowing what it portended.

She flashed to a mountaintop with a red moon falling.

*So be it.*

She reached a tendril of golden fire, frosted with emerald corruption and fueled by the last energies of an ancient mind—and touched the burning sigil.

It ignited as she reached the barge.

She gave herself fully to the map of that brand, letting her body follow the code written inside her. The method, the words, a flow of power beyond her understanding.

Bashaliia dove below the height of the barge, then streaked high again in front of it. He heaved to a sudden stop with a swoop of his huge wings. Ice broke from their tips in a glittering cascade. The sudden halt threw her high off his back into the air, lifting her before the windows of the barge.

Ancient words, written in fire, burst from her lips. She swung her arms high, breaking ice from her body. Her hands clapped above her—the first note of a dreadful song.

She opened herself and screamed into the frigid night. A song of hatred and fury and madness. She had already hardened her power into a weapon, but the ancient sigil inside her turned power into *purpose*.

She stated it loudly, repeating her earlier promise, giving it form and substance.

**Never.**

Her scream struck the barge—and crashed into it. Boards exploded. Draft-iron cables ripped from tethers. The entire barge split in half before her, shattered by her scream, by her power, by the gift of an ancientness that sought redemption.

Below her, Bashaliia screamed, too, lunging higher, neck extended. While they were still bridled together, a fraction of her force blasted out of him. As it did, the steel helm ripped from his skull, spinning and glinting under the starlight into the night.

She smiled coldly, refining her promise.

*Never again.*

She gazed with lowered brows at the ruins of the barge and gave one last surge as she began to fall, casting the last of the fire out of her.

Even empty, she wanted this to never stop.

At the back of her mind, a black abyss wailed the same desire.

She drove her madness through to the barge's forges and ignited their potency with her fury. The explosion was a flaming sun in the dark night.

She savored the destruction.

Then she felt the heat of the blast washing over her. With it came a backlash of fiery madness, striking her at her weakest. She could not stop the storm from filling her, blinding her, spreading to all her now empty places—even down into her dark abyss.

Her head lolled backward as she fell through the night, limp and lost, plummeting into darkness.

Somewhere over the ice, Bashaliia keened and screamed.

She recognized that wail of despair.

The madness had found him, too.

## 94

**DEEP IN THE** Shrivenkeep, Wryth leaned next to Shrive Keres. Before them, the crystal globe of the listening device glowed. A small red blip blinked in stuttering starts and stops, sharing Skerren's message.

The two had been following the details of a battle at a coppery structure deep in the Wastes. Wryth's hands were tight fists. Tension thinned his lips to hard lines. Skerren's forces had invaded a dome and discovered the enemy. More of the infernal bats plagued their efforts—until Skerren dispatched Kalyx.

Wryth had spent months destroying the will of the imprisoned Mýr bat, employing a fiery method developed by a fellow Iflelen—Shrive Vythaas—before the man died. The latest report from Skerren announced the success of Wryth's brutal efforts with the bat.

The enemy had been subdued.

Still, Wryth stared at the crystal globe, at the strange emanations glowing there. It was no longer just the yellow of the bronze artifact and the red of Skerren's barge. A small maelstrom of a dark coppery energy swirled at that same spot.

*Something strange is happening out there.*

While Wryth had been furious at his earlier snubbing, when he had been denied permission to join the kingdom's attack on the Southern Klashe, he now considered it a fortunate boon. He had not heard any word about the success or failure of that endeavor and did not care.

He leaned closer to that tiny swirl on the globe.

*This is all that matters.*

What other wonders might be hidden under that copper dome out in the Wastes? Could there be weapons and knowledge that would far outstrip a lone figure of bronze?

*I should be out there.*

His fists tightened with his desire.

"Another message is coming," Keres said next to him.

Wryth saw it, too. The red blip had restarted its blinking.

Keres studied it closely, not even bothering to record it. After so long, he could read those flashes and pauses as if they were words written in ink.

"What does he say?" Wryth asked.

Keres licked his lips, his brow bunched. "All he says is *She has risen.*"

"What does that mean?"

"I don't know, but he's still sending something. Let me concentrate."

Keres leaned closer to the blinking, as if that would help him draw meaning. Wryth leaned next to him. "Well?"

Keres turned as the crystal globe flared brightly—then exploded with a hint of a distant scream. Wryth felt a stab of fiery pain as he was blown back a step.

Keres fell away, too.

Wryth fingered his face, discovering the source of his agony. A shard of glass pierced his right eye, blinding him on that side. A glancing touch of a fingertip against the crystal seared pain into his skull. He gasped at the agony, at the ruin of his eye.

Keres panted hard next to him, turning his way. A huge dagger of the glass stuck out of his neck. Blood poured across his chest. His mouth opened and closed, like that of a gasping fish.

Keres turned, stumbling for help.

Wryth grabbed his shoulder. "What did Skerren say? At the end?"

Keres struggled to go, his eyes desperate.

Wryth pulled him closer, refusing to let him leave. "Tell me."

Keres mumbled as he sank to his knees, blood surging with each word uttered. Then the Shrive toppled hard to his side, the last of his life pouring over the floor.

Wryth straightened and turned away.

He stared at the wreckage of crystal, marking the end of his hopes. As if mocking him, the bronze bust glowed brighter, warmed by the explosion, as if satisfied by the sacrifice at this altar.

Wryth glared back at it. Keres's last words echoed in his head. They seemed impossible, but Wryth did not doubt them. He focused on the shattered globe, hearing again that distant scream of fury. It only firmed Wryth's conviction that Skerren's last words were true. Skerren had repeated them over and over again until the end.

*She is the* Vyk dyre Rha! *She has risen. She has risen . . .*

# 95

GRAYLIN SEARCHED THROUGH the fiery debris of the Hálendiian barge. Bodies lay among the wreckage, burned, broken, or in pieces. They had all witnessed the destruction of the ship. The splinter of its hull, the explosion of its forges. Parts of the barge had fallen through the dome's door and crashed into flaming pyres.

Daal kept alongside him as he combed through the piles. "She can't be dead."

Graylin nodded. Though it was the hundredth time that Daal had made that statement, Graylin didn't discourage the young man. It helped stoke his own hope.

Still . . .

"Where can she be?" he asked, and turned to Daal. "Are you certain it was Nyx riding that beast?"

Daal nodded, but his face looked as if he hoped he was wrong.

Graylin searched the breadth of the dome. Much of it remained smoky, hiding corners and areas he had not yet hunted.

A handful of raash'ke stirred out there. Two wafted the air, testing their bruised wings. A few more shifted through the smoke, moving like pained shadows, but they were alive. A meager five or six. Daal had told him how Nyx had been trying to get them out of the air. The survivors must be the few who had heeded Nyx's warning, sweeping lower or landing as the debilitating screams of the bat struck.

Before they moved on with their search, the pounding of boots and panting breaths drew Graylin's attention to the tunnel of a copper leg. He grabbed hold of his sword's hilt and shifted closer, ready to defend this space, remembering that a batch of Hálendiian raiders had escaped in that direction. He also recalled that agonized scream from down that tunnel, the one that had drawn the bat.

From the smoky mouth, Darant appeared, flanked by Vikas and Perde. The trio looked exhausted, bloody, and spent.

Graylin crossed to them as they surveyed the fiery destruction.

"Looks like you've been busy," Darant said, shaking blood from his hands with distaste, as if not even wanting to wipe them on his pants.

"The other Hálendiians?" Graylin pressed him. "Commander Ghryss?"

Perde answered. "Seems the bastard choked to death on a couple things. Not that they were that big, mind you, but he still couldn't quite swallow them down."

Darant shook his hands a few more times. "Can't say I'm not a man of my word."

Before Graylin could inquire any further, Jace ran up with Krysh. They both looked excited and hopeful, two emotions far from Graylin's heart at this moment.

"What is it?"

Jace nodded to loosen his tongue. "Shiya has the *turubya* calmed down. It's still shivering some, but it's already settling back to its cradle."

"Once that happens," Krysh said, "she believes she understands what she needs to do."

Despite the hope in those words, Graylin frowned. "Have her hold off for now."

Jace's enthusiasm dimmed. "Still no sign of Nyx?"

A savage cry split the dome, making them all wince and duck. Above, huge black wings carted wide. The monster had returned. The bat swept a tight arc and dove at them.

Graylin waved everyone toward the tunnel. "Get back!"

They all fled, but one member remained behind, still standing, staring up.

"It's Nyx," Daal said.

Graylin skidded to a stop and squinted up. In the claws of the monster, a body hung there, slack and lifeless. He immediately recognized Nyx. Still, his heart clutched.

*Has the bat killed her?*

The beast landed hard into the smoke. Its wings buffeted the pall aside, clearing a space around it. Nyx lay on the floor. The bat leaned over her, balanced on its wingtips. It swept its head low through the air, screaming a warning.

Blood spattered from its head, revealing the wounds there. The steel helm was gone, along with most of the copper needles. A few still glinted from its shaved scalp.

Off to the side, Daal stepped toward the beast.

The bat noted his approach and snapped its neck around, hissing ferally.

"Stay back," Graylin warned.

Daal continued forward. "I must try."

DAAL CROSSED TOWARD the huge Mýr bat. It shifted warily on its wingtips, hunching low over Nyx. He read the defensive posture in that stance.

"You're protecting Nyx," he whispered, seeing a twitch of its wings at her name. "I know that."

He approached, as he did with the raash'ke, leaning on the memories of his ancestors who handled and bonded with such fearsome creatures. Though this bat was from Mýr, it could not be that different. He kept his gaze askance, his head low. He lifted his hands, palms raised.

"I want to help Nyx, too," he assured the beast, emphasizing her name to reach through the madness shining in its eyes.

Daal touched the fire inside him. He had recovered some of his flames, but they remained mere flickers. Worse, he had little true skill with bridle-song. Though he had been altered by the Dreamers into a font of heightened strength, they had not honed any talent of song to match. Instead, he leaned on Nyx's memories that had been shared with him.

He followed her example and hummed softly. He reached into his fire and stirred a golden glow over his raised palms. "Nyx needs me. I will help her."

The bat hissed at him with a frisson of apprehension, but not about his approach.

*You're worried about her, too.*

Daal frowned.

*But why?*

He hummed his hands brighter, while reaching into the shared memories inside him. He found a melody, one that Nyx often sang, one with roots in a lullaby from her father. Something to soothe. He tightened his throat and molded his tones to match that lullaby. To his own ears, his efforts sounded tinny and far from melodic, but it was a fair approximation.

He read the effect. The bat's neck stretched out, and its hissing lowered to a whispery whistle, nearly inaudible, but Daal heard it trying to join him. It was the quietest harmony, like a dream just out of one's grasp.

*You know this. You're struggling to remember.*

Again, a question persisted.

*How does it know this?*

A nose reached to his raised palms, while the bat continued whispering that haunting tune.

Daal fought not to cringe. He stared at the raw scalp of the monster. Blood flowed black from the holes where the copper needles had once stood. A few spikes still poked high.

The soft flaps of that questing nose sniffed at the glow about Daal's finger-tips. As contact was made, he sensed the storm under the ruins of that scalp. It shone with corruption and an emerald fire. But further back, a well of golden light shone, struggling to quash those malignant energies.

Deep inside him, a memory stirred out of Nyx's past, as if drawn up by that golden light.

—*she cradles the tiny bat in her lap and reaches a finger to brush the velvet chin. She lowers the dagger to his throat. She does not want him to feel the sting of this blade, so she keens, a quiet song to her brother to soothe him, stirring a dream of them nestled in slumber . . .*

As this memory stirred, Daal heard that same quiet melody echoing in the bat's whistle now.

"You know this song, don't you," Daal whispered. "You've heard this before."

He now understood why this memory had risen again. He knew why this bat protected her so diligently, even in the storm of madness.

Daal now grasped who this bat truly was.

Not a monster—

"Bashaliia," he said with shock.

The bat shivered away from that name, hissing in confusion and fear.

Daal wouldn't let him go, stepping forward. "You're Bashaliia. *Remember.* You are Nyx's little brother."

The mauled head turned away, as if trying to deny his words.

Daal took another step. "Let me help you. Let me help Nyx."

The bat drew back from him, but then bent down and nudged the limp body toward him, rolling Nyx closer, but not out of its shadow. As the muzzle rose, fiery eyes glared at him, challenging him to prove himself. A glint of poisonous fangs firmed the cost of failure.

Daal crossed low to reach Nyx, dropping to his knees. Her face was pale, her hair frosted with ice. She had been out in the cold for too long. He reached to her hand, expecting the snap of fire that always merged them. But there was nothing. Just the ice of pending death. He rubbed her hands between his palms. He pushed all his fiery energy down his arms and into his fingers.

"Nyx, please wake up."

He pushed his fire into her, forcing her to take it. As he did this, like with Bashaliia, he sensed the madness deep inside her, roiling with emerald fury, trying to burn Nyx away.

He saw her thrashing inside there, ripped and burned at her edges.

*No . . .*

He flashed back to the Mouth, when the horde-mind had torn itself apart after being freed of the spider's control. Unfettered and rudderless, it had needed a new anchor. Nyx had raised a maelstrom as a beacon to draw its pieces together, to preserve its sanity. She had offered herself as a new anchor.

*I must be that for her now.*

Daal closed his eyes and cast his fire into that fiery storm of emerald madness. He gathered his flame and burnished it brighter, a golden beacon in the center of that gale.

*See me.*

He felt her struggling toward him, but the tides had too firm a hold of her. She was still too weak to fight its pull. He dug deeper, emptying more of himself into that flame.

She drew closer, gathering what was left of her own song. Still, at the outer edges, she frayed. The fiery emerald current tore at her, a breath away from ripping her forever into its tide.

He refused to accept this, to lose her to that madness. He poured everything into her. With every breath, with every pump of his heart.

*Take it,* he urged her. *Take all of it.*

Still, Daal sensed that fire alone wasn't enough. She needed more than just *power.* She needed an anchor that was more substantial than any flame.

*Let me be that.*

Daal opened himself fully, offering her not just his power, but all of him. He burned himself atop the pyre he created—until only his heart remained, shining in that flame. With each beat, he cast himself out to her, over and over again.

*We need you.*

I *need you.*


DEEP INSIDE, NYX heard a faint refrain calling to her. She drew closer. It guided her lost ship, a lighthouse in the storm. Its lamp was a flame of pure gold, shining through emerald fires. Its horn was a promise of safe harbor, of the strength of warm arms.

As she closed upon that distant shore, she found clarity coalescing out of madness, a calmness out of chaos. Memory formed out of oblivion, allowing her to remember herself more fully. A word formed inside her, a promise to herself and another.

*Never.*

With this purpose clutched close to her, she swept faster, gathering light to her. But much of it was corrupted, etched deep with emerald. It weighed her down, tried to slow her. But the shine of the lamp ahead burned that sickness away, leaving something even purer afterward.

She rolled like a wave, growing taller, unstoppable, dousing and drowning away the emerald fires around her.

Ahead, a figure stood in that lighthouse, limned against that flame.

She rushed toward that light, toward him.

Remembering all.

Who she was.

Who he was.

She struck that shore, reaching for him, for that safe harbor—and most importantly, the strength of those warm arms.


DAAL FADED AS she rushed toward him. He smiled at her joy and relief. Her golden essence burst against him, throwing him back into his body. He carried her with him.

As the smoky world returned, she was in his arms. He had not seen her move. She was simply there, as if she had always been there, hugging tight to him.

"Thank you," Nyx whispered in his ear.

He pulled her closer with the last beat of his heart.

*You're safe.*

Knowing that, he let go—of her and the world.


NYX HELD DAAL as his head fell to his shoulders and his arms draped to her sides. She felt his weight lean into her and his last breath brush her skin.

*No . . .*

She hugged and shook him. "Daal."

His open eyes stared blindly.

She let go of his body and shifted her hands to his cheeks, drawing his eyes back to her. She sang her grief into a glow, fueling it with his flames.

*I won't let you go.*

The others came rushing up, but Bashaliia hissed them back, protecting the two of them. Nyx sensed the madness there, but it would have to wait.

She reached her gift into Daal, passing through the nothingness that was everything. She swept into his empty spaces, drew energy from those vibrating hard motes. She drew upon his heart and fed it back his fire. She willed it to beat, wrapping it with energy and verve.

But it remained still and dark.

Nyx had made a promise to two—now she added a third. She put all her strength into her demand, her will, her resolve.

**Never.**

Still, she was refused.

"Daal . . . please . . ."

A shadow passed over her. A soft nose nuzzled her crown as Bashaliia sensed her distress. She wanted to rub his ears to reassure him, but she refused to let go of Daal. Still, the reflex to reach to Bashaliia reminded her that *touch* could be more powerful than any gifted song. A simple touch—fingers brushing a cheek, a hand on a shoulder—was often the start of that indescribable, wordless sense of connection, of a wholeness that could only be found in another's heart.

So, she obeyed what she had wanted to do for a long time. She no longer hid it. She pulled Daal to her and kissed him, the most intimate of touches, sharing heat and breath. In the past, she had been wary of touching him, while at the same time desiring it, fueled by the hunger of the dark abyss inside her.

This touch had nothing to do with any darkness.

Only hope.

She warmed her lips with her song, humming her need into him, passing forth a plea—not a demand—the same she had shared with Bashaliia.

*Come back to me.*

She closed her eyes and sang to him, into him. While she never felt his heart begin to beat again, she didn't have to. She knew the truth as she sank into him, merging with him once again, returning to where she belonged. She allowed his fire to wash back and forth between them, warming them both fully back to their bodies.

Once done, she sighed between his lips, offering him no more magic than her heart.

## 96

As Rhaif headed over to the others gathered near the dark tunnel, he spotted movement across the dome's entry. He flinched and ducked, expecting the worst, which considering all that had happened was not unwise. Then he straightened with a smile and hurried to the others.

Ahead of them, Nyx balanced on a leg, leaning on Daal for support. They stood before the giant Mýr bat. Rhaif had heard from Krysh that the beast was Bashaliia in a larger body. Rhaif was not convinced, especially as Perde got too near and the bat lunged at him, snapping fangs at his face.

Nyx scolded both bat and brigand. "Keep back. Both of you. He's still ruled by madness."

As Daal held her, she reached her hands up. Bashaliia lowered his bloody crown to meet her palms. Golden tendrils rose from Nyx's fingertips. The shining strands wafted high, then dove into the open holes where the copper needles had once been.

Rhaif grimaced and held back, not wanting to intrude in what looked like a delicate matter. Nyx bowed her head, and the glow about her bloomed brighter. Rhaif wasn't sure what she was attempting. Then suddenly golden fire burst out of all the holes in the bat's skull. One of the remaining copper needles went flying. For a fleeting moment, emerald fire danced about those holes, too, but it was vanquished by the brighter gold.

Bashaliia collapsed for a breath, wingtips skittering wider, but he caught himself and pushed into Nyx's arms. He keened and fluttered, acting more like his former self.

Daal joined her, and even Perde took a tentative step forward, but then retreated in a clear act of wary cowardice.

Rhaif hurried the last of the way, joining Graylin and Darant. "We've got company," he announced to the two men.

Graylin frowned.

Rhaif pointed up. The broken hull of a ship glided across the opening, slowly circling through the warm mists out in the cold. Though it was fogged by the pall, there was no mistaking the *Sparrowhawk*. The ship was in rough shape, shot through with cannonballs. But it must have defeated the Hálendian ships that had chased after it and was able to return.

Darant craned up and gave a nod of approval. "Good girl."

Rhaif glanced over to the pirate, unsure if he meant the *Hawk* or his daughter Glace.

Graylin turned to Rhaif. "How is Shiya managing?"

"That's why I came over. She's finally tamed the *turubya,* and she thinks she understands what she's supposed to do. But there's two problems."

"What are they?"

"Though she's calmed the crystal orb, it remains unstable. If not employed soon, it may become inoperable."

"How long do we have?"

Rhaif stared up at the dome entrance. "Just be glad the *Sparrowhawk* is here. We have little to no time. The sooner we act the better."

"And the second problem?"

Rhaif shrugged. "Best see for yourself."


GRAYLIN RUBBED HIS chin and studied the rise of the crystal sphere. It had indeed settled down, resting quietly in its cradle. The golden fluid at its heart had returned to a more regular pulsing, but even to his eye, it looked unsteady and tremulous.

*Definitely don't want to wait too long.*

The other challenge was more straightforward. One of the bronze suspension bridges had been damaged, twisted askew by the earlier violent quaking.

He turned to Shiya. "You believe this could be a problem."

"I do not know," she admitted. "Once I energize the *turubya,* it is intended to be dropped down that hole, to fall somewhere near the world's core. The delivery must be precise. It must not strike the walls, or it could be damaged and rendered useless."

He nodded. "And if this suspension doesn't release as intended, it could throw off the angle of its descent."

She simply crossed her arms, her face worried.

Krysh approached with Jace after the two had finished inspecting the bracing. "We may have a solution."

"Which is what?"

Jace lifted his ax. "Brute force."

Graylin frowned. That seemed to be the young man's answer to every challenge of late. "Explain yourself."

"As near as I can tell," Krysh said, "it appears the bridges are calibrated to release at the same time."

Shiya nodded. "That is true."

Jace explained the rest. "The damaged brace could be released *manually*. An ax strike at its housing, where it connects to the cradle, should release it."

Krysh nodded. "The design is simple enough in that regard. But I would not mind more time to test it."

Graylin turned to Shiya.

She turned to the chrysalis. "We must do this now."

Graylin trusted her judgement. There could be no further delay. "We'll need someone to man that brace," he said. "When they see the other bridges release, strike that housing hard and fast."

Jace stepped forward, hefting his ax.

Graylin turned from him and pointed to the strongest among them. "Vikas, would you be willing to do this?"

She nodded and swung to Darant. She gestured firmly, clearly asking for something.

"Aye." The brigand turned to Jace. "She wants your ax, my boy. Guld'guh-lian steel is far stronger than anything we have. Can't risk a mishap, can we?"

Vikas stared down Jace.

With a heavy sigh, he relinquished his weapon with great reluctance. "Be careful with her," he pleaded.

With the matter settled, everyone began moving at once. Daal gathered up the remaining raash'ke. Nyx, with her shin hastily splinted, used Bashaliia to carry Darant and Perde up to the *Sparrowhawk,* to ready the ship for a swift departure.

Graylin kept with Krysh and Rhaif beside Shiya's cocoon. She was already ensconced and sealed inside, waiting on their word.

Across the way, Jace showed Vikas where to hit the housing to release the brace. He seemed to want to go into more detail, but Vikas planted a huge hand on Jace's chest and pushed him ten paces away. She then returned to her post and nodded toward the chrysalis.

Graylin did a final inspection, making sure everyone was clear. Once satisfied, he boomed across the chamber, "We're starting!"

Rhaif put his palm against the cocoon's crystal. Shiya placed her bronze hand over his, then leaned her head back against the copper and closed her eyes.

Graylin held his breath. Nothing seemed to happen for a long stretch. He finally had to let his air out. As he did, the sphere began to glow. A low rumble shook the floor. Down the tunnels, the huge rubber cables vibrated.

The glow of the orb grew brighter. The golden lake at its heart stopped its tremulous pulsing. Rather than remaining amorphous, the pool blinked through a variety of crisp shapes: a pyramid, a cube, a prism, a cone. Some shapes defied the eye. They flashed faster and faster, growing into a blur that looked like a match to the orb: a perfect sphere made of thousands of blended shapes flickering into and out of coherence.

The glow grew into a blaze of shining energy.

Vikas squinted her eyes, but she maintained her post, holding her ax high.

Shiya moaned a single word of warning. "Now."

The blaze exploded outward with a nimbus of wild energies. The force blasted away the braces—except for one.

Vikas, with her ax still above her head, got hit by the same glowing nimbus as it blasted beyond the cradle. She flew far, losing her ax as she hit the floor. The weapon skittered to Jace's toes. Vikas slid farther.

Graylin inhaled to yell at Jace.

But the young man was already moving. He grabbed his ax and followed behind the path of the collapsing nimbus. Ahead, the brace and cradle danced with sparking frazzles of power, but the way was clear. Jace swung his ax two-handed and struck the brace's housing. The Guld'guhlian steel proved its forging and cleaved the bridge free.

At the same time, Jace was blown back, wrapped in that residual energy. His body convulsed through the air and slammed down hard. His skull rang off the copper.

Vikas was already on her feet and rushed to his side.

Graylin turned toward the greater concern.

*Did Jace strike too late?*

Graylin held out one hope. The *turubya* sphere still hung over the open mouth of the pit, suspended by that fiery nimbus. Maybe the timing of the braces' release was not as critical as they had believed. Maybe the bridges just had to drop, allowing the nimbus to take over.

He stared, unblinking. The fiery shine stung his eyes until he could stand it no longer. He blinked. In that fraction of a moment, the orb shot *up* into the dome and hung suspended in the middle. It hovered like a new sun, blinding and stunning to behold—then with the next breath, it slammed down into the hole.

Graylin's eyes still burned with the afterimage of the sphere.

Rhaif shifted toward the pit. "Did we do it? Did we actually do it?"

The answer came with a thunderous slam of steel. A vault door sealed over the hole. Others could be heard closing in succession down its length, until the sound faded away.

Behind them, the crystalline cocoon opened, and Shiya stepped out.

Graylin turned to her, but Shiya addressed Rhaif, touching his elbow tenderly. "It is done."

Vikas waved frantically over by Jace, a reminder that not all had come through unscathed.

NYX HOBBLED ACROSS the dome floor toward Jace and Vikas. She had been in motion as soon as she saw her friend blasted by that ball of destructive energy.

Once close enough, she winced and dropped to a knee next to him. No broken leg was going to keep her from him.

Jace was her only connection to her past. She had lost her dah and brothers, given up her whole life. Nothing of her past remained. Except for Jace. He had been the only true constant throughout all of this.

*I can't lose you.*

Vikas looked at her with concern. The tall woman gestured rapidly in Gynish, fluttering a hand at her throat, then over her chest. "Jace is still breathing. His heart is still beating." Still, Vikas covered her eyes with a shake of her head. "I can't wake him."

Nyx prayed he was just knocked out, but even that could be dangerous.

The others joined them, hovering around.

"Do not move him," Krysh warned. "Not until I examine him."

Shiya spoke up. "We must go. With the *turubya* now seated, this complex will destroy itself to protect against any future tampering."

As if reinforcing her words, the floor jolted hard under them and continued trembling. The dome shook crystal off its wall. All around, the huge cables in the tunnels hummed menacingly.

Nyx shifted closer to Jace. "Let me try to wake him."

"Hurry," Shiya commanded, and turned away. She strode quickly toward one of the tunnels.

Rhaif called after her, "Where are you going?"

She answered without turning, "To retrieve something we will need."

Before more could be asked, she sped away with the preternatural speed of bronze.

Graylin dropped next to Nyx. "You must hurry as Shiya warned."

Nyx nodded and built a glow in her hands. She hovered her palms over Jace's temples and cast glowing tendrils from her fingertips. She glided them into Jace, passing through skin and bones. As soon as she breached his skull, a vast coldness swept into her. She gasped, having never felt such ice. It was far more bitter than even the Wastes, more like brushing against the coldness of the void, the blackness between stars.

Shocked, her song collapsed, and her strands dissolved to mist.

Graylin looked at her. "Well?"

She refused to answer, not until she was sure. She rubbed her palms, still feeling that dread cold. She hummed as she did, rebuilding her song. She stoked it harder, knowing she had to go in there. She sang until the golden tide was strong enough to carry her. She leaned down to his ear and whispered its release. She flowed along with that gold river, sailing through bone as easily as through copper.

As she reached to the contours of his brain, its folds lay dark and quiet. She detected no firing of energy, no sparks of life. The smooth ridges and deep grooves were as quiet as a grave. She risked touching that silent matter—only to again sense the enormity of a void. To her ethereal self, it was not cold.

Only vast and empty.

She shuddered back out of him and into her body.

Graylin had the same question in his eyes.

Nyx stared around. "Jace . . . he's not there at all. There's nothing inside him."

A cough conflicted her judgement.

They all turned as Jace coughed again. He groaned and tried to sit up, thought better of it, then lay back down. "Ow."

"Are you all right?" Krysh asked.

Jace lifted a hand to his forehead. "I think so. Just dizzy."

Rhaif reminded them, "We must get going."

Jace pushed up again, this time successfully, and saw the sealed pit. "Did it work?"

"We can explain later." Graylin helped him to his feet. "Are you truly feeling fit enough to get up to the *Hawk*?"

He squinted, then nodded. "Head feels like it's been kicked by a horse." He shook his fingers. "And my palms still sting from the ax. But yeah, I'm ready to get out of this place."

"Then let's get moving."

Jace noted Nyx looking at him strangely. "What's wrong?"

She shook her head, picturing what she had found inside him. "Nothing."


GRAYLIN AND THE others all gathered in the wheelhouse of the *Sparrow-hawk*. Darant was again at the wheel. Stories had been shared, updating all.

Glace had managed to outmaneuver the other Hálendiian ships by using the power of the new forges: "Only took me strafing over their sodding balloons with our forges at full flame. Burned them right out of the sky. They had no chance."

Graylin suspected there was more to her story, especially with a large portion of the keel and lower hold missing. But detailed explanations could wait.

Darant guided the *Sparrowhawk* away from the copper sprawl below. He aimed them toward the Crèche, where the *Hawk* would undergo another round of repairs. For now, they didn't have to worry about any further Hálendiian raiders.

Darant had kept his promise to Commander Ghryss, to deliver an especially brutal end to the man's life. The bloody act also served to free the tongues of two of his crew—who met far quicker deaths for their help.

From the pair, Darant had learned that the barge and its support ships were the only ones dispatched into the Wastes. The two men had also revealed *how* Graylin's group had been tracked all this time. Apparently, some emanation from Shiya was able to be detected by Iflelen alchymy. Such knowledge was worrisome, but for the moment, as far out in the Wastes as they were, it was not an immediate threat.

Still, the plan was not to spend any more time in the Crèche than necessary. If their group could be tracked, the best course was to keep moving. Fenn had some thoughts on that, but he wanted to do some further calculations.

A door opened behind Graylin with a blast of cold air. The whistling roar from the ruins of the ship followed Shiya as she entered with Rhaif.

"Did you get the devices secured?" Graylin asked as they joined him.

"Bloody things weigh as much as a forge," Rhaif answered. "But we managed. Or rather, Shiya did. I clapped approvingly when she was done."

Nyx limped over with Jace and Krysh. "But what are they?" she asked. "You never said."

Graylin wanted to know, too.

Rhaif smiled. "We're definitely going to need them soon. It's why Shiya told us we had to come out to this site in the Wastes *first*, before traveling to the next one."

Jace pressed him. "Why? What was so important out here?"

Shiya answered, "Cooling units."

Rhaif shrugged. "If we're heading next to the sunblasted side of the Urth, we're going to need more than just new forges."

Darant interrupted them, calling from the maesterwheel, "You might want to come see this."

Graylin headed over with the others.

Darant pointed to their starboard, to where the copper complex still glowed on the broken plains of the Brackenlands. Only now it shone far brighter. From the chasms around its edge, molten rock bubbled and overflowed, spilling out around the dome and its legs.

Darant glanced back at them. "Glad we got out of there when we did."

"Look," Jace said, shifting to keep the view in sight. "I think it's all sinking or melting or something."

Graylin joined him. The entire copper structure was indeed sagging into the Brackenlands. The dome flattened and spread wider, while the limbs sank into the molten rock. Eventually, the intense heat fogged the view, erasing it from sight.

With nothing else to see, Darant turned the ship and swung away. "No one's gonna be trespassing back there anytime soon."

Graylin glanced at Shiya, wondering if her exiting the dome had triggered its final destruction. He remembered how the Root had called her an Axis, confirming she was the key to the facility.

Shiya ignored his look. In fact, she had gone very quiet and still during all of this. She held her head cocked to the side, her brows pinched and frozen.

Rhaif noted the strangeness, too. "Shiya, is something wrong?"

She didn't answer, just continued her long stare.

Rhaif took her hand. "Shiya?"

She finally stirred and patted his fingers, reassuring him. She then faced everyone and announced, "Prince Kanthe wishes you all to know that he is getting married."

※

## 97

WRYTH CROSSED THROUGH the slaughter, being careful where he stepped. Pools of blood covered the marble of the dimly lit palacio. Even the perfume of smoking incense could not mask the smell of split bowel and ripe meat. Bodies sprawled everywhere: cut apart in hallways, slashed across beds, floating in baths turned crimson. Most were pleasure serfs, indentured to servitude. The others were servants and patrons of the palacio.

Most of the latter were legionnaires and knights who had been rewarded access following the campaign to the Southern Klashe. Though the battle had been far from a success, the pretense of victory had to be promulgated. Behind closed doors, the results of that battle had not been as well heralded.

Wryth winced as he continued through the grounds—but not at the brutality and savagery. The ruins of his right eye stabbed with every step. It felt as if that shard of crystal were still imbedded there, but it had been removed eight days ago, along with the remains of his eye. The socket was still packed with a medicant-infused cotton and covered in a leather patch.

Provost Balyn wheezed his rotund form alongside Wryth. The man clutched a scrap of cloth at his nose and spoke through it. "We knew the Southern Klashe would retaliate, but to strike so close to the heart of the kingdom. The legion has been lax in its guardianship."

Wryth scowled. "With a knight's breeches at his ankles and his only weapon being his cock in hand, they could not offer much defense."

"This target, though, makes sense," Treasurer Hesst said, picking his way behind them. "The palacio lies in the shadow of Highmount's walls, buried in one of the six points of its stars. It's remote, exactly opposite the Legionary with its barracks and billets. Plus, they're just pleasure serfs. No one would expect an attack here. It's an insult for sure, but little more than a nuisance."

Balyn had the wherewithal to glare at Hesst for dismissing the slaughter so callously. Still, there was little true heat to his disapproval. He looked more upset to be dragged from his bed at this early hour, as had all the council.

The king's summons had left them no choice. Toranth was already furious, and no one dared goad him any further. They all knew his mood following the campaign in the Klashe. He had thundered and bellowed behind those closed doors. It was estimated they had lost nearly a sixth of their winged forces.

Hesst glanced around as they continued. "Of course, there are plenty of guards here now. Though, they look less grim and more disappointed that they missed their chance at a pleasurable reward."

Wryth did not agree. While some of the legionnaires did appear bored—and a few pocketed treasures left behind by the dead—far more had firm sets to their lips or muttered promises of revenge to each other. It wasn't just serfs who had been slain here, but many of their fellow brothers-in-arms.

Wryth's group finally reached where the king had summoned them. It was the farthest of the palacio's salons, as if Toranth wanted them to view the carnage firsthand before reaching here, to soil their boots and rub their noses in all the blood. The chamber stood at the deepest angle of this point of the wall's star.

Tall doors closed off the room, marking the royal salon of the king.

Only now it would be turned into a makeshift council chamber.

A full fist of Vyrllian knights had been posted at the entry. Though their faces were stained crimson, fury darkened their countenances. Brows were lowered over hard eyes.

The doors were opened for them. They were likely the last to arrive.

Wryth entered ahead of the other two, intending not to be the very last. More knights crowded within the room. Apparently, Toranth was not taking any chances that an assassin might still be hidden on the grounds.

As Wryth entered, a heavy silence greeted him, which was more worrisome than when Toranth blustered. Wryth hurried deeper into the grand salon. The space was draped in velvet, smoky with incense, and lit by an array of gold lanterns. Directly ahead, a large hearth glowed with coals. To the left, a stout table had been set with a flagon of wine and a cold platter of dried fruit, cheeses, and hard breads, a lean repast for when they discussed this attack and how to respond.

Wryth had barely entered when he noted that all the vy-knights in the room had black sigils tattooed on one side of their faces.

All Silvergard.

Wryth's chest clenched, trapping his breath. He suspected the truth, and in another step, it was confirmed.

To his right, a large bed had been stripped of its blankets and furs. At its foot, two women lay in pools of blood, throats slashed to bone, nearly decapitated. Atop the bed, another body was sprawled, naked and exposed, winged by pools of blood.

King Toranth, the Crown'd Lord of Hálendii.

A Klashean sword had been shoved through his mouth, the blade curving down his throat, silencing him forever. The hilt shone brightly above his blue lips.

To the side, Prince Mikaen knelt with his forehead to the bed, his hands clutching hard to his father's arm, his fingers digging deep into the cold flesh.

Wryth knew it must have been the prince who had summoned the council, to keep the death of the king secret until they could all divine a path forward from here.

Captain Thoryn stood next to Mikaen, guarding over the prince's grief.

"What do we do?" Balyn whispered.

No one answered.

Wryth drew no nearer. Even with his one eye, he could plainly see the truth from here. His gaze remained fixed to the hilt of that curved sword. Though it had been scraped and abraded, its pommel showed divots from where gemstones had once adorned it. In his mind's eye, Wryth replaced those rubies and sapphires, returning the sword to its former glory.

Wryth knew this weapon.

It was Prince Paktan's sword—a trophy won by Mikaen weeks ago.

The prince lifted his face from the bed, his cheeks streaked with tears.

All of them feigned.

# 98

ON THE MORNING of the winter's solstice, Kanthe followed alongside Aalia down the center of the vaulted throne room. Crowds cheered and clapped from the packed galleries and arcades to either side. Ahead, the hall's two gold thrones, along with the sweep of gilded wings above them, had been polished and gleamed in the sunlight cast by the rosette window above.

Kanthe stared into that sunny glare. Though only a month had passed since the attack, the window had been mostly replaced, its rosette reset with new stained glass, slowly returning the Illuminated Rose of the Imperium to its full glory.

The same repairs were happening across much of the beleaguered city.

The palace and its throne room had been scrubbed of blood and its blast scars filled. The lower city and docks echoed with the pound of hammers and the endless sawing of wood. The noise continued day and night. And while it should have been grating to the ear, it sounded like hope.

Farther out in the bay, Stone Gods were being returned to pedestals as massive stones were barged into place, ready to be chiseled back to life. Overlooking this work, the town of X'or had been cleared of its wreckage and its baths restored. Kanthe had spent the first quarter of his return in those bloody baths, kept company by Jester and Mead while he healed.

Kanthe glanced to the empty half of his sleeve, pinned back to his elbow. He still felt flashes of pain from his missing arm, but that, too, was fading—if not the nightmares that still struck him at times. But he knew countless others who mourned more than the loss of an arm.

The city had grieved the month long, in ceremonies small and large. Emperor Makar and Prince Jubayr were interred with great pageantry, as befitting their status.

The notable absence to both was Prince Mareesh. He had vanished after the attack, but no one was naïve enough to think this marked the end of his challenge. During long talks on Rami's balcony, his friend had admitted that he could have killed his brother during the battle in the throne room, but he had stayed his hand, choosing to chase Mareesh off instead. Rami still believed his brother could be redeemed. Sadly, Kanthe could not scold that decision. He understood Rami's sentiment all too well, knowing the inner conflict he had with his own brother. Still, he hoped Rami's compassion didn't ruin them in the end.

While Emperor Makar and Prince Jubayr were celebrated and mourned publicly, Aalia grieved them privately, too, descending often into the mausoleum deep beneath the palace. Not even Tazar disturbed those intimate moments. She would tolerate only Rami, who also spent time alone with the dead.

Kanthe appreciated their need for privacy. They were both struggling between grief and guilt—something he recognized all too well.

Kanthe had heard of his father's brutal slaying, and despite what was claimed across Hálendii, he knew it had been no plot by the imperium. Kanthe suspected the true hand that wielded the fatal blade belonged to his brother. Yet, Kanthe also could not dismiss the fear that what had ultimately forced Mikaen's hand was the weight of a gold signet ring. Back on the *Hyperium*, Mikaen had believed Kanthe intended to challenge his birthright and, in turn, the lineage of his children. While any such claims made by the Southern Klashe could be dismissed as a lie, only one person in Hálendii knew the truth—and to remove any future threat, that person had to be silenced forever.

Kanthe suspected such a fate would have eventually come to pass, knowing the friction that had been growing of late between king and prince. Still, Kanthe hated to have played a role in it. Like Aalia and Rami, Kanthe grieved for his father, while guilt further weighed his heart.

Still, after a month, even mourning had to end. Life had to continue, a city had to be restored, a morale had to be bolstered. To that end, this day would host two great pageantries. While Aalia had been widely revered as the new empress, she still had not formally donned the circlet.

She would do so now.

As the two reached the thrones, Kanthe stepped aside and joined Rami. Aalia crossed to the larger of the two seats as the ceremony began, which involved prayers to thirty-three gods, repeated blaring of horns, and a series of lengthy proclamations.

At one point, Rami leaned into him, drowsing off for a moment.

Kanthe straightened him. "Wake up. We've a long day ahead of us still."

"And night," Rami groaned.

The second ceremony would start with the moon's rise, marking the auspicious peak of the solstice. Kanthe stared over to the second, smaller throne, a seat that would be his after he married Aalia this very night.

He matched Rami's groan with one of his own.

Off to the side, near the front of the gathering, he spotted Cassta with her black-draped sisters, looking his way. The young woman's face was stoic, but he swore there was the slimmest smile of amusement, as if she were enjoying his discomfort.

He sighed and turned away.

Finally, a circlet was lifted and carried to the throne by the head cleric of the *Bad'i Chaa,* the House of Wisdom. Aalia removed a veil woven with diamonds from the fall of her black hair, which had been oiled to a mirrored sheen. Her gown was silver, laced with the faintest image in gold of the Haeshan Hawk. Normally, a cape with that sigil would already be gracing her shoulders—but her father's cloak lay wrapped around her brother's body, its gold clasp forever secured to his throat.

The cleric gently rested the circlet of meteoric black iron and its sapphire gems atop her head. Aalia stood as she accepted its weight and responsibility. A beam of sunlight from the broken window struck those jewels and flashed azure shafts across the room.

Thunderous cheering erupted, drowning out the blare of horns.

Aalia stared out across the throngs, her face firm and assured.

Still, Kanthe noted the tremble in her fingers.

As she descended, he crossed and took hold of her hand and clasped those fingers. "You're not alone in this," he whispered. "Know that."

She clutched his arm, leaning on him—but only for a breath. She loosened her hold and stood straighter. He escorted her down the last step, honored to be at her side.

The new empress of the imperium.

After all the dark devastation, Kanthe felt something burn brighter inside him, something he had not felt in a long time.

Hope.


AS THE FIRST of the latterday bells rang, Aalia entered the strategy room atop the Blood'd Tower. She felt lighter after shedding out of her gown and into a simpler *gerygoud* habiliment, which consisted of a short tunic and white robe with splayed sleeves.

She entered with Tazar on her arm. She gave Kanthe a hard stare. She appreciated his support at the ceremony, but she made it clear the marriage to come would be as ceremonial as the finery they would wear. She dreaded having to prepare for that. Still, Tazar had helped her strip out of her gown and proved that a man on his knees could find a greater use for his tongue than simply swearing an oath.

Due to such diligent attention, they were the last to arrive at the small gathering. She crossed to the table with its map of the Southern Klashe. Tazar stepped away to join Llyra, likely to discuss matters of low armies and high affairs.

Kanthe and Rami whispered together to one side of the table, while Pratik and Frell seemed in midargument on the other. They all fell silent when she reached the table and cleared her throat.

"Why have you summoned us all here?" she asked the figure on the far end.

The Augury of Qazen stood in his black robes, with his bronze hidden under paint. Tykhan had asked them to gather in the strategy room, away from any other members of the imperial council, specifically before the wedding.

"I should let you know it is not only *us* in this room," he stated. "But also in attendance, though obviously unseen, are those of our group who reside in the Wastes."

"Nyx and the others?" Kanthe asked.

Tykhan frowned at him for stating the obvious. "They will be listening in, and Shiya will pass to me any of their questions."

Over the past month, the two parties had shared and recounted their respective stories, but Tykhan had insisted on keeping any communications brief and sporadic. While he had taught Shiya how to shield her emanations, he remained wary of exposing themselves too broadly.

Tykhan started, "I've let both groups collect themselves and prepare for what's to come, but as the nuptials are pending, I must raise one last warning to both sides. To let you know *why* I needed the empire readied with a new empress, one married to the rightful heir to the Hálendiian throne. Much depends on this coming to fruition."

"Finally," Aalia stated. "You've been secretive about this long enough."

"True. As you all know, while the party in the Wastes was successful in seating the western hemisphere's *turubya,* the same still must be done on the eastern side."

"Off in the sunblasted Barrens," Rami said. "Won't they—"

Tykhan cut him off with a raised palm. He cocked his head, speaking askance, something he did when addressing those in the Wastes. "No, do not share your path. Not even with me. The fewer who know, the safer you will be."

Tykhan straightened and addressed the room again. "But what I've *not* told anyone until now is that securing and seating the second *turubya* will not be enough to thwart moonfall."

Aalia winced. "Then what else must be done?"

Tykhan stared across the table. "There is a *third* component to all of this." He swept his gaze around the table. "One that will require you all in this room—and the might of the empire."

"To do what?" Kanthe asked.

Tykhan stared the prince down. "To take over the Kingdom of Hálendii."

Kanthe took a step back. "What? Why?"

"I've told you of the great war among the *ta'wyn,* when we fractured between those who wished to honor our creators and those that wanted to usurp this planet for themselves. Those usurpers were led by a betrayer, a Kryst who abandoned our side to lead the other."

"Eligor," Aalia said, remembering the bronze figure in the ancient pages stolen by Frell.

"The *Revn-kree*—those *ta'wyn* who broke from the creators' path—call him the *Rab'almat,* which roughly means the *Lord of Death.*"

Kanthe exhaled in exasperation. "Sounds equally ominous and pompous."

"Do not scoff. His title is apt. He does not care if *any* life survives. Not the Crown, not the beasts of the field, not the green shoots of growth. We *ta'wyn* have no need for any of that. We can thrive on a dead rock devoid of air. That is why the *Revn-kree* want moonfall to happen. It serves as a means to eradicate all life."

Frell spoke up. "But then why didn't the Root in the Wastes destroy the *turubya* long ago? That would have thwarted any future efforts to stop moonfall."

"Because, before his destruction, Eligor forbade it." He stopped to let that sink in. "I suspect it was the madness of isolation, coupled with despair, that drove the Wastes' Root to commit such a heinous act, to defy the dictates left behind by the *Rab'almat.*"

Frell shook his head, still clearly frustrated. "But *why* did Eligor forbid anyone from destroying the *turubya?*"

"As I said, the *ta'wyn* could thrive on a barren rock—but not one shattered to pieces. Destroying a *turubya* risked that happening. Likewise, it remains too early to know how devastating moonfall will be to the Urth. Eligor wanted the *turubya* preserved in case he needed to intervene should moonfall prove too risky to the planet's fundamental structure."

Aalia stared hard at Tykhan, suspecting he was still hiding something. "That's not the only reason Eligor wanted the *turubya* preserved, was it?" she challenged him. "It must have something to do with that *third* task you said we needed to accomplish."

Tykhan smiled. "I chose my empress well."

Aalia scowled. "What is it that we're supposed to do?"

"I mentioned before, at the end of the war, Eligor was defeated, and his broken body whisked away by a handful of *Revn-kree* survivors. The end of this story bears on both parties in the months ahead. Those survivors were led by Eligor's second-in-command, an Axis like Shiya. I believe he, and possibly other *Revn-kree*, guard the second *turubya* within the Barrens. That Axis will be far more dangerous than a half-crazed Root."

Everyone fell silent, knowing how close they had come to defeat in the Wastes. If an Axis and a small army were entrenched in the Barrens, what hope was there for the world?

Still, Aalia refused to bow to despair. "This tale of yours . . . how does it impact us in the Crown?"

"When the *Revn-kree* fled with Eligor's body, there was a piece missing, an important piece." He stared around the table. "The head of Eligor."

Kanthe guessed at the implication. "And that head must be in Hálendii. That's why you want us to invade. To find and destroy the last of him."

"First, it will not require much searching," Tykhan said. "I know exactly where the head of Eligor is hidden."

Kanthe frowned. "Where?"

"Deep in the Shrivenkeep. Preserved in a great instrument of the Iflelen."

Kanthe looked aghast. "How long have they had it?"

"For many centuries."

"Then why haven't you already stolen it?" Frell asked. "You could have destroyed it long ago."

"Because I don't want it destroyed. And the Iflelen have done a masterful job of protecting and preserving it. I saw no reason to intercede until now."

Frell scowled. "I don't understand. Why did you want it preserved? Why don't you want it destroyed?"

"The head alone is harmless. But within that bronze skull is a buried secret. One that will take the ingenuity of a kingdom and an empire to dig out."

"What secret?" Pratik asked.

"When Eligor betrayed us, he stole a component that is necessary to engage and direct the *turubya*. While those two massive spheres will *power* the turning of the Urth, what he stole *controls* them both."

"That's why he forbade the *turubya* from being destroyed," Aalia realized aloud. "He wants mastery over them. A power that could rip the world apart as easily as saving it."

Tykhan gave her a small bow of his head. "Now you understand. For any hope of stopping moonfall, we must secure the kingdom and that head—then discover where Eligor hid what he stole."

"What did he actually take?" Pratik asked. "What does it look like?"

Tykhan shrugged. "I do not know. Such knowledge is well beyond the scope of a menial Root. All I know is that it must be found. Or all is doomed."

Silence settled over the room. Aalia could only imagine how those in the Wastes were handling all of this.

Tykhan lifted a palm. "I will end our communications with the others here. We each know what we must do. To extend this conversation any longer is too great of a risk."

After a long stretch, talk slowly resumed around the table. Aalia remained standing, staring over at Tykhan. She came to another realization and crossed over to keep her words with the Augury private.

"You are no longer open to the others?" she asked.

"Correct."

She nodded. "The party in the Wastes has an *Axis*. While you, as a Root, don't have access to the knowledge we need, she might."

"Possibly."

"You taught Shiya how to silence her emanations, but she remains damaged. Is there any way to restore her?"

"Possibly," he repeated. "But I will not try."

"Why?"

"She is useful enough in her current state to the others. Such efforts could inadvertently damage her further."

Aalia stared hard at him, divining that he wasn't being entirely forthright. "There's another reason you won't try fixing her. What is it?"

He closed his eyes slightly. "When the *Revn-kree* fled, they didn't just hunt down Sleepers to *kill* them—like the one who attacked me. Sometimes, they *replaced* them, too. Burying poisonous seeds among the Sleepers." He sighed. "And I fear, in Shiya's damaged state—"

Aalia understood. "She could be one of those poisonous seeds and not remember it."

Tykhan bowed his head again.

Aalia turned to the window with a worrisome concern, thinking about Mareesh, about poisonous seeds.

*Who else might betray us?*


**FRELL HAD MUCH** to contemplate as he followed Pratik through the ruins of the Abyssal Codex. Aalia had assigned Pratik to oversee the salvage of the great librarie and to manage the Dresh'ri. Such an elevation wasn't well received, but after the last of Zeng's supporters were rooted out and strung up in the gardens, the remaining scholars bowed to her commands.

In small ways like this, Aalia was slowly shifting the Klashean caste structure. She dared not tear it apart too quickly or risk it fraying into chaos. Over in the lower city, during the reconstruction, she had begun to blur the lines among the baseborn castes and the *imri,* as they labored and organized repairs, leaning on imperial pride and a common purpose to fold in her changes.

Even the *Shayn'ra* found common ground with the imperial guards. After fighting shoulder to shoulder during the attempted overthrow, the two factions had established a grudging respect for each other. And while fractious outbreaks still occurred, those were subsiding, too.

Still, despite such progress, Frell had grown troubled of late. It was why he had returned to the librarie. Lantern in hand, he continued down into the depths of the Codex. He followed the central spiral stair, leaving Pratik working above. The stench of smoke lay heavy in his nose.

Still, surprisingly, a large swath of the librarie had been spared. One whole level had miraculously avoided the torch, along with a few isolated islands on other levels. Plus, the Dresh'ri had their own stashes and stacks in their private quarters or scholariums. Pratik had been systematically cataloging what had survived. It served as a reminder that even in the darkest times, knowledge found a way to persist.

Frell finally descended the last curve of the stairs and reached the bottommost level of this inverted subterranean pyramid. He held his lantern higher and crossed to the tall doors, wincing as he pushed into the inner sanctum beyond. He swore he could still hear the dreaded singing of the Venin. It had been etched into his skull. He paused at the threshold and made sure none of the mutilated creatures were hiding in the shadows.

Once satisfied, he headed down the short flight of steps into the room.

Pratik had already cleared out the remains of the two pyres and the bones of the man Frell had tossed into the flames, along with the sacred book. A pang of regret stabbed through him—not at the death, but at the memory of those pages turning to ash.

Still, he took the lesson above to heart.

While the book had been burned here, maybe its wisdom persisted elsewhere.

*I'll keep hunting for it.*

Both to regain that knowledge and to atone for the destruction of that ancient tome.

Frell crossed the room and stepped to the waist-high slab of stone at the back. He raised his lantern, casting its light over the wall behind it. Glowing emerald veins traced through the rock, all appearing to emanate from a drawing above the altar, sketched in soot and black oil.

Frell stared again at the huge full moon rising on the wall. Silhouetted against it was the black beast with outstretched wings, edged by fire. He focused on its dark rider, as hunched as the beast itself. The rider's eyes were stabs of that same vile emerald, glowing with menace.

Frell named the rider. "The Shadow Queen."

He had heard the tale of what had befallen the others in the Wastes. A story of emerald fire and madness, both driven into a winged beast and a small rider.

*Is that what's depicted here?*

A prophecy drawn on stone.

As he stared at those baleful eyes, a fear grew stronger inside him—along with a growing doubt.

*Am I on the right side of this war?*

# 99

NYX RODE BASHALIIA high across the Ameryl Sea. After the talk with the others back in the Crown, she had wanted a moment to herself. She leaned in the saddle that Daal had crafted for her. Her left shin was still in a brace, but after a month, with the winter's solstice upon them, her leg barely pained her.

She closed her eyes and sang to Bashaliia as he wafted into and out of the glowing mists of the Crèche. Her melody was one of her own creation. Though wordless, she started with the music of the swamps: the scissor-song of crickets, the *cronking* of wartoads, the *pluck-crunk* of sprig-frogs, the waddle-splash of mudfish, the silage-belch of bullocks. She folded in the harmony of cracking reeds, the rustling sweep of a breeze through stick-pines, the pattering of a downpour on flat water, and last, the laughs of her brothers as they poled to go fishing.

As her song glowed of home, Bashaliia joined her, echoing her refrain in soft notes and wistful chords. It had been his home, too. She hung with him, sharing their past, warmed by each other. She let the weeks of terror fade and pushed aside what was to come.

She drifted in this moment—until a gust of wind and a stir of mists drew her up in the saddle.

Daal rose atop a raash'ke next to her. His hair swept his cheeks, his eyes bright. He pointed below and called to her. "Graylin! Wants us down! It's almost time!"

She lifted higher in her saddle and waved her acknowledgment.

Daal led the way, drawing her back to the world, to her responsibilities. Bashaliia tracked behind him, trilling with the joy of flight. She felt the rumble of his pleasure between her thighs. Some of it carried into her.

They had all been waiting for this day.

Picking the winter solstice as a goal.

As they swept down, she stared past the crown of Bashaliia's head. Like her, he was recovering. But instead of a leg brace, he wore a helm of leather. Under it, a slather of balms and ointments was helping him heal. She and Floraan had also withdrawn the last of those dreadful copper needles.

She repeated her promise to him.

*Never again.*

She wished the same peace for the Crèche.

Below her, Iskar continued to recover from the raids and assaults. Over the past month, there had been too many trips to the Dreamers with inked bodies wrapped in kelp. Still, some semblance of normalcy had returned. Newcomers from other villages throughout the Crèche had been slowly trickling in, filling the voids left behind, aiding in repairs to help establish themselves here. Others came to see the raash'ke, refusing to believe the miracle until they witnessed it with their own eyes.

For now, both the raash'ke and Pantheans remained skittish of each other. It would take time to reestablish that ancient bond, to learn to trust again.

As Nyx circled to land near Daal's home, she spotted Henna running through a flock of young bats, no larger than crows. They scattered from her footfalls, keening in playful delight. Then she would turn and run the other way, chased by the same flock.

Nyx smiled at such innocent delight and suspected it was the youngest among them who would forge the strongest bond.

*If given enough time . . .*

Daal landed at the edge of Iskar. Nyx alighted in the sand, but she kept her distance. After all that had happened, Bashaliia remained edgy.

Henna spotted her brother and came running up, drawing a score of tiny bats in her wake. Most of the girl's wounds had scabbed and healed over— but not all of them. According to her mother, Henna still had nightmares and insisted on sleeping in her parents' bed.

As Henna rushed to her brother, her path drew too close. Nyx felt the fiery flash inside Bashaliia as he snapped at a passing bat, barely missing its wings, sending it fluttering away in a panic.

"Bashaliia, no . . ."

She ran her fingers through his ruff, down to his skin, and warmed a glow of reassurance in him, tamping down that flash of fire. It had been golden, but for a flicker, she thought she spotted a trickle of emerald. But she couldn't be certain.

Daal glanced at her, worried.

"He's fine," she said. "He's been through a lot."

His shoulders relaxed, trusting her judgement. She wished she had as much confidence in her own assessment. They dismounted and headed to Daal's home. She drew alongside him and slipped her hand into his.

Fire sparked, melding their fingers more closely.

For now, that was as much *touch* as they allowed themselves. She remembered their kiss back at the dome, but after the tumult of their return, pulled in two different directions, they had held off from exploring more.

He glanced at her, a slight smile shadowing his mouth. She had forgotten how, when melded, he could sense her inner self.

He squeezed her fingers, stoking the fire between them. As he did, she felt his desire, the deepening of his breath, the flaring of his pupils, the blood-firming of his passion. But she also felt his restraint, an inner calm that defied her, a well of patience that both warmed her and slightly irritated her.

His smile only deepened.

She felt her cheeks heating up.

Henna burst between them, shoving them apart. Ahead, a pair of bright firepots welcomed them home. Still, the girl's exuberance was not about returning here and all about who awaited them.

"Kalder, you bad boy!" she called as she ran at him.

The vargr had stepped halfway out of the doorway, growling upon hearing their approach. Then he spotted Henna barreling toward him. His eyes got wide. He looked terrified.

Henna leaped headlong at him, wrapping her arms around his neck and hooking her legs over his shoulders. "You get back inside, you naughty boy," she scolded him.

With a weary grunt, the vargr turned and carried her through the draped doorway.

"Maybe I should make that saddle Henna wants," Daal said.

"I don't think we'll be around long enough for that," Nyx said. She meant her words as a jest, but she saw how the sentiment wounded him.

With their mood slightly soured, they pushed through the drape and into the warm room. Chatter and arguing greeted them. Fenn, Jace, and Krysh stood by the cupboard, where maps and charts were pinned to its doors. All three were in a heated discussion.

By the table, Graylin smoked a pipe with Meryk, the two of them waiting for some consensus to be reached.

Graylin nodded to Nyx, giving her a look up and down, making sure she hadn't broken anything else while out of his sight.

Kalder carried Henna over to where a sweetcake was warming on a tray. She unlatched from him and went for a taste, unable to resist. It did smell good. Kalder sighed and returned to Graylin. The vargr must have known the temptation of the cake was going to be the only way to get Henna to let go.

"Did they come to any decision?" Daal asked, waving to the trio.

Nyx crossed to the cupboard. She stared at the various routes mapped on the charts. All of them headed deeper into the Wastes, crossing through it to reach the far side of the Crown. They had all decided not to head back the way they had come. With a war growing over there, the safer path was to swing the other way, avoiding Hálendii and the Klashe entirely.

Still, there were several ways to reach the Barrens—and Frell, Jace, and Krysh had settled on different choices.

"You have to pick one," Nyx warned. "At least for now. We can always shift, depending on whatever we discover."

"True." Krysh placed a hand on Jace's shoulder. "As we're at an impasse, I throw my support to this young man's route."

Jace turned to Fenn. "That's two to your one."

"As a ship's navigator, my vote should count as two, maybe three."

Jace and Krysh frowned at him.

Fenn finally waved dismissively. "I'll concede. For now. We'll have to see how the prevailing winds blow once we're aloft."

"Show me which one," Nyx said.

Jace waved her closer. She shifted next to him, studying him sidelong as she did. He seemed his normal self, as jovial and obsessively focused as always. Still, she couldn't escape that cold emptiness she had felt inside of him. It had been too strange to fully dismiss.

"Here. This one," Jace said, drawing her attention back to the map. He ran a finger through the Wastes and across the Crown to a flagged site deep in the Barrens. "To me, with the direction of winds and expected spring storms, this course makes the most sense."

She nodded, but Fenn stood with his arms crossed. He was staring at the marked path through the Crown. She squinted closer and noted it passed over Bhestya, where Fenn hailed from. He had always been reticent to talk about his past. She wondered if this might be the reason he had argued against this route.

Still, she didn't question it, fearing it might restart the arguments.

As she turned to the table, she noted the wounded look on Daal's face as he stared toward Fenn. The navigator had long forgiven him, but Daal hadn't been able to forgive himself. She knew Daal remained unnerved by his loss of control, how it had nearly killed Fenn. She understood that fear, remembering the feeling of exultant power as she destroyed the Hálendiian barge—and the madness that followed. For her, it had been too easy to free that rage.

But not for Daal.

She knew better, even if he didn't. She crossed to him and brushed a stray strand from his cheek, leaving a trail of fire across his skin, as if trying to burn that fear out of him.

It didn't belong there.

She wondered if the Dreamers had chosen Daal for more than just the gift of bridle-song in his Noorish blood. Had they also been drawn to his kind-heartedness, his calm spirit, his steady compassion? She could still picture Daal burning in the flame of a lighthouse, guiding her out of madness, willing to sacrifice himself.

Down deep, she sensed the truth in this moment.

It shone in his eyes.

The *Oshkapeers* had forged more than a font of power for her. They had granted her a far greater gift.

*The anchor I will need in the days ahead.*

GRAYLIN STAMPED OUT his pipe and stood. "We should all be headed to the plaza. Darant and the others will be disappointed if we aren't there."

Meryk rose with him. "He's right. Floraan should already be waiting for us at the stands."

Graylin got everyone moving, even Kalder. The vargr deserved this as much as anyone. Graylin guided them out to the street.

Once there, Meryk cursed and ducked back inside. He returned a moment later, struggling to fit a circlet of white stone, adorned with gems, atop his head.

During the battle of Iskar, Rhaif had stumbled upon the Reef Farer's circlet. He had clearly planned on keeping the valuable crown—until the village had chosen Meryk as Berent's successor. Only then did Rhaif relinquish his treasure, happy to hand it off to a far worthier Panthean.

Daal smiled and helped his father get the circlet seated securely. "Looks good on you. Like it was always meant to be there."

Meryk pulled his son into a hug that looked capable of breaking ribs, as if trying to squeeze all the embraces a father would miss into this one hold.

Daal finally broke free, wiping at the corners of his eyes. "Gotta go, right?"

Meryk cleared his throat and waved them ahead, not ready to speak quite yet.

They continued across the village, joining the flow of others heading toward the plaza. As they walked, Meryk hooked his arm around his son, still wanting to keep him close, at least for as long as possible.

Daal cast his father an apologetic look.

"It's all right, son," Meryk said. "They're going to need you. We'll be here when you get back."

Graylin stared at the tension in the man's shoulders. His words were light, but the strain to say them was clear.

A month ago, Graylin had explained all to Meryk and Floraan. Graylin could not do otherwise, not when they were stripping Daal from their sides. They had been terrified at learning the truth about moonfall. Still, they had understood the threat and the necessity of their group's task. They had also recognized what would happen if the world started turning. It would mean the end of the Crèche.

Graylin had promised to try to send ships if they were successful, to evacuate the Crèche. But no one truly believed him, least of all himself.

It was Floraan who spoke the simplest truth as she touched Graylin's arm. *No one knows their end. The future remains a mystery until it's written. We'll live as if we have endless days ahead of us—and none. What else can any of us do?*

Graylin and the others finally reached the plaza and crossed through the throngs—made all the easier with a vargr in tow. They climbed the new dais to join Floraan. Daal's mother hugged her son with as much verve and a touch more composure. Women were always tougher than men when it came to matters of expediency and necessity.

They all crossed to rows of seats facing the sea. There was no longer any throne atop the dais, not even for the new Reef Farer. The docks were still being repaired, but headway was significant.

Graylin hoped Darant and his crew proved as resourceful at repairing their ship. The pirate had a long list of overhauls, restorations, modifications, and patch-ups. All to make them ready for a journey across the scorched lands— which included outfitting Shiya's cooling units. She was aboard right now with Rhaif, finishing final adjustments. Thankfully, Darant had a few extra hands, both Noorish and Panthean, several of whom had agreed to travel with them, refilling their depleted crew.

Besides the extra men, Daal had also handpicked and trained five raash'ke, who would be coming with them. Graylin had wanted to bring more bats, but the limits of their food larder had to be considered, especially not knowing if there were any martoks or other beasts to keep the predators fed.

No one wanted a flock of ravenous raash'ke aboard with them.

A murmur rose behind him, respectful and slightly awed.

Graylin turned around and stiffened. Two old Panthean women moved across the dais, walking slowly with canes, one more decrepit than the other. They were dressed in matching gray shifts. Beyond their great age, they looked so much like Ularia that it was uncanny.

Meryk noted his attention, his voice growing reverent. "Nys Playa and Nys Regina," he whispered. "The last of the *Nyssians*. I can't believe they traveled so far for this ceremony."

He and Floraan greeted them and offered them their own seats. The pair accepted them graciously, ending up on either side of Graylin. One looked to be in her eighties and the other well into her nineties, if not beyond.

Graylin nodded to them respectfully, but they must have noted his misgivings and divined the source.

The younger of the two, Nys Playa, patted his knee. "Do not judge our sister Ularia too harshly. She was under much pressure." She offered an amused glint to her eyes. "As you might imagine, we're too old to bear children."

Graylin mumbled that this discussion wasn't necessary.

Nys Playa ignored him and continued, "Desperation makes one hard and mean. As the last of us who could bear children, Ularia was weighted by the history of the Crèche, the responsibility of passing on our heritage. She saw in you hope—and terror."

Graylin turned to the woman, not understanding. "What do you mean?"

"We *Nyssians* know when someone with the proper seed is at hand. It is a gift from the *Oshkapeers*. As you can tell, we are little different in appearance. So it has been since the first of us. The daughters we birth are simply the rebirth of ourselves. We are little changed. Born with the memories of those before us. So it has always been."

Graylin stared between the two women.

"The men we choose to spark our next generations do not give our lineage more than the barest snippet of themselves, bits that might enhance us, but not truly change us. As you might imagine, it is a rarity. But in you, Ularia saw aspects that could nurture our lineage."

"Me?"

"It's what frightened and angered her. Pantheans sadly consider the Noorish to be unworthy, so for her to be stirred toward you—" She shrugged. "It distressed her."

Graylin remembered meeting Ularia atop the dais. She had seemed strangely taken by him. He had attributed it to him being new to the Crèche.

The older of the two, Nys Regina, nudged Graylin with her cane. "Ularia was young. But even my bleary eyes can see you are special. There is more to you than just a stout heart." She lifted her cane enough to point a few rows ahead. "One only has to look at your daughter to know this is true."

"I don't know if Nyx is truly my—"

Regina stared hard at him, her eyes bottomless and ancient, revealing one woman going back ages. "She *is* your daughter, young man. The Dreamers granted us the ability to see the seeds, roots, and branches of a tree. Even yours." The old woman dismissed him with a wave of her cane. "No wonder Ularia was so confounded by you—someone so blind and foolish that he can't see his own daughter standing before him."

Graylin sank back straighter in his seat. He watched Nyx whisper to Daal, her smile bright, so much like her mother's.

If these two were right, Nyx was not just Marayn's daughter.

*She's also mine.*

NYX SAT ON the edge of her chair with Daal on one side and Henna on the other. Kalder lay at Nyx's feet, but Henna had a firm grip on the vargr's ear, as if refusing to let him go.

Around them, the crowd in the plaza anxiously awaited the appearance of Darant and his repaired ship. The entire village had helped this miracle happen in time for the winter's solstice. So, they all wanted to be here to share in the success, especially after so much misery and death.

Nyx stared across the sea as it glowed with the reflection of the mists overhead. Raash'ke plied the skies and skimmed the waves, scribing ripples with their wingtips over the waters.

She hummed under her breath. It was the melody she had shared with Bashaliia, a memory of home distilled into song. She reached to Daal and took his hand. As his fire melted them together, she shared it with him, to let him feel the longing and grief for a home lost, maybe forever.

She wanted him to know she understood the sacrifice he was about to make. He might never see the Crèche again. She turned to him, to let him know he could stay, that he had done enough.

He smiled, his eyes shining with the grief in her song. Still, he gripped her fingers. Not to share his fire, but to simply let her know how he would survive it, how she would.

*Together.*

Horns blew loudly, breaking the bittersweet spell between them. They turned to the seas but still held tight to one another.

A murmur spread through the crowd, then settled to an expectant silence.

Horns blared again, louder now, closer.

People stood, staring off into the fog ahead. The glow of firepots appeared first, accompanied by more horns. Drums began to pound on the shoreline, welcoming and guiding the ship home.

Through the mists, a prow pushed into view, lit from behind. The crowd cheered as the draft-iron sculpture of a dragon reared into view, reflecting the flames of the village, its wings spread wide.

Another round of horns drove the colossal ship into view, forges flaming from its sides and stern. It was Rega sy Noor's ancient ship, reborn again to forge the skies.

Upon returning to the Crèche, the *Sparrowhawk* had been deemed to be too damaged, and another ship lay waiting for them, preserved in ice. Parts of their former ship had been salvaged to patch this older one, including installing the *Hawk*'s maesterwheel at the helm, where it belonged, ready to guide them forward again.

Nyx found the Noorish ship's name to be especially fitting for this next leg of their journey, a trek into the scorched and sunblasted Barrens.

The *Fyredragon*.

# 100

WRYTH STOOD ONCE again in the shadows of the castle's tourney yard, as yet another celebration was underway for Prince Mikaen. Only, on this night of the winter solstice, the prince carried a new title: Highking Mikaen ry Massif, the Crown'd Lord of Hálendii, rightful ruler of all the kingdom and its territories.

Mikaen had been coronated earlier in the day, but the night's festivities had drawn him to the royal balcony overlooking the bonfires, the waving banners, the milling celebrants. He was expected to give a speech, his first as the crowned ruler.

Finally, a trumpet sounded, and Mikaen crossed to the balcony rail. He waited for the cheering and horns to fall silent. He was dressed resplendently in velvet and fur. The jewels of his crown sparked in the firelight—as did his silver mask, now adorned with a single tear inscribed there in honor of his murdered father.

When Mikaen reached the balcony rail, he shrugged back his velvet cape to reveal his children, one under each arm. He smiled broadly and for once sincerely. The love he had for his son and daughter was as authentic as that silver tear was false. He hiked the two babes higher to renewed cheers. His name was chanted for a quarter-bell.

Mikaen waited for it to end, then spoke in a booming voice. "See my shining daughter and bright son! They were born on the morning after my father died! As if the Father Above knew Hálendii had been unjustly aggrieved and blessed our lands with new life."

Wryth scowled, but he still appreciated the sham drama of it all.

He suspected it was Mikaen's love for his children that had ultimately spurred the murder of his father. After the *Hyperium* had returned, Toranth had raged at those in charge, but his animus had fallen heavily upon his son, especially upon learning what had befallen Prince Kanthe. In a fit of rage, the king had blustered that he might yet seek a new queen to bear him a new son, one more deserving of the throne. Those last words, spoken out of anger, likely drove that sword down his throat.

Up on the balcony, Mikaen passed his daughter back to Myella, the new queen consort. He faced the crowd and lifted his son high. The babe squalled loudly. Mikaen gazed up with fatherly pride.

"Hear his cry, my legions! Hear him herald the dawn to come. With the light of the new day, a new era will be born as surely as my son." His voice boomed louder. "It will be a New Dawn! And I will be the New Sun, to bring Hálendii to greater glory!"

The crowd roared again.

Wryth could stand it no longer and turned into the shadows. He knew the coming daybreak wouldn't herald a *New Dawn*—but a *Dark Age.*

And it was already starting.

Before leaving, Wryth had spied the captain of the Silvergard sharing the royal balcony, ever at Mikaen's side. Only now Thoryn wore the laurels of a liege general on his breastplate. His predecessor, Reddak, currently hung outside the Legionary, unidentifiable now, ravaged by crows and flies.

Many others had met similar ends as Mikaen systematically cleared the palace. Toranth's chamberlain, Mallock, was found drowned in his own chamber pot. Provost Balyn had been trampled by horses. The mayor of Azantiia had been skewered from arse to mouth and found floating in a sewage bilge. Treasurer Hesst had been spared the purge, likely because the man knew where all the gold was hidden. And in times of war, such men were worth their weight in the same coinage.

Wryth had also survived, strangely enough due to Prince Kanthe. Wryth had heard what had happened aboard the *Hyperium.* Mikaen was convinced his brother had somehow bewitched one of his crimson-faced Silvergard into aiding his escape. It sounded outlandish, but Wryth knew better than to discourage this belief. As with Treasurer Hesst, Wryth only lived because Mikaen believed he and his fellow Iflelen could be useful, especially when it came to thwarting daemonic witchery.

Still, Wryth remained intrigued by what had happened aboard the *Hyperium,* wondering what had truly transpired. But it had been a long night, and such mysteries could wait until the morning.

As he headed down into the Shrivenkeep, he pondered ways to turn this to his advantage. Distracted by such thoughts—and still dwelling on the catastrophe from a month ago—Wryth found himself standing before the sanctum of the Iflelen. He touched the sigil inscribed on its ebonwood door: the *horn'd snaken* of Lord Đreyk. He could not shake the sense of defeat, both above his head and down here.

As he stood there, he heard a mumbling voice from inside, sounding worried and frustrated.

*Now what?*

With a tired grimace, Wryth pushed inside to find the young acolyte Phenic fussing over a bloodbaerne again. At least this time the child was not struggling to wake. The opposite was true. The boy in front of Phenic lay dead in his cradle, his small features sunken and drained.

"Why haven't you already replaced this one?" Wryth scolded, irritated at yet another problem.

"I . . . I did . . . I mean . . ." Phenic stammered to explain. "This boy . . . I consecrated him into his cradle about midday."

"Preposterous. One this young should have lasted three days, maybe four. You must have done something wrong."

"I swear I didn't. And it's not just this boy." He pointed to the far side. "Another girl was consecrated yesterday, and she is already empty. And I didn't perform her rite."

Wryth waved him back. "Stay here and get this boy removed. I'll go check on the girl."

He headed across the obsidian chamber, intending to pass through the great instrument to reach the far side. As he neared its heart, a pain stabbed into his right eye, a reminder of the crystal globe's blast—and his failure.

He stopped to adjust his eye patch.

This was the first time he had returned to this spot, having little reason to do so before now. He glanced around. The debris had been cleared out and the blood scrubbed away. Even the globe's pedestal had been carted off.

He stared where it had been, unsure if they could ever re-create the globe again. The design had been Skerren's, and from his frantic last message and the explosion, the man was assuredly dead. Especially as Wryth could still hear that distant scream of fury that had seemed to shatter the crystal. He frowned, remembering Skerren's last message.

He whispered it to the quiet room. "She is the *Vyk dyre Rha*! She has risen."

As he finished those words, he noticed the room had gone *too* quiet. All the bloodbaernes had stopped their thumping, not just the two that Phenic had noted.

In the silence, a whisper reached him. "She must be stopped."

Wryth cringed and stumbled back, striking his shoulder against a corner of the great instrument. Before him, the bronze bust glowed brightly, stirring with energy. He remembered it doing so a month ago, too—after the globe had shattered, as if the blast had transferred power to it.

Only now it shone even more brilliantly.

The bust's mouth moved faintly. "Must be stopped . . ."

Wryth took a step closer, balancing between horror and wonder. "Who . . . who are you?"

Bronze lips formed a name. "Kryst Eligor."

Wryth leaned closer—then those bronze eyelids snapped open, shining forth with a brilliant azure fire, like two brilliant suns blazing with infernal energies.

The intensity of that gaze drove him to his knees.

"I will guide you!" the voice boomed, forcing Wryth's brow to the floor.

"To what end?" Wryth asked.

Even with his face lowered, Wryth felt the burn of that gaze.

"To rebuild me."

# ACKNOWLEDGMENTS

A second journey is always more challenging and more fun. It's where you get to stray off the road and explore new trails and discover new characters—but it's also easy to get lost. To honor those who kept me on track, I must thank a group of writers who have stood at my side, many of them for decades: Chris Crowe, Lee Garrett, Matt Bishop, Matt Orr, Chris Riley, Judy Prey, Steve Prey, Caroline Williams, Bryan Wolfe, Sadie Davenport, Igor Poshelyuznyy, Vanessa Bedford, and Lisa Goldkuhl.

Of special acknowledgment, I must also thank the cartographer who crafted this world's maps (all three of them!): Soraya Corcoran. She turned my scribbles and scratches into works of art. Much more of her talent can be found at sorayacorcoran.wordpress.com. And, of course, I must express my thanks, appreciation, and awe to Danea Fidler, the artist who sketched the handsome creatures found throughout the pages of this book. To view more of her skill, do visit her site: daneafidler.com.

On the production side of this creation, I want to thank David Sylvian for all his hard work and dedication in the digital sphere.

Last and most important, none of this would have happened without an astounding team of industry professionals. To everyone at Tor Books—especially president and publisher extraordinaire Devi Pillai, thank you for continuing with me on this journey. Additionally, no book would shine as well without a skilled team behind its marketing and publicity, so I was blessed by the talents of Lucille Rettino, Eileen Lawrence, Stephanie Sarabian, Caroline Perny, Sarah Reidy, Renata Sweeney, and Michelle Foytek. And a big thanks to the team who made this second book in the series look its very best: Heather Saunders, Peter Lutjen, Steve Bucsok, and Rafal Gibek.

Of course, a special shout-out and a big THANKS must go to my editor, William Hinton, who followed me into the Frozen Wastes and helped hone these 230,000 words to their finest sheen. Plus, much thanks to those who furthered his efforts—editorial assistant Oliver Dougherty and copy editor extraordinaire Sona Vogel.

And as always, a big humble bow and thanks to my agents, Russ Galen and Danny Baror (along with his daughter Heather Baror). I wouldn't be the author I am today without such an enthusiastic set of cheerleaders and friends at my back.

Finally, I must stress that any and all errors of fact or detail in this book fall squarely on my own shoulders.

31901069014241